OATHBRINGER

BRANDON SANDERSON

OATHBRINGER

PART TWO

Book Three of
THE STORMLIGHT ARCHIVE

This edition first published in Great Britain in 2019 by Gollancz

First published in Great Britain in 2017 by Gollancz
an imprint of the Orion Publishing Group Ltd
Carmelite House, 50 Victoria Embankment
London EC4Y 0DZ

An Hachette UK Company

1 3 5 7 9 10 8 6 4 2

Illustrations preceding chapters 39 and 58 by Dan dos Santos
Illustrations preceding chapters 8, 15, 25, 27, 33, 67, 99, 108 and 116 by Ben McSweeney
Illustrations preceding chapters 77 and 94 by Miranda Meeks
Illustrations preceding chapters 44 and 104 by Kelley Harris
Maps and illustrations preceding chapters 1, 5, 53, 61, 89 and 120 by Isaac Stewart
Viewpoint icons by Isaac Stewart, Ben McSweeney and Howard Lyon

A CIP catalogue record for this book is
available from the British Library.

ISBN 978 0 575 09337 9

Typeset by Input Data Services Ltd, Somerset

Printed and bound in Great Britain by Clays Ltd, Elcograf S.p.A.

www.brandonsanderson.com
www.gollancz.co.uk

For Alan Layton
Who was cheering for Dalinar
(And me)
Before Stormlight even existed.

CONTENTS

ILLUSTRATIONS

NOTE: *Many illustrations, titles included, contain spoilers for material that comes before them in the book. Look ahead at your own risk.*

ROSHAR

ENDLESS OCEAN

Rall Elorim

RESHI

Kasitor

IRI

RIRA

Kurth

Reshi

Eila

The Misted Mountains

BABATHARNAM

Panatham

MARABETHIA

The Purelake

Shinovar

YULAY

DESH

Fu Nam

ALM

AZIR

AIMIA

Aimian Sea

UEZIER

Azimir

Urithiru

The Valle

Yeddaw

EMUL

GREAT HEX

STEEN

LIAFOR

TASHIKK

Sesemalex Dar

Icewater

TUKAR

MARA

N

LEEWARD

STORMWARD

S

SOUTHERN DEPTHS

STEAMWATER OCEAN

ISLES

Sea

Northgrip

HERDAZ

Mourn's
Vault

Varikev

Ru Parat

Elanar

JAH KEVED

Kholinar

ALETHKAR

UNCLAIMED HILL

TU
BAYLA

Valath

Shulin

Horneater Peaks

BAVLAND

Rathalas

Dawn's
Shadow

TRIAX

Silnasen

Vedenar

Dumadari

Karanak

Shattered
Plain

Tarat Sea

FROSTLANDS

New Natanan

Kharbranth

Longbrow's

Straits

Thaylen City

Kasi

The Shallow Crypts

THAYLENAH

OCEAN OF ORIGINS

FOR HIS ROYAL MAJESTY KING GAVILAR KHOLIN
BY HIS ROYAL HIGH CARTOGRAPHER
ISASIK SHULIN
1167

PART

THREE

Defying Truth, Love Truth

DALINAR • SHALLAN •
KALADIN • ADOLIN

This folio page targets the Thaylen merchant class with styles heavily influenced by the fashion worn by the nobles of Queen Fen Rnamdi's court.

BURDENS

As a Stoneward, I spent my entire life looking to sacrifice myself. I secretly worry that is the cowardly way. The easy way out.

—From drawer 29-5, topaz

The clouds that usually congregated about the base of the Urithiru plateau were absent today, allowing Dalinar to see down along the endless cliffs below the tower's perch. He couldn't see the ground; those cliffs seemed to extend into eternity.

Even with that, he had trouble visualizing how high in the mountains they were. Navani's scribes could measure height using the air somehow, but their numbers didn't satisfy him. He wanted to *see*. Were they really higher than the clouds were over the Shattered Plains? Or did the clouds here in the mountains fly lower?

How contemplative you've grown in your old age, he thought to himself, stepping onto one of the Oathgate platforms. Navani held his arm, though Taravangian and Adrotagia had trailed behind on the ramp up.

Navani looked into his eyes as they waited. 'Still bothered by the latest vision?'

That wasn't what was distracting him at the moment, but he nodded anyway. Indeed, he was worried. Odium. Though the Stormfather had returned to his previous self-confident ways, Dalinar could not shake the memory of the mighty spren whimpering in fright.

Navani and Jasnah had eagerly feasted on his account of meeting the dark god, though they'd chosen not to publish this one for wide dissemination.

'Maybe,' Navani said, 'this was somehow another preplanned event, placed by Honor for you to encounter.'

Dalinar shook his head. 'Odium felt *real*. I truly interacted with him.'

'You can interact with the people in the visions. Just not the Almighty himself.'

'Because, you theorize, the Almighty couldn't create a full simulacrum of a god. No. I saw eternity, Navani . . . a divine vastness.'

He shivered. For now, they had decided to suspend use of the visions. Who knew what risk they'd run by bringing people's minds in and potentially exposing them to Odium?

Of course, who's to say what he can and cannot touch in the real world? Dalinar thought. He looked up again, the sun burning white, the sky a faded blue. He would have thought that being above the clouds would give him more perspective.

Taravangian and Adrotagia finally arrived, followed by Taravangian's strange Surgebinder, the short-haired woman, Malata. Dalinar's guards brought up the rear. Rial saluted him. Again.

'You don't need to salute me each time I look at you, Sergeant,' Dalinar said dryly.

'Just trying ta be extra careful, sir.' The leathery, dark-skinned man saluted one more time. 'Wouldn't want ta be reported for being disrespectful.'

'I didn't mention you by name, Rial.'

'Everyone knew anyway, Brightlord.'

'Imagine that.'

Rial grinned, and Dalinar waved for the man to open his canteen, then sniffed for alcohol. 'It's clean this time?'

'Absolutely! You chastised me last time. Water only.'

'And so you keep the alcohol . . .'

'In my flask, sir,' Rial said. 'Right leg pocket of my uniform. Don't worry though. It's buttoned up tight, and I've completely forgotten it's there. I'll discover it when duty is done.'

'I'm sure.' Dalinar took Navani by the arm and followed Adrotagia and Taravangian.

'You could have someone else assigned to guard you,' Navani whispered to him. 'That greasy man is . . . unfitting.'

'I actually like him,' Dalinar admitted. 'Reminds me of some of my friends from the old days.'

The control building at the center of this platform was shaped like the others – mosaics on the floor, keyhole mechanism in the curved wall. The patterns on the floor, however, were glyphs in the Dawnchant. This building would be identical to one in Thaylen City – and when engaged, it would swap places with that one.

Ten platforms here, ten across the world. The glyphs on the floors indicated that it might somehow be possible to transport directly from one city to another without coming to Urithiru first. They hadn't discovered how that might work, and for now each gate could swap only with its twin – and they had to first be unlocked from both sides.

Navani went straight for the control mechanism. Malata joined her, watching over Navani's shoulder as she fiddled with the keyhole, which was in the center of a ten-pointed star on a metal plate. 'Yes,' Navani said, consulting some notes. 'The mechanism is the same as the one to the Shattered Plains. You need to twist this here . . .'

She wrote something via spanreed to Thaylen City, then ushered them back outside. A moment later, the building itself flashed – a ring of Stormlight running around it, like the afterimage of a firebrand being waved in the dark. Then Kaladin and Shallan emerged from the doorway.

'It worked!' Shallan said as she bounced out, bubbling over with eagerness. In contrast, Kaladin stepped out with a firm gait. 'Transferring only the control buildings, instead of the entire platform, should save us Stormlight.'

'Up until now,' Navani said, 'we've been working the Oathgates at full power for every transfer. I suspect that's not the only mistake we've made in regard to this place and its devices. Anyway, now that you two have unlocked the Thaylen gate on their end, we should be able to use it at will – with the help of a Radiant, of course.'

'Sir,' Kaladin said to Dalinar, 'the queen is prepared to meet with you.'

Taravangian, Navani, Adrotagia, and Malata entered the building, though Shallan started down the ramp back toward Urithiru. Dalinar took Kaladin by the arm as he moved to follow.

'The flight in front of the highstorm went well?' Dalinar asked.

'No problems, sir. I'm confident it will work.'

'Next storm then, soldier, make for Kholinar. I'm counting on you and Adolin to keep Elhokar from doing anything too foolhardy. Be careful. Something strange is going on inside the city, and I can't afford to lose you.'

'Yes, sir.'

'As you fly, wave to the lands along the south fork of the Deathbend River. The parshmen may have conquered them by now, but they actually belong to you.'

'. . . Sir?'

'You're a Shardbearer, Kaladin. That makes you at least fourth dahn, which should be a landed title. Elhokar found you a nice portion along the river that reverted to the crown last year at the death of its brightlord, who had no heir. It's not as large as some, but it is yours now.'

Kaladin looked stunned. 'Are there villages on this land, sir?'

'Six or seven; one town of note. The river is one of the most consistent in Alethkar. It doesn't even dry up in the Midpeace. That's on a good caravan route. Your people will do well.'

'Sir. You know I don't want this burden.'

'If you'd wanted a life without burdens, you shouldn't have said the oaths,' Dalinar said. 'We don't get to choose things like this, son. Just make sure you have a good steward, wise scribes, and some solid men of the fifth and sixth dahns to lead the towns. Personally, I'll count us lucky – you included – if at the end of all this we still *have* a kingdom to burden us.'

Kaladin nodded slowly. 'My family is in northern Alethkar. Now that I've practiced flying with the storms, I'll want to go and fetch them, once I get back from the Kholinar mission.'

'Get that Oathgate open, and you can have as much time as you want. I guarantee, the best thing you can do for your family right now is keep Alethkar from falling.'

By spanreed reports, the Voidbringers were slowly moving northward, and had captured much of Alethkar. Relis Ruthar had tried to gather the remaining Alethi forces in the country, but had been pushed back toward Herdaz, suffering at the hands of the Fused. However, the Voidbringers weren't killing noncombatants. Kaladin's family should be safe enough.

The captain jogged off down the ramp, and Dalinar watched, thinking about his own burdens. Once Elhokar and Adolin returned from the mission to rescue Kholinar, they'd need to get on with Elhokar's highking arrangement. He still hadn't announced that, not even to the highprinces.

A part of Dalinar knew he should simply go forward with it now, naming Adolin highprince and stepping down, but he delayed. This would make a final separation between himself and his homeland. He'd at least like to help recover the capital first.

Dalinar joined the others in the control building, then nodded toward Malata. She summoned her Shardblade and inserted it into the slot. The metal of the plate shifted and flowed, matching the shape of the Blade. They'd run tests, and though the walls of the buildings were thin, you couldn't see the other end of the Shardblade jutting through. The Blade was melding into the mechanism.

Malata pushed against the side of the Blade's hilt. The inner wall of the control building rotated. The floor underneath the mosaics began glowing, illuminating them like stained glass. She stopped her Blade at the proper position, and a flash of light later, they had arrived. Dalinar stepped out of the small building onto a platform in distant Thaylen City, a port on the western coast of a large southern island near the Frostlands.

Here the platform that surrounded the Oathgate had been turned into a sculpture garden – but most of the sculptures lay toppled and broken. Queen Fen waited on the ramp up with her attendants. Shallan had probably told her to wait there in case the room-only transfer didn't work.

The platform was high up in the city, and as Dalinar neared the edge, he saw that it gave an excellent view. The sight of it made Dalinar's breath catch.

Thaylen City was a mountainside metropolis like Kharbranth, placed with its back to a mountain to provide shelter from the highstorms. Though Dalinar had never been to the city before, he'd studied maps, and knew Thaylen City had once included only a section near the center they called the Ancient Ward. This raised portion had a distinctive shape formed by the way the rocks had been carved millennia ago.

The city had long since been built beyond that. A lower section called the Low Ward cluttered the stones around the base of the wall – a wide, squat fortification to the west that ran from the cliffs on one side of the city to the mountain foothills on the other.

Above and behind the Ancient Ward, the city had expanded up a series of steplike tiers. These Loft Wards ended at a majestic Royal Ward at the top of the city, holding palaces, mansions, and temples. The Oathgate platform was on this level, at the northern edge of the city, close to the cliffs down to the ocean.

Once, this place would have been stunning because of its magnificent architecture. Today, Dalinar paused for a different reason. Dozens ... *hundreds* of buildings had fallen in. Entire sections had become rubble when higher structures, smashed by the Everstorm, had slid down on top of them. What had once been one of the finest cities of all Roshar – known for its art, trade, and fine marble – was cracked and broken, like a dinner plate dropped by a careless maid.

Ironically, many more modest buildings at the base of the city – in the wall's shadow – had weathered the storm. But the famous Thaylen docks were out beyond this fortification, on the small western peninsula fronting the city. This area had once been densely developed – likely with warehouses, taverns, and shops. All wood.

They'd been swept away completely. Only smashed ruins remained.

Stormfather. No wonder Fen had resisted his distracting demands. Most of this destruction had been caused by that first full Everstorm; Thaylen City was particularly exposed, with no land to break the storm as it surged across the western ocean. Beyond that, many more of these structures had been of wood, particularly in the Loft Wards. A luxury available to a place like Thaylen City, which up until now had been subject only to the most mild of the stormwinds.

The Everstorm had come five times now, though subsequent passings had – blessedly – been tamer than the first. Dalinar lingered, taking it in, before leading his group to where Queen Fen stood on the ramp with a collection of scribes, lighteyes, and guards. This included her prince consort, Kmakl, an aging Thaylen man with matching mustaches and eyebrows, both drooping down to frame his face. He wore a vest and cap, and was attended by two ardents as scribes.

'Fen ...' Dalinar said softly. 'I'm sorry.'

'We lived too long in luxury, it seems,' Fen said, and he was momentarily surprised by her accent. It hadn't been present in the visions. 'I remember as a child worrying that everyone in other countries would discover how nice things were here, with the mild straits weather and the broken storms. I assumed we'd be swarmed with immigrants someday.'

8

She turned toward her city, and sighed softly.

How would it have been to live here? He tried to imagine living in homes that didn't feel like fortresses. Buildings of wood with broad windows. Roofs needed only for keeping the rain off. He'd heard people joke that in Kharbranth, you had to hang a bell outside to know when the highstorm had arrived, for otherwise you'd miss it. Fortunately for Taravangian, that city's slightly southern orientation had prevented devastation on this scale.

'Well,' Fen said, 'let's do a tour. I think there are a few places worth seeing that are still standing.'

BONDSMITH

> *If this is to be permanent, then I wish to leave record of my husband and children. Wzmal, as good a man as any woman could dream of loving. Kmakra and Molinar, the true gemstones of my life.*
>
> —From drawer 12-15, ruby

T he temple of Shalash,' Fen said, gesturing as they entered.

To Dalinar, it looked much like the others she'd shown them: a large space with a high-domed ceiling and massive braziers. Here, ardents burned thousands of glyphwards for the people, who supplicated the Almighty for mercy and aid. Smoke pooled in the dome before leaking out through holes in the roof, like water through a sieve.

How many prayers have we burned, Dalinar wondered uncomfortably, *to a god who is no longer there? Or is someone else receiving them instead?*

Dalinar nodded politely as Fen recounted the ancient origin of the structure and listed some of the kings or queens who had been crowned here. She explained the significance of the elaborate design on the rear wall, and led them around the sides to view the carvings. It was a pity to see several statues with the faces broken off. How had the storm gotten to them in here?

When they were done, she led them back outside onto the Royal Ward, where the palanquins waited. Navani nudged him.

'What?' he asked softly.

'Stop scowling.'

'I'm not scowling.'

'You're bored.'

'I'm not . . . scowling.'

She raised an eyebrow.

'Six temples?' he asked. 'This city is practically rubble, and we're looking at temples.'

Ahead, Fen and her consort climbed into their palanquin. So far, Kmakl's only part in the tour had been to stand behind Fen and – whenever she said something he thought significant – nod for her scribes to record it in the official histories.

Kmakl didn't carry a sword. In Alethkar, that would indicate the man – at least one of his rank – was a Shardbearer, but that was not the case here. Thaylenah had only five Blades – and three suits of Plate – each held by an ancient family line sworn to defend the throne. Couldn't Fen have taken him on a tour to see those Shards instead?

'Scowling . . .' Navani said.

'It's what they expect of me,' Dalinar said, nodding toward the Thaylen officers and scribes. Near the front, one group of soldiers in particular had watched Dalinar with keen interest. Perhaps this tour's true intent was to give those lighteyes a chance to study him.

The palanquin he shared with Navani was scented like rockbud blossoms. 'The progression from temple to temple,' Navani said softly as their bearers lifted the palanquin, 'is traditional in Thaylen City. Visiting all ten allows a survey of the Royal Ward, and is a not-so-subtle reinforcement of the throne's Vorin piety. They've had trouble with the church in the past.'

'I sympathize. Do you think if I explain I'm a heretic too, she'll stop with all the pomp?'

Navani leaned forward in the small palanquin, putting her freehand on his knee. 'Dear one, if this kind of thing irks you so, we could send a diplomat.'

'I am a diplomat.'

'Dalinar . . .'

'This is my duty now, Navani. I *have* to do my duty. Every time I've ignored it in the past, something terrible has happened.' He took her hands in his. 'I complain because I can be unguarded with you. I'll keep the scowling to a minimum. I promise.'

As their porters skillfully carried them up some steps, Dalinar watched out the palanquin window. This upper section of the city had weathered the storm well enough, as many of the structures here were of thick stone. Still, some had cracked, and a few roofs had fallen in. The palanquin passed a fallen statue, which had broken off at the ankles and toppled from a ledge toward the Loft Wards.

This city was hit harder than any I've had a report about, he thought. *This level of destruction is unique. Is it just all that wood, and the lack of anything to blunt the storm? Or is it more?* Some reports of the Everstorm mentioned no winds, only lightning. Others confusingly reported no rain, but burning embers. The Everstorm varied greatly, even within the same passing.

'It's probably comforting for Fen to do something familiar,' Navani told him quietly as the porters set them down at the next stop. 'This tour is a reminder of days before the city suffered such terrors.'

He nodded. With that in mind, it was easier to bear the thought of yet another temple.

Outside, they found Fen emerging from her palanquin. 'The temple of Battah, one of the oldest in the city. But of course the greatest sight here is the Simulacrum of Paralet, the grand statue that . . .' She trailed off, and Dalinar followed her gaze to the stone feet of the statue nearby. 'Oh. Right.'

'Let's see the temple,' Dalinar urged. 'You said it's one of the oldest. Which are older?'

'Only Ishi's temple is more ancient,' she said. 'But we won't linger there, or here.'

'We won't?' Dalinar asked, noticing the lack of prayer smoke from this roof. 'Is the structure damaged?'

'The structure? No, not the structure.'

A pair of tired ardents emerged and walked down the steps, their robes stained with flecks of red. Dalinar looked to Fen. 'Do you mind if I go up anyway?'

'If you wish.'

As Dalinar climbed the steps with Navani, he caught a scent on the wind. The scent of blood, which reminded him of battle. At the top, the sight inside the doors of the temple was a familiar one. Hundreds of wounded covered the marble floor, lying on simple pallets, painspren reaching out like orange sinew hands between them.

'We had to improvise,' Fen said, stepping up behind him in the doorway, 'after our traditional hospitals filled.'

'So many?' Navani said, safehand to her mouth. 'Can't some be sent home to heal, to their families?'

Dalinar read the answers in the suffering people. Some were waiting to die; they'd bled internally, or had rampant infections, marked by tiny red rotspren on their skin. Others had no homes left, evidenced by the families that huddled around a wounded mother, father, or child.

Storms ... Dalinar felt almost ashamed at how well his people had weathered the Everstorm. When he eventually turned to go, he almost ran into Taravangian, who haunted the doorway like a spirit. Frail, draped in soft robes, the aged monarch was weeping openly as he regarded the people in the temple.

'Please,' he said. '*Please.* My surgeons are in Vedenar, an easy trip through the Oathgates. Let me bring them. Let me ease this suffering.'

Fen pursed her lips to a thin line. She'd agreed to meet, but that didn't make her a part of Dalinar's proposed coalition. But what could she say to a plea like that?

'Your help would be appreciated,' she said.

Dalinar suppressed a smile. She'd conceded one step by letting them activate the Oathgate. This was another one. *Taravangian, you are a gem.*

'Lend me a scribe and spanreed,' Taravangian said. 'I will have my Radiant bring aid immediately.'

Fen gave the necessary orders, her consort nodding for the words to be recorded. As they walked back toward the palanquins, Taravangian lingered on the steps, looking out over the city.

'Your Majesty?' Dalinar asked, pausing.

'I can see my home in this, Brightlord.' He put a trembling hand against the wall of the temple for support. 'I blink bleary eyes, and I see Kharbranth destroyed in war. And I ask, "What must I do to preserve them?"'

'We will protect them, Taravangian. I *vow* it.'

'Yes ... Yes, I believe you, Blackthorn.' He took a long, drawn-out breath, and seemed to wilt further. 'I think . . . I think I shall remain here and await my surgeons. Please go on.'

Taravangian sat down on the steps as the rest of them walked away. At his palanquin, Dalinar looked back up and saw the old man sitting there, hands clasped before himself, liver-spotted head bowed, almost in the attitude of one kneeling before a burning prayer.

Fen stepped up beside Dalinar. The white ringlets of her eyebrows shook in the wind. 'He is far more than people think of him, even after his accident. I've often said it.'

Dalinar nodded.

'But,' Fen continued, 'he acts as if this city is a burial ground. That is *not* the case. We will rebuild from stone. My engineers plan to put walls on the front of each ward. We'll get our feet underneath us again. We just have to get ahead of the storm. It's the sudden loss of labor that really crippled us. Our parshmen . . .'

'My armies could do much to help clear rubble, move stones, and re-build,' Dalinar said. 'Simply give the word, and you will have access to thousands of willing hands.'

Fen said nothing, though Dalinar caught muttered words from the young soldiers and attendants waiting beside the palanquins. Dalinar let his attention linger on them, picking out one in particular. Tall for a Thaylen, the young man had blue eyes, with eyebrows combed and starched straight back alongside his head. His crisp uniform was, nat-urally, cut in the Thaylen style, with a shorter jacket that buttoned tight across the upper chest.

That will be her son, Dalinar thought, studying the young man's fea-tures. By Thaylen tradition, he would be merely another officer, not the heir. The monarchy of the kingdom was not a hereditary position.

Heir or not, this young man was important. He whispered something jeering, and the others nodded, muttering and glaring at Dalinar.

Navani nudged Dalinar and gave him a questioning look.

Later, he mouthed, then turned to Queen Fen. 'So the temple of Ishi is full of wounded as well?'

'Yes. Perhaps we can skip that.'

'I wouldn't mind seeing the lower wards of the city,' Dalinar said. 'Per-haps the grand bazaar I've heard so much about?'

Navani winced, and Fen grew stiff.

'It was . . . by the docks then, was it?' Dalinar said, looking out at the rubble-filled plain before the city. He'd assumed that it would have been in the Ancient Ward, the central part of the city. He should have paid better attention to those maps, apparently.

'I have refreshments set up at the courtyard of Talenelat,' Fen said. 'It was to be the last stop on our tour. Shall we go directly there now?'

Dalinar nodded, and they reboarded the palanquins. Inside, he leaned forward and spoke softly to Navani. 'Queen Fen is not an absolute authority.'

'Even your brother wasn't *absolutely* powerful.'

'But the Thaylen monarch is worse. The councils of merchants and naval officers pick the new monarch, after all. They have great influence in the city.'

'Yes. Where are you going with this?'

'It means she can't accede to my requests on her own,' Dalinar said. 'She can never agree to military aid as long as elements in the city believe that I'm bent on domination.' He found some nuts in an armrest compartment and began munching on them.

'We don't have time for a drawn-out political thaw,' Navani said, waving for him to hand her some nuts. 'Teshav might have family in the city she can lean on.'

'We could try that. Or . . . I have an idea budding.'

'Does it involve punching someone?'

He nodded. To which she sighed.

'They're waiting for a spectacle,' Dalinar said. 'They want to see what the Blackthorn will do. Queen Fen . . . she was the same way, in the visions. She didn't open up to me until I gave her my honest face.'

'Your honest face doesn't *have* to be that of a killer, Dalinar.'

'I'll try not to kill anyone,' he said. 'I just need to give them a lesson. A display.'

A lesson. A display.

Those words caught in his mind, and he found himself reaching back through his memories toward something still fuzzy, undefined. Something . . . something to do with the Rift and . . . and with Sadeas?

The memory darted away, just beneath the surface of his awareness. His subconscious shied from it, and he flinched like he'd been slapped.

In that direction . . . in that direction was *pain*.

'Dalinar?' Navani said. 'I suppose it's *possible* you're right. Perhaps the people seeing you be polite and calm is actually bad for our message.'

'*More* scowls, then?'

She sighed. 'More scowls.'

He grinned.

'Or a grin,' she added. 'From you, one of those can be *more* disturbing.'

The courtyard of Talenelat was a large stone square dedicated to Stonesinew, Herald of Soldiers. Atop a set of steps was the temple itself, but they didn't get a chance to look inside, for the main entrance had collapsed. A large, rectangular stone block – that had once spanned the top of the doorway – rested wedged downward inside it.

Beautiful reliefs covered the walls on the outside, depicting the Herald Talenelat standing his ground alone against a tide of Voidbringers. Unfortunately, these had cracked in hundreds of places. A large black scorch at the top of the wall showed where the strange Everstorm lightning had blasted the building.

None of the other temples had fared this poorly. It was as if Odium had a grudge against this one in particular.

Talenelat, Dalinar thought. *He was the one they abandoned. The one I lost . . .*

'I have some business to attend to,' Fen said. 'With trade to the city disrupted so seriously, I haven't much to offer as victuals. Some nuts and fruit, some salted fish. We've laid them out for you to enjoy. I'll return later so we can conference. In the meantime, my attendants will see to your needs.'

'Thank you,' Dalinar said. They both knew she was making him wait on purpose. It wouldn't be long – maybe a half hour. Not enough to be an insult, but enough to establish that she was still the authority here, no matter how powerful he was.

Even though he wanted some time with her people, he found himself annoyed at the gamesmanship of it. Fen and her consort withdrew, leaving most of the rest behind to enjoy the repast.

Dalinar, instead, decided to pick a fight.

Fen's son would do. He did appear the most critical among those talking. *I don't want to seem the aggressor,* Dalinar thought, positioning himself close to the young man. *And I should pretend I haven't guessed who he is.*

'The temples were nice,' Navani said, joining him. 'But you didn't enjoy them, did you? You wished to see something more militaristic.'

An excellent opening. 'You are right,' he said. 'You there. Captainlord. I'm not one for dallying. Show me the city's wall. *That* is something of real interest.'

'Are you *serious*?' Fen's son said in Thaylen-accented Alethi, words all mashed together.

'Always. What? Are your armies in such bad shape that you'd be embarrassed to let me see them?'

'I'm not going to let an enemy general inspect our defenses.'

'I'm not your enemy, son.'

'I'm not your son, tyrant.'

Dalinar made a big show of looking resigned. 'You've been shadowing me this entire day, soldier, speaking words that I've chosen not to hear. You're close to a line that, if crossed, *will* earn a response.'

The young man paused, showing some measure of restraint. He weighed what he was getting himself into, and decided that the risk was worth the reward. Humiliate the Blackthorn here, and maybe he could save his city – at least as he saw it.

'I regret only,' the man snapped, 'that I didn't speak loudly enough for you to hear the insults, despot.'

Dalinar sighed loudly, then began unbuttoning his uniform jacket, leaving himself in the snug undershirt.

'No Shards,' the young man said. 'Longswords.'

'As you wish.' Fen's son didn't have Shards, though he could have borrowed them if Dalinar insisted. Dalinar preferred this anyway.

The man covered his nervousness by demanding one of his attendants use a rock to draw a ring on the ground. Rial and Dalinar's guards approached, anticipationspren whipping nervously in their wakes. Dalinar waved them back.

'Don't hurt him,' Navani whispered. She hesitated. 'But don't lose either.'

'I'm not going to hurt him,' Dalinar said, handing her his jacket. 'I can't promise the part about losing.' She didn't see – but of course she didn't. He couldn't simply beat this man up. All that would do was prove to the rest of them that Dalinar was a bully.

He strode to the ring and paced it off, to memorize how many steps he could take without being forced out.

'I said longswords,' the young man said, weapon in hand. 'Where's your sword?'

'We'll do this by alternating advantage, three minutes,' Dalinar said. 'To first blood. You may lead off.'

The young man froze. Alternating advantage. The youth would have three minutes armed, against Dalinar unarmed. If Dalinar survived without being bloodied or leaving the ring, he'd have three minutes against his opponent in the reverse: Dalinar armed, the young man unarmed.

It was a ridiculous imbalance, usually only seen in sparring practice, when men trained for situations where they might be unarmed against an armed foe. And then, you'd never use real weapons.

'I . . .' the young man said. 'I'll switch to a knife.'

'No need. Longsword is fine.'

The young man gaped at Dalinar. Songs and stories told of the heroic unarmed man facing down many armed opponents, but in truth, fighting a single armed foe was incredibly difficult.

Fen's son shrugged. 'As much as I'd love to be known as the man who bested the Blackthorn on even terms,' he said, 'I'll take an unfair fight. But have your men here swear an oath that if this goes poorly for you, I'll not be named an assassin. You yourself set these terms.'

'Done,' Dalinar said, looking to Rial and the others, who saluted and said the words.

A Thaylen scribe stood to witness the bout. She counted off the start, and the young man came for Dalinar immediately, swinging like he meant it. Good. If you were going to agree to a fight like this, you shouldn't hesitate.

Dalinar dodged, then dropped into a wrestling stance, though he didn't intend to get close enough to try for a hold. As the scribe counted off the time, Dalinar continued to dodge attacks, hovering around the outside of the ring, careful not to step over the line.

Fen's son – though aggressive – displayed some innate wariness. The young man probably could have forced Dalinar out, but he kept testing instead. He came in again, and Dalinar scrambled away from the flashing sword.

The young man grew concerned and frustrated. Perhaps if it had been cloudy, he would have seen the faint glow of the Stormlight Dalinar was holding.

18

As the countdown drew near the end, the young man grew more frantic. He knew what was coming. Three minutes alone in a ring, unarmed against the Blackthorn. The attacks strayed from hesitant, to determined, to desperate.

All right, Dalinar thought. *Just about now . . .*

The countdown hit ten. The young man came at him with a last-ditch, all-out assault.

Dalinar stood up, relaxed, and held his hands to the sides so that the audience could see him intentionally fail to dodge. Then he stepped *into* the young man's thrust.

The longsword hit him right in the chest, just to the left of his heart. Dalinar grunted at the impact, and the pain, but managed to take the sword in a way that it missed the spine.

Blood filled one of his lungs, and Stormlight rushed to heal him. The young man looked aghast, as if – despite everything – he hadn't expected, or wanted, to land such a decisive blow.

The pain faded. Dalinar coughed, spat blood to the side, then took the young man's hand by the wrist, shoving the sword farther through his chest.

The young man released the sword hilt and scrabbled backward, eyes bulging.

'That was a good thrust,' Dalinar said, voice watery and ragged. 'I could see how worried you were at the end; others might have let their form suffer.'

The queen's son dropped to his knees, staring up as Dalinar stepped closer and loomed over him. Blood seeped around the wound, staining his shirt, until the Stormlight finally had time to heal the external cuts. Dalinar drew in enough that he glowed even in the daylight.

The courtyard had grown silent. Scribes held their mouths, aghast. Soldiers put hands on swords, shockspren – like yellow triangles – shattering around them.

Navani shared a sly smile with him, arms folded.

Dalinar took the sword by the hilt and slid it from his chest. Stormlight rushed to heal the wound.

To his credit, the young man stood up and stammered, 'It's your turn, Blackthorn. I'm ready.'

'No, you blooded me.'

'You let me.'

Dalinar took off his shirt and tossed it at the youth. 'Give me your shirt, and we'll call it even.'

The youth caught the bloody shirt, then looked up at Dalinar in befuddlement.

'I don't want your life, son,' Dalinar said. 'I don't want your city or your kingdom. If I'd *wanted* to conquer Thaylenah, I wouldn't offer you a smiling face and promises of peace. You should know that much from my reputation.'

He turned to the watching officers, lighteyes, and scribes. He'd accomplished his goal. They were in awe of him, afraid. He had them in his hand.

It was shocking, then, to feel his own sudden, stark *displeasure.* For some reason, those frightened faces hit him harder than the sword had.

Angry, ashamed for a reason he still didn't understand, he turned and strode away, up the steps from the courtyard toward the temple above. He waved away Navani when she came to speak with him.

Alone. He needed a moment alone. He climbed to the temple, then turned and sat down on the steps, putting his back against the stone block that had fallen into the doorway. The Stormfather rumbled in the back of his mind. And beyond that sound was . . .

Disappointment. What had he just accomplished? He said he didn't want to conquer this people, but what story did his actions tell? *I'm stronger than you,* they said. *I don't need to fight you. I could crush you without exerting myself.*

Was that what it should feel like to have the Knights Radiant come to your city?

Dalinar felt a twisting nausea deep in his gut. He'd performed stunts like this dozens of times throughout his life – from recruiting Teleb back in his youth, to bullying Elhokar into accepting that Dalinar wasn't trying to kill him, to more recently forcing Kadash to fight him in the practice chamber.

Below, people gathered around Fen's son, talking animatedly. The young man rubbed his chest, as if he'd been the one who'd been struck.

In the back of Dalinar's mind, he heard that same insistent voice. The one he'd heard from the beginning of the visions.

Unite them.

'I'm trying,' Dalinar whispered.

Why couldn't he ever convince anyone peacefully? Why couldn't he get people to listen without first pounding them bloody – or, conversely, shocking them with his own wounds?

He sighed, leaning back and resting his head against the stones of the broken temple.

Unite us. Please.

That was . . . a different voice. A hundred of them overlapping, making the same plea, so quiet he could barely hear them. He closed his eyes, trying to pick out the source of those voices.

Stone? Yes, he had a sensation of chunks of stone in *pain*. Dalinar started. He was hearing the spren of the *temple itself.* These temple walls had existed as a single unit for centuries. Now the pieces – cracked and ruined – hurt. They still viewed themselves as a beautiful set of carvings, not a ruined facade with fallen chunks scattered about. They longed to again be a single entity, unmarred.

The spren of the temple cried with many voices, like men weeping over their broken bodies on a battlefield.

Storms. Does everything I imagine have to be about destruction? About dying, broken bodies, smoke in the air and blood on the stones?

The warmth inside of him said that it did not.

He stood and turned, full of Stormlight, and seized the fallen stone that blocked the doorway. Straining, he shifted the block until he could slip in – squatting – and press his shoulders against it.

He took a deep breath, then *heaved* upward. Stone ground stone as he lifted the block toward the top of the doorway. He got it high enough, then positioned his hands immediately over his head. With a final push, shouting, he pressed with legs, back, and arms together, shoving the block upward with everything he had. Stormlight raged inside him, and his joints popped – then healed – as he inched the stone back into place above the doorway.

He could *feel* the temple urging him onward. It wanted so badly to be whole again. Dalinar drew in more Stormlight, as much as he could hold, draining every gemstone he'd brought.

Sweat streaming across his face, he got the block close enough that it felt *right* again. Power flooded through his arms into it, then seeped across the stones.

The carvings popped back together.

The stone lintel in his hands lifted and settled into place. Light filled the cracks in the stones and knit them back together, and gloryspren burst around Dalinar's head.

When the glow faded, the front wall of the majestic temple – including the doorway and the cracked reliefs – had been restored. Dalinar faced it, shirtless and coated in sweat, feeling twenty years younger.

No, the man he'd been twenty years ago could never have done this.

Bondsmith.

A hand touched his arm; Navani's soft fingers. 'Dalinar ... what did you do?'

'I listened.' The power was good for far, far more than breaking. *We've been ignoring that. We've been ignoring answers right in front of our eyes.*

He looked back over his shoulder at the crowd climbing the steps, gathering around. 'You,' Dalinar said to a scribe. 'You're the one who wrote to Urithiru and sent for Taravangian's surgeons?'

'Y . . . yes, Brightlord,' she said.

'Write again. Send for my son Renarin.'

.·.

Queen Fen found him in the courtyard of the temple of Battah, the one with the large broken statue. Her son – now wearing Dalinar's bloodied shirt tied around his waist, like some kind of girdle – led a crew of ten men with ropes. They'd just gotten the hips of the statue settled back into place; Dalinar drained Stormlight from borrowed spheres, sealing the stone together.

'I think I found the left arm!' a man called from below, where the bulk of the statue had toppled through the roof of a mansion. Dalinar's team of soldiers and lighteyes whooped and rushed down the steps.

'I did not expect to find the Blackthorn shirtless,' Queen Fen said, 'and ... playing sculptor?'

'I can only fix inanimate things,' Dalinar said, wiping his hands on a rag tied at his waist, exhausted. Using this much Stormlight was a new experience for him, and quite draining. 'My son does the more important work.'

A small family left the temple above. Judging by the father's tentative steps, supported by his sons, it seemed the man had broken a leg or two in the most recent storm. The burly man gestured for his sons to step back, took a few steps on his own – and then, his eyes wide, did a short skip.

Dalinar knew that feeling: the lingering effects of Stormlight. 'I should have seen it earlier – I *should* have sent for him the moment I saw those wounded. I'm a fool.' Dalinar shook his head. 'Renarin has the ability to heal. He is new to his powers, as I am to mine, and can best heal those who were recently wounded. I wonder if it's similar to what I'm doing. Once the soul grows accustomed to the wound, it's much harder to fix.'

A single awespren burst around Fen as the family approached, bowing and speaking in Thaylen, the father grinning like a fool. For a moment, Dalinar felt he could *almost* understand what they were saying. As if a part of him were stretching to bond to the man. A curious experience, one he didn't quite know how to interpret.

When they left, Dalinar turned to the queen. 'I don't know how long Renarin will hold out, and I don't know how many of those wounds will be new enough for him to fix. But it is something we could do.'

Men called below, heaving a stone arm out through the window of the mansion.

'I see you've charmed Kdralk as well,' Fen noted.

'He's a good lad,' Dalinar said.

'He was determined to find a way to duel you. I hear you gave him that. You're going to roll over this whole city, charming each person in turn, aren't you?'

'Hopefully not. That sounds like it would take a lot of time.'

A young man came running down from the temple, holding a child with floppy hair who – though his clothing was torn and dusty – was smiling with a broad grin. The youth bowed to the queen, then thanked Dalinar in broken Alethi. Renarin kept blaming the healings on him.

Fen watched them go with an unreadable expression on her face.

'I need your help, Fen,' Dalinar whispered.

'I find it hard to believe you need anything, considering what you've done today.'

'Shardbearers can't hold ground.'

She looked at him, frowning.

'Sorry. That's a military maxim. It . . . never mind. Fen, I have Radiants, yes – but they, no matter how powerful, won't win this war. More importantly, I can't see what I'm missing. *That's* why I need you.

'I think like an Alethi, as do most of my advisors. We consider the war, the conflict, but miss important facts. When I first learned of Renarin's powers, I thought only of restoring people on the battlefield to continue the fight. I need you; I need the Azish. I need a coalition of leaders who see what I don't, because we're facing an enemy that doesn't think like any we've faced before.' He bowed his head to her. 'Please. Join me, Fen.'

'I've already opened that gate, and I'm talking to the councils about giving aid to your war effort. Isn't that what you wanted?'

'Not close, Fen. I want you to *join* me.'

'The difference is?'

'The distinction between referring to it as "your" war, and "our" war.'

'You're relentless.' She took a deep breath, then cut him off as he tried to object. 'I suppose that is what we need right now. All right, Blackthorn. You, me, Taravangian. The first real united Vorin coalition the world has seen since the Hierocracy. It's unfortunate that two of us lead kingdoms that are in ruin.'

'Three,' Dalinar said with a grunt. 'Kholinar is besieged by the enemy. I've sent help, but for now, Alethkar is an occupied kingdom.'

'Wonderful. Well, I think I can persuade the factions in my city to let your troops come and help here. If everything goes well with that, I will write to the Prime of Azir. Maybe that will help.'

'I'm certain it will. Now that you've joined, the Azish Oathgate is the most essential to our cause.'

'Well, they're going to be tricky,' Fen said. 'The Azish aren't as desperate as I am – and frankly, they aren't Vorin. People here, myself included, respond to a good *push* from a determined monarch. Strength and passion, the Vorin way. But those tactics will just make the Azish dig in and rebuff you harder.'

He rubbed his chin. 'Do you have any suggestions?'

'I don't think you'll find it very appealing.'

'Try me,' Dalinar said. 'I'm starting to appreciate that the way I usually do things has severe limitations.'

WINDS AND OATHS

I worry about my fellow Truthwatchers.

—From drawer 8-21, second emerald

The storm did not belong to Kaladin.

He claimed the skies, and to an extent the winds. Highstorms were something different, like a country in which he was a visiting dignitary. He retained some measure of respect, but he also lacked real authority.

While fighting the Assassin in White, Kaladin had traveled with the highstorm by flying at the very front of the stormwall, like a leaf caught in a wave. That method – with the full force of the highstorm raging at his feet – seemed far too risky to use when bringing others. Fortunately, during their trip to Thaylenah, he and Shallan had tested other methods. It turned out he could still draw upon the storm's power while flying above it, so long as he stayed within a hundred feet or so of the stormclouds.

He soared there now, with two bridgemen and Elhokar's chosen team. The sun shone brightly above, and the eternal storm extended in all directions below. Swirling black and grey, lit by sparks of lightning. Rumbling, as if angry at the small group of stowaways. They couldn't see the stormwall now; they'd lagged far behind that. Their angle to Kholinar required them to travel more northward than westward as they cut across the Unclaimed Hills toward northern Alethkar.

There was a mesmerizing beauty to the storm's churning patterns, and Kaladin had to forcibly keep his attention on his charges. There were six of those, which made their team nine in total, counting himself, Skar, and Drehy.

King Elhokar was at the front. They couldn't bring their suits of Shardplate; Lashings didn't work on those. Instead, the king wore thick clothing and a strange kind of glass-fronted mask to block the wind. Shallan had suggested those; they were apparently naval equipment. Adolin came next. Then two of Shallan's soldiers – the sloppy deserters she'd collected like wounded axehound pups – and one maidservant. Kaladin didn't understand why they'd brought those three, but the king had insisted.

Adolin and the others were bundled up as much as the king, which made Shallan look even more odd. She flew in only her blue havah – which she'd pinned to keep it from fluttering too much – with white leggings underneath. Stormlight surged from her skin, keeping her warm, sustaining her.

Her hair streamed behind her, a stark auburn red. She flew with arms outstretched and eyes closed, grinning. Kaladin had to keep adjusting her speed to keep her in line with the others, as she couldn't resist reaching out to feel the wind between her freehand fingers, and waving to windspren as they passed.

How does she smile like that? Kaladin wondered. During their trip through the chasms together, he'd learned her secrets. The wounds she hid. And yet . . . she could simply ignore them somehow. Kaladin had never been able to do that. Even when he wasn't feeling particularly grim, he felt weighed down by his duties or the people he needed to care for.

Her heedless joy made him want to show her how to *really* fly. She didn't have Lashings, but could still use her body to sculpt the wind and dance in the air. . . .

He snapped himself back to the moment, banishing silly daydreams. Kaladin tucked his arms against himself, making a narrower profile for the wind. This made him move up the line of people, so he could renew their Stormlight each in turn. He didn't use Stormlight to maneuver so much as the wind itself.

Skar and Drehy handled their own flight about twenty feet below the group, watching in case anyone dropped for some reason. Lashings renewed, Kaladin maneuvered himself into line between Shallan and King Elhokar. The king stared forward through the mask, as if oblivious to the wondrous storm beneath. Shallan drifted onto her back, beaming as she looked up at the sky, the hem of her pinned skirts rippling and fluttering.

Adolin was a different story. He glanced at Kaladin, then closed his eyes and gritted his teeth. At least he'd stopped flailing each time they hit a change in the winds.

They didn't speak, as their voices would only be lost to the rushing wind. Kaladin's instincts said he could probably lessen the force of the wind while flying – he'd done so before – but there were some abilities he had trouble deliberately reproducing.

Eventually, a line of light flitted from the storm below. It soon looped into a ribbon of light and spun up toward him. 'We just passed the Windrunner River,' Syl said. The words were more of a mental impression than actual sound.

'We're near Kholinar then,' he said.

'She clearly likes the sky,' Syl said, glancing at Shallan. 'A natural. She almost seems like a spren, and I consider that high praise.'

He sighed, and did not look at Shallan.

'Come on . . .' Syl said, zipping around to his other side. 'You need to be with people to be happy, Kaladin. I know you do.'

'I have my bridge crew,' he muttered, voice lost to the winds – but Syl would be able to hear, as he could hear her.

'Not the same. And you know it.'

'She brought her handmaid on a scouting mission. She couldn't go a week without someone to do her hair. You think I'd be interested in that?'

'Think?' Syl said. She took the shape of a tiny young woman in a girlish dress, flying through the sky before him. 'I *know*. Don't think I don't spot you stealing looks.' She smirked.

'Time to stop so we don't overshoot Kholinar,' Kaladin said. 'Go tell Skar and Drehy.'

Kaladin took his charges one at a time, canceling their Lashing forward, replacing it with a half Lashing upward. There was a strange effect to the Lashings that frustrated Sigzil's scientific attempts at terminology. All of his numbers had assumed that once Lashed, a person would be under the influence of both the ground and the Lashing.

That wasn't the case. Once you used a Basic Lashing on someone, their body completely forgot about the pull of the ground, and they fell in the direction you indicated. Partial Lashings worked by making part of the person's weight forget the ground, though the rest continued to be pulled downward. So a half Lashing upward made a person weightless.

Kaladin situated the groups so he could speak to the king, Adolin, and Shallan. His bridgemen and Shallan's attendants hovered a short distance off. Even Sigzil's new explanations had trouble accounting for everything that Kaladin did. He'd somehow made a kind of . . . channel around the group, like in a river. A current, sweeping them along, keeping them closer together.

'It really is beautiful,' Shallan said, surveying the storm, which blanketed everything but the tips of some very distant peaks to their left. Probably the Sunmaker Mountains. 'Like mixing paint – if dark paint could somehow spawn new colors and light within its swirls.'

'So long as I can continue to watch it from a safe distance,' Adolin said. He held Kaladin's arm to keep from drifting away.

'We're close to Kholinar,' Kaladin said. 'Which is good, as we're getting near the back edge of the storm, and I'll soon lose access to its Stormlight.'

'What I feel like I'm about to lose,' Shallan said, looking down, 'is my shoes.'

'Shoes?' Adolin said. 'I lost my *lunch* back there.'

'I can't help imagining something sliding off and dropping into it,' Shallan whispered. 'Vanishing. Gone forever.' She glanced at Kaladin. 'No wisecracks about missing boots?'

'I couldn't think of anything funny.' He hesitated. 'Though that hasn't ever stopped you.'

Shallan grinned. 'Have you ever considered, bridgeman, that *bad* art does more for the world than good art? Artists spend more of their lives making bad practice pieces than they do masterworks, particularly at the start. And even when an artist becomes a master, some pieces don't work out. Still others are somehow just *wrong* until the last stroke.

'You learn more from bad art than you do from good art, as your mistakes are more important than your successes. Plus, good art usually evokes the same emotions in people – most good art is the same *kind* of good. But bad pieces can each be bad in their own unique way. So I'm glad we have bad art, and I'm sure the Almighty agrees.'

'All this,' Adolin said, amused, 'to justify your sense of humor, Shallan?'

'My sense of humor? No, I'm merely trying to justify the creation of Captain Kaladin.'

Ignoring her, Kaladin squinted eastward. The clouds behind them were lightening from deep, brooding black and grey to a more general blandness, the color of Rock's morning mush. The storm was near to ending; what arrived with a fanfare ended with an extended sigh, gales giving way to peaceful rain.

'Drehy, Skar,' Kaladin called. 'Keep everyone in the air. I'm going to go scout below.'

The two gave him salutes, and Kaladin dropped through the clouds, which – from within – looked like dirty fog. Kaladin came out crusted in frost, and rain began pelting him, but it was growing weak. Thunder rumbled softly above.

Enough light seeped through the clouds for him to survey the landscape. Indeed, the city was close, and it was majestic, but he forced himself to look for enemies before marveling. He noted a broad plain before the city – a killing field kept free of trees or large boulders, so that neither could offer cover to an invading army. That was empty, which wasn't unexpected.

The question was who held the city – Voidbringers or humans? He cautiously descended. The place glowed with a sprinkling of Stormlight from cages left out in the storm to recharge the gems. And . . . yes, from guard posts flew Alethi flags, raised now that the worst of the storm had passed.

Kaladin let out a relieved sigh. Kholinar had not fallen, though if their reports were right, all surrounding towns were occupied. In fact, looking closely, he could see that the enemy had begun building stormshelters on the killing field: bunkers from which they could prevent resupply to Kholinar. They were mere foundations of brick and mortar for now. During the times between storms, they were likely guarded – and built up – by large enemy forces.

He finally let himself stare at Kholinar. He knew it was coming, inevitable as a budding yawn; he couldn't keep it down forever. First assess the area for danger, get the lay of the land.

Then gawk.

Storms, that city was beautiful.

He'd flown high above it once in a half dream where he'd seen the Stormfather. That hadn't affected him the way it did to float here, looking over the vast metropolis. He'd seen proper cities now – the warcamps together were probably larger than Kholinar – so it wasn't the size that amazed him, really, but the variety. He was accustomed to functional bunkers, not stone buildings of many shapes and roofing styles.

Kholinar's defining feature, of course, was the windblades: curious rock formations that rose from the stone like the fins of some giant creature mostly hidden beneath the surface. The large curves of stone glittered with red, white, and orange strata, their hues deepened by the rain. He hadn't realized that the city walls were partially constructed on the tops of the outer windblades. There, the lower sections of the walls literally *sprouted* from the ground, while men had built fortifications atop them, evening out the heights and filling spaces between the curves.

Towering over the northern side of the city was the palace complex, which rose high and confident, as if in defiance of the storms. The palace was like a little city unto itself, with bright columns, rotundas, and turrets.

And something was very, *very* wrong with it.

A cloud hung over the palace, a darkness that – at first glance – seemed like nothing more than a trick of the light. Yet the feeling of wrongness persisted, and seemed strongest around a portion at the east of the palace complex. This flat, raised plaza was filled with small buildings. The palace monastery.

The Oathgate platform.

Kaladin narrowed his eyes, then Lashed himself back upward, passing into the clouds. He'd probably let himself gape for too long – he didn't want to start talk of a glowing person in the sky.

Still . . . that city. In Kaladin's heart still lived a country boy who had dreamed of seeing the world.

'Did you see that darkness around the palace?' Kaladin asked Syl.

'Yeah,' she whispered. 'Something's very wrong.'

Kaladin emerged from the clouds and found that his crew had drifted off to the west in the breeze. He Lashed himself toward them, and noticed – for the first time – that his Stormlight was no longer being renewed by the storm.

Drehy and Skar looked visibly relieved when he arrived. 'Kal—' Skar started.

'I know. We don't have much time left. Your Majesty, the city is right below us – and our forces still control the walls. The Parshendi are building storm bunkers and besieging the area, though the bulk of their army probably retreated to nearby towns in anticipation of the storm.'

'The city stands!' Elhokar said. 'Excellent! Captain, take us down.'

'Your Majesty,' Kaladin said. 'If we drop from the sky like this, the enemy scouts *will* see us entering.'

'So?' Elhokar said. 'The need for subterfuge was predicated on a fear that we might have to sneak in. If our forces still hold the city, we can march up to the palace, assert command, and activate the Oathgate.'

Kaladin hesitated. 'Your Majesty, something is ... wrong with the palace. It looks *dark,* and Syl saw it too. I advise caution.'

'My wife and child are inside,' Elhokar said. 'They might be in danger.'

You didn't seem to worry much about them during six years away at war, Kaladin thought.

'Let's go down anyway,' the king said. 'We want to get to the Oathgate as soon as possible . . .' He trailed off, looking from Kaladin to Shallan, to Adolin. 'Don't we?'

'I advise caution,' Kaladin repeated.

'The bridgeman isn't the jumpy type, Your Majesty,' Adolin said. 'We don't know what's going on in the city, or what happened since the reports of chaos and a revolt. Caution sounds good to me.'

'Very well,' Elhokar said. 'This *is* why I brought the Lightweaver. What do you recommend, Brightness?'

'Let's land outside the city,' Shallan said. 'Far enough away that the glow of Stormlight doesn't give us away. We can use illusions to sneak in and find out what is going on without revealing ourselves.'

'Very well,' Elhokar said, nodding curtly. 'Do as she suggests, Captain.'

KHOLINAR

South

East

West

North

a. City Gates
b. Palace
c. Market Row
d. Dueling Arena
e. Theater Square
f. Monastery Dais
g. Sunmaker Park
h. Lanacin Monument
i. Devotary of Insight
j. Impossible Falls
k. Order of Talenelat

Temples
1. Jezerezeh
2. Nalan
3. Chanaranach
4. Vedeledev
5. Pailiah
6. Shalash
7. Battah
8. Kelek
9. Talenelat
10. Ishi

Kholinar Palace Main Level

Monastery Dais

King's Chapel

Sunwalk

Guest Dining
Eastern Gallery

food prep
(Kitchens below)

Guest Quarters

chapels

Grand Entry

Ball-room

Ball-room

Stairs to the Gardens

Garrison

*We can record any secret we wish, and leave it here? How do we know
that they'll be discovered? Well, I don't care. Record that then.*

—From drawer 2-3, smokestone

The enemy army was letting refugees approach the city.

At first, this surprised Kaladin. Wasn't the point of a siege to
prevent people from getting in? And yet, a constant stream of
people was allowed to approach Kholinar. The gates stood closed against
an army invasion, but the side doors – which were still large – were wide
open.

Kaladin handed the spyglass to Adolin. They'd landed in an inconspic-
uous location, then hiked back to the city on foot – but it had been dark
by the time they'd arrived. They'd decided to spend the night outside the
city, hidden by one of Shallan's illusions. Impressively, her Lightweaving
had lasted all night on very little Stormlight.

Now that morning had arrived, they were surveying the city, which
was maybe a mile away. From the outside, their hideout would seem like
merely another knob of stone ground. Shallan couldn't make it trans-
parent from only one side, so they had to see out using a slit that – if
someone walked close by – would be visible.

The illusion felt like a cave – except for the fact that wind and rain went right through it. The king and Shallan had grumbled all morning, complaining of a damp, cold night. Kaladin and his men had slept like stones. There were advantages to having lived through Bridge Four.

'They let refugees in so they can drain the city's resources,' Adolin said, watching through the spyglass. 'A solid tactic.'

'Brightness Shallan,' Elhokar said, accepting the spyglass from Adolin, 'you can give us each illusions, right? We can pretend to be refugees and enter the city easily.'

Shallan nodded absently. She sat sketching near a shaft of light pouring through a small hole in the ceiling.

Adolin turned his spyglass toward the palace, the top of which surmounted the city in the distance. The day was perfectly sunny, bright, and crisp, with only a hint of moisture in the air from the highstorm the day before. There wasn't a cloud in the sky.

But somehow, the palace was still in shadow.

'What could it be?' Adolin said, lowering his spyglass.

'One of *them*,' Shallan whispered. 'The Unmade.'

Kaladin looked back at her. She'd sketched the palace, but it was twisted, with odd angles and distorted walls.

Elhokar studied the palace. 'You were right to recommend caution, Windrunner. My instinct is still to rush in. That's wrong, isn't it? I must be *prudent* and *careful*.'

They gave Shallan time to finish sketches – she claimed to need them for complex illusions. Eventually she stood, flipping pages in her sketchpad. 'All right. Most of us won't need disguises, as nobody will recognize me or my attendants. Same goes for Kaladin's men, I assume.'

'If someone does recognize me,' Skar said, 'it won't cause any problems. Nobody here knows what happened to me at the Shattered Plains.' Drehy nodded.

'All right,' Shallan said, turning to Kaladin and Adolin. 'You two will get new faces and clothing, making you into old men.'

'I don't need a disguise,' Kaladin said. 'I—'

'You spent time with those parshmen earlier in the month,' Shallan said. 'Best to be safe. Besides, you scowl at everyone like an old man anyway. You'll be a great fit.'

Kaladin glowered at her.

'Perfect! Keep it up.' Shallan stepped over and breathed out, and

Stormlight wreathed him. He felt he should be able to take it in, use it – but it resisted him. It was a strange sensation, as if he'd found a glowing coal that gave off no heat.

The Stormlight vanished and he held up a hand, which now appeared wizened. His uniform coat had been changed to a homespun brown jacket. He touched his face, but didn't feel anything different.

Adolin pointed at him. 'Shallan, that is positively *wretched*. I'm impressed.'

'What?' Kaladin looked at his men. Drehy winced.

Shallan wrapped Adolin in Light. He resolved into a sturdy, handsome man in his sixties, with dark brown skin, white hair, and a lean figure. His clothing was no longer ornate, but in good repair. He looked like the kind of old rogue you'd find in a pub, with handy tales about the brilliant things he'd done in his youth. The kind of man that made women think they preferred older men, when in reality they just preferred *him*.

'Oh, now that's unfair,' Kaladin said.

'If I stretch a lie too far, people are more likely to be suspicious,' Shallan said lightly, then stepped over to the king. 'Your Majesty, you're going to be a woman.'

'Fine,' Elhokar said.

Kaladin started. He'd have expected an objection. Judging by the way that Shallan seemed to stifle a quip, she'd been expecting one too.

'You see,' she said instead, 'I don't think you can keep from carrying yourself like a king, so I figure that if you look like a highborn lighteyed woman, it's less likely that you'll be memorable to the guards who—'

'I said it was fine, Lightweaver,' Elhokar said. 'We mustn't waste time. My city and nation are in peril.'

Shallan breathed out again, and the king was transfigured into a tall, stately Alethi woman with features reminiscent of Jasnah's. Kaladin nodded appreciatively. Shallan was right; there was something about the way Elhokar held himself that bespoke nobility. This was an excellent way to deflect people who might wonder who he was.

As they gathered their packs, Syl zipped into the enclosure. She took the shape of a young woman and flitted up to Kaladin, then stepped back in the air – aghast.

'Oh!' she said. 'Wow!'

Kaladin glared at Shallan. 'What did you *do* to me?'

35

'Oh, don't be that way,' she said. 'This will only highlight your excellent personality.'

Don't let her get to you, Kaladin thought. *She wants to get to you.* He hefted his pack. It *didn't* matter what he looked like; it was only an illusion.

But what *had* she done?

He led the way out of their enclosure, and they fell into a line. The rock illusion melted away behind them. Kaladin's men had brought generic blue uniforms with no insignias. They could have belonged to any minor house guard within the Kholin princedom. Shallan's two had on generic brown uniforms, and with Elhokar wearing the dress of a lighteyed woman, they actually looked like a real refugee group. Elhokar would be seen as a brightlady who had fled – without even a palanquin or carriage – before the enemy's advance. She'd brought a few guards, some servants, and Shallan as her young ward. And Kaladin was her . . . what?

Storms. 'Syl,' he growled, 'could I summon you not as a sword, but as a flat, shiny piece of metal?'

'A mirror?' she asked, flying along beside him. 'Hmmm. . . .'

'Not sure if it's possible?'

'Not sure if it's dignified.'

'Dignified? Since when have you cared about dignity?'

'I'm not to be toyed with. I'm a *majestic* weapon to be used only in *majestic* ways.' She hummed to herself and flitted away. Before he could call her back to complain, Elhokar caught up to him.

'Slow down, Captain,' the king said. Even his voice had changed to sound womanly. 'You'll outpace us.'

Reluctantly, Kaladin slowed. Elhokar didn't show what he thought of Kaladin's face; the king kept his eyes forward. He never did think much about other people, so that was normal.

'They call it the Windrunner, you know,' the king said softly. It took Kaladin a moment to realize that Elhokar was referring to the river that ran past Kholinar. Their path took them across it on a wide stone bridge. 'The Alethi lighteyes rule because of *you.* Your order was prominent here, in what was then Alethela.'

'I—'

'Our quest is vital,' Elhokar continued. 'We can't afford to let this city fall. We *cannot* afford mistakes.'

'I assure you, Your Majesty,' Kaladin said, 'I don't intend to make mistakes.'

Elhokar glanced at him, and for a moment Kaladin felt he could see the real king. Not because the illusion was failing, but because of the way Elhokar's lips tightened, his brow creased, and his gaze became so intense.

'I wasn't speaking of you, Captain,' the king said quietly. 'I was referring to my own limitations. When I fail this city, I want to make sure *you* are there to protect it.'

Kaladin looked away, ashamed. Had he really just been thinking of how selfish this man was? 'Your Majesty . . .'

'No,' Elhokar said firmly. 'This is a time to be realistic. A king must do whatever he can for the good of his people, and my judgment has proven . . . deficient. Anything I have "accomplished" in life has been handed to me by my father or my uncle. You are here, Captain, to succeed when I fail. Remember that. Open the Oathgate, see that my wife and child are ushered through it to safety, and return with an army to reinforce this city.'

'I'll do my best, Your Majesty.'

'No,' Elhokar said. 'You'll do what I command. Be extraordinary, Captain. Nothing else will suffice.'

Storms. How was it that Elhokar could give a compliment and yet be insulting at the same time? Kaladin felt a *weight* at hearing words that reminded him of his days in Amaram's army, back when people had first started talking about him, expecting things from him.

Those rumors had become a challenge, creating for everyone the notion of a man who was like Kaladin, but at the same time greater than he could ever be. He'd used that fictional man, relied upon him, to equip his team and to get soldiers transferred to his squad. Without it, he'd never have met Tarah. It was useful to have a reputation, so long as it didn't crush you.

The king dropped back farther into the line. They crossed the killing field under the watchful eyes of bowmen atop the wall. It made Kaladin's back itch, though they were Alethi soldiers. He tried to ignore it by focusing on studying the wall as they stepped into its shadow.

Those strata, he thought, *remind me of the tunnels in Urithiru.* Could there be some connection?

He glanced over his shoulder as Adolin came up to him. The disguised prince winced as he looked at Kaladin.

'Hey,' Adolin said. 'Um . . . wow. That's really distracting.'

Storming woman. 'What do you want?'

'I've been thinking,' Adolin said. 'We'll want a place inside the city to hole up, right? We can't follow either of our original plans – we can't simply stride up to the palace, but we don't want to assault it either. Not until we've done a little scouting.'

Kaladin nodded. He hated the prospect of spending too much time in Kholinar. None of the other bridgemen had gotten far enough to swear the Second Ideal, so Bridge Four would be unable to practice with their powers until he returned. At the same time, the shadowed palace was disquieting. They did need to spend a few days gathering intelligence.

'Agreed,' Kaladin said. 'Do you have any ideas for where we can set up?'

'I've got just the place. Run by people I trust, and close enough to the palace to do some scouting, but far enough away not to get caught in . . . whatever is going on there. Hopefully.' He looked concerned.

'What was it like?' Kaladin asked. 'The thing beneath the tower that you and Shallan fought?'

'Shallan has pictures. You should ask her.'

'I've seen them in the reports Dalinar's scribes gave me,' Kaladin said. 'What was it *like*?'

Adolin turned his blue eyes back to their path. The illusion was so real, it was hard to believe it was actually him – but he did *walk* the same way, with that inborn confidence only a lighteyes had.

'It was . . . wrong,' Adolin finally said. 'Haunting. A nightmare made manifest.'

'Kind of like my face?' Kaladin asked.

Adolin glanced at him, then grinned. 'Fortunately, Shallan covered it up for you with that illusion.'

Kaladin found himself smiling. The way Adolin said things like that made it clear he was joking – and not only at your expense. Adolin made you want to laugh with him.

They drew close to the entrance. Though dwarfed by the main city gates, the side doors were wide enough to admit a cart. Unfortunately, the entrance was blocked by soldiers, and a crowd was accumulating, angerspren boiling on the ground around them. The refugees shook their fists and shouted at being barred entrance.

They'd been letting people in earlier. What was happening? Kaladin glanced at Adolin, then gestured with his chin. 'Check it out?'

'We'll go have a look,' Adolin said, turning toward the others of their group. 'Wait here.'

Skar and Drehy stopped, but Elhokar followed as Kaladin and Adolin continued forward – and so did Shallan. Her servants hesitated briefly, then trailed after her. Storms, the command structure in this expedition was going to be a nightmare.

Elhokar imperiously marched forward and barked at people to move out of his way. Reluctantly, they did – a woman with his bearing was not someone to cross. Kaladin exchanged a wearied glance with Adolin, then both fell in beside the king.

'I demand entry,' Elhokar said, reaching the front of the crowd – which had swelled to some fifty or sixty people, with more steadily arriving.

The small group of guards looked over Elhokar, and their captain spoke. 'How many fighting men can you provide for the city defense?'

'None,' Elhokar snapped. 'They are my *personal* guard.'

'Then, Brightness, you should march them *personally* on to the south and try another city.'

'Where?' Elhokar demanded, the sentiment echoed by many in the crowd. 'There are monsters everywhere, Captain.'

'Word is that there are fewer to the south,' the soldier said, pointing. 'Regardless, Kholinar is full to bursting. You won't find sanctuary here. Trust me. Move on. The city—'

'Who is your superior?' Elhokar cut in.

'I serve Highmarshal Azure, of the Wall Guard.'

'Highmarshal Azure? I've never heard of such a man. Do these people look like they can walk farther? I *command* you to let us enter the city.'

'I'm under orders to only let a set number in each day,' the guard said with a sigh. Kaladin recognized that sense of exasperation; Elhokar could bring it out in the most patient of guards. 'We've passed the limit. You'll need to wait until tomorrow.'

People growled, and more angerspren appeared around them.

'It's not that we're callous,' the guard captain called. 'Will you just *listen*? The city is low on food, and we're running out of room in stormshelters.

Every person we add strains our resources further! But the monsters are focused here; if you flee to the south, you can take refuge there, maybe even get to Jah Keved.'

'Unacceptable!' Elhokar said. 'You've gotten these inane orders from that Azure fellow. Who commands him?'

'The highmarshal has no commander.'

'What?' Elhokar demanded. 'What of Queen Aesudan?'

The guard just shook his head. 'Look, are those two men yours?' He pointed at Drehy and Skar, still standing near the back of the crowd. 'They look like good soldiers. If you assign them to the Wall Guard, I'll give you immediate entry, *and* we'll see that you get a grain ration.'

'Not that one though,' another guard said, nodding toward Kaladin. 'He looks sick.'

'Impossible!' Elhokar demanded. 'I need my guards with me at all times.'

'Brightness . . .' the captain said. Storms, but Kaladin empathized with the poor man.

Syl suddenly grew alert, zipping into the sky as a ribbon of light. Kaladin immediately stopped paying attention to Elhokar and the guards. He searched the sky until he saw figures flying toward the wall in a V formation. There were at least twenty Voidbringers, each trailing a plume of dark energy.

Above, soldiers began to scream. The urgent call of drums followed, and the guard captain cursed in response. He and his men charged in through the open doors, then ran toward the nearest stairs leading up to the wall walk.

'In!' Adolin said as other refugees surged forward. He grabbed the king and towed him inside.

Kaladin fought against the press, refusing to be pushed into the city. He instead craned his neck to look upward, watching the Voidbringers hit the wall. Kaladin's angle at the base was terrible for making sense of the action directly above.

A few men got tossed off the wall farther along. Kaladin took a step toward them, but before he could do anything, they crashed to the ground with strikingly loud impacts. Storms! He was shoved farther toward the city by the crowd, and barely restrained himself from drawing in Stormlight.

Steady, he told himself. *The point is to get in without being seen. You would ruin that by flying to the defense of the city?*

But he was supposed to protect.

'Kaladin,' Adolin called, fighting back through the crowd to where Kaladin stood right outside. 'Come on.'

'They're dominating that wall, Adolin. We should go help.'

'Help how?' Adolin said. He leaned in, speaking softly. 'Summon Shardblades and swing them wildly in the air, like a farmer chasing sky-eels? This is merely a raid to test our defenses. It's not a full-on assault.'

Kaladin drew in a breath, then let Adolin pull him into the city. 'Two dozen of the Fused. They could take this city with ease.'

'Not alone,' Adolin said. 'Everyone knows that Shardbearers can't hold ground – it should be the same for Radiants and those Fused. You need soldiers to take a city. Let's move.'

They went inside and met with the others, then moved away from the walls and gates. Kaladin tried to close his ears to the distant shouts of the soldiers. As Adolin had guessed, the raid ended as abruptly as it had begun, the Fused soaring away from the wall after only a few minutes of fighting. Kaladin sighed, watching them go, then steeled himself and followed with the rest as Adolin led them down a wide thoroughfare.

Kholinar was both more impressive and more depressing from the inside. They passed endless side streets packed with tall, three-story homes built like stone boxes. And storms, the guard at the wall had not been exaggerating. People crowded every street. Kholinar didn't have many alleyways; the stone buildings were built right up against each other in long rows. But people sat in the gutters, clinging to blankets and meager possessions. Too many doors were closed; often on nice days like this, people in the warcamps would leave the thick stormdoors and shutters open to the breeze. Not here. They were locked up tightly, for fear of being overwhelmed by refugees.

Shallan's soldiers pulled tight around her, hands carefully on their pockets. They seemed familiar with the underbelly of city life. Fortunately, she'd accepted Kaladin's pointed suggestion and hadn't brought Gaz.

Where are the patrols? Kaladin thought as they walked through curving streets, up and down slopes. With all these people clogging the streets, surely they needed as many men as possible keeping the peace.

He didn't see anything until they passed out of the section of city nearest the gates and entered a more wealthy area. This part was dominated by larger homes, with grounds marked by iron fences anchored into the stone with hardened crem. Behind *those* were guards, but the streets were devoid of anything similar.

Kaladin felt the gaze of the refugees. The wondering. Was it worth robbing him? Did it matter? Did they have food? Fortunately, the spears Skar and Drehy carried – along with the cudgels held by Shallan's two men – seemed enough to deter any would-be robbers.

Kaladin quickened his pace to catch up to Adolin at the front of their little group. 'Is this safehouse of yours close? I don't like the feeling on these streets.'

'It's a way yet,' Adolin said. 'But I agree. Storms, I should have brought a side sword. Who knew I'd be worried about summoning my Blade?'

'Why can't Shardbearers hold a city?' Kaladin asked.

'Basic military theory,' Adolin said. 'Shardbearers do a great job killing people – but what are they going to do against the population of an entire city? Murder everyone who disobeys? They'd get overwhelmed, Shards or not. Those flying Voidbringers will need to bring in the entire army to take the city. But first they'll test the walls, maybe weaken the defenses.'

Kaladin nodded. He liked to think he knew a great deal about warfare, but the truth was, he didn't have the training of a man like Adolin. He'd participated in wars, but he'd never *run* any.

The farther they got from the walls, the better things seemed to be in the city – fewer refugees, more sense of order. They passed a market that was actually open, and inside he finally spotted a policing force: a tight group of men wearing unfamiliar colors.

This area would have looked nice, under other circumstances. Ridges of shalebark along the street, manicured with a variety of colors: some like plates, others like knobby branches reaching upward. Cultivated trees – which rarely pulled in their leaves – sprouted in front of many of the buildings, gripping the ground with thick roots that melded into the stone.

Refugees huddled in family groups. Here, the buildings were built in large square layouts, with windows facing inward and courtyards at the centers. People crowded into these, turning them into improvised shelters. Fortunately, Kaladin saw no obvious starvation, so the city's food stores hadn't given out yet.

'Did you see that?' Shallan asked softly, joining him.

'What?' Kaladin asked, looking over his shoulder.

'Performers in that market over there, dressed in very odd clothing.' Shallan frowned, pointing down an intersecting street as they passed. 'There's another one.'

It was a man dressed all in white, with strips of cloth that streamed and fluttered as he moved. Head down, he stood on a street corner, leaping back and forth from one position to another. When he looked up and met Kaladin's eyes, he was the first stranger that day who didn't immediately look away.

Kaladin watched until a chull pulling a wagon of storm refuse blocked his view. Then, ahead of them, people started clearing the street.

'To the side,' Elhokar said. 'I'm curious about what this could be.'

They joined the crowds pressed up against the buildings, Kaladin shoving his hands in his pack to protect the large number of spheres he had tucked away in a black purse there. Soon, a strange procession came marching down the center of the street. These men and women were also dressed like performers – their clothes augmented with brightly colored strips of red, blue, or green fabric. They walked past, calling out nonsense phrases. Words Kaladin knew, but which didn't belong together.

'What in Damnation is happening in this city?' Adolin muttered.

'This isn't normal?' Kaladin whispered.

'We have buskers and street performers, but nothing like this. Storms. What are they?'

'Spren,' Shallan whispered. 'They're imitating spren. Look, those are like flamespren, and the ones of white and blue with the flowing ribbons – windspren. Emotion spren too. There's pain, that's fear, anticipation . . .'

'So it's a parade,' Kaladin said, frowning. 'But nobody is having any fun.'

The heads of spectators bowed, and people murmured or . . . prayed? Nearby an Alethi refugee – wrapped in rags and holding a sniveling baby in her arms – leaned against a building. A burst of exhaustionspren appeared above her, like jets of dust rising in the air. Only *these* were bright red instead of the normal brown, and seemed *distorted*.

'This is wrong, wrong, *wrong*,' Syl said from Kaladin's shoulder. 'Oh . . . oh, that spren is from *him*, Kaladin.'

Shallan watched the rising not-exhaustionspren with widening eyes.

She took Adolin by the arm. 'Keep us moving,' she hissed.

He started pushing through the crowd toward a corner where they could cut away from the strange procession. Kaladin grabbed the king by the arm, while Drehy, Skar, and Shallan's two guards instinctively formed up around them. The king let Kaladin pull him away, and a good thing too. Elhokar had been fishing in his pocket, perhaps for a sphere to give the exhausted woman. Storms! In the middle of the crowd!

'Not far now,' Adolin said once they had breathing room on the side street. 'Follow me.'

He led them to a small archway, where the buildings had been built around a shared courtyard garden. Of course, refugees had taken shelter there, many of them huddled in blanket tents that were still wet from the storm the day before. Lifespren bobbed among the plants.

Adolin carefully wound his way through all the people to get to the door he wanted, and then knocked. It was the back door, facing the courtyard instead of the street. Was this a rich person's winehouse, perhaps? It seemed more like a home though.

Adolin knocked again, looking worried. Kaladin stepped up beside him, then froze. On the door was a shiny steel plate with engraved numbers. In it, he could see his reflection.

'Almighty above,' Kaladin said, poking at the scars and bulges on his face, some with open sores. Fake teeth jutted from his mouth, and one eye was higher in his head than the other. His hair grew out in patches, and his nose was *tiny*. 'What did you *do* to me, woman?'

'I've recently learned,' Shallan said, 'that a good disguise *can* be memorable, so long as it makes you memorable for the wrong reason. You, Captain, have a way of sticking in people's heads, and I worried you would do so no matter what face you wore. So I enveloped it with something even *more* memorable.'

'I look like some kind of hideous spren.'

'Hey!' Syl said.

The door finally opened, revealing a short, matronly Thaylen woman in an apron and vest. Behind her stood a burly man with a white beard, cut after the Horneater style.

'What?' she said. 'Who are you?'

'Oh!' Adolin said. 'Shallan, I'll need . . .'

Shallan rubbed his face with a towel from her pack, as if to remove makeup – covering the transformation as his face became his own again. Adolin grinned at the woman, and her jaw dropped.

'Prince *Adolin*?' she said. 'Hurry, hurry. Get in here. It's not safe outside!'

She ushered them in and quickly shut the door. Kaladin blinked at the sphere-lit chamber, its walls lined with bolts of cloth and dummies with half-finished coats on them.

'What is this place?' Kaladin asked.

'Well, I figured we'd want someplace safe,' Adolin said. 'We'd need to stay with someone I'd trust with my life, or *more*.' He looked at Kaladin, then gestured toward the woman. 'So I brought us to my tailor.'

I wish to submit my formal protest at the idea of abandoning the
tower. This is an extreme step, taken brashly.

—From drawer 2-22, smokestone

Secrets.

This city was brimming with them. It was *stuffed* with them, so tightly they couldn't help but ooze out.

The only thing for Shallan to do, then, was punch herself in the face.

That was harder than it seemed. She always flinched. *Come on,* she thought, making a fist. With eyes squeezed shut, she braced herself, then smacked her freehand into the side of her head.

It barely hurt; she simply wasn't capable of hitting herself hard enough. Maybe she could get Adolin to do it for her. He was in the back workroom of the tailor's shop. Shallan had excused herself to step into the front showroom, as she figured the others would react poorly to her trying to actively attract a painspren.

She could hear their voices as they interrogated the polite tailor. 'It started with the riots, Your Majesty,' the woman said in response to a question from Elhokar. 'Or maybe before, with the . . . Well, it's complicated. Oh, I can't believe that you're here. I've had Passion for something to happen, true, but to finally . . . I mean . . .'

'Take a deep breath, Yokska,' Adolin said gently. Even his voice was adorable. 'Once you've taken all this in, we can continue.'

Secrets, Shallan thought. *Secrets caused all of this.*

Shallan peeked into the other room. The king, Adolin, Yokska the tailor, and Kaladin sat inside, all wearing their own faces again. They'd sent Kaladin's men – along with Red, Ishnah, and Vathah – off with the tailor's housemaid to prepare the upper rooms and attic to accommodate guests.

Yokska and her husband would be sleeping on pallets in the back room here; naturally, Elhokar had been given their room. Right now, the small group had arranged a circle of wooden chairs under the heedless watch of tailor's dummies wearing a variety of half-finished coats.

Similar finished coats were displayed around the showroom. They were made in bright colors – even brighter than the Alethi wore at the Shattered Plains – with gold or silver thread, shiny buttons, and elaborate embroidery on the large pockets. The coats didn't close at the front except for a few buttons right below the collar, while the sides flared out, then split into tails at the back.

'It was the execution of the ardent, Brightlord,' Yokska said. 'The queen had her hanged, and . . . Oh! It was so gruesome. Blessed Passion, Your Majesty. I don't want to speak ill of your wife! She must not have realized—'

'Just tell us,' Elhokar said. 'Do not fear reprisal. I must know what the city's people think.'

Yokska trembled. She was a small, plump woman who wore her long Thaylen eyebrows curled in twin ringlets, and was probably very fashionable in that skirt and blouse. Shallan lingered in the doorway, curious as to what the tailor had to say.

'Well,' Yokska continued, 'during the riots, the queen . . . the queen basically vanished. We'd get proclamations from her, now and then, but they often didn't make much sense. It all went wrong at the ardent's death. The city was already in an uproar. . . . She wrote such *awful* things, Your Majesty. About the state of the monarchy, and the queen's faith and . . .'

'And Aesudan condemned her to death,' Elhokar said. Lit by only a few spheres at the center of their circle, his face was half shadowed. It was a most intriguing effect, and Shallan took a Memory for later sketching.

'Yes, Your Majesty.'

'It was the dark spren, obviously, who gave the actual order,' Elhokar said. 'The dark spren that is controlling the palace. My wife would never be so imprudent as to publicly execute an ardent during such parlous times.'

'Oh! Yes, of course. Dark spren. In the palace.' Yokska sounded relieved to have a rationale for not blaming the queen.

Shallan considered, then noticed a pair of fabric scissors on a ledge nearby. She snatched them, then ducked back into the showroom. She pulled her skirt to the side, then stabbed herself in the leg with the scissors.

The sharp pain seared up her leg and through her body.

'Mmmm,' Pattern said. 'Destruction. This . . . this is not normal for you, Shallan. Too far.'

She trembled at the pain. Blood welled from the wound, but she pressed her hand against it to limit its spread.

There! That had done it. Painspren appeared around her, as if crawling out of the ground – like little disembodied hands. They looked skinless, made of sinew. Normally they were bright orange, but these were a sickly green. And they were also *wrong* . . . instead of human hands, these seemed to be from some kind of monster – too distorted, with claws jutting from the sinew.

Shallan eagerly took a Memory, still holding her havah skirt up to keep it from the blood.

'Does that not hurt?' Pattern asked, from where he'd moved onto the wall.

'Of course it does,' Shallan said, her eyes watering. 'That was the point.'

'Mmmm . . .' He buzzed, worried, but he needn't have been, as Shallan had what she wanted. Satisfied, she took in a little Stormlight and healed up, then used some cloth from her satchel to wipe the blood from her leg. She rinsed her hands and the cloth in the washroom basin. She was surprised at the running water; she hadn't thought Kholinar had such things.

She took out her drawing pad and returned to the back room's doorway, where she leaned against the jamb, doing a quick sketch of the strange, twisted painspren. Jasnah would tell her to put down her sketchpad and go sit with the others – but Shallan often paid better attention with a sketchpad in her hands. People who didn't draw never seemed to understand that.

'Tell us about the palace,' Kaladin said. 'The ... dark spren, as His Majesty put it.'

Yokska nodded. 'Oh, yes, Brightlord.'

Shallan glanced up to catch Kaladin's reaction at being called Brightlord, but he didn't show one. His illusory disguise was gone – though Shallan had tucked that sketch away, for possible further use. He'd summoned his Blade earlier in the morning, and he now had eyes as blue as any she'd seen. They hadn't faded yet.

'There was that unexpected highstorm,' Yokska continued. 'And after that, the weather went insane. The rains started going in fits and starts. But oh! When that new storm came, the one with the red lightning, it left a *gloom over the palace.* So nasty! Dark times. I suppose ... suppose those haven't ended.'

'Where were the royal guards?' Elhokar said. 'They should have augmented the Watch, restored order during the rioting!'

'The Palace Guard retreated into the palace, Your Majesty,' Yokska said. 'And she ordered the City Watch to barricade into the barracks. They eventually moved to the palace on the queen's orders. They ... haven't been seen since.'

Storms, Shallan thought, continuing her sketch.

'Oh, I guess I'm jumping about, but I forgot!' Yokska continued. 'In the middle of the rioting, a proclamation came from the queen. Oh, Your Majesty. She wanted to execute the city's parshmen! Well, we all thought she must be – I'm sorry – but we thought she must be mad. Poor things. What have they ever done? That's what we thought. We didn't know.

'Well, the queen posted criers all over the city, proclaiming the parshmen to be Voidbringers. And I must say, about that she was right. Yet it was still so strange. She didn't even seem to notice that half the city was rioting!'

'The dark spren,' Elhokar said, making a fist. '*It* must be blamed, not Aesudan.'

'Were there reports of any strange murders?' Adolin asked. 'Murders, or violence, that came in pairs – a man would die, and then a few days later someone else would be killed in the exact same way?'

'No, Brightlord. Nothing ... nothing like that, though there were many who were killed.'

Shallan shook her head. It was a different Unmade here; another ancient spren of Odium. Religion and lore spoke of them vaguely at best, tending to simplistically conflate them into one evil entity. Navani and Jasnah had begun to research them over the last weeks, but they still didn't know very much.

She finished her sketch of the painspren, then did one of the exhaustionspren they'd seen earlier. She'd managed to glimpse some hungerspren around a refugee on their way. Oddly, those didn't look any different. Why?

Need more information, Shallan thought. *More data.* What was the most embarrassing thing she could think of?

'Well,' Elhokar said, 'though we didn't order the parshmen executed, only exiled, at least that order seems to have reached Aesudan. She must have been free enough from the control of the dark forces to heed our words via spanreed.'

Of course, he didn't mention the logical problems. If the tailor was correct about the dark spren arriving during the Everstorm, then Aesudan had executed the ardent on her own – as that had happened before. Likewise, the order to exile the parshmen would also have come before the Everstorm. And who knew if an Unmade could even influence someone like the queen? The spren in Urithiru had mimicked people, not controlled them.

Yokska did seem to be a little scattered in her retelling of events, so maybe Elhokar could be forgiven for mixing up the timeline. Either way, Shallan needed something embarrassing. *When I spilled wine the first time Father gave me some at a dinner party. No . . . no . . . something more . . .*

'Oh!' Yokska said. 'Your Majesty, you should know. The proclamation requiring the execution of the parshmen . . . well, a coalition of important lighteyes didn't follow it. Then, after that terrible storm, the queen started giving other orders, so the lighteyes went to meet with her.'

'Let me guess,' Kaladin said. 'They never came back from the palace.'

'No, Brightlord, they did not.'

How about when I woke and faced Jasnah, after I'd almost died, and she'd discovered that I'd betrayed her?

Surely remembering *that* event would be enough.

No?

Bother.

'So the parshmen,' Adolin said. '*Did* they get executed?'

'No,' Yokska continued. 'Like I said, everyone was concerned with the riots – save for the servants posting the queen's orders, I suppose. The Wall Guard eventually took action. They restored some measure of order in the city, then rounded up the parshmen and exiled them to the plain outside. And then . . .'

'The Everstorm came,' Shallan said, covertly undoing the button on her safehand sleeve.

Yokska seemed to shrink down in her seat. The others fell silent, which provided the perfect opportunity for Shallan. She took a deep breath, then strolled forward, holding her sketchpad as if distracted. She tripped herself over a roll of cloth on the floor, yelped, and tumbled into the center of the ring of chairs.

She ended up sprawled on the floor, skirts up about her waist – and she wasn't even wearing the leggings today. Her safehand bulged out from between the sleeve buttons, poking into the open *right* in front of not just the king, but Kaladin *and* Adolin.

Perfectly, horribly, *incredibly* mortifying. She felt a deep blush come on, and shamespren dropped around her in a wave. Normally, they took the shape of falling red and white flower petals.

These were like pieces of broken glass.

The men, of course, were more distracted by the position she'd gotten herself into. She squawked, managed to take a Memory of the shamespren, and righted herself, blushing furiously and tucking her hand in her sleeve.

That, she thought, *might be the craziest thing you've ever done. Which is saying a lot.*

She grabbed her sketchbook and bustled away, passing Yokska's white-bearded husband – Shallan still hadn't heard him speak a word – standing in the doorway with a tray of wine and tea. Shallan grabbed the darkest cup of wine and downed it in a single gulp, feeling the stares of the men on her back.

'Shallan?' Adolin piped up. 'Um . . .'

'I'mfinethatwasanexperiment,' she said, ducking into the showroom and throwing herself into a seat placed there for customers. *Storms, that was humiliating.*

She could still see partway into the other room. Yokska's husband walked with his silver tray to the group. He stopped by Yokska – though serving the king first would have been the correct protocol – and rested a hand on her shoulder. She put her own on his.

Shallan flipped open her sketchpad, and was pleased to see more shamespren dropping around her. Still glass. She started a drawing, burying herself in it to keep from thinking about what she'd just done.

'So . . .' Elhokar said in the next room. 'We were talking about the Wall Guard. They obeyed the queen's orders?'

'Well, that was around the time that the highmarshal appeared. I've never seen *him* either. He doesn't come down from the wall much. He restored order, so that's good, but the Wall Guard doesn't have the numbers to police the city *and* watch the wall – so they've taken to watching the wall and mostly leaving us to just . . . survive in here.'

'Who rules now?' Kaladin asked.

'Nobody,' Yokska said. 'Various highlords . . . well, they basically seized sections of the city. Some argued that the monarchy had fallen, that the king – I beg pardon, Your Majesty – had abandoned them. But the real power in the city is the Cult of Moments.'

Shallan looked up from her drawing.

'Those people we saw on the street?' Adolin asked. 'Dressed like spren.'

'Yes, Your Highness,' Yokska said. 'I don't . . . I don't know what to tell you. Spren look strange sometimes in the city, and people think it has to do with the queen, the weird storm, the parshmen . . . They're scared. Some have started claiming they can see a new world coming, a truly strange new world. One ruled by spren.

'The Vorin church has declared the Cult of Moments a heresy, but so many of the ardents were in the palace when it grew dark. Most of those remaining took refuge with one of the highlords who claimed small sections of Kholinar. Those are increasingly isolated, ruling their districts on their own. And then . . . and then there are the fabrials. . . .'

Fabrials. Shallan scrambled to her feet and stuck her head into the next room. 'What about the fabrials?'

'If you use a fabrial,' Yokska said, 'of any sort – from spanreed, to warmer, to painrial – you'll draw *them*. Screaming yellow spren that ride the wind like streaks of terrible light. They shout and swirl about you. That then usually brings the creatures from the sky, the ones with the loose clothing and long spears. They seize the fabrial, and sometimes kill the one trying to use it.'

Storms . . . Shallan thought.

'Have you seen this?' Kaladin asked. 'What did the spren look like? You heard them speak?'

Shallan glanced at Yokska, who had sunk down farther in her seat. 'I think . . . maybe we should give the good tailor a break,' Shallan noted. 'We've shown up on her doorstep out of nowhere, stolen her bedroom, and are now interrogating her. I'm sure the world won't fall apart if we let her have a few minutes to drink her tea and recover.'

The woman looked at Shallan with an expression of pure gratitude.

'Storms!' Adolin said, leaping to his feet. 'Of course you're right, Shallan. Yokska, forgive us, and thank you *so* much for—'

'No need for thanks, Your Highness,' she said. 'Oh, I *did* have Passion that help would come. And here it is! But if it pleases the king, a little rest . . . Yes, a little rest would be *much* appreciated.'

Kaladin grunted and nodded, and Elhokar waved a hand in a way that wasn't *quite* dismissive. More just . . . self-absorbed. The three men left Yokska to rest and joined Shallan in the showroom, where light from the setting sun streamed between the drapes on the front windows. Those would normally be open to show off the tailor's creations, but no doubt they'd lately spent most of their time closed.

The four gathered together to digest what they'd discovered. 'Well?' Elhokar asked, speaking – for once – in a soft, thoughtful tone.

'I want to know what's going on with the Wall Guard,' Kaladin said. 'Their leader . . . none of you have heard of him?'

'Highmarshal Azure?' Adolin asked. 'No. But I've been away for years. There are bound to be many officers in the city who were promoted while the rest of us were at war.'

'Azure might be the one feeding the city,' Kaladin said. 'Someone is providing grain. This place would have eaten itself to starvation without some source of food.'

'At least we've learned something,' Shallan said. 'We know why the spanreeds cut off.'

'The Voidbringers are trying to isolate the city,' Elhokar said. 'They locked down the palace to prevent anyone from using the Oathgate, then cut off communication via spanreeds. They're stalling until they can gather a large enough army.'

Shallan shivered. She held up her sketchpad, showing them the drawings she'd done. 'Something *is* wrong with the city's spren.'

The men nodded as they saw her drawings, though only Kaladin seemed to catch what she'd been doing. He looked from the drawing of the shamespren to her hand, then raised an eyebrow at her.

She shrugged. *Well, it worked, didn't it?*

'Prudence,' the king said softly. 'We mustn't simply rush in and fall to whatever darkness seized the palace, but we also can't afford to be inactive.'

He stood up straighter. Shallan had grown so accustomed to seeing Elhokar as an afterthought – a fault of the way Dalinar, increasingly, had been treating him. But there was an earnest determination to him, and yes, even a regal bearing.

Yes, she thought, taking another Memory of Elhokar. *Yes, you are king. And you* can *live up to your father's legacy.*

'We must have a plan,' Elhokar said. 'I would gladly hear your wisdom on this matter, Windrunner. How should we approach this?'

'Honestly, I'm not sure we should. Your Majesty, it might be best to catch the next highstorm, return to the tower, and report back to Dalinar. He can't reach us with his visions here, and one of the Unmade could very well be beyond our mission's parameters.'

'We don't need Dalinar's permission to act,' Elhokar said.

'I didn't mean—'

'What is my uncle going to do, Captain? Dalinar won't know any more than we will. We either do something about Kholinar ourselves now, or give the city, the Oathgate, *and* my family up to the enemy.'

Shallan agreed, and even Kaladin nodded slowly.

'We should at least scout the city and get a better feel for things,' Adolin noted.

'Yes,' Elhokar said. 'A king needs accurate information to act correctly. Lightweaver, could you take on the look of a messenger woman?'

'Of course,' Shallan said. 'Why?'

'Let us say I were to dictate a letter to Aesudan,' the king said, 'then seal it with the royal seal. You could act the part of a messenger who had come personally from the Shattered Plains, traveling through great hardship to reach the queen to deliver my words. You could present yourself at the palace, and see how the guards there react.'

'That's . . . not a bad idea,' Kaladin said. He sounded surprised.

54

'It could be dangerous,' Adolin said. 'The guards might bring her into the palace itself.'

'I'm the only one here who has confronted one of the Unmade directly,' Shallan said. 'I'm most likely to be able to spot their influence, and I have the resources to get out. I agree with His Majesty – eventually someone must go into the palace and see what is happening there. I promise to back off quickly if my gut says something is happening.'

'Mmmm . . .' Pattern said unexpectedly from her skirts. He generally preferred to remain silent when others were near. 'I will watch and warn. We will be careful.'

'See if you can assess the state of the Oathgate,' the king said. 'Its platform is part of the palace complex, but there are ways up other than through the palace itself. The best thing for the city might be to go in quietly, activate it, and bring in reinforcements, *then* decide how to rescue my family. But do reconnaissance only, for now.'

'And the rest of us just sit around tonight?' Kaladin complained.

'Waiting and trusting those whom you have empowered is the soul of kingship, Windrunner,' Elhokar said. 'But I suspect that Brightness Shallan would not object to your company, and I'd rather have someone watching to help get her out, in an emergency.'

He wasn't exactly correct; she *would* object to Kaladin's presence. Veil wouldn't want him looking over her shoulder, and Shallan wouldn't want him asking questions about that persona.

However, she could find no reasonable objection. 'I want to get a feel for the city,' she said, looking to Kaladin. 'Have Yokska scribe the king's letter, then meet me. Adolin, is there a good spot we could find each other?'

'The grand steps up to the palace complex, maybe?' he said. 'They're impossible to miss, and have a little square out in front of them.'

'Excellent,' Shallan said. 'I'll be wearing a black hat, Kaladin. You can wear your own face, I suppose, now that we're past the Wall Guard. But that slave brand . . .' She reached up to create an illusion to make it vanish from his forehead.

He caught the hand. 'No need. I'll keep my hair down over it.'

'It peeks out,' she said.

'Then let it. In a city full of refugees, nobody is going to care.'

She rolled her eyes, but didn't push. He was probably right. In that uniform, he'd probably just be taken for a slave someone bought, then put in their house guard. Even though the *shash* brand *was* odd.

The king went to prepare his letter, and Adolin and Kaladin stayed in the showroom to talk quietly about the Wall Guard. Shallan headed up the steps. Her own room was a smaller one on the second floor.

Inside were Red, and Vathah, and Ishnah the assistant spy, chatting quietly.

'How much did you eavesdrop on?' Shallan asked them.

'Not much,' Vathah said, thumbing over his shoulder. 'We were too busy watching Ishnah ransack the tailor's bedroom to see if she was hiding anything.'

'Tell me you didn't make a mess.'

'No mess,' Ishnah promised. 'And nothing to report either. The woman might actually be as boring as she seems. The boys did learn some good search procedures though.'

Shallan walked past the small guest bed and looked out the window at a daunting view down a city street. So many homes, so many people. Intimidating.

Fortunately, Veil wouldn't see it that way. There was only one problem.

I can't work with this team, she thought, *without them eventually asking questions.* This Kholinar mission would bring it to a head, as Veil hadn't flown with them.

She'd been dreading this. And . . . kind of . . . anticipating it? 'I need to tell them,' she whispered.

'Mmm,' Pattern said. 'It's good. Progress.'

Rather, she'd been backed into a corner. Still, it had to be done eventually. She walked to her pack and removed a white coat and a hat, which folded up on its side. 'Some privacy, boys,' she said to Vathah and Red. 'Veil needs to get dressed.'

They looked from the coat to Shallan, then back. Red slapped the side of his head and laughed. 'You're *kidding*. Well, I feel like an idiot.'

She'd expected Vathah to feel betrayed. Instead he nodded – as if this made perfect sense. He saluted her with one finger, then the two men retreated.

Ishnah lingered. Shallan had – after some debate – decided to bring the woman. Mraize had vetted her, and in the end, Veil needed the training.

'You don't look surprised about this,' Shallan said as she started changing.

'I was suspicious when Veil . . . when you told me to go on this mission,' she said. 'Then I saw the illusions, and guessed.' She paused. 'I had it reversed. I thought Brightness Shallan was the persona. But the spy – *that's* the false identity.'

'Wrong,' Shallan said. 'They're both equally false.' Once dressed, she flipped through her sketchbook and found a drawing of Lyn in her scouting uniform. Perfect. 'Go tell Brightlord Kaladin I'm already out and exploring, and that he should meet me in about an hour.'

She climbed out the window and dropped one story to the ground, relying on her Stormlight to keep her legs from breaking. Then she struck off down the street.

I returned to the tower to find squabbling children, instead of proud knights. That's why I hate this place. I'm going to go chart the hidden undersea caverns of Aimia; find my maps in Akinah.

—From drawer 16-16, amethyst

V eil enjoyed being in a proper city again, even if it was half feral. Most cities lived on the very edge of civilization. Everyone talked about towns and villages out in the middle of nowhere as if they were uncivilized, but she'd found people in those places pleasant, even-tempered, and comfortable with their quieter way of life.

Not in cities. Cities balanced on the edge of sustainability, always one step from starvation. When you pressed so many people together, their cultures, ideas, and stenches rubbed off on one another. The result wasn't civilization. It was contained chaos, pressurized, bottled up so it couldn't escape.

There was a *tension* to cities. You could breathe it, feel it in every step. Veil loved it.

Once a few streets from the tailor's shop, she pulled down the brim of her hat and held up a page from her sketchbook as if consulting a map. This covered her as she breathed out Stormlight, transforming her features and hair to match those of Veil, instead of Shallan.

No spren came, screaming to warn of what she'd done. So Lightweaving was different from using fabrials. She'd been fairly certain it was safe, as they'd worn disguises into the city, but she'd wanted to be away from the tailor's shop in case.

Veil strolled down the thoroughfare, long coat rippling around her calves. She decided immediately that she liked Kholinar. She liked how the city rolled across its hills, a lumpy blanket of buildings. She liked how it smelled of Horneater spices in one gust of wind, then of Alethi steamed crabs in the next. Admittedly, those probably weren't proper crabs today, but cremlings.

That part she didn't like. These poor people. Even in this more affluent area, she could barely walk a quarter block without having to weave around huddles of people. The midblock courtyards were clogged with what had probably been normal villagers not long ago, but who were now impoverished wretches.

There wasn't much wheeled traffic on the streets. Some palanquins ringed by guards. No carriages. Life, however, did not stop for a war – or even for a second Aharietiam. There was water to draw, clothes to clean. Women's work mostly, as she could see from the large groups of men standing around. With no one really in charge in the city, who would pay men to work forges? To clean streets or chip crem? Even worse, in a city this size, much of the menial labor would have been done by parshmen. Nobody would be eager to leap in to take their place.

The bridgeboy is right though, Veil thought, loitering at an intersection. *The city* is *still being fed.* A place like Kholinar could consume itself quickly, once the food or water ran out.

No, cities were not civilized places. No more than a whitespine was domesticated just because it had a collar around its neck.

A small group of cultists dressed as rotspren limped down the street, the wet red paint on their clothing evocative of blood. Shallan considered these people extreme and alarming, probably crazy, but Veil wasn't convinced. They were too theatrical – and there were too many of them – for all to be truly deranged. This was a fad. A way of dealing with unexpected events and giving some shape to lives that had been turned upside down.

That didn't mean they weren't dangerous. A group of people all trying to impress one another was always more dangerous than the lone psychopath. So she gave the cultists a wide berth.

Over the next hour, Veil surveyed the city while wending her way in the general direction of the palace. The area with the tailor's shop was the most normal. It had a good functioning market, which she intended to investigate further when not pressed for time. It had parks, and though these had been appropriated by the crowds, the people in them were lively. Family groups – even communities transplanted from outer villages – doing the best they could.

She passed bunkerlike mansions of the wealthy. Several had been ransacked: gates broken down, window shutters cracked, grounds draped with blankets or shanties. Some lighteyed families, it seemed, hadn't maintained enough guards to withstand the riots.

Anytime Veil's path took her closer to the city walls, she entered sections of the city that were the most cramped, and the most despondent. Refugees just sitting on the streets. Vacant eyes, ragged clothing. People without homes or community.

The closer she drew to the palace though, the emptier the city became. Even the unfortunates who populated the streets near the walls – where the Voidbringers were raiding – knew to stay away from this area.

That made the homes of the wealthy here in the palace district seem . . . out of place. In normal times, living close to the palace would have been a privilege, and every large compound here had private walls that sheltered delicate gardens and ostentatious windows. But now, Veil felt the wrongness of the area as a prickling sensation on her skin. The families living here must have felt it, but they stubbornly remained in their mansions.

She peeked through the iron gate of one such mansion, and found soldiers on sentry duty: men in dark uniforms whose colors and heraldry she couldn't discern. In fact, when one glanced at her, she couldn't make out his eyes. It was probably just a trick of the light, but . . . storms. The soldiers had a wrongness about them; they moved oddly, rushing in bursts, like prowling predators. They didn't stop to talk to each other as they passed.

She backed away and continued down the street. The palace was right ahead. Straight on in front of it were the wide steps where she'd meet Kaladin, but she had some time left. She slipped into a park nearby, the first she'd seen in the city that wasn't clogged with refugees. Towering stumpweight trees – bred over time for height and spread of leaves – gave a shadowed canopy.

Away from potential prying eyes, she used Stormlight to overlay Veil's features and clothing with those of Lyn. A stronger, more sturdy build, a blue scout's uniform. The hat became a black rain hat, of the type often worn during the Weeping.

She left the park as Veil playing a part. She tried to keep this distinction sharp in her mind. She was *still Veil*. Merely in disguise.

Now, to see what she could find out about the Oathgate. The palace was built on a rise overlooking the city, and she slipped through the streets to its eastern side, where she indeed found the Oathgate platform. It was covered in buildings, and was as high as the palace – maybe twenty feet up. It connected to the main palace by a covered walkway that rested atop a small wall.

They built that walkway right over the ramp, she thought with displeasure. The only other paths up onto the platform were sets of steps cut into the rock, and those were guarded by people in spren costumes.

Veil watched from a safe distance. So the cult was involved in this somehow? Above on the platform, smoke trailed from a large fire, and Veil could hear sounds rising from that direction. Were those . . . screams?

The whole place was unnerving, and she shivered, then retreated. She found Kaladin leaning against the base of a statue in a square before the palace steps. Soulcast out of bronze, the statue depicted a figure in Shardplate rising as if from waves.

'Hey,' she said softly. 'It's me. Do you like the boots on this outfit?' She raised her foot.

'Do we have to keep bringing that up?'

'I was giving you a passcode, bridgeboy,' she said. 'To prove I'm who I say I am.'

'Lyn's face made that clear,' he said, handing her the king's letter, inside a sealed envelope.

I like him, Veil thought. An . . . odd thought, in how much stronger that feeling was to Veil than it had been to Shallan. *I like that brooding sense he has about him, those dangerous eyes.*

Why did Shallan focus so much on Adolin? He was nice, but also bland. You couldn't tease him without feeling bad, but Kaladin, he glared at you in the most satisfying of ways.

The part of her that was still Shallan, deep down, was bothered by this line of thinking. So instead, Veil turned her attention to the palace. It was a grand structure, but more like a fortress than she'd pictured. Very Alethi. The bottom floor was a massive rectangle, with the short side facing toward the storm. The upper levels were successively thinner, and a dome rose from the center of the building.

From up close, she couldn't make out exactly where the sunlight stopped and the shadow began. Indeed, the air of darkness felt ... different from how Urithiru had when the dark spren was there. She kept feeling that she wasn't seeing it all. When she'd glance away and look back, she could *swear* that something was different. Had that planter moved, the one running along the grand entry steps? Or ... had that door always been painted blue?

She took a Memory, then looked away and back, and took another Memory. She wasn't certain what good it would do, as she'd had trouble drawing the palace earlier.

'Do you see them?' Kaladin whispered. 'The soldiers, standing between the pillars?'

She hadn't. The front of the palace – at the top of the long set of stairs – was set with pillars. Looking closer into the shadows, she saw men in there, gathered beneath the overhang supported by the columns. They stood like statues, their spears upright, never moving.

Anticipationspren rose around Veil, and she jumped. While two of the spren looked normal – like flat streamers – the others were wrong. They waved long, thin tendrils that looked like lashes to whip a servant.

She shared a glance with Kaladin, then took a Memory of the spren.

'Shall we?' Kaladin asked.

'I shall. You stay here.'

He glanced at her.

'If something goes wrong, I'd rather you be ready out here to come in and help. Best not to potentially get us both stuck in the grip of one of the Unmade. I'll shout if I need you.'

'And if you can't shout? Or if I can't hear you?'

'I'll send Pattern.'

Kaladin folded his arms, but nodded. 'Fine. Just be careful.'

'I'm always careful.'

He raised an eyebrow at her, but he was thinking of Shallan. Veil wasn't as foolhardy.

The climb up those steps seemed to take far too long. For a moment she could have sworn they stretched into the sky, toward the eternal void. And then she was atop them, standing before those pillars.

A group of guards approached her.

'I have a message from the king!' she said, holding it up. 'To be delivered directly to Her Majesty. I've traveled all the way from the Shattered Plains!'

The guards didn't break stride. One opened a door into the palace while the others formed up behind Veil, prodding her forward. She swallowed, sweat chilling her brow, and let them force her to that door. That maw . . .

She walked into a grand entryway, marked by marble and a brilliant sphere chandelier. No Unmade. No darkness waiting to consume her. She breathed out, though she *could* feel something. That phantom eeriness was indeed stronger here. The *wrongness*. She jumped when one of the soldiers put his hand on her shoulder.

A man in a captainlord's knots left a small room beside the grand chamber. 'What is this?'

'Messenger,' a soldier said. 'From the Shattered Plains.' Another plucked the letter from her fingers and handed it toward the captainlord. She could see their eyes now, and they seemed ordinary – darkeyed grunts, lighteyed officer.

'Who was your commander there?' the captain asked her, looking over the letter, then squinting at the seal. 'Well? I served on the Plains for a few years.'

'Captain Colot,' she said, naming the officer who had joined the Windrunners. He wasn't Lyn's actual commander, but he did have scouts in his team.

The captainlord nodded, then handed the letter to one of his men. 'Take it to Queen Aesudan.'

'I was supposed to deliver it in person,' Veil said, though she itched to be out of this place. To flee madly, if she were being honest. She had to stay. Whatever she learned here would be of—

One of the soldiers ran her through.

It happened so quickly, she was left gaping at the sword blade protruding through her chest – wet with her blood. He yanked the weapon back out, and Veil collapsed with a groan. She reached for Stormlight, by instinct.

No . . . no, do as . . . as Jasnah did . . .

Pretend. Feign. She stared up at the men in horror, in betrayal, pain-spren rising around her. One soldier jogged off with the message, but the captain merely walked back toward his post. Not one of the rest said a word as she bled all over the floor, her vision fading . . .

She let her eyes close, then took in a short, sharp breath of Stormlight. Just a tiny amount, which she kept within, holding her breath. Enough to keep her alive, heal the wounds inside . . .

Pattern. Please don't go. Don't do anything. Don't hum, don't buzz. Quiet. Stay quiet.

One of the soldiers picked her up and slung her over his shoulder, then carried her through the palace. She dared cracking a single eye, and found the wide hallway here was lined with dozens upon dozens of soldiers. Just . . . standing there. They were alive; they'd cough, or shift position. Some leaned back against the wall, but they all kind of stayed in place. Human, but *wrong.*

The guard carrying her passed a floor-to-ceiling mirror rimmed in a fancy bronze frame. In it, she glimpsed the guard with Lyn thrown over his shoulder. And beyond that, deep within the mirror, something turned – the normal image fading – and looked toward Shallan with a sudden and surprised motion. It looked like a shadow of a person, only with white spots for eyes.

Veil quickly closed her peeking eye. Storms, what had *that* been?

Don't shift. Stay perfectly still. Don't even breathe. Stormlight allowed her to survive without air.

The guard carried her down some steps, then opened a door and walked down a few more. He dropped her none too gently onto the stone and tossed her hat on top of her, then turned and left, closing a door behind him.

Veil waited as long as she could stand before opening her eyes and finding herself in darkness. She took a breath, and nearly choked at the rotten, musty stench. Dreading and suspecting what she might find, she drew in Stormlight and made herself glow.

She'd been dropped beside a small line of corpses. There were seven of them, three male and four female, wearing fine clothing – but covered in rotspren, their flesh chewed at by cremlings.

Holding in a scream, she scrambled to her feet. Perhaps ... perhaps these were some of those lighteyes who'd come to the palace to talk to the queen?

She snatched her hat and scrambled to the steps. This was the wine cellar, a stone vault cut right into the rock. At the door she finally heard Pattern, who had been talking, though his voice had seemed distant.

'Shallan? I felt what you told me. Don't go. Shallan, are you well? Oh! The destruction. You destroy some things, but seeing others destroyed upsets you. Hmmmm. . . .' He seemed pleased to have figured it out.

She focused on his voice, something familiar. Not the memory of a sword protruding from her own chest, not the callous way she'd been dumped here and left to rot, not the line of corpses with exposed bones, haunted faces, chewed-out eyes ...

Don't think. Don't see it.

She shoved it all away, and rested her forehead against the door. Then she carefully eased it open and found an empty stone hallway beyond, with more steps leading upward.

There were too many soldiers that way. She put on a new illusion, of a servant woman from her sketchbook. Maybe that would be less suspicious. It covered the blood, at least.

She didn't head back upstairs, but instead took a separate path farther into the tunnels. This turned out to be the Kholin mausoleum, which was lined with another kind of corpse: old kings turned to statues. Their stone eyes chased her down empty tunnels until she found a door that, judging from the sunlight underneath, led out into the city.

'Pattern,' she whispered. 'Check for guards outside.'

He hummed and slid under the door, then returned a moment later. 'Mmm . . . There are two.'

'Go back, then along the wall slowly to the right,' she said, infusing him.

He did so, sliding under the door. A sound she'd created rose from him as he moved away, imitating the captainlord's voice from above, calling for the guards. It wasn't perfect, as she hadn't sketched the man, but it seemed to work as she heard booted feet move off.

She slipped out, and found herself at the base of the rise that the palace sat upon, a cliff of some twenty feet above her. The guards were distracted, walking to her right, so Veil slipped onto a street nearby, then ran for a short time, thankful to finally have a chance to work off some of her energy.

She collapsed in the shadow of a hollow building, with the windows broken open and the door missing. Pattern scooted along the ground nearby, joining her. The guards didn't seem to have noticed her.

'Go find Kaladin,' she said to Pattern. 'Bring him here. Warn him that soldiers might be watching him from the palace, and they might come for him.'

'Mmmm.' Pattern slid away from her. She huddled against herself, back to a stone wall, her coat still covered in blood. After a nerve-racking wait, Kaladin stepped onto the street, then hurried up to her. 'Storms!' he said, kneeling beside her. Pattern slipped off his coat, humming happily. 'Shallan, what happened to you?'

'Well,' she said, 'as a connoisseur of things that have killed me, I think a *sword* happened.'

'Shallan . . .'

'The evil force that rules the palace did not think highly of someone coming with a letter from the king.' She smiled at him. 'You could say, um, it made that point quite clear.'

Smile. I need you to smile.

I need what happened to be all right. Something that can simply roll off me. Please.

'Well . . .' Kaladin said. 'I'm glad we . . . took a stab at this anyway.' He smiled.

It was all right. Just another day, another infiltration. He helped her to her feet, then looked to check on her wound, and she slapped his hand. The cut was *not* in an appropriate location.

'Sorry,' he said. 'Surgeon's instincts. Back to the hideout?'

'Yes, please,' she said. 'I'd rather not be killed again today. It's quite draining. . . .'

BINDER OF GODS

The disagreements between the Skybreakers and the Windrunners have grown to tragic levels. I plead with any who hear this to recognize you are not so different as you think.

—From drawer 27-19, topaz

Dalinar reached into the dark stone shaft where he'd hidden the assassin's Honorblade. It was still there; he felt the hilt under the lip of stone.

He expected to feel more upon touching it. Power? A tingling? This was a weapon of Heralds, a thing so ancient that common Shardblades were young by comparison. Yet, as he slipped it free and stood up, the only thing he felt was his own anger. This was the weapon of the assassin who had killed his brother. The weapon used to terrorize Roshar, murder the lords of Jah Keved and Azir.

It was shortsighted of him to see such an ancient weapon merely as the sword of the Assassin in White. He stepped out into the larger room next door, then regarded the sword in the light of the spheres he had placed on a stone slab there. Sinuous and elegant, this was the weapon of a king. Jezerezeh'Elin.

'There are some who assumed you were one of the Heralds,' Dalinar noted to the Stormfather, who rumbled in the back of his mind. 'Jezerezeh, Herald of Kings, Father of Storms.'

Men say many foolish things, the Stormfather replied. *Some name Kelek Stormfather, others Jezrien. I am neither of them.*

'But Jezerezeh *was* a Windrunner.'

He was before Windrunners. He was Jezrien, a man whose powers bore no name. They were simply him. The Windrunners were named only after Ishar founded the orders.

'Ishi'Elin,' Dalinar said. 'Herald of Luck.'

Or of mysteries, the Stormfather said, *or of priests. Or of a dozen other things, as men dubbed him. He is now as mad as the rest. More, perhaps.*

Dalinar lowered the Honorblade, looking eastward toward the Origin. Even through the stone walls, he knew that was where to find the Stormfather. 'Do you know where they are?'

I have told you. I do not see all. Only glimpses in the storms.

'Do you *know* where they *are?*'

Only one, he said with a rumble. *I . . . have seen Ishar. He curses me at night, even as he names himself a god. He seeks death. His own. Perhaps that of every man.*

It clicked. 'Stormfather!'

Yes?

'Oh. Uh, that was a curse. . . . Never mind. Tezim, the god-priest of Tukar? Is it him? Ishi, Herald of Luck, is the man who has been waging war against Emul?'

Yes.

'For what purpose?'

He is insane. Do not look for meaning in his actions.

'When . . . when were you thinking of informing me of this?'

When you asked. When else would I speak of it?

'When you thought of it!' Dalinar said. 'You know things that are important, Stormfather!'

He just rumbled his reply.

Dalinar took a deep breath, trying to calm himself. Spren did not think like men. Anger would not change what the Stormfather told him. But what would?

'Did you know about my powers?' Dalinar asked. 'Did you know that I could heal the stone?'

I knew it once you did it, the Stormfather said. *Yes, once you did it, I always knew.*

'Do you know what else I can do?'

Of course. Once you discover it, I will know.

'But—'

Your powers will come when you are ready for them, not before, the Stormfather said. *They cannot be hurried or forced.*

But do not look toward the powers of others, even those who share your Surges. Their lot is not yours, and their powers are small, petty things. What you did in reknitting those statues was a mere trifle, a party trick.

Yours is the power Ishar once held. Before he was Herald of Luck, they called him Binder of Gods. He was the founder of the Oathpact. No Radiant is capable of more than you. Yours is the power of Connection, of joining men and worlds, minds and souls. Your Surges are the greatest of all, though they will be impotent if you seek to wield them for mere battle.

The words washed over Dalinar, seeming to press him backward with their force. When the Stormfather was done, Dalinar found himself out of breath, a headache coming on. He reflexively drew in Stormlight to heal it, and the small chamber dimmed. That stopped the pain, but it did nothing for his cold sweat.

'Are there others like me out there?' he finally asked.

Not right now, and there can ever be only three. One for each of us.

'Three?' Dalinar said. 'Three spren who make Bondsmiths. You . . . and Cultivation are two?'

The Stormfather actually laughed. *You would have a difficult time making* her *your spren. I should like to see you try it.*

'Then who?'

My siblings need not concern you.

They seemed of compelling concern, but Dalinar had learned when to avoid pressing an issue. That would only cause the spren to withdraw.

Dalinar took the Honorblade in a firm grip, then collected his spheres, one of which had gone dun. 'Have I ever asked how you renew these?' Dalinar held up the sphere, inspecting the ruby at the center. He'd seen these loose, and had always been surprised by how small they actually were. The glass made them look far larger.

Honor's power, during a storm, is concentrated in one place, the Stormfather said. *It pierces all three realms and brings Physical, Cognitive, and*

Spiritual together momentarily in one. The gemstones, exposed to the wonder of the Spiritual Realm, are lit by the infinite power there.

'Could you renew this sphere, now?'

I . . . do not know. He sounded intrigued. *Hold it forth.*

Dalinar did so, and felt something happen, a tugging on his insides, like the Stormfather straining against their bond. The sphere remained dun.

It is not possible, the Stormfather said. *I am close to you, but the power is not – it still rides the storm.*

That was far more than he usually got from the Stormfather. He hoped he could remember it exactly to repeat to Navani – of course, if the Stormfather was listening, he'd correct Dalinar's mistakes. The Stormfather hated to be misquoted.

Dalinar stepped out into the hallway to meet Bridge Four. He held up the Honorblade – a powerful, world-changing artifact. But, like the Shardblades modeled after it, the weapon was useless if he left it hidden.

'This,' he said to the men of Bridge Four, 'is the Honorblade your captain recovered.'

The twenty-odd men gathered closer, their curious faces reflecting in the metal.

'Anyone who holds this,' Dalinar said, 'will immediately gain the powers of a Windrunner. Your captain's absence is interrupting your training. Perhaps this, though only one can use it at a time, can mitigate that.'

They gaped at the weapon, so Dalinar held it out toward Kaladin's first lieutenant – the bearded older bridgeman named Teft.

Teft reached out, then drew his hand back. 'Leyten,' he barked. 'You're our storming armorer. You take the thing.'

'Me?' a stocky bridgeman said. 'That's not armor.'

'Close enough.'

'I . . .'

'Airsick lowlanders,' Rock the Horneater said, shoving forward and taking the weapon. 'Your soup is cold. That is idiom for "You are all stupid."'

The Horneater hefted it, curious, and his eyes bled to a glassy blue.

'Rock?' Teft asked. 'You? Holding a weapon?'

'I am not going to swing this thing,' Rock said, rolling his eyes. 'I will keep him safe. This is all.'

'It's a Shardblade,' Dalinar warned. 'You've trained on those, correct?'

'We have, sir,' Teft said. 'Doesn't mean one of this lot won't storming cut their own feet off. But . . . I suppose we can use this to heal it if they do. Sigzil, come up with a rotation so we can practice.'

Heal . . . Dalinar felt stupid. He'd missed it again. Anyone holding this Blade had the powers of a Radiant. Did that mean they could use Stormlight to heal themselves? If so, that might be a valuable extra use of the weapon.

'Don't let anyone know you have this,' Dalinar told them. 'I assume you can learn to dismiss and summon it like an ordinary Shardblade. See what you can discover, then report to me.'

'We'll put it to good use, sir,' Teft promised.

'Good.' The clock fabrial on his forearm dinged, and Dalinar stifled a sigh. She'd learned to make it ding? 'If you'll all excuse me, I have to prepare for an appointment with an emperor a thousand miles away.'

⁘

A short time later, Dalinar stood on his balcony. Hands clasped behind his back, he stared out toward the Oathgate transport platforms.

'I did a great deal of business with the Azish when I was younger,' Fen said from behind him. 'This might not work, but it is a *much* better plan than traditional Alethi strutting.'

'I don't like him going alone,' Navani replied.

'By all reports,' Fen said dryly, 'he got stabbed through the chest, lifted a stone roughly the weight of ten men, then started putting my city back together one rock at a time. I think he'll be fine.'

'No amount of Stormlight will help if they simply imprison him,' Navani said. 'We could be sending him to become a hostage.'

They were arguing for his benefit. He had to understand the risks. And he did. He walked over to give Navani a light kiss. He smiled at her, then turned and extended his hand toward Fen, who gave him a paper packet, like a large envelope.

'This is it, then?' he asked. 'All three are in here?'

'They're marked with appropriate glyphs,' Navani said. 'And the spanreed is inside too. They've promised to speak in Alethi during the meeting – you won't have an interpreter from our side, as you insist on going alone.'

71

'I do,' Dalinar said, starting toward the door. 'I want to try Fen's suggestion.'

Navani quickly rose and took his arm with her freehand.

'I assure you,' he said. 'I will be safe.'

'No you won't. But this is no different from a hundred other times you've ridden off to battle. Here.' She handed him a small box sheathed in cloth.

'Fabrial?'

'Lunch,' she said. 'There's no telling when those people will feed you.'

She'd wrapped it in a glyphward. Dalinar cocked his eyebrow at it, and she shrugged. *Can't hurt, right?* that seemed to say. She took him in an embrace, held on an extra moment – more than another Alethi might – then stepped back. 'We'll be watching the spanreed. One hour with no communication, and we're coming for you.'

He nodded. He couldn't write to them of course, but he could flip the reed on and off to send signals, an old general's trick for when you lacked a scribe.

A short time later, he strode out onto Urithiru's western plateau. Crossing it on his way to the Oathgate, he passed men marching in formations, sergeants shouting orders, runners carrying messages. Two of his Shardbearers – Rust and Serugiadis, men who had the Plate only – practiced with massive Shardbows, launching thick arrows hundreds of yards toward a large straw target that Kaladin had placed for them on a nearby mountainside.

A significant number of the common soldiers sat around holding spheres, staring at them intently. Word had spread that Bridge Four was recruiting. He'd lately noticed numerous men in the hallways holding a sphere 'for luck.' Dalinar even passed a group out here who were talking about *swallowing* spheres.

The Stormfather rumbled with displeasure. *They go about this backward. Foolish men. They can't draw in Light and become Radiant; they first must be approaching Radiance, and look for Light to fulfill the promise.*

Dalinar barked at the men to get back to training, and to *not* swallow any spheres. They obeyed with a scrambling rush, shocked to find the Blackthorn looming over them. He shook his head, then continued. His path, unfortunately, took him through a mock battle. Two blocks of spearmen pressed against each other on the plateau, straining and grunting, training to hold their formations under stress. Though they carried blunt practice spears, this was mostly shield work.

Dalinar saw the warning signs of things going too far. Men were shouting with real acrimony, and angerspren were boiling at their feet. One of the lines wavered, and instead of pulling back, their opponents rammed their shields against them repeatedly.

Green and white on one side, black and maroon on the other. Sadeas and Aladar. Dalinar cursed and approached the men, shouting for them to pull back. Soon, his call was taken up by captains and commanders. The rear ranks of the two practice blocks pulled away – leaving the contestants at the center to devolve into a brawl.

Dalinar shouted, and Stormlight shimmered along the stones before him. Those who hadn't gotten caught up in the fighting jumped back. The rest got stuck in the Stormlight, which glued them to the ground. This caused all but the most furious to stop their fighting.

He pulled the last few apart and pushed them down, sticking them by their seats to the stone next to their angerspren. The men thrashed, then saw him and froze, looking appropriately chagrined.

I remember being that wrapped up in battle, Dalinar thought. *Is it the Thrill?* He couldn't remember feeling it for . . . for a long time. He would have the men questioned to determine whether any could feel it.

Dalinar let the Stormlight evaporate away like luminescent steam. Aladar's officers withdrew their group in an orderly fashion, shouting for the men to start calisthenics. The soldiers from Sadeas's army, however, spat at the ground and heaved themselves to their feet, retreating in sullen bunches, cursing and muttering.

They're getting worse, Dalinar thought. Under Torol Sadeas, they'd been slovenly and sadistic, but still soldiers. Yes, they tended to brawl, but they'd been quick to obey in battle. So they'd been effective, just not exemplary.

The new Sadeas banner flew above these men. Meridas Sadeas – Amaram – had changed the glyphpair's design, as was traditional: Sadeas's squat tower had elongated, and the hammer had changed to an axe.

Despite his reputation for running a crisp army, it was obvious he was having trouble controlling these men. He'd never commanded a force this large – and perhaps the murder of their highprince had upset the men to the point that there was nothing Amaram could do.

Aladar hadn't been able to provide anything of substance about Torol's murder. The investigation was supposed to be ongoing . . . but there were no leads. The spren hadn't done it, but they had no idea who had.

I'll need to take action about those soldiers, Dalinar thought. *They need something to tire them out, keep them from getting into fights. . . .*

Perhaps he had just the thing. He considered that as he finally made his way up the ramp to the proper Oathgate platform, then crossed the empty field to the control building. Jasnah waited within, reading a book and making notes. 'What took you?' she asked.

'Almost had a riot out on the parade ground,' he said. 'Two training formations got interlocked and started bashing one another.'

'Sadeas?'

Dalinar nodded.

'We'll have to do something about them.'

'I've been thinking. Maybe some hard labor – strictly supervised – in a ruined city might be just the thing.'

Jasnah smiled. 'How convenient that we're currently providing exactly such assistance to Queen Fen. Work Sadeas's troops to exhaustion, assuming we can keep them under control there.'

'I'll start with small batches, to be certain we're not sending more trouble Fen's direction,' Dalinar said. 'Have you had any news from the king's infiltration team at Kholinar?' As anticipated, the Stormfather was unable to reach anyone on the team to bring them into a vision – nor would Dalinar dare risk it – but they'd sent several spanreeds with Elhokar and Shallan.

'None. We'll keep watch and tell you the moment we get any sort of response.'

Dalinar nodded, and shoved down his worry for Elhokar and his son. He had to trust that they'd eventually either accomplish their task, or find a way to report what was stopping them.

Jasnah summoned her Shardblade. Odd how natural it looked to see Jasnah with a sword. 'You ready?'

'I am.'

The Reshi girl, Lift, had obtained permission from the Azish court to unlock the Oathgate on their side. The emperor was – at long last – willing to meet with Dalinar in the flesh.

Jasnah engaged the device, rotating the inner wall, the floor shimmering.

Light flashed outside, and immediately, stuffy heat surged in through the doorways. Apparently a season of summer was well under way in Azir.

It *smelled* different here. Of exotic spices and more subtle things like unfamiliar woods.

'Good luck,' Jasnah said as he stepped out of the room. It flashed behind him as she returned to Urithiru, leaving him to meet the Azish imperial court on his own.

65

VERDICT

Now that we abandon the tower, can I finally admit that I hate this place? Too many rules.

—From drawer 8-1, amethyst

Memories churned in Dalinar's head as he walked down a long corridor outside the Oathgate control building in Azimir, which was covered by a magnificent bronze dome. The Grand Market, as it was called, was an enormous indoor shopping district. That would prove inconvenient when Dalinar needed to use the full Oathgate.

He couldn't see any of the market currently; the control building – which had been treated as some kind of monument in the market – was now surrounded by a wooden set of walls, and a new corridor. Empty of people, it was lit by sphere lamps along the walls. Sapphires. Coincidence, or a gesture of respect to a Kholin visitor?

At the end, the hallway opened into a small room populated by a line of Azish soldiers. They wore plated mail, with colorful caps on their heads, greatshields, and very long-handled axes with small heads. The whole group jumped as Dalinar entered, and then shied back, weapons held threateningly.

Dalinar held his arms out to the sides, packet from Fen in one hand, food bundle in the other. 'I am unarmed.'

They spoke quickly in Azish. He didn't see the Prime or the little Radiant, though the people in patterned robes were viziers and scions – both were, essentially, Azish versions of ardents. Except here, the ardents were involved in the government far more than was proper.

A woman stepped forward, the many layers of her long, extravagant robes rustling as she walked. A matching hat completed the outfit. She was important, and perhaps planned to interpret for him herself.

Time for my first attack, Dalinar thought. He opened the packet that Fen had given him and removed four pieces of paper.

He presented them to the woman, and was pleased at the shock in her eyes. She hesitantly took them, then called to some of her companions. They joined her before Dalinar, which made the guards distinctly anxious. A few had drawn triangular kattari, a popular variety of short sword here in the west. He'd always wanted one.

The ardents withdrew behind the soldiers, speaking animatedly. The plan was to exchange pleasantries in this room, then for Dalinar to immediately return to Urithiru – whereupon they intended to lock the Oathgate from their side. He wanted more. He intended to *get* more. Some kind of alliance, or at least a meeting with the emperor.

One of the ardents started reading the papers to the others. The writing was in Azish, a funny language made of little markings that looked like cremling tracks. It lacked the elegant, sweeping verticals of the Alethi women's script.

Dalinar closed his eyes, listening to the unfamiliar language. As in Thaylen City, he had a moment of feeling he could almost understand. Stretching, he felt that meaning was close to him.

'Would you help me understand?' he whispered to the Stormfather.

What makes you think I can?

'Don't be coy,' Dalinar whispered. 'I've spoken new languages in the visions. You can make me speak Azish.'

The Stormfather rumbled in discontent. *That wasn't me,* he finally said. *It was you.*

'How do I use it?'

Try touching one of them. With Spiritual Adhesion, you can make a Connection.

Dalinar regarded the group of hostile guards, then sighed, waving and miming the act of dumping a drink into his mouth. The soldiers exchanged sharp words, then one of the youngest was pushed forward with a canteen. Dalinar nodded in thanks, then – as he took a drink from the water bottle – grabbed the young man by the wrist and held on.

Stormlight, the rumbling in his mind said.

Dalinar pressed Stormlight into the other man, and felt something – like a friendly sound coming from another room. All you had to do was get in. After a careful shove, the door opened, and sounds twisted and undulated in the air. Then, like music changing keys, they modulated from gibberish to sense.

'Captain!' cried the young guard that Dalinar held. 'What do I do? He's got me!'

Dalinar let go, and fortunately his understanding of the language persisted. 'I'm sorry, soldier,' Dalinar said, handing back the canteen. 'I didn't mean to alarm you.'

The young soldier stepped back among his fellows. 'The warlord speaks *Azish?*' He sounded as surprised as if he'd met a talking chull.

Dalinar clasped his hands behind his back and watched the ardents. *You insist on thinking of them as ardents,* he told himself, *because they can read, both male and female.* But he was no longer in Alethkar. Despite those bulky robes and large hats, the Azish women wore nothing on their safehands.

Sunmaker, Dalinar's ancestor, had argued that the Azish had been in need of civilizing. He wondered if anyone had believed that argument even in those days, or if they'd all seen it for the rationalization it was.

The viziers and scions finished reading, then turned toward Dalinar, lowering the pages he'd given them. He had heeded Queen Fen's plan, trusting that he couldn't bully his way through Azir with a sword. Instead, he had brought a different kind of weapon.

An essay.

'Do you truly speak our language, Alethi?' the lead vizier called. She had a round face, dark brown eyes, and a cap covered in bright patterns. Her greying hair came out the side in a tight braid.

'I've had the opportunity to learn it recently,' Dalinar said. 'You are Vizier Noura, I assume?'

'Did Queen Fen really write this?'

'With her own hand, Your Grace,' Dalinar said. 'Feel free to contact Thaylen City to confirm.'

They huddled to consult again in quiet tones. The essay was a lengthy but compelling argument for the economic value of the Oathgates to the cities that hosted them. Fen argued that Dalinar's desperation to forge an alliance made for the perfect opportunity to secure beneficial and lasting trade deals through Urithiru. Even if Azir had no plans to fully join the coalition, they should negotiate use of the Oathgates and send a delegation to the tower.

It spent a lot of words saying what was obvious, and was exactly the sort of thing Dalinar had no patience for. Which, hopefully, would make it perfect for the Azish. And if it wasn't quite sufficient . . . well, Dalinar knew never to go into battle without fresh troops in reserve.

'Your Highness,' Noura said, 'as impressed as we are that you cared to learn our language – and even considering the compelling argument presented here – we think it best if . . .'

She trailed off as Dalinar reached in his packet and withdrew a second sheaf of papers, six pages this time. He held them up before the group like a raised banner, then proffered them. A nearby guard jumped back, making his mail jingle.

The small chamber grew quiet. Finally, a guard accepted the papers and took them to the viziers and scions. A shorter man among them began reading quietly – this one was an extended treatise from Navani, talking about the wonders they'd discovered in Urithiru, formally inviting the Azish scholars to visit and share.

She made clever arguments about the importance of new fabrials and technology in fighting the Voidbringers. She included diagrams of the tents she'd made to help them fight during the Weeping, and explained her theories for floating towers. Then, with Dalinar's permission, she offered a gift: detailed schematics that Taravangian had brought from Jah Keved, explaining the creation of so-called half-shards, fabrial shields that could withstand a few blows from Shardblades.

The enemy is united against us, went her essay's final argument. *They have the unique advantages of focus, harmony, and memories that extend far into the past. Resisting them will require our greatest minds, whether Alethi, Azish, Veden, or Thaylen. I freely give state secrets, for the days of hoarding knowledge are gone. Now, we either learn together or we fall individually.*

The viziers finished, then they passed around the schematics, studying them for an extended time. When the group looked back at Dalinar, he could see that their attitude was changing. Remarkably, this was *working*.

Well, he didn't know much about essays, but he had an instinct for combat. When your opponent was gasping for breath, you didn't let him get back up. You rammed your sword right into his throat.

Dalinar reached into his packet and removed the last paper inside: a single sheet written on front and back. He held it up between his first two fingers. The Azish watched it with wide eyes, as if he'd revealed a glowing gemstone of incalculable wealth.

This time Vizier Noura herself stepped forward and took it. ' "Verdict," ' she read from the top. ' "By Jasnah Kholin." '

The others pushed through the guards, gathering around, and began reading it to themselves. Though this was the shortest of the essays, he heard them whispering and marveling over it.

'Look, it incorporates all *seven* of Aqqu's Logical Forms!'

'That's an allusion to the *Grand Orientation*. And . . . storms . . . she quotes Prime Kasimarlix in three successive stages, each escalating the same quote to a different level of Superior Understanding.'

One woman held her hand to her mouth. 'It's written entirely in a single rhythmic meter!'

'Great *Yaezir*,' Noura said. 'You're *right*.'

'The allusions . . .'

'Such wordplay . . .'

'The *momentum* and *rhetoric* . . .'

Logicspren burst around them in the shape of little stormclouds. Then, practically as one, the scions and viziers turned to Dalinar.

'This is a work of *art*,' Noura said.

'Is it . . . persuasive?' Dalinar asked.

'It provokes further consideration,' Noura said, looking to the others, who nodded. 'You actually came alone. We are shocked by that – aren't you worried for your safety?'

'Your Radiant,' Dalinar said, 'has proven to be wise for one so young. I am certain I can depend on her for my safety.'

'I don't know that I'd depend on her for anything,' said one of the men, chuckling. 'Unless it's swiping your pocket change.'

'All the same,' Dalinar said, 'I have come begging you to trust me. This seemed the best proof of my intentions.' He spread his hands to the sides. 'Do not send me back immediately. Let us talk as allies, not men in a battlefield tent of parley.'

'I will bring these essays before the Prime and his formal council,' Vizier Noura finally said. 'I admit he seems fond of you, despite your inexplicable invasion of his dreams. Come with us.'

That would lead him away from the Oathgate, and any chance he had at transferring home in an emergency. But that was what he'd been hoping for.

'Gladly, Your Grace.'

∴

They walked along a twisting path through the dome-covered market – which was now empty, like a ghost town. Many of the streets ended at barricades manned by troops.

They'd turned the Azimir Grand Market into a kind of reverse fortress, intended to protect the city from whatever might come through the Oathgate. If troops left the control building, they would find themselves in a maze of confusing streets.

Unfortunately for the Azish, the control building alone was *not* the gate. A Radiant could make this entire *dome* vanish, replaced with an army in the middle of Azimir. He'd have to be delicate about how he explained that.

He walked with Vizier Noura, followed by the other scribes, who passed the essays around again. Noura didn't make small talk with him, and Dalinar maintained no illusions. This trip through the dark indoor streets – with packed market buildings and twisting paths – was meant to confuse him, should he try to remember the way.

They eventually climbed up to a second level and left through a doorway out onto a ledge along the outside rim of the dome. Clever. From up here, he could see that the ground-floor exits from the market were barricaded or sealed off. The only clear way out was up that flight of steps, onto this platform around the circumference of the large bronze dome, then down another set of steps.

From this upper ramp, he could see some of Azimir – and was relieved by how little destruction he saw. Some of the neighborhoods on the west side of the city seemed to have collapsed, but all in all, the city had weathered the Everstorm in good shape. Most of the structures were stone here, and the grand domes – many overlaid with reddish-gold bronze – reflected the sunlight like molten marvels. The people wore colorful clothing, of patterns that scribes could read like a language.

This summer season was warmer than he was accustomed to. Dalinar turned east. Urithiru lay somewhere in that direction, in the border mountains – far closer to Azir than to Alethkar.

'This way, Blackthorn,' Noura said, starting down the wooden ramp. It was constructed upon a woodwork lattice. Seeing those wooden stilts, Dalinar had a moment of surreal memory. It vaguely reminded him of something, of perching above a city and looking down at wooden lattices. . . .

Rathalas, he thought. *The Rift.* The city that had rebelled. Right. He felt a chill, and the pressure of something hidden trying to thrust itself into his consciousness. There was more to remember about that place.

He walked down the ramp, and took it as a mark of respect that two entire divisions of troops surrounded the dome. 'Shouldn't those men be on the walls?' Dalinar asked. 'What if the Voidbringers attack?'

'They've withdrawn through Emul,' Noura said. 'Most of that country is on fire by now, due to either the parshmen or Tezim's armies.'

Tezim. Who was a Herald. *Surely he wouldn't side with the enemy, would he?* Perhaps the best thing they could hope for was a war between the Voidbringers and the armies of a mad Herald.

Rickshaws waited for them below. Noura joined him in one. It was novel, being pulled by a man acting like a chull. Though it was faster than a palanquin, Dalinar found it far less stately.

The city was laid out in a very orderly manner. Navani had always admired that. He watched for more signs of destruction, and while he found few, a different oddity struck him. Masses of people standing in clumps, wearing colorful vests, loose trousers or skirts, and patterned caps. They shouted about unfairness, and though they looked angry, they were surrounded by logicspren.

'What's all this?' Dalinar asked.

'Protestors.' She looked to him, and obviously noted his confusion. 'They've lodged a formal complaint, rejecting an order to exit the city and work the farms. This gives them a one-month period to make their grievances known before being forced to comply.'

'They can simply *disobey* an imperial order?'

'I suppose you'd merely march everyone out at swordpoint. Well, we don't do things that way here. There are processes. Our people aren't slaves.'

Dalinar found himself bristling; she obviously didn't know much about Alethkar, if she assumed all Alethi darkeyes were like chulls to be herded around. The lower classes had a long and proud tradition of rights related to their social ranking.

'Those people,' he said, realizing something, 'have been ordered to the fields because you lost your parshmen.'

'Our fields haven't yet been planted,' Noura said, eyes growing distant. 'It's like they knew the very best time to cripple us by leaving. Carpenters and cobblers must be pressed into manual labor, just to prevent a famine. We might feed ourselves, but our trades and infrastructure will be devastated.'

In Alethkar, they hadn't been as fixated on this, as reclaiming the kingdom was more pressing. In Thaylenah, the disaster had been physical, the city ravaged. Both kingdoms had been distracted from a more subversive disaster, the economic one.

'How did it happen?' Dalinar asked. 'The parshmen leaving?'

'They gathered in the storm,' she said. 'Leaving homes and walking right out into it. Some reports said the parshmen claimed to hear the beating of drums. Other reports – these are all very contradictory – speak of spren guiding the parshmen.

'They swarmed the city gates, threw them open in the rain, then moved out onto the plain surrounding the city. The next day, they demanded formal economic redress for improper appropriation of their labors. They claimed the subsection of the rules exempting parshmen from wages was extralegal, and put a motion through the courts. We were negotiating – a bizarre experience, I must say – before some of their leaders got them marching off instead.'

Interesting. Alethi parshmen had acted Alethi – immediately gathering for war. The Thaylen parshmen had taken to the seas. And the Azish parshmen ... well, they'd done something quintessentially Azish. They had lodged a complaint with the government.

He had to be careful not to dwell on how amusing that sounded, if only because Navani had warned him not to underestimate the Azish.

Alethi liked to joke about them – insult one of their soldiers, it was said, and he'd submit a form requesting an opportunity to swear at you. But that was a caricature, likely about as accurate as Noura's own impression of his people always doing everything by the sword and spear.

Once at the palace, Dalinar tried to follow Noura and the other scribes into the main building – but soldiers instead gestured him toward a small outbuilding.

'I was hoping,' he called after Noura, 'to speak with the emperor in person.'

'Unfortunately, this petition cannot be granted,' she said. The group left him and strode into the grand palace itself, a majestic bronze building with bulbous domes.

The soldiers sequestered him in a narrow chamber with a low table at the center and nice couches along the sides. They left him inside the small room alone, but took up positions outside. It wasn't quite a prison, but he obviously wasn't to be allowed to roam either.

He sighed and sat on a couch, dropping his lunch to the table beside some bowls of dried fruit and nuts. He took the spanreed out and sent a brief signal to Navani that meant *time*, the agreed sign that he was to be given another hour before anyone panicked.

He rose and began pacing. How did men suffer this? In battle, you won or lost based on strength of arms. At the end of the day, you knew where you stood.

This endless talking left him so uncertain. Would the viziers dismiss the essays? Jasnah's reputation seemed to be powerful even here, but they'd seemed less impressed by her argument than by the way she expressed it.

You've always worried about this, haven't you? the Stormfather said in his mind.

'About what?'

That the world would come to be ruled by pens and scribes, not swords and generals.

'I . . .' *Blood of my fathers.* That was true.

Was that why he insisted on negotiating himself? Why he didn't send ambassadors? Was it because deep down, he didn't trust their gilded words and intricate promises, all contained in documents he couldn't read? Pieces of paper that were somehow harder than the strongest Shardplate?

'The contests of kingdoms are supposed to be a *masculine* art,' he said. 'I should be able to do this myself.'

The Stormfather rumbled, not truly in disagreement. Just in . . . amusement?

Dalinar finally settled onto one of the couches. Might as well eat something . . . except his cloth-wrapped lunch lay open, crumbs on the table, the wooden curry box empty save for a few drips. What on Roshar?

He slowly looked up at the other couch. The slender Reshi girl perched not on the seat, but up on the backrest. She wore an oversized Azish robe and cap, and was gnawing on the sausage Navani had packed with the meal, to be cut into the curry.

'Kind of bland,' she said.

'Soldier's rations,' Dalinar said. 'I prefer them.'

''Cuz you're bland?'

'I prefer not to let a meal become a distraction. Were you in here all along?'

She shrugged, continuing to eat his food. 'You said something earlier. About men?'

'I . . . was beginning to realize that I'm uncomfortable with the idea of scribes controlling the fates of nations. The things women write are stronger than my military.'

'Yeah, that makes sense. Lots of boys is afraid of girls.'

'I'm not—'

'They say it changes when you grow up,' she said, leaning forward. 'I wouldn't know, because I ain't going to grow. I figured it out. I just gotta stop eatin'. People that don't eat, don't get bigger. Easy.'

She said it all around mouthfuls of his food.

'Easy,' Dalinar said. 'I'm sure.'

'I'm gonna start *any* day now,' she said. 'You want that fruit, or . . .'

He leaned forward, pushing the two bowls of dried fruit toward her. She attacked them. Dalinar leaned back in the seat. This girl seemed so out of place. Though she was lighteyed – with pale, clear irises – that didn't matter as much in the west. The regal clothing was too big on her, and she didn't take care to keep her hair pulled back and tucked up under the cap.

This entire room – this entire city, really – was an exercise in ostentation. Metal leaf coated domes, the rickshaws, even large portions of the walls of this room. The Azish owned only a few Soulcasters, and famously one could make bronze.

The carpeting and couches displayed bright patterns of orange and red. The Alethi favored solid colors, perhaps some embroidery. The Azish preferred their decorations to look like the product of a painter having a sneezing fit.

In the middle of it all was this girl, who looked so simple. She swam through ostentation, but it didn't stick to her.

'I listened to what they're sayin' in there, tight-butt,' the girl said. 'Before comin' here. I think they're gonna deny you. They gots a *finger.*'

'I should think they have many fingers.'

'Nah, this is an *extra* one. Dried out, looks like it belonged to some gramma's gramma, but it's actually from an *emperor.* Emperor Snot-a-Lot or—'

'Snoxil?' Dalinar asked.

'Yeah. That's him.'

'He was Prime when my ancestor sacked Azimir,' Dalinar said with a sigh. 'It's a relic.' The Azish could be a superstitious lot, for all their claims about logic and essays and codes of law. This relic was probably being used during their discussions as a reminder of the last time the Alethi had been in Azir.

'Yeah, well, all I know is he's *dead,* so he ain't got to worry about . . . about . . .'

'Odium.'

The Reshi girl shivered visibly.

'Could you go and talk to the viziers?' Dalinar asked. 'Tell them that you think supporting my coalition is a good idea? They listened to you when you asked to unlock the Oathgate.'

'Nah, they listened to Gawx,' she said. 'The geezers that run the city don't like me much.'

Dalinar grunted. 'Your name is Lift, right?'

'Right.'

'And your order?'

'More food.'

'I meant your order of Knights Radiant. What powers do you have?'

'Oh. Um . . . Edgedancer? I slip around and stuff.'

'Slip around.'

'It's real fun. Except when I run into things. Then it's only kinda fun.'

Dalinar leaned forward, wishing – again – he could go in and talk to all those fools and scribes.

No. For once, trust in someone else, Dalinar.

Lift cocked her head. 'Huh. You smell like her.'

'Her?'

'The crazy spren who lives in the forest.'

'You've met the *Nightwatcher*?'

'Yeah . . . You?'

He nodded.

They sat there, uncomfortable, until the young girl handed one of her bowls of dried fruit toward Dalinar. He took a piece and chewed it in silence, and she took another.

They ate the entire bowl, saying nothing until the door opened. Dalinar jumped. Noura stood in the doorway, flanked by other viziers. Her eyes flickered toward Lift, and she smiled. Noura didn't seem to think as poorly of Lift as the little girl indicated.

Dalinar stood up, feeling a sense of dread. He prepared his arguments, his pleas. They had to—

'The emperor and his council,' Noura said, 'have decided to accept your invitation to visit Urithiru.'

Dalinar cut off his objection. Did she say *accept*?

'The Prime of Emul has almost reached Azir,' Noura said. 'He brought the Sage with him, and they should be willing to join us. Unfortunately, following the parshman assault, Emul is a fraction of what it once was. I suspect he will be eager for any and every source of aid, and will welcome this coalition of yours.

'The prince of Tashikk has an ambassador – his brother – in the city. He'll come as well, and the princess of Yezier is reportedly coming in person to plead for aid. We'll see about her. I think she simply believes Azimir will be safer. She lives here half the year anyway.

'Alm and Desh have ambassadors in the city, and Liafor is always eager to join whatever we do, as long as they can cater the storming meetings. I can't speak for Steen – they're a tricky bunch. I doubt you want Tukar's priest-king, and Marat is overrun. But we can bring a good sampling of the empire to join your discussions.'

'I . . .' Dalinar stammered. 'Thank you!' It was actually *happening*! As they'd hoped, Azir was the linchpin.

'Well, your wife writes a good essay,' Noura said.

He started. 'Navani's essay was the one that convinced you? Not Jasnah's?'

'Each of the three arguments were weighed favorably, and the reports from Thaylen City are encouraging,' Noura said. 'That had no small part in our decision. But while Jasnah Kholin's writing is every bit as impressive as her reputation suggests, there was something . . . more authentic about Lady Navani's plea.'

'She is one of the most authentic people I know.' Dalinar smiled like a fool. 'And she is good at getting what she wants.'

'Let me lead you back to the Oathgate. We will be in contact about the Prime's visit to your city.'

Dalinar collected his spanreed and bade farewell to Lift, who stood on the back of the couch and waved to him. The sky looked brighter as the viziers accompanied him back to the dome that housed the Oathgate. He could hear them speaking eagerly as they entered the rickshaws; they seemed to be embracing this decision with gusto, now that it had been made.

Dalinar passed the trip quietly, worried that he might say something brutish and ruin things. Once they entered the market dome, he did take the opportunity to mention to Noura that the Oathgate could be used to transport everything there, including the dome itself.

'I'm afraid that it's a larger security threat than you know,' he finished saying to her as they reached the control building.

'What would it do,' she said, 'if we built a structure halfway across the plateau perimeter? Would it slice the thing in two? What if a person is half on, half off?'

'That we don't know yet,' Dalinar said, fumbling the spanreed on and off in a pattern to send the signal that would bring Jasnah back through the Oathgate to fetch him.

'I'll admit,' Noura said softly as the other viziers chatted behind, 'I'm . . . not pleased at being overruled. I am the emperor's loyal servant, but I do *not* like the idea of your Radiants, Dalinar Kholin. These powers are dangerous, and the ancient Radiants turned traitor in the end.'

'I will convince you,' Dalinar said. 'We will prove ourselves to you. All I need is a chance.'

The Oathgate flashed, and Jasnah appeared inside. Dalinar bowed to Noura in respect, then stepped backward into the building.

'You are not what I expected, Blackthorn,' Noura said.

'And what did you expect?'

'An animal,' she said frankly. 'A half-man creature of war and blood.'

Something about that struck him. *An animal . . .* Echoes of memories shuddered inside of him.

'I was that man,' Dalinar said. 'I've merely been blessed with enough good examples to make me aspire to something more.' He nodded to Jasnah, who repositioned her sword, rotating the inner wall to initiate the transfer and take them back to Urithiru.

Navani waited outside the building. Dalinar stepped out and blinked at the sunlight, chilled by the mountain cold. He smiled broadly at her, opening his mouth to tell her what her essay had done.

An animal . . . An animal reacts when it is prodded . . .

Memories.

You whip it, and it becomes savage.

Dalinar stumbled.

He vaguely heard Navani crying out, yelling for help. His vision spun, and he fell to his knees, feeling an overwhelming nausea. He clawed at the stone, groaning, breaking fingernails. Navani . . . Navani was calling for a healer. She thought he'd been poisoned.

It wasn't that. No, it was far, far worse.

Storms. He *remembered.* It came crashing down on him, the weight of a thousand boulders.

He remembered what had happened to Evi. It had started in a cold fortress, in highlands once claimed by Jah Keved.

It had ended at the Rift.

STRATEGIST

ELEVEN YEARS AGO

Dalinar's breath misted as he leaned on the stone windowsill. In the room behind him, soldiers set up a table with a map on it.

'See there,' Dalinar said, pointing out the window. 'That ledge down there?'

Adolin, now twelve years old – nearly thirteen – leaned out the window. The outside of the large stone keep bulged here at the second floor, which would make scaling it challenging – but the stonework provided a convenient handhold in the form of a ledge right below the window.

'I see it,' Adolin said.

'Good. Now watch.' Dalinar gestured into the room. One of his guards pulled a lever, and the stonework ledge retracted into the wall.

'It moved!' Adolin said. 'Do that again!'

The soldier obliged, using the lever to make the ledge stick out, then retract again.

'Neat!' Adolin said. So full of energy, as always. If only Dalinar could harness that for the battlefield. He wouldn't need Shards to conquer.

'Why did they build that, do you think?' Dalinar asked.

'In case people climb it! You could make them drop back down!'

'Defense against Shardbearers,' Dalinar said, nodding. 'A fall this far would crack their Plate, but the fortress also has interior corridor sections that are too narrow to maneuver in properly with Plate and Blade.'

Dalinar smiled. Who knew that such a gem had been hiding in the highlands between Alethkar and Jah Keved? This solitary keep would provide a nice barrier if true war ever did break out with the Vedens.

He gestured for Adolin to move back, then shuttered the window and rubbed his chilled hands. This chamber was decorated like a lodge, hung with old forgotten greatshell trophies. At the side, a soldier stoked a flame in the hearth.

The battles with the Vedens had wound down. Though the last few fights had been disappointing, having his son with him had been an absolute delight. Adolin hadn't gone into battle, of course, but he'd joined them at tactics meetings. Dalinar had at first assumed the generals would be annoyed at the presence of a child, but it was hard to find little Adolin annoying. He was so earnest, so interested.

Together, he and Adolin joined a few of Dalinar's lesser officers at the room's table map. 'Now,' Dalinar said to Adolin, 'let's see how well you've been paying attention. Where are we now?'

Adolin leaned over, pointing at the map. 'This is our new keep, which you won for the crown! Here's the old border, where it used to be. Here's the *new* border in blue, which we won back from those thieving Vedens. They've held our land for *twenty years*.'

'Excellent,' Dalinar said. 'But it's not merely land we've won.'

'Trade treaties!' Adolin said. 'That's the point of the big ceremony we had to do. You and that Veden highprince, in formal dress. We won the right to trade for *tons* of stuff for cheap.'

'Yes, but that's not the most important thing we won.'

Adolin frowned. 'Um . . . horses . . .'

'No, son, the most *important* thing we've won is legitimacy. In signing this new treaty, the Veden king has recognized Gavilar as the rightful king of Alethkar. We've not just defended our borders, we've forestalled a greater war, as the Vedens now acknowledge our right to rule – and won't be pressing their own.'

Adolin nodded, understanding.

It was gratifying to see how much one could accomplish in both politics and trade by liberally murdering the other fellow's soldiers. These last years full of skirmishes had reminded Dalinar of why he lived. More, they'd given him something new. In his youth, he'd warred, then spent the evenings drinking with his soldiers.

Now he had to explain his choices, vocalize them for the ears of an eager young boy who had questions for everything – and expected Dalinar to know the answers.

Storms, it was a challenge. But it felt good. *Incredibly* good. He had no intention of ever returning to a useless life spent wasting away in Kholinar, going to parties and getting into tavern brawls. Dalinar smiled and accepted a cup of warmed wine, surveying the map. Though Adolin had been focused on the region where they were fighting the Vedens, Dalinar's eyes were instead drawn to another section.

It included, written in pencil, the numbers he'd requested: projections of troops at the Rift.

'*Viim cachi eko!*' Evi said, stepping into the room, holding her arms tight to her chest and shivering. 'I had thought central Alethkar was cold. Adolin Kholin, where is your jacket?'

The boy looked down, as if suddenly surprised that he wasn't wearing it. 'Um . . .' He looked to Teleb, who merely smiled, shaking his head.

'Run along, son,' Dalinar said. 'You have geography lessons today.'

'Can I stay? I don't want to leave you.'

He wasn't speaking merely of today. The time was approaching when Adolin would go to spend part of the year in Kholinar, to drill with the swordmasters and receive formal training in diplomacy. He spent most of the year with Dalinar, but it was important he get *some* refinement in the capital.

'Go,' Dalinar said. 'If you pay attention in your lesson, I'll take you riding tomorrow.'

Adolin sighed, then saluted. He hopped off his stool and gave his mother a hug – which was un-Alethi, but Dalinar suffered the behavior. Then he was out the door.

Evi stepped up to the fire. 'So cold. What possessed someone to build a fortress way up here?'

'It's not that bad,' Dalinar said. 'You should visit the Frostlands in a season of winter.'

'You Alethi cannot understand cold. Your bones are frozen.'

Dalinar grunted his response, then leaned down over the map. *I'll need to approach from the south, march up along the lake's coast. . . .*

'The king is sending a message via spanreed,' Evi noted. 'It's being scribed now.'

Her accent is fading, Dalinar noticed absently. When she sat down in a chair by the fire, she supported herself with her right hand, safehand tucked demurely against her waist. She kept her blonde hair in Alethi braids, rather than letting it tumble about her shoulders.

She'd never be a great scribe – she didn't have the youthful training in art and letters of a Vorin woman. Besides, she didn't like books, and preferred her meditations. But she'd tried hard these last years, and he was impressed.

She still complained that he didn't see Renarin enough. The other son was unfit for battle, and spent most of his time in Kholinar. Evi spent half the year back with him.

No, no, Dalinar thought, writing a glyph on the map. *The coast is the expected route.* What then? An amphibious assault across the lake? He'd need to see if he could get ships for that.

A scribe eventually entered bearing the king's letter, and everyone but Dalinar and Evi left. Evi held the letter and hesitated. 'Do you want to sit, or—'

'No, go ahead.'

Evi cleared her voice. '"Brother,"' the letter began, '"the treaty is sealed. Your efforts in Jah Keved are to be commended, and this should be a time of celebration and congratulations. Indeed, on a personal note, I wish to express my pride in you. The word from our best generals is that your tactical instincts have matured to full-fledged strategic genius. I never counted myself among their ranks, but to a man, they commend you as their equal.

'"As I have grown to become a king, it seems you have found your place as our general. I'm most interested to hear your own reports of the small mobile team tactics you've been employing. I would like to speak in person at length about all of this – indeed, I have important revelations of my own I would like to share. It would be best if we could meet in person. Once, I enjoyed your company every day. Now I believe it has been three years since we last spoke face to face."'

'But,' Dalinar said, interrupting, 'the Rift needs to be dealt with.'

Evi broke off, looking at him, then back down at the page. She continued reading. '"Unfortunately, our meeting will have to wait a few storms longer. Though your efforts on the border have certainly helped solidify our power, I have failed to dominate Rathalas and its renegade leader with politics.

'"I must send you to the Rift again. You are to quell this faction. Civil war could tear Alethkar to shreds, and I dare not wait any longer. In truth, I wish I'd listened when we spoke – so many years ago – and you challenged me to send you to the Rift.

'"Sadeas will gather reinforcements and join you. Please send word of your strategic assessment of the problem. Be warned, we are certain now that one of the other highprinces – we don't know who – is supporting Tanalan and his rebellion. He may have access to Shards. I wish you strength of purpose, and the Heralds' own blessings, in your new task. With love and respect, Gavilar."'

Evi looked up. 'How did you know, Dalinar? You've been poring over those maps for weeks – maps of the Crownlands and of Alethkar. You *knew* he was going to assign you this task.'

'What kind of strategist would I be if I couldn't foresee the next battle?'

'I thought we were going to relax,' Evi said. 'We were going to be done with the killing.'

'With the momentum I have? What a waste that would be! If not for this problem in Rathalas, Gavilar would have found somewhere else for me to fight. Herdaz again, perhaps. You can't have your best general sitting around collecting crem.'

Besides. There would be men and women among Gavilar's advisors who worried about Dalinar. If anyone was a threat to the throne, it would be the Blackthorn – particularly with the respect he'd gained from the kingdom's generals. Though Dalinar had decided years ago that he would never do such a thing, many at court would think the kingdom safer if he were kept away.

'No, Evi,' he said as he made another notation, 'I doubt we will ever settle back in Kholinar again.'

He nodded to himself. That was the way to get the Rift. One of his mobile bands could round and secure the lake's beach. He could move the entire army across it then, attacking far faster than the Rift expected.

Satisfied, he looked up. And found Evi crying.

The sight stunned him, and he dropped his pencil. She tried to hold it back, turning toward the fire and wrapping her arms around herself, but the sniffles sounded as distinct and disturbing as breaking bones.

Kelek's breath . . . he could face soldiers and storms, falling boulders and dying friends, but nothing in his training had ever prepared him to deal with these soft tears.

'Seven years,' she whispered. 'Seven *years* we've been out here, living in wagons and waystops. Seven years of murder, of chaos, of men crying to their wounds.'

'You married—'

'Yes, I *married a soldier*. It's my fault for not being strong enough to deal with the consequences. Thank you, Dalinar. You've made that very clear.'

This was what it was like to feel helpless. 'I . . . thought you were growing to like it. You now fit in with the other women.'

'The other women? Dalinar, they make me feel *stupid*.'

'But . . .'

'Conversation is a *contest* to them,' Evi said, throwing her hands up. '*Everything* has to be a contest to you Alethi, always trying to show up everyone else. For the women it's this awful, unspoken game to prove how witty they each are. I've thought . . . maybe the only answer, to make you proud, is to go to the Nightwatcher and ask for the blessing of intelligence. The Old Magic can change a person. Make something great of them—'

'Evi,' Dalinar cut in. 'Please, don't speak of that place or that creature. It's blasphemous.'

'You say that, Dalinar,' she said. 'But no one actually cares about religion here. Oh, they make sure to point out how superior their beliefs are to mine. But who actually ever worries about the Heralds, other than to swear by their names? You bring ardents to battle merely to Soulcast rocks into grain. That way, you don't have to stop *killing* each other long enough to find something to eat.'

Dalinar approached, then settled down into the other seat by the hearth. 'It is . . . different in your homeland?'

She rubbed her eyes, and he wondered if she'd see through his attempt to change the subject. Talking about her people often smoothed over their arguments.

'Yes,' she said. 'True, there are those who don't care about the One or the Heralds. They say we shouldn't accept Iriali or Vorin doctrines as our own. But Dalinar, many *do* care. Here . . . here you just pay some ardent to burn glyphwards for you and call it done.'

Dalinar took a deep breath and tried again. 'Perhaps, after I've seen to the rebels, I can persuade Gavilar not to give me another assignment. We could travel. Go west, to your homeland.'

'So you could kill my people instead?'

'No! I wouldn't—'

'They'd attack you, Dalinar. My brother and I are exiles, if you haven't forgotten.'

He hadn't seen Toh in a decade, ever since the man had gone to Herdaz. He reportedly liked it quite well, living on the coast, protected by Alethi bodyguards.

Evi sighed. 'I'll never see the sunken forests again. I've accepted that. I will live my life in this harsh land, so dominated by wind and cold.'

'Well, we could travel someplace warm. Up to the Steamwater. Just you and I. Time together. We could even bring Adolin.'

'And Renarin?' Evi asked. 'Dalinar, you have *two* sons, in case you have forgotten. Do you even care about the child's condition? Or is he nothing to you now that he can't become a soldier?'

Dalinar grunted, feeling like he'd taken a mace to the head. He stood up, then walked toward the table.

'What?' Evi demanded.

'I've been in enough battles to know when I've found one I can't win.'

'So you flee?' Evi said. 'Like a coward?'

'The coward,' Dalinar said, gathering his maps, 'is the man who delays a necessary retreat for fear of being mocked. We'll go back to Kholinar after I deal with the rebellion at the Rift. I'll promise you at least a year there.'

'Really?' Evi said, standing up.

'Yes. You've won this fight.'

'I . . . don't feel like I've won. . . .'

'Welcome to war, Evi,' Dalinar said, heading toward the door. 'There are no unequivocal wins. Just victories that leave fewer of your friends dead than others.'

He left and slammed the door behind him. Sounds of her weeping chased him down the steps, and shamespren fell around him like flower petals. *Storms, I don't deserve that woman, do I?*

Well, so be it. The argument was her fault, as were the repercussions. He stomped down the steps to find his generals, and continue planning his return assault on the Rift.

Normal Painspren

Altered Painspren

The painspren in Kholinar are a sickly
green color, with long claws and oddly
distorted proportions (even more than usual).

They respond to pain as readily as ever.

Shamespren have transformed from
their usual manifestations as falling blossoms
to shards of broken glass.

The sense of embarrassment itself
appears unaffected.

Curiously, the hungerspren
appear to be unchanged.

MISHIM

This generation has had only one Bondsmith, and some blame the divisions among us upon this fact. The true problem is far deeper. I believe that Honor himself is changing.

—From drawer 24-18, smokestone

A day after being murdered in a brutal fashion, Shallan found that she was feeling much better. The sense of oppression had left her, and even her horror seemed distant. What lingered was that single glimpse she'd seen in the mirror: a glimmer of the Unmade's presence, beyond the plane of the reflection.

The mirrors in the tailor's shop didn't show such proclivities; she had checked every one. Just in case, she'd given a drawing of the thing she'd seen to the others, and warned them to watch.

Today, she strolled into the little kitchen, which was beside the rear workroom. Adolin ate flatbread and curry while King Elhokar sat at the room's table, earnestly . . . writing something? No, he was *drawing*.

Shallan rested fond fingers on Adolin's shoulder and enjoyed his grin in response. Then she rounded to peek over the king's shoulder. He was doing a map of the city, with the palace and the Oathgate platform. It wasn't half bad.

'Anyone seen the bridgeman?' Elhokar asked.

'Here,' Kaladin said, strolling in from the workroom. Yokska, her husband, and her maid were out shopping for more food, using spheres that Elhokar had provided. Food was apparently still for sale in the city, if you had the spheres to pay.

'I,' Elhokar said, 'have devised a plan for how to proceed in this city.'

Shallan shared a look with Adolin, who shrugged. 'What do you suggest, Your Majesty?'

'Thanks to the Lightweaver's excellent reconnaissance,' the king said, 'it is evident my wife is being held captive by her own guards.'

'We don't know that for certain, Your Majesty,' Kaladin said. 'It sounded like the queen has succumbed to whatever is affecting the guards.'

'Either way, she is in need of rescue,' Elhokar said. 'Either we must sneak into the palace for her and little Gavinor, or we must rally a military force to help us capture the location by strength of arms.' He tapped his map of the city with his pen. 'The Oathgate, however, remains our priority. Brightness Davar, I want you to investigate this Cult of Moments. Find out how they're using the Oathgate platform.'

Yokska had confirmed that each night, some members of the cult set a blazing fire on top of the platform. They guarded the place all hours of the day.

'If you could join whatever ritual or event they are performing,' the king said, 'you would be within feet of the Oathgate. You could transport the entire plateau to Urithiru, and let our armies there deal with the cult.

'In case that is not viable, Adolin and I – in the guise of important lighteyes from the Shattered Plains – shall contact the lighteyed houses in the city who maintain private guard forces. We shall gather their support, perhaps revealing our true identities, and put together an army for assaulting the palace, if needed.'

'And me?' Kaladin asked.

'I don't like the sound of this Azure person. See what you can find out about him and his Wall Guard.'

Kaladin nodded, then grunted.

'It's a good plan, Elhokar,' Adolin said. 'Nice work.'

A simple compliment probably should not have made a king beam like it did. Elhokar even drew a gloryspren – and notably, it didn't seem different from ordinary ones.

'But there is something we have to face,' Adolin continued. 'Have you listened to the list of charges that ardent – the one who got executed – made against the queen?'

'I . . . Yes.'

'Ten glyphs,' Adolin said, 'denouncing Aesudan's excess. Wasting food while people starved. Increasing taxes, then throwing lavish parties for her ardents. Elhokar, this started long before the Everstorm.'

'We can . . . ask her,' the king said. 'Once she is safe. Something must have been wrong. Aesudan was always proud, and always ambitious, but never gluttonous.' He eyed Adolin. 'I know that Jasnah says I shouldn't have married her – that Aesudan was too hungry for power. Jasnah never understood. I *needed* Aesudan. Someone with strength . . .' He took a deep breath, then stood up. 'We mustn't waste time. The plan. Do you agree with it?'

'I like it,' Shallan said.

Kaladin nodded. 'It's too general, but it's at least a line of attack. Additionally, we need to trace the grain in the city. Yokska says the lighteyes provide it, but she also says the palace stores are closed.'

'You think someone has a Soulcaster?' Adolin asked.

'I think this city has too many secrets,' Kaladin said.

'Adolin and I shall ask the lighteyes, and see if they know,' Elhokar said, then looked to Shallan. 'The Cult of Moments?'

'I'll get on it,' she said. 'I need a new coat anyway.'

⁘

She slipped out of the building again as Veil. She wore the trousers and her coat, though that now had a hole in the back. Ishnah had been able to wash the blood off, but Veil still wanted to replace it. For now, she covered the hole with a Lightweaving.

Veil sauntered down the street, and found herself feeling increasingly confident. Back in Urithiru, she'd still been struggling to get her coat on straight, so to speak. She winced as she thought of her trips through the bars, making a fool of herself. You didn't need to *prove* how much you could drink in order to look tough – but that was the sort of thing you couldn't learn without wearing the coat, living in it.

She turned toward the market, where she hoped to get a feel for Kholinar's people. She needed to know how they thought before she could begin to understand how the Cult of Moments had come to be, and therefore how to infiltrate it.

This market was very different from those at Urithiru, or the night markets of Kharbranth. First off, this one was obviously ancient. These worn, weathered shops felt like they'd been here for the first Desolation. These were stones smoothed by the touch of a million fingers, or indented by the press of thousands of passing feet. Awnings bleached by the progression of day after day.

The street was wide, and not crowded. Some stalls were empty, and the remaining merchants didn't shout at her as she passed. These seemed effects of the smothered sensation everyone felt – the feeling of a city besieged.

Yokska served only men, and Veil wouldn't have wanted to reveal herself to the woman anyway. So she stopped at a clothier and tried on some new coats. She chatted with the woman who ran the accounts – her husband was the actual tailor – and got some suggestions on where to look for a coat matching her current one, then stepped back out onto the street.

Soldiers in light blue patrolled here, the glyphs on their uniforms proclaiming them to be of House Velalant. Yokska had described their brightlord as a minor player in the city until so many lighteyes had vanished into the palace.

Veil shivered, remembering the line of corpses. Adolin and Elhokar were fairly certain those were the remnants of a distant Kholin and his attendants – a man named Kaves, who had often tried to gain power in the city. Neither were sad to see him go, but it whispered of a continuing mystery. More than thirty people had gone to meet with the queen, many more powerful than Kaves. What had happened to them?

She passed an assortment of vendors peddling the usual range of necessities and curiosities, from ceramics to dining wares, to fine knives. It was nice to see that here, the soldiers had imposed some semblance of order. Perhaps rather than fixating on the closed stalls, Veil should have appreciated how many were still open.

The third clothing shop finally had a coat she liked, of the same style as her old one – white and long, past her knees. She paid to have it taken in, then casually asked the seamstress about the city's grain.

The answers led her one street over to a grain station. It had formerly been a Thaylen bank, with the words *Secure Keeps* across the top in Thaylen and the women's script. The proprietors had long ago fled – moneylenders seemed to have a sixth sense for impending danger, the way some animals could sense a storm hours before it arrived.

The soldiers in light blue had appropriated it, and the vaults now protected precious grain. People waited in line outside, and at the front, soldiers doled out enough lavis for one day's flatbread and gruel.

It was a good sign – if a distinct and terrible reminder of the city's situation. She would have applauded Velalant's kindness, save for his soldiers' blatant incompetence. They shouted at everyone to stay in line, but didn't do anything to enforce the order. They did have a scribe watching to make sure nobody got in line twice, but they didn't exclude people who were *obviously* too well-to-do to need the handout.

Veil glanced around the market, and noted people watching from the crannies and hollows of abandoned stalls. The poor and unwanted, those destitute beyond even the refugees. Tattered clothing, dirty faces. They watched like spren drawn by a powerful emotion.

Veil settled down on a low wall beside a drainage trough. A boy huddled nearby, watching the line with hungry eyes. One of his arms ended in a twisted, unusable hand: three fingers mere nubs, the other two crooked.

She fished in her trouser pocket. Shallan didn't carry food, but Veil knew the importance of having something to chew on. She could have sworn she'd tucked something in while getting ready. . . . There it was. A meat stick, Soulcast but flavored with sugar. Not quite large enough to be a sausage. She bit off an end, then wagged the rest toward the urchin.

The boy sized her up, probably trying to determine her angle. Finally he crept over and took the offering, quickly stuffing the whole thing into his mouth. He waited, eyeing her to see if she had more.

'Why don't you get in line?' Veil asked.

'They got rules. Gotta be a certain age. And if you're too poor, they shove ya out of line.'

'For what reason?'

The boy shrugged. 'Don't need one, I guess. They say you've already been through, 'cept you haven't.'

'Many of those people . . . they're servants from wealthy homes, aren't they?'

The urchin nodded.

Storming lighteyes, Veil thought as she watched. Some of the poor were shoved out of line for one infraction or another, as the urchin had claimed. The others waited patiently, as it was their job. They'd been sent by wealthy homes to collect food. Many bore the lean, strong look of house guards, though they didn't wear uniforms.

Storms. Velalant's men really had no idea how to do this. *Or maybe they know* exactly *what they're doing,* she thought. *And Velalant is just keeping the local lighteyes happy and ready to support his rule, should the winds turn his way.*

It made Veil sick. She fished out a second meat stick for the urchin, then started to ask him how far Velalant's influence reached – but the kid was gone in a heartbeat.

The grain distribution ended, and a lot of unhappy people called out in despair. The soldiers said they'd do another handout in the evening, and counseled people to line up and wait. Then the bank closed its doors.

But where did Velalant *get* the food? Veil rose and continued through the market, passing pools of angerspren. Some looked like the normal pools of blood; others were more like tar, pitch-black. When the bubbles in these popped, they showed a burning red within, like embers. Those vanished as people settled down to wait – and exhaustionspren appeared instead.

Her optimism about the market evaporated. She passed crowds milling about, looking lost, and read depression in people's eyes. Why try to pretend life could go on? They were doomed. The Voidbringers were going to rip this city apart – if they didn't simply let everyone starve.

Someone needed to do something. *Veil* needed to do something. Infiltrating the Cult of Moments suddenly seemed too abstract. Couldn't she do something directly for these poor people? Except . . . she hadn't even been able to save her own family. She had no idea what Mraize had done with her brothers, and she refused to think about them. How would she save an entire city?

She shouldered through the crowd, seeking freedom, suddenly feeling trapped. She needed out. She—

What was that sound?

Shallan pulled up short, turning, *hearing.* Storms. It couldn't be, could it? She drifted toward the sound, that *voice.*

'You say that, my dear man,' it proclaimed, 'but *everyone* thinks they know the moons. How could they not? We live beneath their gaze each night. We've known them longer than our friends, our wives, our children. And yet . . . and yet . . .'

Shallan pushed through the milling crowd to find him sitting on the low wall around a storm cistern. A metal brazier burned before him, emitting thin lines of smoke that twisted in the wind. He was dressed, strangely, in a soldier's uniform – Sadeas's livery, with the coat unbuttoned and a colored scarf around his neck.

The traveler. The one they called the King's Wit. Angular features, a sharp nose, hair that was stark black.

He was *here*.

'There are still stories to tell.' Wit leaped to his feet. Few people were paying attention. To them, he was just another busker. 'Everyone knows that Mishim is the cleverest of the three moons. Though her sister and brother are content to reign in the sky – gracing the lands below with their light – Mishim is always looking for a chance to escape her duty.'

Wit tossed something into the brazier, producing a bright green puff of smoke the color of Mishim, the third and slowest of the moons.

'This story takes place during the days of Tsa,' Wit continued. 'The grandest queen of Natanatan, before that kingdom's fall. Blessed with grand poise and beauty, the Natan people were famous across all of Roshar. Why, if you'd lived back then, you'd have viewed the east as a place of great culture, not an empty wasteland!

'Queen Tsa, as you've doubtless heard, was an architect. She designed high towers for her city, built to reach ever upward, grasping toward the sky. One night, Tsa rested in her greatest tower, enjoying the view. So it was that Mishim, that clever moon, happened to pass in the sky close by. (It was a night when the moons were large, and these – everyone knows – are nights when the moons pay special attention to the actions of mortals.)

'"Great Queen!" Mishim called. "You build such fine towers in your grand city. I enjoy viewing them each night as I pass."'

Wit dropped powder into the brazier, this time in clumps that caused two lines of smoke – one white, one green – to stream upward. Shallan stepped forward, watching the smoke curl. The marketgoers slowed, and began to gather.

'Now,' Wit said, thrusting his hands into the smoke lines, twisting them so that the smoke swirled and contorted, giving the sense of a green moon spinning in the center, 'Queen Tsa was hardly ignorant of Mishim's crafty ways. The Natans were never fond of Mishim, but rather revered the great Nomon.

'Still, one does not ignore a moon. "Thank you, Great Celestial One," Tsa called. "Our engineers labor ceaselessly to erect the most splendid of mortal accomplishments."

'"Almost they reach to my domain," Mishim called. "One wonders if you are trying to obtain it."

'"Never, Great Celestial One. My domain is this land, and the sky is yours."'

Wit thrust his hand high in his smoke, drawing the line of white into the shape of a straight pillar. His other hand swirled a pocket of green above it, like a whirlpool. A tower and a moon.

That can't be natural, can it? Shallan thought. *Is he Lightweaving?* Yet she saw no Stormlight. There was something more . . . organic about what he did. She couldn't be completely certain it was supernatural.

'As always, Mishim was hatching a scheme. She loathed being hung in the sky each night, far from the delights of the world below, and the pleasures that only mortals know. The next night, Mishim again passed Queen Tsa in her tower. "It is a pity," Mishim said, "that you cannot see the constellations from up close. For they are truly beautiful gemstones, shaped by the finest of gem cutters."

'"It *is* a pity," Tsa said. "But all know that the eyes of a mortal would burn to see such a lofty sight."

'On the next night, Mishim tried again. "It is a pity," she said, "that you cannot converse with the starspren, as they tell delightsome stories."

'"It *is* a pity," Tsa agreed. "But everyone knows that the language of the heavens would drive a mortal mad."

'The next night, Mishim tried a third time. "It is a pity that you cannot see the beauty of your kingdom from above. For the pillars and domes of your city are radiant."

'"It *is* a pity," Tsa agreed. "But those sights are meant for the great ones of heaven, and to behold them myself would be blasphemous."'

Wit dropped another powder into the brazier, bringing up yellow-gold smoke. By now, dozens of people had gathered to watch. He swept his hands to the sides, sending the smoke spraying out in a flat plane. Then it crept upward again in lines – forming towers. A city?

He continued to swirl with one hand, drawing the green smoke up into a ring that – with a thrust of his hand – he sent spinning across the top of the yellow-golden city. It was *remarkable*, and Shallan found her jaw dropping. This was an image that *lived*.

Wit glanced to the side, where he'd put his pack. He started, as if surprised. Shallan cocked her head as he quickly recovered, jumping back into the story so fast that it was easy to miss his lapse. But now, as he spoke, he searched the audience with careful eyes.

'Mishim,' he said, 'was not finished. The queen was pious, but the moon was crafty. I will leave it to you to decide which is the more powerful. The fourth night, as Mishim passed the queen, she tried a different ploy.

'"Yes," Mishim said, "your city is grand, as only a god can see from above. That is why it is so, so sad that one of the towers has a flawed roof."'

Wit swept to the side, destroying the lines of smoke that made up the city. He let the smoke dwindle, the powders he'd thrown running out, all save the line of green.

'"*What?*" Tsa said. "A flawed tower? *Which one?*"

'"It is but a minor blemish," Mishim said. "Do not let it worry you. I appreciate the effort your craftsmen, however incompetent, put into their work." She continued on her way, but knew that she had trapped the queen.

'Indeed, on the next night, the beautiful queen stood waiting on her balcony. "Great One of the Heavens!" Tsa called. "We have inspected the roofs, and cannot find the imperfection! Please, *please* tell me which tower it is, so I can break it down."

'"I cannot say," Mishim said. "To be mortal is to be flawed; it is not right to expect perfection of you."

'This only made the queen more worried. On the next night, she asked, "Great One of the Sky, *is* there a way that I could visit the heavens? I will close my ears to the stories of the starspren and turn my eyes away from the constellations. I would look only upon the flawed works of my people, not the sights meant for you, so that I may see with my own eyes what must be fixed."

'"It is a forbidden thing that you ask," Mishim said, "for we would have to trade places, and hope that Nomon does not notice." She said it with much glee, though hidden, for this request was the very thing she desired.

'"I will feign that I am you," Tsa promised. "And I will do all that you do. We will switch back once I am done, and Nomon will never know."'

Wit grinned broadly. 'And so, the moon and the woman traded places.' His raw enthusiasm for the story was infectious, and Shallan found herself smiling.

They were at war, the city was falling, but all she wanted to do was listen to the end of this story.

Wit used powders to send up four different smoke lines – blue, yellow, green, and intense orange. He swirled them together in a transfixing vortex of hues. And as he worked, his blue eyes fell on Shallan. They narrowed, and his smile became sly.

He just recognized me, she realized. *I'm still wearing Veil's face. But how . . . how did he know?*

When he finished his swirling colors, the moon had become white, and the single straight tower he made by swiping up in the smoke was instead pale green.

'Mishim came down among the mortals,' he proclaimed, 'and Tsa climbed the heavens to sit in the place of the moon! Mishim spent the remaining hours of the night drinking, and courting, and dancing, and singing, and doing all the things she had watched from afar. She lived frantically during her few hours of freedom.

'In fact, she was so captivated that she forgot to return, and was shocked by the dawning of sunlight! She hurriedly climbed to the queen's high tower, but Tsa had already set, and the night had passed.

'Mishim now knew not only the delights of mortality, but the anxiety as well. She passed the day in great disquiet, knowing that Tsa would be trapped with her wise sister and solemn brother, spending the day in the place where moons rest. When night again came, Mishim hid inside the tower, expecting that Salas would call out and chide her for her appetites. Yet Salas passed without comment.

'Surely, when Nomon rose, he would lash out against her foolishness. Yet Nomon passed without comment. Finally, Tsa rose in the sky, and Mishim called to her. 'Queen Tsa, mortal, what has happened? My siblings did not call to me. Did you somehow go undiscovered?'

'"No," Tsa replied. "Your siblings knew me as an impostor immediately."

'"Then let us trade places quickly!" Mishim said. "So that I may tell them lies and placate them."

'"They are placated already," Tsa said. "They think I am delightful. We spent the daylight hours feasting."

'"Feasting?" Her siblings had never feasted with her before.

'"We sang sweet songs together."

'"Songs?" Her siblings had never sung with her before.

'"It is truly wonderful up here," Tsa said. "The starspren tell amazing tales, as you promised, and the gemstone constellations are grand from up close."

'"Yes. I love those stories, and those sights."

'"I think," Tsa said, "that I might stay."'

Wit let the smoke fail until only a single line of green remained. It shrank down, dwindling, almost out. When he spoke, his voice was soft.

'Mishim,' he said, 'now knew another mortal emotion. Loss.

'The moon began to panic! She thought of her grand view from up so high, where she could see all lands and enjoy – if from afar – their art, buildings, and songs! She remembered the kindness of Nomon and the thoughtfulness of Salas!'

Wit made a swirl of white smoke, and pushed it slowly to his left, the new moon Tsa close to setting.

'"Wait!" Mishim said. "Wait, Tsa! Your word is broken! You spoke to the starspren and gazed upon the constellations!"'

Wit caught the smoke ring with one hand, somehow making it stay, swirling in one place.

'"Nomon said that I could," Tsa explained. "And I was not harmed."

'"You broke your word nonetheless!" Mishim cried. "You must come back to earth, mortal, for our bargain is at an end!"'

Wit let the ring hang there.

Then vanish.

'To Mishim's eternal relief, Tsa relented. The queen climbed back down into her tower, and Mishim scrambled up into the heavens. With great pleasure, she sank toward the horizon. Though just before she set, Mishim heard a song.'

Oddly, Wit added a small line of blue smoke to the brazier.

'It was a song of laughter, of beauty. A song Mishim had never heard! It took her long to understand that song, until months later, she passed in the sky at night and saw the queen in the tower again. Holding a child with skin that was faintly blue.

'They did not speak, but Mishim knew. The queen had tricked her. Tsa had *wanted* to spend one day in the heavens, to know Nomon for a night. She had given birth to a son with pale blue skin, the color of Nomon himself. A son born of the gods, who would lead her people to glory. A son who bore the mantle of the heavens.

'And that is why to this day, the people of Natanatan have skin of a faintly blue shade. And it is why Mishim, though still crafty, has never again left her place. Most importantly, it is the story of how the moon came to know the one thing that before, only mortals had known. Loss.'

The last line of blue smoke dwindled, then went out.

Wit didn't bow for applause or ask for tips. He sat back down on the cistern wall that had been his stage, looking exhausted. People waited, stunned, until a few started yelling for more. Wit remained silent. He bore their requests, their pleas, then their curses.

Slowly, the audience drifted away.

Eventually, only Shallan stood before him.

Wit smiled at her.

'Why that story?' she asked. 'Why now?'

'I don't give the meanings, child,' he said. 'You should know that by now. I just tell the tale.'

'It was beautiful.'

'Yes,' he said. Then he added, 'I miss my flute.'

'Your what?'

He hopped up and began gathering his things. Shallan slipped forward and glanced inside his pack, catching sight of a small jar, sealed at the top. It was mostly black, but the side pointed toward her was instead white.

Wit snapped the pack closed. 'Come. You look like you could use the opportunity to buy me something to eat.'

My research into the cognitive reflections of spren at the tower has been deeply illustrative. Some thought that the Sibling had withdrawn from men by intent – but I find counter to that theory.

—From drawer 1-1, first zircon

Wit led Shallan to a squat tavern that was so grown over with crem, it gave the impression of having been molded from clay. Inside, a fabrial ceiling fan hung motionless; starting it up would have drawn the attention of the strange screaming spren.

Despite the large signs outside offering chouta for sale, the place was empty. The prices raised Shallan's eyebrows, but the scents emanating from the kitchen were inviting. The innkeeper was a short, heavyset Alethi man with a paunch so thick he looked like a big chull egg. He scowled as Wit entered.

'You!' he said, pointing. 'Storyteller! You were supposed to draw customers here! The place would be full, you said!'

'My tyrannical liege, I believe you misunderstood.' Wit gave a flowery bow. 'I said that you would be full. And you are. Of what, I did not say, as I did not wish to sully my tongue.'

'Where are my patrons, you idiot!'

Wit stepped to the side, holding out his hands toward Shallan. 'Behold, mighty and terrible king, I have recruited you a subject.'

The innkeeper squinted at her. 'Can she pay?'

'Yes,' Wit said, holding up Shallan's purse and poking through it. 'She'll probably leave a tip too.'

With a start, Shallan felt at her pocket. Storms, she'd even kept her hand on that purse most of the day.

'Take the private room then,' the innkeeper said. 'It's not like anyone else is using it. Idiot bard. I'll expect a good performance out of you tonight!'

Wit sighed, tossing Shallan her purse. He seized his pack and brazier, leading her to a chamber beside the main dining room. As he ushered her in, he raised a fist toward the innkeeper. 'I've had enough of your oppression, tyrant! Secure your wine well this evening, for the revolution will be swift, vengeful, and intoxicated!'

Closing the door behind him, Wit shook his head. 'That man really should know better by now. I have no idea why he continues to put up with me.' He set his brazier and pack by the wall, then settled at the room's dining table, where he leaned back and put his boots up on the seat next to him.

Shallan sat at the table more delicately, Pattern slipping off her coat and across to dimple the tabletop next to her. Wit didn't react to the spren.

The room was nice, with painted wood panels set into the walls and rockbuds along a ledge near the small window. The table even had a yellow silk tablecloth. The room was obviously meant for lighteyes to enjoy private dining, while unsavory darkeyes ate out in the main chamber.

'That's a nice illusion,' Wit said. 'You got the back of the head right. People always flub the back. You've broken character though. You're walking like a prim lighteyes, which looks silly in that costume. You'll only be able to pull off a coat and hat if you *own* them.'

'I know,' she said, grimacing. 'The persona . . . fled once you recognized me.'

'Shame about the dark hair. Your natural red would be arresting with the white coat.'

'This guise is supposed to be less memorable than that.'

He glanced at the hat, which she'd set on the table. Shallan blushed.

She felt like a girl nervously showing her first drawings to her tutor.

The innkeeper entered with drinks, a mild orange, as it was still early in the day. 'Many thanks, my liege,' Wit said. 'I vow to compose another song about you. One without so many references to the things you've mistaken for young maidens ...'

'Storming idiot,' the man said. He set the drinks on the table, and didn't notice that Pattern rippled out from under one. The innkeeper bustled out, closing the door.

'Are you one of them?' Shallan blurted out. 'Are you a Herald, Wit?'

Pattern hummed softly.

'Heavens no,' Wit said. 'I'm not stupid enough to get mixed up in religion again. The last seven times I tried it were all disasters. I believe there's at least one god still worshipping me by accident.'

She eyed him. It was always hard to tell which of Wit's exaggerations were supposed to mean something and which were confusing distractions. 'Then what *are* you?'

'Some men, as they age, grow kinder. I am not one of those, for I have seen how the cosmere can mistreat the innocent – and that leaves me disinclined toward kindness. Some men, as they age, grow wiser. I am not one of those, for wisdom and I have always been at cross-purposes, and I have yet to learn the tongue in which she speaks. Some men, as they age, grow more cynical. I, fortunately, am not one of those. If I were, the very air would warp around me, sucking in all emotion, leaving only scorn.'

He tapped the table. 'Other men ... other men, as they age, merely grow stranger. I fear that I *am* one of those. I am the bones of a foreign species left drying on the plain that was once, long ago, a sea. A curiosity, perhaps a reminder, that all has not always been as it is now.'

'You're ... old, aren't you? Not a Herald, but as old as they are?'

He slid his boots off the chair and leaned forward, holding her eyes. He smiled in a kindly way. 'Child, when they were but babes, I had already lived dozens of lifetimes. "Old" is a word you use for worn shoes. I'm something else entirely.'

She trembled, looking into those blue eyes. Shadows played within them. Shapes moved, and were worn down by time. Boulders became dust. Mountains became hills. Rivers changed course. Seas became deserts.

'Storms,' she whispered.

'When I was young . . .' he said.

'Yes?'

'I made a vow.'

Shallan nodded, wide-eyed.

'I said I'd always be there when I was needed.'

'And you have been?'

'Yes.'

She breathed out.

'It turns out I should have been more specific, as "there" is technically anywhere.'

'It . . . what?'

'To be honest, "there" has – so far – been a random location that is of absolutely no use to anyone.'

Shallan hesitated. In an instant, whatever she seemed to have sensed in Wit was gone. She flopped back in her seat. 'Why am I talking to *you* of all people?'

'Shallan!' he said, aghast. 'If you were talking to someone else, they wouldn't be me.'

'I happen to know plenty of people who aren't you, Wit. I even *like* some of them.'

'Be careful. People who aren't me are prone to spontaneous bouts of sincerity.'

'Which is bad?'

'Of course! "Sincerity" is a word people use to justify their chronic dullness.'

'Well, *I* like sincere people,' Shallan said, raising her cup. 'It's delightful how surprised they look when you push them down the stairs.'

'Now, that's unkind. You shouldn't push people down the stairs for being sincere. You push people down the stairs for being *stupid*.'

'What if they're sincere *and* stupid?'

'Then you run.'

'I quite like arguing with them instead. They do make me look smart, and Vev knows I need the help. . . .'

'No, no. You should *never* debate an idiot, Shallan. No more than you'd use your best sword to spread butter.'

'Oh, but I'm a scholar. I enjoy things with curious properties, and stupidity is *most* interesting. The more you study it, the further it flees – and yet the more of it you obtain, the less you understand about it!'

Wit sipped his drink. 'True, to an extent. But it can be hard to spot, as – like body odor – you never notice your own. That said . . . put two smart people together, and they *will* eventually find their common stupidity, and in so doing become idiots.'

'Like a child, it grows the more you feed it.'

'Like a fashionable dress, it can be fetching in youth, but looks particularly bad on the aged. And unique though its properties may be, stupidity is frighteningly common. The sum total of stupid people is somewhere around the population of the planet. Plus one.'

'Plus one?' Shallan asked.

'Sadeas counts twice.'

'Um . . . he's dead, Wit.'

'What?' Wit sat up straight.

'Someone murdered him. Er . . . we don't know who.' Aladar's investigators had continued hunting the culprit, but the investigation had stalled by the time Shallan left.

'Someone offed old Sadeas, and I *missed* it?'

'What would you have done? Helped him?'

'Storms, no. I'd have *applauded.*'

Shallan grinned and let out a deep sigh. Her hair had reverted to red – she'd let the illusion lapse. 'Wit,' she said, 'why are you here? In the city?'

'I'm not completely sure.'

'Please. Could you just answer?'

'I did – and I was honest. I can know where I'm supposed to be, Shallan, but not always what I'm supposed to do there.' He tapped the table. 'Why are *you* here?'

'To open the Oathgate,' Shallan said. 'Save the city.'

Pattern hummed.

'Lofty goals,' Wit said.

'What's the point of goals, if not to spur you to something lofty?'

'Yes, yes. Aim for the sun. That way if you miss, at least your arrow will fall far away, and the person it kills will likely be someone you don't know.'

The innkeeper chose that moment to arrive with some food. Shallan didn't feel particularly hungry; seeing all those starving people outside had stolen her appetite.

The small plates held crumbly cakes of Soulcast grain topped with a single steamed cremling – a variety known as a skrip, with a flat tail, two large claws, and long antennae. Eating cremlings wasn't uncommon, but it wasn't particularly fine dining.

The only difference between Shallan's meal and Wit's was the sauce – hers sweet, his spicy, though his had the sauce in a cup at the side. Food supplies were tight, and the kitchen wasn't preparing both masculine and feminine dishes.

The innkeeper frowned at her hair, then shook his head and left. She got the impression he was accustomed to oddities around Wit.

Shallan looked down at her food. Could she give this to someone else? Someone who deserved it more than she did?

'Eat up,' Wit said, rising and walking to the small window. 'Don't waste what you're given.'

Reluctantly, she did as he instructed. It wasn't particularly good, but it wasn't terrible. 'Aren't you going to eat?' she asked.

'I'm smart enough not to follow my own advice, thank you very much.' He sounded distracted. Outside the window, a procession from the Cult of Moments was passing.

'I want to learn to be like you,' Shallan said, feeling silly as she said it.

'No you don't.'

'You're funny, and charming, and—'

'Yes, yes. I'm so storming clever that half the time, even *I* can't follow what I'm talking about.'

'—and you change things, Wit. When you came to me, in Jah Keved, you changed everything. I want to be able to do that. I want to be able to change the world.'

He didn't seem at all interested in his food. *Does he eat?* she wondered. *Or is he . . . like some kind of spren?*

'Who came with you to the city?' he asked her.

'Kaladin. Adolin. Elhokar. Some of our servants.'

'King Elhokar? Here?'

'He's determined to save the city.'

'Most days, Elhokar has trouble saving face, let alone cities.'

'I like him,' Shallan said. 'Despite his . . . Elhokarness.'

'He does grow on you, I suppose. Like a fungus.'

'He really wants to do what is right. You should hear him talk about it lately. He wants to be remembered as a good king.'

'Vanity.'

'You don't care about how you'll be remembered?'

'I'll remember myself, which is enough. Elhokar though, he worries about the wrong things. His father wore a simple crown because he needed no reminder of his authority. Elhokar wears a simple crown because he worries that something more lavish might make people look at it, instead of at him. He doesn't want the competition.'

Wit turned away from his inspection of the hearth and chimney. 'You want to change the world, Shallan. That's well and good. But be careful. The world predates you. She has seniority.'

'I'm a Radiant,' Shallan said, shoving another forkful of crumbly, sweet bread into her mouth. 'Saving the world is in the job description.'

'Then be wise about it. There are two kinds of important men, Shallan. There are those who, when the boulder of time rolls toward them, stand up in front of it and hold out their hands. All their lives, they've been told how great they are. They assume the world itself will bend to their whims as their nurse did when fetching them a fresh cup of milk.

'Those men end up squished.

'Other men stand to the side when the boulder of time passes, but are quick to say, "See what I did! I made the boulder roll there. Don't make me do it again!"

'These men end up getting everyone else squished.'

'Is there not a third type of person?'

'There is, but they are oh so rare. These know they can't stop the boulder. So they walk beside it, study it, and bide their time. Then they shove it – ever so slightly – to create a deviation in its path.

'These are the men . . . well, these are the men who actually change the world. And they terrify me. For men never see as far as they think they do.'

Shallan frowned, then looked at her empty plate. She hadn't thought she was hungry, but once she'd started eating . . .

Wit walked past and deftly lifted her plate away, then swapped it with his full one.

'Wit . . . I can't eat that.'

'Don't be persnickety,' he said. 'How are you going to save the world if you starve yourself?'

'I'm *not* starving myself.' But she took a little bite to satisfy him. 'You make it sound like having the power to change the world is a bad thing.'

'Bad? No. Abhorrent, depressing, ghastly. Having power is a terrible burden, the worst thing imaginable, except for every other alternative.' He turned and studied her. 'What is *power* to you, Shallan?'

'It's . . .' Shallan cut at the cremling, separating it from its shell. 'It's what I said earlier – the ability to change things.'

'Things?'

'Other people's lives. Power is the ability to make life better or worse for the people around you.'

'And yourself too, of course.'

'I don't matter.'

'You should.'

'Selflessness is a Vorin virtue, Wit.'

'Oh, bother *that*. You've got to live life, Shallan, *enjoy* life. Drink of what you're proposing to give everyone else! That's what I do.'

'You . . . do seem to enjoy yourself a great deal.'

'I like to live every day like it's my last.'

Shallan nodded.

'And by that I mean lying in a puddle of my own urine, calling for the nurse to bring me more pudding.'

She almost choked on a bite of cremling. Her cup was empty, but Wit walked past and put his in her hand. She gulped it down.

'Power is a knife,' Wit said, taking his seat. 'A terrible, dangerous knife that can't be wielded without cutting yourself. We joked about stupidity, but in reality most people aren't stupid. Many are simply *frustrated* at how little control they have over their lives. They lash out. Sometimes in spectacular ways . . .'

'The Cult of Moments. They reportedly claim to see a transformed world coming upon us.'

'Be wary of anyone who claims to be able to see the future, Shallan.'

'Except you, of course. Didn't you say you can see where you need to be?'

'Be wary,' he repeated, 'of *anyone* who claims to be able to see the future, Shallan.'

Pattern rippled on the table, not humming, only changing more quickly, forming new shapes in a rapid sequence. Shallan swallowed. To her surprise, her plate was empty again. 'The cult has control of the

Oathgate platform,' she said. 'Do you know what they do up there every night?'

'They feast,' Wit said softly, 'and party. There are two general divisions among them. The common members wander the streets, moaning, pretending to be spren. But others up on the platform actually *know* the spren – specifically, the creature known as the Heart of the Revel.'

'One of the Unmade.'

Wit nodded. 'A dangerous foe, Shallan. The cult reminds me of a group I knew long ago. Equally dangerous, equally foolish.'

'Elhokar wants me to infiltrate them. Get onto that platform and activate the Oathgate. Is it possible?'

'Perhaps.' Wit settled back. 'Perhaps. I can't make the gate work; the spren of the fabrial won't obey me. You have the proper key, and the cult takes new members eagerly. Consumes them, like a fire needing new logs.'

'How? What do I do?'

'Food,' he said. 'Their proximity to the Heart drives them to feast and celebrate.'

'Drinking in life?' she said, quoting his sentiment from earlier.

'No. Hedonism has never been enjoyment, Shallan, but the opposite. They take the wonderful things of life and indulge until they lose savor. It's listening to beautiful music, performed so loud as to eliminate all subtlety – taking something beautiful and making it carnal. Yet their feasting does give you an opening. I've brushed against their leaders – despite my best efforts. Bring them food for the revel, and I can get you in. A warning, however, simple Soulcast grain won't satisfy them.'

A challenge, then. 'I should get back to the others.' She looked up to Wit. 'Would you ... come with me? Join us?'

He stood, then walked to the door and pressed his ear against it. 'Unfortunately, Shallan,' he said, glancing at her, 'you're not why I am here.'

She took a deep breath. 'I *am* going to learn how to change the world, Wit.'

'You already know how. Learn *why*.' He stepped back from the door and pressed himself against the wall. 'Also, tell the innkeeper I disappeared in a puff of smoke. It will drive him crazy.'

'The inn—'

The door opened suddenly, swinging inward. The innkeeper entered, and hesitated as he found Shallan sitting alone at the table. Wit slipped deftly around the door and out behind the man, who didn't notice.

'Damnation,' the innkeeper said, searching around. 'I don't suppose he's going to work tonight?'

'I have no idea.'

'He said he'd treat me like a king.'

'Well, he's keeping that promise . . .'

The innkeeper took the plates, then bustled out. Conversations with Wit had a way of ending in an odd manner. And, well, starting in an odd manner. Odd all around.

'Do you know anything about Wit?' she asked Pattern.

'No,' Pattern said. 'He feels like . . . mmm . . . one of us.'

Shallan fished in her pouch for some spheres – Wit had stolen a few, she noted – as a tip for the poor innkeeper. Then she made her way back to the tailor's shop, planning how to use her team to get the requisite food.

FREE MEAL, NO STRINGS

The wilting of plants and the general cooling of the air is disagreeable, yes, but some of the tower's functions remain in place. The increased pressure, for example, persists.

—From drawer 1-1, second zircon

Kaladin drew in a small amount of Stormlight and stoked the tempest within. That little storm raged inside him, rising from his skin, haunting the space behind his eyes and making them glow. Fortunately – though he stood in a busy market square – this tiny amount of Stormlight wouldn't be enough for people to see in the bright sunlight.

The storm was a primal dance, an ancient song, an eternal battle that had raged since Roshar was new. It wanted to be used. He acquiesced, kneeling to infuse a small stone. He Lashed it upward just enough to make it tremble, but not enough to send it zipping into the air.

The eerie screams came soon after. People started to shout in panic. Kaladin ducked away, exhaling his Stormlight and becoming – hopefully – merely another bystander. He crouched with Shallan and Adolin behind a planter. This plaza – with pillared archways on all four sides, sheltering what had once been a great variety of shops – was several blocks away from the tailor's shop.

People squeezed into buildings or slipped out onto other streets. The slow ones simply huddled down beside the walls, hands over their heads. The spren arrived as two lines of bright yellow-white, twisting about one another above the plaza. Their inhuman screeches were awful. Like ... like the sound of a wounded animal, dying alone in the wilderness.

Those weren't the spren he'd seen while traveling with Sah and the other parshmen. That one had seemed more akin to a windspren; these looked like vivid yellow spheres crackling with energy. They didn't seem to be able to pinpoint the rock directly, and spun over the courtyard as if confused, still screaming.

A short time later, a figure descended from the sky. A Voidbringer in loose red and black clothing that rippled and churned in the breeze. He carried a spear and a tall, triangular shield.

That spear, Kaladin thought. Long, with a slender point for puncturing armor, it was like a horseman's lance. He found himself nodding. That would be an excellent weapon for using in flight, where you'd need extra reach to attack men on the ground, or even enemies soaring around you.

The spren ceased screaming. The Voidbringer looked about, fluttering through the air, then glared at the spren and said something. Again, they seemed confused. They'd sensed Kaladin's use of Stormlight – likely interpreted it as a fabrial being used – but now couldn't pinpoint the location. Kaladin had used such a small amount of Stormlight, the rock had lost its charge almost immediately.

The spren dispersed, vanishing as emotion spren often did. The Voidbringer lingered, surrounded by dark energy, until horns nearby announced the Wall Guard approaching. The creature finally shot back into the air. People who had been hiding scuttled away, looking relieved to have escaped with their lives.

'Huh,' Adolin said, standing. He wore an illusion, imitating – as per Elhokar's instructions – Captainlord Meleran Khal, Teshav's youngest son, a powerfully built balding man in his thirties.

'I can hold Stormlight as long as I want without drawing attention,' Kaladin said. 'The moment I Lash something, they come screaming.'

'And yet,' Adolin said, glancing at Shallan, 'the disguises draw no attention.'

'Pattern says we're quieter than him,' Shallan said, thumbing toward

Kaladin. 'Come on, let's get back. Don't you boys have an appointment tonight?'

⁂

'A party,' Kaladin said, pacing back and forth in the tailor shop's showroom. Skar and Drehy leaned by the doorway, each with a spear in the crook of his arm.

'*This* is what they're like,' Kaladin said. 'Your city is practically burning. What should you do? Throw a *party*, obviously.'

Elhokar had suggested parties as a way of contacting the city's lighteyed families. Kaladin had laughed at the idea, assuming that there wouldn't be such a thing. Yet, with minimal searching, Adolin had scrounged up *half a dozen* invitations.

'Good darkeyed people slave away, growing and preparing food,' Kaladin said. 'But the lighteyes? They have so much storming time they have to *make up* things to do.'

'Hey Skar,' Drehy said. 'You ever go out drinking, even when at war?'

'Sure,' Skar said. 'And back in my village, we'd have a dance in the stormshelter twice a month, even while boys were off fighting in border skirmishes.'

'It's not the same,' Kaladin said. 'You taking their side?'

'Are there sides?' Drehy asked.

A few minutes later, Adolin came tromping down the stairs and grinning like a fool. He was wearing a ruffled shirt under a powder-blue suit with a jacket that didn't close all the way and tails at the back. Its golden embroidery was the finest the shop could provide.

'Please tell me,' Kaladin said, 'that you didn't bring us to live with your tailor because you wanted a new wardrobe.'

'Come on, Kal,' Adolin said, inspecting himself in a showroom mirror. 'I need to look the part.' He checked his cuffs and grinned again.

Yokska came out and looked him over, then dusted his shoulders. 'I think it pulls too tightly through the chest, Brightlord.'

'It's wonderful, Yokska.'

'Take a deep breath.'

It was like she was a storming surgeon, the way she lifted his arm and felt at his waist, muttering to herself. Kaladin had seen his father give physicals that were less invasive.

123

'I thought that straight coats were still the style,' Adolin said. 'I have a folio out of Liafor.'

'Those aren't up to date,' Yokska said. 'I was in Liafor last Midpeace, and they're moving *away* from military styles. But they made those folios to sell uniforms at the Shattered Plains.'

'Storms! I had *no idea* how unfashionable I was being.'

Kaladin rolled his eyes. Adolin saw that in the mirror, but just turned around, giving a bow. 'Don't worry, bridgeboy. You can continue to wear clothing to match your scowl.'

'You look like you tripped and fell into a bucket of blue paint,' Kaladin said, 'then tried to dry off with a handful of parched grass.'

'And you look like what the storm leaves behind,' Adolin said, passing by and patting Kaladin on the shoulder. 'We like you anyway. Every boy has a favorite stick he found out in the yard after the rains.'

Adolin stepped over to Skar and Drehy, clasping hands with each of them in turn. 'You two looking forward to tonight?'

'Depends on how the food is in the darkeyed tent, sir,' Skar said.

'Swipe me something from the inner party,' Drehy said. 'I hear they've got storming good pastries at those fancy lighteyes parties.'

'Sure. You need anything, Skar?'

'The head of my enemy, fashioned into a tankard for drinking,' Skar said. 'Barring that, I'll take a pastry or seven.'

'I'll see what I can do. Keep your ears open for any good taverns that are still open. We can go out tomorrow.' He strode past Kaladin and tied on a side sword.

Kaladin frowned, looking to him, then to his bridgemen, then back at Adolin. 'What?'

'What what?' Adolin asked.

'You're going to go out drinking with bridgemen?' Kaladin said.

'Sure,' Adolin said. 'Skar, Drehy, and I go way back.'

'We spent some time keeping His Highness from falling into chasms,' Skar said. 'He repaid us with a bit of wine and good conversation.'

The king entered, wearing a more muted version of the same style of uniform. He bustled past Adolin, heading toward the stairs. 'Ready? Excellent. Time for new faces.'

The three stopped by Shallan's room, where she was sketching and humming to herself, surrounded by creationspren. She gave Adolin a kiss that was more intimate than Kaladin had seen from the two of them before, then changed him back into Meleran Khal. Elhokar became an older man, also bald, with pale yellow eyes. General Khal, one of Dalinar's highest officers.

'I'm fine,' Kaladin said as she eyed him. 'Nobody is going to recognize me.'

He wasn't sure what it was, but wearing another face like that . . . to him it felt like lying.

'The scars,' Elhokar said. 'We need you not to stand out, Captain.'

Reluctantly, Kaladin nodded, and allowed Shallan to add a Lightweaving to his head to make the slave brands vanish. Then, she handed each of them a sphere. The illusions were tied to the Stormlight inside of those – if the sphere ran out, their false faces would vanish.

The group set out, Skar and Drehy joining them, spears at the ready. Syl flitted out from an upper window of the shop, soaring on ahead of them along the street. Kaladin had tested summoning her as a Blade earlier, and that hadn't drawn the screamers, so he felt well-armed.

Adolin immediately started joking with Skar and Drehy. Dalinar wouldn't have liked to hear they'd gone out drinking. Not because of any specific prejudice, but there was a command structure to an army. Generals weren't supposed to fraternize with the rank and file; it threw wrinkles into how armies worked.

Adolin could get away with things like that. As he listened, Kaladin found himself feeling ashamed of his earlier attitude. The truth was, he was feeling pretty good these days. Yes, there was a war, and yes, the city was seriously stressed – but ever since he'd found his parents alive and well, he'd been feeling better.

That wasn't so uncommon a feeling for him. He felt good lots of days. Trouble was, on the bad days, that was hard to remember. At those times, for some reason, he felt like he had *always* been in darkness, and always *would* be.

Why was it so hard to remember? Did he have to keep slipping back down? Why couldn't he stay up here in the sunlight, where everyone else lived?

It was nearing evening, maybe two hours from sunset. They passed several plazas like the one where they'd tested his Surgebinding. Most had been turned into living space, with people crowding in. Just sitting and waiting for whatever would happen next.

Kaladin trailed a little behind the others, and when Adolin noticed, he excused himself from the conversation and dropped back. 'Hey,' he said. 'You all right?'

'I'm worried that summoning a Shardblade would make me stand out too much,' Kaladin said. 'I should have brought a spear tonight.'

'Maybe you should let me teach you how to use a side sword. You're pretending to be head of our bodyguards tonight, and you're lighteyed today. It looks strange for you to walk around without a side sword.'

'Maybe I'm one of those punchy guys.'

Adolin stopped in place and grinned at Kaladin. 'Did you just say *"punchy guys"*?'

'You know, ardents who train to fight unarmed.'

'Hand to hand?'

'Hand to hand.'

'Right,' Adolin said. 'Or "punchy guys," as everyone calls them.'

Kaladin met his eyes, then found himself grinning back. 'It's the academic term.'

'Sure. Like swordy fellows. Or spearish chaps.'

'I once knew a real axalacious bloke,' Kaladin said. 'He was great at psychological fights.'

'Psychological fights?'

'He could really get inside someone's head.'

Adolin frowned as they walked. 'Get inside . . . Oh!' Adolin chuckled, slapping Kaladin on the back. 'You talk like a girl sometimes. Um . . . I mean that as a compliment.'

'Thanks?'

'But you *do* need to practice the sword more,' Adolin said, growing excited. 'I know you like the spear, and you're good with it. Great! But you're not simply a spearman anymore; you're going to be an irregular. You won't be fighting in a line, holding a shield for your buddies. Who knows what you'll be facing?'

'I trained a little with Zahel,' Kaladin said. 'I'm not *completely* useless with a sword. But . . . part of me doesn't see the point.'

'You'll be better if you practice with a sword, trust me. Being a good duelist is about knowing one weapon, and being a good foot soldier

– that's probably more about training than it is about *any* single weapon. But you want to be a great *warrior*? For that you need to be able to use the best tool for the job. Even if you're never going to use a sword, you'll fight people who do. The best way to learn how to defeat someone wielding a weapon is to practice with it yourself.'

Kaladin nodded. He was right. It was strange to look at Adolin in that bright outfit, stylish and glittering with golden thread, and hear him speak real battle sense.

When I was imprisoned for daring to accuse Amaram, he was the only light-eyes who stood up for me.

Adolin Kholin was simply a good person. Powder-blue clothing and all. You couldn't hate a man like him; storms, you kind of *had* to like him.

Their destination was a modest home, by lighteyed standard. Tall and narrow, at four stories high it could have housed a dozen darkeyed families.

'All right,' Elhokar said as they drew near. 'Adolin and I will feel out the lighteyes for potential allies. Bridgemen, chat with those in the dar-keyed guard tent, and see if you can discover anything about the Cult of Moments, or other oddities in the city.'

'Got it, Your Majesty,' Drehy said.

'Captain,' he said to Kaladin, 'you'll go to the lighteyed guard tent. See if you can—'

'—find out anything about this Highmarshal Azure person,' Kaladin said. 'From the Wall Guard.'

'Yes. We will plan to stay relatively late, as intoxicated party guests might share more than sober ones.'

They broke, Adolin and Elhokar presenting invitations to the doorman, who let them in – then gestured Drehy and Skar toward the darkeyed guards' feast, happening in a tent set up on the grounds.

There was a separate tent for people who were lighteyed but not land-owners. Privileged, but not good enough to get in the doors to the actual party. In his role as a lighteyed bodyguard, that would be the place for Kaladin – but for some reason the thought of going in there made him feel sick.

Instead he whispered to Skar and Drehy – promising to be back soon – and borrowed Skar's spear, just in case. Then Kaladin left, walking the block. He'd return to do as told by Elhokar. But while there was enough light, he thought he'd maybe survey the wall and see if he could get an idea of the Wall Guard's numbers.

More, he wanted to walk a little longer. He strolled to the foot of the nearby city wall, counting guard posts on top, looking at the large lower portion that was a natural part of the local rock. He rested his hand on the smooth, strata-lined formation of stone.

'Hey!' a voice called. 'Hey, you!'

Kaladin sighed. A squad of soldiers from the Wall Guard was patrolling here. They considered this road around the city – next to the foot of the wall – to be their jurisdiction, but they didn't patrol any farther inward.

What did they want? He wasn't doing anything wrong. Well, running would only stir up a ruckus, so he dropped his spear and turned around, extending his arms out to the sides. In a city full of refugees, certainly they wouldn't harass one man too much.

A squad of five tromped over to him, led by a man with a wispy dark beard and bright, light blue eyes. The man took in Kaladin's uniform, with no insignia, and glanced at the fallen spear. Then he looked at Kaladin's forehead and frowned.

Kaladin raised his hands to the brands there, which he could feel. But Shallan had put an illusion over those. Hadn't she?

Damnation. He's going to assume I'm a deserter.

'Deserter, I assume?' the soldier asked sharply.

Should have just gone to the storming party.

'Look,' Kaladin said. 'I don't want trouble. I just—'

'Do you want a meal?'

'A . . . meal?'

'Free food for deserters.'

That's unexpected.

Reluctantly, he lifted the hair from his forehead, testing to see that the brands were still visible. Mostly, the hair prevented one from seeing the details.

The soldiers started visibly. Yes, they could see the brands. Shallan's illusion had worn off for some reason? Hopefully the other disguises fared better.

'A lighteyes with a *shash* brand?' their lieutenant asked. 'Storms, friend. You've got to have *some* story.' He slapped Kaladin on the back and pointed toward their barracks ahead. 'I'd love to hear it. Free meal, no strings. We won't press you into service. I give my oath.'

Well, he'd wanted information about the leader of the Wall Guard, hadn't he? What better place to get it than from these men?

Kaladin picked up his spear and let them lead him away.

HIGHMARSHAL AZURE

Something is happening to the Sibling. I agree this is true, but the division among the Knights Radiant is not to blame. Our perceived worthiness is a separate issue.

—From drawer 1-1, third zircon

The Wall Guard's barracks smelled like home to Kaladin. Not his father's house – which smelled of antiseptic and the flowers his mother crushed to season the air. His *true* home. Leather. Boiling stew. Crowded men. Weapon oil.

Spheres hung on the walls, white and blue. The place was big enough to house two platoons, a fact confirmed by the shoulder patches he saw. The large common room was filled with tables, and a few armorers worked in the corner, sewing jerkins or uniforms. Others sharpened weapons, a rhythmic, calming sound. These were the noises and scents of an army well maintained.

The stew didn't smell anywhere near as good as Rock's; Kaladin had been spoiled by the Horneater's cooking. Still, when one of the men went to fetch him a bowl, he found himself smiling. He settled onto a long wooden bench, near a fidgety little ardent who was scribing glyphwards onto pieces of cloth for the men.

Kaladin instantly loved this place, and the state of the men spoke highly of Highmarshal Azure. He would likely be some middling officer who had been thrust into command during the chaos of the riots, which made him all the more impressive. Azure had secured the wall, gotten the parshmen out of the city, and seen to the defense of Kholinar.

Syl zipped around the rafters as soldiers called out questions about the newcomer. The lieutenant who had found him – his name was Noromin, but his men called him Noro – answered readily. Kaladin was a deserter. He had a *shash* brand, an ugly one. You should see it. Sadeas's mark. On a *lighteyes* no less.

The others in the barrack found this curious, but not worrisome. Some even cheered. Storms. Kaladin couldn't imagine any force of Dalinar's soldiers being so welcoming of a deserter, let alone a dangerous one.

Considering that, Kaladin now picked out another undercurrent in the room. Men sharpening weapons that had chips in them. Armorers repairing cuts in leather – cuts made by lances in battle. Conspicuously empty seats at most of the tables, with cups set at them.

These men had suffered losses. Not huge ones yet. They could still laugh. But storms, there was a tension to this room.

'So,' Noro said. '*Shash* brand?'

The rest of the squad settled in, and a short man with hair on the backs of his hands set a bowl of thick stew and flatbread in front of Kaladin. Standard fare, with steamed tallow and cubed meat. Soulcast, of course, and lacking flavor – but hearty and nutritious.

'I had a squabble,' Kaladin said, 'with Highlord Amaram. I felt he'd gotten some of my men killed needlessly. He disagreed.'

'Amaram,' said one of the men. 'You aim high, friend.'

'I know Amaram,' the man with hairy hands said. 'I did secret missions for him, back in my operative days.'

Kaladin looked at him, surprised.

'Best to ignore Beard,' Lieutenant Noro said. 'It's what the rest of us do.'

'Beard' didn't have a beard. Maybe the hairy hands were enough. He nudged Kaladin. 'It's a good story. I'll tell it to you sometime.'

'You can't just brand a lighteyed man a slave,' Lieutenant Noro said. 'You need a highprince's permission. There's more to this story.'

'There is,' Kaladin said. Then he continued eating his stew.

'Oooh,' said a tall member of the squad. 'Mystery!'

Noro chuckled, then waved at the room. 'So what do you think?'

'You said you weren't going to press me,' Kaladin said between bites.

'I'm not pressing you, but you won't find a place out there in the city where you'll eat as well as you do here.'

'Where do you get it?' Kaladin asked, spooning the stew into his mouth. 'You can't use Soulcasters. The screamers will come after you. Stockpile? I'm surprised one of the highlords in the city hasn't tried to appropriate it.'

'Astute,' Lieutenant Noro said with a smile. He had a disarming way about him. 'That's a Guard secret. But in here there's always a stew bubbling and bread baking.'

'It's my recipe,' Beard added.

'Oh please,' the tall man said. 'You're a cook now too, Beard?'

'A *chef*, thank you very much. I learned that flatbread recipe from a Horneater mystic at the top of a mountain. The real *story* is how I got there. . . .'

'It's where you landed, obviously,' the tall soldier said, 'after someone in your last squad *kicked* you.'

The men laughed. It felt warm in here, on this long bench, a well-laid fire burning steadily in the corner. Warm and friendly. As Kaladin ate, they gave him some space, chatting among themselves. Noro . . . he seemed less a soldier and more a chummy merchant trying to sell you earrings for your beloved. He dropped very obvious dangling hints for Kaladin. Reminders of how well-fed they were, of how good it was to be part of a squad. He spoke of warm beds, of how they didn't have to go on watch duty *that* often. Of playing cards while the highstorm blew.

Kaladin got a second bowl of stew, and as he settled back into his place, he realized something with a shock.

Storms. They're all *lighteyes, aren't they?*

Every person in the room, from the cook to the armorers, to the soldiers doing dishes. In a group like this, everyone had a secondary duty, like armoring or field surgery. Kaladin hadn't noticed their eyes. The place had felt so natural, so comfortable, that he'd assumed they were all dark-keyed like him.

He knew that most lighteyed soldiers weren't high officers. He'd been told that they were basically just people – he'd been told it over and over. Somehow, sitting in that room finally made the fact real to him.

'So, Kal . . .' Lieutenant Noro asked. 'What do you think? Maybe reenlist? Give this another try?'

'Aren't you afraid I'll desert?' Kaladin asked. 'Or worse, that I can't control my temper? I might be dangerous.'

'Not as dangerous as being short manned,' Beard said. 'You know how to kill people? That's good enough for us.'

Kaladin nodded. 'Tell me about your commander. That will be a big part of any group. I only just got into town. Who *is* this Highmarshal Azure?'

'You can meet him yourself!' Beard said. 'He does rounds every night around dinner time, checking on each barracks.'

'Um, yes,' Noro said.

Kaladin eyed him. The lieutenant seemed uncomfortable.

'The highmarshal,' Noro said quickly, 'is *incredible*. We lost our former commander during the riots, and Azure led a group who held the wall when the Cult of Moments tried – in the chaos – to seize the city gates.'

'He fought like a Voidbringer,' another squad member said. 'I was there. We were almost overwhelmed, then Azure joined us, holding aloft a gleaming Shardblade. He rallied our numbers, inspired even the wounded to keep fighting. Storms. Felt like we had spren at our backs, holding us up, helping us fight.'

Kaladin narrowed his eyes. 'You don't say . . .'

He pried more from them as he finished his bowl. They had nothing but praise for Azure, though the man hadn't displayed any other . . . odd abilities that Kaladin could discover. Azure was a Shardbearer, maybe a foreigner, who had been previously unknown to the Guard – but with the fall of their commander, and the subsequent disappearance of their highlord patron at the palace, Azure had ended up in command.

There was something else. Something they weren't saying. Kaladin helped himself to a third bowl of stew, more to delay to see if the highmarshal really would make an appearance or not.

Soon, a disturbance near the door sent men standing up. Kaladin followed suit, turning. A senior officer entered wearing a glittering chain and a bright tabard, accompanied by attendants, inspiring a round of salutes. The highmarshal wore an appropriately azure cloak – a lighter shade than the traditional Kholin blue – with a mail coif down around the neck and a helm carried in hand.

She was also a she.

Kaladin blinked in surprise, and heard a gasp from Syl up above. The highmarshal was of average height for an Alethi woman, maybe just under, and wore her hair straight and short, reaching halfway down her cheeks. Her eyes were orange, and she wore a side sword with a glistening silver basket hilt. That wasn't Alethi design. Was it the aforementioned Shardblade? It did have an otherworldly look about it, but why wear it instead of dismissing it?

Regardless, the highmarshal was lean and grim, and had a couple of serious scars on her face. She wore gloves on both hands.

'The highmarshal is a *woman*?' Kaladin hissed.

'We don't talk about the marshal's secret,' Beard said.

'Secret?' Kaladin said. 'It's pretty *storming* obvious.'

'We don't talk about the marshal's secret,' Beard repeated, and the others nodded. 'Hush, all right?'

Hush about it? Storms. This sort of thing simply didn't *happen* in Vorin society. Not like in the ballads and stories. He'd been in three armies, and had never seen a woman holding a weapon. Even the Alethi scouts carried only knives. He'd half expected a riot when he'd armed Lyn and the others, although for Radiants, Jasnah and Shallan had already supplied precedent.

Azure told the men they could sit down. One of the men offered her a bowl of stew, and she accepted. The men cheered after she took a bite and complimented the cook.

She handed the bowl to one of her attendants, and things returned to normal – men chatting, working, eating. Azure walked to speak with the various officers. First the platoon leader, who would be a captain. The other lieutenants next.

When she stopped at their table, she took in Kaladin with a discerning gaze.

'Who's the new recruit, Lieutenant Noro?' she asked.

'This is Kal, sir!' Noro said. 'Found him haunting the street outside. Deserter, with a *shash* brand.'

'On a lighteyes? Storms, man. Who did you kill?'

'It's not the one that I killed that got me my brands, sir. It's the one I didn't kill.'

'That has the sound of a practiced explanation, soldier.'

'That's because it is.'

Kaladin figured she, at last, would push for more information. She merely grunted. He couldn't place her age, though the scars probably made her look older than she really was.

'You joining up?' she said. 'We have food for you.'

'Frankly, sir, I don't know. On one hand, I can't believe nobody cares about my past. On the other, you're obviously desperate, which also makes me reluctant.'

She turned toward Lieutenant Noro. 'You haven't shown him?'

'No, sir. We just got some stew in him.'

'I'll do it. Kal, come with me.'

⁘

Whatever they wanted to show him was at the top of the wall, as they hiked him up an enclosed stone stairwell. Kaladin wanted to learn more about the supposed 'secret' that Azure was a woman. But when he asked, Lieutenant Noro shook his head quickly and made a hushing motion.

Soon they'd assembled atop the fortifications. The Kholinar wall was a powerful defensive structure, reportedly over sixty feet tall at points, with a wide wall walk on the top, ten feet across. The wall rolled across the landscape, enclosing all of Kholinar. It had actually been built *on top* of the outer windblades, fitting onto them like an inverted crown, the raised portions matching crevasses between windblades.

The wall was interrupted by guard towers every three hundred feet or so. These large structures were big enough to house squads, perhaps entire platoons, on watch.

'Guessing from that brand,' Azure said to him, 'you were in one of the armies that recruits in the north. You joined up to fight on the Shattered Plains, didn't you? But Sadeas used that army up north to funnel him veterans, plus maybe seize some land now and then from rival highprinces. You ended up fighting other Alethi, scared farmboys, instead of shipping off to avenge the king. Something like that?'

'Something like that,' Kaladin admitted.

'Damnation me if I blame a man for deserting that,' Azure said. 'I don't hold it against you, soldier.'

'And the brand?'

Azure pointed northward. Night had finally fallen, and in the distance, Kaladin could see a glow.

'They advance back into place after each storm,' Azure said softly. 'And camp a portion of their army out there. That's good battle sense, to prevent us from being resupplied – and to make sure we don't know when they'll attack. Nightmares, Kal. A real *Voidbringer* army.

'If that were an Alethi force, the people in this city wouldn't have much to worry about. Sure, there would be casualties on the wall, but no would-be king of Alethkar is going to burn and pillage the capital. But those *aren't* Alethi. They're monsters. At best, they'll enslave the entire populace. At worst . . .' She let the thought dangle, then looked at him. 'I'm *glad* you have a brand. It says you're dangerous, and we have narrow confines up here on the wall. We can't simply press every eligible man; I need real soldiers, men who know what they're doing.'

'So that's why I'm here?' Kaladin asked. 'To see that?'

'I want you to think,' Azure said. 'I tell the men – this Wall Guard, this is *redemption*. If you fight here, nobody will care what you did before. Because they know if we fall, this city and this nation will be no more.

'*Nothing* matters, except holding this wall when that assault comes. You can go hide in the city and pray that we are strong enough without you. But if we aren't, you'll be no more than another corpse. Up here, you can fight. Up here, you have a *chance*.

'We won't press you. Walk away tonight. Lie down and think about what is coming; imagine another night when men are up here dying, bleeding for you. Think about how powerless you'll feel if the monsters get in. Then when you come back tomorrow, we'll get you a Wall Guard patch.'

It was a potent speech. Kaladin glanced to Syl, who landed on his shoulder, then took a long look at the lights on the horizon.

Are you out there, Sah? Did they bring you and the others here? What of Sah's little daughter, who had collected flowers and clutched playing cards like a treasured toy? Was Khen there, the parshwoman who had demanded Kaladin retain his freedom, despite being angry at him for the entire trip?

Winds send that they hadn't been dragged further into this mess.

He joined the others in clattering back down the stairwell. Afterward, Noro and the rest of the squad bade him a happy farewell, as if certain he'd return. And he probably would, though not for the reasons they assumed.

He went back to the mansion and forced himself to chat with some of the guards at the lighteyed tent, though he learned nothing, and his brands made something of a stir among them. Adolin and Elhokar finally emerged, *their* illusions intact. So what was wrong with Kaladin's? The sphere Shallan had given him was still infused.

Kaladin gathered Drehy and Skar, then joined the king and Adolin as they started the walk home.

'What has you so thoughtful, Captain?' Elhokar asked.

'I think,' Kaladin said, eyes narrowed, 'I might have found us another Radiant.'

71
A SIGN OF
HUMANITY

ELEVEN YEARS AGO

There weren't enough boats for an amphibious attack on Rathalas, so Dalinar was forced to use a more conventional assault. He marched down from the west – having sent Adolin back to Kholinar – and assigned Sadeas and his forces to come in from the east. They converged toward the Rift.

Dalinar spent much of the trip passing through pungent smoke trails from the incense Evi burned in a small censer attached to the side of her carriage. A petition to the Heralds to bless her marriage.

He often heard her weeping inside the vehicle, though whenever she left it she was perfectly composed. She read letters, scribed his responses, and took notes at his meetings with generals. In every way, she was the perfect Alethi wife – and her unhappiness crushed his soul.

Eventually they reached the plains around the lake, crossing the riverbed – which was dry, except during storms. The rockbuds drank so fully of the local water supply, they'd grown to enormous sizes. Some were taller than a man's waist, and the vines they produced were as thick as Dalinar's wrist.

He rode alongside the carriage – his horse's hooves beating a familiar rhythm on the stones beneath – and smelled incense. Evi's hand reached out of her carriage's side window, and she placed another glyphward into the censer. He didn't see her face, and her hand retreated quickly.

Storming woman. An Alethi would be using this as a ploy to guilt him into bending. But she wasn't Alethi, for all her earnest imitations. Evi was far too genuine, and her tears were real. She sincerely thought their spat back in the Veden fortress boded ill for their relationship.

That bothered him. More than he wanted to admit.

A young scout jogged up to give him the latest report: The vanguard had secured his desired camp ground near the city. There had been no fighting yet, and he hadn't expected any. Tanalan would not abandon the walls around the Rift to try to control ground beyond bowshot.

It was good news, but Dalinar still wanted to snap at the messenger – he wanted to snap at *someone*. Stormfather, this battle couldn't come soon enough. He restrained himself and sent the messenger woman away with a word of thanks.

Why did he care so much about Evi's petulance? He'd never let his arguments with Gavilar bother him. Storms, he'd never let his arguments with *Evi* bother him this way before. It was strange. He could have the accolades of men, fame that stretched across a continent, but if she didn't admire him, he felt that he had somehow failed. Could he really ride into combat feeling like this?

No. He couldn't.

Then do something about it. As they wound through the plain of rock-buds, he called to the driver of Evi's carriage, having him stop. Then, handing his horse's reins to an attendant, he climbed into the carriage.

Evi bit her lip as he settled down on the seat across from her. It smelled nice within – the incense was fainter here, while the crem dust of the road was blocked by wood and cloth. The cushions were plush, and she had some dried fruit in a dish, even some chilled water.

'What is wrong?' she demanded.

'I was feeling saddle sore.'

She cocked her head. 'Perhaps you could request a salve—'

'I want to talk, Evi,' Dalinar said with a sigh. 'I'm not actually sore.'

'Oh.' She pulled her knees up against her chest. In here, she had undone and rolled back her safehand sleeve, displaying her long, elegant fingers.

'Isn't this what you wanted?' Dalinar said, looking away from the safe-hand. 'You've been praying nonstop.'

'For the Heralds to soften your heart.'

'Right. Well, they've done that. Here I am. Let's talk.'

'No, Dalinar,' she said, reaching across to fondly touch his knee. 'I wasn't praying for myself, but for those of your countrymen you are planning to kill.'

'The rebels?'

'Men no different from you, who happened to be born in another city. What would *you* have done, had an army come to conquer your home?'

'I'd have fought,' Dalinar said. 'As they will. The better men will dominate.'

'What gives you the right?'

'My sword.' Dalinar shrugged. 'If the Almighty wants us to rule, we'll win. If He doesn't, then we'll lose. I rather think He wants to see which of us is stronger.'

'And is there no room for mercy?'

'Mercy landed us here in the first place. If they don't want to fight, they should give in to our rule.'

'But—' She looked down, hands in her lap. 'I'm sorry. I don't want another argument.'

'I do,' Dalinar said. 'I like it when you stand up for yourself. I like it when you *fight*.'

She blinked tears and looked away.

'Evi . . .' Dalinar said.

'I hate what this does to you,' she said softly. 'I see beauty in you, Dalinar Kholin. I see a great man struggling against a terrible one. And sometimes, you get this look in your eyes. A horrible, terrifying nothingness. Like you have become a creature with no heart, feasting upon souls to fill that void, dragging painspren in your wake. It haunts me, Dalinar.'

Dalinar shifted on the carriage seat. What did that even mean? A 'look' in his eyes? Was this like when she'd claimed that people stored bad memories in their skin, and needed to rub them off with a stone once a month? Westerners had some curiously superstitious beliefs.

'What would you have me do, Evi?' he asked softly.

'Have I won again?' she said, sounding bitter. 'Another battle where I've bloodied you?'

'I just . . . I need to know what you want. So I can understand.'

'Don't kill today. Hold back the monster.'

'And the rebels? Their brightlord?'

'You spared that boy's life once before.'

'An obvious mistake.'

'A sign of *humanity*, Dalinar. You asked what I want. It is foolish, and I *can* see there is trouble here, that you have a duty. But . . . I do not wish to see you kill. Do not feed *it*.'

He rested his hand on hers. Eventually the carriage slowed again, and Dalinar stepped out to survey an open area not clogged by rockbuds. The vanguard waited there, five thousand strong, assembled in perfect ranks. Teleb did like to put on a good show.

Across the field, outside of bowshot, a wall broke the landscape with – seemingly – nothing to protect. The city was hidden in the rift in the stone. From the southwest, a breeze off the lake brought the fecund scent of weeds and crem.

Teleb strode up, wearing his Plate. Well, Adolin's Plate.

Evi's Plate.

'Brightlord,' Teleb said, 'a short time ago, a large guarded caravan left the Rift. We hadn't the men to besiege the city, and you had ordered us not to engage. So I sent a scout team to tail them, men who know the area, but otherwise let the caravan escape.'

'You did well,' Dalinar said, taking his horse from a groom. 'Though I'd have liked to know who was bringing supplies to the Rift, that might have been an attempt to draw you away into a skirmish. However, gather the vanguard now and bring them in behind me. Pass the word to the rest of the men. Have them form ranks, just in case.'

'Sir?' Teleb asked, shocked. 'You don't want to rest the army before attacking?'

Dalinar swung into the saddle and rode past him at a trot, heading toward the Rift. Teleb – usually so unflappable – cursed and shouted orders, then hurried to the vanguard, gathering them and marching them hastily behind Dalinar.

Dalinar made sure not to get too far ahead. Soon he approached the walls of Rathalas, where the rebels had gathered, primarily archers. They wouldn't be expecting an attack so soon, but of course Dalinar wouldn't camp for long outside either, not exposed to the storms.

Do not feed it.

Did she know that he considered this hunger inside of him, the bloodlust, to be something strangely external? A companion. Many of his officers felt the same. It was natural. You went to war, and the Thrill was your reward.

Dalinar's armorers arrived, and he climbed out of the saddle and stepped into the boots they provided, then held out his arms, letting them quickly strap on his breastplate and other sections of armor.

'Wait here,' he told his men, then climbed back onto his horse and set his helm on his pommel. He walked his horse out onto the killing field, summoning his Shardblade and resting it on his shoulder, reins in the other hand.

Years had passed since his last assault on the Rift. He imagined Gavilar racing ahead of him, Sadeas cursing from behind them and demanding 'prudence.' Dalinar picked his way forward until he was about halfway to the gates. Any closer and those archers were likely to start shooting; he was already well within their range. He stilled his horse and waited.

There was some discussion on the walls; he could see the agitation among the soldiers. After about thirty minutes of him sitting there, his horse calmly licking the ground and nibbling at the grass that peeked out, the gates finally creaked open. A company of infantrymen poured out, accompanying two men on horseback. Dalinar dismissed the bald one with the purple birthmark across half his face; he was too old to be the boy Dalinar had spared.

It had to be the younger man riding the white steed, cape streaming behind him. Yes, he had an eagerness to him, his horse threatening to outstrip his guards. And the way he stared daggers at Dalinar . . . this was Brightlord Tanalan, son of the old Tanalan, whom Dalinar had bested after falling down into the Rift itself. That furious fight across wooden bridges and then in a garden suspended from the side of the chasm.

The group stopped about fifty feet from Dalinar.

'Have you come to parley?' called the man with the birthmark on his face.

Dalinar walked his horse closer so he wouldn't have to shout. Tanalan's guards raised shields and spears.

Dalinar inspected them, then the fortifications. 'You've done well here. Polemen on the walls to push me off, should I come in alone. Netting draped down at the top, which you can cut free to entangle me.'

'What do you want, tyrant?' Tanalan snapped. His voice had the typical nasal accent of the Rifters.

Dalinar dismissed his Blade and swung free of his horse, Plate grinding on stone as he hit the ground. 'Walk with me a moment, Brightlord. I promise not to harm you unless I'm attacked first.'

'I'm supposed to take your word?'

'What did I do, the last time we were together?' Dalinar asked. 'When I had you in my hand, how did I act?'

'You robbed me.'

'And?' Dalinar asked, meeting the younger man's violet eyes.

Tanalan measured him, tapping one finger against his saddle. Finally he dismounted. The man with the birthmark put a hand on his shoulder, but the youthful brightlord pulled free.

'I don't see what you hope to accomplish here, Blackthorn,' Tanalan said, joining Dalinar. 'We have nothing to say to one another.'

'What do I want to accomplish?' Dalinar said, musing. 'I'm not certain. My brother is normally the talker.' He started walking along the corridor between the two hostile armies. Tanalan lingered, then jogged to catch up.

'Your troops look good,' Dalinar said. 'Brave. Arrayed against a stronger force, yet determined.'

'They have strong motivation, Blackthorn. You murdered many of their fathers.'

'It will be a pity to destroy them in turn.'

'Assuming you can.'

Dalinar stopped and turned to regard the shorter man. They stood on a too-quiet field, where even the rockbuds and the grass had the sense to withdraw. 'Have I ever lost a battle, Tanalan?' Dalinar asked softly. 'You know my reputation. Do you think it exaggerated?'

The younger man shifted, looking over his shoulder toward where he had left his guards and advisors. When he looked back, he was more resolved. 'Better to die trying to bring you down than to surrender.'

'You'd better be sure of that,' Dalinar said. 'Because if I win here, I'm going to have to make an example. I'll *break* you, Tanalan. Your sorry, weeping city will be held up before all who would defy my brother. Be *absolutely* certain you want to fight me, because once this starts, I will be forced to leave only widows and corpses to populate the Rift.'

The young nobleman's jaw slowly dropped. 'I . . .'

'My brother attempted words and politics to bring you into line,'

Dalinar said. 'Well, I'm good at only one thing. He builds. I destroy. But because of the tears of a good woman, I have come – against my better judgment – to offer you an alternative. Let's find an accommodation that will spare your city.'

'An accommodation? You *killed my father*.'

'And someday a man will kill me,' Dalinar said. 'My sons will curse his name as you curse mine. I hope *they* don't throw away thousands of lives in a hopeless battle because of that grudge. You want vengeance. Fine. Let's duel. Me and you. I'll lend you a Blade and Plate, and we'll face each other on equal grounds. I win, and your people surrender.'

'And if I beat you, will your armies leave?'

'Hardly,' Dalinar said. 'I suspect they'll fight harder. But they won't have me, and you'll have won your father's Blade back. Who knows? Maybe you'll defeat the army. You'll have a better storming chance, at least.'

Tanalan frowned at Dalinar. 'You aren't the man I thought you were.'

'I'm the same man I've always been. But today . . . today that man doesn't want to kill anyone.'

A sudden fire inside him raged against those words. Was he really going to such lengths to *avoid* the conflict he'd been so anticipating?

'One of your own is working against you,' Tanalan suddenly said. 'The loyal highprinces? There's a traitor among them.'

'I'd be surprised if there weren't several,' Dalinar said. 'But yes, we know that one has been working with you.'

'A pity,' Tanalan said. 'His men were here not an hour ago. A little earlier and you'd have caught them. Maybe they'd have been forced to join me, and their master would have been pulled into the war.' He shook his head, then turned and walked back toward his advisors.

Dalinar sighed in frustration. A dismissal. Well, there had never been much of a chance that this would work. He walked back to his horse and pulled himself up into the saddle.

Tanalan mounted as well. Before riding back to his city, the man gave Dalinar a salute. 'This is unfortunate,' he said. 'But I see no other way. I cannot defeat you in a duel, Blackthorn. To try would be foolish. But your offer is . . . appreciated.'

Dalinar grunted, pulled on his helm, then turned his horse.

'Unless . . .' Tanalan said.

'Unless?'

'Unless, of course, this was really a ruse all along, a scheme arranged by your brother, you, and me,' Tanalan said. 'A . . . false rebellion. Intended to trick disloyal highprinces into revealing themselves.'

Dalinar raised his faceplate and turned back.

'Perhaps my outrage was feigned,' Tanalan said. 'Perhaps we have been in touch since your attack here, all those years ago. You *did* spare my life, after all.'

'Yes,' Dalinar said, feeling a sudden surge of excitement. 'That would explain why Gavilar didn't immediately send our armies against you. We were in collusion all along.'

'What better proof, than the fact that we just had this strange battlefield conversation?' Tanalan looked over his shoulder at the body of his men on the wall. 'My men must be thinking it very odd. It will make sense when they hear the truth – that I was telling you about the envoy that had been here, delivering weapons and supplies to us from one of your secret enemies.'

'Your reward, of course,' Dalinar said, 'would be legitimacy as a highlord in the kingdom. Perhaps that highprince's place.'

'And no fighting today,' Tanalan said. 'No deaths.'

'No deaths. Except perhaps for the actual traitors.'

Tanalan looked to his advisors. The man with the birthmark nodded slowly.

'They headed east, toward the Unclaimed Hills,' Tanalan said, pointing. 'A hundred soldiers and caravaneers. I think they were planning to stay for the night in the waystop at a town called Vedelliar.'

'Who was it?' Dalinar asked. 'Which highprince?'

'It might be best if you find out for yourself, as—'

'*Who?*' Dalinar demanded.

'Brightlord Torol Sadeas.'

Sadeas? 'Impossible!'

'As I said,' Tanalan noted. 'Best if you see for yourself. But I will testify before the king, assuming you keep your side of our . . . accord.'

'Open your gates to my men,' Dalinar said, pointing. 'Stand down your soldiers. You have my word of honor for your safety.'

With that, he turned and trotted back toward his forces, passing into a corridor of men. As he did, Teleb ran up to meet him. 'Brightlord!' he said. 'My scouts have returned from surveying that caravan. Sir, it—'

'Was from a highprince?'

'Undoubtedly,' Teleb said. 'They couldn't determine which one, but they claim to have seen someone in *Shardplate* among them.'

Shardplate? That made no sense.

Unless that is how he's planning to see that we lose, Dalinar thought. *That might not have been a simple supply caravan – it could be a flanking force in disguise.*

A single Shardbearer hitting the back of his army while it was distracted could do incredible damage. Dalinar didn't believe Tanalan, not completely. But . . . storms, if Sadeas secretly *had* sent one of his Shardbearers to the battlefield, Dalinar couldn't just send a simple team of soldiers to deal with him.

'You have command,' he said to Teleb. 'Tanalan is going to stand down; have the vanguard join the locals on the fortifications, but do not displace them. Camp the rest of the army back in the field, and keep our officers out of Rathalas. This isn't a surrender. We're going to pretend that he was on our side all along, so he can save face and preserve his title. Horinar, I want a company of a hundred elites, our fastest, ready to march with me immediately.'

They obeyed, asking no questions. Runners dashed with messages, and the entire area became a hive of motion, men and women hastening in all directions.

One person stood still in the midst of it, hands clasped hopefully at her breast. 'What happened?' Evi asked as he trotted his horse toward her.

'Go back to our camp and compose a message to my brother saying that we may have brought the Rift to our side without bloodshed.' He paused, then added, 'Tell him not to trust anyone. One of our closest allies may have betrayed us. I'm going to go find out.'

The Edgedancers are too busy relocating the tower's servants and farmers to send a representative to record their thoughts in these gemstones.

I'll do it for them, then. They are the ones who will be most displaced by this decision. The Radiants will be taken in by nations, but what of all these people now without homes?

—From drawer 4-17, second topaz

T his city had a heartbeat, and Veil felt she could hear it when she closed her eyes.

She crouched in a dim room, hands touching the smooth stone floor, which had been eroded by thousands upon thousands of footfalls. If stone met a man, stone might win – but if stone met *humanity*, then no force could preserve it.

The city's heartbeat was deep within these stones, old and slow. It had yet to realize something dark had moved in. A spren as ancient as it was. An urban disease. People didn't speak of it; they avoided the palace, mentioned the queen only to complain about the ardent who had been killed. It was like standing in a highstorm and griping that your shoes were too tight.

A soft whistling drew Veil's attention. She looked up and scanned the small loading dock around her, occupied only by herself, Vathah, and their wagon. 'Let's go.'

Veil eased the door open and entered the mansion proper. She and Vathah wore new faces. Hers was a version of Veil with too large a nose and dimpled cheeks.

His was the face of a brutish man Shallan had seen in the market. Red's whistle meant the coast was clear, so they strode down the hallway without hesitation.

This extravagant stone mansion had been built around a square, skylit atrium, where manicured shalebark and rockbuds flourished, bobbing with lifespren. The atrium went up four stories, with walkways around each level. Red was on the second, whistling as he leaned on the balustrade.

The real showpiece of the mansion, however, wasn't the garden, but waterfalls. Because not a single one of them was actually water.

They *had* been, once. But sometime long ago, someone had mixed far too much wealth with far too much imagination. They had hired Soulcasters to transform large fountains of water that had been poured from the top level, four stories up. They'd been Soulcast into other materials right as the water splashed to the floor.

Veil's path took her along rooms to her left, with an overhang of the first floor's atrium balcony overhead. A former waterfall spilled down to her right, now made of crystal. The shape of flowing water crashed forever onto the stone floor, where it blossomed outward in a wave, brilliant and glistening. The mansion had changed hands dozens of times, and people called it Rockfall – despite the newest owner's attempt over the last decade to rename it the incredibly boring Hadinal Keep.

Veil and Vathah hurried along, accompanied by Red's reassuring whistling. The next waterfall was similar in shape, but made instead from polished dark stumpweight wood. It looked strangely natural, almost like a tree *could* have grown in that shape, poured from above and running down in an undulating column, splashing outward at the base.

They soon passed a room to their left, where Ishnah was talking with the current mistress of Rockfall. Each time the Everstorm struck, it left destruction – but in an oddly distinct way from a highstorm. Everstorm lightning had proven its greatest danger. The strange red lightning didn't merely set fires or scorch the ground; it could break through rock, causing blasts of fragmenting stone.

One such strike had broken a gaping hole in the side of this ancient, celebrated mansion. It had been patched with an unsightly wooden wall that would be covered with crem, then finally bricked over. Brightness Nananav – a middle-aged Alethi woman with a bun of hair practically as tall as she was – gestured at the boarded-up hole, and then at the floor.

'You'll make them match the others,' Nananav said to Ishnah, who wore the guise of a rug merchant. 'I won't stand for them to be even a *shade* off. When you return with the repaired rugs, I'm going to set them beside the ones in other rooms to check!'

'Yes, Brightness,' Ishnah said. 'But the damage is much worse than I—'

'These rugs were woven in *Shinovar*. They were made by a blind man who trained *thirty years* with a master weaver before being allowed to produce his own rugs! He died after finishing my commission, so there are *no others* like these.'

'I'm well aware, as you've told me three times now. . . .'

Veil took a Memory of the woman; then she and Vathah slipped past the room, continuing along the atrium. They were supposedly part of Ishnah's staff, and wouldn't be suffered to wander about freely. Red – noting that they were on their way – started to head back to rejoin Ishnah. He'd have been excused to visit the privy, but would be missed if he was gone too long.

His tune cut off.

Veil opened a door and pulled Vathah inside, heart thrumming as – right outside – a pair of guards walked down the stairwell from the second level.

'I still say we should be doing this at night,' Vathah whispered.

'They have this place guarded like a fort at night.'

The change of the guard was in midmorning, so Veil and the others had come just before that. Theoretically, this meant the guards would be tired and bored after an uneventful night.

Veil and Vathah had entered a small library lit by a few spheres in a goblet on the table. Vathah eyed them, but didn't move – this infiltration was about far more than a few chips. Veil set down her pack and rummaged until she got out a notebook and charcoal pencil.

Veil took a deep breath, then let Shallan bleed back into existence. She quickly sketched Nananav from the glimpse earlier.

'I'm still amazed you were both of them, all along,' Vathah said. 'You don't act anything like one another.'

'That's rather the point, Vathah.'

'I wish I'd picked it out myself.' He grunted, scratching the side of his head. 'I like Veil.'

'Not me?'

'You're my boss. I'm not supposed to like you.'

Straightforward, if rude. At least you always knew where you stood with him. He listened at the door, then cracked it open, tracking the guards. 'All right. We go up the stairs, then come back along the second-floor walkway. We grab the goods, stuff them in the dumbwaiter, and make for the exit. Storms. I wish we could do this when nobody was awake.'

'What would be the fun of that?' Shallan finished her drawing with a flourish, then stood, poking Vathah in the side. 'Admit it. You're enjoying this.'

'I'm as nervous as a new recruit on his first day at war,' Vathah said. 'My hands shake, and I swear every noise means someone spotted us. I feel *sick*.'

'See?' Shallan said. 'Fun.' She pushed beside him and glanced out through the cracked door. Storming guards. They'd set up in the atrium nearby. They could undoubtedly hear the real Nananav's voice from there, so if Shallan strolled out wearing the woman's face, that would certainly cause alarm.

Time to get creative. Pattern buzzed as she considered. Make the waterfalls flow again? Illusions of strange spren? No ... no, nothing so theatrical. Shallan was letting her sense of the dramatic run away with her.

Stay simple, as she'd done before. Veil's way. She closed her eyes and breathed out, pressing the Light into Pattern, Lightweaving only sound – that of Nananav calling the guards into the room where she was lecturing Ishnah. Why come up with a new trick when the old ones worked fine? Veil didn't feel the need to improvise merely to be different.

Pattern carried the illusion away, and the sound lured the guards off down the hall. Shallan led Vathah out of the library, then around the corner and up the steps. She breathed out Stormlight, which washed over her, and became Veil fully. Then Veil became the woman who was not *quite* Veil, with the dimples. And then, layered on top of that, she became Nananav.

Arrogant. Talkative. Certain that everyone around her was just *looking* for a reason not to do things properly. As they stepped onto the next floor, she adopted a calm, measured gait, eyeing the banister. When had that last been polished?

'I don't find this fun,' Vathah said, walking beside her. 'But I do like it.'

'Then it's fun.'

'Fun is winning at cards. This is something else.'

He'd taken to his role earnestly, but she really should look at getting more refined servants. Vathah was like a hog in human clothing, always grunting and mulling about.

Why shouldn't she be served by the best? She was a *Knight Radiant*. She shouldn't have to put up with barely human deserters who looked like something Shallan would draw after a hard night drinking, and maybe while holding the pencil with her teeth.

The role is getting to you, a part of her whispered. *Careful.* She glanced about for Pattern, but he was still below.

They stopped at a second-floor room, locked tightly. The plan was for Pattern to open it, but she didn't have the patience to wait. Besides, a master-servant was walking along.

He gave a bow when he saw Nananav.

'*That* is your bow?' Nananav said. 'That quick bob? Where did they teach you that?'

'My apologies, Brightness,' the man said, bowing more deeply.

'I could cut your legs off at the knees,' Nananav said. 'Then maybe you'd at least *appear* properly penitent.' She rapped on the door. 'Open this.'

'Why – ' He broke off, perhaps realizing she was not in a mood for complaints. He hurried forward and undid the combination lock on the door, then pulled it open for her, letting out air that smelled of spice.

'You may go do penance for your insult to me,' Nananav said. 'Climb to the roof and sit there for exactly one hour.'

'Brightness, if I have offended—'

'*If?*' She pointed. 'Go!'

He gave another bow – barely sufficient – and ran off.

'You might be overdoing that, Brightness,' Vathah said, rubbing his chin. 'She has a reputation for being difficult, not *insane*.'

'Shut up,' Nananav said, striding into the room.

The mansion's larder.

Racks of dried sausages covered one wall. Sacks of grain were stacked in the back, and boxes filled with longroots and other tubers covered the floor. Bags of spices. Small jugs of oil.

Vathah pulled the door closed, then hurriedly began stuffing sausages in a sack. Nananav wasn't so hasty. This was a good place to keep it all, nice and locked up. Taking it elsewhere seemed ... well, a crime.

Maybe she could move into Rockfall, act the part. And the former lady of the house? Well, she was an inferior version, obviously. Just deal with her, take her place. It would feel *right*, wouldn't it?

With a chill, Veil let one layer of illusion drop. Storms ... Storms. What had *that* been?

'Not to give *offense*, Brightness,' Vathah said, putting his sack of sausages in the dumbwaiter, 'but you can stand there and supervise. Or you can storming help, and get twice as much food along with half as much ego.'

'Sorry,' Veil said, grabbing a sack of grain. 'That woman's head is a frightening place.'

'Well, I did say that Nananav is notoriously difficult.'

Yeah, Veil thought. *But I was talking about Shallan.*

They worked quickly, filling the large dumbwaiter – which was needed to take in large shipments from the delivery room below. They got all of the sausages, most of the longroots, and a few sacks of grain. Once the dumbwaiter was full, the two of them lowered the thing to the ground floor. They waited by the door, and fortunately Red started whistling. The ground floor was clear again. Not trusting herself with Nananav's face, she stayed Veil as the two hurried out. Pattern waited outside, and he hummed, climbing her trousers.

On their way down, they passed a waterfall made of pure marble. Shallan would have loved to linger and marvel at the artful Soulcasting. Fortunately, Veil was running this operation. Shallan ... Shallan got lost in things. She'd get focused on details, or stick her head in the clouds and dream about the big picture. That comfortable middle, that safe place of moderation, was unfamiliar ground to her.

They descended the steps, then joined Red at the damaged room and helped him carry a rolled-up carpet to the loading bay. She had Pattern quietly open the lock to the dumbwaiter down here, then sent him away to decoy a few servants who had been bringing wood into the bay. They pursued an image of a feral mink with a key in its mouth.

Together, Veil, Red, and Vathah unrolled the rug, filled it with sacks of food from the dumbwaiter, then rolled it back up and heaved it into their waiting wagon. The guards at the gate shouldn't notice a few extra-bulgy carpets.

They fetched a second carpet, repeated the process, then started back. Veil, however, paused in the loading bay, right by the door. What was that on the ceiling? She cocked her head at the strange sight of pools of liquid, dripping down.

Angerspren, she realized. *Collecting there and then boiling through the floor.* The larder was directly above them.

'Run!' Veil said, spinning and bolting back toward the wagon. A second later, someone upstairs started shouting.

Veil scrambled into the wagon's seat, then slapped the chull with the steering reed. Her team, joined by Ishnah, charged back into the room and leapt into the wagon, which started moving. Step. By. Protracted. Step.

Veil . . . Shallan slapped the large crab on the shell, urging it forward. But chulls went at chull speed. The wagon eased out into the courtyard, and ahead the gates were already closing.

'Storms!' Vathah said. He looked over his shoulder. 'Is this part of the "fun"?'

Behind them, Nananav burst out of the building, her hair wobbling. 'Stop them! Thieves!'

'Shallan?' Vathah asked. 'Veil? Whoever you are? Storms, they have *crossbows!*'

Shallan breathed out.

The gates clanged shut ahead of them. Armed guards entered the small courtyard, weapons ready.

'Shallan!' Vathah cried.

She stood on the wagon, Stormlight swirling around her. The chull pulled to a stop, and she confronted the guards. The men stumbled to a halt, jaws dropping.

Behind, Nananav broke the silence. 'What are you idiots doing? Why . . .'

She trailed off, then pulled up short as Shallan turned to look at her. Wearing the woman's face.

Same hair. Same features. Same clothing. Mimicked right down to the attitude, with nose in the air. Shallan/Nananav raised her hands to the side, and spren burst from the ground around the wagon. Pools of blood, shimmering the wrong color, and boiling far too violently. Pieces of glass that rained down. Anticipationspren, like thin tentacles.

Shallan/Nananav let her image distort, features sliding off her face, dripping down like paint running down a wall. Ordinary Nananav screamed and fled back toward the building. One of the guards loosed his crossbow, and the bolt took Shallan/Nananav right in the head.

Bother.

Her vision went dark for a moment, and she had a flash of panic remembering her stabbing in the palace. But why should she care if actual painspren joined the illusory ones around her? She righted herself and looked back toward the soldiers, her face melting, the crossbow bolt sticking from her temple.

The guards ran.

'Vathah,' she said, 'plesh open sha gate.' Her mouth didn't work right. How odd.

Vathah didn't move, so she glared at him.

'Gah!' he shouted, scrambling back and stumbling across one of the rugs in the bed of the wagon. He fell down beside Red, who was surrounded by fearspren, like globs of goo. Even Ishnah looked as if she'd seen a Voidbringer.

Shallan let the illusions go, all of them, right down to Veil. Just normal, everyday Veil. 'Itsh all right,' Veil said. 'Jush illushionsh. Go, open sha gatesh.'

Vathah heaved himself out of the wagon and ran for the gates.

'Um, Veil?' Red said. 'That crossbow bolt . . . the blood is staining your outfit.'

'I wash going to shrow it away regardlesh,' she said, settling back down, growing more comfortable as Pattern rejoined the wagon and scuttled across the seat to her. 'I've got a new outfit almosht ready.'

At this rate, she'd have to buy them in bulk.

They maneuvered the wagon out the gates, then picked up Vathah. No guards gave pursuit, and Veil's mind . . . drifted as they pulled away.

That . . . that crossbow bolt *was* getting annoying. She couldn't feel her safehand. Bother. She poked at the bolt; it seemed that her Stormlight had healed her head *around* the wound. She gritted her teeth and tried to pull it out, but the thing was jammed in there. Her vision blurred again.

'I'm going to need shome help, boysh,' she said, pointing at it and drawing in more Stormlight.

She blacked out entirely when Vathah pulled it free. She came to a short time later, slumped in the front seat of the wagon. When she brushed the side of her head with her fingers, she found no hole.

'You worry me sometimes,' Vathah said, steering the chull with a reed.

'I do what needs to be done,' Veil said, relaxing back and setting her feet up on the front of the wagon. Was it only her imagination, or did the people lining the streets today look hungrier than they had previous days? Hungerspren buzzed about the heads of the people, like black specks, or little flies of the type you could find sometimes on rotting plants. Children cried in the laps of exhausted mothers.

Veil turned away, ashamed, thinking of the food she had hidden in the wagon. How much good could she do with all of that? How many tears could she dry, how many of the hungry cries of children could she silence?

Steady . . .

Infiltrating the Cult of Moments was a greater good than feeding a few mouths now. She needed this food to buy her way in. To investigate . . . the Heart of the Revel, as Wit had called it.

Veil didn't know much of the Unmade. She'd never paid attention to the ardents on important matters, let alone when they spoke of old folk-tales and stories of Voidbringers. Shallan knew little more, and wanted to find a book about the subject, of course.

Last night, Veil had returned to the inn where Shallan had met with the King's Wit, and while he hadn't been there, he'd left a message for her.

I'm still trying to get you a contact among the cult's highers. Everyone I talk to merely says, 'Do something to get their attention.' I would, but I'm certain that violating the city's indecency laws would be unwise, even considering the lack of a proper watch.

Do something to get their attention. They seemed to have their fingers in everything, in this city. Kind of like the Ghostbloods. Watching secretly.

Maybe she didn't need to wait for Wit. And maybe she could solve two problems at once.

'Take us to the Ringington Market,' she said to Vathah, naming the market closest to the tailor's shop.

'Aren't we going to unload the food before we return the wagon to that merchant?'

'Of course we are,' she said.

He eyed her, but when she didn't explain further, he turned the wagon as she directed. Veil took her hat and coat from the back of the wagon and pulled them on, then covered the bloodstains on her shirt with a Lightweaving.

She had Vathah pull up to a specific building in the market. When they stopped, refugees peeked into the wagon bed, but saw only rugs – and they scattered when Vathah glared at them.

'Guard the wagon,' Veil said, digging out a small sack of food. She hopped down and went sauntering toward the building. The roof had been ruined by the Everstorm, making it a perfect place for squatters. She found Grund inside the main room, as usual.

She'd returned several times during her time in the city, getting information from Grund – who was the grimy little urchin she'd bribed with food on her first day in the market. He seemed to always be hanging around here, and Veil was well aware of the value of having a local urchin to ply for information.

Today, he was alone in the room. The other beggars were out hunting food. Grund drew on a little board with charcoal, using his one good hand, the deformed one hidden in his pocket. He perked up as soon as he saw her. He'd stopped running away; it seemed that city urchins got concerned when someone was actively looking for them.

That changed when they knew you had food.

He tried to look uninterested until Veil dropped the sack in front of him. A sausage peeked out. Then, his dark eyes practically bulged out of his face.

'An entire *sack*?' Grund asked.

'It was a good day,' Veil said, squatting down. 'Any news for me on those books?'

'Nope,' he said, poking the sausage – as if to see whether she'd suddenly snatch it back. 'I ain't heard nothing.'

'Let me know if you do. In the meantime, do you know of anyone who could use a little extra food? People who are particularly nice or deserving, but who get overlooked by the grain rationing?'

He eyed her, trying to determine her angle.

'I've got extra to give away,' Veil explained.

'You're going to *give* them *food*.' He said it as if it was as rational as making cremlings fall from the sky.

'Surely I'm not the first. The palace used to give food to the poor, didn't it?'

'That's a thing that kings do. Not regular people.' He looked her up and down. 'But you aren't regular people.'

'I'm not.'

'Well ... Muri the seamstress has always been nice to me. She's got lots of kids. Having trouble feedin' them. She has a hovel over by the old bakery that burned down on that first Evernight. And the refugee kids that live in the park over on Moonlight Way. They're just little, you know? Nobody to watch for them. And Jom, the cobbler. He broke his arm ... You wanna write this down or something?'

'I'll remember.'

He shrugged and gave her an extensive list. She thanked him, then reminded him to keep looking for the book she'd asked for. Ishnah had visited some booksellers on Shallan's orders, and one had mentioned a title called *Mythica*, a newer volume that spoke of the Unmade. The bookseller had owned a copy, but his shop had been robbed during the riots. Hopefully, someone in the underground knew where his goods had gone.

Veil had a spring to her step as she walked back to the wagon. The cult wanted her to get their attention? Well, she'd get their attention. She doubted Grund's list was unbiased, but stopping right in the middle of the market and heaving out sacks seemed likely to incite a riot. This was as good a method to give away the food as any.

Muri the seamstress proved to indeed be a woman with many children and little means of feeding them. The children in the park were right where Grund had indicated. Veil left a heap of food for them, then walked away as they scrambled up to it in amazement.

By the fourth stop, Vathah had figured it out. 'You're going to give it all away, aren't you?'

'Not all,' Veil said, lounging in her seat as they rolled toward the next destination.

'What about paying the Cult of Moments?'

'We can always steal more. First, my contact says we have to get their attention. I figure, a crazy woman in white riding through the market throwing out sacks of food is bound to do that.'

'You've got the crazy part right, at least.'

Veil slipped her hand back into a rolled-up carpet, and pulled out a sausage for him. 'Eat something. It'll make you feel better.'

He grumbled, but took it and bit at the end.

By the evening, the cart was empty. Veil wasn't certain if she could get the cult's attention this way, but storms did it feel good to be *doing* something. Shallan could go off and study books, talk plots, and scheme. Veil would worry about the people who were actually starving.

She didn't give it *all* away though. She let Vathah keep his sausage.

I am worried about the tower's protections failing. If we are not safe from the Unmade here, then where?

—From drawer 3-11, garnet

'Stuff it, Beard,' Ved said. 'You did *not* meet the Blackthorn.'

'I did!' the other soldier said. 'He complimented me on my uniform, and gave me his own knife. For valor.'

'Liar.'

'Be careful,' Beard said. 'Kal might stab you if you keep interrupting a good story.'

'Me?' Kaladin said, walking with the others of the squad on patrol. 'Don't bring me into this, Beard.'

'Look at him,' Beard said. 'He's got *hungry* eyes, Ved. He wants to hear the end of the story.'

Kaladin smiled with the others. He had joined the Wall Guard officially upon Elhokar's orders, and had promptly been added to Lieutenant Noro's squad. It felt almost . . . cheap to be part of the group so quickly, after the effort it had been to forge Bridge Four.

Still, Kaladin liked these men, and enjoyed their banter as they ran their patrol beat along the inside base of the wall. Six men was a lot for a simple patrol, but Azure wanted them to stay in groups. Along with Beard, Ved, and Noro, the squad included a heavyset man named Alaward and a friendly man named Vaceslv – Alethi, but with obvious Thaylen heritage. The two kept trying to get Kaladin to play cards with them.

It was an uncomfortable reminder of Sah and the parshmen.

'Well, you won't believe what happened next,' Beard continued. 'The Blackthorn told me . . . Oh, storm it. You're not listening, are you?'

'Nope,' Ved said. 'Too busy looking at that.' He nodded back at something they'd passed.

Beard snickered. 'Ha! Will you look at that roosting chicken? Who does he think he's impressing?'

'Storming waste of skin,' Ved agreed.

Kal grinned, glanced over his shoulder, looking for whoever Beard and Ved had spotted. Must be someone silly to provoke such a strong . . .

It was Adolin.

The prince lounged on the corner, wearing a false face and a yellow suit after the new fashionable style. He was guarded by Drehy, who stood several inches taller, happily munching on some chouta.

'Somewhere,' Beard said solemnly, 'a kingdom is without its banners because that fellow bought them all up and made coats out of them.'

'Where do they think up these things?' Vaceslv asked. 'I mean . . . storms! Do they just say, "You know what I need for the apocalypse? You know what would be *really* handy? A new *coat.* Extra sequins."'

They passed Adolin – who nodded toward Kaladin, then looked away. That meant all was well, and Kaladin could continue with the guards. A shake of the head would have been the sign to extricate himself and return to the tailor's shop.

Beard continued to snicker. 'When in the service of the merchant lords of Steen,' he noted, 'I once had to swim across an entire vat of dye in order to save the prince's daughter. When I was done, I *still* wasn't as colorful as that preening cremling.'

Alaward grunted. 'Storming highborns. Useless for anything but giving bad orders and eating twice as much food as an honest man.'

'But,' Kaladin said, 'how can you say that? I mean, he's lighteyed. Like us.' He winced. Did that sound fake? *It sure is nice being lighteyed as I, of course, have light eyes – like you, my eyes are lighter than the dark eyes of darkeyes*. He had to summon Syl several times a day to keep his eye color from changing.

'Like us?' Beard said. 'Kal, what crevasse have you been living in? Are the middlers actually *useful* where you come from?'

'Some,' Kaladin said.

Beard and Ved – well, the whole squad, except Noro – were tenners: men of the tenth dahn, lowest ranking in the lighteyed stratification system. Kaladin hadn't ever paid much attention; to him, lighteyes had always just been lighteyes.

These men saw the world very differently. Middlers were anyone better than eighth dahn, but who weren't quite highlords. They might as well have been another species, for how the squadsmen thought of them – particularly those of the fifth and sixth dahn who didn't serve in the military.

How was it that these men somehow naturally ended up surrounding themselves with others of their own rank? They married tenners, drank with tenners, joked with tenners. They had their own jargon and traditions. There was an entire world represented here that Kaladin had never seen, despite it residing right next door to him.

'Some middlers *are* useful,' Kaladin said. 'Some of them are good at dueling. Maybe we could go back and recruit that guy. He was wearing a sword.'

The others looked at him like he was mad.

'Kal, my kip,' Beard said. 'Kip' was a slang word that Kaladin hadn't quite figured out yet. 'You're a good fellow. I like how you see the best in folks. You haven't even learned to ignore me yet, which most folks decide to do after our first meal together.

'But you've *got* to learn to see the world for how it is. You can't go around trusting middlers, unless they're good officers like the highmarshal. Men like that one back there, they'll strut about telling you everything you should do – but put them on the wall during an attack, and they'll wet themselves yellower than that suit.'

'They have parties,' Ved agreed. 'Best thing for them, really. Keeps them out of our business.'

What a strange mix of emotions. On one hand, he wanted to tell them about Amaram and rant about the injustices done – repeatedly – to those he loved. At the same time . . . they were mocking *Adolin Kholin*, who had a shot at the title of best swordsman in all of Alethkar. Yes, his suit was a little bright – but if they would merely spend five minutes talking to him, they'd see he wasn't so bad.

Kaladin trudged along. It felt wrong to be on patrol without a spear, and he instinctively sought out Syl, who rode the winds above. He'd been given a side sword to carry at his right, a truncheon to carry at his left, and a small round shield. The first thing the Wall Guard had taught him was how to draw the sword by reaching down with his right hand – not lowering his shield – and pulling it free of the sheath.

They wouldn't use sword or truncheon when the Voidbringers finally assaulted; there were proper pikes up above for that. Down here was a different matter. The large road – it rounded the city alongside the wall – was clear and clean, maintained by the Guard. But most of the streets that branched off it were crowded with people. Nobody but the poorest and most wretched wanted to be this close to the walls.

'How is it,' Ved said, 'those refugees can't get it through their heads that we're the only thing separating them from the army outside?'

Indeed, many of those they passed on side streets watched the patrol with outright hostility. At least nobody had thrown anything at them today.

'They see that we're fed,' Noro replied. 'They smell food from our barracks. They're not thinking with their heads, but with their stomachs.'

'Half of those belong to the cult anyway,' Beard noted. 'One of these days, I'll have to infiltrate that. Might have to marry their high priestess, but let me tell you, I'm *terrible* in a harem. Last time, the other men grew jealous of me taking all the priestess's attention.'

'She laughed so hard at your offering she got distracted, eh?' Ved asked.

'Actually, there's a story about—'

'Calm it, Beard,' the lieutenant said. 'Let's get ready for the delivery.' He shifted his shield to his other hand, then took out his truncheon. 'Get intimidating, everybody. Truncheons only.'

The group pulled out their wooden cudgels. It felt wrong to have to defend themselves from their own people – brought back memories of being in Amaram's army, bivouacking near towns. Everyone had always *talked* about the glories of the army and the fight on the Shattered Plains. And yet, once towns got done gawking, they transitioned to hostility with remarkable speed. An army was the sort of thing everyone wanted to have, so long as it was off doing important things elsewhere.

Noro's squad met up with another from their platoon – with two squads on the wall for duty, two squads off, and two down here patrolling, they were around forty strong. Together, the twelve men formed up to guard a slow, chull-pulled wagon that left one of their larger barrack warehouses. It carried a mound of closed sacks.

Refugees crowded around, and Kaladin brandished his truncheon. He had to use his shield to shove a man who got too close. Fortunately, this caused others to back away, instead of rushing the wagon.

They rolled inward only one street before stopping at a city square. Syl flitted down and rested on his shoulder. 'They . . . they look like they *hate* you.'

'Not me,' Kaladin whispered. 'The uniform.'

'What . . . what will you do if they actually attack?'

He didn't know. He hadn't come to this city to fight the populace, but if he refused to defend the squad . . .

'Storming Velalant is late,' Ved grumbled.

'A little more time,' Noro said. 'We'll be fine. The good people know this food goes to them eventually.'

Yes, after they wait hours in line at Velalant's distribution stations.

Farther into the city – obscured by the gathering crowds – a group of people approached in stark violet, with masks obscuring their faces. Kaladin watched uncomfortably as they started whipping their own forearms. Drawing painspren, which climbed from the ground around them, like hands missing the skin. Except these were too large, and the wrong color, and . . . and didn't seem human.

'I prayed to the spren of the night and they came to me!' a man at their forefront shouted, raising hands high. 'They rid me of my pain!'

'Oh no . . .' Syl whispered.

'Embrace them! The spren of changes! The spren of a new storm, a new land. A new people!'

Kaladin took Noro by the arm. 'Sir, we need to retreat. Get this grain back to the warehouse.'

'We have orders to . . .' Noro trailed off as he glanced at the increasingly hostile crowd.

Fortunately, a group of some fifty men in blue and red rounded a corner and began shoving aside refugees with rough hands and barked shouts. Noro's sigh was almost comically loud. The angry crowd broke away as Velalant's troops surrounded the grain shipment.

'Why do we do this in the daytime?' Kaladin asked one of their officers. 'And why don't you simply come to our warehouse and escort it from there? Why the display?'

A soldier moved him – politely, but firmly – back from the wagon. The troops surrounded it and marched it away, the crowd flowing after them.

When they got back to the wall, Kaladin felt like a man seeing land after swimming all the way to Thaylenah. He pressed his palm against the stone, feeling its cool, rough grain. Drawing a sense of safety from it, much as he would draw out Stormlight. It would have been easy to fight that crowd – they were basically unarmed. But while training prepared you for the mechanics of the fight, the emotions were another thing entirely. Syl huddled on his shoulder, staring back along the street.

'This is all the queen's fault,' Beard muttered softly. 'If she hadn't killed that ardent . . .'

'Stop with that,' Noro said sharply. He took a deep breath. 'My squad, we're on the wall next. You have half an hour to grab a drink or a nap, then assemble at our station above.'

'And storms be praised for that!' Beard said, heading straight for the stairwell, obviously planning to get to the station above, then relax. 'I'll happily take some time staring down an enemy army, thank you very much.'

Kaladin joined Beard in climbing. He still didn't know where the man had gotten his nickname. Noro was the only one in the squad who wore a beard, though his wasn't exactly inspiring. Rock would have laughed it to shame and euthanized it with a razor and some soap.

'Why do we pay off the highlords, Beard?' Kaladin asked as they climbed. 'Velalant and his type are pretty useless, from what I've seen.'

'Yeah. We lost the *real* highlords in the riots or to the palace. But the highmarshal knows what to do. I suspect that if we didn't share with people like Velalant, we'd have to fight *them* off from seizing the grain. At least this way, people are eventually getting fed, and we can watch the wall.'

They talked like that a lot. Holding the city wall was their job, and if they looked too far afield – tried too hard to police the city or bring down the cult – they'd lose their focus. The city had to stand. Even if it burned inside, it had to stand. To an extent, Kaladin agreed. The army couldn't do everything.

It still hurt.

'When are you going to tell me how we make all that food?' Kaladin whispered.

'I . . .' Beard looked around in the stairwell. He leaned in. 'I don't know, Kal. But first thing that Azure did when he took command? Had us attack the low monastery, by the eastern gates, away from the palace. I know men from other companies who were on that assault. The place had been overrun by rioters.'

'They had a Soulcaster, didn't they?'

Beard nodded. 'Only one in the city that wasn't at the palace when it . . . you know.'

'But how do we use it without drawing the screamers?' Kaladin asked.

'Well,' Beard said, and his tone shifted. 'I can't tell you all the secrets, but . . .' He launched into a story about the time Beard himself had learned to use a Soulcaster from the king of Herdaz. Maybe he wasn't the best source of information.

'The highmarshal,' Kaladin interrupted. 'Have you noticed the odd thing about her Shardblade? No gemstone on the pommel or crossguard.'

Beard eyed him, lit by the stairwell's window slits. Calling the highmarshal a 'she' always provoked a response. 'Maybe that's why *the highmarshal* never dismisses it,' Beard said. 'Maybe it's broken somehow?'

'Maybe,' Kaladin said. Aside from his fellow Radiants' Blades, he'd seen one Shardblade before that didn't have a gemstone on it. The Blade of the Assassin in White. An Honorblade, which granted Radiant powers to whoever held it. If Azure held a weapon that let her have the power of Soulcasting, perhaps that explained why the screamers hadn't found out yet.

They finally emerged onto the top of the wall, stepping into sunlight. The two of them stopped there, looking inward over the flowing city – with the breaching windblades and rolling hills. The palace, ever in gloom, dominated the far side. The Wall Guard barely patrolled the section of wall that passed behind it.

'Did you know anyone in the Palace Guard ranks?' Kaladin asked. 'Are any of the men in there still in contact with families out here or anything?'

Beard shook his head. 'I got close a little while back. I heard voices, Kal. Whispering to me to join them. The highmarshal says we have to close our ears to those. They can't take us unless we listen.' He rested his hand on Kaladin's shoulder. 'Your questions are honest, Kal. But you worry too much. We need to focus on the wall. Best not to talk too much about the queen, or the palace.'

'Like we don't talk about Azure being a woman.'

'Her secret' – Beard winced – 'I mean, the highmarshal's secret is ours to guard and protect.'

'We do a storming poor job of that, then. Hopefully we're better at defending the wall.'

Beard shrugged, hand still on Kaladin's shoulder. For the first time, Kaladin noticed something. 'No glyphward.'

Beard glanced at his arm, where he wore the traditional white armband that you'd tie a glyphward around. His was blank. 'Yeah,' he said, shoving his hand in his coat pocket.

'Why not?' Kaladin said.

Beard shrugged. 'Let's just say, I know a lot about telling which stories have been made up. Nobody's watching over us, Kal.'

He trudged off toward their muster station: one of the tower structures that lined the wall. Syl stood up on Kaladin's shoulder, then walked up – as if on invisible steps – through the air to stand even with his eyes. She looked after Beard, her girlish dress rippling in wind that Kaladin couldn't feel. 'Dalinar thinks God isn't dead,' she said. 'Just that the Almighty – Honor – was never actually God.'

'You're part of Honor. Doesn't that offend you?'

'Every child eventually realizes that her father isn't actually God.' She looked at him. 'Do you think anybody is watching? Do you really think there isn't anything out there?'

Strange question to answer, to a little bit of a divinity.

Kaladin lingered in the doorway to the guard tower. Inside, the men of his squad – Platoon Seven, Squad Two, which didn't have the same ring to it as Bridge Four – laughed and banged about as they gathered equipment.

'I used to take the terrible things that had happened to me,' he said, 'as proof that there was no god. Then in some of my darkest moments, I took my life as proof there *must* be something up there, for only *intentional* cruelty could offer an explanation.'

He took a deep breath, then looked toward the clouds. He had been delivered up to the sky, and had found magnificence there. He'd been given the power to protect and defend.

'Now,' he said. 'Now I don't know. With all due respect, I think Dalinar's beliefs sound too convenient. Now that one deity has proven faulty, he insists the Almighty must never have *been* God? That there must be something else? I don't like it. So . . . maybe this simply isn't a question we can ever answer.'

He stepped into the fortification. It had broad doorways on either side leading in from the wall, while slits along the outward side provided archer positions, as did the roof. To his right stood racks of weapons and shields, and a table for mess. Above that, a large window looked out at the city beyond, where those inside could get specific orders via signal flags from below.

He was sliding his shield onto a rack when the drums sounded, calling the alarm. Syl zipped up behind him like string suddenly pulled taut.

'Assault on the wall!' Kaladin shouted, reading the drumbeats. 'Equip up!' He scrambled across the room and seized a pike from the line on the wall. He tossed it to the first man who came, then continued distributing as the men scrambled to obey the signals. Lieutenant Noro and Beard handed out shields – rectangular full shields in contrast to the small round patrolling shields they'd carried below.

'Form up!' Kaladin shouted, right before Noro did it.

Storms. I'm not their commander. Feeling like an idiot, Kaladin took his own pike and balanced the long pole, carrying it out beside Beard, who carried only a shield. On the wall, the four squads formed a bristling formation of pikes and overlapping shields. Some of the men in the center – like Kaladin and Noro – held only a pike, gripping it two-handed.

Sweat trickled down Kaladin's temples. He'd been trained briefly in pike blocks during his time in Amaram's army. They were used as a counter to heavy cavalry, which was a newer development in Alethi warfare. He couldn't imagine that they'd be terribly effective atop a wall. They were great for thrusting outward toward an enemy block of troops, but it was difficult for him to keep the pike pointed upward. It didn't balance well that way, but how else were they to fight the Fused?

The other platoon that shared a station with them formed up on the tower's top, holding bows. Hopefully, the arrow cover mixed with the defensive pike formation would be effective. Kaladin finally saw the Fused streaking through the air – approaching another section of the wall.

Men in his platoon waited, nervous, adjusting glyphwards or repositioning shields. The Fused clashed distantly with others of the Wall Guard; Kaladin could barely make out yells. The drumbeats from the drummers' stations were a holding beat, telling everyone to remain in their own section.

Syl came zipping back, moving agitatedly, sweeping one way, then the other. Several men in the formation leaned out, as if wanting to break away and go charging to where their fellows were fighting.

Steady, Kaladin thought, but cut himself off from saying it. He wasn't in command here. Captain Deedanor, the platoon leader, hadn't arrived yet – which meant Noro was the ranking officer, with seniority over the other squad lieutenants. Kaladin gritted his teeth, straining, forcibly keeping himself from giving any kind of order until – blessedly – Noro spoke up.

'Now, don't you break away, Hid,' the lieutenant called. 'Keep your shields together, men. If we rush off now, we'll be easy pickings.'

The men reluctantly pulled back into formation. Eventually, the Fused streaked away. Their strikes never lasted long; they would hit hard, testing reaction times at various places along the wall – and they often broke into and searched the towers nearby. They were preparing for a true assault, and – Kaladin figured – also trying to find out how the Wall Guard was feeding itself.

The drums signaled for the squads to stand down, and the men of Kaladin's platoon lethargically trudged back to their tower. A sense of frustration accompanied them. Pent-up aggression. All of that anxiety, the rush of the battle, only to stand around and sweat while other men died.

Kaladin helped rack up the weapons, then got himself a bowl of stew and joined Lieutenant Noro, who was waiting on the wall right outside the tower. A messenger used signal flags to indicate to others down in the city that Noro's platoon hadn't engaged.

'You have my apologies, sir,' Kaladin said softly. 'I'll see it doesn't happen again.'

'Um . . . it?'

'I preempted you earlier,' Kaladin said. 'Gave orders when it was your place.'

'Oh! Well, you're quite quick off the cuff, Kal! Eager for combat, I'd say.'

'Perhaps, sir.'

'You want to prove yourself to the team,' Noro said, rubbing his wispy beard. 'Well, I like a man with enthusiasm. Keep your head, and I suspect you'll end up as a squadleader before too long.' He said it like a proud parent.

'Permission, sir, to be excused from duty? There might be wounded that need my attention farther along the wall.'

'Wounded? Kal, I know you said you had some field medicine training – but the army's surgeons will be there already.'

Right, they'd have actual surgeons.

Noro clapped him on the shoulder. 'Go in and eat your stew. There will be enough action later. Don't run too fast toward danger, all right?'

'I'll . . . try to remember that, sir.'

Still, there was nothing to do but walk back into the tower, Syl alighting on his shoulder, and sit down to eat his stew.

SWIFTSPREN

Today, I leaped from the tower for the last time. I felt the wind dance around me as I fell all the way along the eastern side, past the tower, and to the foothills below. I'm going to miss that.

—From drawer 10-1, sapphire

Veil leaned her head to look in through the window of the old, broken shop in the market. Grund the urchin sat in his usual place, carefully stripping down an old pair of shoes for the hogshide. As he heard Veil, he dropped his tool and reached for a knife with his good hand.

He saw that it was her, then caught the package of food she tossed to him. It was smaller this time, but actually had some fruit. Very rare in the city these days. The urchin pulled the bag of food close, closing his dark green eyes, looking . . . reserved. What an odd expression.

He's still suspicious of me, she thought. *He's wondering what I'll someday demand of him for all this.*

'Where are Ma and Seland?' Veil asked. She had prepared packages for the two women who stayed here with Grund.

'Moved out to the old tinker's place,' Grund said. He thumbed upward, toward the sagging ceiling. 'Thought this place was getting too dangerous.'

'You sure you don't want to do the same?'

'Nah,' he said. 'I can finally move without kicking someone.'

She left him and shoved her hands in her pockets, wearing her new coat and hat against the cool air. She'd hoped that Kholinar would prove to be warmer, after so long on the Shattered Plains or Urithiru. But it was cold here too, suffering a season of winter weather. Perhaps the arrival of the Everstorm was to be blamed.

She checked in on Muri next, the former seamstress with three daughters. She was of second nahn, high ranking for a darkeyes, and had run a successful business in a town near Revolar. Now she trolled the water ditches following storms for the corpses of rats and cremlings.

Muri always had some gossip that was amusing but generally pointless. Veil left about an hour later and made her way out of the market, dropping her last package in the lap of a random beggar.

The old beggar sniffed the package, then whooped with excitement. 'The Swiftspren!' he said, nudging one of the other beggars. 'Look, the Swiftspren!' He cackled, digging into the package, and his friend roused from his sleep and snatched some flatbread.

'Swiftspren?' Veil asked.

'That's you!' he said. 'Yup, yup! I *heard* of you. Robbing rich folk all through the city, you do! And nobody can stop you, 'cuz you're a *spren*. Can walk through walls, you can. White hat, white coat. Don't always appear the same, do ya?'

The beggar started stuffing his face. Veil smiled – her reputation was spreading. She'd enhanced it by sending Ishnah and Vathah out, wearing illusions to look like Veil, giving away food. Surely, the cult couldn't ignore her much longer. Pattern hummed as she stretched, exhaustionspren – all of the corrupted variety – spinning about her in the air, little red whirlwinds. The merchant she'd stolen from earlier had chased her away himself, and had been nimble for his age.

'Why?' Pattern asked.

'Why what?' Veil asked. 'Why is the sky blue, the sun bright? Why do storms blow, or rains fall?'

'Mmmm . . . Why are you so happy about feeding so few?'

'Feeding these few is something we can do.'

'So is jumping from a building,' he said – frank, as if he didn't understand the sarcasm he used. 'But we do not do this. You lie, Shallan.'

'Veil.'

'Your lies wrap other lies. Mmm . . .' He sounded drowsy. Could spren get drowsy? 'Remember your Ideal, the truth you spoke.'

She shoved hands in her pockets. Evening was coming, the sun slipping toward the western horizon. As if it were running from the Origin and the storms.

It was the individual touch, the light in the eyes of people she gave to, that really excited her. Feeding them felt so much more *real* than the rest of the plan to infiltrate the cult and investigate the Oathgate.

It's too small, she thought. That was what Jasnah would say. *I'm thinking too small.*

Along the street, she passed people who whimpered and suffered. Far too many hungerspren in the air, and fearspren at nearly every corner. She had to do *something* to help.

Like throwing a thimbleful of water onto a bonfire.

She stood at an intersection, head bowed, as the shadows grew long, reaching toward night. Chanting broke her out of her trance. How long had she been standing there?

Flickering light, orange and primal, painted a street to her left. No sphere glowed that color. She walked toward it, pulling off her hat and sucking in Stormlight. She released it in a puff, then stepped through, trailing tendrils that wrapped around her and transformed her shape.

People had gathered, as they usually did, when the Cult of Moments paraded. Swiftspren broke through them, wearing the costume of a spren from her notes – notes she'd lost to the sea. A spren shaped like a glowing arrowhead that wove through the sky around skyeels.

Golden tassels streamed from her back, long, with arrowhead shapes at the ends. Her entire front was wrapped in cloth that trailed behind, her arms, legs, and face covered. Swiftspren flowed among the cultists, and drew stares even from them.

I have to do more, she thought. *I have to think grander schemes.*

Could Shallan's lies help her be something more than a broken girl from rural Jah Keved? A girl who was, deep down, terrified that she had *no idea* what she was doing.

The cultists chanted softly, repeating the words of the leaders at the front.

'Our time has passed.'

'Our time has passed.'

'The spren have come.'

'The spren have come.'

'Give them our sins.'

'Give them our sins. . . .'

Yes . . . she could feel it. The freedom these people felt. It was the peace of surrender. They coursed down the street, proffering their torches and lanterns toward the sky, wearing the garb of spren. Why worry? Embrace the release, embrace the transition, embrace the coming of storm and spren.

Embrace the end.

Swiftspren breathed in their chants and saturated herself with their ideas. She became them, and she could *hear* it, whispering in the back of her mind.

Surrender.

Give me your passion. Your pain. Your love.

Give up your guilt.

Embrace the end.

Shallan, I'm not your enemy.

That last one stood out, like a scar on a beautiful man's face. Jarring.

She came to herself. Storms. She'd initially thought that this group might lead her up to the revel on the Oathgate platform, but . . . she'd let herself be carried away by the darkness. Trembling, she stopped in place.

The others stopped around her. The illusion – the sprenlike tassels behind her – continued to stream, even when she wasn't walking. There was no wind.

The cultists' chanting broke off, and corrupted awespren exploded around several of their heads. Soot-black puffs. Some fell to their knees. To them – wrapped in streaming cloth, face obscured, ignoring wind and gravity – she would look like an actual spren.

'There are spren,' Shallan said to the gathered crowd, using Lightweaving to twist and warp her voice, 'and there are *spren*. You followed the dark ones. They whisper for you to abandon yourselves. *They lie.*'

The cultists gasped.

'We do not want your devotion. When have spren ever demanded your *devotion*? Stop dancing in the streets and be *men* and *women* again. Strip off those idiotic costumes and return to your families!'

They didn't move quickly enough, so she sent her tassels streaming upward, curling about one another, lengthening. A powerful light flashed from her.

'Go!' she shouted.

They fled, some throwing off their costumes as they went. Shallan waited, trembling, until she was alone. She let the glow vanish and shrouded herself in blackness, then stepped off the street.

When she emerged from the blackness, she looked like Veil again. Storms. She'd ... she'd become one of them so *easily*. Was her mind so quickly corrupted?

She wrapped her arms around herself, trailing through streets and markets. Jasnah would have been strong enough to keep going with them until reaching the platform. And if these hadn't been allowed up – most that wandered the streets weren't privileged enough to join the feast – then she'd have done something else. Perhaps take the place of one of the feast guards.

Truth was, she *enjoyed* the thievery and feeding the people. Veil wanted to be a hero of the streets, like in the old stories. That had corrupted Shallan, preventing her from going forward with something more logical.

But she'd never been the logical one. That was Jasnah, and Shallan *couldn't* be her. Maybe ... maybe she could become Radiant and ...

She huddled against a wall, arms wrapped around herself. Sweating, trembling, she went looking for light. She found it down a street: a calm, level glow. The friendly light of spheres, and with it a sound that seemed impossible. Laughter?

She chased it, hungry, until she reached a gathering of people singing beneath Nomon's azure gaze. They'd overturned boxes, gathering in a ring, while one man led the boisterous songs.

Shallan watched, hand on the wall of a building, Veil's hat held limply in her gloved safehand. Shouldn't that laughter have been more desperate? How could they be so happy? How could they sing? In that moment, these people seemed like strange beasts, beyond her understanding.

Sometimes she felt like a thing wearing a human skin. She was that thing in Urithiru, the Unmade, who sent out puppets to feign humanity.

It's him, she noticed absently. *Wit's leading the songs.*

He hadn't left her any more messages at the inn. Last time she'd visited, the innkeeper complained that he'd moved out, and had coerced her to pay Wit's tab.

Veil pulled on her hat, then turned and trailed away down the small market street.

.•.

She turned herself back into Shallan right before she reached the tailor's shop. Veil let go reluctantly, as she kept wanting to go track down Kaladin in the Wall Guard. He wouldn't know her, so she could approach him, pretend to get to know him. Maybe flirt a little . . .

Radiant was aghast at that idea. Her oaths to Adolin weren't complete, but they were important. She respected him, and enjoyed their time training together with the sword.

And Shallan . . . what did Shallan want again? Did it matter? Why bother worrying about her?

Veil finally let go. She folded her hat and coat, then used an illusion to disguise them as a satchel. She layered an illusion of Shallan and her havah over the top of her trousers and shirt, then strolled inside, where she found Drehy and Skar playing cards and debating which kind of chouta was best. There were different kinds?

Shallan nodded to them, then – exhausted – started up the steps. A few hungerspren, however, reminded her that she hadn't saved anything for herself from the day's thievery. She put away her clothing, then hiked down to the kitchen.

Here she found Elhokar drinking from a single cup of wine into which he'd dropped a sphere. That red-violet glow was the room's only light. On the table before him was a sheet of glyphs: names of the houses he had been approaching, through the parties. He'd crossed out some of the names, but had circled the others, writing down numbers of troops they might be able to provide. Fifty armsmen here, thirty there.

He raised the glowing cup to her as she gathered some flatbread and sugar. 'What is that design on your skirt? It . . . seems familiar to me.'

She glanced down. Pattern, who usually clung to her coat, had been replicated in the illusion on the side of her havah. 'Familiar?'

Elhokar nodded. He didn't seem drunk, just contemplative. 'I used to see myself as a hero, like you. I imagined claiming the Shattered Plains in my father's name. Vengeance for blood spilled. It doesn't even matter now, does it? That we won?'

'Of course it matters,' Shallan said. 'We have Urithiru, and we defeated a large army of Voidbringers.'

He grunted. 'Sometimes I think that if I merely *insist* long enough, the world will transform. But wishing and expecting is of the Passions. A heresy. A good Vorin worries about transforming themselves.'

Give me your passion. . . .

'Have you any news about the Oathgate or the Cult of Moments?' Elhokar asked.

'No. I have some thoughts about getting up there though. New ones.'

'Good. I might have troops for us soon, though their numbers will be smaller than I'd hoped. We depend upon your reconnaissance, however. I would know what is happening on that platform before I march troops onto it.'

'Give me a few more days. I'll get onto the platform, I promise.'

He took a drink of his wine. 'There are few people remaining to whom I can still be a hero, Radiant. This city. My son. Storms. He was a baby when I last saw him. He'd be three now. Locked in the palace . . .'

Shallan set down her food. 'Wait here.' She fetched her sketchpad and pencils from a shelf in the showroom, then returned to Elhokar and settled down. She placed some spheres out for light, then started drawing.

Elhokar sat at the table across from her, lit by the cup of wine. 'What are you doing?'

'I don't have a proper sketch of you,' Shallan said. 'I want one.'

Creationspren started to appear around her immediately. They seemed normal, though they were so odd anyway, it could be hard to tell.

Elhokar *was* a good man. In his heart, at least. Shouldn't that matter most? He moved to look over her shoulder, but she was no longer sketching from sight.

'We'll save them,' Shallan whispered. 'You'll save them. It will be all right.'

Elhokar watched silently as she filled in the shading and finished the picture. Once she lifted her pencil, Elhokar reached past her and rested his fingers on the page. It depicted Elhokar kneeling on the ground, beaten down, clothing ragged. But he looked upward, outward, chin raised. He wasn't beaten. No, this man was noble, *regal*.

'Is that what I look like?' he whispered.

'Yes.' *It's what you could be, at least.*

'May I . . . may I have it?'

She lacquered the page, then handed it to him.

'Thank you.' Storms. He almost seemed to be in tears!

Feeling embarrassed, she gathered her supplies and her food, then hurried out of the kitchen. Back in her rooms, she met Ishnah, who was grinning. The short, darkeyed woman had been out earlier, wearing Veil's face and clothing.

She held up a slip of paper. 'Someone handed me this today, Brightness, while I was giving away food.'

Frowning, Shallan took the note.

Meet us at the borders of the revel in two nights, the day of the next Everstorm, it read. *Come alone. Bring food. Join the feast.*

ELEVEN YEARS AGO

Dalinar left the horse.

Horses were too slow.

A misty fog blew off the lake, reminding him of that day long ago when he, Gavilar, and Sadeas had first attacked the Rift.

The elites who accompanied him were the product of years of planning and training. Primarily archers, they wore no armor, and were trained for long-distance running. Horses were magnificent beasts; the Sunmaker famously had used an entire company of cavalry. Over a short distance, their speed and maneuverability had been legendary.

Those possibilities intrigued Dalinar. Could men be trained to fire bows from horseback? How devastating would that be? What about a charge of horses bearing men with spears, like the legends spoke of during the Shin invasion?

For today, however, he didn't need horses. Men were better suited for long-distance running, not to mention being much better at scrambling over broken hillsides and uneven rocks. This company of elites could outrun any harrying force he'd yet to meet. Though archers, they were proficient with the sword. Their training was unparalleled, and their stamina legendary.

Dalinar hadn't trained with them personally, as he didn't have time to practice running thirty miles a day. Fortunately, he had Plate to make up the difference. Clad in his armor, he led the charging force over scrub and rock, past reeds that released hairlike inner strands to shiver on the breeze until he drew near. Grass, tree, and weed took fright at his approach.

Two fires burned inside him. First the energy of the Plate, lending power to each step. The second fire was the Thrill. Sadeas, a traitor? Impossible. He had supported Gavilar all along. Dalinar trusted him.

And yet . . .

I thought myself trustworthy, Dalinar thought, leading the charge down a hillside, a hundred men flooding behind him. *Yet I almost turned on Gavilar.*

He would see for himself. He would find out whether this 'caravan' that had brought supplies to the Rift actually had a Shardbearer in its ranks or not. But the possibility that he had been betrayed – that Sadeas could have been working against them all along – drove Dalinar to a kind of focused madness. A clarity only the Thrill bestowed.

It was the focus of a man, his sword, and the blood he would spill.

The Thrill seemed to transform within him as he ran, soaking into his tiring muscles, saturating him. It became a power unto itself. So, when they crested a hillside some distance south of the Rift, he felt somehow *more* energetic than when he'd left.

As his company of elites jogged up, Dalinar pulled to a stop, armored feet grinding on stone. Ahead, down the hill and at the mouth of a canyon, a frantic group was scrambling to arms. The caravan. Its scouts must have spotted the approach of Dalinar's force.

They'd been setting up camp, but left their tents, running for the canyon, where they'd be able to avoid being flanked. Dalinar roared, summoning his Blade, ignoring the fatigue of his men as he dashed down the hillside.

The soldiers wore forest green and white. Sadeas's colors.

Dalinar reached the bottom of the hill and stormed through the now-abandoned camp. He swept past the stragglers, slicing out with Oathbringer, dropping them, their eyes burning.

Wait.

His momentum wouldn't *let* him stop now. Where was the enemy Shardbearer?

Something is wrong.

Dalinar led his men into the canyon after the soldiers, following the enemy along a wide path up the side. He raised Oathbringer high as he ran.

Why would they put on Sadeas's colors if they're a secret *envoy bringing contraband supplies?*

Dalinar stopped in place, his soldiers swarming around him. Their path had taken them about fifty feet up from the bottom of the canyon, on the south side of a steep incline. He saw no sign of a Shardbearer as the enemy gathered above. And . . . those uniforms . . .

He blinked. That . . . that was wrong.

He shouted an order to pull back, but the sound of his voice was overwhelmed by a sudden roar. A sound like thunder, accompanied by a dreadful clatter of rock against rock. The ground quivered, and he turned in horror to find a landslide tumbling down the steep side of the ravine to his right – directly above where he had led his men.

He had a fraction of a moment to take it in before the rocks pounded him in a terrible crash.

Everything spun, then grew black. Still he was pounded, rolled, *crushed.* An explosion of molten sparks briefly flashed in his eyes, and something hard smacked him on the head.

Finally it ended. He found himself lying in blackness, his head pounding, thick warm blood running down his face and dripping from his chin. He could feel the blood, but not see it. Had he been blinded?

His cheek was pressed against a rock. No. He wasn't blind; he'd been buried. And his helm had shattered. He shifted with a groan, and something illuminated the stones around his head. Stormlight seeping from his breastplate.

Somehow he'd survived the landslide. He lay facedown, prone, buried. He shifted again, and from the corner of his eye saw a rock sink, threatening to crush sideways into his skull. He lay still, his head thundering with pain. He flexed his left hand and found that gauntlet broken, his forearm plate too. But his right-hand armor still worked.

This . . . this was a trap. . . .

Sadeas was not a traitor. This had been designed by the Rift and its highlord to lure Dalinar in, then drop stones to crush him. Cowards. They'd tried something like that in Rathalas long ago too. He relaxed, groaning softly.

No. Can't lie here.

Maybe he could pretend to be dead. That sounded so appealing he closed his eyes and started to drift.

A fire ignited inside him.

You have been betrayed, Dalinar. Listen. He heard voices – men picking through the wreckage of the rockslide. He could make out their nasal accent. Rifters.

Tanalan sent you here to die!

Dalinar sneered, opening his eyes. Those men wouldn't let him hide in this tomb of stone, feigning death. He carried Shards. They would find him to recover their prize.

He braced himself, using his Plated shoulder to keep the rock from rolling against his exposed head, but did not otherwise move. Eventually the men above started speaking eagerly; from their words, they'd found his armor's cape sticking out through the stone, the glyphs of *khokh* and *linil* stark on the blue background.

Stones scraped, and the burden upon him lightened. The Thrill built to a crescendo. The stone near his head rolled back.

Go.

Dalinar heaved with his Plated feet and shifted a boulder with his still-armored hand, opening enough space that he could stand up straight. He ripped free of the tomb and stumbled upright into open air, stones clattering.

The Rifters cursed and scrambled backward as he leaped out of the hole, boots grinding against stones. Dalinar growled, summoning his Blade.

His armor was in worse shape than he'd assumed. Sluggish. Broken in four separate places.

All around him, Tanalan's men's eyes seemed to *glow*. They gathered and grinned at him; he could see the Thrill thick in their expressions. His Blade and leaking Plate reflected in their dark eyes.

Blood streaming down the side of his face, Dalinar grinned back at them.

They rushed to attack.

⁘

Dalinar saw only red.

He partially came to himself as he found himself pounding a man's head repeatedly against the stones. Behind him lay a pile of corpses with burned eyes, piled high around the hole where Dalinar had stood, fighting against them.

He dropped the head of the corpse in his hands and breathed out, feeling ... What did he feel? Numb, suddenly. Pain was a distant thing. Even anger was nebulous. He looked down at his hands. Why was he using those, and not his Shardblade?

He turned to the side, where Oathbringer protruded from a rock where he'd stabbed it. The ... gemstone on the pommel was cracked. That was right. He couldn't dismiss it; something about the crack had interfered.

He stumbled to his feet, looking around for more foes, but none came to challenge him. His armor ... someone had broken the breastplate while fighting him, and he felt at a stab wound on his chest. He barely remembered that.

The sun was low on the horizon, plunging the canyon into shadows. Around him, discarded bits of clothing flapped in the breeze, and bodies lay still. Not a sound, not even cremling scavengers.

Drained, he bound the worst of his wounds, then grabbed Oathbringer and set it on his shoulder. Never had a Shardblade felt so heavy.

He started walking.

Along the way, he discarded pieces of Shardplate, which grew too heavy. He'd lost blood. Far too much.

He focused on the steps. One after another.

Momentum. A fight was all about *momentum*.

He didn't dare take the obvious route, in case he encountered more Rifters. He crossed through the wilderness, vines writhing beneath his feet and rockbuds sprouting after he passed.

The Thrill returned to urge him on. For this walk *was* a fight. A battle. Night fell, and he threw off his last piece of Shardplate, leaving only the neck brace. They could regrow the rest of it from that, if they had to.

Keep. Moving.

In that darkness, shadowed figures seemed to accompany him. Armies made of red mist at the corners of his vision, charging forces that fell to dust and then sprouted from shadow again, like surging ocean waves in a constant state of disintegration and rebirth. Not just men, but eyeless horses. Animals locked in struggle, stifling the life from one another. Shadows of death and conflict to propel him through the night.

He hiked for an eternity. Eternity was nothing when time had no meaning. He was actually surprised when he approached the light of the Rift, from torches held by soldiers on the walls. His navigation by the moons and stars had been successful.

He stalked through the darkness toward his own camp on the field. There was another army here. Sadeas's actual soldiers; they'd arrived ahead of schedule. Another few hours, and Tanalan's ploy wouldn't have worked.

Dalinar dragged Oathbringer behind him; it made a soft scraping sound as it cut a line in the stone. He numbly heard soldiers talking by the bonfire ahead, and one called something out. Dalinar ignored them, each step relentless, as he passed into their light. A pair of young soldiers in blue crowed their challenges until cutting off and lowering spears, gaping.

'Stormfather,' one of them said, stumbling back. 'Kelek and the Almighty himself!'

Dalinar continued through camp. Noise stirred at his passing, men crying of visions of the dead and of Voidbringers. He made for his command tent. The eternity it took to get there seemed the same length as the others. How could he cross so many miles in the same time as it took to go the few feet to a simple tent? Dalinar shook his head, seeing red at the sides of his vision.

Words broke through the canvas of the tent. 'Impossible. The men are spooked. They . . . No, it's simply not *possible*.'

The flaps burst apart, revealing a man with fine clothing and wavy hair. Sadeas gaped, then stumbled to the side, holding the flap for Dalinar, who did not break stride. He walked straight in, Oathbringer slicing a ribbon in the ground.

Inside, generals and officers gathered by the grim light of a few sphere lanterns. Evi, comforted by Brightness Kalami, was weeping, though Ialai studied the table full of maps. All eyes turned toward Dalinar.

'How?' Teleb asked. 'Blackthorn? We sent a team of scouts to inform you as soon as Tanalan turned on us and cast our soldiers off his walls. Our force reported all men lost, an ambush . . .'

Dalinar hefted Oathbringer and slammed it down into the stone ground beside him, then sighed at finally being able to release the burden. He placed his palms on the sides of the battle table, hands crusted in blood. His arms were covered in it too.

'You sent the same scouts,' he whispered, 'who first spied on the caravan, and reported seeing a Shardbearer leading it?'

'Yes,' Teleb said.

'Traitors,' Dalinar said. 'They're working with Tanalan.' He couldn't have known that Dalinar would parley with him. Instead, the man had somehow bribed away members of the army, and had intended to use their reports to coax Dalinar into a hurried ride to the south. Into a trap.

It had all been set in motion before Dalinar had spoken to Tanalan. Planned well in advance.

Teleb barked out orders for the scouts to be imprisoned. Dalinar leaned down over the battle maps on the table. 'This is a map for a siege,' he whispered.

'We . . .' Teleb looked to Sadeas. 'We figured that the king would want time to come down himself. To, um, avenge you, Brightlord.'

'Too slow,' Dalinar said, his voice ragged.

'Highprince Sadeas proposed . . . another option,' Teleb said. 'But the king—'

Dalinar looked to Sadeas.

'They used my name to betray you,' Sadeas said, then spat to the side. 'We will suffer rebellions like this time and time again unless they *fear* us, Dalinar.'

Dalinar nodded slowly. 'They must bleed,' he whispered. 'I want them to suffer for this. Men, women, children. They must know the punishment for broken oaths. *Immediately.*'

'Dalinar?' Evi stood up. 'Husband?' She stepped forward, toward the table.

Then he turned toward her, and she stopped. Her unusual, pale Westerner skin grew even more starkly white. She stepped backward, pulling her hands toward her chest, and gaped at him, horrified, fearspren growing up from the ground around her.

Dalinar glanced toward a sphere lantern, which had a polished metal surface. The man who looked back seemed more Voidbringer than man, face crusted over with blackened blood, hair matted with it, blue eyes wide, jaw clenched. He was sliced with what seemed to be a hundred wounds, his padded uniform in tatters.

'You shouldn't do this,' Evi said. 'Rest. Sleep, Dalinar. Think about this. Give it a few days.'

So tired . . .

'The entire kingdom thinks us weak, Dalinar,' Sadeas whispered. 'We took too long to put this rebellion down. You have never listened to me before, but listen now. You want to prevent this sort of thing from happening again? You *must* punish them. Every one.'

'Punish them . . .' Dalinar said, the Thrill rising again. Pain. Anger. Humiliation. He pressed his hands against the map table to steady himself. 'The Soulcaster that my brother sent. She can make two things?'

'Grain and oil,' Teleb said.

'Good. Set her to work.'

'More food supplies?'

'No, oil. As much as we have gemstones for. Oh, and someone take my wife to her tent so she may recover from her unwarranted grief. Everyone else, gather round. In the morning, we make Rathalas an example. I promised Tanalan that his widows would weep for what I did here, but that is too merciful for what they've done to me.

'I intend to so thoroughly ruin this place that for ten generations, nobody will *dare* build here for fear of the spirits who will haunt it. We will make a *pyre* of this city, and there shall be no weeping for its passing, for *none will remain to weep.*'

ELEVEN YEARS AGO

Dalinar agreed to change clothing. He washed his face and arms, and let a surgeon look at his wounds.

The red mist was still there, coloring his vision. He would *not* sleep. It wouldn't let him.

About an hour after he'd arrived in camp, he trudged back to the command tent, cleaned but not particularly refreshed.

The generals had drawn up a new set of battle plans to take the city walls, as instructed by Sadeas. Dalinar inspected and made a few changes, but told them to suspend making plans to march down into the city and clear it. He had something else in mind.

'Brightlord!' a messenger woman said, arriving at the tent. She stepped in. 'An envoy is leaving the city. Flying the flag of truce.'

'Shoot them dead,' Dalinar said calmly.

'Sir?'

'Arrows, woman,' Dalinar said. 'Kill anyone who comes out of the city, and leave their bodies to rot.'

'Um, yes, Brightlord.' The messenger ducked away.

Dalinar looked up toward Sadeas, who still wore his Shardplate, glittering in the spherelight. Sadeas nodded in approval, then gestured to the side. He wanted to speak in private.

Dalinar left the table. He should hurt more. Shouldn't he? Storms . . .

he was so numb, he could barely feel anything, aside from that burning within, simmering deep down. He stepped with Sadeas out of the tent.

'I've been able to stall the scribes,' Sadeas whispered, 'as you ordered. Gavilar doesn't know that you live. His orders from before were to wait and lay siege.'

'My return supersedes his distant orders,' Dalinar said. 'The men will know that. Even Gavilar wouldn't disagree.'

'Yes, but why keep him ignorant of your arrival?'

The last moon was close to setting. Not long until morning. 'What do you think of my brother, Sadeas?'

'He's exactly what we need,' Sadeas said. 'Hard enough to lead a war; soft enough to be beloved during peace. He has foresight and wisdom.'

'Do you think he could do what needs to be done here?'

Sadeas fell silent. 'No,' he finally said. 'No, not now. I wonder if *you* can either. This will be more than just death. It will be complete destruction.'

'A lesson,' Dalinar whispered.

'A display. Tanalan's plan was clever, but risky. He knew his chances of winning here depended upon removing you and your Shards from the battle.' He narrowed his eyes. 'You thought those soldiers were mine. You actually believed I'd betray Gavilar.'

'I worried.'

'Then know this, Dalinar,' Sadeas said, low, his voice like stone grinding stone. 'I would cut out my own heart before betraying Gavilar. I have no interest in being king – it's a job with little praise and even less amusement. I mean for this kingdom to stand for centuries.'

'Good,' Dalinar said.

'Honestly, I worried that *you* would betray him.'

'I almost did, once. I stopped myself.'

'Why?'

'Because,' Dalinar said. 'There has to be someone in this kingdom capable of doing what needs to be done, and it can't be the man sitting on the throne. Continue to hold the scribes back; it will be better if my brother can reasonably disavow what we're about to do.'

'Something will leak out soon,' Sadeas said. 'Between our two armies, there are too many spanreeds. Storming things are getting so cheap, most of the officers can afford to buy a pair to manage their households from a distance.'

Dalinar strode back into the tent, Sadeas following. Oathbringer still sat where he'd stuck it into the stones, though an armorer had replaced the gemstone for him.

He pulled the Blade from the rock. 'Time to attack.'

Amaram turned from where he stood with the other generals. 'Now, Dalinar? At night?'

'The bonfires on the wall should be enough.'

'To take the wall fortifications, yes,' Amaram said. 'But Brightlord, I don't relish fighting down into those vertical streets in the night.'

Dalinar shared a look with Sadeas. 'Fortunately, you won't have to. Send the word for the men to prepare the oil and flaming brands. We march.'

Highmarshal Perethom took the orders and began organizing specifics. Dalinar lifted Oathbringer on his shoulder. *Time to bring you home.*

In under a half hour, men charged the walls. No Shardbearers led this time; Dalinar was too weak, and his Plate was in shambles. Sadeas never did like exposing himself too early, and Teleb couldn't rush in alone.

They did it the mundane way, sending men to be crushed by stones or impaled by arrows as they carried ladders. They broke through eventually, securing a section of the wall in a furious, bloody fight.

The Thrill was an unsatisfied lump inside Dalinar, but he was wrung out, worn down. So he continued to wait until finally, Teleb and Sadeas joined the fight and routed the last of the defenders, sending them down from the walls toward the chasm of the city itself.

'I need a squad of elites,' Dalinar said softly to a nearby messenger. 'And my own barrel of oil. Have them meet me inside the walls.'

'Yes, Brightlord,' the young boy said, then ran off.

Dalinar strode across the field, passing fallen men bloody and dead. They'd died almost in ranks where waves of arrows had struck. He also passed a cluster of corpses in white, where the envoy had been slaughtered earlier. Warmed by the rising sun, he passed through the now-open gates of the wall and entered the ring of stone that surrounded the Rift.

Sadeas met him there, faceplate up, cheeks even redder than normal from exertion. 'They fought like Voidbringers. More vicious than last time, I'd say.'

'They know what is coming,' Dalinar said, walking toward the cliff edge. He stopped halfway there.

'We checked it for a trap this time,' Sadeas noted.

Dalinar continued forward. The Rifters had gotten the better of him twice now. He should have learned the first time. He stopped at the edge of the cliff, looking down at a city built on platforms, rising up along the widening sides of the rift of stone. It was little wonder they thought so highly of themselves as to resist. Their city was grand, a monument of human ingenuity and grit.

'Burn it,' Dalinar said.

Archers gathered with arrows ready to ignite, while other men rolled up barrels of oil and pitch to give extra fuel.

'There are thousands of people in there, sir,' Teleb said softly from his side. 'Tens of thousands.'

'This kingdom must know the price of rebellion. We make a statement today.'

'Obey or die?' Teleb asked.

'The same deal I offered you, Teleb. You were smart enough to take it.'

'And the common people in there, the ones who didn't get a chance to choose a side?'

Sadeas snorted from nearby. 'We will prevent more deaths in the future by letting every brightlord in this kingdom know the punishment for disobedience.' He took a report from an aide, then stepped up to Dalinar. 'You were right about the scouts who turned traitor. We bribed one to turn on the others, and will execute the rest. The plan was apparently to separate you from the army, then hopefully kill you. Even if you were simply delayed, the Rift was hoping their lies would prompt your army into a reckless attack without you.'

'They weren't counting on your swift arrival,' Dalinar said.

'Or your tenacity.'

The soldiers unplugged barrels of oil, then began dropping them down, soaking the upper levels of the city. Flaming brands followed – starting struts and walkways on fire. The very foundations of this city were flammable.

Tanalan's soldiers tried to organize a fight back out of the Rift, but they'd surrendered the high ground, expecting Dalinar to do as he had before, conquering and controlling.

He watched as the fires spread, flamespren rising in them, seeming larger and more . . . angry than normal. He then walked back – leaving a solemn Teleb – to gather his remaining elites. Captainlord Kadash had fifty for him, along with two barrels of oil.

'Follow,' Dalinar said, walking around the Rift on its east side, where the fracture was narrow enough to cross on a short bridge.

Screams below. Then cries of pain. Calls for mercy. People flooded from buildings, shouting in terror, fleeing on walkways and steps toward the basin below. Many buildings burned, trapping others inside.

Dalinar led his squad along the northern rim of the Rift until they reached a certain location. His armies waited here to kill any soldiers who tried to break out, but the enemy had concentrated their assault on the other side, then been mostly beaten back. The fires hadn't reached up here yet, though Sadeas's archers had killed several dozen civilians who had tried to flee in this direction.

For now, the wooden ramp down into the city was clear. Dalinar led his group down one level to a location he remembered so well: the hidden door set into the wall. It was metal now, guarded by a pair of nervous Rifter soldiers.

Kadash's men shot them down with shortbows. That annoyed Dalinar; all of this fighting, and nothing with which to feed the Thrill. He stepped over one of the corpses, then tried the door, which was no longer hidden. It was still locked tight. Tanalan had decided to go with security instead of secrets, this time.

Unfortunately for them, Oathbringer had come home. Dalinar easily cut off the steel hinges. He stepped back as the door slammed forward onto the walkway, shaking the wood.

'Light those,' he said, pointing to the barrels. 'Roll them down and burn out anyone hiding inside.'

The men hurried to obey, and soon the tunnel of rock had fitful black smoke pouring from it. Nobody tried to flee, though he thought he heard cries of pain inside. Dalinar watched as long as he could, until soon the smoke and heat drove him back.

The Rift behind him was becoming a pit of darkness and fire. Dalinar retreated up the ramp to the stones above. Archers lit the final walkways and ramps behind him. It would be long before people decided to resettle here. Highstorms were one thing, but there was a more terrible force upon the land. And it carried a Shardblade.

Those screams ... Dalinar passed lines of soldiers who waited along the northern rim in silent horror; many wouldn't have been with Dalinar and Gavilar during the early years of their conquest, when they'd allowed pillaging and ransacking of cities. And for those who did remember . . . well, he'd often found an excuse to stop things like this before.

He drew his lips to a line, and shoved down the Thrill. He would *not* let himself enjoy this. That single sliver of decency he could keep back.

'Brightlord!' a soldier said, waving to him. 'Brightlord, you must see this!'

Just below the cliff here – one tier down into the city – was a beautiful white building. A palace. Farther out along the walkways, a group of people fought to reach the building. The wooden walkways were on fire, and preventing their access. Shocked, Dalinar recognized Tanalan the younger from their encounter earlier.

Trying to get into his home? Dalinar thought. Figures darkened the building's upper windows; a woman and children. *No. Trying to get to his family.*

Tanalan hadn't been hiding in the saferoom after all.

'Throw a rope,' Dalinar said. 'Bring Tanalan up here, but shoot down the bodyguards.'

The smoke billowing out of the Rift was growing thick, lit red by the fires. Dalinar coughed, then stepped back as his men let down a rope to the platform below, a section that wasn't burning. Tanalan hesitated, then took it, letting Dalinar's men haul him up. The bodyguards were sent arrows when they tried to climb up a nearby burning ramp.

'Please,' Tanalan said, clothing ashen from the smoke, as he was hauled up over the stone rim. 'My family. *Please.*'

Dalinar could hear them screaming below. He whispered an order, and his elites pushed back the regular Kholin troops from the area, opening up a wide half-circle against the burning rift, where only Dalinar and his closest men were able to observe the captive.

Tanalan slumped on the ground. 'Please . . .'

'I,' Dalinar said softly, 'am an animal.'

'What—'

'An animal,' Dalinar said, 'reacts as it is prodded. You whip it, and it becomes savage. With an animal, you can start a tempest. Trouble is, once it's gone feral, you can't just whistle it back to you.'

'Blackthorn!' Tanalan screamed. 'Please! My *children.*'

'I made a mistake years ago,' Dalinar said. 'I will not be so foolish again.'

And yet . . . those screams.

Dalinar's soldiers seized Tanalan tightly as Dalinar turned from the man and walked back to the pit of fire. Sadeas had just arrived with a company of his own men, but Dalinar ignored them, Oathbringer still held against his shoulder. Smoke stung Dalinar's nose, his eyes watering. He couldn't see across the Rift to the rest of his armies; the air warped with heat, colored red.

It was like looking into Damnation itself.

Dalinar released a long breath, suddenly feeling his exhaustion even more deeply. 'It is enough,' he said, turning toward Sadeas. 'Let the rest of the people of the city escape out the mouth of the canyon below. We have sent our signal.'

'What?' Sadeas said, hiking over. 'Dalinar—'

A loud series of cracks interrupted him. An entire section of the city nearby collapsed into the flames. The palace – and its occupants – crashed down with it, a tempest of sparks and splintering wood.

'No!' Tanalan shouted. '*NO!*'

'Dalinar . . .' Sadeas said. 'I prepared a battalion below, with archers, per your orders.'

'My orders?'

'You said to 'Kill anyone who comes out of the city and leave their bodies to rot.' I had men stationed below; they've launched arrows in at the city struts, burned the walkways leading down. This city burns from both directions – from underneath and from above. We can't stop it now.'

Wood cracked as more sections of city collapsed. The Thrill surged, and Dalinar pushed it away. 'We've gone too far.'

'Nonsense! Our lesson won't mean much if people can merely walk away.' Sadeas glanced toward Tanalan. 'Last loose end is this one. We don't want him getting away again.' He reached for his sword.

'I'll do it,' Dalinar said. Though the concept of more death was starting to sicken him, he steeled himself. This was the man who had betrayed him.

Dalinar stepped closer. To his credit, Tanalan tried to leap to his feet and fight. Several elites shoved the traitor back down to the ground, though Captainlord Kadash himself was just standing at the side of the city, looking down at the destruction. Dalinar could feel that heat, so terrible. It mirrored a sense within him. The Thrill . . . incredibly . . . was *not satisfied*. Still it thirsted. It didn't seem . . . didn't seem it *could* be satiated.

Tanalan collapsed, blubbering.

'You should not have betrayed me,' Dalinar whispered, raising Oathbringer. 'At least this time, you didn't hide in your hole. I don't know who you let take cover there, but know they are dead. I took care of that with barrels of fire.'

Tanalan blinked, then started laughing with a frantic, crazed air. 'You don't know? How could you not know? But you killed our messengers. You poor fool. You poor, *stupid* fool.'

Dalinar seized him by the chin, though the man was still held by his soldiers. '*What?*'

'She came to us,' Tanalan said. 'To plead. How could you have missed her? Do you track your own family so poorly? The hole you burned . . . we don't hide there anymore. Everyone knows about it. Now it's a prison.'

Ice washed through Dalinar, and he grabbed Tanalan by the throat and held, Oathbringer slipping from his fingers. He strangled the man, all the while demanding that he retract what he'd said.

Tanalan died with a smile on his lips. Dalinar stepped back, suddenly feeling too weak to stand. Where was the Thrill to bolster him? 'Go back,' he shouted at his elites. 'Search that hole. Go . . .' He trailed off.

Kadash was on his knees, looking woozy, a pile of vomit on the rock before him. Some elites ran to try to do as Dalinar said, but they shied away from the Rift – the heat rising from the burning city was incredible.

Dalinar roared, standing, pushing toward the flames. However, the fire was too intense. Where he had once seen himself as an unstoppable force, he now had to admit exactly how small he was. Insignificant. Meaningless.

Once it's gone feral, you can't just whistle it back to you.

He fell to his knees, and remained there until his soldiers pulled him – limp – away from the heat and carried him to his camp.

⁂

Six hours later, Dalinar stood with hands clasped behind his back – partially to hide how badly they were shaking – and stared at a body on the table, covered in a white sheet.

Behind him in the tent, some of his scribes whispered. A sound like swishing swords on the practice field. Teleb's wife, Kalami, led the discussion; she thought that Evi must have defected. What else could explain why the burned corpse of a highprince's wife had been found in an enemy safehouse?

It fit the narrative. Showing uncharacteristic determination, Evi had drugged the guard protecting her. She'd snuck away in the night. The scribes wondered how long Evi had been a traitor, and if she'd helped recruit the group of scouts who had betrayed Dalinar.

He stepped forward, resting his fingers on the smooth, too-white sheet. *Fool woman.* The scribes didn't know Evi well enough. She hadn't been a traitor – she'd gone to the Rift to plead for them to surrender. She'd seen in Dalinar's eyes that he wouldn't spare them. So, Almighty help her, she'd gone to do what she could.

Dalinar barely had the strength to stand. The Thrill had abandoned him, and that left him broken, pained.

He pulled back the corner of the sheet. The left side of Evi's face was scorched, nauseating, but the right side had been down toward the stone. It was oddly untouched.

This is your fault, he thought at her. *How dare you do this? Stupid, frustrating woman.*

This was *not* his fault, *not* his responsibility.

'Dalinar,' Kalami said, stepping up. 'You should rest.'

'She didn't betray us,' Dalinar said firmly.

'I'm sure eventually we'll know what—'

'She did *not* betray us,' Dalinar snapped. 'Keep the discovery of her body quiet, Kalami. Tell the people . . . tell them my wife was slain by an assassin last night. I will swear the few elites who know to secrecy. Let everyone think she died a hero, and that the destruction of the city today was done in retribution.'

Dalinar set his jaw. Earlier today, the soldiers of his army – so carefully trained over the years to resist pillaging and the slaughter of civilians – had burned a city to the ground. It would ease their consciences to think that first, the highlady had been murdered.

Kalami smiled at him, a knowing – even self-important – smile. His lie would serve a second purpose. As long as Kalami and the head scribes *thought* they knew a secret, they'd be less likely to dig for the true answer.

Not my fault.

'Rest, Dalinar,' Kalami said. 'You are in pain now, but as the highstorm must pass, all mortal agonies will fade.'

Dalinar left the corpse to the ministrations of others. As he departed, he strangely heard the screams of those people in the Rift. He stopped, wondering what it was. Nobody else seemed to notice.

Yes, that was distant screaming. In his head, maybe? They all seemed children to his ears. The ones he'd abandoned to the flames. A chorus of the innocent pleading for help, for mercy.

Evi's voice joined them.

The Taker of Secrets

Sja-anat, creator and corrupter - unique among the Unmade.

Creator

Her twisted creations are her beloved children.

Her admiration of the spren of our world inspires her.

Corrupter

She seeks the Children of Honor and the Children of Cultivation.

With one touch she corrupts.

Sja-anat

Something must be done about the remnants of Odium's forces. The parsh, as they are now called, continue their war with zeal, even without their masters from Damnation.

—From drawer 30-20, first emerald

Kaladin dashed across the street. 'Wait!' he shouted. 'One more here!'

Ahead, a man with a thin mustache struggled to close a thick wooden door. It stuck partway open, however, giving just enough time for Kaladin to slip through.

The man swore at him, then pulled the door shut. Made of dark stumpweight wood, it made a muffled *thunk*. The man did up the locks, then stepped back and let three younger men place a thick bar into the settings.

'Cutting that close, armsman,' the mustachioed man said, noting the Wall Guard patch on Kaladin's shoulder.

'Sorry,' Kaladin said, handing the man a few spheres as a cover charge. 'But the storm is still a few minutes away.'

'Can't be too careful with this new storm,' the man said. 'Be glad the door got stuck.'

Syl sat on the hinges, legs hanging over the sides. Kaladin doubted it had been luck; sticking people's shoes to the stone was a classic winds-pren trick. Still, he did understand the doorman's hesitance. Everstorms didn't *quite* match up with scholarly projections. The previous one had arrived hours earlier than anyone had guessed it would. Fortunately, they tended to blow in slower than highstorms. If you knew to watch the sky, there was time to find shelter.

Kaladin ran his hand through his hair and started deeper into the wine-house. This was one of those fashionable places that – while technically a stormshelter – was used only by rich people who had come to spend the storm enjoying themselves. It had a large common room and thick walls of stone blocks. No windows, of course. A bartender kept people liquored near the back, and a number of booths ringed the perimeter.

He spotted Shallan and Adolin sitting in a booth at the side. She wore her own face, but Adolin looked like Meleran Khal, a tall, bald man around Adolin's height. Kaladin lingered, watching Shallan laugh at something Adolin said, then poke him – with her safehand – in the shoulder. She seemed completely enthralled by him. And good for her. Everyone deserved something to give them light, these days. But . . . what about the glances she shot him on occasion, times when she didn't quite seem to be the same person? A different smile, an almost wicked look to her eyes . . .

You're seeing things, he thought to himself. He strode forward and caught their attention, settling into the booth with a sigh. He was off duty, and free to visit the city. He'd told the others he'd find his own shel-ter for the storm, and only had to be back in time for evening post-storm patrol.

'Took you long enough, bridgeboy,' Adolin said.

'Lost track of time,' Kaladin said, tapping the table. He hated being in stormshelters. They felt too much like prisons.

Outside, thunder announced the Everstorm's arrival. Most people in the city would be inside their homes, the refugees instead in public stormshelters.

This for-pay shelter was sparsely occupied, only a few of the tables or booths in use. That would give privacy to talk, fortunately, but it didn't bode well for the proprietor. People didn't have spheres to waste.

'Where's Elhokar?' Kaladin asked.

'Elhokar is working on last-minute plans through the storm,' Adolin said. 'He's decided to reveal himself tonight to the lighteyes he's chosen. And . . . he's done a good job, Kal. We'll at least have some troops because of this. Fewer than I'd like, but *something.*'

'And maybe another Knight Radiant?' Shallan asked, glancing at Kaladin. 'What have you found?'

He quickly caught them up on what he'd learned: The Wall Guard might have a Soulcaster, and was *definitely* producing food somehow. It had seized emerald stores in the city – a fact he'd recently discovered.

'Azure is . . . tough to read,' Kaladin finished. 'She visits the barracks every night, but never talks about herself. Men report seeing her sword cut through stone, but it has no gemstone. I think it might be an Honor-blade, like the weapon of the Assassin in White.'

'Huh,' Adolin said, sitting back. 'You know, that would explain a lot.'

'My platoon has dinner with her tonight, after evening patrol,' Kaladin said. 'I intend to see what I can learn.'

A serving girl came for orders, and Adolin bought them wine. He knew about lighteyed drinks and – without needing to be told – ordered something without a touch of alcohol for Kaladin. He'd be on duty later. Adolin did get Shallan a cup of violet, to Kaladin's surprise.

As the serving girl left with the order, Adolin reached out toward Kaladin. 'Let me see your sword.'

'My sword?' Kaladin said, glancing toward Syl, who was huddling near the back of the booth and humming softly to herself. A way of ignoring the sounds of the Everstorm, which rumbled beyond the stones.

'Not *that* sword,' Adolin said. 'Your side sword.'

Kaladin glanced down to where the sword stuck out beside his seat. He'd almost forgotten he was wearing the thing, which was a relief. The first few days, he'd bumped the sheath into everything. He unbuckled it and set it on the table for Adolin.

'Good blade,' the prince said. 'Well maintained. It was in this condition when they assigned it to you?'

Kaladin nodded. Adolin drew it and held it up.

'It's a little small,' Shallan noted.

'It's a one-handed sword, Shallan. Close-range infantry weapon. A longer blade would be impractical.'

'Longer . . . like Shardblades?' Kaladin asked.

'Well, yes, they break all kinds of rules.' Adolin waved the sword through a few motions, then sheathed it. 'I like this highmarshal of yours.'

'It's not even *her* weapon,' Kaladin said, taking it back.

'You boys done comparing your swords?' Shallan asked. 'Because I've found something.' She thumped a large book onto the table. 'One of my contacts finally tracked down a copy of Hessi's *Mythica*. It's a newer book, and has been poorly received. It attributes distinct personalities to the Unmade.'

Adolin lifted the cover, peeking in. 'So . . . anything about swords in it?'

'Oh hush,' she said, and batted his arm in a playful – and somewhat nauseating – way.

Yes, it was uncomfortable to watch the two of them. Kaladin liked them both . . . just not together. He forced himself to look around the room, which was occupied by lighteyes trying to drink away the sounds of the storm. He tried not to think of refugees who would be packed into stuffy public shelters, clutching their meager possessions and hoping some of what they were forced to leave behind would survive the storm.

'The book,' Shallan said, 'claims there were nine Unmade. That matches the vision Dalinar saw, though other reports speak of ten Unmade. They're likely ancient spren, primal, from the days before human society and civilization.

'The book claims the nine rampaged during the Desolations, but says not all were destroyed at Aharietiam. The author insists that some are active today; I find her vindicated – obviously – by what we've experienced.'

'And there's one of these in the city,' Adolin said.

'I think . . .' Shallan said. 'I think there might be *two*, Adolin. Sja-anat, the Taker of Secrets, is one. Again, Dalinar's visions mention her. Sja-anat's touch corrupted other spren – and we're seeing the effects of that here.'

'And the other one?' Adolin asked.

'Ashertmarn,' Shallan said softly. She slipped a little knife from her satchel and began to absently carve at the top of the table. 'The Heart of the Revel. The book has less to say on him, though it speaks of how he leads people to indulge in excess.'

'Two Unmade,' Kaladin said. 'Are you sure?'

'Sure as I can be. Wit confirmed the second, and the way the queen acted leading up to the riots seems an obvious sign. As for the Taker of Secrets, we can see the corrupted spren ourselves.'

'How do we fight two?' Kaladin asked.

'How do we fight *one?*' Adolin said. 'In the tower, we didn't so much fight the thing as frighten it off. Shallan can't even say how she did that. What does the book say about fighting them?'

'Nothing.' Shallan shrugged, blowing at her little carving on the table. It was of a corrupted gloryspren in the shape of a cube, which another patron had attracted. 'The book says if you see a spren the wrong color, you're supposed to immediately move to another town.'

'There's *kind of* an army in the way,' Kaladin said.

'Yes, amazingly your stench hasn't cleared them out yet.' Shallan started leafing through her book.

Kaladin frowned. Comments like that were part of what confused him about Shallan. She seemed perfectly friendly one moment, then she'd snap at him the next, while pretending it was merely part of normal conversation. But she didn't talk like that to others, not even in jest.

What is wrong with you, woman? he thought. They'd shared something intimate, in the chasms back on the Shattered Plains. A highstorm huddled together, and words. Was she embarrassed by that? Was that the reason she snapped at him sometimes?

If that was so, how did one explain the other times, when she watched him and grinned? When she winked, in a sly way?

'Hessi reports stories of the Unmade not only corrupting spren, but corrupting *people*,' Shallan was saying. 'Maybe that's what's happening with the palace. We'll know more after infiltrating the cult tonight.'

'I don't like you going alone,' Adolin said.

'I won't be alone. I'll have my team.'

'One washwoman and two deserters,' Kaladin said. 'If Gaz is anything to judge by, Shallan, you shouldn't put too much trust in those men.'

Shallan raised her chin. 'At least *my* soldiers knew when to get away from the warcamps, as opposed to just standing around letting people fling arrows at them.'

'We trust you, Shallan,' Adolin said, eyeing Kaladin as if to say, *Drop it.* 'And we really need a look at that Oathgate.'

'What if I can't open it?' Shallan asked. 'What then?'

'We have to retreat back to the Shattered Plains,' Kaladin said.

'Elhokar won't leave his family.'

'Then Drehy, Skar, and I rush the palace,' Kaladin said. 'We fly in at night, enter through the upper balcony, grab the queen and the young prince. We do it all right before the highstorm comes, then the lot of us fly back to Urithiru.'

'And leave the city to fall,' Adolin said, drawing his lips to a line.

'Can the city hold?' Shallan asked. 'Maybe until we can get back with a real army, marched out here?'

'That would take months,' Adolin said. 'And the Wall Guard is ... what? Four battalions?'

'Five in total,' Kaladin said.

'Five thousand men?' Shallan asked. 'So few?'

'That's large for a city garrison,' Adolin said. 'The point of fortifications is to let a small number hold against a much larger force. But the enemy has an unexpected advantage. Voidbringers who can fly, and a city infested with their allies.'

'Yeah,' Kaladin said. 'The Wall Guard is earnest, but they won't be able to withstand a dedicated assault. There are tens of thousands of parshmen out there – and they're close to attacking. We don't have much time left. The Fused will sweep in to secure portions of the wall, and their armies will follow. If we're going to hold this city, we'll need Radiants and Shardbearers to even the odds.'

Kaladin and Shallan shared a look. Their Radiants were not a battle-ready group, not yet. Storms. His men had barely taken to the skies. How could they be expected to fight those creatures who flew so easily upon the winds? How could he protect this city *and* protect his men?

They fell silent, listening to the room shake with the sounds of thunder outside. Kaladin finished his drink, wishing it were one of Rock's concoctions instead, and flicked away an odd cremling that he spotted clinging to the side of the bench. It had a multitude of legs, and a bulbous body, with a strange tan pattern on its back.

Disgusting. Even with the stresses to the city, the proprietor could at least keep this place clean.

※

Once the storm finally blew itself out, Shallan stepped from the wine-house, holding Adolin's arm. She watched Kaladin hurry off toward the barracks for evening patrol.

She should probably be equally eager to get going. She still had to steal some food today – enough to satisfy the Cult of Moments when she approached them later in the evening. That should be easy enough. Vathah had taken to planning operations under Ishnah's guidance, and was proving quite proficient.

Still, she lingered, enjoying Adolin's presence. She wanted to be here, with him, before it was time to be Veil. *She* . . . well, she didn't much care for him. Too clean-cut, too oblivious, too *expected*. She was fine with him as an ally, but wasn't the least bit interested romantically.

Shallan held his arm, walking with him. People already moved through the city, cleaning up – more so they could scavenge than out of civic duty. They reminded her of cremlings that emerged after a storm to feast on the plants. Indeed, nearby, ornamental rockbuds spat out vines in clusters beside doorways. A splatter of green vines and unfurling leaves, set against the brown city canvas.

One patch nearby had been struck – and burned away – by the Everstorm's red lightning.

'I need to show you the Impossible Falls sometime,' Adolin said. 'If you watch them from the right angles, it looks like the water is flowing down along the tiers, then somehow right up onto the top again. . . .'

As they walked, she had to step over a dead mink sticking half out of a broken tree trunk. Not the most romantic of strolls, but it *was* good to hold on to Adolin's arm – even if he had to wear a false face.

'Hey!' Adolin said. 'I didn't get to look through the sketchbook. You said you were going to show me.'

'I brought the wrong one, remember? I had to carve on the table.' She grinned. 'Don't think I missed you going up and paying for the damage when I wasn't looking.'

He grunted.

'People carve on bar tables. It happens *all the time*.'

'Sure, sure. It was a good carving too.'

'And you still think I shouldn't have done it.' She squeezed his arm. 'Oh, Adolin Kholin. You *are* your father's son. I won't do it again, all right?'

He was blushing. 'I,' he said, 'was promised sketches. I don't care if it's the wrong sketchbook. I feel like I haven't seen any of your pictures for ages.'

'There's nothing good in this one,' she said, digging in her satchel. 'I've been distracted lately.'

He still made her hand it over, and secretly she was pleased. He started flipping through the more recent pictures, and though he noted the ones of strange spren, he idled most on the sketches of refugees she'd done for her collection. A mother with her daughter, sitting in shadow, but with her face looking toward the horizon and the hints of a rising sun. A thick-knuckled man sweeping the area around his pallet on the street. A young woman, lighteyed and hanging out a window, hair drifting free, wearing only a nightgown with her hand tied in a pouch.

'Shallan,' he said, 'these are amazing! Some of the best work you've ever done.'

'They're just quick sketches, Adolin.'

'They're beautiful,' he said, looking at another, where he stopped. It was a picture of him in one of his new suits.

Shallan blushed. 'Forgot that was there,' she said, trying to get the sketchbook back. He lingered on the picture, then finally succumbed to her prodding and handed it back. She let out a sigh of relief. It wasn't that she'd be *embarrassed* if he saw the sketch of Kaladin on the next page – she did sketches of all kinds of people. But best to end on the picture of Adolin. Veil had been seeping through on that other one.

'You're getting better, if that's possible.'

'Maybe. Though I don't know how much I can credit myself with the progress. *Words of Radiance* says that a lot of Lightweavers were artists.'

'So the order recruited people like you.'

'Or the Surgebinding made them better at sketching, giving them an unfair advantage over other artists.'

'I have an unfair advantage over other duelists. I have had the finest training since childhood. I was born strong and healthy, and my father's wealth gave me some of the best sparring partners in the world. My build gives me reach over other men. Does that mean I don't deserve accolades when I win?'

'You don't have *supernatural* help.'

'You still had to work hard. I know you did.' He put his arm around her, pulling her closer as they walked. Other Alethi couples kept their distance in public, but Adolin had been raised by a mother with a fondness for hugs. 'You know, there's this thing my father complains about. He asked what the use of Shardblades was.'

'Um . . . I think they're pretty obviously for cutting people up. Without cutting them, actually. So—'

'But why only swords? Father asks why the ancient Radiants never made tools for the people.' He squeezed her shoulder. 'I *love* that your powers make you a better artist, Shallan. Father was wrong. The Radiants *weren't* just soldiers! Yes, they created incredible weapons, but they also created incredible art! And maybe once this war is done, we can find other uses for their powers.'

Storms, his enthusiasm could be intoxicating. As they walked toward the tailor's shop, she was loath to part with him, though Veil did need to get on with her day's work.

I can be anyone, Shallan thought, noticing a few joyspren blowing past, like a swirl of blue leaves. *I can become anything.* Adolin deserved someone far better than her. Could she . . . become that someone? Craft for him the perfect bride, a woman that looked and acted as befitted Adolin Kholin?

It wouldn't be her. The real her was a bruised and sorry thing, painted up all pretty, but inside a horrid mess. She already put a face over that for him. Why not go a few steps farther? Radiant . . . Radiant could be his perfect bride, and she *did* like him.

The thought made Shallan feel cold inside.

Once they were close enough to the tailor's shop that she didn't worry about him being safe as he walked back on his own, Shallan forced herself to pull out of his grip. She held his hand a moment with her freehand. 'I need to be going.'

'You aren't to meet the cult until sunset.'

'I need to steal some food first to pay them.'

Still, he held to her hand. 'What do you do out there, Shallan? Who do you become?'

'Everyone,' she said. Then she reached up and kissed him on the cheek. 'Thank you for being you, Adolin.'

'Everyone else was taken already,' he mumbled.

Never stopped me.

He watched her until she ducked around a corner, heart thumping. Adolin Kholin in her life was like a warm sunrise.

Veil started to seep out, and she was forced to acknowledge that sometimes she preferred the storm and the rain to the sun.

She checked at the drop point, inside a corner of a building that was now rubble. Here, Red had deposited a pack that contained Veil's outfit. She grabbed it and went hunting a good place to change.

The end of the world had come, but that seemed most true after a storm. Refuse strewn about, people who hadn't gotten to shelters moaning from fallen shacks or alongside streets.

It was like each storm tried to wipe them off Roshar, and they only remained through sheer grit and luck. Now, with two storms, it was even worse. If they defeated the Voidbringers, would the Everstorm remain? Had it begun to erode their society in a way that – win the war or not – would eventually end with them all swept out to sea?

She felt her face changing as she walked, draining Stormlight from her satchel. It rose in her like a flaring flame, before dimming to an ember as she became the people from the sketches Adolin had seen.

The poor man who tried doggedly to keep the area around his little pallet clean, as if to try to maintain some control over an insane world.

The lighteyed girl who wondered what had happened to the joy of adolescence. Instead of her wearing her first havah to a ball, her family was forced to take in dozens of relatives from neighboring towns, and she spent the days locked away because the streets weren't safe.

The mother with a child, sitting in darkness, looking toward the horizon and a hidden sun.

Face after face. Life after life. Overpowering, intoxicating, alive. Breathing, and crying, and laughing, and being. So many hopes, so many lives, so many dreams.

She unbuttoned her havah up the side, then let it fall. She dropped her satchel, which thumped from the heavy book inside. She stepped forward in only her shift, safehand uncovered, feeling the wind on her skin. She was still wearing an illusion, one that didn't disrobe, so nobody could see her.

Nobody could see her. Had anyone *ever* seen her? She stopped on the street corner, wearing shifting faces and clothing, enjoying the sensation of freedom, clothed yet naked skin shivering at the wind's kiss.

Around her, people ducked away into buildings, frightened.

Just another spren, Shallan/Veil/Radiant thought. *That's what I am. Emotion made carnal.*

She lifted her hands to the sides, exposed, yet invisible. She breathed the breaths of a city's people.

'Mmm . . .' Pattern said, unweaving himself from her discarded dress. 'Shallan?'

'Maybe,' she said, lingering.

Finally, she let herself slip fully into Veil's persona. She immediately shook her head and fetched the clothing and satchel. She was lucky it hadn't been stolen. Foolish girl. They didn't have time for prancing around from poem to poem.

Veil found a secluded location beside a large gnarled tree whose roots spread all the way along the wall in either direction. She quickly rearranged her underclothing, then put on her trousers and did up her shirt. She pulled on her hat, checked herself in a hand mirror, then nodded.

Right, then. Time to meet up with Vathah.

He was waiting at the inn where Wit had once stayed. Radiant retained hope that she'd meet him again there, for a more thorough interrogation. In the private room, away from the eyes of the fretting innkeeper, Vathah laid out a couple of spheres to light the maps he'd purchased. They detailed the manor she intended to hit this afternoon.

'They call it the Mausoleum,' Vathah explained as Veil sat. He showed her an artist's sketch he'd purchased, which was of the building's grand hall. 'Those statues are all Soulcast, by the way. They're favored servants of the house, turned to storming stone.'

'It's a sign of honor and respect among lighteyes.'

'It's *creepy*,' Vathah said. 'When I die, burn my corpse up right good. Don't leave me staring for eternity while your descendants sip their tea.'

Veil nodded absently, placing Shallan's sketchbook on the table. 'Pick an alias from this. This map says the larder is on the outside wall. Time is tight, so we might want to do this one the easy way. Have Red make a distraction, then use Shallan's Blade to cut us an opening right in to the food.'

'You know, they're said to have *quite* the fortune at the Mausoleum. The Tenet family riches are . . .' He trailed off as he saw her expression. 'No riches, then.'

'We get the food to pay the cult, then we get out.'

'Fine.' He settled on the image of the man sweeping around his pallet, staring at it. 'You know, when you reformed me from banditry, I figured I was done with stealing.'

'This is different.'

'Different how? We stole mostly food back then too, Brightness. Just wanted to stay alive and forget.'

'And do you still want to forget?'

He grunted. 'No, suppose I don't. Suppose I sleep a little better now at night, don't I?'

The door opened and the innkeeper bustled in, holding drinks. Vathah yelped, though Veil turned with a droll expression. 'I believe,' she said, 'I wanted to not be interrupted.'

'I brought drinks!'

'Which is an interruption,' Veil said, pointing out the door. 'If we're thirsty, we'll ask.'

The innkeeper grumbled, then backed out the door, carrying his tray. *He's suspicious,* Veil thought. *He thinks we were up to something with Wit, and wants to find out what.*

'Time to move these meetings to another location, eh, Vathah?' She looked back at the table.

And found someone else sitting there.

Vathah was gone, replaced by a bald man with thick knuckles and a well-kept smock. Shallan glanced at the picture on the table, then at the drained sphere beside it, then back at Vathah.

'Nice,' she said. 'But you forgot to do the back of the head, the part not in the drawing.'

'What?' Vathah asked, frowning.

She showed him the hand mirror.

'Why'd you put his face on me?'

'I didn't,' Veil said, standing. 'You panicked and this happened.'

Vathah prodded at his face, still looking in the mirror, confused.

'I'll bet the first few times are always accidents,' Veil said. She tucked the mirror away. 'Gather this stuff up. We'll do the mission as planned, but tomorrow you're relieved of infiltration duty. I'll want you practicing with your Stormlight instead.'

'Practicing . . .' He finally seemed to get it, his brown eyes opening widely. 'Brightness! I'm no storming *Radiant*.'

'Of course not. You're probably a squire – I think most orders had them. You might become something more. I think Shallan was making illusions off and on for years before she said the oaths. But then, it's all kind of muddled in her head. I had my sword when I was very young, and . . .'

208

She took a deep breath. Fortunately, Veil hadn't lived through those days.

Pattern hummed in warning.

'Brightness . . .' Vathah said. 'Veil, you really think that I . . .'

Storms, he seemed like he was going to *cry*.

She patted him on the shoulder. 'We don't have time to waste. The cult will be waiting for me in four hours, and expect a nice payment of food. You going to be all right?'

'Sure, sure,' he said. The illusion finally dropped, and the image of Vathah himself so emotional was even more striking. 'I can do this. Let's go steal from some rich people and give to some crazy people instead.'

THE REVEL

> *A coalition has been formed among scholar Radiants. Our goal is to deny the enemy their supply of Voidlight; this will prevent their continuing transformations, and give us an edge in combat.*
>
> —From drawer 30-20, second emerald

Veil had exposed herself.

That nagged at her as the wagon – filled with spoils from the robbery – rolled toward the appointed meeting place with the cult. She nestled in the back, against a bag of grain, feet up on a paper-wrapped haunch of cured pork.

'Swiftspren' was Veil, as she was the one who had been seen distributing the food. Therefore, to enter this revel, she would have to go as herself.

The enemy knew what she looked like. Should she have created a new persona, a false face, to not expose Veil?

But Veil is a false face, a part of her said. *You could always abandon her.*

She strangled that part of her, smothered it deep. Veil was too real, too vital, to abandon. Shallan would be easier.

First moon was up by the time they reached the steps to the Oathgate platform. Vathah rolled the wagon into place, and Veil hopped off, coat rippling around her. Two guards here were dressed as flamespren, with golden and red tassels. Their muscular builds, and those two spears set near the steps, hinted these men might have been soldiers before joining the cult.

A woman bustled between them, wearing a flat white mask with eyeholes but no mouth or other features. Veil narrowed her eyes; the mask reminded her of Iyatil, Mraize's master in the Ghostbloods. But it was a very different shape.

'You were told to come alone, Swiftspren,' the woman said.

'You expected me to unload all of this on my own?' Veil waved to the back of the wagon.

'We can handle it,' the woman said smoothly, stepping over as one of the guards held up a torch – not a sphere lamp – and the other lowered the wagon's tailgate. 'Mmmm …'

Veil turned sharply. That hum …

The guards started unloading the food.

'You can take all but the two bags marked with red,' Veil said, pointing. 'I need those for my rounds visiting the poor.'

'I wasn't aware this was a negotiation,' the cultist said. 'You asked for this. You've been leaving whispers through the city that you want to join the revel.'

Wit's work, apparently. She'd have to thank him.

'Why are you here?' the cultist asked, sounding curious. 'What is it you want, Swiftspren, so-called hero of the markets?'

'I just … keep hearing this voice. It says that this is the end, that I should give in to it. Embrace the time of spren.' She turned toward the Oathgate platform; an orange glow was rising from the top. 'The answers are up there, aren't they?'

From the corner of her eye, she saw the three nod to one another. She'd passed some kind of test.

'You may climb the steps to enlightenment,' the cultist in white told her. 'Your guide will meet you at the top.'

She tossed her hat to Vathah and met his eyes. Once the unloading was through, he'd pull away and set up a few streets farther off, where he could watch the edge of the Oathgate platform. If she had trouble, she would throw herself off, counting on Stormlight to heal her after falling.

She started up the steps.

٭

Kaladin normally liked the feeling of the city after a storm. Clean and fresh, washed of grime and refuse.

He'd done evening patrol, checking over their beat to see everything was all right following the storm. Now he stood on the top of the wall, waiting for the rest of his squad, who were still stowing their equipment. The sun had barely set, and it was time for dinner.

Below, he picked out buildings newly scarred from lightning strikes. A pod of corrupted windspren danced past, trailing intense red light. Even the smell of the air was wrong somehow. Moldy and sodden.

Syl sat quietly on his shoulder until Beard and the others piled into the stairwell. He finally joined them, walking down below to the barrack, where both platoons – his and the one they shared the space with – were gathering for dinner. Roughly twenty of the men from the other platoon would be on wall duty tonight, but everyone else was present.

Not long after Kaladin arrived, the two platoon captains called their men to muster. Kaladin fell into line between Beard and Ved, and together they saluted as Azure stepped into the doorway. She was arrayed for battle as always, with her breastplate, chain, and cloak.

Tonight, she decided to do a formal inspection. Kaladin held attention with the others as she walked down their lines and commented quietly to the two captains. She looked over a few swords, and asked several of the men if they needed anything. Kaladin felt as if he'd stood in similar lines a hundred times, sweating and hoping that the general would find everything in order.

They always did. This wasn't the type of inspection that was intended to actually find problems – this was a chance for the men to show off for their highmarshal. They swelled as she told them they 'just might be the finest platoons of fighting men I've ever had the privilege of leading.' Kaladin was certain he'd heard those exact words from Amaram.

Trite or not, the words inspired the men. They gave the highmarshal shouts of approval once they were given leave to break ranks. Perhaps the number of 'finest platoons' in the army went up during times of war, when everyone craved a morale boost.

Kaladin walked to the officers' table. It hadn't taken much work to get himself invited to dine with the highmarshal. Noro really wanted him promoted to lieutenant, and most of the others were too intimidated by Azure to sit at her table.

The highmarshal hung her cloak and strange sword on a peg. She kept her gloves on, and though he couldn't see her chest because of the breast-plate, that face and build were obviously female. She was also very Alethi, with the skin tone and hair, her eyes a glimmering light orange.

She must have spent time as a mercenary out west, Kaladin thought. Sigzil had once told him that women fought in the west, particularly among mercenaries.

The meal was simple curried grain. Kaladin took a bite, well acquainted by now with the aftertaste of Soulcast grain. A lingering staleness. The curry helped, but the cooks had used the boiled-off starch of the grain to thicken it, so it had some of the same flavor.

He'd been placed relatively far from the center of the table, where Azure conversed with the two platoon captains. Eventually, one excused himself to use the privy.

Kaladin thought for a moment, then picked up his plate and moved down the table to settle into the open spot.

※

Veil reached the top of the platform, entering what felt like a little village. The monastery structures here were much smaller – yet far nicer – than the ones on the Shattered Plains had been. A cluster of fine stonework structures with slanted, wedge-shaped roofs, the points toward the Origin.

Ornamental shalebark grew around the bases of most of the buildings, cultivated and carved into swirling patterns. Veil took a Memory for Shallan, but her focus was on the firelight coming from farther inward. She couldn't see the control building. All of these other structures were in the way. She *could* see the palace off to her left, glowing in the night with windows lit. It connected to the Oathgate platform by a covered walkway called the Sunwalk. A small group of soldiers, visible in the darkness only as shadows, guarded the way across.

Close to her – at the top of the steps – a rotund man sat along a shalebark ridge. He had short hair and light green eyes, and gave her an affable grin. 'Welcome! I'm your guide tonight, for your first time at the revel! It can be . . . ah, disorienting.'

Those are ardent robes, Veil noted. Ripped, stained from what appeared to be a variety of foods.

'Everyone who comes up here,' he said, hopping off his seat, 'is reborn. Your name is now ... um ...' He pulled a piece of paper from his pocket. 'Where did I write that? Well, suppose it isn't important. Your name is Kishi. Doesn't that sound nice? Good job getting up here. This is where you'll find the real fun in the city.'

He shoved his hands back in his pockets and looked down one of the roadways, then his shoulders slumped. 'Anyway,' he said. 'Let's get going. Lots of reveling to do tonight. Always so much reveling to be done ...'

'And you are?'

'Me? Oh, um, Kharat is what they named me. I think? I forget.' He ambled forward without waiting to see if she followed.

She did, eager to get to the center. However, just past the first building, she reached the revel – and had to stop to take it in. A bonfire burned right on the ground, flames crackling and whipping in the wind, bathing Veil in heat. Corrupted flamespren, vivid blue and somehow more jagged, danced inside of it. Tables lined the walkway here, piled with food. Candied meats, stacks of flatbread crusted with sugar, fruits and pastries.

A variety of people passed by, occasionally scooping food off the tables with their bare hands. They laughed and shouted. Many had been ardents, marked by brown robes. Others were lighteyes, though their clothing had ... decayed? It seemed a fitting word for these suits with missing jackets, havah dresses whose skirts were ragged from brushing the ground. Safehand sleeves ripped off at the shoulder and discarded somewhere.

They moved like fish in a school, flowing from right to left. She picked out soldiers, both lighteyed and dark, in the remnants of uniforms. They seemed to take no note of her or Kharat standing to the side.

She'd have to cut through the stream of people to get farther inward to the Oathgate control building. She started to do so, but Kharat took her by the arm, steering her to join the flow of people.

'We have to stay to the outer ring,' he said. 'No going inward for us, nope. Be happy. You get ... you get to enjoy the end of the world in style. ...'

She reluctantly let herself be pulled along. It was probably best to do a round of the platform anyway. However, not long after starting, she began to hear the voice.

Let go.

Give up your pain.
Feast. Indulge.
Embrace the end.

Pattern hummed on her coat, his sound lost to the many people laughing and drinking. Kharat stuck his fingers into some kind of creamy dessert, taking it by the handful. His eyes had glazed over, and he muttered to himself as he pushed the food into his mouth. Though others laughed and even danced, most showed that same glassy look.

She could feel Pattern's vibrations on her coat. It seemed to counteract the voices, clearing her head. Kharat handed her a cup of wine he'd scooped from a table. Who set this all up? Where were the servants?

There was just *so much* food. Tables and tables of it. People moved in buildings they passed, engaging in other carnal delights. Veil tried to slip across the stream of revelers, but Kharat kept hold of her.

'Everyone wants to go inward their first time,' he said. 'You aren't allowed. Enjoy this. Enjoy the feeling. It's not our fault, right? We didn't fail her. We were only doing what she asked. Don't cause a storm, girl. Nobody wants that. . . .'

He hung on to Veil's arm. So instead she waited until they passed another building, and tugged him that way.

'Going to find a partner?' he asked, numb. 'Sure. That's allowed. Assuming you can find anyone still sober enough to care . . .'

They entered the building, which had once been a place for meditation, filled with individual rooms. It smelled sharply of incense, and each alcove had its own brazier for burning prayers. Those were now occupied for another sort of experience.

'I just want to rest a moment,' she told Kharat, peeking into an empty room. It had a window. She could slip out that, maybe. 'It's all so overwhelming.'

'Oh.' He looked over his shoulder toward the revel passing outside. His left hand was still coated with sweet paste.

Veil stepped into the chamber. When he tried to follow, she said, 'I need a moment alone.'

'I'm supposed to keep watch on you,' he said, and prevented her from closing the door.

'Then watch,' she said and settled down on the bench inside the cell. 'From a distance.'

He sighed and sat down on the floor of the hallway.

Now what? *A new face,* she thought. *What did he name me?* Kishi. It meant Mystery. She used a Memory she'd drawn earlier in the day, that of a woman from the market. In her mind, Shallan added touches to the clothing. A havah, ragged like the others, an exposed safehand.

It would do. She wished she could sketch it, but she could make this work. Now, what to do about her guard?

He probably hears voices, she thought. *I can use that.* She pressed her hand to Pattern, and wove sound.

'Go,' she whispered, 'hang on the wall of the hallway outside, next to him.'

Pattern softly hummed his reply. She closed her eyes, and could faintly hear the words she'd woven to be whispered near Kharat.

Indulge.

Get something to drink.

Join the revel.

'You going to just sit there?' Kharat called in to her.

'Yes.'

'I'm going to get something to drink. Don't leave.'

'Fine.'

He rose, then jogged out. By the time he got back, she had attached an illusion of Veil to a ruby mark, then left it there. It showed Veil resting on the bench, eyes closed, snoring softly.

Kishi passed Kharat in the hallway, stepping with glassy eyes. He didn't spare her a second glance, and instead settled down in the hallway with a large cup of wine to watch Veil.

Kishi joined the revel outside. A man there laughed and grabbed at her safehand, as if to pull her toward one of the rooms. Kishi dodged him and slipped farther inward, flowing through the stream of people. This 'outer ring' seemed to round the entire Oathgate platform.

The secrets were farther toward the center. Nobody forbade Kishi as she left the flow of the outer ring, stepping between two buildings, heading inward.

⁘

The others stopped their small talk, and the officers' table grew very still as Kaladin settled down across from Azure.

The highmarshal laced her gloved hands before herself. 'Kal, was it?' she said. 'The lighteyed man with slave brands. How are you finding your time in the Wall Guard?'

'It's a well-run army, sir, and strangely welcoming of one such as myself.' He then nodded over the highmarshal's shoulder. 'I've never seen someone treat a Shardblade so casually. You just hang it on a peg?'

The others at the table watched with obviously held breaths.

'I'm not particularly worried about anyone taking her,' Azure said. 'I trust these men.'

'It's still remarkable,' Kaladin said. 'Foolhardy, even.'

Across the table, two places down from Azure, Lieutenant Noro raised his hands silently toward Kaladin in a pleading way. *Don't screw this up, Kal!*

But Azure smiled. 'I never did get an explanation for that *shash* brand, soldier.'

'I never gave a proper one, sir,' Kaladin said. 'I'm not fond of the memories that earned me the scar.'

'How did you end up in this city?' Azure asked. 'Sadeas's lands are far to the north. There are several armies of Voidbringers between here and there, by report.'

'I flew. How about you, sir? You couldn't have been in the city long before the siege began; nobody talks of you earlier than that time. They say you appeared right when the Guard needed you.'

'Perhaps I was always here, but merely blended in.'

'With those scars? They may not spell out danger as explicitly as mine, but they'd have been memorable.'

The rest of the table – lieutenants and the platoon captain – stared at Kaladin slack-jawed. Perhaps he was pushing too hard, acting too far above his station.

He'd never been good at acting his station though.

'Perhaps,' Azure said, 'one shouldn't be questioning my arrival. Be thankful someone was here when the city needed them.'

'I *am* thankful,' Kaladin said. 'Your reputation with these men commends you, Azure, and extreme times can excuse a great deal. Eventually though, you'll need to come clean. These men deserve to know who – exactly – is commanding them.'

'And what about you, Kal?' She took a spoonful of curry and rice

– men's food, which she ate with gusto. 'Do they deserve to know your past? Shouldn't you come clean?'

'Perhaps.'

'I am your commanding officer, you realize. You *should* answer me when I ask questions.'

'I've given answers,' Kaladin said. 'If they aren't the ones you want, then perhaps your questions aren't very good.'

Noro gasped audibly.

'And you, Kal? You make statements, dripping with implications. You want answers? Why not just *ask*?'

Storms. She was right. He'd been dancing around serious questions. Kaladin looked her in the eyes. 'Why won't you let anyone talk about the fact that you're a woman, Azure? Noro, don't faint. You'll embarrass us all.'

The lieutenant thumped his forehead against the table, groaning softly. The captainlord, with whom Kaladin hadn't interacted much, had gone red-faced.

'They came up with this game on their own,' Azure said. 'They're Alethi, so they need an excuse for why they're listening to a woman giving military orders. Pretending there's some mystery focuses them on that, instead of on masculine pride. I find the entire thing silly.' She leaned forward. 'Tell me honestly. Did you come here chasing me?'

Chasing you? Kaladin cocked his head.

Drums sounded in the near distance.

It took a moment for them, even Kaladin, to register what that meant. Then Kaladin and Azure threw themselves back from the bench at nearly the same time. 'To arms!' Kaladin shouted. 'There's an attack on the wall!'

∴

The next ring inward on the Oathgate platform was filled with people crawling.

Kishi stood at the perimeter, watching a multitude of men and women in ragged finery crawl past her, giggling, moaning, or gasping. Each seemed in the thrall of a different emotion, and each stared with an openly maddened expression. She thought she recognized a few from the descriptions of lighteyes who had disappeared into the palace, though in their state, it was hard to tell.

A woman with long hair dragging on the ground looked toward her, grinning with clenched teeth and bleeding gums. She crawled, one hand after another, her havah shredded, faded. She was followed by a man wearing rings glowing with Stormlight, in contrast to his ripped clothing. He giggled incessantly.

The food on the tables here rotted, and was infested with decayspren. Kishi wavered at the edge of the ring. She should have kept to the outer ring; she didn't belong here. There was food aplenty behind her. Laughter and reveling. It seemed to pull her back, inviting her to join the eternal, beautiful walk.

Within that ring, time wouldn't matter. She could forget Shallan, and what she'd done. Just . . . just give in . . .

Pattern hummed. Veil gasped, letting Kishi burst from her, Lightweaving collapsing. Storms. She had to be away from this place. It was doing things to her brain. Strange things, even for *her*.

Not yet. She pulled her coat tight, then picked her way across the street full of crawling people. No bonfire lit her way, only the moon overhead and the light of the jewelry the people wore.

Storms. Where had they all gone for the storm? Their moaning, chittering, and babbling chased her as she crossed the street, then hurried down a dark pathway between two monastery buildings, inward. Toward the control building, which should be right ahead.

The voices in her head combined from whispers to a kind of surging rhythm. A thumping of impressions, followed by a pause, followed by another surge. Almost like . . .

She stepped between the buildings and entered a moonlit square, colored violet from Salas above. Instead of the control building, she found an overgrown mass. Something had covered the entire structure, like the Midnight Mother had enveloped the gemstone pillar beneath Urithiru.

The dark mass pulsed and throbbed. Black veins as thick as a man's leg ran from it and melded with the ground nearby. A heart. It beat an irregular rhythm, *bum-ba-ba-bum* instead of the common *ba-bum* of her own heartbeat.

Give in.

Join the revel.

Shallan, listen to me.

She shook herself. That last voice had been different. She'd heard it before, hadn't she?

She looked to the side, and found her shadow on the ground, pointed the wrong way, toward the moonlight instead of away from it. The shadow crept up the wall, with eyes that were white holes, glowing faintly.

I'm not your enemy. But the heart is a trap. Take caution.

Distantly, drums started sounding on the top of the wall. The Voidbringers were attacking.

It all threatened to overwhelm her. The thumping heart, the strange processions in rings around it, the drums and the panic that the Fused were coming for *her* because she'd been *seen*.

Veil seized control. She'd accomplished her goal, she'd scouted the area, and she had information about the Oathgate. It was time to get out.

She turned and – forcibly – put on Kishi's face. She crossed the stream of crawling, moaning people. She flowed back into the outer ring of revelers, before slipping out.

She didn't check on her guide. She walked to the rim of the Oathgate platform and, without a look back, leaped off.

*Our revelation is fueled by the theory that the Unmade can perhaps
be captured like ordinary spren. It would require a special prison. And
Melishi.*

—From drawer 30-20, third emerald

K aladin charged up the stairwell beside Highmarshal Azure, the
sound of drums breaking the air like echoes of thunder from the
departed storm. He counted the beats.

Storms. That's my section under assault.

'Damnation these creatures!' Azure muttered. 'I'm missing something.
Like white on black ...' She glanced at Kaladin. 'Just tell me. Who are
you?'

'Who are *you?*'

The two burst out of the stairwell onto the wall's top, entering a scene
of chaos. The soldiers on duty had lit the enormous oil lamps on the tops
of the towers, giving light to the dark walls. Fused swooped between
them, trailing dark violet light, attacking with long, bloodied lances.

Men lay screaming on the ground or huddled in pairs, holding up
shields as if trying to hide from the nightmares above.

Kaladin and Azure exchanged a look, then nodded to one another.
Later.

She broke left and Kaladin dashed right, shouting for men to form up. Syl spun around his head, concerned, anxious. Kaladin scooped a shield off the ground and seized a soldier by the arm, towing him around and locking shields. A swooping lance *clanged* off the metal, sending a jolt through Kaladin. The Voidbringer flew past.

Pained, Kaladin ignored the wounded and bleeding who crawled with corrupted painspren. He pulled the scattered remnants of the Eighth Platoon back together while his own men stumbled to a halt outside the stairwell. These were their friends, the people with whom they shared a barrack.

'To your right and up!' Syl shouted.

Kaladin set himself and used his shield to push aside the lance of a Voidbringer who soared past. A second Voidbringer followed, wearing a long skirt of rippling crimson cloth. The way she flew was almost mesmerizing. . . . Right up until her lance pinned Captain Deedanor against the wall's battlements, then lifted him and tossed him over.

He screamed as he plummeted toward the ground below. Kaladin almost broke rank and ran for him, but held himself in the line by force. He reached, by instinct, for the Stormlight in his pouch – but held himself back. Using it for Lashing would attract screamers, and in this darkness, even drawing in a small amount would reveal him for what he was. The Fused would all attack him together; he would risk undermining the mission to save the entire city.

Today, he protected best through discipline, order, and keeping a level head. 'Squads One and Two, with me!' he shouted. 'Vardinar, you've got Five and Six; have your men hand out pikes, then grab bows and get to the tower's top. Noro, take squads Three and Four and set up on the wall walk just past the tower. My men will hold here on this side. Go, *go!*'

Nobody voiced a complaint as they scrambled to do as he said. Kaladin heard shouts from the highmarshal farther down the wall, but didn't have a chance to see how she was doing. As his two squads finally got a proper shield wall mounted, a human corpse slammed down onto the wall walk nearby. It had been dropped from very high up – or perhaps it had been Lashed into the sky and had only now fallen. Most of the wounded men were archers from the Eighth Platoon; it looked like they'd been swept from the top of the tower.

We can't fight these things, Kaladin thought. The Voidbringers attacked in sweeping dives, coming in from all directions. It was impossible to maintain a normal formation beneath that assault.

Syl shifted into the shape of a girl and looked at him questioningly. He shook his head. He *could* fight without Stormlight. He'd protected people long before he could fly.

He started to call out orders, but a Fused passed by, slapping at their pikes with a large shield. Before the men could get them reoriented, another *crashed* down into the center of them, sending soldiers stumbling. A violet glow steamed from the creature's body as it swept around with its lance, wielding it like an oversized staff.

Kaladin ducked by instinct, trying to maneuver his pike. The Fused grinned as the formation disintegrated. It was male, reminiscent of a Parshendi, with layered plates of chitin armor creeping down across its forehead and rising from cheeks that were marbled black and red.

Kaladin leveled his pike, but the creature lunged along it and pressed its hand against Kaladin's chest. He felt himself grow lighter, but also suddenly begin to fall backward.

The creature had *Lashed* him.

Kaladin fell back, like he was toppling off a ledge, falling along the wall toward a group of his men. The Fused wanted Kaladin to crash into them, but it had made a mistake.

The sky was *his*.

Kaladin responded immediately to the Lashing, and reoriented himself in the blink of an eye. *Down* became the direction he was falling: along the walkway, toward the towering guard post. His men seemed to be stuck to the side of a cliff, turning toward him, horrified.

Kaladin was able to shove against the stone with the end of his pike, moving him to the side so he whooshed past his men instead of crashing into them. Syl joined him as a ribbon, and he twisted, falling feet-first along the walkway toward the guard tower below.

He was able to nudge himself so he fell right into the open doorway. He dropped the pike, then caught the lip of the doorway as he passed through it. He stopped with a jarring lurch, arms protesting with pain, but that maneuver slowed him enough. When he swung and let go, he dropped through the room – past the dining table, which seemed glued to the wall – and landed on the opposite wall, inside the building. He stepped over to the other doorway, which looked out onto the walk where he'd positioned Noro's squad. Beard and Ved held pikes toward the sky, looking anxious.

'Kaladin!' Syl said. 'Above!'

He looked upward and out the doorway he'd come through. The Voidbringer who had Lashed him came soaring downward, carrying a lance. It curved to bypass the tower, preparing to whip around and attack Beard and the men on the other side.

Kaladin growled and dashed along the inside wall of the tower, pulled himself up past the table, then *hurled* himself out a window.

He crashed into the Voidbringer in midair, shoving the creature's lance to the side.

'Leave. My. Men. *Alone!*'

Kaladin clung to the clothing of the monster, spinning in the air dozens of feet above the dark city, sparkling with the light of spheres in windows or lanterns. The Voidbringer Lashed them higher, falsely assuming that the more height it had, the more advantage it would gain over Kaladin.

Holding tightly with his left hand, wind whipping around them, Kaladin reached out with his right hand and summoned Syl as a long knife. She appeared immediately, and Kaladin shoved the diminutive Shardblade into the creature's stomach.

The Voidbringer grunted and looked at him with deep, glowing red eyes. It dropped its lance and began to claw at Kaladin while spinning itself in the air, trying to throw him free.

They can survive wounds, Kaladin thought, gritting his teeth as the thing gripped at his neck. *Like Radiants. That Voidlight sustains them.*

Kaladin still refrained from drawing in his own Stormlight. He suffered the Fused's Lashings as it spun them in the air, shouting in a language Kaladin didn't understand. He tried to maneuver the Shardknife and cut the thing's spine. The weapon was insanely sharp, but for the moment, leverage and disorientation were bigger factors.

The Voidbringer grunted, then Lashed itself – with Kaladin hanging on – back downward toward the wall. They fell quickly, a double or triple Lashing, spiraling and screaming toward the wall walk.

Kaladin! Syl's voice, in his head. *I sense something . . . something about its power. Cut upward, toward the heart.*

The city, the battle, the sky – all became a blur. Kaladin forced his Blade farther into the creature's chest, pushing it upward, seeking . . .

The Shardknife struck something brittle and hard.

The Fused's red eyes winked out.

Kaladin twisted, putting the corpse beneath him and the wall walk. They hit hard, and he bounced off the corpse, then hit the stones with a *crack*. He groaned, eyes flashing with pain, and was forced – by instinct – to take in a breath of Stormlight to heal the damage of the fall.

That Light flowed through him, reknitting bones, repairing organs. It was used up in a moment, and he forced himself not to draw in more, instead pushing himself up and shaking his head.

The Voidbringer stared sightlessly from the wall walk beside him. It was dead.

Ahead, the other Fused began streaking away in retreat, leaving a broken and battered group of guards. Kaladin stumbled to his feet; his section of the wall was empty, save for the dead and the dying. He didn't recognize any; he'd hit the wall some fifty feet away from his platoon's position.

Syl landed on his shoulder and patted him on the side of the head. Painspren littered the wall, crawling this way and that, in the shape of hands without skin.

This city is doomed, Kaladin thought as he knelt by one of the wounded and quickly prepared a bandage by slicing up a fallen cloak. *Storms. We might all be doomed. We're not anywhere near ready to fight these things.*

It looked like Noro's squad, at least, had survived. They jogged down the wall and gathered around the Voidbringer Kaladin had killed, nudging it with the butts of their pikes. Kaladin tied off a tourniquet, then moved to another man, whose head he wrapped.

Soon, army surgeons flooded the wall. Kaladin stepped back, bloodied – but more angry than tired. He turned to Noro, Beard, and the others, who had gathered around him.

'You killed one,' Beard said, feeling at his arm with the empty glyphward. 'Storms. You actually *killed* one, Kal.'

'How many have you brought down?' Kaladin asked, realizing that he'd never asked. 'How many has the Wall Guard killed during the assaults these last weeks?'

His men shared glances.

'Azure drove a few off,' Noro said. 'They're afraid of her Shardblade. But as for Voidbringers killed . . . this would be the first, Kal.'

Storms. Even worse, the one he'd killed would be reborn. Unless the Heralds set up their prison again, Kaladin couldn't ever really kill one of the Fused.

'I need to talk to Azure,' he said, striding down the wall walk. 'Noro, report.'

'None fallen, sir, though Vaceslv took a gash to the chest. He's with the surgeons, and should pull through.'

'Good. Squad, you're with me.'

He found Azure surveying the Eighth Platoon's losses near their guard tower. She had her cloak off and held oddly in one hand, wrapped around her forearm, with part of it draping down below. Her unsheathed Shard-blade glittered, long and silvery.

Kaladin stepped up to her, the sleeve of his uniform stained dark with the blood of the Voidbringer he'd killed. Azure looked tired, and she gestured with her sword outward. 'Have a look.'

Lights lit the horizon. Sphere lights. Thousands upon thousands of them – far more than he'd seen on previous nights. They blanketed the landscape.

'That's the entire enemy army,' Azure said. 'I'd bet my red life on it. Somehow, they marched them *through* that storm earlier today. It won't be long now. They'll have to attack before the next highstorm. A few days at most.'

'I need to know what's going on here, Azure,' Kaladin said. 'How are you getting food for this army?'

She drew her lips to a line.

'He killed one, Highmarshal,' Beard whispered from behind him. 'Storms . . . he took one of them down. Grabbed on like he was mounting a storming horse, then rode the bastard through the sky.'

The woman studied him, and reluctantly Kaladin summoned Syl as a Shardblade. Noro's eyes bulged, and Ved nearly fainted – though Beard just grinned.

'I'm here,' Kaladin said, resting the Sylblade on his shoulder, 'on orders from King Elhokar and the Blackthorn. It's my job to save Kholinar. And it's time you started talking to me.'

She smiled at him. 'Come with me.'

Ba-Ado-Mishram has somehow Connected with the parsh people.
as Odium once did. She provides Voidlight and facilitates forms of
power. Our strike team is going to imprison her.

—From drawer 30-20, fourth emerald

G rund wasn't at his normal spot inside the corner of the broken
shop.

The place hadn't fared well during the Everstorm; the ceiling was sagging even *more,* and a snarl of tree branches had been blown in through the window, littering the floor. Veil frowned, calling his name. After fleeing the Oathgate platform, she'd met up with Vathah, who had been waiting as instructed.

She'd sent Vathah back to report to the king, and probably should have gone herself. But she hadn't been able to shake the eerie disquiet of her trip through the revel. Going back home would have left her too much time to think.

Veil wanted to be out working instead. Monsters and Voidbringers were something she couldn't comprehend, but starving children ... she could do something about that. She'd taken the two remaining sacks of food and gone to help the city's people.

If she could find them.

'Grund?' Veil repeated, leaning farther in through the window. Before, he'd always been up at this time. Perhaps he'd finally moved out of the building, like all the others had. Or maybe he hadn't gotten back from the stormshelter yet, following the Everstorm.

She turned to leave, but Grund finally stumbled into the room. The little urchin tucked his malformed hand into his pocket and scowled at her. That was odd. He normally seemed so happy when she arrived.

'What's wrong?' she asked.

'Nothin',' he said. 'Thought you was someone else.' He gave her a grin.

Veil fished a few pieces of flatbread from her bag. 'Not much today, I'm afraid. I wanted to make sure to stop by though. The information you gave us on that book was very helpful.'

He licked his lips, holding out his hands. She tossed him the flatbread, and he took an eager bite. 'What do you need next?'

'Nothing right now,' Veil said.

'Come on. There has to be something I can do to help. Something you want, right?'

Too desperate, Veil thought. *What is beneath the surface here? What have I missed?*

'I'll consider,' she said. 'Grund, is everything all right?'

'Right. Sure, everything is great!' He paused. 'Unless it shouldn't be?'

Pattern hummed softly on Veil's coat. She agreed.

'I'll stop by again in a few days. Should have a big haul then.' Veil tipped her hat to the urchin, then slipped back into the market. It was late, but people lingered. Nobody wanted to be alone on days after the Everstorm came. Some looked toward the wall, where those Fused had attacked. But that sort of thing happened almost daily, so it didn't cause too much of a stir.

Veil drew more attention than she'd have wanted. She'd exposed herself to them, given up her face.

'Grund tells lies, doesn't he?' Pattern whispered.

'Yeah. I'm not sure why, or what about.'

As she wove into the market, she put her hand before her face, changing it with a wave of the fingers. She took her hat off, folded it, and covertly Lightwove it to look like a waterskin. Each was a little change that nobody would notice. She tucked her hair into her coat, made it look shorter, then finally closed her coat and changed the clothing underneath.

When she took off the coat and folded it up, she was no longer Veil, but a market guard she'd drawn earlier.

Rolled coat under her arm, she lingered at a corner and waited to see if anyone passed, looking for Veil. She didn't spot anyone, though her training with Ishnah at spotting tails wasn't yet extensive. She threaded her way back through the crowd to Grund's shop again. She lingered near the wall, then eased toward the window, listening.

'. . . Told you we shouldn't have given her the book,' a voice was saying inside.

'This is pathetic,' another said. 'Pathetic! That was the best you could do?'

She heard a grunt, and a whimper. *That's Grund.* Veil cursed softly, scrambling around to look in through the window. A group of thugs was chewing on the flatbread she'd brought. Grund lay in the corner, whimpering and holding his stomach.

Veil felt a flash of rage, and angerspren immediately boiled around her, pools that sprayed red and orange. She shouted at the men and dashed for the doorway. They immediately scattered, though one slammed a cudgel onto Grund's head with a sickening *crunch*.

By the time she reached Grund, the men had vanished farther into the building. She heard the door in the back slam closed. Pattern appeared in her hand as a Shardblade, but Stormfather! She couldn't give chase – not and leave the poor child here.

Veil dismissed Pattern and knelt, aghast at the bloody wound in Grund's head. It was bad. The skull was broken, bleeding . . .

He blinked, dazed. 'V . . . Veil?'

'Storms, Grund,' she whispered. 'I . . .' What could she do? 'Help? Help, somebody! There's a wounded child in here!'

Grund whimpered, then whispered something. Veil leaned close, feeling useless.

'Hate . . .' Grund whispered. 'Hate you.'

'It's all right,' Veil said. 'They're gone now. They . . . they ran. I'll help.' Bandage. She cut at her shirttails with her knife.

'Hate you,' Grund whispered.

'It's me, Grund. Not those others.'

'Why couldn't you leave me alone?' he whispered. 'They killed them all. My friends. Tai . . .'

Veil pressed the cloth against his head wound, and he winced. Storms. 'Quiet. Don't exert yourself.'

'Hate you,' he repeated.

'I brought you food, Grund.'

'You drew *them*,' he hissed. 'You strutted around, throwing food. You thought people wouldn't notice?' He closed his eyes. 'Had to sit all day, wait for . . . for you. My *life* was waiting for you. If I wasn't here when you came, or if I tried to hide the food, they beat me.'

'How long?' she whispered, feeling her confidence shake.

'Since the first day, you storming woman. Hate . . . hate you . . . Others too. We all . . . hate you . . .'

She sat with him as his breathing slowed, then cut off. Finally she knelt back, bloodied cloth in her hands.

Veil could handle this. She'd seen death. It . . . it was life . . . on the street . . . and . . .

Too much. Too much for one day.

Shallan blinked tears from the corners of her eyes. Pattern hummed. 'Shallan,' he said. 'The boy, he spoke of the others. Others?'

Storms! She threw herself to her feet and pushed out into the night, dropping Veil's hat and coat in her haste. She ran for Muri – the mother who had once been a seamstress. Shallan shoved through the market until she reached the packed tenement where the seamstress lived. She crossed the common room, then breathed a sigh of relief as she found Muri alive, inside her small room. The woman was hurriedly tossing clothing into a sack, her eldest daughter clutching a similar one.

She looked up, saw Shallan – who still looked like Veil – and cursed to herself. 'You.' The frown lines and scowl were unfamiliar. She'd always seemed so pleasant.

'You know already?' Shallan asked. 'About Grund?'

'Grund?' Muri snapped. 'All I know is that the Grips are angry about something. I'm not going to take a chance.'

'The Grips?'

'How oblivious are you, woman? The gang in charge of this area has had toughs watching us all for when you next arrived. The one watching me met with another, and they had a quiet argument, then took off. I heard my name. So I'm leaving.'

'They took the food I gave you, didn't they? Storms, they *killed* Grund!'

Muri stopped, then shook her head. 'Poor kid. Better you than he.' She cursed, gathering her sacks and shoving her children toward the common room. 'We always had to sit here, waiting for you and your storming sack of goodies.'

'I'm . . . I'm sorry.'

Muri left into the night with her children. Shallan watched them go, feeling numb. Empty. She quietly sank down in Muri's deserted room, still holding the cloth with Grund's blood.

We are uncertain the effect this will have on the parsh. At the very least, it should deny them forms of power. Melishi is confident, but Naze-daughter-Kuzodo warns of unintended side effects.

—From drawer 30-20, fifth emerald

M y name is Kaladin,' he said, standing in the barrack common room – which had been emptied at the high-marshal's order. Noro's squad had remained by Kaladin's request, and Azure had invited in Battalionlord Hadinar – a stocky, bejowled fellow, one of Azure's primary officers. The only other person in the room was the fidgety ardent who painted glyphwards for the platoon.

Soft blue spherelight bathed the table where most of them sat. Kaladin stood instead, washing the blood from his hands with a damp rag at a water basin.

'Kaladin,' Azure mused. 'A regal name. What's your house?'

'They just call me Stormblessed. If you need proof of my orders from the king, it can be arranged.'

'Let's pretend, for the sake of conversation, that I believe you,' Azure said. 'What do you want from us?'

'I need to know how you're using a Soulcaster without drawing the attention of the screaming spren. The secret might be essential to my work to save the city.'

Azure nodded, then rose and walked toward the back of the barrack. She used a key to open the back room. Kaladin had glanced in there before though. It only held some supplies.

The rest of them followed Azure into the room, where she slipped a small hook between two stones and threw a hidden latch. This let her remove a stone, revealing a handle. She heaved, pulling open a doorway. The light of a few handheld spheres revealed a small corridor that ran down the middle of the city wall.

'You cut a tunnel in one of the *windblades*, sir?' Beard asked, shocked.

'This has been here longer than any of us have been alive, soldier,' Battalionlord Hadinar said. 'It is a quick, secret way between posts. There are even a few hidden stairwells up to the top.'

They had to go single file inside. Beard followed behind Kaladin, scrunched up against him in the confines. 'Um, so Kal, you . . . you know the Blackthorn?'

'Better than most.'

'And . . . ahem . . . you know—'

'That the two of you never went swimming together in the Purelake?' Kaladin said. 'Yes, though I suspect the rest of the squad guessed that, Beard.'

'Yeah,' he said, glancing back at the others. He exhaled softly. 'I figured you'd never believe the truth, since it was actually the Azish emperor. . . .'

This corridor, cut through the stone, reminded Kaladin of the strata of Urithiru. They reached a trapdoor in the floor, which Azure opened with a key. A short trip down a ladder – which had a dumbwaiter beside it, with ropes and pulleys – led them to a large room filled with sacks of grain. Kaladin held up a sphere, revealing a jagged wall with chunks cut out of it in a distinctly uneven way.

'I come down here every night or so,' Azure said, pointing with a gloved hand, 'and cut out blocks with my Blade. I have nightmares about the city collapsing down on us, but I don't know of another way to get enough stone – at least not without drawing even more attention.'

On the other side of the chamber, they found yet another locked door. Azure knocked twice, then opened this one, revealing a smaller room occupied by an aged female ardent. She knelt beside a stone block, and wore a distinctive fabrial on her hand – one that glowed powerfully with light from the emeralds it contained.

The woman had an inhuman look to her; she seemed to be growing vines under her skin, and they peeked out around her eyes, growing from the corners and spreading down her face like runners of ivy.

She stood and bowed to Azure. A real Soulcaster. So . . . Azure wasn't doing it herself? 'How?' Kaladin asked. 'Why didn't the screamers come for you?'

Azure pointed at the sides of the room, and for the first time Kaladin noticed the walls were covered in reflective metal plates. He frowned and rested his fingers against one, and found it cool to the touch. This wasn't steel, was it?

'Soon after the strangeness at the palace began,' Azure said, 'a man pulled a chull cart up to the front of our barrack. He had these sheets of metal in the back. He was . . . an odd fellow. I've had interactions with him before.'

'Angular features?' Kaladin guessed. 'Quick with an insult. Silly and straight, somehow all at once?'

'You know him, I see,' Azure said. 'He warned us to only Soulcast inside a room lined with this metal. So far as we can tell, it prevents the screamers from sensing us. Unfortunately, it also blocks spanreeds from contacting the outside.

'We keep poor Ithi and her sister working nonstop, trading off the Soulcaster. Feeding the entire city would be an impossible task for the two of them, but we've been able to at least keep our army strong, with some to spare.'

Damnation, Kaladin thought, inspecting the reflective walls. This wasn't going to help him use his powers without notice.

'All right, Stormblessed,' Azure said. 'I've opened our secrets to you. Now you'll tell me how the king could expect *one man*, even a Shard-bearer, to be able to save this city.'

'There's a device in Kholinar,' he said, 'of ancient design. It can instantly transport large groups of people across great distances.' He turned toward Azure and the others. 'The Kholin armies wait to join us here. All we need to do is activate the device – something that only a select few people can do.'

The soldiers looked stunned – all but Azure, who perked up. 'Really? You're serious?'

Kaladin nodded.

'Great! Let's get this thing working! Where is it?'

Kaladin took a deep breath. 'Well, that happens to be the problem. . . .'

Surely this will bring – at long last – the end to war that the Heralds promised us.

—From drawer 30-20, final emerald

She huddled someplace. She'd forgotten where.

For a while, she'd been . . . everybody. A hundred faces, cycling one after another. She searched them for comfort. Surely she could find *someone* who didn't hurt.

All the nearby refugees had fled, naming her a spren. They left her with those hundred faces, in silence, until her Stormlight died off.

That left only Shallan. Unfortunately.

Darkness. A candle snuffed out. A scream cut off. With nothing to see, her mind provided images.

Her father, his face turning purple as she strangled him, singing a lullaby.

Her mother, dead with burned eyes.

Tyn, run through by Pattern.

Kabsal, shaking on the floor as he succumbed to poison.

Yalb, the incorrigible sailor from *Wind's Pleasure*, dead in the depths of the sea.

An unnamed coachman, murdered by members of the Ghostbloods.

Now Grund, his head opened up.

Veil had tried to help these people, but had succeeded only in making their lives worse. The lie that was Veil became suddenly manifest. She *hadn't* lived on the streets and she *didn't* know how to help people. Pretending to have experience didn't mean she actually did.

Veil had always thought to herself that Shallan could handle the big picture, the Voidbringers and the Unmade. Now she had to confront the truth that she had *no idea* what to do. She couldn't get to the Oathgate. It was guarded by an ancient spren that could get inside her brain.

The whole city was depending on her, but she hadn't even been able to save a little beggar boy. As she curled up on the floor, Grund's death seemed a shadow of everything else, of her good intentions turned arrogant.

Everywhere she trod, death haunted her. Every face she wore was a lie to pretend she could stop it.

Couldn't she be somebody who didn't hurt, just once?

Light pushed shadows before it, long and slender. She blinked, momentarily transfixed. How many days had it been since she'd seen light? A figure stepped into the common room outside her little hole of a chamber. She was still in the long room Muri had lived in.

She sniffled softly.

The newcomer brought his light to her doorway, then carefully stepped inside and settled down across from her, his back against the wall. The room was narrow enough that his legs stretched out and touched the wall beside her. She had hers drawn up, knees against her chest, head resting on them.

Wit didn't speak. He put his sphere on the floor, and let her have the silence.

'I should have known better,' she finally whispered.

'Perhaps,' Wit said.

'Giving out so much food only drew predators. Foolish. I should have focused on the Oathgate.'

'Again, perhaps.'

'It's so hard, Wit. When I wear Veil's face . . . I . . . I have to think like her. Seeing the larger scope grows difficult when she takes over. And I *want* her to take over, because she's not me.'

'The thieves who killed that child have been seen to,' Wit said.

She looked up at him.

'When some of the men in the market heard what had happened,'Wit continued, 'they finally formed the militia they'd been talking about. They rushed the Grips, forcing them to give up the murderer, then disperse. I apologize for not acting sooner; I had been distracted by other tasks. You'll be pleased to know that some of the food you gave away was still in their base.'

'Was it worth that boy's life?' Shallan whispered.

'I cannot judge the worth of a life. I would not dare to attempt it.'

'Muri said it would be better if I were dead.'

'As *I* lack the experience to decide the worth of a life, I sincerely doubt that she has somehow obtained it. You tried to help the people of the market. You mostly failed. This is life. The longer you live, the more you fail. Failure is the mark of a life well lived. In turn, the only way to live without failure is to be of no use to anyone. Trust me, I've practiced.'

She sniffled, looking away. 'I have to become Veil to escape the memories, but I don't have the experience that she pretends to have. I haven't lived her life.'

'No,' Wit said softly. 'You've lived a harsher one, haven't you?'

'Yet still, somehow, a naive one.' She drew in a deep, ragged breath. She had to stop this. She knew she had to get over the tantrum and go back to the tailor's shop.

She'd do it. She'd shove all this into the back of her mind, with everything else she ignored. They could all fester together.

Wit settled back. 'Have you heard the story of the Girl Who Looked Up?'

Shallan didn't reply.

'It's a story from long ago,' Wit said. He cupped his hands around the sphere on the floor. 'Things were different in that time. A wall kept out the storms, but everyone ignored it. All but one girl, who looked up one day, and contemplated it.'

'Why is there a wall?' Shallan whispered.

'Oh, so you *do* know it? Good.' He leaned down, blowing at the crem dust on the floor. It swirled up, making a figure of a girl. It gave the brief impression of her standing before a wall, but then disintegrated back into dust. He tried again, and it swirled a little higher this time, but still fell back to dust.

'A little help?' he asked. He pushed a bag of spheres across the ground toward Shallan.

Shallan sighed, then picked up the bag and drew in the Stormlight. It started to rage within her, demanding to be used, so she stood up and breathed out, Weaving it into an illusion she'd done once before. A pristine village, and a young girl standing and looking upward, toward an impossibly tall wall in the distance.

The illusion made the room seem to vanish. Somehow, Shallan painted the walls and ceiling in precisely the right way, making them disappear into the landscape – become part of it. She hadn't made them invisible; they were merely covered up in a way that made it seem Shallan and Wit were standing in another place.

This was ... this was more than she'd ever done before. But was *she* really doing it? Shallan shook her head and stepped up beside the girl, who wore long scarves.

Wit stepped up on the other side. 'Hmmm,' he said. 'Not bad. But it's not dark enough.'

'What?'

'I thought you knew the story,' Wit said, tapping the air. The color and light bled from her illusion, leaving them standing in the darkness of night, lit only by a frail set of stars. The wall was an enormous blot before them. 'In these days, there was no light.'

'No light ...'

'Of course, even without light, people still had to live, didn't they? That's what people do. I hasten to guess it's the *first* thing they learn how to do. So they lived in the darkness, farmed in the darkness, ate in the darkness.' He waved behind him. People stumbled about in the village, feeling their way to different activities, barely able to see by the starlight.

In this context, strange though it seemed, some pieces of the story as she'd told it made sense. When the girl went up to people and asked, 'Why is there a wall?' it was obvious why they found it so easy to ignore.

The illusion followed Wit's words as the girl in the scarves asked several people about the wall. *Don't go beyond it, or you shall die.*

'And so,' Wit said, 'she decided that the only way she'd find answers would be to climb the wall herself.' He glanced at Shallan. 'Was she stupid or bold?'

'How should I know?'

'Wrong answer. She was both.'

'It *wasn't* stupid. If nobody asked questions, then we would never learn anything.'

'What of the wisdom of her elders?'

'They offered no explanation for why she shouldn't ask about the wall! No rationalization, no justification. There's a difference between listening to your elders and just being as frightened as everyone else.'

Wit smiled, the sphere in his hand lighting his face. 'Funny, isn't it, how so many of our stories start the same way, but have opposing endings? In half, the child ignores her parents, wanders out into the woods, and gets eaten. In the other half she discovers great wonders. There aren't many stories about the kids who say, 'Yes, I shall not go into the forest. I'm glad my parents explained that is where the monsters live.''

'Is that what you're trying to teach me, then?' Shallan snapped. 'The fine distinction between choosing for yourself and ignoring good advice?'

'I'm a terrible teacher.' He waved his hand as the girl reached the wall after a long hike. She started to climb. 'Fortunately, I am an *artist*, and not a teacher.'

'People learn things from art.'

'Blasphemy! Art is not art if it has a *function*.'

Shallan rolled her eyes.

'Take this fork,' Wit said. He waved his hand. Some of her Stormlight split off from her, spinning above his hand and making an image of a floating fork in the darkness. 'It has a use. Eating. Now, if it were to be ornamented by a master artisan, would that change its function?' The fork grew intricate embossing in the form of growing leaves. 'No, of course not. It has the same use, ornamented or not. The *art* is the part that serves no purpose.'

'It makes me happy, Wit. That's a purpose.'

He grinned, and the fork disappeared.

'Weren't we in the middle of a story about a girl climbing a wall?' Shallan asked.

'Yes, but that part takes *forever*,' he said. 'I'm finding things to occupy us.'

'We could just skip the boring part.'

'Skip?' Wit said, aghast. '*Skip* part of a *story*?'

Shallan snapped her fingers, and the illusion shifted so that they stood atop the wall in the darkness. The girl in the scarves finally – after toiling many days – pulled herself up beside them.

'You wound me,' Wit said. 'What happens next?'

'The girl finds *steps*,' Shallan said. 'And the girl realizes that the wall wasn't to keep something in, but to keep her and her people out.'

'Because?'

'Because we're monsters.'

Wit stepped over to Shallan, then quietly folded his arms around her. She trembled, then twisted, burying her face in his shirt.

'You're not a monster, Shallan,' Wit whispered. 'Oh, child. The *world* is monstrous at times, and there are those who would have you believe that you are terrible by association.'

'I am.'

'No. For you see, it flows the other direction. You are not worse for your association with the world, but it is better for its association with *you*.'

She pressed against him, shivering. 'What do I do, Wit?' she whispered. 'I know . . . I know I shouldn't be in so much pain. I had to . . .' She took a deep breath. 'I had to kill them. I *had* to. But now I've said the words, and I can't ignore it anymore. So I should . . . should just die too, for having done it. . . .'

Wit waved to the side, toward where the girl in the scarves still overlooked a new world. What was that long pack she had set down beside her?

'So you remember,' Wit said gently, 'the rest of the story?'

'It's not important. We found the moral already. The wall kept people out.'

'Why?'

'Because . . .' What had she told Pattern before, when she'd been showing him this story?

'Because,' Wit said, pointing, 'beyond the wall was God's Light.'

It burst alight in a sudden explosion: a brilliant and powerful brightness that lit the landscape beyond the wall. Shallan gasped as it shone over them. The girl in the scarves gasped in turn, and saw the world in all its colors for the first time.

'She climbed down the steps,' Shallan whispered, watching the girl run down the steps, scarves streaming behind her. 'She hid among the creatures who lived on this side. She sneaked up to the Light and she brought it back with her. To the other side. To the . . . to the land of shadows . . .'

'Yes indeed,' Wit said as the scene played out, the girl in the scarves slipping up to the grand source of light, then breaking off a little piece in her hand.

An incredible chase.

The girl climbing the steps frantically.

A crazed descent.

And then . . . light, for the first time in the village, followed by the coming of the storms – boiling over the wall.

'The people suffered,' Wit said, 'but each storm brought light renewed, for it could never be put back, now that it had been taken. And people, for all their hardship, would never choose to go back. Not now that they could *see*.'

The illusion faded, leaving the two of them standing in the common room of the building, Muri's little chamber off to the side. Shallan pulled back, ashamed at having wept on his shirt.

'Do you wish,' Wit asked, 'that you could go back to not being able to see?'

'No,' she whispered.

'Then live. And let your failures be part of you.'

'That sounds . . . that sounds an awful lot like a moral, Wit. Like you're trying to do something *useful*.'

'Well, as I said, we all fail now and then.' He swept his hands to the sides, as if brushing something away from Shallan. Stormlight curled out from her right and left, swirling, then forming into two identical versions of Shallan. They stood with ruddy hair, mottled faces, and sweeping white coats that belonged to someone else.

'Wit . . .' she started.

'Hush.' He walked up to one of the illusions, inspecting it, tapping his chin with his index finger. 'A lot has happened to this poor girl, hasn't it?'

'Many people have suffered more and they get along fine.'

'Fine?'

Shallan shrugged, unable to banish the truths she'd spoken. The distant memory of singing to her father as she strangled him. The people she'd failed, the problems she'd caused. The illusion of Shallan to the left gasped, then backed up against the wall of the room, shaking her head. She collapsed, head down against her legs, curling up.

242

'Poor fool,' Shallan whispered. 'Everything she tries only makes the world worse. She was broken by her father, then broke herself in turn. She's worthless, Wit.' She gritted her teeth, found herself sneering. 'It's not really her fault, but she's still worthless.'

Wit grunted, then pointed at the second illusion, standing behind them. 'And that one?'

'No different,' Shallan said, tiring of this game. She gave the second illusion the same memories. Father. Helaran. Failing Jasnah. Everything.

The illusory Shallan stiffened. Then set her jaw and stood there.

'Yes, I see,' Wit said, strolling up to her. 'No different.'

'What are you doing to my illusions?' Shallan snapped.

'Nothing. They're the same in every detail.'

'Of course they're not,' Shallan said, tapping the illusion, feeling it. A sense pulsed through her from it, memories and pain. And ... and something smothering them ...

Forgiveness. For herself.

She gasped, pulling her finger back as if it had been bitten.

'It's terrible,' Wit said, stepping up beside her, 'to have been hurt. It's unfair, and awful, and horrid. But Shallan ... it's okay to live on.'

She shook her head.

'Your other minds take over,' he whispered, 'because they look so much more appealing. You'll never control them until you're confident in returning to the one who birthed them. Until *you* accept being *you*.'

'Then I'll never control it.' She blinked tears.

'No,' Wit said. He nodded toward the version of her still standing up. 'You will, Shallan. If you do not trust yourself, can you trust me? For in you, I see a woman more wonderful than any of the lies. I promise you, that woman is *worth* protecting. *You* are worth protecting.'

She nodded toward the illusion of herself still standing. 'I can't be her. She's just another fabrication.'

Both illusions vanished. 'I see only one woman here,' Wit said. 'And it's the one who is standing up. Shallan, that has always been you. You just have to admit it. Allow it.' He whispered to her. 'It's all right to hurt.'

He picked up his pack, then unfolded something from inside it. Veil's hat. He pressed the hat into her palm.

Shockingly, morning light was shining in the doorway. Had she been here all night, huddled in this hole of a room?

'Wit?' she asked. 'I . . . I can't do it.'

He smiled. 'There are certain things I know, Shallan. This is one of them. You *can*. Find the balance. Accept the pain, but *don't accept that you deserved it.*'

Pattern hummed in appreciation of that. But, it wasn't as easy as Wit said. She took in a breath, and felt . . . a shiver run through her. Wit collected his things, pack over his shoulder. He smiled, then stepped out into the light.

Shallan released her breath, feeling foolish. She followed Wit out into the light, emerging into the market, which hadn't quite woken up yet. She didn't see Wit outside, but that was no surprise. He had a way of being where he shouldn't, but not being where you'd expect.

Carrying Veil's hat, she walked the street, feeling odd to be herself in trousers and coat. Red hair, but a safehand glove. Should she hide?

Why? This felt . . . fine. She walked all the way back to the tailor's shop and peeked in. Adolin sat at a table inside, bleary-eyed.

He stood upright. 'Shallan? We were worried! Vathah said you should have come back!'

'I—'

He embraced her, and she relaxed into him. She felt . . . better. Not well yet. It was all still there. But something about Wit's words . . .

I see only one woman here. The one who is standing up.

Adolin still held her for a time, as if he needed to reassure himself. 'I know you're fine, of course,' he said. 'I mean, you're basically unkillable, right?' Finally, he pulled back – still holding her shoulders – and looked down at her outfit. Should she explain?

'Nice,' Adolin said. 'Shallan, that's *sharp*. The red on white.' He stepped back, nodding. 'Did Yokska make that for you? Let me see the hat on you.'

Oh, Adolin, she thought, pulling on the hat.

'The jacket is a hair too loose,' Adolin said. 'But the style is a really good match. Bold. Crisp.' He cocked his head. 'Would look better with a sword at your waist. Maybe . . .' He trailed off. 'Do you hear that?'

She turned, frowning. It sounded like marching. 'A parade this early?'

They looked out at the street and found Kaladin approaching along with what seemed to be an army of five or six hundred men, wearing the uniforms of the Wall Guard.

Adolin sighed softly. 'Of course. He's probably their leader now or something. Storming bridgeboy.'

Kaladin marched his men right up to the front of the tailor's shop. She and Adolin stepped out to meet him, and she heard Elhokar scrambling down the steps inside, shouting at what he'd apparently seen out the window.

Kaladin was speaking softly with a woman in armor, helm under her arm, face crossed by a pair of scars. Highmarshal Azure was younger than Shallan had expected.

The soldiers grew hushed as they saw Adolin, then the king, who was already dressed.

'So *that's* what you meant,' Azure said to Kaladin.

'Stormblessed?' Elhokar asked. 'What is this?'

'You've been wanting an army to attack the palace, Your Majesty,' Kaladin said. 'Well, we're ready.'

As the duly appointed keepers of the perfect gems, we of the Else-callers have taken the burden of protecting the ruby nicknamed Honor's Drop. Let it be recorded.

—From drawer 20-10, zircon

Adolin Kholin washed his face with a splash of cold water, then rubbed it clean with a washrag. He was tired – he'd spent much of the night fretting about Shallan's failure to return. Below, in the shop proper, he could hear the others stomping about as they made last-minute preparations for the assault.

An assault on the *palace*, his home for many years. He took a deep breath.

Something was wrong. He fidgeted, checking his belt knife, the emergency bandages in his pocket. He checked the glyphward Shallan had made him at his request – *determination* – wrapped around his forearm. Then he finally realized what was bothering him.

He summoned his Shardblade.

It was thick at the base, as wide as a man's palm, and the front waved like the ripples of a moving eel. The back had small crystalline protrusions growing out of it. No sheath could hold a weapon like this, and no mortal sword could imitate it – not without growing unusably heavy.

You *knew* a Shardblade when you saw one. That was the point.

Adolin held the weapon before him in the lavatory, looking at his reflection in the metal. 'I don't have my mother's necklace,' he said, 'or any of the other traditions I used to follow. I never really needed those. I've only ever needed you.'

He took a deep breath. 'I guess ... I guess you used to be alive. The others say they can hear your screaming if they touch you. That you're dead, yet somehow still in pain. I'm sorry. I can't do anything about that, but ... thank you. Thank you for assisting me all these years. And if it helps, I'm going to use you to do something good today. I'll try to always use you that way.'

He felt better as he dismissed the Blade. Of course, he carried another weapon: his belt knife, long and thin. A weapon intended for stabbing armored men.

It had felt so *satisfying* to shove it through Sadeas's eye. He still didn't know whether to feel ashamed or proud. He sighed, checked himself in the mirror, then made another quick decision.

When he walked down the steps to the main room a short time later, he was wearing his Kholin uniform. His skin missed the softer silk and better form of the tailored outfit, but he found he walked taller in this one. Despite the fact that a part of him, deep down, worried he didn't deserve to bear his father's glyphs any longer.

He nodded to Elhokar, who was speaking with the strange woman known as Highmarshal Azure. 'My scouts have been driven back,' she said. 'But they saw enough, Your Majesty. The Voidbringer army *is* here, in its strength. They'll attack today or tomorrow for certain.'

'Well,' Elhokar said. 'I suppose I understand why you did what you had to in taking control of the Guard. I can't very well have you hanged as a usurper. Good work, Highmarshal.'

'I ... appreciate that?'

Shallan, Kaladin, Skar, and Drehy were standing with a palace map. They needed to memorize the layout. Adolin and Elhokar, of course, already knew it. Shallan had chosen not to change out of the fetching white outfit she'd been wearing earlier. It would be more functional for an assault than a skirt. Storms, there was something about a woman in trousers and a coat.

Elhokar left Azure to take reports from some of her men. Nearby in the room, a few lighteyed men saluted him – the highlords he and Adolin had revealed themselves to the night before. All they'd needed to do was walk away from the spheres powering their illusions, and their true faces had become manifest.

Some of these men were opportunists, but many were loyalists. They'd brought some hundred men-at-arms with them – not as many as Kaladin had brought from the Wall Guard, but still, Elhokar seemed proud of what he had done in gathering them. As well he should.

Together, he and Adolin joined the Radiants near the front of the shop. Elhokar waved for the highlords to join them, then spoke firmly. 'Is everyone clear?' Elhokar asked.

'Storm the palace,' Kaladin said. 'Seize the Sunwalk, cross to the Oathgate platform, hold it while Shallan tries to drive away the Unmade like she did in Urithiru. Then we activate the Oathgate, and bring troops to Kholinar.'

'The control building is *completely* overgrown with that black heart, Your Majesty,' Shallan said. 'I don't truly know how I drove away the Midnight Mother – and I certainly don't know that I'll be able to do the same here.'

'But you're willing to try?' the king asked.

'Yes.' She took a deep breath. Adolin squeezed her on the shoulder reassuringly.

'Windrunner,' the king said. 'The duty I give you and your men is to get Queen Aesudan and the heir to safety. If the Oathgate works, we take them that way. If not, you must fly them out of the city.'

Adolin glanced at the highlords, who seemed to be taking all of this – the arrival of Knights Radiant, the king's decision to storm his own palace – in stride. He knew a little of how they felt. Voidbringers, Everstorm, corrupted spren in the city . . . eventually, you stopped being shocked at what happened to you.

'Are we sure this path across the Sunwalk is the best way?' Kaladin asked, pointing at the map Drehy was holding. He moved his finger from the palace's eastern gallery, along the Sunwalk onto the Oathgate platform.

Adolin nodded. 'It's the best way to the Oathgate. Those narrow steps up the outside of that plateau would be murder to storm. Our best chance is to go up the palace's front steps, bring down the doors with our Shardblades, and fight through the entryway to the eastern gallery. From there, you can go up to the right to reach the king's quarters, or go straight across the Sunwalk.'

'I don't relish fighting along this corridor,' Kaladin said. 'We have to assume that the Fused will join the battle on the side of the Palace Guard.'

'It's possible I can distract them, if they do come,' Shallan said.

Kaladin grunted and didn't complain further. He saw, as Adolin did. This wasn't going to be an easy fight – there were a lot of choke points the defenders could use. But what else could they do?

In the distance, drums had begun sounding. From the walls. Kaladin looked toward them.

'Another raid?' one of the highlords asked.

'Worse,' Kaladin said as, behind them, Azure cursed softly. 'That's the signal that the city's under attack.'

Azure pushed out the front doors of the tailor's shop, and the rest of them followed. Most of the six hundred men here belonged to the Wall Guard, and some stepped toward the distant walls, gripping spears and shields.

'Steady, men,' Azure called. 'Your Majesty, the bulk of my soldiers are dying on the wall in a hopeless fight. I'm here because Stormblessed convinced me that the *only* way to help them is to take that palace. So if we're going to do it, the time is *now*.'

'We march, then!' Elhokar said. 'Highmarshal, Brightlords, pass the word to your forces. Organize ranks! We march on the palace at my command!'

Adolin turned as some Fused coursed through the sky along the distant wall. Enemy Surgebinders. Storms. He shook his head and hurried over to Yokska and her husband. They had watched all this – the arrival of an army on their doorstep, the preparations for an assault – with bewilderment.

'If the city holds,' Adolin said, 'you'll be fine. But if it falls ...' He took a deep breath. 'Reports from other cities indicate that there won't be wholesale slaughter. The Voidbringers are here to occupy, not exterminate. I'd still suggest you prepare to flee the city and make your way to the Shattered Plains.'

'The *Shattered Plains*?' Yokska asked, aghast. 'But Brightlord, that's hundreds and hundreds of miles!'

'I know,' he said, wincing. 'Thank you so much for taking us in. We're going to do what we can to stop this.'

Nearby, Elhokar approached the timid ardent who had come with Azure. He had been hurriedly painting glyphwards for the soldiers, and jumped as Elhokar took him by the shoulder and shoved an object into his hand.

'What's this?' the ardent asked, nervous.

'It's a spanreed,' Elhokar said. 'A half hour after my army marches, you are to contact Urithiru and warn them to get their forces ready to transfer here, via the Oathgate.'

'I can't use a fabrial! The screamers—'

'Steady, man! The enemy may be too preoccupied by their attack to notice you. But even if they do, you *must* take the risk. Our armies must be ready. The fate of the city could depend upon this.'

The ardent nodded, pale.

Adolin joined the troops, calming his nerves by force. Just another battle. He'd been in dozens, if not hundreds of those. But storms, he was used to empty fields of stone, not streets.

Nearby, a small group of guardsmen chatted softly. 'We'll be fine,' one of them was saying. He was a shorter man, clean-shaven, though he had strikingly hairy arms. 'I tell you, I saw my own death up there on the wall. She streaked toward me, lance held right toward my heart. I looked in those red eyes, and I saw myself dying. Then ... he was there. He shot from the tower window like an arrow and crashed into the Voidbringer. That spear was meant for my life, and he changed fate, I tell you. I swear, he was *glowing* when he did it. ...'

We're entering an era of gods, Adolin thought.

Elhokar raised his Shardblade high and gave the command. They marched through the city, passing worried refugees. Rows of buildings with doors shut tight, as if in preparation for a storm. Eventually, the palace rose before the army like an obsidian block. The very stones seemed to have changed color.

Adolin summoned his Shardblade, and the sight of it seemed to give comfort to the men nearby. Their march took them toward the northern section of the city, near the city wall. Here, the Fused were visible, attacking the troops. A strange *thumping* started, and Adolin took it as another set of drums – until a *head* crested the top of the wall nearest them.

Storms! It had an enormous stone wedge of a face that reminded him of that of some greatshell beast, though its eyes were just red spots glowing from deep within.

The monster pulled itself up by one arm. It didn't seem quite as tall as the city walls, but it was still enormous. Fused buzzed about as it swatted along the wall – spraying defenders like cremlings – then smashed a guard tower.

Adolin realized that he, along with much of their force, had stopped to stare at the daunting sight. The ground trembled as stones tumbled down a few blocks away, smashing into buildings.

'Keep moving!' Azure called. 'Storms! They're trying to get in and beat us to the palace!'

The monster ripped apart the guard tower, then with a casual flip tossed a boulder the size of a horse toward them. Adolin gaped, feeling powerless as the rock inexorably hurtled toward him and the troops.

Kaladin rose into the air on a streak of light.

He hit the stone and rolled with it, twisting and tumbling in the air. His glow diminished severely.

The boulder lurched. It somehow *changed momentum*, tossed away from Kaladin like a pebble flicked off the table. It crested the city wall, narrowly missing the monster that had thrown it. Adolin faintly heard spren begin to scream, but that was drowned out by the sounds of rock falling and people on the streets shouting.

Kaladin renewed himself with Stormlight from his pack. He was carrying most of the gemstones they'd brought from Urithiru, a wealth from the emerald reserve, to use in their mission and in opening the Oathgate.

Drehy rose into the air beside him, then Skar, who had Lashed Shallan upward as well. Adolin knew she was basically immortal, but it was still strange to see her here, on the front lines.

'We'll distract the Fused,' Kaladin shouted to Adolin, pointing at a group of figures flying through the air in their direction. 'And – if we can – we'll seize the Sunwalk. Get in through the palace, and meet with us in the eastern gallery!'

They zipped off. In the near distance, the monster started pounding on the gates there, cracking and splintering the wood.

'Forward!' Azure yelled.

Adolin charged, running up beside Elhokar and Azure. They reached the palace grounds and surged up the steps. At the top, soldiers in very similar uniforms – black and a darker blue, but still Kholin – withdrew, shutting the palace's front doors.

'King's Guard,' Adolin shouted, pointing at a group of men in red who had been designated as Elhokar's honor guard. 'Be sure to watch the king's flanks as he cuts! Don't let the enemy strike at him as the door falls!'

Men crowded up the steps, taking positions along the front of the palace's front porch. They held spears, though some were lighteyed. Adolin, Azure, and Elhokar each went to a separate door atop the steps. Here, the front of the palace roof – held up by thick columns – shielded them from the stones that the creature was flinging.

Teeth gritted, Adolin rammed his Blade into the crack between the thick wooden palace door and the wall. He swiped upward quickly, cutting through both hinges and the bar that had been thrown on the inside. After another slice down the other side freed the door, he stepped back into position. It fell inward with a crash.

Immediately, the enemy soldiers inside rammed spears outward, hoping to catch Adolin. He danced back, and didn't dare swing. Wielding a Shardblade with one hand was a challenge, even when you didn't have to worry about hitting your own men.

He skipped to the side and let the Wall Guard attack the doorway. Adolin, instead, moved over beside a group of soldiers who had come with Highlord Urimil. Here, Adolin cut through a section of the wall, making an improvised doorway that the soldiers shoved open. He moved down the long porch, opening another, then a third.

That done, he peeked in on Elhokar, who had stepped through his felled door, and was now inside the palace. He swept about himself with his Blade in a one-handed grip, shield held in the other. He opened a pocket in the enemy soldiers, having killed dozens already.

Careful, Elhokar, Adolin thought. *Remember, you don't have Plate.* Adolin pointed at a platoon of soldiers. 'Reinforce the King's Guard, and make sure he doesn't get overwhelmed. If he does, shout for me.'

They saluted, and Adolin stepped back. Azure had cut down her door, but her Shardblade wasn't as long as the other two. She was leading a more conservative attack, cutting the ends off spears as they rammed out toward her men. As he watched, she stabbed an enemy soldier who tried to push through. Remarkably, his eyes didn't burn, though his skin did go a strange ashen grey as he died.

Blood of my fathers, Adolin thought. *What's wrong with her Blade?*

Even with all the opened doorways, getting into the palace was slow going. The men inside had formed shield-wall rings around the doorways, and the fighting mostly happened with men using short spears to stab at each other. Some platoons of Wall Guard brought in longer pikes to break the ranks of defenders, preparing for a surge.

'You men ever flank-shielded a Shardbearer?' Adolin said to the nearest squad of soldiers.

'No sir,' said one of the men. 'But we've done the training. . . .'

'It'll have to do,' Adolin said, taking his Blade in two hands. 'I'm going in that center hole. Stay close and keep the spears off my sides. I'll be careful not to catch you in my sweeps.'

'Yes, sir!' their squadleader said.

Adolin took a deep breath, then approached the opening. The interior bristled with spears. Like the proverbial whitespine's den.

At Adolin's instruction, a soldier on his side faced his men and did a countdown with one hand. As the last finger dropped, the soldiers at the doorway fell back. Adolin charged through into the palace entry hall, with its marble floors and high vaulted ceilings.

The enemy thrust a dozen spears at him. He ducked low, taking a slice on the shoulder as he did a two-handed sweep, cutting a group of soldiers at the knees. The enemy dropped, their legs ruined by the Shardblade.

Four men followed him in and raised shields at his sides. Adolin attacked forward, hacking the fronts off spears, cutting at hands. Storms . . . the men he fought were too silent. They'd cry in pain if stabbed, or grunt with exertion, but they otherwise seemed muted – as if the darkness smothered their emotions.

Adolin took his Blade in an overhead grip and fell into Stonestance, swiping down with precise cuts, felling man after man in a careful, controlled set of strikes. His soldiers protected his flanks, while the wide reach of the Blade protected his front.

Eyes burned. The shield line wavered. 'Fall back three steps!' Adolin shouted to his men, then transitioned to Windstance and swept outward with wide, flowing sweeps.

In the passion and beauty of dueling, he sometimes forgot how *terrible* a weapon Shardblades were. Here, as he rampaged among the faltering line, it was all too obvious. He killed eight men in a moment, and completely destroyed the defensive line.

'Go!' he shouted, pointing with his Blade. Men surged through the doorway and seized the ground just inside the entry hall. Nearby, Elhokar stood tall, his narrow Shardblade glittering as he called commands. Soldiers fell, dying and cursing – the true sounds of battle. The price of conflict.

The enemy finally broke, falling back through the entry hall – which was too large to hold – toward the narrower hallway leading to the eastern gallery.

'Pull out the wounded!' Azure called, stepping in. 'Seventh Company, hold that far side of the room, make sure they don't try to rush back in. Third Company, sweep the wings and make sure there aren't any surprises.'

Curiously, Azure had removed her cloak and wrapped it half around her left arm. Adolin had never seen anything like it; perhaps she was accustomed to fighting in Plate.

Adolin got some water, then let a surgeon bandage the shallow cut he'd taken. Though the depths of the palace felt like caverns, this entryway was glorious. Walls of marble, polished and reflective. Grand staircases, and a bright red rug down the center. He'd burned that as a child once, playing with a candle.

Cut bandaged, he joined Azure, Elhokar, and several of the highlords, who were studying the wide corridor that led to the eastern gallery. The enemy had formed an excellent shield wall here. They'd settled in, and men in the second rank had crossbows ready and waiting.

'That's going to be crimson to break,' Azure said. 'We'll fight for every inch.'

Outside, the crashing at the gate finally grew silent.

'They're in,' Adolin guessed. 'That breach isn't far from here.'

Highlord Shaday grunted. 'Maybe our enemies will turn against one another? Can we hope the Voidbringers and the Palace Guard will start fighting each other?'

'No,' Elhokar said. 'The forces that have darkened the palace belong to the enemy who now fights quickly to reach us. They know the danger the Oathgate presents.'

'Agreed,' Adolin said. 'This palace will soon be swarming with parsh-man troops.'

'Gather your men,' Elhokar said to the group. 'Azure has command of the assault. Highmarshal, you *must* clear this hallway.'

One of the highlords looked at the woman and cleared his throat, but then decided not to say anything.

Grim, Azure commanded archers to use shortbows to try to soften the enemy. But that shield wall was built to hold out against arrows, so Azure gave the order, and her men advanced against the fortified enemy.

Adolin looked away as the corridor became a meat grinder, crossbow bolts smacking against men in waves. The Wall Guard had shields too, but they had to risk advancing, and a crossbow could *punch*.

Adolin had never been good at this part of battlefield fighting. Storm it, he wanted to be at the front, leading the charge. The rational part of him knew that would be stupid. You didn't risk your Shardbearers in such a charge, not unless they had Plate.

'Your Majesty,' an officer called to Elhokar, crossing the entryway. 'We found an oddity.'

Elhokar nodded for Adolin to take care of it, and – glad for the distraction – he jogged over to meet up with the man. 'What?'

'Closed door to the palace garrison,' the man said, 'rigged to lock from the *outside*.'

Curious. Adolin hiked after the man, passing an improvised triage station where a couple of surgeons knelt among painspren, seeing to men who had been wounded in the initial assault. They'd be far busier once the push down the hallway was finished.

To the west of the entryway was the palace garrison, a large housing for soldiers. A group of Azure's men were studying the door – which had indeed been rigged to lock shut from the outside with a metal bar. Judging from the splintered wood, whatever was inside had tried to get out.

'Open it,' Adolin said, summoning his Shardblade.

The soldiers cautiously lifted aside the bar, then eased open the door, one holding out some spheres for light. They didn't find monsters, but a group of dirty men in Palace Guard uniforms. They had gathered at the noise outside, and at seeing Adolin, a few of them fell to their knees, letting out relieved praises to the Almighty.

'Your Highness?' said a younger Alethi man with captain's knots on his shoulder. 'Oh, Prince Adolin. It *is* you. Or is this . . . is this somehow a cruel deception?'

'It's me,' Adolin said. 'Sidin? Storms, man! I barely recognize you through that beard. What happened?'

'Sir! Something's wrong with the queen. First she killed that ardent, and then *executed* Brightlord Kaves. . . .' He took a deep breath. 'We're traitors, sir.'

'She culled the Guard, sir,' another man said. 'Locked us in here because we wouldn't obey. Practically forgot about us.'

Adolin breathed out a relieved sigh. The fact that the entire Guard hadn't simply gone along with her . . . well, it lifted a burden from his shoulders, one he hadn't realized he'd been carrying.

'We're taking back the palace,' Adolin said. 'Gather your men, Sidin, and meet up with the surgeons in the main entryway. They'll look you over, get you some water, take your reports.'

'Sir!' Sidin said. 'If you're storming the palace, we want to join you.' Many of the others nodded.

'Join us? You've been locked in here for weeks, men! I don't expect that you're fit for combat.'

'Weeks?' Sidin said. 'Surely it's only been a few days, Brightlord.' He scratched at a beard that seemed to argue with that sentiment. 'We've only eaten . . . what, three times since being thrown in here?'

Several of the others nodded.

'Take them to the surgeons,' Adolin said to the scouts who had fetched him. 'But . . . get spears for the ones who claim to be strong enough to hold them. Sidin, your men will be reserves. Don't push yourselves too hard.'

Back in the main entryway, Adolin passed a surgeon working on a man in a Palace Guard uniform. To the surgeons, it didn't matter if you were an enemy – they were helping any who needed their attention. That was fine, but this man stared up with glazed eyes, and didn't cry or groan like a wounded man should. He only whispered to himself.

I know him *too*, Adolin realized, searching for the name. *Dod? That's it. That's what we called him, anyway.*

He reported to the king what he'd found. Ahead, Azure's men were making a final push to claim the hallway. They'd left dozens dying, staining the carpet a darker shade of red. Adolin had the distinct sense that he could *hear* something. Over the din of the fighting, over the shouts of men echoing against the walls. A quiet voice that somehow cut to his soul.

Passion. Sweet passion.

The Palace Guard finally relinquished the hallway, retreating through two sets of broad double doors at the other end. Those would lead to the eastern gallery; the doors weren't very defensible, but the enemy was obviously trying to buy as much time as possible.

Some soldiers cleared bodies out of the way, preparing the way for Adolin and Elhokar to cut down the doors. The wood, however, started shaking before they could strike. Adolin backed up, presenting his Blade in Windstance by habit, ready to strike at what came through.

The door opened, revealing a glowing figure.

'Stormfather . . .' Adolin whispered.

Kaladin shone with a powerful brilliance, his eyes beacons of blue, streaming with Stormlight. He gripped a glowing metallic spear that was easily twelve feet long. Behind him, Skar and Drehy also glowed brilliantly, looking little like the affable bridgemen who had protected Adolin on the Shattered Plains.

'The gallery is secure,' Kaladin said, Stormlight puffing from his lips. 'The enemy you pushed back has fled up the steps. Your Majesty, I suggest you send Azure's men onto the Sunwalk to hold it.'

Adolin ducked into the eastern gallery, followed by a flood of soldiers, Azure calling commands. Straight ahead was the entrance to the Sunwalk, an open-sided walkway. On it, Adolin was surprised to see not only guard corpses, but three prominent bodies in blue. Kaladin, Skar, Drehy. Illusions?

'Worked better than fighting them off,' Shallan said, stepping up to his side. 'The flying ones are distracted by the fighting at the city wall, so they left the moment they thought the bridgemen had fallen.'

'We pushed another force of Palace Guards back into the monastery first,' Kaladin said, pointing. 'We're going to need an army to scrape them out.'

Azure looked to Elhokar, who nodded, so she started giving the commands. Shallan clicked her tongue, prodding at Adolin's bandaged shoulder, but he assured her it was nothing serious.

The king strode through the gallery, then looked up the broad stairs.

'Your Majesty?' Kaladin called.

'I'm going to lead a force up to the royal chambers,' Elhokar said. 'Someone needs to find out what happened to Aesudan, what happened to this whole storming city.'

The glow faded from Kaladin's eyes, his Stormlight running low. His clothing seemed to droop, his feet settling more solidly on the ground. He suddenly seemed a man again, and Adolin found that more relaxing.

'I'll go with him,' Kaladin said softly to Adolin, handing him the pack of emeralds, after picking out two brilliant ones for himself. 'Take Skar and Drehy, and get Shallan to the Unmade.'

'Sounds good,' Adolin said. He picked out some soldiers to go with the king: a platoon from the Wall Guard, a handful of the armsmen the highlords had brought. And – after some thought – he added Sidin and half a platoon of the men who had been imprisoned in the palace.

'Those troops refused the queen's orders,' Adolin said to Elhokar, nodding to Sidin. 'They seem to have resisted the influence of whatever's going on in here, and they'll know the palace better than the Wall Guard.'

'Excellent,' Elhokar said, then started up the steps. 'Don't wait for us. If Brightness Davar is successful, go right to Urithiru and bring our armies back.'

Adolin nodded, then gave Kaladin a quick salute – tapping his wrists together with hands in fists. The Bridge Four salute. 'Good luck, bridgeboy.'

Kaladin smiled, his silvery spear vanishing as he gave the salute back, then hustled after the king. Adolin jogged over to Shallan, who was staring along the Sunwalk. Azure had claimed it with her soldiers, but hadn't advanced onto the Oathgate platform beyond.

Adolin rested his hand on Shallan's shoulder.

'They're there,' she whispered. 'Two of them, this time. Last night, Adolin . . . I had to run. The revel was getting inside my head.'

'I've heard it,' he said, resummoning his Blade. 'We'll face it together. Like last time.'

Shallan took a deep breath, then summoned Pattern as a Shardblade. She held the Blade before herself in a common stance.

'Good form,' Adolin said.

'I had a good teacher.'

They advanced across the Sunwalk, passing fallen enemy soldiers – and a single dead Fused, pinned to a cleft in the rock by what appeared to be his own lance. Shallan lingered at the corpse, but Adolin pulled her along until they reached the monastery proper. Azure's soldiers advanced at his command, engaging Palace Guards here to secure a path toward the center.

As they waited, Adolin stepped up to the edge of the plateau and surveyed the city. His home.

It was falling.

The nearest gate had been broken completely open, and parshmen flooded through it toward the palace. Others had taken the walls via ladder crews, and those were pushing down into the city at other points, including near the palace gardens.

That enormous stone monstrosity moved along the wall on the inside, reaching up and slapping at guard towers. A large group of people in varied costumes had surged down Talan Way, passing along one of the windblades. The Cult of Moments? He couldn't be certain what part they'd played, but parshmen were flooding the city in that direction as well.

We can fix this, Adolin thought. *We can bring our armies in, hold the palace hill, push back to the walls.* They had dozens of Shardbearers. They had Bridge Four and other Surgebinders. They *could* save this city.

He just needed to get them here.

Soon, Azure approached with a platoon of thirty men. 'The pathway inward is secure, though a knot of the enemy still holds the very center. I've spared a few men to scour nearby buildings. It looks like the people you mentioned – the ones who were reveling last night – are slumbering inside. They don't move, even when we prod them.'

Adolin nodded, then led the way toward the center of the plateau, Shallan and Azure following. They passed battle lines of Azure's soldiers, who were holding the streets. He soon saw the main force of the enemy, collected on a path between monastery buildings, barring the way to the Oathgate's control building.

Spurred by the urgency of Kholinar's predicament, Adolin took point and swept among the enemy, burning their eyes with his Blade. He broke their line, though one straggler almost got in a lucky strike. Skar, fortunately, seemed to appear out of nowhere; the bridgeman caught the blow with his shield, then rammed a spear through the guardsman's chest.

'How many is that I owe you now?' Adolin asked.

'I wouldn't think to keep count, Brightlord,' Skar said with a grin, glowing light puffing from his lips.

Drehy joined them, and they chased the routed enemy past the King's Chapel, finally reaching the control building. Adolin had always known it as the Circle of Memories, merely another part of the monastery. As Shallan had warned, it was overgrown with a dark mass that pulsed and throbbed, like a pitch-black heart. Dark veins spread from it like roots, pulsating in time with the heart.

'Storms . . .' Drehy whispered.

'All right,' Shallan said, walking forward. 'Guard this area. I'll see what I can do.'

The enemy makes another push toward Feverstone Keep. I wish we knew what it was that had them so interested in that area. Could they be intent on capturing Rall Elorim?

—From drawer 19-2, third topaz

Kaladin charged up the broad stairs, followed by some fifty soldiers.

Stormlight pulsed within him, lending a spring to each step. The Fused had taken time to come attack him on the Sunwalk, and had left soon after Shallan had created her ruse. He could only assume that the city assault was consuming the enemy's attention, which meant he might be able to use his powers without drawing immediate reprisal.

Elhokar led the way, brilliant Shardblade carried in a two-handed grip. They twisted around at a landing and charged up another flight. Elhokar didn't seem to care that each step took them farther from the bulk of their army.

'Up the stairs,' he said softly to Syl. 'Check for an ambush on each floor.'

'Yessir, commander sir, Radiant sir,' she said, and zipped off. A moment later she zipped back down. 'Lots of men on the third floor, but they're backing away from the stairwell. Doesn't look like an ambush.'

Kaladin nodded, then slowed Elhokar with a touch on the arm. 'We have a reception waiting,' Kaladin said. He pointed at a squad of soldiers. 'It seems the king lost his guards somewhere. You're now them. If we get into combat, keep His Majesty from being surrounded.' He pointed at another group. 'You men are . . . Beard?'

'Yes, Kal?' the stocky guardsman said. He hesitated, then saluted. 'Um, sir?' Behind him were Noro, Ved, Alaward, and Vaceslv . . . Kaladin's entire squad from the Wall Guard.

Noro shrugged. 'Without the captain, we don't have a proper platoon leader. Figured we should stick with you.'

Beard nodded and rubbed at the glyphward wrapping his right arm. *Fortune*, it read.

'Good to have you,' Kaladin said. 'Try to keep me from being flanked, but give me space if you can.'

'Don't crowd you,' Lieutenant Noro said, 'and don't let anyone else crowd you either. Can do, sir.'

Kaladin looked to the king and nodded. The two of them took the last few steps up to the landing to emerge into a broad stone hallway, carpeted down the center but otherwise unornamented. Kaladin had expected the palace to be more lavish, but it appeared that even here – in the seat of their power – the Kholins preferred buildings that felt like bunkers. Funny, after hearing them complain that their fortresses on the Shattered Plains lacked comfort.

Syl was right. A platoon of enemy soldiers had formed up down the hall, holding halberds or crossbows, but seemed content to wait. Kaladin prepared Stormlight; he could paint the walls with a power that would cause crossbow bolts to veer aside in their flight, but it was far from a perfect art. It was the power he understood the least.

'Do you not see me?' Elhokar bellowed. 'Do you not know your monarch? Are you so far consumed by the touch of the spren that you would kill your *own king*?'

Storms . . . those soldiers barely seemed to be breathing. At first they didn't move – then a few looked backward, down the hallway. Was that a distant voice?

The palace soldiers immediately broke formation and retreated. Elhokar set his jaw, then led the way after them. Each step made Kaladin more anxious. He didn't have the troops to properly hold their retreat; all he could do was post a pair of men at each intersection, with instructions to yell if they saw someone coming down the cross hallways.

They passed a corridor lined with statues of the Heralds. Nine of them, at least. One was missing. Kaladin sent Syl ahead to watch, but that left him feeling even more exposed. Everyone but him seemed to know the way, which made sense, but it made him feel carried along on some sort of tide.

They finally reached the royal chambers, marked by a broad set of doors, open and inviting. Kaladin stopped his men thirty feet from the opening, near a corridor that split off to the left.

Even from here, he could see that the chamber beyond the doors finally displayed some of the lavish ornamentation he had expected. Rich carpets, too much furniture, everything covered in embroidery or gilding.

'There are soldiers down that smaller hallway to the left,' Syl said, zipping back to him. 'There isn't a single one in the room ahead, but . . . Kaladin, *she's* in there. The queen.'

'I can hear her,' Elhokar said. 'That's her voice, singing.'

I know that tune, Kaladin thought. Something about her soft song was familiar. He wanted to advise caution, but the king was already hurrying forward, a worried squad of men following.

Kaladin sighed, then arranged his remaining men; half stayed back to watch their retreat, and the other half formed up at the left hallway to stare down the Palace Guard. Storms. If this went wrong he'd have a bloodbath on his hands, with the king trapped in the middle.

Still, this *was* why they'd come up here. He followed the queen's song and entered the room.

．◆．

Shallan stepped up to the dark heart. Even though she hadn't studied human anatomy as much as she'd have liked – her father thought it unfeminine – in the sunlight, she could easily see that it was the wrong shape.

This isn't a human heart, she decided. *Maybe it's a parshman heart.* Or, well, a giant, dark violet spren in the shape of one, growing over the Oathgate control building.

'Shallan,' Adolin said. 'We're running out of time.'

His voice brought to her an awareness of the city around her. Of soldiers skirmishing only one street over. Of distant drums going quiet, one at a time, as guard posts on the wall fell. Of smoke in the air, and a soft, high-pitched roar that seemed the echoes of thousands upon thousands of people shouting in the chaos of a city being conquered.

She tried Pattern first, stabbing him into the heart as a Shardblade. The mass simply split around the Blade. She slashed with it, and the spren cut, then sealed up behind. So. Time to try what she'd done in Urithiru.

Trembling, Shallan closed her eyes and pressed her hand against the heart. It *felt* real, like warm flesh. Like in Urithiru, touching the thing let her sense it. Feel it. *Know* it.

It tried to sweep her away.

⁘

The queen sat at a vanity beside the wall.

She was much as Kaladin had anticipated. Younger than Elhokar, with long dark Alethi hair, which she was combing. Her song had fallen away to a hum.

'Aesudan?' Elhokar asked.

She looked away from the mirror, then smiled broadly. She had a narrow face, with prim lips painted a deep red. She rose from the seat and glided to him. 'Husband! So it *was* you I heard. You have returned at last? Victorious over our enemies, your father avenged?'

'Yes,' Elhokar said, frowning. He moved to step toward her, but Kaladin grabbed him by the shoulder and held him back.

The queen focused on Kaladin. 'New bodyguard, dear one? Far too scruffy; you should have consulted me. You have an image to maintain.'

'Where is Gav, Aesudan? Where is my son?'

'He's playing with friends.'

Elhokar looked to Kaladin, and gestured to the side with his chin. *See what you can find*, it seemed to say.

'Keep alert,' Kaladin whispered, then began picking through the room. He passed the remnants of lavish meals only partially eaten. Pieces of fruit each with a single bite taken out of them. Cakes and pastries. Candied meats on sticks. It looked like it should have rotted, based on the decayspren he noticed, but it hadn't.

'Dear one,' Elhokar said, keeping his distance from the queen, 'we heard that the city has seen . . . trouble lately.'

'One of my ardents tried to refound the Hierocracy. We really should keep better watch on who joins them; not every man or woman is proper for service.'

'You had her executed.'

'Of course. She tried to overthrow us.'

Kaladin picked around a pile of musical instruments of the finest wood, sitting in a heap.

Here, Syl's voice said in his mind. *Across the room. Behind the dressing screen.*

He passed the balcony to his left. If he remembered right – though the story had been told so often, he had heard a dozen differing versions – Gavilar and the assassin had fallen off that ledge during their struggles.

'Aesudan,' Elhokar said, his voice pained. He stepped forward, extending his hand. 'You're not well. Please, come with me.'

'Not well?'

'There's an evil influence in the palace.'

'Evil? Husband, what a fool you are at times.'

Kaladin joined Syl and glanced behind the dressing screen, which had been pushed back against the wall to section off a small cubby. Here a child – two or three years old – huddled and trembled, clutching a stuffed soldier. Several spren with soft red glows were picking at him like cremlings at a corpse. The boy tried to turn his head, and the spren pulled on the back of his hair until he looked up, while others hovered in front of his face and took horrific shapes, like horses with melting faces.

Kaladin reacted with swift, immediate *rage*. He growled, seizing the Sylblade from the air, forming a small dagger from mist. He drove the dagger forward and caught one of the spren, pinning it to the wall's wooden paneling. He had never known a Shardblade to cut a spren before, but this worked. The thing screamed in a soft voice, a hundred hands coming from its shape and scraping at the Blade, at the wall, until it seemed to *rip* into a thousand tiny pieces, then faded.

The other three red spren streaked away in a panic. In his hands, Kaladin felt Syl *tremble,* then groan softly. He released her, and she took the shape of a small woman. 'That was ... that was *terrible*,' she whispered, floating over to land on his shoulder. 'Did we ... just *kill* a spren?'

'The thing deserved it,' Kaladin said.

Syl just huddled on his shoulder, wrapping her arms around herself.

The child sniffled. He was dressed in a little uniform. Kaladin glanced back at the king and queen – he'd lost track of their conversation, but they spoke in hissing, furious tones.

'Oh, Elhokar,' the queen was saying. 'You were ever so oblivious. Your father had grand plans, but you . . . all you ever wanted to do was sit in his shadow. It was for the best that you went off to play war.'

'So you could stay here and . . . and do *this*?' Elhokar said, waving toward the palace.

'I continued your father's work! I found the secret, Elhokar. Spren, ancient spren. You can *bond* with them!'

'Bond . . .' Elhokar's mouth worked, as if he couldn't understand the very word he spoke.

'Have you seen my Radiants?' Aesudan asked. She grinned. 'The Queen's Guard? I've done what your father could not. Oh, he found one of the ancient spren, but he could never discover how to bond it. But I, *I* have solved the riddle.'

In the dim light of the royal chambers, Aesudan's eyes glittered. Then started to glow a deep red.

'Storms!' Elhokar said, stepping back.

Time to go. Kaladin reached down to try to pick up the child, but the boy screamed and scrambled away from him. That, finally, drew the king's attention. Elhokar rushed over, throwing aside the dressing screen. He gasped, then knelt beside his son.

The child, Gavinor, scooted away from his father, crying.

Kaladin looked back to the queen. 'How long have you been planning this?'

'Planning for my husband's return?'

'I'm not talking to you. I'm talking to the thing beyond you.'

She laughed. 'Yelig-nar serves me. Or do you speak of the Heart of the Revel? Ashertmarn has no will; he is merely a force of consumption, mindless, to be harnessed.'

Elhokar whispered something to his son. Kaladin couldn't hear the words, but the child stopped weeping. He looked up, blinked away tears, and finally let his father pick him up. Elhokar cradled the child, who in turn clutched his stuffed soldier. It wore blue armor.

'Out,' Kaladin said.

'But . . .' The king looked toward his wife.

'Elhokar,' Kaladin said, gripping the king's shoulder. 'Be a hero to the one you can save.'

The king met his eyes, then nodded, clutching the young child. He started toward the door, and Kaladin followed, keeping his eyes on the queen.

She sighed loudly, stepping after them. 'I feared this.'

They rejoined their soldiers, then began to retreat down the hallway.

Aesudan stopped in the doorway to the king's chambers. 'I have outgrown you, Elhokar. I have taken the gemstone into me, and have harnessed Yelig-nar's power.' Something started to twist around her, a black smoke, blown as if from an unseen wind.

'Double time,' Kaladin said to his men, drawing in Stormlight. He could feel it coming; he'd sensed where this would go the moment they'd started up the steps.

It was almost a relief when, at last, Aesudan shouted for her soldiers to attack.

⁘

Give it all to me, the voices whispered in Shallan's mind. *Give me your passion, your hunger, your longing, your loss. Surrender it. You are what you feel.*

Shallan swam in it, lost, like in the depths of the ocean. The voices beset her from all sides. When one whispered that she was pain, Shallan became a weeping girl, singing as she twisted a chain tight around a thick neck. When another whispered that she was hunger, she became an urchin on the street, wearing rags for clothing.

Passion. Fear. Enthusiasm. Boredom. Hatred. Lust.

She became a new person with every heartbeat. The voices seemed thrilled by this. They assaulted her, growing to a frenzy. Shallan was a thousand people in a moment.

But which one was her?

All of them. A new voice. Wit's?

'Wit!' she screamed, surrounded by snapping eels in a dark place. 'Wit! Please.'

You're all of them, Shallan. Why must you be only one emotion? One set of sensations? One role? One life?

'They rule me, Wit. Veil and Radiant and all the others. They're *consuming* me.'

Then be ruled as a king is ruled by his subjects. Make Shallan so strong, the others must bow.

'I don't know if I can!'

The darkness thrummed and surged.

And then . . . withdrew?

Shallan didn't feel as if she'd changed anything, but still the darkness retreated. She found herself kneeling on the cold stones outside the control building. The enormous heart became sludge, then melted away, almost seeming to crawl, sending out runners of dark liquid before itself.

'You did it!' Adolin said.

I did?

'Secure that building,' Azure commanded her soldiers. Drehy and Skar glowed nearby, looking grim, fresh blood on their clothing. They'd been fighting.

Shallan stood up on shaky feet. The small, circular structure in front of her seemed insignificant compared to the other monastery buildings, but it was the key to everything.

'This is going to be tricky, Azure,' Adolin said. 'We're going to have to fight back down into the city, push the enemy out. Storms, I hope my father has our armies ready.'

Shallan blinked, dazed. She couldn't help feeling she'd failed. That she hadn't done *anything*.

'The first transfer will be only the control building,' Adolin said. 'After that, she'll swap the entire platform – buildings and all. We'll want to move our army back into the palace before that happens.' Adolin turned, surveying the path back. 'What is taking the king so long?'

Shallan stepped into the control building. It looked much as the one she'd discovered at the Shattered Plains – though better maintained, and its tile mosaics on the floor were of fanciful creatures. An enormous beast with claws, and fur like a mink. Something that looked like a giant fish. On the walls, lanterns shone with gemstones – and between them hung full-length mirrors.

Shallan walked toward the keyhole control device, summoning Pattern as a Blade. She studied him, then looked up at herself in one of the mirrors hanging on the wall.

Someone else stood in the mirror. A woman with black hair that fell to her waist. She wore archaic clothing, a sleeveless, flowing gown that was more of a tunic, with a simple belted waist. Shallan touched her face. Why had she put this illusion on?

The reflection didn't mimic her motions, but pressed forward, raising hands against the glass. The reflected room faded and the figure distorted, and became a jet-black shadow with white holes for eyes.

Radiant, the thing said, mouthing the words. *My name is Sja-anat. And I am not your enemy.*

•‧•

Kaladin's men charged down the steps in their escape, though the back ranks bunched up in the hallway around the stairwell. Behind, the Queen's Guard set up and lowered crossbows. Sylspear held high, Kaladin stepped between the two groups and pooled Stormlight into the ground, drawing the bolts downward. He was unpracticed with this power, and unfortunately, some of the bolts still slammed into shields, even heads.

Kaladin growled, then drew in a deep breath of Stormlight, bursting alight – the glow of his skin shining on the walls and ceiling of the palace hallway. The queen's soldiers shied back before the light as if it were something physical.

Distantly, he heard the screaming spren react to what he'd done. He Lashed himself in precisely the right way to rise a few feet off the ground, then float there. The queen's soldiers blinked against the light, as if it were somehow too strong for their eyes. At last, the captain of the rearguard called the final withdrawal, and the rest of Kaladin's men rushed down the stairs. Only Noro's squad lingered.

Some of the queen's soldiers began to test forward at him, so he dropped to the floor and started down the steps at a run. Beard and the rest of the squad joined him, followed by the queen's soldiers, unnaturally silent.

Unfortunately, Kaladin heard something else echoing up the stairwell from down below. The sounds of men clashing, and of familiar singing.

Parshendi songs.

'Rearguard!' Kaladin shouted. 'Form up on the steps; orient toward the upper floor!'

His soldiers obeyed, turning and leveling spears and shields at the descending enemy. Kaladin Lashed himself upward and twisted so that he hit the ceiling feet-first. He ducked and ran – passing over the heads of his men in the high stairwell – until he reached the ground floor.

The first ranks of his soldiers clashed with parshman troops in the eastern gallery. But the enemy had penned them into the stairwell, so most of his troops couldn't get down to the fight.

Kaladin released his Lashing, dropping and twisting to land in a tempest of light before the parshman ranks. Several of his men groaned and cried as they fell, bloodied, to the enemy spears. Kaladin felt his rage flare, and he lowered the Sylspear. It was time to begin the work of death.

Then he saw the face of the parshman in front of him.

It was Sah. Former slave. Cardplayer. Father.

Kaladin's friend.

❖

Shallan regarded the figure in the mirror. It *had* spoken. 'What are you?'

They call me the Taker of Secrets, the figure said. *Or they once did.*

'One of the Unmade. Our enemies.'

We were made, then unmade, she agreed. *But no, not an enemy!* The figure turned humanlike again, though the eyes remained glowing white. It pressed its hands against the glass. *Ask my son. Please.*

'You're of *him*. Odium.'

The figure glanced to the sides, as if frightened. *No. I am of me. Now, only of me.*

Shallan considered, then looked at the keyhole. By using Pattern in that, she could initiate the Oathgate.

Don't do it, Sja-anat pled. *Listen, Radiant. Listen to my plea. Ashertmarn fled on purpose. It is a trap. I was compelled to touch the spren of this device, so it will not function as you wish.*

❖

Kaladin's will to fight evaporated.

He'd been stoked with energy, ready to enter the battle and protect his men. But ...

Sah recognized him and gasped, then grabbed his companion – Khen – one of the others Kaladin knew – and pointed. The parshwoman cursed, and the group of them scrambled away from the steps – leaving dead human soldiers.

In the opening provided, Kaladin's men pushed down off the steps into

270

the grand hall. They surged around Kaladin as – stunned – he lowered his spear.

The large, pillared hall became a scene of utter chaos. Azure's soldiers rushed in from the Sunwalk, meeting the parshmen who came up the stairs from the back of the palace – they'd likely broken in through the gardens there. The king held his son, standing amid a group of soldiers in the very center. Kaladin's men managed to get down off the steps, and behind them rushed the Queen's Guard.

It all churned into a melee. Battle lines disintegrated, and platoons shattered, men fighting alone or in pairs. It was a battlefield commander's nightmare. Hundreds of men mixing and screaming and fighting and dying.

Kaladin saw them. *All* of them. Sah and the parshmen, fighting to keep their freedom. The guardsmen who had been rescued, fighting for their king. Azure's Wall Guard, terrified as their city fell around them. The Queen's Guard, convinced they were loyally following orders.

In that moment, Kaladin lost something precious. He'd always been able to trick himself into seeing a battle as *us* against *them*. Protect those you love. Kill everyone else. But . . . but they didn't deserve death.

None of them did.

He locked up. He froze, something that hadn't happened to him since his first days in Amaram's army. The Sylspear vanished in his fingers, puffing to mist. How could he fight? How could he kill people who were just doing the best they could?

'Stop!' he finally bellowed. '*Stop it! Stop killing each other!*'

Nearby, Sah rammed Beard through with a spear.

'*STOP! PLEASE!*'

Noro responded by running through Jali – one of the other parshmen Kaladin had known. Ahead, Elhokar's ring of guards fell, and a member of the Queen's Guard managed to ram the point of a halberd into the king's arm. Elhokar gasped, dropping his Shardblade from pained fingers, holding his son close with his other arm.

The Queen's Guardsman pulled back, eyes widening – as if seeing the king for the first time. One of Azure's soldiers cut the guardsman down in his moment of confusion.

Kaladin screamed, tears streaming from his eyes. He begged them to just stop, to listen.

They couldn't hear him. Sah – gentle Sah, who had only wanted to protect his daughter – died by Noro's sword. Noro, in turn, got his head split by Khen's axe.

Noro and Sah fell beside Beard, whose dead eyes stared sightlessly – his arm stretched out, glyphward soaking up his blood.

Kaladin slumped to his knees. His Stormlight seemed to frighten off the enemies; everyone stayed away from him. Syl spun around him, begging for him to listen, but he couldn't hear her.

The king . . . he thought, numb. *Get* . . . *get to Elhokar* . . .

Elhokar had fallen to his knees. In one arm he held his terrified son, in the other hand he held . . . a sheet of paper? A sketch?

Kaladin could almost hear Elhokar stuttering the words.

Life . . . *life before death* . . .

The hair on Kaladin's neck rose. Elhokar started to glow softly.

Strength . . . *before weakness* . . .

'Do it, Elhokar,' Kaladin whispered.

Journey. Journey before . . .

A figure emerged from the battle. A tall, lean man – so, so familiar. Gloom seemed to cling to Moash, who wore a brown uniform like the parshmen. For a heartbeat the battle pivoted on him. Wall Guard behind him, broken Palace Guard before.

'Moash, no . . .' Kaladin whispered. He couldn't move. Stormlight bled from him, leaving him empty, exhausted.

Lowering his spear, Moash ran Elhokar through the chest.

Kaladin screamed.

Moash pinned the king to the ground, shoving aside the weeping child prince with his foot. He placed his boot against Elhokar's throat, holding him down, then pulled the spear out and stabbed Elhokar through the eye as well.

He held the weapon in place, carefully waiting until the fledgling glow around the king faded and flickered out. The king's Shardblade appeared from mist and clanged to the ground beside him.

Elhokar, king of Alethkar, was dead.

Moash pulled the spear free and glanced at the Shardblade. Then he kicked it aside. He looked at Kaladin, then quietly made the Bridge Four salute, wrists tapped together. The spear he held dripped with Elhokar's blood.

The battle broke. Kaladin's men had been all but obliterated; the remnants escaped along the Sunwalk. A member of the Queen's Guard scooped up the young prince and carried him away. Azure's men limped back before the growing parshman armies.

The queen descended the stairs, wreathed in black smoke, eyes glowing red. She'd transformed, strange crystal formations having pierced her skin like carapace. Her chest was glowing bright with a gemstone, as if it had replaced her heart. It shone through her dress.

Kaladin turned from her and crawled toward the king's corpse. Nearby, a member of the Queen's Guard finally took notice of him, seizing him by the arm.

And then . . . light. Glowing Stormlight flooded the chamber as twin Radiants exploded out from the Sunwalk. Drehy and Skar swept through the enemy, driving them back with sweeping spears and Lashings.

A second later, Adolin grabbed Kaladin under the arms and heaved him backward. 'Time to go, bridgeboy.'

Don't tell anyone. I can't say it. I must whisper. I foresaw this.

—From drawer 30-20, a particularly small emerald

Adolin shoved down the emotion of seeing Elhokar's dead body. It was one of the first battlefield lessons his father had taught him.

Grieve later.

Adolin pulled Kaladin out along the Sunwalk while Skar and Drehy guarded their retreat, encouraging the last of the Wall Guard to run – or limp – to safety.

Kaladin stumbled along. Though he didn't appear wounded, he stared with a glazed-over look. Those were the eyes of a man who bore the kinds of wounds you couldn't fix with bandages.

They eventually poured out of the Sunwalk onto the Oathgate platform, where Azure's soldiers held firm, her surgeons running to help the wounded who had escaped the bloodbath in the eastern gallery. Skar and Drehy dropped down to the platform, guarding the way onto the Sunwalk, to prevent the Queen's Guard or parshmen from following.

Adolin stumbled to a stop. From this vantage he could see the city.

Stormfather.

Tens of thousands of parshmen flooded in through the broken gates or across the nearby sections of wall. Figures glowing with dark light zipped through the air. Those seemed to be gathering in formations nearby, perhaps for an assault on the Oathgate platform.

Adolin took it all in, and admitted the terrible truth. His city was lost.

'All forces, hold the platform,' he heard himself saying. 'But pass the word. I'm going to take us to Urithiru.'

'Sir!' a soldier said. 'Civilians are crowding the base of the platform, trying to get up the steps.'

'Let them!' Adolin shouted. 'Get as many people up here as you can. Hold against any enemy who tries to reach the platform top, but don't engage them if they don't press. We're abandoning the city. Anyone not on the platform in ten minutes will be left behind!'

Adolin hurried toward the control building. Kaladin followed, dazed. *After what he's been through,* Adolin thought, *I wouldn't have expected that anything could faze him. Not even Elhokar's . . .*

Storms. Grieve later.

Azure stood guard in the doorway to the control building, holding the pack full of gemstones. Hopefully, those would be enough to get everyone to safety.

'Brightness Davar told me to clear everyone else out,' the highmarshal said. 'Something's wrong with the device.'

Adolin cursed under his breath and stepped inside. Shallan knelt on the ground before a mirror, looking at herself. Behind, Kaladin stepped in, then settled down on the floor, placing his back to the wall.

'Shallan,' Adolin said. 'We need to go. *Now.*'

'But—'

'The city has fallen. Transfer the entire platform, not just the control building. We need to get as many people as we can to safety.'

'My men on the wall!' Azure said.

'They're dead or routed,' Adolin said, gritting his teeth. 'I don't like it any more than you do.'

'The king—'

'The king is *dead.* The queen has joined the enemy. I'm ordering our retreat, Azure.' Adolin locked gazes with the woman. 'We gain nothing by dying here.'

She drew her lips to a line, but didn't argue further.

'Adolin,' Shallan whispered, 'the heart was a trick. I didn't chase it off

– it left on purpose. I think . . . I think the Voidbringers *intentionally* left Kaladin and his men alone after only a brief fight. They let us come here because the Oathgate is trapped.'

'How do you know?' Adolin asked.

Shallan cocked her head. 'I'm speaking to her.'

'Her?'

'Sja-anat. The Taker of Secrets. She says that if we engage the device, we'll be caught in a disaster.'

Adolin took a deep breath.

'Do it anyway,' he said.

·.·

Do it anyway.

Shallan understood the implication. How could they trust an ancient spren of Odium? Perhaps Shallan really *had* driven the black heart away, and – in a panic to keep the humans from escaping – Sja-anat was now stalling.

Shallan looked away from the pleading figure in the mirror. The others couldn't see her – she'd confirmed this with Azure already.

'Pattern?' she whispered. 'What do you think?'

'Mmmm . . .' he said quietly. 'Lies. So many lies. I don't know, Shallan. I cannot tell you.'

Kaladin slumped by the wall, staring sightlessly, as if he were dead inside. She couldn't recall ever seeing him in such a state.

'Get ready.' Shallan stood up, summoning Pattern as a Blade.

Trust is not mine, said the figure in the mirror. *You will not give my children a home. Not yet.*

Shallan pushed the Blade into the lock. It melded to match Pattern's shape.

I will show you, Sja-anat said. *I will try. My promise is not strong, for I cannot know. But I will try.*

'Try what?' Shallan asked.

Try not to kill you.

With those words haunting her, Shallan engaged the Oathgate.

*My spren claims that recording this will be good for me, so here I go.
Everyone says I will swear the Fourth Ideal soon, and in so doing, earn
my armor. I simply don't think that I can. Am I not supposed to want
to help people?*

—From drawer 10-12, sapphire

D alinar Kholin stood at attention, hands behind his back, one wrist gripping the other. He could see so far from his balcony at Urithiru – but it was endless miles of nothing. Clouds and rock. So much and so little, all at once.

'Dalinar,' Navani said, stepping up and resting her hands on his arm. 'Please. At least come inside.'

They thought he was sick. They thought his collapse on the Oathgate platform had been caused by heart troubles, or fatigue. The surgeons had suggested rest. But if he stopped standing up straight, if he let it bow him down, he worried the memories would crush him.

The memories of what he'd done at the Rift.

The crying voices of children, begging for mercy.

He forced his emotions down. 'What news,' he said, embarrassed by how his voice trembled.

'None,' Navani said. 'Dalinar . . .'

Word had come from Kholinar via spanreed, one that somehow still worked. An assault on the palace, an attempt to reach the Oathgate.

Outside, the gathered Kholin, Aladar, and Roion armies clogged one of Urithiru's Oathgate platforms, waiting to be taken to Kholinar to join the battle. But nothing happened. Time seeped away. It had been four hours since the first communication.

Dalinar closed his mouth, eyes ahead, and stared at the expanse. At attention, like a soldier. That was how he would wait. Even though he'd never *really* been a soldier. He'd commanded men, ordered recruits to stand in line, inspected ranks. But he himself . . . he'd skipped all of that. He'd waged war in a bloodthirsty riot, not a careful formation.

Navani sighed, patting him on the arm, then returned to their rooms to sit with Taravangian and a small collection of scribes and highprinces. Awaiting news from Kholinar.

Dalinar stood in the breeze, wishing he could empty his mind, rid himself of memories. Go back to being able to pretend he was a good man. Problem was, he'd given in to a kind of fancy, one everyone told about him. They said the Blackthorn had been a terror on the battlefield, but still honest. Dalinar Kholin, he would fight you fair, they said.

Evi's cries, and the tears of murdered children, spoke the truth. Oh . . . oh, *Almighty above.* How could he live with this pain? So fresh, restored anew? But why pray? There was no Almighty watching. If there had been – and if he'd had a shred of justice to him – Honor would have long ago purged this world of the fraud that was Dalinar Kholin.

And I had the gall to condemn Amaram for killing one squad of men to gain a Shardblade. Dalinar had burned an entire city for less. Thousands upon thousands of people.

'Why did you bond me?' Dalinar whispered to the Stormfather. 'Shouldn't you have picked a man who was just?'

Just? Justice is what you brought to those people.

'That was not justice. That was a massacre.'

The Stormfather rumbled. *I have burned and broken cities myself. I can see . . . yes, I see a difference now. I see pain now. I did not see it before the bond.*

Would Dalinar lose his bond now, in exchange for making the Stormfather increasingly aware of human morality? Why *had* these cursed memories returned? Couldn't he have continued for a little longer without them? Long enough to forge the coalition, to prepare the defense of humankind?

That was the coward's route. Wishing for ignorance. The coward's route he'd obviously taken – though he could not yet remember his visit to the Nightwatcher, he knew what he'd asked for. Relief from this awful burden. The ability to lie, to pretend he had not done such horrible things.

He turned away and walked back into his rooms. He didn't know how he'd face this – bear this burden – but today, he needed to focus on the salvation of Kholinar. Unfortunately, he couldn't make battle plans until he knew more about the city's situation.

He entered the common room, where the core of his government had gathered. Navani and the others sat on some couches around the spanreed, waiting. They'd laid out battle maps of Kholinar, talked over strategies, but then . . . hours had passed with no news.

It felt so frustrating to just sit here, ignorant. And it left Dalinar with too much time to think. To remember.

Instead of sitting with the others, Taravangian had taken his normal place: a seat before the warming fabrial in the corner. Legs aching and back stiff, Dalinar walked over and finally let himself sit, groaning softly as he took the seat beside Taravangian.

Before them, a bright red ruby glowed with heat, replacing a fire with something safer but far more lifeless.

'I'm sorry, Dalinar,' Taravangian finally said. 'I'm sure news will come soon.'

Dalinar nodded. 'Thank you for what you did when the Azish came to tour the tower.'

The Azish had arrived yesterday for an initial tour, but Dalinar had been recovering from the sudden return of his memories. Well . . . truth was, he was *still* recovering. He'd welcomed them, then retired, as Taravangian had offered to lead the tour. Navani said the Azish dignitaries had all been charmed by the elderly king, and planned to return soon for a more in-depth meeting about the possibility of a coalition.

Dalinar leaned forward, staring at the heating fabrial. Behind, Aladar and General Khal conversed – for probably the hundredth time – on how to recover the Kholinar walls, if they were lost by the time the Oathgate started working.

'Have you ever come to the sudden realization,' Dalinar said softly, 'that you're not the man everyone thinks you are?'

'Yes,' Taravangian whispered. 'More daunting, however, are similar moments: when I realize I'm not the man *I* think of myself as being.'

Stormlight swirled in the ruby. Churning. Trapped. Imprisoned.

'We spoke once,' Dalinar said, 'of a leader forced to either hang an innocent man or free three murderers.'

'I remember.'

'How does one live after making a decision like that? Particularly if you eventually discover you made the wrong choice?'

'This is the sacrifice, isn't it?' Taravangian said softly. 'Someone must bear the responsibility. Someone must be dragged down by it, ruined by it. Someone must stain their soul so others may live.'

'But you're a good king, Taravangian. You didn't murder your way to your throne.'

'Does it matter? One wrongly imprisoned man? One murder in an alley that a proper policing force could have stopped? The burden for the blood of those wronged must rest somewhere. I am the sacrifice. *We,* Dalinar Kholin, are the sacrifices. Society offers us up to trudge through dirty water so others may be clean.' He closed his eyes. 'Someone has to fall, that others may stand.'

The words were similar to things Dalinar had said, and thought, for years. Yet Taravangian's version was somehow twisted, lacking hope or life.

Dalinar leaned forward, stiff, feeling old. The two didn't speak for a long period until the others started to stir. Dalinar stood, anxious.

The spanreed was writing. Navani gasped, safehand to her lips. Teshav turned pale, and May Aladar sat back in her seat, looking sick.

The spanreed cut off abruptly and dropped to the page, rolling as it landed.

'What?' Dalinar demanded. 'What does it say?'

Navani looked to him, then glanced away. Dalinar shared a look with General Khal, then Aladar.

Dread settled on Dalinar like a cloak. *Blood of my fathers.* 'What does it say?' he pled.

'The ... the capital has fallen, Dalinar,' Navani whispered. 'The ardent reports that Voidbringer forces have seized the palace. He ... he cut off after only a few sentences. It looks like they found him, and . . .'

She squeezed her eyes shut.

'The team you sent,' Teshav continued, 'has apparently failed, Bright-lord.' She swallowed. 'The remnants of the Wall Guard have been captured and imprisoned. The city has fallen. There is no word on the king, Prince Adolin, or the Radiants. Brightlord . . . the message cuts off there.'

Dalinar sank back down into his chair.

'Almighty above,' Taravangian whispered, grey eyes reflecting the glow of the heating fabrial. 'I am so, *so* sorry, Dalinar.'

Good night, dear Urithiru. Good night, sweet Sibling. Good night, Radiants.

—From drawer 29-29, ruby

T he Oathgate's control building shook like it had been hit by a boulder. Adolin stumbled, then fell to his knees.

The shaking was followed by a distinct *ripping* sound, and a blinding flash of light.

His stomach lurched.

He fell through the air.

Shallan screamed somewhere nearby.

Adolin struck a hard surface, and the impact was so jarring that he rolled to the side. That caused him to tumble off the edge of a white stone platform.

He fell into something that gave way beneath him. Water? No, it didn't feel right. He twisted in it – not a liquid, but *beads*. Thousands upon thousands of glass beads, each smaller than a Stormlight sphere.

Adolin thrashed, panicked as he sank. He was dying! He was going to die and suffocate in this sea of endless beads. He—

Someone caught his hand. Azure pulled him up and helped him back onto the platform, beads rolling from his clothing. He coughed, feeling that he had been drowning, though he'd gotten only a few beads in his mouth.

Stormfather! He groaned, looking around. The sky overhead was wrong. Pitch-black, it was streaked with strange clouds that seemed to stretch forever into the distance – like roads in the sky. They led toward a small, distant sun.

The ocean of beads extended in every direction, and tiny lights hovered above them – thousands upon thousands, like candle flames. Shallan stepped over, kneeling beside him. Nearby, Kaladin was standing up, shaking himself. This circular stone platform was like an island in the ocean of beads, roughly where the control building had been.

Hovering in the air were two enormous spren – they looked like stretched-out versions of people, and stood some thirty feet tall, like sentinels. One was pitch-black in coloring, the other red. He thought them statues at first, but their clothing rippled in the air, and they shifted, one turning eyes down to look at him.

'Oh, this is bad,' someone said nearby. 'So very, very bad.'

Adolin looked and found the speaker to be a creature in a stiff black costume, with a robe that seemed – somehow – to be made of stone. In place of its head was a shifting, changing ball of lines, angles, and impossible dimensions.

Adolin jumped to his feet, scrambling back. He almost collided with a young woman with blue-white skin, pale as snow, wearing a filmy dress that rippled in the wind. Another spren stood beside her, with ashen brown features that seemed to be made of tight cords, the thickness of hair. She wore ragged clothing, and her eyes had been scratched out, like a canvas that someone had taken a knife to.

Adolin looked around, counting them. Nobody else was here on the landing. Those two enormous spren in the sky, and the three smaller ones on the platform. Adolin, Shallan, Kaladin, and Azure.

It seemed the Oathgate had only taken those who had been inside the control building. But *where* had it taken them?

Azure looked up at the sky. 'Damnation,' she said softly. 'I *hate* this place.'

THE END OF

Part Three

INTERLUDES

❖

VENLI • MEM • SHELER

Odium's grand purpose for Venli meant turning her into a showpiece.

'Then, the humans waged a war of extermination against us,' she told the assembled crowd. 'My sister tried to negotiate, to explain that we had no blame for the assassination of their king. They would not listen. They saw us only as slaves to be dominated.'

The wagon upon which she stood wasn't a particularly inspiring dais, but it was better than the pile of boxes she'd used in the last town. At least her new form – envoyform – was tall, the tallest she'd ever worn. It was a form of power, and brought strange abilities, primarily the ability to speak and understand all languages.

That made it perfect for instructing the crowds of Alethi parshmen. 'They fought for *years* to exterminate us,' she said to Command. 'They could not suffer slaves who could think, who could resist. They worked to crush us, lest we inspire a revolution!'

The people gathered around the wagon bore thick lines of marbling – of red and either black or white. Venli's own white and red was far more delicate, with intricate swirls.

She continued, speaking triumphantly to the Rhythm of Command, telling these people – as she'd told many others – her story. At least the version of it that Odium had instructed her to tell.

She told them she'd personally discovered new spren to bond, creating a form that would summon the Everstorm. The story left out that Ulim had done much of the work, giving her the secrets of stormform. Odium obviously wanted to paint the listeners as a heroic group, with Venli their brave leader. The listeners were to be the foundation myth of his growing empire: the last of the old generation, who had fought bravely against the Alethi, then sacrificed themselves to free their enslaved brothers and sisters.

Hauntingly, the narrative said that Venli's people were now extinct, save herself.

The former slaves listened, rapt by her narrative. She told it well; she should, given how often she'd related it these last weeks. She ended with the call to action, as specifically instructed.

'My people have passed, joining the eternal songs of Roshar,' she said. 'The day now belongs to you. We had named ourselves "listeners" because of the songs we heard. These are your heritage, but you are not to merely listen, but sing. Adopt the rhythms of your ancestors and build a nation here! You must *work*. Not for the slavers who once held your minds, but for the future, for your children! And for us. Those who died that you might exist.'

They cheered to the Rhythm of Excitement. That was good to hear, even if it was an inferior rhythm. Venli heard something better now: new, powerful rhythms that accompanied forms of power.

Yet ... hearing those old rhythms awakened something in her. A memory. She put her hand to the pouch at her belt.

How like the Alethi these people act, she thought. She had found humans to be ... stern. Angry. Always walking about with their emotions worn openly, prisoners to what they felt. These former slaves were similar. Even their jokes were Alethi, often biting toward those to whom they were closest.

At the conclusion of her speech, an unfamiliar Voidspren ushered the people back to work. She'd learned there were three levels in the hierarchy of Odium's people. There were these common singers, who wore the ordinary forms Venli's people had used. Then there were those called Regals, like herself, who were distinguished by forms of power – created by bonding one of several varieties of Voidspren. At the top were the Fused – though she had trouble placing spren like Ulim and others. They obviously outranked the common singers, but what of the Regals?

She saw no humans in this town; those had been rounded up or chased off. She'd overheard some Fused saying that human armies still fought in western Alethkar, but this eastern section was completely singer controlled – remarkable, considering how the humans greatly outnumbered the singers. The Alethi collapse was due in part to the Everstorm, in part to the arrival of the Fused, and in part to the fact that the Alethi had repeatedly conscripted eligible men for their wars.

Venli settled down on the back of the cart, and a femalen singer brought her a cup of water, which she took gladly. Proclaiming yourself as the savior of an entire people was thirsty work.

The singer woman lingered. She wore an Alethi dress, with the left hand covered up. 'Is your story really true?'

'Of course it is,' Venli said to Conceit. 'You doubt?'

'No, of course not! It's just . . . it's hard to imagine. Parshmen *fighting*.'

'Call yourselves singers, not parshmen.'

'Yes. Um, of course.' The femalen held her hand to her face, as if embarrassed.

'Speak to the rhythms to express apology,' Venli said. 'Use Appreciation to thank someone for correction, or Anxiety to highlight your frustration. Consolation if you are truly contrite.'

'Yes, Brightness.'

Oh, Eshonai. They have so far to go.

The woman scampered away. That lopsided dress looked ridiculous. There was no reason to distinguish between the genders except in mateform. Humming to Ridicule, Venli hopped down, then walked through the town, head high. The singers wore mostly workform or nimbleform, though a few – like the femalen who had brought the water – wore scholarform, with long hairstrands and angular features.

She hummed to Fury. Her people had spent *generations* struggling to discover new forms, and here these people were given a dozen different options? How could they value that gift without knowing the struggle? They gave Venli deference, bowing like humans, as she approached the town's mansion. She had to admit there was something very satisfying about that.

'What are *you* so smug about?' Rine demanded to Destruction when Venli stepped inside. The tall Fused waited by the window, hovering – as always – a few feet off the ground, his cloak hanging down and resting on the floor.

Venli's sense of authority evaporated. 'I can't help but feel as if I'm among babes, here.'

'If they are babes, you are a toddler.'

A second Fused sat on the floor amid the chairs. That one never spoke. Venli didn't know the femalen's name, and found her constant grin and unblinking eyes . . . upsetting.

Venli joined Rine by the window, looking out at the singers who populated the village. Working the land. Farming. Their lives might not have changed much, but they had their songs back. That meant everything.

'We should bring them human slaves, Ancient One,' Venli said to Subservience. 'I fear that there is too much land here. If you really want these villages to supply your armies, they'll need more workers.'

Rine glanced at her. She'd found that if she spoke to him respectfully – and if she spoke in the ancient tongue – her words were less likely to be dismissed.

'There are those among us who agree with you, child,' Rine said.

'You do not?'

'No. We will need to watch the humans constantly. At any moment, any of them could manifest powers from the enemy. We killed him, and yet he fights on through his Surgebinders.'

Surgebinders. Foolishly, the old songs spoke highly of them. 'How can they bind spren, Ancient One?' she asked to Subservience. 'Humans don't . . . you know . . .'

'So timid,' he said to Ridicule. 'Why is mentioning gemhearts so difficult?'

'They are sacred and personal.' Listener gemhearts were not gaudy or ostentatious, like those of greatshells. Clouded white, almost the color of bone, they were beautiful, intimate things.

'They're a part of you,' Rine said. 'The dead bodies taboo, the refusal to talk of gemhearts – you're as bad as those out there, walking around with one hand covered.'

What? *That* was unfair. She attuned Fury.

'It . . . shocked us when it first happened,' Rine eventually said. 'Humans don't have gemhearts. How could they bond spren? It was unnatural. Yet somehow, their bond was *more powerful than ours*. I always said the same thing, and believe it even more strongly now: We must exterminate them. Our people will never be safe on this world as long as the humans exist.'

Venli felt her mouth grow dry. Distantly, she heard a rhythm. The Rhythm of the Lost? An inferior one. It was gone in a moment.

Rine hummed to Conceit, then turned and barked a command to the crazy Fused. She scrambled to her feet and loped after him as he floated out the door. He was probably going to confer with the town's spren. He'd give orders and warnings, which he usually only did right before they left one town for another. Despite having unpacked her things, working under the assumption she'd be here for the night, now Venli suspected they would soon be moving on.

She went to her room on the second floor of the mansion. As usual, the *luxury* of these buildings astounded her. Soft beds you felt you would sink into. Fine woodworking. Blown-glass vases and crystal sconces on the walls for holding spheres. She'd always hated the Alethi, who had acted like they were benevolent parents encountering wild children to be educated. They had pointedly ignored the culture and advancements of Venli's people, eyeing only the hunting grounds of the greatshells that they – because of translation errors – decided must be the listeners' gods.

Venli felt at the beautiful swirls in the glass of a wall sconce. How had they colored some of it white, but not all of it? Whenever she encountered things like this, she had to remind herself forcefully that the Alethi being *technologically* superior did not make them *culturally* superior. They'd simply had access to more resources. Now that the singers had access to artform, they would be able to create works like this too.

But still . . . it was so beautiful. Could they really *exterminate* the people who had created such beautiful and delicate swirls in the glass? The decorations reminded her of her own pattern of marbling.

The pouch at her waist started vibrating. She wore a listener's leather skirt below a tight shirt, topped with a looser overshirt. Part of Venli's place was to show the singers that someone like them – not some distant, fearsome creature from the past – had brought the storms and freed the singers.

Her eyes lingered on the sconce, and then she dumped out her pouch on the room's stumpweight desk. Spheres bounced free, along with a larger number of uncut gemstones, which her people had used instead.

The little spren rose from where it had been hiding among the light. It looked like a comet when it moved, though sitting still – as it did now – it only glowed like a spark.

'Are you one of them?' she asked softly. 'The spren that move in the sky some nights?'

It pulsed, sending off a ring of light that dissipated like glowing smoke. Then it began zipping through the room, looking at things.

'The room isn't any different from the last one you looked at,' she said to Amusement.

The spren zipped to the wall sconce, where it let off a pulse in awe, then moved to the identical one on the opposite side of the door.

Venli moved to gather her clothing and writings from the drawers in the dresser. 'I don't know why you stay with me. It can't be comfortable in that bag.'

The spren zipped past her, looking in the drawer that she'd opened.

'It's a *drawer*,' she said.

The spren peeked out, then pulsed in a quick blinking succession.

That's Curiosity, she thought, recognizing the rhythm. She hummed it to herself as she packed her things, then hesitated. Curiosity was an old rhythm. Like . . . Amusement, which she'd attuned moments ago. She could hear the normal rhythms again.

She looked at the little spren. 'Is this your doing?' she demanded to Irritation.

It shrank, but pulsed to Resolve.

'What are you hoping to accomplish? Your kind betrayed us. Go find a human to bother.'

It shrank further. Then pulsed to Resolve again.

Bother. Down below, the door slammed open. Rine was back already. 'In the pouch,' she hissed to Command. 'Quickly.'

MEM

There was art to doing laundry.

Sure, everyone knew the basics, just like every child could hum a tune. But did they know how to relax the fibers of a stubborn seasilk dress by returning it to a warm brine, then restore its natural softness by rinsing it and brushing with the grain? Could they spot the difference between a mineral dye from Azir and a floral dye from the Veden slopes? You used different soaps for each one.

Mem toiled at her canvas – which was, in this case, a pair of vivid red trousers. She scooped some powder soap – hog fat based, mixed with fine abrasive – and rubbed at a stain on the leg. She wetted the trousers again, then with a fine brush she worked in the soap.

Oil stains were challenging enough, but this man had gotten blood on the same spot. She had to get the stain out without fading that fine Mycalin red – they got it from a slug on the shores of the Purelake – or ruining the cloth. Mraize did like his clothing to look sharp.

Mem shook her head. What *was* this stain? She had to go through four soaps, then try some of her drying powder, before she got it to budge, and then she moved on to the rest of the suit. Hours passed. Clean this spot, rinse that shirt. Hang it up for all to see. She didn't notice the time until the other Veden washwomen started to leave in clumps, returning to their homes, some of which were empty and cold, their husbands and sons dead in the civil war.

The need for clean clothing outlived disasters. The end of the world could come, but that would only mean more bloodstains to wash. Mem finally stepped back before her drying racks, hands on hips, basking in the accomplishment of a day's work well done.

Drying her hands, Mem went to check on her new assistant, Pom, who was washing underclothes. The dark-skinned woman was obviously of mixed blood, both Easterner and Westerner. She was finishing an under-shirt, and didn't say anything as Mem stepped up beside her.

Storms, why hasn't anyone snatched her up? Mem thought as the gor-geous woman rubbed the shirt, then dunked it, then rubbed it again. Women like Pom didn't usually end up as washgirls, though she did tend to stare daggers at any man who got too close. Maybe that was it.

'Well done,' Mem said. 'Hang that to dry and help me gather the rest of this.' They piled clothing in baskets, then made the short hike through the city.

Vedenar still smelled like smoke to Mem. Not the good smoke of bak-eries, but rather of the enormous pyres that had burned outside on the plain. Her employer lived near the markets, in a large townhome beside some rubble – a lingering reminder of when siege weapons had rained boulders upon Vedenar.

The two washwomen passed guards at the front and headed up the steps. Mem insisted on not using the servants' entrance. Mraize was one of the few who humored her.

'Keep close,' she said to Pom, who dallied once they were inside. They hurried down a long, unornamented corridor, then up a staircase.

People said that servants were invisible. Mem had never found that to be true, particularly around people like Mraize. Not only did the house steward notice if someone so much as moved a candlestick, Mraize's friends were the type who kept careful track of everyone near them. Two of them stood in a doorway Mem passed, a man and woman speaking quietly. Both wore swords, and though they didn't interrupt their conver-sation as the washwomen passed, they watched.

Mraize's quarters were at the top of a staircase. He wasn't there today – he appeared on occasion to drop off dirty clothing, then gallivanted off someplace to find new types of crem to stain his shirts. Mem and Pom went into his den first – he kept his evening jackets there.

Pom froze in the doorway.

'Stop dallying,' Mem reminded her, covering a smile. After stark, empty hallways and stairwells, this overstuffed den *was* a little overwhelming. She'd marveled too, her first time here. A mantel covered in curiosities, each in its own glass display. Deep rugs from Marat. Five paintings of the finest skill, each of a different Herald.

'You were right,' Pom said from behind.

'Of course I was right,' Mem said, setting down her basket in front of the corner wardrobe. 'Mraize – remember, he doesn't want to be called 'master' – is of the finest and most refined taste. He employs *only* the best of—'

She was interrupted by a ripping sound.

It was a sound that inspired terror. The sound of a seam splitting, or of a delicate chemise tearing as it caught on part of a washtub. It was the sound of disaster incarnate. Mem turned to find her new assistant standing on a chair, *attacking* one of Mraize's paintings with a knife.

A piece of Mem's brain stopped working. A whine escaped from the back of her throat and her vision grew dark.

Pom was . . . she was *destroying one of Mraize's paintings.*

'I've been looking for that,' Pom said, stepping back and putting hands on hips, still standing on the chair.

Two guards burst into the room, perhaps drawn by the noise. They looked at Pom and their jaws dropped. In turn, she flipped her knife about in her hand and pointed it threateningly at the men.

Then, horror of horrors, *Mraize himself* appeared behind the soldiers, wearing an evening jacket and slippers. 'What is this ruckus?'

So *refined.* Yes, his face looked like it had seen the wrong side of a sword a couple of times. But he had exquisite taste in clothing and – of course – in garment-care professionals.

'Ah!' he said, noticing Pom. 'Finally! The masterpiece of the Oilsworn was all it took, was it? Excellent!' Mraize shoved out the confused guards, then pulled the door shut. He didn't even seem to notice Mem. 'Ancient One, would you care for something to drink?'

Pom narrowed her eyes at him, then hopped off the chair. She walked quickly to Mraize and used one hand on his chest to push him aside. She pulled open the door.

'I know where Talenelat is,' Mraize said.

Pom froze.

'Yes . . . let's have that drink, shall we?' Mraize asked. 'My *babsk* has been eager to speak with you.' He glanced at Mem. 'Is that my Azish cavalrylord's suit?'

'Um . . . yes . . .'

'You got the aether out of it?'

'The . . . what?'

He strode over and pulled the red trousers out of the basket to inspect them. 'Mem, you are an absolute genius. Not every hunter carries a spear, and this is proof indeed. Go to Condwish and tell him I approve a three-firemark bonus for you.'

'Th-thank you, Mraize.'

'Go collect your bonus, and leave,' Mraize said. 'Note that you will need to find a new washgirl to help you, after today.'

E*shonai would have loved this,* Venli thought as she flew hundreds of feet in the air. Rine and the other Fused carried her by means of linked harnesses. It made her feel like a sack of grain being hauled to market, but it gave her quite an amazing view.

Endless hills of stone. Patches of green, often in the shadows of hillsides. Thick forests snarled with undergrowth to present a unified front against the storms.

Eshonai would have been thrilled; she'd have begun drawing maps, talking about the places she could go.

Venli, on the other hand, spent most of these trips feeling sick to her stomach. Normally she didn't have to suffer for long; towns were close together here in Alethkar. Yet today, her ancestors flew her past many occupied towns without stopping.

Eventually, what first appeared to be another ridge of stones resolved into the walls of a large city, easily twice the size of one of the domes at the Shattered Plains.

Stone buildings and reinforced towers. Marvels and wonders. It had been years since she'd seen Kholinar – only that once, when they'd executed King Gavilar. Now, smoke rose in patches throughout the city, and many of the guard towers had been shattered. The city gates lay broken. Kholinar, it seemed, had been conquered.

Rine and his companions zipped through the air, raising fists toward other Fused. They surveyed the city, then soared out beyond the wall and landed near a bunker outside the city. They waited as Venli undid her harness, then lifted into the air again just high enough that the bottoms of their long cloaks brushed the stones.

'Am I finished with my work, Ancient One?' Venli asked to Subservience. 'Is that why you finally brought me here?'

'Done?' Rine said to Ridicule. 'Child, you haven't even begun. Those little villages were practice. Today, your true labor begins.'

SHELER

'Y ou have three choices,' the Herdazian general said.

He had dark brown skin the color of a weathered stone, and there was a hint of grey in the thin mustache on his upper lip. He stepped up to Sheler, then put his hands to his sides. Remarkably, some men affixed manacles *to the general's own wrists*. What on Roshar?

'Pay attention,' the general said. 'This is important.'

'To the manacles?' Sheler said in Herdazian. Life on the border had forced him to learn the language. 'What is going on here? Do you realize the *trouble* you're in for taking me captive?' Sheler started to stand, but one of the Herdazian soldiers forced him down so hard, his knees rapped against the hard stone floor of the tent.

'You have *three* choices.' The general's manacles clinked as he twisted his hands in them. 'First, you can choose the sword. Now, that might be a clean death. A good beheading rarely hurts. Unfortunately, it won't be a headsman who gets the chance with you. We'll give the sword to the women you abused. Each gets a hack, one after another. How long it goes on will depend on them.'

'This is *outrageous*!' Sheler said. 'I'm a lighteyes of the fifth dahn! I'm cousin to the highlord himself, and—'

'Second option,' the general said, 'is the hammer. We break your legs and arms, then hang you from the cliff by the ocean. You might last until the storm that way, but it will be miserable.'

Sheler struggled to no avail. Captured by *Herdazians*. Their general wasn't even a lighteyes!

The general twisted his hands, then pulled them apart. The manacles clinked to the ground. Nearby, several of his officers grinned, while others groaned. A scribe had tapped off the time, and gave an accounting of the seconds the escape had taken.

The general accepted the applause of several men, then thumped another – a loser in the betting – on his back. Sheler almost seemed forgotten for a moment. Finally, the general turned back to him. 'I wouldn't take the hammer, if I were you. But there's a third option: the hog.'

'I *demand* the right of ransom!' Sheler said. 'You *must* contact my high-prince and accept payment based on my rank!'

'Ransom is for men caught in battle,' the general said. 'Not bastards caught robbing and murdering civilians.'

'My homeland is under invasion!' Sheler shouted. 'I was gathering resources so we might mount a resistance!'

'A resistance is *not* what we caught you mounting.' The general kicked at the manacles by his feet. 'Choose one of the three options. I don't have all day.'

Sheler licked his lips. How had he ended up in this situation? His homeland gone crazy, the parshmen rampaging, his men scattered by *flying* monsters? Now this? The dirty Herdazians obviously weren't going to listen to reason. They . . .

Wait.

'Did you say *hog*?' Sheler asked.

'It lives down by the shore,' the Herdazian general said. 'That's your third option. We grease you, and you wrestle the hog. It's fun for the men to watch. They need sport now and then.'

'And if I do this, you won't kill me?'

'No, but this isn't as easy as you think. I've tried it myself, so I can speak with authority.'

Crazy Herdazians. 'I choose the hog.'

'As you wish.' The general picked up the manacles and handed them to his officer.

'Thought you'd fail these ones for sure,' the officer said. 'The merchant claimed they're from the best Thaylen locksmiths.'

'Doesn't matter how good the lock is, Jerono,' the general said with a grin, 'if the cuffs are loose.' What a ridiculous little man – too-wide smile, a flat nose, a missing tooth. Why, Highlord Amaram would have—

Sheler was jerked to his feet by the chains, then pulled through the camp of Herdazian soldiers on the Alethi border. There were more refugees here than actual fighting men! Give Sheler a single company, and he could rout this entire force.

His insufferable captors led him down an incline, past the cliffs and toward the shore. Soldiers and refugees alike gathered above, jeering and calling. Obviously, the Herdazian general was too frightened to actually *kill* an Alethi officer. So they would humiliate him by making him wrestle a pig. They'd have a good laugh, then send him away smarting.

Idiots. He'd come back with an army.

One man locked Sheler's chain to a metal loop on the stones. Another approached with a pitcher of oil. They poured it over Sheler's head; he sputtered as the liquid ran down his face. 'What is that *stench*?'

Above, someone blew a horn.

'I'd say "good luck," boss,' the Herdazian soldier told Sheler as his companion ran off, 'but I've got three marks on you not lasting a full minute. Still, who knows. When the general was chained down here, he got out in less.'

The ocean started to churn.

'Of course,' the soldier said, 'the general likes this kind of thing. He's a little weird.'

The soldier dashed back up the bank, leaving Sheler locked in place, doused in pungent oil, and gaping as an enormous claw broke the surface of the ocean.

Perhaps 'the hog' was more of a nickname.

Venli's little spren – whom she'd named Timbre – peeked around the room, looking in each corner and shadowed place, like she did each time Venli let her out of the pouch.

Days had passed since Venli had first arrived at Kholinar. And, as Rine had warned, this was her true labor. Venli now gave her presentation a dozen times each day, speaking to groups of singers brought out of the city for the purpose. She wasn't allowed into Kholinar herself. They kept her sequestered in this stormshelter outside, which they called the hermitage.

Venli hummed to Spite as she leaned against the window, annoyed by the incarceration. Even the window had only been installed – cut by a Shardblade and set with thick stormshutters – after her repeated requests. The city outside called to her. Majestic walls, beautiful buildings. It reminded her of Narak ... which, actually, her people hadn't built. In living there, the listeners had profited from the labors of ancient humans, as modern humans had profited from the enslaved singers.

Timbre floated over to her, then hovered by the window, as if to sneak out and look around outside.

'No,' Venli said.

Timbre pulsed to Resolve, then inched forward in the air.

'Stay inside,' Venli said to Command. 'They're watching for spren like you. Descriptions of your kind, and others, have been spread all through the city.'

The little spren backed away, pulsing to Annoyance, before settling in the air beside Venli.

Venli rested her head on her arms. 'I feel like a relic,' she whispered. 'Already I seem like a cast-off ruin from a nearly forgotten day. Are you the reason I feel like that, suddenly? I only get this way when I let you out.'

Timbre pulsed to Peace. Upon hearing that, something stirred deep within Venli: the Voidspren that occupied her gemheart. That spren couldn't think, not like Ulim or the higher Voidspren. It was a thing of emotions and animal instincts, but the bond with it granted Venli her form of power.

She started to wonder. So many of the Fused were obviously unhinged; perhaps their inordinately long lives had taken a toll on their psyches. Wouldn't Odium need new leaders for his people? If she proved herself, could she claim a place among them?

New Fused. New . . . gods?

Eshonai had always worried about Venli's thirst for power, and had cautioned her to control her ambitions. Even Demid, at times, had been worried for her. And now . . . and now they were all dead.

Timbre pulsed to Peace, then to Pleading, then back to Peace.

'I can't,' Venli said to Mourning. 'I can't.'

Pleading. More insistent. The Rhythm of the Lost, of Remembrance, and then Pleading.

'I'm the wrong one,' Venli said to Annoyance. 'I can't do this, Timbre. I can't resist him.'

Pleading.

'I *made* this happen,' she said to Fury. 'Don't you realize that? I'm the one who *caused all this*. Don't plead to me!'

The spren shrank, her light diminishing. Yet she still pulsed to Resolve. Idiot spren. Venli put a hand to her head. Why . . . why was she not more angry about what had happened to Demid, Eshonai, and the others? Could Venli really think about joining the Fused? Those monsters insisted her people were gone, and rebuffed her questions about the thousands of listeners who had survived the Battle of Narak. Were they all . . . *all* being turned into Fused? Shouldn't Venli be thinking about that, not her ambitions?

A form changes the way you think, Venli. Everyone knew that. Eshonai had lectured – incessantly, as had been her way – about not letting the form dictate one's actions. *Control the form, don't let it control you.*

But then, Eshonai had been exemplary. A general and a hero. Eshonai had done her duty.

All Venli had ever wanted was power.

Timbre suddenly pulsed with a flash of light, and zipped away under the bed, terrified.

'Ah,' Venli said to Mourning, looking past the city at the sudden darkening of the sky. The Everstorm. It came about every nine days, and this was the second since her arrival. 'So that's why they didn't bring an evening batch to listen to me.'

She folded her arms, took a deep breath, and hummed to Resolve until she lost track and shifted unconsciously to the Rhythm of Destruction. She didn't close the window. He didn't like that. Instead, she closed her eyes and listened to the thunder. Lightning flashed beyond her eyelids, red and garish. The spren in her *leaped* to feel it, and she grew excited, the Rhythm of Destruction swelling inside her.

Her people might be gone, but this . . . this *power* was worth it. How could she not embrace this?

How long can you keep being two people, Venli? She seemed to hear Eshonai's voice. *How long will you vacillate?*

The storm hit, wind blasting through the window, lifting her . . . and she entered some kind of vision. The building vanished, and she was tossed about in the storm – but she knew that after it passed, she wouldn't be hurt.

Venli eventually dropped onto a hard surface. She hummed to Destruction and opened her eyes, finding herself standing on a platform hanging high in the sky, far above Roshar, which was a blue and brown globe below. Behind her was a deep, black nothingness marred only by a tiny blip that could have been a single star.

That yellow-white star expanded toward her at an awesome speed, swelling, growing, until it overwhelmed her with an incredible flame. She felt her skin melting, her flesh burning away.

You are not telling the story well enough, Odium's voice declared, speaking the ancient tongue. *You grow restless. The Fused inform me of it. This will change or you will be destroyed.*

'Y-yes . . . Lord.' Speaking burned away her tongue. She could no

FOUR

Defy! Sing Beginnings!

ADOLIN • SHALLAN • KALADIN • DALINAR •
NAVANI • SZETH • TARAVANGIAN • VENLI

88

VOICES

EIGHT YEARS AGO

Gavilar was starting to look worn.

Dalinar stood at the back of the king's den, listening with half an ear. The king spoke with the heirs of the highprinces, staying to safe topics, like Gavilar's plans for various civic projects in Kholinar.

He's looking so old, Dalinar thought. *Grey before his time. He needs something to revitalize him.* A hunt, maybe?

Dalinar didn't need to participate in the meeting; his job was to loom. Occasionally, one of the younger men would glance toward the perimeter of the room, and see the Blackthorn there in shadow. Watching.

He saw fires reflected in their eyes, and heard the weeping of children in the back of his mind.

Don't be weak, Dalinar thought. *It's been almost three years.*

Three years, living with what he'd done. Three years, wasting away in Kholinar. He'd assumed it would get better.

It was only getting worse.

Sadeas had carefully spun news of the Rift's destruction to the king's advantage. He'd called it regrettable that the Rifters had forced Kholin action by killing Dalinar's wife, and named it unfortunate that the city had caught fire during the fighting. Gavilar had publicly censured

Dalinar and Sadeas for 'losing the city to flames,' but his denunciation of the Rifters had been far more biting.

The implication was clear. Gavilar didn't *want* to unleash the Blackthorn. Even he couldn't predict what kind of destruction Dalinar would bring. Obviously, such measures were a last resort – and these days, everyone was careful to give him plenty of other options.

So efficient. All it had cost was one city. And possibly Dalinar's sanity.

Gavilar suggested to the gathered lighteyes that they light a fire in the hearth, for warmth. Well, that was the signal that he could leave. Dalinar could not *stand* fire. The scent of smoke smelled like burning skin, and the crackling of flames reminded him only of her.

Dalinar slipped out the back door, stepping into a hallway on the third floor, heading toward his own rooms. He had moved himself and his sons into the royal palace. His own keep reminded him too much of her.

Storms. Standing in that room – looking at the fear in the eyes of Gavilar's guests – had made the pain and memories particularly acute today. He was better on some days. Others . . . felt like today. He needed a stiff drink from his wine cabinet.

Unfortunately, as he rounded through the curved corridor, he smelled incense in the air. Coming from his rooms? Renarin was burning it again.

Dalinar pulled up, as if he'd run up against something solid, then turned on his heel and walked away. It was too late, unfortunately. That scent . . . that was *her* scent.

He strode down to the second floor, passing bloodred carpets, pillared hallways. Where to get something to drink? He couldn't go out into the city, where people acted so terrified of him. The kitchens? No, he wouldn't go begging to one of the palace chefs – who would in turn tiptoe to the king and whisper that the Blackthorn had been at the violets again. Gavilar complained at how much Dalinar drank, but what else did soldiers do when not at war? Didn't he deserve a little relaxation, after all he'd done for this kingdom?

He turned toward the king's throne room, which – as the king was using his den instead – would be empty today. He went in through the servants' entrance and stepped into a small staging room, where food was prepared before being delivered to the king. Using a sapphire sphere for light, Dalinar knelt and rummaged in one of the cupboards. Usually they kept some rare vintages here for impressing visitors.

The cupboards were empty. Damnation. He found nothing but pans, trays, and cups. A few bags of Herdazian spices. He fumed, tapping the counter. Had Gavilar discovered that Dalinar was coming here, and moved the wine? The king thought him a drunkard, but Dalinar indulged only on occasion. On bad days. Drink quieted the sounds of people crying in the back of his mind.

Weeping. Children burning. Begging their fathers to save them from the flames. And Evi's voice, accompanying them all . . .

When was he going to escape this? He was becoming a coward! Nightmares when he tried to sleep. Weeping in his mind whenever he saw fire. Storms take Evi for doing this to him! If she'd acted like an adult instead of a child – if she'd been able to face *duty* or just *reality* for once – she wouldn't have gotten herself killed.

He stomped into the corridor and strode right into a group of young soldiers. They scrambled to the sides of the hallway and saluted. Dalinar tipped his head toward their salutes, trying to keep the thunder from his expression.

The consummate general. That was who he was.

'Father?'

Dalinar pulled up sharply. He'd completely missed that Adolin was among the soldiers. At fifteen, the youth was growing tall and handsome. He got the former from Dalinar. Today, Adolin wore a fashionable suit with far too much embroidery, and boots that were topped by silver.

'That's not a standard-issue uniform, soldier,' Dalinar said to him.

'I know!' Adolin said. 'I had it specially tailored!'

Storms . . . His son was becoming a fop.

'Father,' Adolin said, stepping up and making an eager fist. 'Did you get my message? I've got a bout set up with Tenathar. Father, he's *ranked*. It's a step toward winning my Blade!' He beamed at Dalinar.

Emotions warred inside of Dalinar. Memories of good years spent with his son in Jah Keved, riding or teaching him the sword.

Memories of her. The woman from whom Adolin had inherited that blond hair and that smile. So genuine. Dalinar wouldn't trade Adolin's sincerity for a hundred soldiers in proper uniforms.

But he also couldn't face it right now.

'Father?' Adolin said.

'You're in uniform, soldier. Your tone is too familiar. Is this how I taught you to act?'

Adolin blushed, then put on a stronger face. He didn't wilt beneath the stern words. When censured, Adolin only *tried harder*.

'Sir!' the young man said. 'I'd be proud if you'd watch my bout this week. I think you'll be pleased with my performance.'

Storming child. Who could deny him? 'I'll be there, soldier. And will watch with pride.'

Adolin grinned, saluted, then dashed back to join the others. Dalinar walked off as quickly as he could, to get away from that hair, that wonderful – haunting – smile.

Well, he needed a drink now more than ever. But he would *not* go begging to the cooks. He had another option, one that he was certain even his brother – sly though Gavilar was – wouldn't have considered. He went down another set of steps and reached the eastern gallery of the palace, now passing ardents with shaved heads. It was a sign of his desperation that he came all the way out here, facing their condemning eyes.

He slipped down the stairwell into the depths of the building, entering halls that led toward the kitchens in one direction, the catacombs in the other. A few twists and turns led him out onto the Beggars' Porch: a small patio between the compost heaps and the gardens. Here, a group of miserable people waited for the offerings Gavilar gave after dinner.

Some begged of Dalinar, but a glare made the rag-clothed wretches pull back and cower. At the back of the porch, he found Ahu huddled in the shadows between two large religious statues, their backs facing the beggars, their hands spread toward the gardens.

Ahu was an odd one, even for a crazy beggar. With black, matted hair and a scraggly beard, his skin was dark for an Alethi. His clothing was mere scraps, and he smelled worse than the compost.

Somehow he always had a bottle with him.

Ahu giggled at Dalinar. 'Have you seen me?'

'Unfortunately.' Dalinar settled on the ground. 'I have smelled you too. What are you drinking today? It had better not be water this time, Ahu.'

Ahu wagged a stout, dark bottle. 'Dunno what it is, little child. Tastes good.'

Dalinar tried a sip and hissed. A burning wine, no sweetness to it at all. A white, though he didn't recognize the vintage. Storms . . . it smelled intoxicating.

Dalinar took a chug, then handed the bottle back to Ahu. 'How are the voices?'

'Soft, today. They chant about ripping me apart. Eating my flesh. Drinking my blood.'

'Pleasant.'

'Hee hee.' Ahu snuggled back against the branches of the hedge-wall, as if they were soft silk. 'Nice. Not bad at all, little child. What of your noises?'

In reply, Dalinar reached out his hand. Ahu gave him the bottle. Dalinar drank, welcoming the fuzzing of mind that would quiet the weeping.

'*Aven begah,*' Ahu said. 'It's a fine night for my torment, and no telling the skies to be still. Where is my soul, and who is this in my face?'

'You're a strange little man, Ahu.'

Ahu cackled his response and waved for the wine. After a drink, he returned it to Dalinar, who wiped off the beggar's spittle with his shirt. Storm Gavilar for pushing him to this.

'I like you,' Ahu said to Dalinar. 'I like the pain in your eyes. Friendly pain. Companionable pain.'

'Thanks.'

'Which one got to you, little child?' Ahu asked. 'The Black Fisher? The Spawning Mother, the Faceless? Moelach is close. I can hear his wheezing, his scratching, his scraping at time like a rat breaking through walls.'

'I have no idea what you're talking about.'

'Madness,' Ahu said, then giggled. 'I used to think it wasn't my fault. But you know, we can't escape what we did? *We* let them in. *We* attracted them, befriended them, took them out to dance and courted them. It is *our fault.* You open yourself to it, and you pay the price. They ripped my brain out and made it dance! I watched.'

Dalinar paused, the bottle halfway to his lips. Then he held it out to Ahu. 'Drink this. You need it.'

Ahu obliged.

Sometime later, Dalinar stumbled back to his rooms, feeling downright *serene* – thoroughly smashed and without a crying child to be heard. At the door, he stopped and looked back down the corridor. Where . . . He couldn't remember the trip back up from the Beggars' Porch.

He looked down at his unbuttoned jacket, his white shirt stained with dirt and drink. *Um . . .*

A voice drifted through the closed door. Was that Adolin inside? Dalinar started, then focused. Storms, he'd come to the wrong door.

Another voice. Was that Gavilar? Dalinar leaned in.

'I'm worried about him, Uncle,' Adolin's voice said.

'Your father never adjusted to being alone, Adolin,' the king replied. 'He misses your mother.'

Idiots, Dalinar thought. He didn't miss Evi. He wanted to be *rid* of her.

Though . . . he did ache now that she was gone. Was that why she wept for him so often?

'He's down with the beggars again,' another voice said from inside. Elhokar? That little boy? Why did he sound like a man? He was only . . . how old? 'He tried the serving room again first. Seems he forgot he drank that all last time. Honestly, if there's a bottle hidden in this palace anywhere, that drunken fool will find it.'

'My father is *not* a fool!' Adolin said. 'He's a great man, and you owe him your—'

'Peace, Adolin,' Gavilar said. 'Both of you, hold your tongues. Dalinar is a soldier. He'll fight through this. Perhaps if we go on a trip we can distract him from his loss. Maybe Azir?'

Their voices . . . He had just rid himself of Evi's weeping, but hearing this dragged her back. Dalinar gritted his teeth and stumbled to the proper door. Inside, he found the nearest couch and collapsed.

SEA OF ORACLES

X Kholinar

I rode that mandra from here to Celebrant, so you owe me those silver pieces after all.

Candlemore

Salavashi Trench

SEA OF ORACLES

SEA OF ORACLES

I met Smolderbrand. Stole this map from her.

Smolderbrand Channel

Celebrant

Celebrant Channel

North Hallen Channel

Nor Channel

Emberdark Channel

South Hallen Channel

Emberdark

The Burning Gardens

THE GLASSWATER DEEP

THE LUMINOUS SHALLOWS

Spren fishing is illegal here, but their jail is nicer than most.

Ravizadth

I hate this lake.

X Thayler City

THAYLEN SEA

Avoid at all costs.

Caretaker of Laughter

Salumon the Third Tower

DAMNATION

My research into the Unmade has convinced me that these things were not simply 'spirits of the void' or 'nine shadows who moved in the night.' They were each a specific kind of spren, endowed with vast powers.

—From Hessi's *Mythica,* page 3

Adolin had never bothered imagining what Damnation might look like.

Theology was for women and scribes. Adolin figured he'd try to follow his Calling, becoming the best swordsman he could. The ardents told him that was enough, that he didn't need to worry about things like Damnation.

Yet here he was, kneeling on a white marble platform with a black sky overhead, a cold sun – if it could even be called that – hanging at the end of a roadway of clouds. An ocean of shifting glass beads, clattering against one another. Tens of thousands of flames, like the tips of oil lamps, hovering above that ocean.

And the spren. Terrible, awful spren swarmed in the ocean of beads, bearing a multitude of nightmare forms. They twisted and writhed, howling with inhuman voices. He didn't recognize any of the varieties.

'I'm dead,' Adolin whispered. 'We're dead, and this is Damnation.'

But what of the pretty, blue-white spren girl? The creature with the stiff robe and a mesmerizing, impossible symbol instead of a head? What of the woman with the scratched-out eyes? And those two enormous spren standing overhead, with spears and—

Light exploded to Adolin's left. Kaladin Stormblessed, pulling in power, floated into the air. Beads rattled, and every monster in the writhing throng turned – as if one – to fixate upon Kaladin.

'Kaladin!' the spren girl shouted. 'Kaladin, they feed on Stormlight! You'll draw their attention. *Everything's* attention.'

'Drehy and Skar . . .' Kaladin said. 'Our soldiers. Where are they?'

'They're still on the other side,' Shallan said, standing up beside Adolin. The creature with the twisted head took her arm, steadying her. 'Storms, they might be safer than we are. We're in Shadesmar.'

Some of the lights nearby vanished. Candles' flames being snuffed out.

Many spren swam toward the platform, joining an increasingly large group that churned around it, causing a ruckus in the beads. The majority of them were long eel-like things, with ridges along their backs and purple antennae that squirmed like tongues and seemed to be made of thick liquid.

Beneath them, deep in the beads, something enormous shifted, causing beads to roll off one another in piles.

'Kaladin!' the blue girl shouted. 'Please!'

He looked at her, and seemed to see her for the first time. The Light vanished from him, and he dropped – hard – to the platform.

Azure held her thin Shardblade, gaze fixed on the things swimming through the beads around their platform. The only one who didn't seem frightened was the strange spren woman with the scratched-out eyes and the skin made of rough cloth. Her eyes . . . they weren't empty sockets. Instead she was like a portrait where the eyes had been scraped off.

Adolin shivered. 'So . . .' he said. 'Any idea what is happening?'

'We're not dead,' Azure growled. 'They call this place Shadesmar. It's the realm of thought.'

'I peek into this place when I Soulcast,' Shallan said. 'Shadesmar overlaps the real world, but many things are inverted here.'

'I passed through it when I first came to your land about a year ago,' Azure added. 'I had guides then, and I tried to avoid looking at too much crazy stuff.'

'Smart,' Adolin said. He put his hand to the side to summon his own Shardblade.

The woman with the scratched eyes stretched her head toward him in an unnatural way, then *screeched* with a loud, piercing howl.

Adolin stumbled away, nearly colliding with Shallan and her ... her spren? Was that Pattern?

'That is your sword,' Pattern said in a perky voice. He had no mouth that Adolin could see. 'Hmmm. She is quite dead. I don't think you can summon her here.' He cocked his bizarre head, looking at Azure's Blade. 'Yours is different. Very curious.'

The thing deep beneath their platform shifted again.

'That is probably bad,' Pattern noted. 'Hmmm ... yes. Those spren above us are the souls of the Oathgate, and that one deep beneath us is likely one of the Unmade. It must be very large on this side.'

'So what do we do?' Shallan asked.

Pattern looked in one direction, then the other. 'No boat. Hmmm. Yes, that *is* a problem, isn't it?'

Adolin spun around. Some of the eel-like spren climbed onto the platform, using stumpy legs that Adolin had missed earlier. Those long purple antennae stretched toward him, wiggling. . . .

Fearspren, he realized. Fearspren were little globs of purple goo that looked exactly like the tips of those antennae.

'We need to get off this platform,' Shallan said. 'Everything else is secondary. Kaladin ...' She trailed off as she glanced toward him.

The bridgeman knelt on the stone, head bowed, shoulders slumped. Storms ... Adolin had been forced to carry him away from the battle, numb and broken. Looked like that emotion had caught up to him again.

Kaladin's spren – Adolin could only guess that was the identity of the pretty girl in blue – stood beside him, one hand resting protectively on his back. 'Kaladin's not well,' she said.

'I have to be well,' Kaladin said, his voice hoarse as he climbed back to his feet. His long hair fell across his face, obscuring his eyes. Storms. Even surrounded by monsters, the bridgeman could look intimidating. 'How do we get to safety? I can't fly us without attracting attention.'

'This place is the inverse of your world,' Azure said. She stepped back from a long antenna exploring in her direction. 'Where there are larger bodies of water on Roshar, we will have land here, correct?'

'Mmm,' Pattern said, nodding.

'The river?' Adolin asked. He tried to orient himself, looking past the thousands of floating lights. 'There.' He pointed at a lump he could barely spot in the distance. Like a long island.

Kaladin stared at it, frowning. 'Can we swim in these beads?'

'No,' Adolin said, remembering what it had felt like to fall into this ocean. 'I . . .'

The beads rattled and clacked against one another as the large thing surged beneath. In the near distance, a single spire of rock broke the surface, tall and black. It emerged like a mountain peak slowly lifting from the sea, beads rattling in waves around it. As it grew to the height of a building, a *joint* appeared. Storms. It wasn't a spire or a mountain . . . it was a claw.

More emerged in other directions. An enormous hand was reaching slowly upward through the glass beads. Deep beneath them a heartbeat began sounding, rattling the beads.

Adolin stumbled back, horrified, and nearly slipped into the bead ocean. He kept his balance, barely, and found himself face-to-face with the woman with scratches for eyes. She stared at him, completely emotionless, as if waiting for him to try to summon his Shardblade so she could scream again.

Damnation. No matter what Azure said, he was certainly in Damnation.

∻

'What do I do?' Shallan whispered. She knelt on the white stone of the platform, searching among the beads. Each gave her an impression of an object in the Physical Realm. A dropped shield. A vase from the palace. A scarf.

Nearby, hundreds of little spren – like little orange or green *people*, only a few inches tall – were climbing among the spheres. She ignored those, searching for the soul of something that would help.

'Shallan,' Pattern said, kneeling. 'I don't think . . . I don't think Soulcasting will accomplish anything? It will change an object in the other realm, but not here.'

'What *can* I do here?' Those spines or claws or whatever rose around them, inevitable, deadly.

Pattern hummed, hands clasped before him. His fingers were too smooth, as if they were chiseled of obsidian. His head shifted and changed, going through its sequence – the spherical mass was never the same, yet somehow still always felt like him.

'My memory . . .' he said. 'I don't remember.'

Stormlight, Shallan thought. Jasnah had told her to never enter Shadesmar without Stormlight. Shallan pulled a sphere from her pocket – she still wore Veil's outfit. The beads nearby reacted, trembling and rolling toward her.

'Mmmm . . .' Pattern said. 'Dangerous.'

'I doubt staying here will be better,' Shallan said. She sucked in a little Stormlight, only one mark's worth. As before, the spren didn't seem to notice her use of Stormlight as much as they had Kaladin's. She rested her freehand against the surface of the ocean. Beads stopped rolling and instead clicked together beneath her hand. When she pushed down, they resisted.

Good first step, she thought, drawing in more Stormlight. The beads pressed around her hand, gathering, rolling onto one another. She cursed, worried that she'd soon just have a big pile of beads.

'Shallan,' Pattern said, poking at one of the beads. 'Perhaps this?'

It was the soul of the shield she'd felt earlier. She moved the sphere to her gloved safehand, then pressed her other hand to the ocean. She used that bead's soul as a guide – much like she used a Memory as a guide for doing a sketch – and the other beads obediently rolled together and locked into place, forming an imitation of the shield.

Pattern stepped out onto it, then jumped up and down happily. Her shield held him without sinking, though he seemed as heavy as an ordinary person. Good enough. Now she just needed something big enough to hold them all. Preferably, as she considered, two somethings.

'You, sword lady!' Shallan said, pointing at Azure. 'Help me over here. Adolin, you too. Kaladin, see if you can brood this place into submission.'

Azure and Adolin hurried over.

Kaladin turned, frowning. 'What?'

Don't think about that haunted look in his eyes, Shallan thought. *Don't think about what you've done in bringing us here, or how it happened. Don't think, Shallan.*

Her mind went blank, like it did in preparation for drawing, then locked on to her task.

Find a way out.

'Everybody,' she said, 'those flames are the souls of people, while these spheres represent the souls of objects. Yes, there are huge philosophical implications in that. Let's try to ignore them, shall we? When you touch a bead, you should be able to sense what it represents.'

Azure sheathed her Shardblade and knelt, feeling at the spheres. 'I can ... Yes, there's an impression to each one.'

'We need the soul of something long and flat.' Shallan plunged her hands into the spheres, eyes closed, letting the impressions wash over her.

'I can't sense anything,' Adolin said. 'What am I doing wrong?' He sounded overwhelmed, but don't think about that.

Look. Fine clothing that hadn't been taken out of its trunk in a long, long time. So old that it saw the dust as part of itself.

Withering fruit that understood its purpose: decompose and stick its seeds to the rock, where they could hopefully weather storms long enough to sprout and gain purchase.

Swords, recently swung and glorying in their purpose fulfilled. Other weapons belonged to dead men, blades that had the faintest inkling that they'd failed somehow.

Living souls bobbed around, a swarm of them entering the Oathgate control chamber. One brushed Shallan. Drehy the bridgeman. For a brief moment she *felt* what it was like to be him. Worried for Kaladin. Panicked that nobody was in charge, that he would have to take command. He wasn't a commander. You couldn't be a rebel if you were in charge. He liked being told what to do – that way he could find a method to do it with style.

Drehy's worries caused her own to bubble up. *The bridgemen's powers will fade without Kaladin,* she thought. *What of Vathah, Red, and Ishnah? I didn't*—

Focus. Something reached out from the back of her mind, grabbed those thoughts and feelings, and yanked them into the darkness. Gone.

She brushed a bead with her fingers. A large door, like a keep's gate. She grabbed the sphere and shifted it to her safehand. Unfortunately, the next bead she touched was the palace *itself.* Momentarily stunned by the majesty of it, Shallan gaped. She held the entire palace in her *hand.*

Too large. She dropped it and kept searching.

Trash that still saw itself as a child's toy.

A goblet that had been made from melted-down nails, taken from an old building.

There. She seized hold of a sphere and pressed Stormlight into it. A building rose before her, made entirely out of beads: a copy of the Oathgate control building. She managed to make its top rise only a few feet above the surface, most of the building sinking into the depths. The rooftop was within reach.

'On top of it!' she shouted.

She held the replica in place as Pattern scrambled onto the roof. Adolin followed, trailed by that ghostly spren and Azure. Finally, Kaladin picked up his pack and walked with his spren onto the rooftop.

Shallan joined them with the aid of a hand from Adolin. She clutched the sphere that was the soul of the building, and tried to make the bead structure move through the sea like a raft.

It resisted, sitting there motionless. Well, she had another plan. She scurried to the other side of the roof and stretched down, held by Pattern, to touch the sea again. She used the soul of the large door to make another standing platform. Pattern jumped down, followed by Adolin and Azure.

Once they'd all piled precariously on the door, Shallan let go of the building. It crashed down behind them, beads falling in a tumult, frightening some of the little green spren crawling among the beads nearby.

Shallan reconstructed the building on the other side of the door, with only the rooftop showing. They filed across.

They progressed like that – following building with door and door with building – inching toward that distant land. Each iteration took Stormlight, though she could reclaim some from each creation before it collapsed. Some of the eel-like spren with the long antennae followed them, curious, but the rest of the varieties – and there were dozens – let them pass without much notice.

'Mmm . . .' Pattern said. 'Much emotion on the other side. Yes, this is good. It distracts them.'

The work was tiring and tedious, but step by step, Shallan moved them away from the frothing mess of the city of Kholinar. They passed the frightened lights of souls, the hungry spren who feasted on the emotions from the other side.

'Mmm . . .' Pattern whispered to her. 'Look, Shallan. The lights of souls are no longer disappearing. People must be surrendering in Kholinar. I know you do not like the destruction of your own.'

That *was* good, but not unexpected. The parshmen had never massacred civilians, though she couldn't say for certain what happened to Azure's soldiers. She hoped fervently they were able to either escape or surrender.

Shallan had to edge her group frighteningly close to two of the spines that had emerged from the depths. Those gave no sign of having noticed them. Beyond, they reached a calmer space out among the beads. A place where the only sound came from the clacking of glass.

'She corrupted them,' Kaladin's spren whispered.

Shallan took a break, wiping her brow with a handkerchief from her satchel. They were distant enough that the lights of souls in Kholinar were just a general haze of light.

'What was that, spren?' Azure asked. 'Corrupted?'

'That's why we're here. The Oathgate – do you remember those two spren in the sky? Those two are the gateway's soul, but the red coloring . . . They must be His now. That's why we ended up here, instead of going to Urithiru.'

Sja-anat, Shallan thought, *said she was supposed to kill us. But that she'd try not to.*

Shallan wiped her brow again, then got back to work.

⁘

Adolin felt useless.

All his life, he had understood. He'd taken easily to dueling. People naturally seemed to like him. Even in his darkest moment – standing on the battlefield and watching Sadeas's armies retreat, abandoning him and his father – he'd *understood* what was happening to him.

Not today. Today he was just a confused little boy standing in Damnation.

Today, Adolin Kholin was nothing.

He stepped onto another copy of the door. They had to huddle together while Shallan dismissed the rooftop behind, sending it crashing down, then squeezed past everyone to raise another copy of the building.

Adolin felt small. So very small. He started toward the rooftop. Kaladin, however, remained standing on the door, staring sightlessly. Syl, his spren, tugged his hand.

'Kaladin?' Adolin asked.

Kaladin finally shook himself and gave in to Syl's prodding. He walked onto the rooftop. Adolin followed, then took Kaladin's pack – deliberately but firmly – and swung it over his own shoulder. Kaladin let him. Behind, the doorway shattered back into the ocean of beads.

'Hey,' Adolin said. 'It will be all right.'

'I survived Bridge Four,' Kaladin growled. 'I'm strong enough to survive this.'

'I'm pretty sure you could survive anything. Storms, bridgeboy, the Almighty used some of the same stuff he put into Shardblades when he made you.'

Kaladin shrugged. But as they walked onto the next platform, his expression grew distant again. He stood while the rest of them moved on. Almost like he was waiting for their bridge to dissolve and dump him into the sea.

'I couldn't make them see,' Kaladin whispered. 'I couldn't ... couldn't protect them. I'm supposed to be able to *protect* people, aren't I?'

'Hey,' Adolin said. 'You really think that strange spren with the weird eyes is my sword?'

Kaladin started and focused on him, then scowled. 'Yes, Adolin. I thought that was clear.'

'I was just wondering.' Adolin glanced over his shoulder and shivered. 'What do you think about this place? Have you ever heard of anything like it?'

'Do you *have* to talk right now, Adolin?'

'I'm frightened. I talk when I'm frightened.'

Kaladin glared at him as if suspecting what Adolin was doing. 'I know little of this place,' he finally answered. 'But I think it's where spren are born....'

Adolin kept him talking. As Shallan created each new platform, Adolin would lightly touch Kaladin on the elbow or shoulder and the bridgeman would step forward. Kaladin's spren hovered nearby, but she let Adolin guide the conversation.

Slowly they approached the strip of land, which turned out to be made of a deep, glassy black stone. Kind of like obsidian. Adolin got Kaladin across onto the land, then settled him with his spren. Azure followed, her shoulders sagging. In fact, her ... her *hair* was fading. It was the strangest thing; Adolin watched it dim from Alethi jet-black to a faint grey as she sat down. Must be another effect of this strange place.

How much did she know of Shadesmar? He'd been so focused on Kaladin, he hadn't thought to interrogate her. Unfortunately, he was so tired right now, he was having trouble thinking straight.

Adolin stepped back onto the platform as Pattern stepped off. Shallan looked as if she was about to collapse. She stumbled, and the platform ruptured. He managed to grab her, and fortunately they only fell to waist-deep in the beads before their feet touched ground. The little balls of glass seemed to slide and move too easily, not supporting their weight.

Adolin had to practically haul Shallan through the tide of beads up onto the bank. There, she toppled backward, groaning and closing her eyes.

'Shallan?' he asked, kneeling beside her.

'I'm fine. It just took . . . concentration. Visualization.'

'We need to find another way back to our world,' Kaladin said, seated nearby. 'We can't rest. They're fighting. We need to help them.'

Adolin surveyed his companions. Shallan lay on the ground; her spren had joined her, lying in a similar posture and looking up at the sky. Azure slumped forward, her small Shardblade across her lap. Kaladin continued to stare at nothing with haunted eyes, his spren hovering behind him, worried.

'Azure,' Adolin said, 'is it safe here, on this land?'

'As safe as anywhere in Shadesmar,' she said tiredly. 'The place can be dangerous if you attract the wrong spren, but there isn't anything we can do about that.'

'Then we camp here.'

'But –' Kaladin said.

'We camp,' Adolin said. Gentle, but firm. 'We can barely stand up straight, bridgeman.'

Kaladin didn't argue further. Adolin scouted up the bank, though each step felt like it was weighted with stone. He found a small depression in the glassy stone and – with some urging – got the rest of them to move to it.

As they made improvised beds from their coats and packs, Adolin looked one last time at the city, standing witness to the fall of his birthplace.

Storms, he thought. *Elhokar . . . Elhokar is dead.*

Little Gav had been taken, and Dalinar was planning to abdicate. Third in line was . . . Adolin himself.

King.

REBORN

I have done my best to separate fact from fiction, but the two blend like mixing paint when the Voidbringers are involved. Each of the Unmade has a dozen names, and the powers ascribed to them range from the fanciful to the terrifying.

—From Hessi's *Mythica*, page 4

Szeth-son-son . . .
      Szeth-son . . .
      Szeth, Truthless . . .
Szeth. Just Szeth.

Szeth of Shinovar, once called the Assassin in White, had been reborn. Mostly.

The Skybreakers whispered of it. Nin, Herald of Justice, had restored him following his defeat in the storm. Like most things, death had not been Szeth's to claim. The Herald had used a type of fabrial to heal his body before his spirit departed.

It had *almost* taken too long, however. His spirit hadn't properly reattached to his body.

Szeth walked with the others out onto the stone field before their small fortress, which overlooked the Purelake. The air was humid, almost like that of his homeland, though it didn't smell earthy or alive. It smelled of seaweed and wet stone.

There were five other hopefuls, all of them younger than Szeth. He was shortest among them, and the only one who kept his head bald. He couldn't grow a full head of hair, even if he didn't shave it.

The other five kept their distance from him. Perhaps it was because of the way he left a glowing afterimage when he moved: a sign of his soul's improper reattachment. Not all could see it, but these could. They were close enough to the Surges.

Or maybe they feared him because of the black sword in a silver sheath that he wore strapped to his back.

Oh, it's the lake! the sword said in his mind. It had an eager voice that didn't sound distinctly feminine or masculine. *You should draw me, Szeth! I would love to see the lake. Vasher says there are magic fish here. Isn't that interesting?*

'I have been warned, sword-nimi,' Szeth reminded the weapon, 'not to draw you except in the case of extreme emergency. And only if I carry much Stormlight, lest you feed upon my soul.'

Well, I wouldn't do that, the sword said. It made a huffing sound. *I don't think you're evil at all, and I only destroy things that are evil.*

The sword was an interesting test, given him by Nin the Herald – called Nale, Nalan, or Nakku by most stonewalkers. Even after weeks of carrying this black sword, Szeth did not understand what the experience was to teach him.

The Skybreakers arranged themselves to watch the hopefuls. There were some fifty here, and that didn't count the dozens who were supposedly out on missions. So *many*. An entire order of Knights Radiant had survived the Recreance and had been watching for the Desolation for two thousand years, constantly replenishing their numbers as others died of old age.

Szeth would join them. He would accept their training, as Nin had promised him he would receive, then travel to his homeland of Shinovar. There, he would bring justice to the ones who had falsely exiled him.

Do I dare bring them judgment? a part of him wondered. *Dare I trust myself with the sword of justice?*

The sword replied. *You? Szeth, I think you're super trustworthy. And I'm a good judge of people.*

'I was not speaking to you, sword-nimi.'

I know. But you were wrong, and so I had to tell you. Hey, the voices seem quiet today. That's nice, isn't it?

Mentioning it brought the whispers to Szeth's attention. Nin had not healed Szeth's madness. He'd called it an effect of Szeth's connection to the powers, and said that he was hearing trembles from the Spiritual Realm. Memories of the dead he'd killed.

He no longer feared them. He had died and been forced to return. He had failed to join the voices, and now they ... they had no power over him, right?

Why, then, did he still weep in the night, terrified?

One of the Skybreakers stepped forward. Ki was a golden-haired woman, tall and imposing. Skybreakers clothed themselves in the garb of local lawkeepers – so here, in Marabethia, they wore a patterned shoulder cloak and a colorful skirtlike wrap. Ki wore no shirt, merely a simple cloth tied around her chest.

'Hopefuls,' she said in Azish, 'you have been brought here because a full Skybreaker has vouched for your dedication and solemnity.'

She's boring, the sword said. *Where did Nale go?*

'You said he was boring too, sword-nimi,' Szeth whispered.

That's true, but interesting things happen around him. We need to tell him that you should draw me more often.

'Your first training has already been completed,' Ki said. 'You traveled with the Skybreakers and joined them in one of their missions. You have been evaluated and deemed worthy of the First Ideal. Speak it. You know the Words.'

Vasher always drew me, the sword said, sounding resentful.

'Life before death,' Szeth said, closing his eyes. 'Strength before weakness. Journey before destination.'

The other five belted it out. Szeth whispered it to the voices that called to him from the darkness. Let them see. He would bring justice to those who had caused this.

He'd hoped that the first oath would restore his ability to draw upon Stormlight – something he had lost along with his previous weapon. However, when he removed a sphere from his pocket, he was unable to access the Light.

'In speaking this ideal,' Ki said, 'you are officially pardoned for any past misdeeds or sins. We have paperwork signed by proper authorities for this region.

'To progress further among our ranks, and to learn the Lashings, you will need a master to take you as their squire. Then may you speak the Second Ideal. From there, you will need to impress a highspren and form a bond — becoming a full Skybreaker. Today you will take the first of many tests. Though we will evaluate you, remember that the final measure of your success or failure belongs to the highspren. Do you have any questions?'

None of the other hopefuls said anything, so Szeth cleared his throat. 'There are five Ideals,' he said. 'Nin told me of this. You have spoken them all?'

'It's been centuries since anyone mastered the Fifth Ideal,' Ki said. 'One becomes a full Skybreaker by speaking the Third Ideal, the Ideal of Dedication.'

'We can . . . know what the Ideals are?' Szeth asked. For some reason, he'd thought they would be hidden from him.

'Of course,' Ki said. 'You will find no games here, Szeth-son-Neturo. The First Ideal is the Ideal of Radiance. You have spoken it. The second is the Ideal of Justice, an oath to seek and administer justice.

'The Third Ideal, the Ideal of Dedication, requires you to have first bonded a highspren. Once you have, you swear to dedicate yourself to a greater truth — a code to follow. Upon achieving this, you will be taught Division, the second — and more dangerous — of the Surges we practice.'

'Someday,' another Skybreaker noted, 'you may achieve the Fourth Ideal: the Ideal of Crusade. In this, you choose a personal quest and complete it to the satisfaction of your highspren. Once successful, you become a master like ourselves.'

Cleanse Shinovar, Szeth thought. That would be his quest. 'What is the Fifth Ideal?' he asked.

'The Ideal of Law,' Ki said. 'It is difficult. You must become law, become truth. As I said, it has been centuries since that was achieved.'

'Nin told me we were to *follow* the law — something external, as men are changeable and unreliable. How can we become the law?'

'Law must come from somewhere,' another of the Skybreaker masters said. 'This is not an oath you will swear, so don't fixate upon it. The first three will do for most Skybreakers. I was of the Third Ideal for two decades before achieving the Fourth.'

When nobody else asked further questions, experienced Skybreakers began Lashing the hopefuls into the air.

'What is happening?' Szeth asked.

'We will carry you to the place of the test,' Ki said, 'as you cannot move with your own Stormlight until you swear the Second Ideal.'

'Do I belong with these youths?' Szeth said. 'Nin treated me as something different.' The Herald had taken him on a mission to Tashikk, hunting Surgebinders from other orders. A heartless act that Nin had explained would prevent the coming of the Desolation.

Except that it had not. The Everstorm's return had convinced Nin he was wrong, and he'd abandoned Szeth in Tashikk. Weeks had passed there until Nin had returned to collect him. The Herald had dropped Szeth here at the fortress, then had vanished into the sky again, this time off to 'seek guidance.'

'The Herald,' Ki said, 'originally thought that you might skip to the Third Ideal because of your past. He is no longer here, however, and we cannot judge. You'll have to follow the same path as everyone else.'

Szeth nodded. Very well.

'No further complaints?' Ki asked.

'It is orderly,' Szeth said, 'and you have explained it well. Why would I complain?'

The others seemed to like this response, and Ki herself Lashed him into the sky. For a moment he felt the freedom of flight – reminding him of his first days, holding an Honorblade long ago. Before he'd become Truthless.

No. You were never Truthless. Remember that.

Besides, this flight was not truly his. He continued falling upward until another Skybreaker caught him and Lashed him downward, counteracting the first effect and leaving him hovering.

A pair of Skybreakers took him, one under each arm, and the entire group soared through the air. He couldn't imagine they'd done this sort of thing in the past, as they'd remained hidden for so many years. But they didn't seem to care about secrecy anymore.

I like it up here, the sword said. *You can see everything.*

'Can you actually see things, sword-nimi?'

Not like a man. You *see all kinds of things, Szeth. Except, unfortunately, how useful I am.*

*I should point out that although many personalities and motives are
ascribed to them, I'm convinced that the Unmade were still* spren. *As
such, they were as much manifestations of concepts or divine forces
as they were individuals.*

—From Hessi's *Mythica,* page 7

Kaladin remembered cleaning crem off the bunker floor while in
Amaram's army.

That sound of chisel on stone reminded Kal of his mother.
He knelt on kneepads and scraped at the crem, which had seeped in
under doors or had been tracked in on the boots of soldiers, creating an
uneven patina on the otherwise smooth floor. He wouldn't have thought
that soldiers would care that the ground wasn't level. Shouldn't he be
sharpening his spear, or . . . or oiling something?

Well, in his experience, soldiers spent little time doing soldier things.
They instead spent ages walking places, waiting around, or – in his case
– getting yelled at for walking around or waiting in the wrong places.
He sighed as he worked, using smooth even strokes, like his mother had
taught him. Get underneath the crem and push. You could lift it up in
flat sections an inch or more wide. Much easier than chipping at it from
above.

A shadow darkened the door, and Kal glanced over his shoulder, then hunkered down farther. *Great.*

Sergeant Tukks walked to one of the bunks and settled down, the wood groaning under his weight. Younger than the other sergeants, he had features that were . . . off somehow. Perhaps it was his short stature, or his sunken cheeks.

'You do that well,' Tukks said.

Kal continued to work, saying nothing.

'Don't feel so bad, Kal. It's not unusual for a new recruit to pull back. Storms. It's not so uncommon to freeze in *battle*, let alone on the practice field.'

'If it's so common,' Kal muttered, 'why am *I* being punished?'

'What, this? A little cleaning duty? Kid, this isn't punishment. This is to help you fit in.'

Kal frowned, leaning back and looking up. 'Sergeant?'

'Trust me. Everyone was waiting for you to get a dressing-down. The longer you went without one, the longer you were going to feel like the odd man out.'

'I'm scraping floors because I *didn't* deserve to be punished?'

'That, and for talking back to an officer.'

'He wasn't an officer! He was just a lighteyes with—'

'Better to stop that kind of behavior *now*. Before you do it to someone who matters. Oh, don't glower, Kal. You'll understand eventually.'

Kal attacked a particularly stubborn knob of crem near the leg of a bunk.

'I found your brother,' Tukks noted.

Kaladin's breath caught.

'He's in the Seventh,' Tukks said.

'I need to go to him. Can I be transferred? We weren't supposed to be split apart.'

'Maybe I can get him moved here, to train with you.'

'He's a messenger! He's not supposed to train with the spear.'

'Everyone trains, even the messenger boys,' Tukks said.

Kal gripped his chisel tightly, fighting down the urge to stand up and go looking for Tien. Didn't they understand? Tien couldn't hurt *cremlings.* He'd catch the things and usher them outside, talking to them like pets. The image of him holding a spear was ludicrous.

Tukks took out some fathom bark and started chewing. He leaned back on the bunk and put his feet up on the footboard. 'Make sure you get that spot to your left.'

Kaladin sighed, then moved to the indicated place.

'Do you want to talk about it?' Tukks asked. 'The moment when you froze during practice?'

Stupid crem. Why did the Almighty make it?

'Don't be ashamed,' Tukks continued. 'We practice so you can freeze now, instead of when it will get you killed. You face down a squad, knowing they want to kill you even though they've never met you. And you hesitate, thinking it can't possibly be true. You can't possibly be here, preparing to fight, to bleed. Everyone feels that fear.'

'I wasn't afraid of getting hurt,' Kal said softly.

'You won't get far if you can't admit to a little fear. Emotion is good. It's what defines us, makes us—'

'I wasn't afraid of getting hurt.' Kaladin took a deep breath. 'I was afraid of *making* someone hurt.'

Tukks twisted the bark in his mouth, then nodded. 'I see. Well, that's another problem. Not unusual either, but a different matter indeed.'

For a time, the only sound in the large barrack was that of chisel on stone. 'How do you do it?' Kal finally asked, not looking up. 'How can you hurt people, Tukks? They're just poor darkeyed slobs like us.'

'I think about my mates,' Tukks said. 'I can't let the lads down. My squad is my family now.'

'So you kill someone else's family?'

'Eventually, we'll be killing shellheads. But I know what you mean, Kal. It's hard. You'd be surprised how many men look in the face of an enemy and find that they're simply not capable of hurting another person.'

Kal closed his eyes, letting the chisel slip from his fingers.

'It's good you aren't so eager,' Tukks said. 'Means you're sane. I'll take ten unskilled men with earnest hearts over one callous idiot who thinks this is all a game.'

The world doesn't make sense, Kal thought. His father, the consummate surgeon, told him to avoid getting too wrapped up in his patients' emotions. And here was a career killer, telling him *to* care?

Boots scraped on stone as Tukks stood up. He walked over and rested one hand on Kal's shoulder. 'Don't worry about the war, or even the battle.

Focus on your squadmates, Kal. Keep *them* alive. Be the man *they* need.'
He grinned. 'And get the rest of this floor scraped. I think when you come
to dinner, you'll find the rest of the squad more friendly. Just a hunch.'

That night, Kaladin discovered that Tukks was right. The rest of the
men *did* seem more welcoming, now that he'd been disciplined. So Kal
held his tongue, smiled, and enjoyed the companionship.

He never told Tukks the truth. When Kal had frozen on the practice
field, it hadn't been out of fear. He'd been very sure he *could* hurt someone.
In fact, he'd realized that he could kill, if needed.

And that was what had terrified him.

⁂

Kaladin sat on a chunk of stone that looked like melted obsidian. It grew
right out of the ground in Shadesmar, this place that didn't seem real.

The distant sun hadn't shifted in the sky since they'd arrived. Nearby,
one of the strange fearspren crawled along the banks of the sea of glass
beads. As big as an axehound, but longer and thinner, it looked vaguely
like an eel with stumpy legs. The purple feelers on its head wiggled and
shifted, flowing in his direction. When it didn't sense anything in him
that it wanted, it continued along the bank.

Syl didn't make any noise as she approached, but he caught sight of
her shadow coming up from behind – like other shadows here, it pointed
toward the sun. She sat down on the lump of glass next to him, then
thumped her head sideways, resting it on his arm, her hands in her lap.

'Others still asleep?' Kaladin asked.

'Yup. Pattern's watching over them.' She wrinkled her nose. 'Strange.'

'He's nice, Syl.'

'That's the strange part.'

She swung her legs out in front of her, barefoot as usual. It seemed
odder here on this side where she was human size. A small flock of spren
flew above them, with bulbous bodies, long wings, and flowing tails. Instead of a head, each one had a golden ball floating right in front of the
body. That seemed familiar. . . .

Gloryspren, he thought. It was like the fearspren, whose antennae manifested in the real world. Only part of the actual spren showed there.

'So . . .' Syl said. 'Not going to sleep?'

Kaladin shook his head.

'Now, I might not be an *expert* on humans,' she said. 'For example, I still haven't figured out why only a handful of your cultures seem to worship me. But I do think I heard somewhere that you have to sleep. Like, every night.'

He didn't respond.

'Kaladin . . .'

'What about you?' he said, looking away, along the isthmus of land that marked where the river was in the real world. 'Don't you sleep?'

'Have I ever needed sleep?'

'Isn't this your land? Where you come from? I figured you'd . . . I don't know . . . be more mortal here.'

'I'm still a spren,' she said. 'I'm a little piece of God. Did you miss the part about worshipping me?'

When he didn't reply, she poked him in the side. 'You were supposed to say something sarcastic there.'

'Sorry.'

'We don't sleep; we don't eat. I think we might feed off humans, actually. Your emotions. Or you thinking about us, maybe. It all seems very complicated. In Shadesmar, we can think on our own, but if we go to your realm, we need a human bond. Otherwise, we're practically as mindless as those gloryspren.'

'But how did you make the transition?'

'I . . .' She adopted a distant expression. 'You called for me. Or, no, I knew that you would *someday* call for me. So I transferred to the Physical Realm, trusting that the honor of men lived, unlike what my father always said.'

Her father. The *Stormfather*.

It was so strange to be able to feel her head on his arm. He was accustomed to her having very little substance.

'Could you transfer again?' Kaladin asked. 'To carry word to Dalinar that something might be wrong with the Oathgates?'

'I don't think so. You're here, and my bond is to you.' She poked him again. 'But this is all a distraction from the real problem.'

'You're right. I need a weapon. And we'll need to find food somehow.'

'Kaladin . . .'

'Are there trees on this side? This obsidian might make a good spearhead.'

She lifted her head from his arm and looked at him with wide, worried eyes.

'I'm fine, Syl,' he said. 'I just lost my focus.'

'You were basically catatonic.'

'I won't let it happen again.'

'I'm not *complaining*.' She wrapped her arms around his right arm, like a child clinging to a favored toy. Worried. Frightened. 'Something's wrong inside you. But I don't know what.'

I've never locked up in real combat, he thought. *Not since that day in training, when Tukks had to come talk to me.* 'I . . . was just surprised to find Sah there,' he said. 'Not to mention Moash.'

How do you do it? How can you hurt people, Tukks. . . .

She closed her eyes and leaned against him without letting go of his arm.

Eventually he heard the others stirring, so he extricated himself from Syl's grasp and went to join them.

WATER
WARM AS BLOOD

The most important point I wish to make is that the Unmade are still among us. I realize this will be contentious, as much of the lore surrounding them is intertwined with theology. However, it is clear to me that some of their effects are common in the world – and we simply treat them as we would the manifestations of other spren.

—From Hessi's *Mythica,* page 12

The Skybreaker test was to take place in a modest-sized town on the north border of the Purelake. Some people lived *in* the lake, of course, but sane society avoided that.

Szeth landed – well, *was* landed – near the center of the town square, along with the other hopefuls. The main bulk of the Skybreakers either remained in the air or settled onto the cliffs around the town.

Three masters landed near Szeth, as did a handful of younger men and women who could Lash themselves. The group being tested today would include hopefuls like Szeth – who needed to find a master and swear the Second Ideal – and squires who had achieved that step already, but now needed to attract a spren and speak the Third Ideal.

It was a varied group; the Skybreakers didn't seem to care for ethnicity or eye color. Szeth was the only Shin among them, but the others included Makabaki, Reshi, Vorins, Iriali, and even one Thaylen.

A tall, strong man in a Marabethian wrap and an Azish coat hefted himself from his seat on a porch. 'It took you long enough!' he said in Azish, striding toward them. 'I sent for you hours ago! The convicts have escaped into the lake; who knows how far they've gotten by now! They will kill again if not stopped. Find and deal with them – you'll know them by the tattoos on their foreheads.'

The masters turned to the squires and hopefuls; some of the more eager among them immediately went running toward the water. Several that could Lash took to the sky.

Szeth lingered, along with four of the others. He stepped up to Ki, in her shoulder cloak of a high judge of Marabethia.

'How did this man know to send for us?' Szeth asked.

'We have been expanding our influence, following the advent of the new storm,' she replied. 'The local monarchs have accepted us as a unifying martial force, and have given us legal authority. The city's high minister wrote to us via spanreed, pleading for help.'

'And these convicts?' a squire asked. 'What do we know of them, and our duty here?'

'This group of convicts escaped the prison there along the cliffs. The report says they are dangerous murderers. Your task is to find the guilty and execute them. We have writs ordering their deaths.'

'All of those who escaped are guilty?'

'They are.'

At that, several of the other squires left, hurrying to prove themselves. Still, Szeth lingered. Something about the situation bothered him. 'If these men are murderers, why were they not executed before?'

'This area is populated by Reshi idealists, Szeth-son-Neturo,' Ki said. 'They have a strange, nonviolent attitude, even toward criminals. This town is charged with holding prisoners from all across the region, and Minister Kwati is paid tribute to maintain these facilities. Now that the murderers have escaped, mercy is withdrawn. They are to be executed.'

That was enough for the last two squires, who took to the sky to begin their search. And Szeth supposed it was enough for him as well.

These are Skybreakers, he thought. *They wouldn't knowingly send us after innocents.* He could have taken their implied approval at the start. Yet . . . something bothered him. This was a test, but of what? Was it merely about the speed with which they could dispatch the guilty?

He started toward the waters.

'Szeth-son-Neturo,' Ki called to him.

'Yes?'

'You walk on stone. Why is this? Each Shin I have known calls stone holy, and refuses to set foot on it.'

'It cannot be holy. If it truly were, Master Ki, it would have burned me away long ago.' He nodded to her, then stepped into the Purelake.

The water was warmer than he'd remembered. It wasn't deep at all – reportedly, even in the very center of the lake the water wouldn't reach higher than a man's thighs, save for the occasional sinkhole.

You are far behind those others, the sword said. *You're never going to catch anyone at this rate.*

'I knew a voice like yours once, sword-nimi.'

The whispers?

'No. A single one, in my mind, when I was young.' Szeth shaded his eyes, looking across the glistening lake. 'I hope things go better this time.'

The flying squires would catch anyone in the open, so Szeth would need to search for less obvious criminals. He only needed one . . .

One? the sword said. *You're not being ambitious enough.*

'Perhaps. Sword-nimi, do you know why you were given to me?'

Because you needed help. I'm good at helping.

'But why me?' Szeth continued trudging through the water. 'Nin said I was never to let you leave my presence.'

It seemed like more of a burden than an aid. Yes, the sword was a Shardblade – but one he'd been cautioned about drawing.

The Purelake seemed to extend forever, wide as an ocean. Szeth's steps startled schools of fish, which would follow behind him for a bit, occasionally nipping at his boots. Gnarled trees poked from the shallows, gorging themselves on the water while their roots grasped the many holes and furrows in the lake bed. Rock outcrops broke the lake near the coast, but inward the Purelake grew placid, more *empty*.

Szeth turned parallel to the shore.

You're not going the same way as the others.

That was true.

Honestly, Szeth, I have to be frank. You aren't good at slaying evil. We haven't killed anyone while you've held me.

'I wonder, sword-nimi. Did Nin-son-God give you to me so I could practice resisting your encouragements, or because he saw me as equally bloodthirsty? He did call us a good match.'

I'm not bloodthirsty, the sword said immediately. *I just want to be useful.*

'And not bored?'

Well, that too. The sword made some soft hums, imitating a human deep in thought. *You say you killed many people before we met. But the whispers . . . you didn't take pleasure in destroying those who needed to be destroyed?*

'I am not convinced that they needed to be destroyed.'

You killed them.

'I was sworn to obey.'

By a magic rock.

He had explained his past to the sword several times now. For some reason, it had difficulty understanding – or remembering – certain things. 'The Oathstone had no magic. I obeyed because of honor, and I sometimes obeyed evil or petty men. Now I seek a higher ideal.'

But what if you pick the wrong thing to follow? Couldn't you end up in the same place again? Can't you just find evil, then destroy it?

'And what is evil, sword-nimi?'

I'm sure you can spot it. You seem smart. If increasingly kind of boring.

Would that he could continue in such monotony.

Nearby, a large twisted tree rose from the bank. Several of the leaves along one branch were pulled in, seeking refuge inside the bark; someone had disturbed them. Szeth didn't give overt indication that he'd noticed, but angled his walk so that he stepped beneath the tree. Part of him hoped the man hiding in the tree had the sense to stay hidden.

He did not. The man leaped for Szeth, perhaps tempted by the prospect of obtaining a fine weapon.

Szeth sidestepped, but without Lashings he felt slow, awkward. He escaped the slashes of the convict's improvised dagger, but was forced back toward the water.

Finally! the sword said. *All right, here's what you have to do. Fight him and win, Szeth.*

The criminal rushed him. Szeth caught the hand with the dagger, twisting to use the man's own momentum to send him stumbling into the lake.

Recovering, the man turned toward Szeth, who was trying to read what he could from the man's ragged, sorry appearance. Matted, shaggy hair.

Reshi skin bearing many lesions. The poor fellow was so filthy, beggars and street urchins would find him distasteful company.

The convict passed his knife from one hand to the other, wary. Then he rushed Szeth again.

Szeth caught the man by the wrist once more and spun him around, the water splashing. Predictably, the man dropped his knife, which Szeth plucked from the water. He dodged the man's grapple, and in a moment had one arm around the convict's neck. Szeth raised the knife and – before he formed conscious thought – pressed the blade against the man's chest, drawing blood.

He managed to pull back, preventing himself from killing the convict. Fool! He needed to question the man. Had his time as Truthless made him such an eager killer? Szeth lowered the knife, but that gave the man an opening to twist and pull them both down into the Purelake.

Szeth splashed into water warm as blood. The criminal landed on top and forced Szeth under the surface, slamming his hand against the stony bottom and making him drop the knife. The world became a distorted blur.

This isn't *winning*, the sword said.

How ironic it would be to survive the murder of kings and Shardbearers only to die at the hands of a man with a crude knife. Szeth almost let it happen, but he knew fate was not finished with him yet.

He threw off the criminal, who was weak and scrawny. The man tried to grab the knife – which was clearly visible beneath the surface – while Szeth rolled the other direction to gain some distance. Unfortunately, the sword on his back got caught between the stones of the lake bottom, and that caused him to jerk back to the water. Szeth growled and – with a heave – ripped himself free, breaking the sword's harness strap.

The weapon sank into the water. Szeth splashed to his feet, turning to face the winded, dirty convict.

The man glanced at the submerged, silver sword. His eyes glazed, then he grinned wickedly, *dropped* his knife, and dove for the sword.

Curious. Szeth stepped back as the convict came up looking gleeful, holding the weapon.

Szeth punched him across the face, his arm leaving a faint afterimage. He grabbed the sheathed sword, ripping it from the weaker man's hands. Though the weapon often seemed too heavy for its size, it now felt light

342

in his fingers. He stepped to the side and swung it – sheath and all – at his enemy.

The weapon struck the convict's back with a sickening crunch. The poor man splashed down into the lake and fell still.

I suppose that will do, the sword said. *Really, you should have just used me in the first place.*

Szeth shook himself. Had he killed the fellow after all? Szeth knelt and pulled him up by his matted hair. The convict gasped, but his body didn't move. Not dead, but paralyzed.

'Did someone work with you in your escape?' Szeth asked. 'One of the local nobility, perhaps?'

'What?' the man sputtered. 'Oh, Vun Makak. What have you done to me? I can't feel my arms, my legs . . .'

'Did *anyone* from the outside help you?'

'No. Why . . . why would you ask?' The man sputtered. 'Wait. Yes. Who do you want me to name? I'll do whatever you say. Please.'

Szeth considered. *Not working with the guards then, or the minister of the town.* 'How did you get out?'

'Oh, Nu Ralik . . .' the man said, crying. 'We shouldn't have killed the guard. I just wanted . . . wanted to see the sun again. . . .'

Szeth dropped the man back into the water. He stepped onto the shore and sat down on a rock, breathing deeply. Not long ago, he had danced with a Windrunner at the front of a storm. Today, he fought in shallow water against a half-starved man.

Oh, how he missed the sky.

That was cruel, the sword said. *Leaving him to drown.*

'Better than feeding him to a greatshell,' Szeth said. 'That happens to criminals in this kingdom.'

Both are cruel, the sword said.

'You know of cruelty, sword-nimi?'

Vivenna used to tell me that cruelty is only for men, as is mercy. Only we can choose one or the other, and beasts cannot.

'You count yourself as a man?'

No. But sometimes she talked like she did. And after Shashara made me, she argued with Vasher, saying I could be a poet or a scholar. Like a man, right?

Shashara? That sounded like Shalash, the Eastern name for the Herald

Shush-daughter-God. So perhaps this sword's origin was with the Heralds.

Szeth rose and walked up the coast, back toward the town.

Aren't you going to search for other criminals?

'I needed only one, sword-nimi, to test what has been told to me and to learn a few important facts.'

Like how smelly convicts are?

'That is indeed part of the secret.'

He passed the small town where the master Skybreakers waited, then hiked up the hillside to the prison. The dark block of a structure overlooked the Purelake, but the beautiful vantage was wasted; the place had barely any windows.

Inside, the smell was so foul, he had to breathe through his mouth. The body of a single guard had been left in a pool of blood between cells. Szeth almost tripped over it – there was no light in the place, save for a few sphere lamps in the guard post.

I see, he thought, kneeling beside the fallen man. *Yes.* This test was indeed a curious one.

Outside, he noted some of the squires returning to the town with corpses in tow, though none of the other hopefuls seemed to have found anyone. Szeth picked his way carefully down the rocky slope to the town, careful not to drag the sword. Whatever Nin's reasons for entrusting him with the weapon, it was a holy object.

At the town, he approached the beefy nobleman, who was trying to make small talk with Master Ki – failing spectacularly. Nearby, other members of the town were debating the ethics of simply executing murderers, or holding them and risking this. Szeth inspected the dead convicts, and found them as dirty as the one he had fought, though two weren't nearly as emaciated.

There was a prison economy, Szeth thought. *Food went to those in power while others were starved.*

'You,' Szeth said to the nobleman. 'I found only one body above. Did you really have a *single* guard posted to watch all these prisoners?'

The nobleman sneered at him. 'A Shin stonewalker? Who are you to question me? Go back to your stupid grass and dead trees, little man.'

'The prisoners were free to create their own hierarchy,' Szeth continued. 'And nobody watched to see they didn't make weapons, as I faced one with a knife. These men were mistreated, locked in darkness, not given enough food.'

'They were criminals. *Murderers.*'

'And what happened to the money you were sent to administrate this facility? It certainly didn't go toward proper security.'

'I don't have to listen to this!'

Szeth turned from him to Ki. 'Do you have a writ of execution for this man?'

'It is the first we obtained.'

'*What?*' the nobleman said. Fearspren boiled up around him.

Szeth undid the clasp on the sword and drew it.

A rushing sound, like a thousand screams.

A wave of power, like the beating of a terrible, stunning wind.

Colors changed around him. They deepened, growing darker and more vibrant. The city nobleman's cloak became a stunning array of deep oranges and blood reds.

The hair on Szeth's arms stood on end and his skin spiked with a sudden incredible pain.

DESTROY!

Liquid darkness flowed from the Blade, then melted to smoke as it fell. Szeth screamed at the pain in his arm even as he slammed the weapon through the chest of the blubbering nobleman.

Flesh and blood puffed instantly into black smoke. Ordinary Shardblades burned only the eyes, but this sword somehow consumed the entire body. It seemed to sear away even the man's *soul.*

EVIL!

Veins of black liquid crept up Szeth's hand and arm. He gaped at them, then gasped and rammed the sword back into its silvery sheath.

He fell to his knees, dropping the sword and raising his hand, fingers bent and tendons taut. Slowly, the blackness evaporated from his flesh, the awful pain easing. The skin of his hand, which had already been pale, had been bleached to grey-white.

The sword's voice sank to a deep muttering in his mind, its words slurring. It struck him as sounding like the voice of a beast falling into a stupor after having gorged itself. Szeth breathed deeply. Fumbling at his pouch, he saw that several spheres inside were completely drained. *I will need far more Stormlight if I'm to ever try that again.*

The surrounding townspeople, squires, and even master Skybreakers regarded him with uniform horror. Szeth picked up the sword and struggled to his feet, before fastening the sword's clasp. Holding the sheathed weapon in both hands, he bowed to Ki. 'I have dealt,' he said, 'with the worst of the criminals.'

'You have done well,' she said slowly, glancing at where the nobleman had stood. There wasn't even a stain on the stones. 'We will wait and make certain the other criminals have been killed or captured.'

'Wise,' Szeth said. 'Could I . . . beg something to drink? I suddenly find myself very thirsty.'

⁘

By the time all the escapees had been accounted for, the sword was stirring again. It had never fallen asleep, if a sword could do such a thing. Rather, it had mumbled in his mind until it slowly became lucid.

Hey! the sword said as Szeth sat on a low wall alongside the city. *Hey, did you* draw *me?*

'I did, sword-nimi.'

Great job! Did we . . . did we destroy lots of evil?

'A great and corrupt evil.'

Wow! I'm impressed. You know, Vivenna never drew me even once? She carried me for a long time too. Maybe a couple of days even?

'And how long have I been carrying you?'

At least an hour, the sword said, satisfied. *One, or two, or ten thousand. Something like that.*

Ki approached, and he returned her water canteen. 'Thank you, Master Ki.'

'I have decided to take you as my squire, Szeth-son-Neturo,' she said. 'In all honesty, there was an argument among us over who would have the privilege.'

He bowed his head. 'I may swear the Second Ideal?'

'You may. Justice will serve you until you attract a spren and swear to a more specific code. During my prayers last night, Winnow proclaimed the highspren are watching you. I won't be surprised if it takes mere months before you achieve the Third Ideal.'

Months. No, he would not take months. But he did not swear quite yet.

Instead, he nodded toward the prison. 'Pardon, master, a question. You knew this breakout would happen, didn't you?'

'We suspected. One of our teams investigated this man and discovered how he was using his funds. When the call came, we were not surprised. It provided a perfect testing opportunity.'

'Why not deal with him earlier?'

'You must understand our purpose and our place, a fine point difficult for many squires to grasp. That man had *not yet broken a law*. His duty was to imprison the convicts, which he had done. He was allowed to judge if his methods were satisfactory or not. Only once he failed, and his charges had escaped, could we mete out justice.'

Szeth nodded. 'I swear to seek justice, to let it guide me, until I find a more perfect Ideal.'

'These Words are accepted,' Ki said. She removed a glowing emerald sphere from her pouch. 'Take your place above, squire.'

Szeth regarded the sphere, then – trembling – breathed in the Stormlight. It returned to him in a rush.

The skies were his once again.

93

KATA

Taxil mentions Yelig-nar, named Blightwind, in an oft-cited quote. Though Jasnah Kholin has famously called its accuracy into question, I believe it.

—From Hessi's *Mythica*, page 26

When Adolin woke up, he was still in the nightmare.

The dark sky, glass ground, the strange creatures. He had a crick in his neck and a pain in his back; he'd never mastered the 'sleep anywhere' skill the grunts bragged about.

Father could have slept on the ground, a part of him thought. *Dalinar is a true soldier.*

Adolin thought again of the jolt he'd felt when ramming his dagger through Sadeas's eye and into his brain. Satisfaction and shame. Strip away Adolin's nobility, and what was left? A duelist when a world needed generals? A hothead who couldn't even take an insult?

A murderer?

He threw off his coat and sat up, then jumped and gasped as he found the woman with the scratched-out eyes looming over him. 'Ishar's soul!' Adolin cursed. 'Do you have to stay so close?'

She didn't move. Adolin sighed, then changed the dressing on his shallow shoulder cut, using bandages from his pocket. Nearby, Shallan

348

and Azure catalogued their meager supplies. Kaladin trudged over to join them. Had the bridgeboy slept?

Adolin stretched, then – accompanied by his ghostly spren – walked down the short slope to the ocean of glass beads. A few lifespren floated nearby; on this side, their glowing green motes had tufts of white hair that rippled as they danced and bobbed. Perhaps they were circling plants by the riverbank in the Physical Realm? Those small dots of light swimming above the rock might be the souls of fish. How did that work? In the real would, they'd be in the water, so shouldn't they be *inside* the stone?

He knew so little, and felt so overwhelmed. So *insignificant*.

A fearspren crawled up out of the ocean of beads, purple antenna pointing at him. It scuttled closer until Adolin picked up some beads and threw one at the spren, which scuttled back into the ocean and lurked there, watching him.

'What do you think of all this?' Adolin asked the woman with the scratched-out eyes. She didn't respond, but he often talked to his sword without it responding.

He tossed up one of the beads and caught it. Shallan could tell what each represented, but all he got was a dull impression of . . . something red?

'I'm being childish, aren't I?' Adolin asked. 'So, forces moving in the world now make me look insignificant. That's no different from a child growing up and realizing his little life isn't the center of the universe. Right?'

Problem was, his little life *had* been the center of the universe, growing up. *Welcome to being the son of Dalinar storming Blackthorn.* He hurled the sphere into the sea, where it skittered against its fellows.

Adolin sighed, then started a morning kata. Without a sword, he fell back on the first kata he'd ever learned – an extended sequence of stretches, hand-to-hand moves, and stances to help loosen his muscles.

The forms calmed him. The world was turning on its head, but familiar things were still familiar. Strange, that he should have to come to that revelation.

About halfway through, he noticed Azure standing on the bank. She walked down the slope and fell into line beside him, doing the same kata. She must have known it already, for she kept pace with him exactly.

They stepped back and forth along the rocks, sparring with their own shadows, until Kaladin approached and joined them. He wasn't as practiced, and cursed under his breath as he got a sequence wrong – but he'd obviously done it before too.

He must have learned it from Zahel, Adolin realized.

The three moved together, their breathing controlled, scraping boots on the glass. The sea of beads rolling against itself began to sound soothing. Even rhythmic.

The world is the same as it's always been, Adolin thought. *These things we're finding – monsters and Radiants – aren't new. They were only hidden. The world has always been like this, even if I didn't know it.*

And Adolin . . . he was still himself. He had all the same things to be proud of, didn't he? Same strengths? Same accomplishments?

Same flaws too.

'Are you three *dancing*?' a voice suddenly piped up.

Adolin immediately spun around. Shallan had settled on the slope above them, still wearing her white uniform, hat, and single glove. He found himself grinning stupidly. 'It's a warm-up kata,' he explained. 'You—'

'I know what it is. You tried to teach it to me, remember? I just thought it odd to see you all down here like that.' She shook her head. 'Weren't we going to plan how to get out of here?'

Together, they started up the slope, and Azure fell into step beside Adolin. 'Where did you learn that kata?'

'From my swordmaster. You?'

'Likewise.'

As they approached their camp in the small nestlike depression in the obsidian ground, something felt off to Adolin. Where was his sword, the woman with the scratched-out eyes?

He stepped back and spotted her standing on the coast, looking at her feet.

'All right,' Shallan said, drawing him back. 'I made a list of our supplies.' She gestured with a pencil toward the items – which were arrayed on the ground – as she spoke. 'One bag of gemstones from the emerald reserve. I used roughly half of our Stormlight in our transfer to Shadesmar and crossing the sea of beads. We have my satchel, with charcoal, reed pens, brushes, ink, lacquer, some solvents, three sketchpads, my sharpening knife, and one jar of jam I'd stowed inside for an emergency snack.'

'Wonderful,' Kaladin said. 'I'm sure a pile of brushes will be useful in fighting off Voidspren.'

'Better than your tongue, which is notably dull lately. Adolin has his side knife, but our only real weapon is Azure's Shardblade. Kaladin brought the bag of gemstones inside his pack, which fortunately also contained his travel rations: three meals of flatbread and jerked pork. We also have a water jug and three canteens.'

'Mine is half empty,' Adolin noted.

'Mine too,' Azure said. 'Which means we have maybe one day's worth of water and three meals for four people. Last time I crossed Shadesmar, it took four weeks.'

'Obviously,' Kaladin said, 'we have to get back through the Oathgate into the city.'

Pattern hummed, standing behind Shallan. He seemed like a statue; he didn't shift his weight or move in small ways like a human would. Kaladin's spren was different. She always seemed to be moving, slipping this way or that, girlish dress rippling as she walked, her hair swaying.

'Bad,' Pattern said. 'The spren of the Oathgate are *bad* now.'

'Do we have any other options?' Kaladin said.

'I remember . . . some,' Syl said. 'Much more than I used to. Our land, every land, is three realms. The highest is the Spiritual, where gods live – there, all things, times, and spaces are made into one.

'We're now in the Cognitive Realm. Shadesmar, where spren live. You are from the Physical Realm. The only way I know of to transfer there is to be pulled by human emotions. That won't help you, as you're not spren.'

'There's another way to transfer between realms,' Azure said. 'I've used it.'

Her hair had recovered its dark coloring, and it seemed to Adolin that her scars had faded. Something about her was downright strange. She seemed almost like a spren herself.

She bore his scrutiny, looking from him to Kaladin, to Shallan. Finally she sighed deeply. 'Story time?'

'Yes, please,' Adolin replied. 'You've traveled in this place before?'

'I'm from a far land, and I came to Roshar by crossing this place, Shadesmar.'

'All right,' Adolin said. 'But why?'

'I came chasing someone.'

'A friend?'

'A criminal,' she said softly.

'You're a soldier though,' Kaladin said.

'Not really. In Kholinar, I merely stepped up to do a job nobody else was doing. I thought perhaps the Wall Guard would have information on the man I'm hunting. Everything went wrong, and I got stuck.'

'When you arrived in our land,' Shallan said, 'you used an Oathgate to get from Shadesmar to the Physical Realm?'

'No.' Azure laughed, shaking her head. 'I didn't know of those until Kal told me about them. I used a portal between realms. Cultivation's Perpendicularity, they call it. On your side, it's in the Horneater Peaks.'

'That's hundreds of miles from here,' Adolin said.

'There's supposedly another perpendicularity,' Azure said. 'It's unpredictable and dangerous, and appears randomly in different places. My guides warned against trying to hunt it.'

'Guides?' Kaladin said. 'Who were these guides?'

'Why, spren of course.'

Adolin glanced toward the distant city they'd left, where there had been fearspren and painspren aplenty.

'Not like those,' Azure said, laughing. 'People spren, like these two.'

'Which raises a question,' Adolin said, pointing as the spren with the strange eyes rejoined them. 'That's the soul of my Shardblade. Syl is Kaladin's, and Pattern Shallan's. So . . .' He pointed at the weapon at her belt. 'Tell us honestly, Azure. Are you a Knight Radiant?'

'No.'

Adolin swallowed. *Say it.* 'You're a Herald then.'

She laughed. 'No. What? A Herald? Those are basically *gods,* right? I'm no figure from mythology, thank you very much. I'm just a woman who has been constantly out of her league since adolescence. Trust me.'

Adolin glanced at Kaladin. He didn't seem convinced either.

'Really,' Azure said. 'There's no spren here for my Blade because it's flawed. I can't summon or dismiss it, like you can yours. She's a handy weapon, but a pale copy of what you carry.' She patted it. 'Anyway, when I last crossed this place, I hired a ship to convey me.'

'A ship?' Kaladin said. 'Sailed by whom?'

'Spren. I hired it at one of their cities.'

'Cities?' Kaladin looked toward Syl. 'You have *cities?*'

'Where did you think we lived?' Syl said, amused.

'Lightspren are usually guides,' Azure continued. 'They like to travel, to see new places. They sail all across Roshar's Shadesmar, peddling goods, trading with other spren. Um . . . you're supposed to watch out for Cryptics.'

Pattern hummed happily. 'Yes. We are very famous.'

'What about using Soulcasting?' Adolin looked to Shallan. 'Could you make us supplies?'

'I don't think it would work,' Shallan replied. 'When I Soulcast, I change an object's soul here in this realm, and it reflects in the other world. If I changed one of these beads, it might become something new in the Physical Realm – but it would still be a bead to us.'

'Food and water aren't impossible to find here,' Azure said, 'if you can make it to a port city. The spren don't need these things, but humans living on this side – and there are some – need a constant supply. With that Stormlight of yours, we can trade. Maybe buy passage to the Horneater Peaks.'

'That would take a long time,' Kaladin said. 'Alethkar is falling *right now,* and the Blackthorn needs us. It—'

He was interrupted by a haunting screech. It was reminiscent of sheets of steel grinding against one another. It was met by others, echoing in unison. Adolin spun toward the sounds, shocked by their intensity. Syl put her hands to her lips, and Pattern cocked his strange head.

'What was *that*?' Kaladin demanded.

Azure hurriedly began shoving their supplies into Kaladin's pack. 'You remember before we slept, how I said we'd be fine unless we attracted the wrong spren?'

'. . . Yes?'

'We should get moving. *Now.*'

Types of Wine

In order of Strength

Violet

Pink

Blue

Orange

Sapphire

Yellow

Red

Auburn

Strongest — *Spiced sandalwood aroma.*

Complex notes of berry & lemon.

Nutty taste with hints of honey.

Flavorful with an earthy, pleasant burn.

Spicy taste with an earthy aroma.

Bold, deep without guilt.

Floral. Aids alertness & vigour.

Fruity with notes of ginger.

Weakest

I've had milk more intoxicati[ng] than this.

Made from fermented lavis grain. Depending on the infusions, this traditionally tastes most like whiskey

Made from fermented fruit, and is similar to th[e] grape wines we're used to.

Cider

It serves the Cultured Vorin well to be versed in the diverse beers, mudbeers, ciders, juices, and lagers of other cultures.

Cider is served chilled, if possible. Horneater lager should not be drunk in the presence of enemies.

Winespren

Winespren are quite rare. Reported only in foreign nations.

What? Rare? I see these all the time.

Responsible for tha[t] embarrassing tatt[oo] of mine.

Horneater Lage[r]

SEVEN YEARS AGO

Dalinar stumbled as he swept everything from the dresser, up-ending a bowl of hot soup. He didn't want *soup*. He yanked out drawers, dumping clothing to the ground, steam curling from the spilled broth.

They'd done it again! They'd taken his bottles. How *dare* they! Couldn't they hear the weeping? He roared, then grabbed his trunk, overturning it. A flask rolled out along with the clothing. Finally! Something they hadn't found.

He slurped down the dregs it contained, and groaned. The weeping echoed around him. Children dying. Evi begging for her life.

He needed more.

But . . . wait, did he need to be presentable? The hunt? Was that today?

Stupid man, he thought. The last of the hunts had been weeks ago. He'd convinced Gavilar to come with him out into the wilderness, and the trip had gone well. Dalinar had been presentable – sober, commanding even. A figure right from the storming songs. They'd discovered those parshmen. They'd been so *interesting*.

For a time, away from civilization, Dalinar had felt like himself. His old self.

He hated that person.

Growling, he dug in his large wardrobe. This fort on the eastern rim of

Alethkar was the first mark of civilization on their trip home. It had given Dalinar access, again, to the necessities of life. Like wine.

He barely heard the rap on his door as he flung coats out of the wardrobe. When he looked over, he saw two youths standing there. His sons. Angerspren boiled around him. Her hair. Her judgmental eyes. How many lies about him had she stuffed into their heads?

'What?' Dalinar roared.

Adolin stood his ground. Almost seventeen now, fully a man. The other one, the invalid, cringed down. He looked younger than his . . . what . . . twelve years? Thirteen?

'We heard the commotion, *sir*,' Adolin said, jutting out his chin. 'We thought you might need help.'

'I need nothing! Out! *GET OUT!*'

They scrambled away.

Dalinar's heart raced. He slammed the wardrobe and pounded his fists on the bedside table, toppling the sphere lamp. Puffing, groaning, he fell to his knees.

Storms. They were only a few days' march from the ruins of Rathalas. Was that why the screaming was louder today?

A hand fell on his shoulder. 'Father?'

'Adolin, so help me—' Still kneeling, Dalinar turned, then cut off. It wasn't Adolin, but the other one. Renarin had returned, timid as always, his spectacled eyes wide and his hand trembling. He held something out.

A small bottle. 'I . . .' Renarin swallowed. 'I got you one, with the spheres the king gave me. Because you always go through what you buy so quickly.'

Dalinar stared at that bottle of wine for an endless moment. 'Gavilar hides the wine from me,' he mumbled. 'That's why none is left. I . . . couldn't possibly . . . have drunk it all. . . .'

Renarin stepped in and hugged him. Dalinar flinched, bracing as if for a punch. The boy clung to him, not letting go.

'They talk about you,' Renarin said, 'but they're wrong. You just need to rest, after all the fighting you did. I know. And I miss her too.'

Dalinar licked his lips. 'What did she tell you?' he said, voice ragged. 'What did your mother say about me?'

'The only honest officer in the army,' Renarin said, 'the honorable

356

soldier. Noble, like the Heralds themselves. Our father. The greatest man in Alethkar.'

What stupid words. Yet Dalinar found himself weeping. Renarin let go, but Dalinar grabbed him, pulling him close.

Oh, Almighty. Oh God. Oh God, please . . . I've started to hate my sons. Why hadn't the boys learned to hate him back? They should hate him. He *deserved* to be hated.

Please. Anything. I don't know how to get free of this. Help me. Help me . . .

Dalinar wept and clung to that youth, that child, as if he were the only real thing left in a world of shadows.

INESCAPABLE VOID

Yelig-nar had great powers, perhaps the powers of all Surges compounded in one. He could transform any Voidbringer into an extremely dangerous enemy. Curiously, three legends I found mention swallowing a gemstone to engage this process.

—From Hessi's *Mythica,* page 27

K aladin marched at speed through Shadesmar, trying – with difficulty – to control the simmering dissatisfaction inside of him.

'Mmmm ...' Pattern said as another screech sounded behind them. 'Humans, you must stop your emotions. They are very inconvenient here.'

The group hiked southward, along the narrow line of land that overlaid the river in the real world. Shallan was the slowest of them, and had difficulty keeping up, so they'd agreed she should hold a little Stormlight. It was either that, or let the screeching spren reach them.

'What are they like?' Adolin said to Azure, puffing as they marched. 'You said those sounds were from angerspren? Boiling pools of blood?'

'That's the part you see in the Physical Realm,' Azure said. 'Here ... that's merely their saliva, pooling as they drool. They're nasty.'

'And dangerous,' Syl said. She scampered along the obsidian ground, and didn't seem to get tired. 'Even to spren. But how did we draw them? Nobody was angry, right?'

Kaladin tried again to smother his frustration.

'I wasn't feeling anything other than tired,' Shallan said.

'I felt overwhelmed,' Adolin said. 'Still do. But not angry.'

'Kaladin?' Syl said.

He looked at the others, then down at his feet. 'It just feels like . . . like we're abandoning Kholinar. And only I *care*. You were talking about how to get food, find a way to the Horneater Peaks, this perpendicularity or whatever. But we're *abandoning* people to the Voidbringers.'

'I care too!' Adolin said. 'Bridgeboy, that was my *home*. It—'

'I know,' Kaladin snapped. He took a breath, forcing himself to calm. 'I know, Adolin. I *know* it's not rational to try to get back through the Oathgate. We don't know how to work it from this side, and besides, it's obviously been corrupted. My emotions are irrational. I'll try to contain them. I promise.'

They fell silent.

You're not angry at Adolin, Kaladin thought forcefully. *You're not actually angry at* anyone. *You're just looking for something to latch on to. Something to feel.*

Because the darkness was coming.

It fed off the pain of defeat, the agony of losing men he'd tried to protect. But it could feed off anything. Life going well? The darkness would whisper that he was only setting himself up for a bigger fall. Shallan glances at Adolin? They must be whispering about him. Dalinar sends him to protect Elhokar? The highprince must want to get rid of Kaladin.

He'd failed at that, regardless. When Dalinar heard that Kholinar had fallen . . .

Get out, Kaladin thought, squeezing his eyes shut. *Get out, get out, get out!*

It would continue until numbness seemed preferable. Then that numbness would claim him and make it hard to do anything at all. It would become a sinking, inescapable void from within which everything looked washed out. Dead.

Within that dark place, he'd wanted to betray his oaths. Within that dark place, he'd given the king up to assassins and murderers.

Eventually, the screeches faded into the distance. Syl guessed that the angerspren had been drawn into the beads, off toward Kholinar and the powerful emotions there. The group continued their hike. There was only one way to go: south, along the narrow peninsula of obsidian running through the bead ocean.

'When I traveled here last time,' Azure said, 'we passed numbers of peninsulas like this one. They always had lighthouses at the ends. We stopped at them sometimes for supplies.'

'Yes . . .' Syl said, nodding. 'I remember those. It's useful for ships to note where land juts into the beads. There should be one at the end of this one . . . though it looks loooong. We'll have to hike it for several days.'

'At least it's a goal,' Adolin said. 'We travel south, get to the lighthouse, and hope to catch a ship there.'

There was an insufferable spring to his step, like he was actually *excited* by this terrible place. Idiot Adolin, who probably didn't even understand the consequences of—

Stop it. STOP IT. He helped you.

Storms. Kaladin hated himself when he got like this. When he tried to empty his mind, he drifted toward the void of darkness. But when he instead let himself think, he started remembering what had happened in Kholinar. Men he loved, killing each other. Awful, terrifying perspective.

He could see too many sides. Parshmen angry at being enslaved for years, attempting to overthrow a corrupt government. Alethi protecting their homes from invading monsters. Elhokar trying to save his son. The palace guards trying to keep their oaths.

Too many eyes to see through. Too many emotions. Were these his only two options? Pain or oblivion?

Fight it.

Their hike continued, and he tried to turn his attention to his surroundings instead of his thoughts. The thin peninsula wasn't barren, as he'd first assumed. Growing along its edges were small, brittle plants that looked like ferns. When he asked, Syl told him they grew exactly like plants in the Physical Realm.

Most were black, but occasionally they had vibrant colors, blended together like stained glass. None grew higher than his knees, and most only reached his ankles. He felt terrible whenever he brushed one and it crumpled.

The sun didn't seem to change position in the sky, no matter how long they walked. Through spaces between the clouds, he saw only blackness. No stars, no moons. Eternal, endless darkness.

⁘

They camped for what should have been the night, then hiked all the next day. Kholinar vanished into the distance behind, but still they kept going: Azure at the front, then Pattern, Syl, and Kaladin, with Shallan and Adolin at the back, Adolin's spren trailing them. Kaladin would have preferred to take the rearguard, but if he tried, Adolin positioned himself to the back again. What did the princeling think? That Kaladin would lag behind, if not minded?

Syl walked beside him, mostly quiet. Being back on this side troubled her. She'd look at things, like the occasional colorful plant, and cock her head as if trying to remember. 'It's like a dream from the time when I was dead,' she'd said when he prompted her.

They camped another 'night,' then started walking again. Kaladin skipped breakfast – their rations were basically gone. Besides, he welcomed the grumbling stomach. It reminded him that he was alive. Gave him something to think about, other than the men he'd lost . . .

'Where did you live?' he asked Syl, still carrying his pack, hiking along the seemingly infinite peninsula. 'When you were young, on this side?'

'It was far to the west,' she said. 'A grand city, ruled by honorspren! I didn't like it though. I wanted to travel, but Father kept me in the city, especially after . . . you know . . .'

'I'm not actually sure that I do.'

'I bonded a Knight Radiant. Haven't I told you of him? I remember . . .' She closed her eyes as she walked, chin up, as if basking in a wind he could not feel. 'I bonded him soon after I was born. He was an elderly man, kindly, but he *did* fight. In one battle. And he died. . . .'

She blinked open her eyes. 'That was a long time ago.'

'I'm sorry.'

'It's all right. I wasn't ready though for the bond. Spren normally weather the death of their Radiant, but I . . . I lost myself when I lost him. It all turned out to be morbidly fortuitous, because soon after, the Recreance happened. Men forsook their oaths, which killed my siblings. I survived, for I didn't have a bond then.'

'And the Stormfather locked you away?'

'Father assumed I'd been killed with the others. He found me, asleep, after what must have been ... wow, a thousand years on your side. He woke me and took me home.' She shrugged. 'After that, he wouldn't let me leave the city.' She took Kaladin by the arm. 'He was foolish, as were the other honorspren born after the Recreance. They knew something bad was coming, but wouldn't do anything. And I heard you calling, even from so far away. . . .'

'The Stormfather let you out?' Kaladin said, stunned by the confessions. This was more than he'd found out about her since ... since forever.

'I snuck away,' she said with a grin. 'I gave up my mind and joined your world, hiding among the windspren. We can barely see them on this side. Did you know that? Some spren live mostly in your realm. I suppose the wind is always there somewhere, so they don't fade like passions do.' She shook her head. 'Oh!'

'Oh?' Kaladin asked. 'Did you remember something?'

'No! Oh!' She pointed, hopping up and down. 'Look!'

In the distance, a bright yellow light glowed like a spark in the otherwise dim landscape.

A lighthouse.

Yelig-nar is said to consume souls, but I can't find a specific explanation. I'm uncertain this lore is correct.

—From Hessi's *Mythica,* page 51

On the day of the first meeting of monarchs at Urithiru, Navani made each person – no matter how important – carry their own chair. The old Alethi tradition symbolized each chief bringing important wisdom to a gathering.

Navani and Dalinar arrived first, stepping off the lift and walking toward the meeting room near the top of Urithiru. Her chair was sensible but comfortable, made of Soulcast wood with a padded seat. Dalinar had tried to bring a stool, but she'd insisted that he do better. This wasn't a battlefield strategy tent, and forced austerity wouldn't impress the monarchs. He'd eventually selected a sturdy wooden chair of thick stumpweight, with wide armrests but no padding.

He'd quietly spent the trip up watching floors pass. When Dalinar was troubled, he went silent. His brow would scrunch up in thought, and to everyone else, it looked like he was scowling.

'They got out, Dalinar,' Navani said to him. 'I'm sure they did. Elhokar and Adolin are safe, somewhere.'

He nodded. But even if they had survived, Kholinar had fallen. Was that why he seemed so haunted?

No, it was something else. Ever since he'd collapsed after visiting Azir, it seemed that something in Dalinar had snapped. This morning, he had quietly asked her to lead the meeting. She worried, deeply, for what was happening to him. And for Elhokar. And for Kholinar . . .

But storms, they had worked so hard to forge this coalition. She would *not* let it collapse now. She'd already grieved for a daughter, but then that daughter had returned to her. She *had* to hope the same for Elhokar – at the very least, so she could keep functioning while Dalinar mourned.

They settled their chairs in the large meeting room, which had a clear view out flat glass windows overlooking mountains. Servants had already set out refreshment along the curved side wall of the half-circle room. The tiled floor was inlaid with the image of the Double Eye of the Almighty, complete with Surges and Essences.

Bridge Four piled into the room after them. Many had brought simple seats, but the Herdazian had stumbled onto the lift with a chair so grand – inlaid with embroidered blue cloth and silver – it was almost a throne.

They settled their chairs behind hers with a fair bit of squabbling, and then attacked the food without waiting for permission. For a group that was essentially one step from being lighteyed Shardbearers, they were an unruly and raucous bunch.

Bridge Four had, characteristically, taken the news of their leader's potential fall with laughter. *Kaladin is tougher than a wind-tossed boulder, Brightness,* Teft had told her. *He survived Bridge Four, he survived the chasms, and he'll survive this.*

She had to admit their optimism was heartening. But if the team had survived, why hadn't they returned during the latest highstorm?

Steady, Navani thought to herself, regarding the bridgemen, who were surrounded by laughterspren. One of those men currently carried Jezerezeh's Honorblade. She couldn't tell which; the Blade could be dismissed like an ordinary Shardblade, and they swapped it among themselves in order to be unpredictable.

Soon, the others began arriving on different lifts, and Navani watched carefully. The chair-carrying tradition was, in part, a symbol of equality – but Navani figured she might be able to learn something about the monarchs from their choices. Being a human was about making sense of chaos, finding meaning among the random elements of the world.

First to arrive was the young Azish Prime. His tailor had done a wonderful job making his regal costume fit; it would have been easy for the youth to look like a child swimming in those stately robes and that headdress. He carried a very ornate throne, covered in loud Azish patterns, and each of his closest advisors helped by holding it with one hand.

The large contingent settled in, and others flooded in behind, including three representatives of kingdoms subject to Azir: the prime of Emul, the princess of Yezier, and the ambassador from Tashikk. All brought chairs that were *faintly* inferior to that of the Azish Prime.

A balancing act went on here. Each of the three monarchies gave just enough respect to the Prime so as not to embarrass him. They were his subjects in name only. Still, Navani should be able to focus her diplomacy efforts on the Prime. Tashikk, Emul, and Yezier would fall in line. Two were historically closest with the Azish throne, and the third – Emul – was in no position to stand on its own after the war with Tukar and the Voidbringer assault had basically broken the princedom into pieces.

The Alethi contingent arrived next. Renarin, who seemed terrified that something had happened to his brother, brought a simple chair. Jasnah had outdone him by actually bringing a padded stool – she and Dalinar could be painfully similar. Navani noticed with annoyance that Sebarial and Palona weren't with the other highprinces. Well, at least they hadn't shown up bearing massage tables.

Notably, Ialai Sadeas ignored the requirement that she carry her own chair. A scarred guardsman placed a sleek, lacquered chair down for her – stained so dark a maroon, it might as well have been black. She met Navani's eyes as she sat, cold and confident. Amaram was technically highprince, but he was still in Thaylenah, working alongside his soldiers to rebuild the city. Navani doubted Ialai would have let him represent them at this meeting anyway.

It seemed so long ago when Ialai and Navani had huddled together at dinners, conspiring on how to stabilize the kingdom their husbands were conquering. Now, Navani wanted to seize the woman and shake her. *Can't you stop being petty for one storming minute?*

Well, as had been happening for so long now, the other highprinces would defer either to Kholin or to Sadeas. Letting Ialai participate was a calculated risk. Forbid her, and the woman *would* find a way to sabotage the proceedings. Let her in, and hopefully she'd start to see the importance of this work.

At least Queen Fen and her consort seemed committed to the coalition. They set their chairs by the glass window, backs to the storms, as the Thaylens often joked. Their wooden chairs were high-backed, painted blue, and upholstered a pale nautical white. Taravangian – bearing a nondescript chair of wood with no padding – asked to join them. The old man had insisted on carrying his own chair, though Navani had specifically excused him, Ashno of Sages, and others with a frail bearing.

Adrotagia sat with him, as did his Surgebinder. She didn't go join Bridge Four ... and, curiously, Navani realized she still thought of the woman as *his* Surgebinder.

The only other person of note was Au-nak, the Natan ambassador. He represented a dead kingdom that had been reduced to a single city-state on the eastern coast of Roshar with a few other cities as protectorates.

For a moment, it all seemed too much for Navani. The Azish Empire, with all its intricacies. The countermovement among the Alethi highprinces. Taravangian, who was somehow king of Jah Keved – the second-largest kingdom on Roshar. Queen Fen and her obligation to the guilds in her city. The Radiants – like the little Reshi who was currently outeating the huge Horneater bridgeman, almost as if it were a contest.

So much to think about. *Now* was when Dalinar stepped back?

Calm, Navani thought at herself, taking a deep breath. *Order from chaos. Find the structure here and start building upon it.*

Everyone had naturally arranged themselves into a circle, with monarchs at the front and highprinces, viziers, interpreters, and scribes radiating out from them. Navani stood up and strode into the center. Just as everyone was quieting, Sebarial and his mistress finally sauntered in. They made right for the food, and had apparently forgotten chairs entirely.

'I,' she said as the room hushed again, 'know of no other conference like this in the history of Roshar. Perhaps they were common in the days of the Knights Radiant, but certainly nothing like it has occurred since the Recreance. I would like to both welcome *and* thank you, our noble guests. Today we make history.'

'It only took a Desolation to cause it,' Sebarial said from the food table. 'The world should end more often. It makes everyone so much more accommodating.'

The various interpreters whispered translations to their charges. Navani found herself wondering if it was too late to have him tossed off the tower. You could do it – the sheer side of Urithiru, facing the Origin, was straight all the way down. She could watch Sebarial fall practically to the bottom of the mountains, if she wanted.

'We,' Navani said sharply, 'are here to discuss the future of Roshar. We must have a unified vision and goal.'

She glanced around the room as people considered. *He's going to talk first,* she thought, noticing the prime of Emul shifting in his seat. His name was Vexil the Wise, but people often referred to the Makabaki princes and primes by their country, much as Alethi highprinces were often referred to by their house name.

'The course is obvious, isn't it?' Emul said through an interpreter, though Navani understood his Azish. He bowed in his seat to the Azish child emperor, then continued. 'We must reclaim my nation from the hands of the traitor parshmen; then we must conquer Tukar. It is completely unreasonable to allow this insane man, who claims to be a god, to continue bereaving the glorious Azish Empire.'

This is going to get difficult, Navani thought as a half dozen other people started to speak at once. She raised her freehand. 'I will do my best to moderate fairly, Your Majesties, but do realize that I am only one person. I depend upon you all to facilitate the discussion, rather than trying to talk over one another.'

She nodded at the Azish Prime, hoping he'd take the floor. A translator whispered her words into the Prime's left ear; then Noura the vizier leaned forward and spoke quietly into the other, undoubtedly giving instructions.

They'll want to see how this plays out, Navani decided. *One of the others will speak next. They'll want to contrast the Emuli position, to assert themselves.*

'The throne recognizes the prime of Emul,' the little emperor finally said. 'And, er, we are aware of his desires.' He paused and looked around. 'Um, anyone else have a comment?'

'My brother the prince wishes to address you,' said the tall, refined representative from Tashikk, who wore a flowery suit of yellow and gold rather than his people's traditional wrap. A scribe whispered to him as a spanreed scratched out the message Tashikk's prince wanted conveyed to the gathering.

He'll contradict Emul, Navani thought. *Point us in another direction. Toward Iri maybe?*

'We of Tashikk,' the ambassador said, 'are more interested in the discovery of these glorious portals. The Alethi have invited us here and told us we're part of a grand coalition. We would respectfully inquire how often we will have use of these gates, and how to negotiate tariffs.'

Immediately, the room exploded with conversation.

'Our gate,' Au-nak said, 'in our *historical homeland* is being used without our permission. And while we thank the Alethi for securing it for us—'

'If there is to be war,' Fen said, 'then it's a bad time to be discussing tariffs. We should just agree to free trade.'

'Which would help your merchants, Fen,' Sebarial called. 'How about asking them to help the rest of us out with some free wartime supplies?'

'Emul –' the Emuli Prime began.

'Wait,' the Yezier princess said. 'Shouldn't we be concerned about Iri and Rira, who seem to have completely fallen in with the enemy?'

'Please,' Navani said, interrupting the mess of conversations. '*Please.* Let's do this in an orderly way. Perhaps before deciding where to fight, we could discuss how to best equip ourselves against the enemy threat?' She looked to Taravangian. 'Your Majesty, can you tell us more about the shields your scholars in Jah Keved are creating?'

'Yes. They . . . they are strong.'

'. . . How strong?' Navani prompted.

'Very strong. Er, yes. Strong enough.' He scratched his head and looked at her helplessly. 'How . . . how strong do you need them to be?'

She drew in a deep breath. He wasn't having a good day. Her mother had been like that, lucid on some days, barely cognizant on others.

'The half-shards,' Navani said, addressing the room, 'will give us an edge against the enemy. We have given the plans to the Azish scholars; I'm looking forward to pooling our resources and studying the process.'

'Could it lead to Shardplate?' Queen Fen asked.

'Possibly,' Navani said. 'But the more I study what we've discovered here in Urithiru, the more I've come to realize that our image of the ancients having fantastic technology was deeply flawed. An exaggeration at best, perhaps a fancy.'

'But Shards . . .' Fen said.

'Manifestations of spren,' Jasnah explained. 'Not fabrial technology. Even the gemstones we discovered, containing words of ancient Radiants during the days when they left Urithiru, were crude – if used in a way we hadn't yet explored. All this time we've been assuming that we lost great technology in the Desolations, but it seems we are far, far more advanced than the ancients ever were. It is the process of bonding spren that we lost.'

'Not lost,' the Azish Prime said. '*Abandoned.*'

He looked toward Dalinar, who sat in a relaxed posture. Not slumped, but not stiff either – a posture that somehow read as, 'I'm in control here. Don't pretend otherwise.' Dalinar loomed over a room even when trying to be unobtrusive. That furrowed brow darkened his blue eyes, and the way he rubbed his chin evoked the image of a man contemplating whom to execute first.

The attendees had arranged their seats roughly in a circle, but most of them faced Dalinar, who sat by Navani's chair. After everything that had happened, they didn't trust him.

'The ancient oaths are spoken once more,' Dalinar said. 'We are again Radiant. This time, we will not abandon you. I vow it.'

Noura the vizier whispered in the Azish Prime's ear, and he nodded before speaking. 'We are still *very* concerned about the powers in which you dabble. These abilities . . . who is to say that the Lost Radiants were wrong in abandoning them? They were frightened of something, and they locked these portals for a reason.'

'It is too late to turn back from this now, Your Majesty,' Dalinar said. 'I have bonded the Stormfather himself. We must either use these abilities, or crumple beneath the invasion.'

The Prime sat back, and his attendants seemed . . . concerned. They whispered among themselves.

Bring order from the chaos, Navani thought. She gestured toward the bridgemen and Lift. 'I understand your concern, but surely you have read our reports of the oaths these Radiants follow. Protection. Remembering the fallen. Those oaths are proof that our cause is just, our Radiants trustworthy. The powers are in safe hands, Your Majesty.'

'I think,' Ialai declared, 'we should stop dancing around and patting ourselves on the back.'

Navani spun to face Ialai. *Don't sabotage this*, she thought, meeting the woman's eyes. *Don't you dare.*

'We are here,' Ialai continued, 'to focus our attention. We should be discussing where to invade to gain the best position for an extended war. Obviously, there is only one answer. Shinovar is a bounteous land. Their orchards grow without end; the land is so mild that even the grass has grown relaxed and fat. We should seize that land to supply our armies.'

The others in the room nodded as if this were a perfectly acceptable line of conversation. With one targeted arrow, Ialai Sadeas proved what everyone whispered – that the Alethi were building a coalition to conquer the world, not just protect it.

'The Shin mountains present a historical problem,' said the Tashikki ambassador. 'Attacking across or through them is basically impossible.'

'We have the Oathgates now,' Fen said. 'Not to bring up that particular problem again, but has anyone investigated whether the Shin one can be opened? Having Shinovar as a redoubt, difficult to invade conventionally, would help secure our position.'

Navani cursed Ialai softly. This would only reinforce the Azish worry that the gates were dangerous. She tried to rein the discussion in, but it slipped away from her again.

'We need to know what the Oathgates do!' Tashikk was saying. 'Could the Alethi not share with us everything they've discovered regarding them?'

'What about your people?' Aladar shot back. 'They are the great traders in information. Could you share with us your secrets?'

'All Tashikki information is freely available.'

'At a huge price.'

'We need—'

'But *Emul*—'

'This whole thing is going to be a mess,' Fen said. 'I can see it already. We need to be able to trade freely, and Alethi greed could destroy this.'

'*Alethi* greed?' Ialai demanded. 'Are you trying to see how far you can push us? Because I assure you Dalinar Kholin will *not* be intimidated by a bunch of merchants and bankers.'

'Please,' Navani said into the growing uproar. 'Quiet.'

Nobody seemed to notice. Navani breathed out, then cleared her mind.

Order from chaos. How could she bring order to this chaos? She stopped fretting, and tried to listen to them. She studied the chairs they'd brought, the tone of their voices. Their fears, hidden behind what they demanded or requested.

The shape of it started to make sense to her. Right now, this room was full of building materials. Pieces of a fabrial. Each monarch, each kingdom, was one piece. Dalinar had gathered them, but he hadn't *formed* them.

Navani stepped up to the Azish Prime. People quieted as, shockingly, she bowed to him.

'Your Excellency,' she said, upon rising. 'What would you say is the Azish people's greatest strength?'

He glanced at his advisors as her words were translated, but they gave him no answer. Rather, they seemed curious to know what he'd say.

'Our laws,' he finally replied.

'Your famed bureaucracy,' Navani said. 'Your clerks and scribes – and by extension, the great information centers of Tashikk, the timekeepers and stormwardens of Yezier, the Azish legions. You are the greatest organizers on Roshar. I've long envied your orderly approach to the world.'

'Perhaps this is why your essay was so well received, Brightness Kholin,' the emperor said, sounding completely sincere.

'In light of your skill, I wonder. Would anyone in this room complain if a specific task were assigned to your scribes? We need procedures. A code of how our kingdoms are to interact, and how we're to share resources. Would you of Azir be willing to create this?'

The viziers looked shocked, then immediately began talking to one another in hushed, excited tones. The looks of delight on their faces were enough proof that yes indeed, they'd be willing.

'Now, wait,' Fen interjected. 'Are you talking of laws? That we all have to follow?' Au-nak nodded eagerly in agreement.

'More *and* less than laws,' Navani said. 'We need codes to guide our interactions – as proven by today. We must have procedures on how we hold meetings, how to give each person a turn. How we share information.'

'I don't know if Thaylenah can agree to even that.'

'Well, surely you'd want to see what the codes contained first, Queen Fen,' Navani said, strolling toward her. 'After all, we *are* going to need to administrate trade through the Oathgates. I wonder, who has excellent expertise in shipping, caravans, and trade in general . . . ?'

'You'd give that to *us*?' Fen asked, completely taken aback.

'It seems logical.'

Sebarial choked softly on the snacks he'd been eating, and Palona pounded him on the back. He'd wanted that job. *That will teach you to show up late to my meeting and make only wisecracks*, Navani noted.

She glanced at Dalinar, who seemed worried. Well, he always seemed worried lately.

'I'm not giving you the Oathgates,' Navani said to Fen. 'But someone has to oversee trade and supplies. It would be a natural match for the Thaylen merchants – so long as a fair agreement can be reached.'

'Huh,' Fen said, settling back. She glanced at her consort, who shrugged.

'And the Alethi?' the petite Yezier princess asked. 'What of you?'

'Well, we do excel at one thing,' Navani said. She looked to Emul. 'Would you accept help from our generals and armies to help you secure what is left of your kingdom?'

'By every Kadasix that has ever been holy!' Emul said. 'Yes, of course! Please.'

'I have several scribes who are experts in fortification,' Aladar suggested from his seat behind Dalinar and Jasnah. 'They could survey your remaining territory and give you advice on securing it.'

'And recovering what we've lost?' Emul asked.

Ialai opened her mouth to speak, perhaps to extol the virtues of Alethi warmongering again.

Jasnah cut her off, speaking decisively. 'I propose we entrench ourselves first. Tukar, Iri, Shinovar . . . each of these looks tempting to attack, but what good will that do if we stretch ourselves too far? We should focus on securing our lands as they now stand.'

'Yes,' Dalinar said. 'We shouldn't be asking ourselves, 'Where should we strike?' but instead, 'Where will our enemy strike next?"'

'They've secured three positions,' Highprince Aladar said. 'Iri, Marat . . . and Alethkar.'

'But you sent an expedition,' Fen said. 'To reclaim Alethkar.'

Navani caught her breath, glancing at Dalinar. He nodded slowly.

'Alethkar has fallen,' Navani said. 'The expedition failed. Our homeland is overrun.'

Navani had expected this to prompt another burst of conversation, but instead it was greeted only by stunned silence.

Jasnah continued for her. 'The last of our armies have retreated into Herdaz or Jah Keved, harried and confused by enemies who can fly – or by the sudden attacks of shock troops of parshmen. Our only holdouts are on the southern border, by the sea. Kholinar has fallen completely; the Oathgate is lost to us. We've locked it on our side, so that it cannot be used to reach Urithiru.'

'I'm sorry,' Fen said.

'My daughter is correct,' Navani said, trying to project strength while admitting that they had become a nation of refugees. 'We should apply our efforts *first* toward making sure no more nations fall.'

'My homeland –' the prime of Emul began.

'No,' Noura said in thickly accented Alethi. 'I'm sorry, but no. If the Voidbringers had wanted your last nibble of land, Vexil, they'd have taken it. The Alethi can help you secure what you have, and it seems generous of them to do so. The enemy brushed past you to gather in Marat, conquering only what was necessary on the way. Their eyes are turned elsewhere.'

'Oh my!' Taravangian said. 'Could they . . . be coming for me?'

'It does seem a reasonable assumption,' Au-nak said. 'The Veden civil war left the country in ruin, and the border between Alethkar and Jah Keved is porous.'

'Maybe,' Dalinar said. 'I've fought on that border. It's not as easy a battlefield as it would seem.'

'We must defend Jah Keved,' Taravangian said. 'When the king gave me the throne, I promised I'd care for his people. If the Voidbringers attack us . . .'

The worry in his voice gave Navani an opportunity. She stepped back into the center of the room. 'We won't allow that to happen, will we?'

'I will send troops to your aid, Taravangian,' Dalinar said. 'But one army can be construed as an invading force, and I am not intending to invade my allies, even in appearance. Can we not mortar this alliance with a show of solidarity? Will anyone else help?'

The Azish Prime regarded Dalinar. Behind him, the viziers and scions conducted a private conversation by writing on pads of paper. When they finished, Vizier Noura leaned forward and whispered to the emperor, who nodded.

'We will send five battalions to Jah Keved,' he said. 'This will prove an important test of mobility through the Oathgates. King Taravangian, you will have the support of Azir.'

Navani released a long breath in relief.

She gave leave for the meeting to take a pause, so that people could enjoy refreshment – though most would probably spend it strategizing or relaying events to their various allies. The highprinces became a flurry of motion, breaking into individual houses to converse.

Navani settled down in her seat beside Dalinar.

'You've promised away a great deal,' he noted. 'Giving Fen control of trade and supply?'

'Administration is different from control,' Navani said. 'But either way, did you think you were going to make this coalition work without giving something up?'

'No. Of course not.' He stared outward. That haunted expression made her shiver. *What did you remember, Dalinar? And what did the Nightwatcher do to you?*

They needed the Blackthorn. *She* needed the Blackthorn. His strength to quiet the sick worry inside of her, his will to forge this coalition. She took his hand in hers, but he stiffened, then stood up. He did that whenever he felt he was growing too relaxed. It was as if he was looking for danger to face.

She stood up beside him. 'We need to get you out of the tower,' she decided. 'To get a new perspective. Visit someplace new.'

'That,' Dalinar said, voice hoarse, 'would be good.'

'Taravangian was speaking of having you tour Vedenar personally. If we're going to send Kholin troops into the kingdom, it would make sense for you to get a feel for the situation there.'

'Very well.'

The Azish called for her, asking for clarification on what direction she wanted them to take with their coalition bylaws. She left Dalinar, but couldn't leave off worrying about him. She'd have to burn a glyphward today. A dozen of them, for Elhokar and the others. Except . . . part of the problem was that Dalinar claimed nobody was watching the prayers as they burned, sending twisting smoke to the Tranquiline Halls. Did she believe that? Truly?

Today, she'd taken a huge step toward unifying Roshar. Yet she felt more powerless than ever.

RIINO

Of the Unmade, Sja-anat was most feared by the Radiants. They spoke extensively of her ability to corrupt spren, though only 'lesser' spren – whatever that means.

—From Hessi's *Mythica,* page 89

Kaladin remembered holding a dying woman's hand.

It had been during his days as a slave. He remembered crouching in the darkness, thick forest underbrush scratching his skin, the night around him too quiet. The animals had fled; they knew something was wrong.

The other slaves didn't whisper, shift, or cough in their hiding places. He'd taught them well.

We have to go. Have to move.

He tugged on Nalma's hand. He'd promised to help the older woman find her husband, who had been sold to another household. That wasn't supposed to be legal, but you could get away with doing all kinds of things to slaves with the right brands, especially if they were foreign.

She resisted his tug, and he could understand her hesitance. The underbrush was safe, for the moment. It was also too obvious. The brightlords had chased them in circles for days, getting closer and closer. Stay here, and the slaves would be captured.

He tugged again, and she passed the signal to the next slave, all the way down the line. Then she clung to his hand as he led them – as quietly as he could – toward where he remembered a game trail.

Get away.

Find freedom. Find honor again.

It had to be out there somewhere.

The snapping sound of the trap closing sent a jolt through Kaladin. A year later, he'd still wonder how he missed stepping in it himself.

It got Nalma instead. She yanked her hand from his as she screamed.

Hunters' horns moaned in the night. Light burst from newly un-shielded lanterns, showing men in uniforms among the trees. The other slaves broke, bursting out of the underbrush like game for sport. Next to Kaladin, Nalma's leg was caught in a fierce steel trap – a thing of springs and jaws that they wouldn't even use on a beast, for fear of ruining the sport. Her tibia jutted through her skin.

'Oh, Stormfather,' Kaladin whispered as painspren writhed around them. 'Stormfather!' He tried to stanch the blood, but it spurted between his fingers. 'Stormfather, no. Stormfather!'

'Kaladin,' she said through clenched teeth. 'Kaladin, *run* . . .'

Arrows cut down several of the fleeing slaves. Traps caught two others. In the distance, a voice called, 'Wait! That's my property you're cutting down.'

'A necessity, Brightlord,' a stronger voice said. The local highlord. 'Unless you want to encourage more of this behavior.'

So much blood. Kaladin uselessly made a bandage as Nalma tried to push him away, to make him run. He took her hand and held it instead, weeping as she died.

After killing the others, the brightlords found him still kneeling there. Against reason, they spared him. They said it was because he hadn't run with the others, but in truth they'd needed someone to bear warning to the other slaves.

Regardless of the reason, Kaladin had lived.

He always did.

∴

There was no underbrush here in Shadesmar, but those old instincts served Kaladin well as he crept toward the lighthouse. He'd suggested that he scout ahead, as he didn't trust this dark land. The others had agreed. With Lashings, he could get away most easily in an emergency – and neither Adolin nor Azure had experience scouting. Kaladin didn't mention that most of *his* practice sneaking had come as a runaway slave.

He focused on staying low to the ground, trying to use rifts in the black stone to hide his approach. Fortunately, stepping silently wasn't difficult on this glassy ground.

The lighthouse was a large stone tower topped by an enormous bonfire. It threw a flagrant orange glow over the point of the peninsula. Where did they get the *fuel* for that thing?

He drew closer, accidentally startling a burst of lifespren, which shot up from some crystalline plants, then floated back down. He froze, but heard no sounds from the lighthouse.

Once he got a little closer, he settled down to watch for a while, to see if he could spot anything suspicious. He sorely missed the diaphanous form Syl had in the Physical Realm; she could have reported back to the others what he'd seen, or even scouted into the building herself, invisible to all but the right eyes.

After a short time, something crawled out of the beads of the ocean near him: a round lurglike creature with a fat, bulbous body and squat legs. About the size of a toddler, it hopped close to him, then tipped the entire top half of its head backward. A long tongue shot up in the air from the gaping mouth; it began to flap and wave.

Storms. An anticipationspren? They looked like streamers on his side, but those . . . those were waving *tongues*? What other simple, stable parts of his life were complete lies?

Two more anticipationspren joined the first, clustering near him and deploying their long, wagging tongues. He kicked at them. 'Shoo.' Deceptively solid, they refused to budge, so he tried calming himself, hoping it would banish them. Finally, he just continued forward, his three bothersome attendants hopping behind. That sorely undermined the stealth of his approach, making him more nervous – which in turn made the anticipationspren even more eager to stick with him.

He managed to reach the wall of the tower, where he might have expected the heat of the enormous fire to be oppressive. Instead, he could barely feel it. Notably, the flames caused his shadow to behave normally, extending behind him instead of pointing toward the sun.

He took a breath, then glanced up through the open-shuttered window, into the ground floor of the lighthouse.

Inside, he saw an old Shin man – with furrowed, wrinkled skin and a completely bald head – sitting in a chair, reading by spherelight. A human? Kaladin couldn't decide if that was a good sign or not. The old man began to turn a page in his book, then froze, looking up.

Kaladin ducked down, heart thumping. Those stupid anticipationspren continued to crowd nearby, but their tongues shouldn't be visible through the window –

'Hello?' an accented voice called from inside the lighthouse. 'Who's out there? Show yourself!'

Kaladin sighed, then stood up. So much for his promise to do some stealthy reconnaissance.

⁘

Shallan waited with the others in the shadow of a strange rock growth. It looked something like a mushroom made from obsidian, the height of a tree; she thought she'd seen its like before, during one of her glimpses into Shadesmar. Pattern said it was alive, but 'very, very slow.'

The group waited, pensive, as Kaladin scouted. She hated sending him alone, but Shallan knew nothing about that sort of work. Veil did. But Veil . . . still felt broken, from what had happened in Kholinar. That was dangerous. Where would Shallan hide now? As Radiant?

Find the balance, Wit had said. *Accept the pain, but don't accept that you deserved it. . . .*

She sighed, then got out her sketchbook and started drawing some of the spren they'd seen.

'So,' Syl said, sitting on a rock nearby and swinging her legs. 'I've always wondered. Does the world look weird to you, or normal?'

'Weird,' Pattern said. 'Mmm. Same as for everyone.'

'I guess neither of us technically have eyes,' Syl said, leaning back and looking up at the glassy canopy of their tree-mushroom shelter. 'We're each a bit of power made manifest. We honorspren mimic Honor himself. You Cryptics mimic . . . weird stuff?'

'The fundamental underlying mathematics by which natural phenomena occur. Mmm. Truths that explain the fabric of existence.'

'Yeah. Weird stuff.'

Shallan lowered her pencil, looking with dissatisfaction at the attempt she'd made at drawing a fearspren. It looked like a child's scribble.

Veil was seeping out.

That has always been you, Shallan. You just have to admit it. Allow it.

'I'm trying, Wit,' she whispered.

'You all right?' Adolin asked, kneeling beside her, putting his hand on her back, then rubbing her shoulders. Storms, that felt good. They'd walked *entirely* too far these last few days.

He glanced at her sketchpad. 'More ... what did you call it? Abstractionalism?'

She snapped the sketchpad closed. 'What is taking that bridgeman so long?' She glanced over her shoulder, which interrupted Adolin. 'Don't stop,' she added, 'or I will murder you.'

He chuckled and continued working at her shoulders. 'He'll be fine.'

'You were worried about him yesterday.'

'He's got battle fatigue, but an objective will help with that. We have to watch him when he's sitting around doing nothing, not when he's got a specific mission.'

'If you say so.' She nodded toward Azure, who stood by the coast, staring across the ocean of beads. 'What do you make of her?'

'That uniform is well tailored,' Adolin said, 'but the blue doesn't work with her skin. She needs a lighter shade. The breastplate is overly much, like she's trying to prove something. I do like the cape though. I've always wanted to justify wearing one. Father gets away with it, but I never could.'

'I wasn't asking for a wardrobe assessment, Adolin.'

'Clothing says a lot about people.'

'Yeah? What happened to the fancy suit you got in Kholinar?'

He looked down – which stopped the massaging of shoulders for an unacceptable count of three, so she growled at him.

'It didn't fit me anymore,' he said, resuming the massage. 'But you do raise an important problem. Yes, we need to find food and drink. But if I have to wear the same uniform this entire trip, you won't have to murder me. I'll commit suicide.'

Shallan had almost forgotten that she was hungry. How odd. She sighed, closing her eyes and trying not to melt *too* much into the feeling of his touch.

379

'Huh,' Adolin said a short time later. 'Shallan, what do you suppose that is?'

She followed his nod and spotted an odd little spren floating through the air. Bone-white and brown, it had wings extending to the sides and long tresses for a tail. In front of its body hovered a cube.

'Looks like those gloryspren we saw earlier,' she noted. 'Only the wrong color. And the shape of the head is . . .'

'Corrupted!' Syl said. 'That's one of Odium's!'

⋰

As he stepped inside the lighthouse, Kaladin's instincts drove him to check to either side of the doorway for anyone waiting in ambush. The room seemed empty save for furniture, the Shin man, and some strange pictures on the walls. The place smelled of incense and spices.

The Shin man snapped his book closed. 'Cutting it close, aren't you? Well, let us begin! We haven't much time.' He stood up, proving himself to be rather short. His odd clothing had puffed out portions on the arms, the trousers very tight. He walked to a door at the side of the chamber.

'I should fetch my companions,' Kaladin said.

'Ah, but the very *best* readings happen at the beginning of the high-storm!' The man checked a small device that he took from his pocket. 'Only two minutes off.'

A highstorm? Azure had said they didn't need to worry about those in Shadesmar.

'Wait,' Kaladin said, stepping after the little man – who had entered a room built up against the base of the lighthouse. It had large windows, but its main feature was a small table at the center. That held something lumpish covered by a black cloth.

Kaladin found himself . . . curious. That was good, after the darkness of the last few days. He stepped in, glancing to the sides again. One wall contained a picture of people kneeling before a bright white mirror. Another was a cityscape at dusk, with a group of low houses clustered before an enormous wall that had light glowing beyond it.

'Well, let's begin!' the man said. 'You have come to witness the extraordinary, and I shall provide it. The price is a mere two marks of Stormlight. You shall be greatly rewarded in kind – both in dreams and luster!'

'I should really get my friends. . . .' Kaladin said.

The man whipped the cloth off the table, revealing a large crystalline globe. It glowed with a powerful light, bathing the room in luminescence. Kaladin blinked against it. Was that Stormlight?

'Are you balking at the price?' the man said. 'What is the money to you? Potential? If you never spend it, you gain nothing by having it. And the witness of what is to come will far recompense you for small means expended!'

'I . . .' Kaladin said, raising his hand against the light. 'Storms, man. I have no idea what you're talking about.'

The Shin man frowned, face lit from below like the globe. 'You came here for a fortune, didn't you? To the Rii Oracle? You wish me to see the unwalked paths – during the highstorm, when realms blend.'

'A fortune? You mean *foretelling the future*?' Kaladin felt a bitter taste in his mouth. 'The future is *forbidden*.'

The old man cocked his head. 'But . . . isn't this why you came to see me?'

'Storms, no. I'm looking for passage. We heard that ships come by here.'

The old man rubbed the bridge of his nose and sighed. 'Passage? Why didn't you say so? And I was really enjoying the speech. Ah well. A ship? Let me check my calendars. I think supplies are coming soon. . . .'

He bustled past Kaladin, muttering to himself.

Outside, the sky rippled with light. The clouds *shimmered*, gaining a strange, ethereal luminescence. Kaladin gaped, then glanced back at the little man, who had fetched a ledger from a side table.

'That . . .' Kaladin said. 'Is that what a highstorm looks like on this side?'

'Hmmm? Oh, new, are you? How have you gotten into Shadesmar, but not seen a storm pass? Did you come directly from the perpendicularity?' The old man frowned. 'Not a lot of people coming through there anymore.'

That *light*. The bright sphere on the table – as large as a man's head, and glowing with a milky light – shifted colors, matching the pearlescent ripples above. There was no gemstone inside that globe. And the light seemed different. Transfixing.

'Here now,' the man said as Kaladin stepped forward, 'don't touch that. It's only for *properly trained* fo—'

Kaladin rested his hand on the sphere.

And felt himself get carried away by the storm.

⁂

Shallan and the others dodged for cover, but too slowly. The strange spren flitted right under their small canopy.

Overhead, the clouds started to ripple with a vibrant set of colors.

The corrupted gloryspren *landed* on Shallan's arm. *Odium suspects that you survived,* a voice said in her mind. That . . . that was the voice of the Unmade from the mirror. Sja-anat. *He thinks something strange happened to the Oathgate because of our influence – we've never managed to Enlighten such powerful spren before. It's believable that something odd might happen. I lied, and said I think you were sent far, far from the point of transfer.*

He has minions in this realm, and they will be told to hunt you. So take care. Fortunately, he doesn't know that you're a Lightweaver – he thinks you are an Elsecaller for some reason.

I will do what I can, but I'm not sure he trusts me any longer.

The spren fluttered away.

'Wait!' Shallan said. 'Wait, I have questions!'

Syl tried to snatch it, but it dodged and was soon out over the ocean.

⁂

Kaladin rode the storm.

He'd done this before, in dreams. He'd even spoken to the Stormfather.

This felt different. He rode in a shimmering, rippling surge of colors. Around him, the clouds streamed past at incredible speed, coming alight with those colors. Pulsing with them, as if to a beat.

He couldn't feel the Stormfather. He couldn't see a landscape beneath him. Just shimmering colors, and clouds that faded into . . . light.

Then a figure. Dalinar Kholin, kneeling someplace dark, surrounded by nine shadows. A flash of glowing red eyes.

The enemy's champion was coming. Kaladin knew in that moment – an overpowering sensation thrumming through him – that Dalinar was in terrible, *terrible* danger. Without help, the Blackthorn was doomed.

'Where!' Kaladin screamed to the light as it began to fade. 'When! How do I reach him!'

The colors diminished.

'*Please!*'

He saw a flash of a vaguely familiar city. Tall, built along the stones, it had a distinctive pattern of buildings at the center. A wall and an ocean beyond.

Kaladin dropped to his knees in the fortuneteller's room. The little Shin man batted Kaladin's hand from the glowing sphere. ' – rtune seers like myself. You'll ruin it, or . . .' He trailed off, then took Kaladin's head, turning it toward him. 'You *saw something*!'

Kaladin nodded weakly.

'How? Impossible. Unless . . . you're *Invested*. What Heightening are you?' He squinted at Kaladin. 'No. Something else. Merciful Domi . . . A Surgebinder? It has begun again?'

Kaladin stumbled to his feet. He glanced at the large globe of light, which the lighthouse keeper covered up again with the black cloth, then put his hand to his forehead, which had begun thumping with pain. What had *that* been? His heart still raced with anxiety.

'I . . . I need to go get my friends,' he said.

❖

Kaladin sat in the main room of the lighthouse, in the chair Riino – the Shin lighthouse keeper – had occupied earlier. Shallan and Adolin negotiated with him on the other side of the room, Pattern looming over Shallan's shoulder and making the fortuneteller nervous. Riino had food and supplies for trade, though it would cost them infused spheres. Apparently, Stormlight was the only commodity that mattered on this side.

'Charlatans like him aren't uncommon, where I come from,' Azure said, resting with her back against the wall near Kaladin. 'People who claim to be able to see the future, living off people's hopes. Your society was right to forbid them. The spren do likewise, so his kind have to live off in places like this, hoping people will be desperate enough to come to them. Probably gets some business with each ship that comes through.'

'I saw something, Azure,' Kaladin said, still trembling. 'It was real.' His limbs felt drained, like the aftereffect of lifting weights for a long period.

'Maybe,' Azure said. 'Those types use dusts and powders that grant euphoria, making you *think* you've seen something. Even the gods of my land catch only glimpses of the Spiritual Realm – and in all my life, I've only met one human I believe truly understood it. And he might actually be a god. I'm not sure.'

'Wit,' Kaladin said. 'The man that brought you the metal that protected your Soulcaster.'

She nodded.

Well, Kaladin *had* seen something. *Dalinar* . . .

Adolin walked over and handed Kaladin a squat metal cylinder. He used a device – provided by the Shin man – to break open the top. There were some fish rations inside. Kaladin poked at the chunks with his finger, then inspected the container.

'Canned food,' Azure noted. 'It's extremely convenient.'

Kaladin's stomach rumbled, so he dug into the fish with the spoon Adolin provided. The meat tasted salty, but was good – far better than something Soulcast. Shallan joined them, trailed by Pattern, while the lighthouse keeper bustled off to fetch some supplies they'd traded for. The man glanced at the doorway, where the spren of Adolin's Blade stood, silent like a statue.

Out through the room's window, Kaladin could see Syl standing on the coast, watching out over the sea of beads. *Her hair doesn't ripple here,* he thought. In the Physical Realm it often waved as if being brushed by an unseen breeze. Here, it acted like the hair of a human.

She hadn't wanted to enter the lighthouse for some reason. What was that about?

'The lighthouse keeper says a ship will be arriving any time now,' Adolin said. 'We should be able to buy passage.'

'Mmm,' Pattern said. 'The ship is going to Celebrant. Mmm. A city on the island.'

'Island?'

'It's a lake on our side,' Adolin said. 'Called the Sea of Spears, in the southeast of Alethkar. By the ruins . . . of Rathalas.' He drew his lips to a line and glanced away.

'What?' Kaladin asked.

'Rathalas was where my mother was killed,' Adolin said. 'Assassinated by rebels. Her death drove my father into a fury. We almost lost him to the despair.' He shook his head, and Shallan rested her hand on his arm.

'It's ... not a pleasant event to think about. Sadeas burned the city to the ground in retribution. My father gets a strange, distant expression whenever someone mentions Rathalas. I think he blames himself for not stopping Sadeas, even though he was mad with grief at the time, wounded and incoherent from an attempt on his own life.'

'Well, there's still a spren city on this side,' Azure said. 'But it's in the wrong direction. We need to be heading west – toward the Horneater Peaks – not south.'

'Mmm,' Pattern said. 'Celebrant is a prominent city. In it, we could find passage wherever we wish to go. And the lighthouse keeper doesn't know when a ship going the right way might pass here.'

Kaladin put his fish down, then gestured at Shallan. 'Can I have some paper?'

She let him have a sheet from her sketchpad. With an unpracticed hand, he drew out the buildings he'd seen in his momentary ... whatever it had been. *I've seen this pattern before. From above.*

'That's Thaylen City,' Shallan said. 'Isn't it?'

That's right, Kaladin thought. He'd only visited once, opening the city's Oathgate. 'I saw this, in the vision I explained to you.' He glanced at Azure, who seemed skeptical.

Kaladin could still feel his emotion from the vision, that thrumming sense of anxiety. The sure knowledge that Dalinar was in grave danger. Nine shadows. A champion who would lead the enemy forces ...

'The Oathgate in Thaylen City is open and working,' Kaladin said. 'Shallan and I saw to that. And since the Oathgate in Kholinar brought us to Shadesmar, theoretically another – one that isn't corrupted by the Unmade – could get us back.'

'Assuming I can figure out how to work it on this side,' Shallan said. 'That's a pretty daunting assumption.'

'We should try to reach the perpendicularity in the Peaks,' Azure said. 'It's the only sure way back.'

'The lighthouse keeper says he thinks something strange is happening there,' Shallan said. 'Ships from that direction have never ended up arriving.'

Kaladin rested his fingers on the sketch he'd done. He *needed* to get to Thaylen City. It didn't matter how. The darkness inside him seemed to retreat.

He had a purpose. A goal. Something to focus on other than the people he'd lost in Kholinar.

Protect Dalinar.

Kaladin returned to eating his fish, and the group settled in to wait for the ship. It took a few hours, during which the clouds steadily faded in color, before growing plain white again. On the other side, the highstorm had completed its passing.

Eventually, Kaladin saw something out on the horizon, beyond where Syl sat on the rocks. Yes, that was a ship, sailing in from the west. Except . . . it didn't have a sail. Had he even felt wind in Shadesmar? He didn't think so.

The ship crashed through the ocean of beads, surging toward the lighthouse. It employed no sail, no mast, and no oars. Instead, it was pulled from the front by an elaborate rigging attached to a group of incredible spren. Long and sinuous, they had triangular heads and floated on multiple sets of rippling wings.

Storms . . . they pulled the ship like chulls. Flying, majestic chulls with undulating bodies. He'd never seen anything like it.

Adolin grunted from where he stood by the window. 'Well, at least we'll be traveling in style.'

Lore suggested leaving a city if the spren there start acting strangely.
Curiously, Sja-anat was often regarded as an individual, when others
– like Moelach or Ashertmarn – were seen as forces.

—From Hessi's *Mythica*, page 90

S zeth of Shinovar left the Skybreaker fortress with the twenty
other squires. The sun approached the clouded horizon to the
west, gilding the Purelake red and gold. Those calm waters,
strangely, now sprouted dozens of long wooden poles.

Of various heights ranging from five to thirty feet, these poles appeared to have been jammed into fissures in the lake bottom. Each had
an odd knobby shape at the top.

'This is a test of martial competence,' Master Warren said. The Azish
man looked strange in the garb of a Marabethian lawkeeper, chest bare
and shoulders draped with the short, patterned cloak. The Azish were
normally so proper, overly encumbered with robes and hats. 'We must
train to fight, if the Desolation truly has begun.'

Without Nin's guidance to confirm, they spoke of the Desolation in
'if's and 'might's.

'Each pole is topped with a group of bags bearing powders of a different color,' Warren continued. 'Fight by throwing those – you cannot

use other weapons, and you cannot leave the contest area marked by the poles.

'I will call time over when the sun sets. We will tally the number of times each squire's uniform was marked by one of the bags of powder. You lose four points for each different color on your uniform, and an additional point for each repeated hit from a color. The winner is the one who has lost the fewest points. Begin.'

Szeth drew in Stormlight and Lashed himself into the air with the others. Though he didn't care if he won arbitrary tests of competence, the chance to dance the Lashings – for once without needing to cause death and destruction – called to him. This would be like those days in his youth, spent training with the Honorblades.

He soared upward about thirty feet, then used a half Lashing to hover. Yes, the tops of the poles each bore a collection of small pouches tied on by strings. He Lashed himself past one, snatching a pouch, which let out a puff of pink dust as it came off in his hand. He now saw why the squires had been told to wear a white shirt and trousers today.

'Excellent,' Szeth said as the other squires scattered, grabbing pouches.

What? the sword asked. Szeth carried it on his back, tied securely in place, at an angle from which he could not draw the weapon. *I don't understand. Where is the evil?*

'No evil today, sword-nimi. Just a *challenge*.'

He hurled the pouch at one of the other squires, hitting her square in the shoulder, and the resulting dust colored her shirt in that spot. Notably, the master had said that only color on the *uniform* would be counted, so holding the pouches and dusting one's own fingers was fine. Similarly, hitting each other in the face gained no advantage.

The others took quickly to the game; soon pouches were being flung in all directions. Each pole bore only a single color, encouraging competitors to move about to hit others with as many colors as possible. Joret tried hovering in one spot anyway, dominating one pole to prevent others from hitting him with its color. Sitting still made him a target, however, and his uniform was quickly covered in spots.

Szeth dove, then pulled himself up with an expert Lashing so that he swooped, skimming the surface of the Purelake. He grabbed a pole as he passed, bending it out of Cali's reach as she went by above.

I'm down too low, Szeth realized as bags of dust fell toward him. *Too easy a target.*

He twisted back and forth, executing a complex maneuver that manipulated both Lashings and the wind of his passing. Pouches smacked the water near him.

He pulled upward. Lashing wasn't like the flight of a swallow – instead, it was like tying oneself to strings, a puppet to be yanked about. It was easy to lose control, as evidenced by the awkward motions of the newer squires.

As Szeth gained height, Zedzil fell in behind him, holding a pouch in each hand. Szeth added a second Lashing upward, then a third. His Stormlight lasted so much longer than it had before – he could only assume that Radiants were more efficient than those who used Honorblades for the powers.

He shot upward like an arrow, windspren joining and twisting around him. Zedzil followed, but when he tried to throw a pouch at Szeth, the wind was too great. The pouch fell backward immediately, striking Zedzil on his own shoulder.

Szeth dropped into a dive, and Zedzil followed until Szeth snatched a green bag from a pole and tossed it over his shoulder, hitting Zedzil again. The younger man cursed, then shot away to find easier prey.

Still, this combat proved to be a surprising challenge. Szeth had rarely fought in the air itself, and this contest felt similar to when he'd battled the Windrunner in the skies. He twisted among the poles, dodging pouches – even snatching one from the air before it hit him – and found he was *enjoying* himself.

The screams from the shadows seemed dim, less pressing. He wove between thrown pouches, dancing above a lake painted by the hues of a setting sun, and smiled.

Then immediately felt guilty. He had left tears, blood, and terror in his wake like a personal seal. He had destroyed monarchies, families – innocent and guilty alike. He could not be *happy.* He was only a tool of retribution. Not redemption, for he dared not believe in such.

If he was to be forced to keep living, it should not be a life that anyone would ever envy.

You think like Vasher, the sword said in his head. *Do you know Vasher?*

*He teaches swords to people now, which is funny because VaraTreledees always
says Vasher isn't any good with the sword.*

Szeth rededicated himself to the fight, not for joy but for practicality.
Unfortunately, his momentary distraction earned him his first hit. A dark
blue pouch struck, its circle stark on his white shirt.

He growled, soaring upward with a pouch in each hand. He flung
them with precision, hitting one squire in the back, then another in the
leg. Nearby, four of the older squires flew in formation. They would chase
an isolated squire, swarming him or her with a flurry of eight pouches,
often scoring six or seven hits while rarely getting hit themselves.

As Szeth zoomed past, they fixated on him, perhaps because his
uniform was nearly pristine. He immediately Lashed himself upward –
canceling his lateral Lashing – to try to get above the pack. These were
well practiced with their powers, however, and not so easily put off.

If he continued straight upward, they'd merely chase him until he ran
out of Stormlight. Already his reserves were low, as each squire had only
been given enough to last through the contest. If he double- or triple-
Lashed himself too often, he'd run out early.

The sun was slipping inch by inch out of sight. Not much time left; he
simply needed to last.

Szeth dove to the side, moving quickly and erratically. Only one of
the pack chasing him chanced a throw; the others knew to wait for a
better shot. Szeth's swoop took him straight toward a pole, but it held no
pouches. Fari looked like he had gathered them all up to hoard the color.

So Szeth grabbed the pole itself.

He pushed it to the side, bending it until it snapped, leaving him with
a pole some ten feet long. He lightened it with a partial Lashing upward,
then tucked it under his arm.

A quick glance over the shoulder showed that the four teammates were
still tailing him. The one who had thrown earlier had grabbed two new
pouches and was catching up to the others with a double Lashing.

Make a stand, the sword suggested. *You can take them.*

For once, Szeth agreed. He zoomed down until he was near the water,
his passing causing a trail of ripples on the surface. Younger squires
dodged out of his way, flinging dust bags, but missing because of his
speed.

He deliberately Lashed himself to the side in a smooth, predictable turn. It was exactly the opportunity the pack had been waiting for, and they started throwing at him. But he was no frightened child, to be intimidated and overwhelmed by superior numbers. He was the Assassin in White. And this was but a game.

Szeth spun and began batting the pouches away with his staff. He even managed to hit the last one back into the face of the leader of the group, a man named Ty.

It wouldn't count as a mark, but the dust got in Ty's eyes, causing him to blink and slow. The group expended most of their pouches, which let Szeth – Lashed now directly toward them – get close.

And nobody should *ever* let him get too close.

He dropped his staff and grabbed a squire by her shirt, using her as a shield from an opportunist outside the group, who was throwing crimson bags. Szeth spun with her, then kicked her toward a companion. They slammed together, trailing streaks of red dust. He grabbed another squire from the pack, trying to Lash him away.

The man's body resisted the Lashing, however. People bearing Stormlight were more difficult to Lash – something Szeth was only now coming to understand. He could, however, Lash himself backward, hauling the man with him. When he let go, the squire had trouble adjusting to the change in momentum, and jolted in the air, letting himself get hit by a half dozen bags from outsiders.

Szeth zipped away, running dangerously low on Stormlight. Only another few minutes . . .

Beneath him, Ty called to the others, pointing up at Szeth. The obvious current winner. Only one strategy made sense at this point.

'Get him!' Ty shouted.

Oh, good! the sword said.

Szeth Lashed himself downward – which proved wise, as many of the squires shot up past him, assuming he'd try to stay high. No, his best defense while outnumbered was confusion. He got among them, a storm of pouches targeting him. Szeth did what he could to avoid them, zipping one way, then the other – but there were too many attacks. The poorly aimed ones were the most dangerous, as moving out of the way of a well-placed attack almost always took him into the path of an errant one.

One pouch struck his back, followed by a second. A third hit his side.

Dust flew all around as the squires hit each other too. That was his hope: that even as he took hits, they would take more.

He soared up, then dove again, causing the others to dodge like sparrows before a hawk. He flew along the water, scattering fish in the waning light, then shot upward to—

His Stormlight ran out.

His glow vanished. The tempest within died. Before the sun could set, the cold took him. Szeth arced in the air, and was *pummeled* with a dozen different pouches. He dropped through the cloud of multicolored dust, leaving an afterimage from his loosely fastened spirit.

He splashed into the Purelake.

Fortunately, he hadn't been too high, so the landing was only mildly painful. He hit the bottom of the shallow lake; then when he stood up, the others hit him with another round of pouches. No mercy from *this* group.

The last sliver of the sun vanished, and Master Warren shouted an end to the test. The others streaked away, their Stormlight conspicuous in the dimming light.

Szeth stood waist-deep in water.

Wow, the sword said. *I kind of feel bad for you.*

'Thank you, sword-nimi. I . . .'

What were those two spren floating nearby, shaped as small *slits* in the air? They separated the sky, like wounds in skin, exposing a black field full of stars. When they moved, the substance of reality bent around them.

Szeth bowed his head. He no longer ascribed to spren any particular religious significance, but he could still be in awe of these. He might have lost this contest, but he seemed to have impressed the highspren.

Or *had* he lost? What *exactly* had the rules been?

Thoughtful, he ducked under the water, swimming in the shallow lake back toward the bank. He climbed out, water streaming from his clothing as he walked up to the others. The masters had brought out bright sphere lanterns, along with food and refreshment. A Tashikki squire was recording the points while two masters adjudicated what counted as a 'hit' and what did not.

Szeth suddenly felt frustrated by their games. Nin had promised him the opportunity to cleanse Shinovar. What time was there for games? The moment had come for him to ascend to a rank beyond all of this.

He walked up to the masters. 'I am sorry to have won this contest, as I did the one with the prison.'

'You?' Ty said, incredulous. Ty had five spots on him. Not bad. 'You got hit at *least* two dozen times.'

'I believe,' Szeth replied, 'that the rules stated the winner was the one with the fewest marks on his uniform.' He held his hands to the side, showing his white clothing, washed clean during his swim.

Warren and Ki shared a look. She nodded with a hint of a smile.

'There is always one,' Warren said, 'who notices that. Remember that while loopholes are to be exploited, Szeth-son-Neturo, they are dangerous to rely upon. Still, you have done well. Both in your performance, and in seeing this hole in the rules.' He glanced into the night, squinting at the two highspren, who seemed to have made themselves visible to Warren as well. 'Others agree.'

'He used a weapon,' one of the older squires said, pointing. 'He broke the rules!'

'I used a pole to block pouches,' Szeth said. 'But I did not attack anyone with it.'

'You attacked me!' said the woman he'd thrown at someone else.

'Physical contact was not forbidden, and I cannot help it if you are unable to control your Lashings when I release you.'

The masters didn't object. Indeed, Ki leaned in to Warren. 'He is beyond the skill of these. I hadn't realized . . .'

Warren looked back to him. 'You shall soon have your spren, gauging by this performance.'

'Not soon,' Szeth said. 'Right now. I shall say the Third Ideal this night, choosing to follow the law. I—'

'*No,*' a voice interrupted.

A figure stood up on the low wall surrounding the order's stone courtyard. Skybreakers gasped, holding up lanterns, illuminating a man with dark Makabaki skin highlighted by a white crescent birthmark on his right cheek. Unlike the others, he wore a striking uniform of silver and black.

Nin-son-God, Nale, Nakku, Nalan – this man had a hundred different names and was revered across all Roshar. The Illuminator. The Judge. A founder of humankind, defender against the Desolations, a man ascended to divinity.

The Herald of Justice had returned.

'Before you swear, Szeth-son-Neturo,' Nin said, 'there are things you need to understand.' He looked across the Skybreakers. 'Things you all must understand. Squires, masters, gather our gemstone reserves and mobile packs. We will leave most of the squires. They leak Stormlight too much, and we have a long way to go.'

'Tonight, Just One?' Ki asked.

'Tonight. It is time for you to learn the two greatest secrets that I know.'

MANDRAS

They appear to come in a variety of sizes.

They move with a sinuous grace, but unlike skyeels I don't know if the mandras really need to obey any rules of physics.

The wings move in a regular rhythm, but they do not appear to be the source of either locomotion or lift.

The shape of the head is exactly the same as the luckspren that can be found accompanying greatshells. I am sure it's no coincidence that they're the same as those ~~that fly~~ beside skyeels.

The process by which the sailors steer is incredible to watch. Each mandra is harnessed with a rig of pulleys on each side. To steer in the desired direction, the pulleys' ropes are shortened on the corresponding side and then retied to the cleats on the ship's railing.

REACHERS

Nergaoul was known for driving forces into a battle rage, lending them great ferocity. Curiously, he did this to both sides of a conflict. Voidbringer and human. This seems common of the less self-aware spren.

—From Hessi's *Mythica*, page 121

When Kaladin awoke on the ship in Shadesmar, the others were already up. He sat, bleary-eyed on his bunk, listening to beads crash outside the hull. There almost seemed . . . a pattern or rhythm to them? Or was he imagining things?

He shook his head, standing and stretching. He had slept fitfully, slumber interrupted by thoughts of his men dying, of Elhokar and Moash, of worries for Drehy and Skar. The darkness blanketed his feelings, making him lethargic. He hated that he was the last to rise. That was always a bad sign.

He used the facilities, then forced himself to climb up the steps. The vessel had three levels. The bottom was the hold. The next level, the lower deck, was for the cabins, where the humans had been given a spot for them all to share.

The uppermost deck was open to the sky, and was populated by spren. Syl said they were lightspren, but the common name was Reachers. They looked like humans with strange bronze skin – metallic, as if they were living statues. Both men and women wore rugged jackets and trousers. Actual human clothing, not merely imitations of it like Syl wore.

They didn't carry weapons other than knives, but the ship had wicked harpoons clipped in racks at the sides of the deck. Seeing those made Kaladin infinitely more comfortable; he knew exactly where to go for a weapon.

Syl stood near the bow, watching out over the sea of beads again. He almost missed spotting her at first because her dress was red, instead of its normal white-blue. Her hair had changed to black, and ... and her skin was *flesh colored* – tan, like Kaladin's. What on Roshar?

He crossed the deck toward her, stumbling as the ship crashed through a swell in the beads. Storms, and Shallan said this was *more* smooth than some boats she'd been on? Several Reachers passed, calmly managing the large riggings and harnesses that attached to the spren who pulled the craft.

'Ah, human,' one of the Reachers said as Kaladin passed. That was the captain, wasn't it? Captain Ico? He resembled a Shin man, with large, childlike eyes made of metal. He was shorter than the Alethi, but sturdy. He wore the same tan clothing as the others, sporting a multitude of buttoned pockets.

'Come with me,' Ico told Kaladin, then crossed the deck without waiting for a response. They didn't speak much, these Reachers.

Kaladin sighed, then followed the captain back to the stairwell. A line of copper plating ran down the inside wall of the stairwell – and Kaladin had seen a similar ornamentation on the deck. He'd assumed it was decorative, but as the captain walked, he rested his fingers on the metal in an odd way.

Touching a plate with the tips of his fingers, Kaladin felt a distinct vibration. They passed the quarters of the ordinary spren sailors. They didn't sleep, but they did seem to enjoy their breaks from work, swinging quietly in hammocks, often reading.

It didn't bother him to see male Reachers with books – spren were obviously similar to ardents, who were outside of common understandings of male and female. At the same time ... spren, reading? How odd.

When they reached the hold, the captain turned on a small oil lamp – so far as Kaladin could tell, he didn't use a flaming brand to create the fire.

How did it work? It seemed foolhardy to use fire for light with so much wood and cloth around.

'Why not use spheres for light?' Kaladin asked him.

'We have none,' Ico said. 'Stormlight fades too quickly on this side.'

That was true. Kaladin's team carried several larger unset gemstones, which would hold Stormlight for weeks – but the smaller spheres would run out after a week or so without seeing a storm. They'd been able to trade the chips and marks to the lighthouse keeper in exchange for barter supplies – mostly cloth – to buy passage on this ship.

'The lighthouse keeper wanted the Stormlight,' Kaladin said. 'He kept it in some kind of globe.'

Captain Ico grunted. 'Foreign technology,' he said. 'Dangerous. Draws the wrong spren.' He shook his head. 'At Celebrant, the moneychangers have perfect gemstones that can hold the light indefinitely. Similar.'

'Perfect gemstones? Like, the Stone of Ten Dawns?'

'I don't know of this thing. Light in a perfect stone doesn't run out, so you can give Stormlight to the moneychangers. They use devices to transfer it from smaller gemstones to their perfect ones. Then they give you credit to spend in the city.'

The hold was closely packed with barrels and boxes that were lashed to the walls and floor. Kaladin could barely squeeze through. Ico selected a rope-handled box from a stack, then asked Kaladin to pull it out as Ico resettled the boxes that had been atop it, then relashed them.

Kaladin spent the time thinking about perfect gemstones. Did such a thing exist on his side? If there really *were* flawless stones that could hold Stormlight without ever running out, that seemed important to know. It could mean the difference between life and death for Radiants during the Weeping.

Once Ico was done resettling the cargo, he gestured for Kaladin to help him pick up the box they'd removed. They maneuvered it out of the hold and up onto the top deck. Here, the captain knelt and opened the box, which revealed a strange device that looked a little like a coatrack – although only about three feet tall. Made entirely of steel, it had dozens of small metal prongs extending from it, like the branches of a tree – only it had a metal basin at the very bottom.

Ico fished in a pocket and took out a small box, from which he removed a handful of glass beads like those that made up the ocean. He placed one of them into a hole in the center of the device, then waved toward Kaladin. 'Stormlight.'

'For what?'

'For you to live.'

'Are you threatening me, Captain?'

Ico sighed and regarded him with a suffering expression. Very human in its nature. It seemed the look of a man talking to a child. The spren captain waved his hand, insistent, so Kaladin took a diamond mark from his pocket.

Cradling the sphere in one hand, Ico touched the glass bead he'd put in the fabrial. 'This is a soul,' he said. 'Soul of water, but very cold.'

'Ice?'

'Ice from a high, high place,' he said. 'Ice that has never melted. Ice that has never known warmth.' The light in Kaladin's sphere dimmed as Ico concentrated. 'You know how to manifest souls?'

'No,' Kaladin said.

'Some of your kind do,' he said. 'It is rare. Rare among us too. The gardeners among the cultivationspren are best at it. I am unpracticed.'

The ocean bead expanded and grew cloudy, looking like ice. Kaladin got a distinct sense of *coldness* from it.

Ico handed back the diamond mark, now partially drained, then dusted off his hands and stood up, pleased.

'What does it do?' Kaladin asked.

Ico nudged the device with his foot. 'It gets cold now.'

'Why?'

'Cold makes water,' he said. 'Water collects in that basin. You drink, and don't die.'

Cold makes water? It didn't seem to be making any water that Kaladin could see. Ico hiked off to survey the spren steering the ship, so Kaladin knelt beside the device, trying to understand. Eventually, he spotted drops of water collecting on the 'branches' of the device. They ran down the metal and gathered in the basin.

Huh. When the captain had said – during their initial negotiations – that he could provide water for human passengers, Kaladin had assumed the ship would have some barrels in the hold.

The device took about a half hour to make a small cup of water, which Kaladin drank as a test – the basin had a spigot and a detachable tin cup.

The water was cool but flavorless, unlike rainwater. How did coldness make water though? Was this melting ice in the Physical Realm somehow, and bringing it here?

As he was sipping the water, Syl walked over – her skin, hair, and dress still colored like those of a human. She stopped next to him, placed her hands on her hips, and went into full pout.

'What?' Kaladin asked.

'They won't let me ride one of the flying spren.'

'Smart.'

'Insufferable.'

'Why on Roshar would you look at one of those things and think, "You know what, I need to get on its back"?'

Syl looked at him as if he were crazy. 'Because they can *fly*.'

'So can you. Actually, so can I.'

'You don't fly, you fall the wrong way.' She unfolded her arms so that she could fold them immediately again and huff loudly. 'You're telling me you're not even curious what it's like to climb on one of those things?'

'Horses are bad enough. I'm not about to get onto something that doesn't even have *legs*.'

'Where's your sense of adventure?'

'I dragged it out back and clubbed it senseless for getting me into the army. What have you done to your skin and hair, by the way?'

'It's a Lightweaving,' she said. 'I asked Shallan, because I didn't want rumors of an honorspren spreading from the ship's crew.'

'We can't waste Stormlight on something like that, Syl.'

'We used a mark that was running out anyway!' she said. 'So it was worthless to us; it would have been depleted by the time we arrived. So it's wasting nothing.'

'What if there's an emergency?'

She stuck her tongue out at him, then at the sailors at the front of the ship. Kaladin returned the little tin cup to its place on the side of the device, then settled with his back to the ship railing. Shallan sat across the deck near the flying spren, doing sketches.

'You should go talk to her,' Syl said, sitting next to him.

'About wasting Stormlight?' Kaladin said. 'Yes, perhaps I should. She does seem inclined to be frivolous with who she expends it for.'

Syl rolled her eyes.

'What?'

'Don't go lecture her, silly. Chat with her. About life. About fun things.' Syl nudged him with her foot. 'I know you want to. I can *feel* that you do. Be glad I'm the wrong kind of spren, or I would probably be licking your forehead or something to get at your emotions.'

The ship surged against a wave of beads. The souls of things in the physical world.

'Shallan is betrothed to Adolin,' Kaladin said.

'Which isn't an oath,' Syl said. 'It's a promise to maybe make an oath sometime.'

'It's still not the sort of thing you play around with.'

Syl rested her hand on his knee. 'Kaladin. I'm your spren. It's my *duty* to make sure that you're not alone.'

'Is that so? Who decided?'

'I did. And don't give me excuses about not being lonely, or about "only needing your brothers in arms." You can't lie to me. You feel dark, sad. You need something, someone, and she makes you feel better.'

Storms. It felt like Syl and his emotions were double-teaming him. One smiled with encouragement, while the other whispered terrible things. That he'd always be alone. That Tarah had been right to leave him.

He filled another cup with as much water as he could get from the basin, then carried it toward Shallan. The pitching of the ship almost made him dump the cup overboard.

Shallan glanced up as he eased down beside her, his back resting against the deck's railing. He handed her the cup. 'It makes water,' he said, thumbing at the device. 'By getting cold.'

'Condensation? How fast does it go? Navani would be interested in that.' She sipped the water, holding it in her gloved safehand – which was strange to see on her. Even when they'd traveled the bottoms of the chasms together, she'd worn a very formal havah.

'You walk like they do,' she said absently, finishing her sketch of one of the flying beasts.

'They?'

'The sailors. You keep your balance well. You'd have been at home as a sailor yourself, I suspect. Unlike some others.' She nodded toward Azure, who stood across the deck, holding on to the railing for dear life and occasionally shooting distrusting glares at the Reachers. Either she did not like being on a ship, or she did not trust the spren. Perhaps both.

'May I?' Kaladin asked, nodding toward Shallan's sketch. She shrugged, so he took the sketchpad and studied her pictures of the flying beasts. As always, they were excellent. 'What does the text say?'

'Just some theorizing,' she said, flipping back a page in her notebook. 'I lost my original of this picture, so this is kind of crude. But have you ever seen something like these arrowhead spren here?'

'Yeah . . .' Kaladin said, studying her drawing of a skyeel flying with arrowhead spren moving around it. 'I've seen them near greatshells.'

'Chasmfiends, skyeels, anything else that should be heavier than it actually is. Sailors call them luckspren on our side.' She gestured with the cup toward the front of the ship, where sailors managed the flying beasts. 'They call these "mandras," but the arrowhead shapes on their heads are the same shape as luckspren. These are bigger, but I think they – or something like them – help skyeels fly.'

'Chasmfiends don't fly.'

'They kind of do, mathematically. Bavamar did the calculations on Reshi greatshells, and found they should be crushed by their own weight.'

'Huh,' Kaladin said.

She started to get excited. 'There's more. Those mandras, they *vanish* sometimes. Their keepers call it "dropping." *I* think they must be getting pulled into the Physical Realm. It means you can never use only one mandra to pull a ship, no matter how small that ship. And you can't take them – or most other spren – too far from human population centers on our side. They waste away and die for reasons people here don't understand.'

'Huh. So what do they eat?'

'I'm not sure,' Shallan said. 'Syl and Pattern talk about feeding off emotions, but there's something else that . . .' She trailed off as Kaladin flipped to the next page in her notebook. It seemed like an attempt at drawing Captain Ico, but was incredibly juvenile. Basically just a stick figure.

'Did Adolin get hold of your sketchbook?' he asked.

She snatched the book from him and closed it. 'I was just trying out a different style. Thanks for the water.'

'Yes, I had to walk all the way from over there. At least seven steps.'

'Easily ten,' Shallan said. 'And on this precarious deck. Very dangerous.'

'Practically as bad as fighting the Fused.'

'Could have stubbed your toe. Or gotten a splinter. Or pitched over the side and been lost to the depths, buried by a thousand thousand beads and the weight of the souls of an infinite number of forgotten objects.'

'Or . . . that.'

'Highly unlikely,' Shallan agreed. 'They keep this deck well maintained, so there really aren't any splinters.'

'With my luck, I'd find one anyway.'

'I had a splinter once,' Shallan noted. 'It eventually got out of hand.'

'You . . . you did *not* just say that.'

'Yes, you obviously imagined it. What a sick, sick mind you have, Kaladin.'

Kaladin sighed, then nodded to the sailors. 'They do walk about barefoot. Have you noticed that? Something about the copper lines set into the deck.'

'The copper vibrates,' Shallan said. 'And they keep touching it. I think they might be using it to communicate somehow.'

'That would explain why they don't talk much,' Kaladin said. 'I'd have expected them to watch us a little more than they do. They don't seem that curious about us.'

'Which is odd, considering how interesting Azure is.'

'Wait. Just Azure?'

'Yes. In that polished breastplate and striking figure, with her talk of chasing bounties and traveling worlds. She's deeply mysterious.'

'I'm mysterious,' Kaladin said.

'I used to think you were. *Then* I found out you don't like good puns – it's truly possible to know *too* much about somebody.'

He grunted. 'I'll try to be more mysterious. Take up bounty hunting.' His stomach growled. 'Starting with a bounty on lunch, maybe.'

They'd been promised two meals a day, but considering how long it had taken Ico to remember they needed water, perhaps he should ask.

'I've been trying to track our speed,' Shallan said, flipping through her notebook. She went quickly through the pages, and he could see that – oddly – they alternated between expert renditions and comically bad ones.

She landed on a map she'd made of this region in Shadesmar. Alethi rivers were now peninsulas, and the Sea of Spears was an island, with the city named Celebrant on the western side. The river peninsulas meant that in order to get to the city, the ship had to swing to the west. Shallan had marked their path with a line.

'It's hard to gauge our progress, but I'd guess that we're moving faster than the average ship in our world. We can go directly where we want without worrying about the winds, for one thing.'

'So . . . two more days?' Kaladin asked, guessing based on her marks.

'More or less. Quick progress.'

He moved his fingers down, toward the bottom of her map. 'Thaylen City?' he asked, tapping one point she'd marked.

'Yes. On this side, it will be on the edge of a lake of beads. We can guess the Oathgate will reflect there as a platform, like the one we left in Kholinar. But how to activate it . . .'

'I want to try. Dalinar is in danger. We *need* to get to him, Shallan. In Thaylen City.'

She glanced at Azure, who maintained that was the wrong direction to go. 'Kaladin . . . I don't know if we can trust what you saw. It's dangerous to presume you know the future—'

'I didn't see the future,' Kaladin said quickly. 'It wasn't like that. It was like soaring the sky with the Stormfather. I just know . . . I *know* I have to get to Dalinar.'

She still seemed skeptical. Perhaps he'd told them too much of the lighthouse keeper's theatrics.

'We'll see, once we get to Celebrant.' Shallan closed her map, then squirmed, glancing back at the railing they'd been leaning against. 'Do you suppose they have chairs anywhere? These railings aren't very comfortable for sitting against.'

'Probably not.'

'What do you even call these things?' Shallan said, tapping the railing. 'A deck wall?'

'No doubt they've made up some obscure nautical word,' Kaladin said. 'Everything on a ship has odd names. Port and starboard instead of left and right. Galley instead of kitchen. Nuisance instead of Shallan.'

'There was a name . . . railing? Deck guard? No, wale. It's called a wale.' She grinned. 'I don't really like how it feels to sit against this wale, but I'm sure I'll eventually get over it.'

He groaned softly. 'Really?'

'Vengeance for calling me names.'

'Name. One name. And it was more a declaration of fact than an attack.'

She punched him lightly in the arm. 'It's good to see you smiling.'

'That was smiling?'

'It was the Kaladin equivalent. That scowl was almost jovial.' She smiled at him.

Something felt warm within him at being near her. Something felt *right*. It wasn't like with Laral, his boyhood crush. Or even like with Tarah, his first real romance. It was something different, and he couldn't define it. He only knew he didn't want it to stop. It pushed back the darkness.

'Down in the chasms,' he said, 'when we were trapped together, you talked about your life. About . . . your father.'

'I remember,' she said softly. 'In the darkness of the storm.'

'How do you do it, Shallan? How do you keep smiling and laughing? How do you keep from fixating on the terrible things that have happened?'

'I cover them up. I have this uncanny ability to hide away anything I don't want to think about. It . . . it's getting harder, but for most things I can just . . .' She trailed off, staring straight ahead. 'There. Gone.'

'Wow.'

'I know,' she whispered. 'I'm crazy.'

'No. No, Shallan! I wish I could do the same.'

She looked at him, brow wrinkling. '*You're* crazy.'

'How nice would it be, if I could simply shove it all away? Storms.' He tried to imagine it. Not spending his life worrying about the mistakes he'd made. Not hearing the constant whispers that he wasn't good enough, or that he'd failed his men.

'This way, I'll never face it,' Shallan said.

'It's better than being unable to function.'

'That's what I tell myself.' She shook her head. 'Jasnah said that power is an illusion of perception. Act like you have authority, and you often will. But pretending fragments me. I'm *too* good at pretending.'

'Well, whatever you're doing, it's obviously working. If I could smother these emotions, I'd do so eagerly.'

She nodded, but fell silent, then resisted all further attempts to draw her into conversation.

*I am convinced that Nergaoul is still active on Roshar. The accounts
of the Alethi 'Thrill' of battle align too well with ancient records –
including the visions of red mist and dying creatures.*

—From Hessi's *Mythica,* page 140

Dalinar remembered almost everything now. Though he still
hadn't recovered the details of his meeting with the Nightwatcher, the rest was as fresh as a new wound, dripping blood
down his face.

There had been so many more holes in his mind than he'd realized.
The Nightwatcher had ripped apart his memories like the fabric of an
old blanket, then sewn a new quilt out of it. In the intervening years he'd
thought himself mostly whole, but now all those scars had been ripped
free and he could see the truth.

He tried to put all of that out of his mind as he toured Vedenar, one
of the great cities of the world, known for its amazing gardens and lush
atmosphere. Unfortunately, the city had been devastated by the Veden
civil war, then the subsequent arrival of the Everstorm. Even along the
sanitized path he walked for the tour, they passed scorched buildings,
piles of rubble.

He couldn't help but think of what he'd done to Rathalas. And so, Evi's tears accompanied him. The cries of dying children.

Hypocrite, they said. *Murderer. Destroyer.*

The air smelled of salt and was filled with the sounds of waves smashing on cliffs outside the city. How did they live with that constant roaring? Did they never know peace? Dalinar tried to listen politely as Taravangian's people led him into a garden, full of low walls overgrown with vines and shrubs. One of few that hadn't been destroyed in the civil war.

The Vedens loved ostentatious greenery. Not a subtle people, all brimming with passion and vice.

The wife of one of the new Veden highprinces eventually led Navani off to inspect some paintings. Dalinar was instead led to a small garden square, where some Veden lighteyes were chatting and drinking wine. A low wall on the eastern side here allowed for the growth of all kinds of rare plants in a jumble, which was the current horticultural fashion. Lifespren bobbed among them.

More small talk? 'Excuse me,' Dalinar said, nodding toward a raised gazebo. 'I'm going to take a moment to survey the city.'

One of the lighteyes raised his hand. 'I can show—'

'No thank you,' Dalinar said, then started up the steps to the gazebo. Perhaps that had been too abrupt. Well, at least it fit his reputation. His guards had the sense to remain below, at the foot of the steps.

He reached the top, trying to relax. The gazebo gave him a nice view of the cliffs and the sea beyond. Unfortunately, it let him see the rest of the city – and storms, it was *not* in good shape. The walls were broken in places, the palace nothing more than rubble. Huge swaths of the city had burned, including many of the platelike terraces that had been Veden showpieces.

Out beyond – on the fields north of the city – black scars on the rock still showed where heaps of bodies had been burned following the war. He tried to turn away from all that and look out at the peaceful ocean. But he could smell smoke. That wasn't good. In the years following Evi's death, smoke had often sent him descending into one of his worse days.

Storms. I'm stronger than this. He *could* fight it. He wasn't the man he'd been all those years ago. He forced his attention toward the stated purpose of visiting the city: surveying the Veden martial capabilities.

Many of the living Veden troops were barracked in storm bunkers right inside the city walls. From reports he'd heard earlier, the civil war had brought incredible losses. Even *baffling* ones. Many armies would break after suffering ten percent casualties, but here – reportedly – the Vedens had continued fighting after losing more than *half* their numbers.

Perhaps they'd been driven mad by the persistent crashing of those waves. And . . . what else did he hear?

More phantom weeping. Taln's palms! Dalinar drew a deep breath, but smelled only smoke.

Why must I have these memories? he thought, angry. *Why did they suddenly return?*

Mixing with those emotions was a growing fear for Adolin and Elhokar. Why hadn't they sent word? If they'd escaped, wouldn't they have flown to safety – or at the very least, found a spanreed? It seemed ridiculous to assume multiple Radiants and Shardbearers were trapped in the city, unable to flee. But the alternative was to worry that they hadn't survived. That he'd sent them to die.

Dalinar tried to stand, straight-backed and at attention, beneath the weight of it all. Unfortunately, he knew too well that if you locked your knees and stood *too* straight, you risked fainting. Why was it that trying to stand tall should make you so much more likely to fall?

His guards at the base of the stone hill parted to let Taravangian – in his characteristic orange robes – shuffle through. The old man carried an enormous diamond-shaped kite shield, large enough to cover his entire left side. He climbed up to the gazebo, then sat down on one of the benches, panting.

'Did you want to see one of these, Dalinar?' he asked after a moment, holding out the shield.

Glad for the distraction, Dalinar took the shield, hefting it. 'Half-shard?' he said, noting a steel box – with a gemstone inside – fastened to the inner surface.

'Indeed,' Taravangian said. 'Crude devices. There are legends of metal that can block a Shardblade. A metal that falls from the sky. Silver, but somehow lighter. I should like to see that, but for now we can use these.'

Dalinar grunted.

'You know how they make fabrials, don't you?' Taravangian asked. 'Enslaved spren?'

'Spren can't be "enslaved" any more than a chull can.'

The Stormfather rumbled distantly in his mind.

'That gemstone,' Taravangian said, 'imprisons the kind of spren that gives things substance, the kind that holds the world together. We have entrapped in that shield something that, at another time, might have blessed a Knight Radiant.'

Storms. He couldn't deal with a philosophical problem like this today. He tried to change the topic. 'You seem to be feeling better.'

'It's a good day for me. I feel better than I have recently, but that can be dangerous. I'm prone to thinking about mistakes I've made.' Taravangian smiled in his kindly way. 'I try to tell myself that at the very least, I made the best choice I could, with the information I had.'

'Unfortunately, I'm certain I *didn't* make the best choices I could,' Dalinar said.

'But you wouldn't change them. If you did, you'd be a different person.'

I did change them, Dalinar thought. *I erased them. And I did become a different person.* Dalinar set the shield beside the old man.

'Tell me, Dalinar,' Taravangian said. 'You've spoken of your disregard for your ancestor, the Sunmaker. You called him a tyrant.'

Like me.

'Let us say,' Taravangian continued, 'you could snap your fingers and change history. Would you make it so that the Sunmaker lived longer and accomplished his desire, uniting all of Roshar under a single banner?'

'Turn him into *more* of a despot?' Dalinar said. 'That would have meant him slaughtering his way all across Azir and into Iri. Of course I wouldn't wish that.'

'But what if it left you, today, in command of a completely unified people? What if *his* slaughter let *you* save Roshar from the Voidbringer invasion?'

'I . . . You'd be asking me to consign millions of innocents to the pyre!'

'Those people are long dead,' Taravangian whispered. 'What are they to you? Numbers in a scribe's footnote. Yes, the Sunmaker was a monster. However, the current trade routes between Herdaz, Jah Keved, and Azir were forged by his tyranny. He brought culture and science back to Alethkar. Your modern Alethi cultural eruption can be traced *directly* back to what he did. Morality and law are built upon the bodies of the slain.'

'I can't do anything about that.'

'No, no. Of course you can't.' Taravangian tapped the half-shard shield. 'Do you know *how* we capture spren for fabrials, Dalinar? From spanreeds to heatrials, it's all the same. You lure the spren with something it loves. You give it something familiar to draw it in, something it knows deeply. In that moment, it becomes your slave.'

I . . . I really *can't think about this right now.* 'Excuse me,' Dalinar said, 'I need to go check on Navani.'

He strode from the gazebo and down the steps, bustling past Rial and his other guards. They followed, towed in his wake like leaves after a strong gust of wind. He entered the city, but didn't go looking for Navani. Perhaps he could visit the troops.

He walked back along the street, trying to ignore the destruction. Even without it though, this city felt *off* to him. The architecture was very like Alethi architecture, nothing like the flowery designs of Kharbranth or Thaylenah – but many buildings had plants draping and dangling from every window. It was strange to walk along streets full of people who looked Alethi but spoke a foreign tongue.

Eventually Dalinar reached the large stormshelters right inside the city walls. Soldiers had set up tent cities next to them, temporary bivouacs they could tear down and carry into one of the loaflike bunkers for storms. Dalinar found himself growing calmer as he walked among them. This was familiar; this was the peace of soldiers at work.

The officers here welcomed him, and generals took him on tours of the bunkers. They were impressed by his ability to speak their language – something he'd gained early in his visit to the city, using his Bondsmith abilities.

All Dalinar did was nod and ask the occasional question, but somehow he felt like he was accomplishing something. At the end, he entered a breezy tent near the city gates, where he met with a group of wounded soldiers. Each had survived when his entire platoon had fallen. Heroes, but not the conventional type. It took being a soldier to understand the heroism of simply being willing to continue after all your friends had died.

The last in line was an elderly veteran who wore a clean uniform and a patch for a defunct platoon. His right arm was missing, his jacket sleeve tied off, and a younger soldier led him up to Dalinar. 'Look, Geved. The Blackthorn himself! Didn't you always say you wanted to meet him?'

The older man had one of those stares that made him seem like he could see right through you. 'Brightlord,' he said, and saluted. 'I fought your army at Slickrock, sir. Brightlord Nalanar's second infantry. Storming fine battle that was, sir.'

'Storming fine indeed,' Dalinar said, saluting him back. 'I figured your forces had us at three different points.'

'Those were good times, Brightlord. Good times. Before everything went wrong . . .' His eyes glazed over.

'What was it like?' Dalinar asked softly. 'The civil war, the battle here, at Vedenar?'

'It was a nightmare, sir.'

'Geved,' the younger man said. 'Let's go. They have food—'

'Didn't you hear him?' Geved said, pulling his remaining arm out of the boy's grip. 'He *asked*. Everyone dances around me, ignoring it. Storms, sir. The civil war was a *nightmare*.'

'Fighting other Veden families,' Dalinar said, nodding.

'It wasn't that,' Geved said. 'Storms! We squabble as much as you do, sir. Pardon that. But I ain't ever felt bad fighting my own. It's what the Almighty wants, right? But that battle . . .' He shuddered. 'Nobody would stop, Brightlord. Even when it should have been done. They just kept right on fighting. Killing because they *felt* like killing.'

'It burned in us,' another wounded man said from by the food table. The man wore an eye patch and looked like he hadn't shaved since the battle. 'You know it, Brightlord, don't you? That river inside of you, pulling your blood all up into your head and making you love each swing. Making it so that you can't stop, no matter how tired you are.'

The Thrill.

It started to glow inside Dalinar. So familiar, so warm, and so *terrible*. Dalinar felt it stir, like . . . like a favorite axehound, surprised to hear its master's voice after so long.

He hadn't felt it in what seemed like an eternity. Even back on the Shattered Plains, when he'd last felt it, it had seemed to be weakening. Suddenly that made sense. It wasn't that he'd been learning to overcome the Thrill. Instead, it had left him.

To come here.

'Did others of you feel this?' Dalinar asked.

'We all did,' another of the men said, and Geved nodded. 'The officers . . .

they rode about with teeth clenched in rictus grins. Men shouted to keep the fight, maintain the momentum.'

It's all about momentum.

Others agreed, talking about the remarkable haze that had covered the day.

Losing any sense of peace he'd gained from the inspections, Dalinar excused himself. His guards raced to keep up as he fled – moving even faster as a newly arrived messenger called to him, saying he was needed back at the gardens.

He wasn't ready. He didn't want to face Taravangian, or Navani, or especially Renarin. Instead, he climbed the city wall. Inspect . . . inspect the fortifications. That was why he'd come.

From the top, he could again see those large sections of the city, burned and broken in the war.

The Thrill called to him, distant and thin. No. *No.* Dalinar marched along the wall, passing soldiers. To his right, waves crashed against the rocks. Shadows moved in the shallows, beasts two or three times as big as a chull, their shells peeking from the depths between waves.

It seemed that Dalinar had been four people in his life. The bloodlusty warrior, who killed wherever he was pointed, and the consequences could go to Damnation.

The general, who had feigned distinguished civility – when secretly, he'd longed to get back on the battlefield so he could shed more blood.

Third, the broken man. The one who paid for the actions of the youth.

Then finally, the fourth man: most false of them all. The man who had given up his memories so he could pretend to be something better.

Dalinar stopped, resting one hand on the stones. His guards assembled behind him. A Veden soldier approached from the other direction along the wall, calling out in anger. 'Who are you? What are you doing up here?'

Dalinar squeezed his eyes shut.

'You! Alethi. Answer me. Who let you scale this fortification?'

The Thrill stirred, and the animal inside him wanted to lash out. A fight. He needed a *fight.*

No. He fled again, hurrying down a tight, constricting stone stairwell. His breathing echoed against the walls, and he nearly stumbled and tripped down the last flight.

He burst out onto the street, sweating, surprising a group of women carrying water. His guards piled out after him. 'Sir?' Rial asked. 'Sir, are you . . . Is everything . . . ?'

Dalinar sucked in Stormlight, hoping it would drive away the Thrill. It didn't. It seemed to complement the sensation, driving him to act.

'Sir?' Rial said, holding out a canteen that smelled of something strong. 'I know you said I shouldn't carry this, but I did. And . . . and you might need it.' Dalinar stared at that canteen. A pungent scent rose to envelop him. If he drank that, he could forget the whispers. Forget the burned city, and what he'd done to Rathalas. And to Evi.

So easy . . .

Blood of my fathers. Please. No.

He spun away from Rial. He needed rest. That was all, just rest. He tried to keep his head up and slow his pace as he marched back toward the Oathgate.

The Thrill nipped at him from behind.

If you become that first man again, it will stop hurting. In your youth, you did what needed to be done. You were stronger then.

He growled, spinning and flinging his cloak to the side, looking for the voice that had spoken those words. His guards shied back, gripping their spears tightly. The beleaguered inhabitants of Vedenar scurried away from him.

Is this leadership? To cry each night? To shake and tremble? Those are the actions of a child, not a man.

'Leave me alone!'

Give me your pain.

Dalinar looked toward the sky and let out a raw bellow. He charged through the streets, no longer caring what people thought when they saw him. He needed to be *away* from this city.

There. The steps up to the Oathgate. The people of this city had once made a garden out of its platform, but that had been cleared away. Ignoring the long ramp, Dalinar took the steps two at a time, Stormlight lending him endurance.

At the top, he found a cluster of guards in Kholin blue standing with Navani and a smattering of scribes. She immediately strode over. 'Dalinar, I tried to ward him off, but he was insistent. I don't know what he wants.'

'He?' Dalinar asked, puffing from his near run.

Navani gestured toward the scribes. For the first time, Dalinar noticed that several among them wore the short beards of ardents. But those blue robes? What were those?

Curates, he thought, *from the Holy Enclave in Valath.* Technically, Dalinar himself was a head of the Vorin religion – but in practice, the curates guided church doctrine. The staves they bore were wound with gemstones, more ornate than he'd expected. Hadn't most of that pomp been done away with at the fall of the Hierocracy?

'Dalinar Kholin!' one said, stepping forward. He was young for an ardentia leader, perhaps in his early forties. His square beard was streaked with a few lines of grey.

'I am he,' Dalinar said, shrugging off Navani's touch to his shoulder. 'If you would speak with me, let us retire to a place more private—'

'Dalinar Kholin,' the ardent said, louder. 'The council of curates declares you a heretic. We cannot tolerate your insistence that the Almighty is not God. You are hereby proclaimed excommunicate and anathema.'

'You have no right—'

'We have *every* right! The ardents must watch the lighteyes so that you steer your subjects well. That is *still* our duty, as outlined in the Covenants of Theocracy, witnessed for centuries! Did you really think we would ignore what you've been preaching?'

Dalinar gritted his teeth as the stupid ardent began outlining Dalinar's heresies one by one, demanding that he deny them. The man stepped forward, close enough now that Dalinar could smell his breath.

The Thrill stirred, sensing a fight. Sensing blood.

I'm going to kill him, a part of Dalinar thought. *I have to run now, or I will kill this man.* It was as clear to him as the sun's light.

So he ran.

He dashed to the Oathgate control building, frantic with the need to escape. He scrambled up to the keyhole, and only then remembered that he didn't have a Shardblade that could operate this device.

Dalinar, the Stormfather rumbled. *Something is wrong. Something I cannot see, something hidden to me. What are you sensing?*

'I *have* to get away.'

I will not be a sword to you. We spoke of this.

Dalinar growled. He felt something he could touch, something beyond places. The power that bound worlds together. *His* power.

Wait, the Stormfather said. *This is not right!*

Dalinar ignored him, reaching beyond and pulling power through. Something bright white manifested in his hand, and he rammed it into the keyhole.

The Stormfather groaned, a sound like thunder.

The power made the Oathgate work, regardless. As his guards called his name outside, Dalinar flipped the dial that would make only the small building transport – not the entire plateau – then pushed the keyhole around the outside of the room, using the power as a handhold.

A ring of light flashed around the structure, and cold wind poured in through the doorways. He stumbled out onto a platform before Urithiru. The Stormfather pulled back from him, not breaking the bond, but withdrawing his favor.

The Thrill flooded in to replace it. Even this far away. Storms! Dalinar couldn't escape it.

You can't escape yourself, Dalinar, Evi's voice said in his mind. *This is who you are. Accept it.*

He couldn't run. Storms . . . he couldn't run.

Blood of my fathers. Please. Please, help me.

But . . . to whom was he praying?

He staggered down from the platform in a daze, ignoring questions from soldiers and scribes alike. He made his way to his room, increasingly desperate to find a way – any way – to hide from Evi's condemning voice.

In his rooms, he pulled a book off the shelf. Bound in hogshide, with thick paper. He held *The Way of Kings* as if it were a talisman that would drive back the pain.

It did nothing. Once this book had saved him, but now it seemed useless. He couldn't even read its words.

Dropping the book, he stumbled out of the room. No conscious thought led him to Adolin's chambers or drove him to ransack the younger man's room. But he found what he'd hoped, a bottle of wine kept for a special occasion. Violet, prepared in its strength.

This represented that third man he'd been. Shame, frustration, and days spent in a haze. Terrible times. Times he'd given up part of his soul in order to forget.

But storms, it was either this or start killing again. He raised the bottle to his lips.

DEADEYE

Moelach is very similar to Nergaoul, though instead of inspiring a battle rage, he supposedly granted visions of the future. In this, lore and theology align. Seeing the future originates with the Unmade, and is from the enemy.

—From Hessi's *Mythica*, page 143

Adolin tugged at the jacket, standing in Captain Ico's cabin. The spren had lent the room to him for a few hours.

The jacket was too short, but was the biggest the spren had. Adolin had cut off the trousers right below the knees, then tucked the bottoms into his long socks and tall boots. He rolled the sleeves of the jacket up to match, approximating an old style from Thaylenah. The jacket still looked too baggy.

Leave it unbuttoned, he decided. *The rolled sleeves look intentional that way.* He tucked his shirt in, pulled the belt tight. Good by contrast? He studied it in the captain's mirror. It needed a waistcoat. Those, fortunately, weren't *too* hard to fake. Ico had provided a burgundy coat that was too small for him. He removed the collar and sleeves, stitched the rough edges under, then slit it up the back.

He was just finishing it up with some laces on the back when Ico checked in on him. Adolin buttoned on the improvised waistcoat, threw on the jacket, then presented himself with hands at his sides.

'Very nice,' Ico said. 'You look like an honorspren going to a Feast of Light.'

'Thanks,' Adolin said, inspecting himself in the small mirror. 'The jacket needs to be longer, but I don't trust myself to let down the hems.'

Ico studied him with metal eyes – bronze, with holes for the pupils, like Adolin had seen done for some statues. Even the spren's hair appeared sculpted in place. Ico could almost have been a Soulcast king from an age long past.

'You were a ruler among your kind, weren't you?' Ico asked. 'Why did you leave? The humans we get here are refugees, merchants, or explorers. Not kings.'

King. Was Adolin a king? Surely his father would decide not to continue with the abdication, now that Elhokar had passed.

'No answer?' Ico said. 'That is fine. But you *were* a ruler among them. I can read it in you. Highborn status is important to humans.'

'Maybe a little too important, eh?' Adolin said, adjusting the neck scarf he'd made from his handkerchief.

'That is true,' Ico said. 'You are all human – and so none of you, regardless of birth, can be trusted with oaths. A contract to travel, this is fine. But humans will betray trust if it is given to them.' The spren frowned, then seemed to grow embarrassed, glancing away. 'That was rude.'

'Rudeness doesn't necessarily imply untruth though.'

'I did not mean an insult, regardless. You are not to be blamed. Betraying oaths is simply your nature, as a human.'

'You don't know my father,' Adolin said. Still, the conversation left him uncomfortable. Not because of Ico's words – spren tended to say odd things, and Adolin didn't take offense.

More, he felt his own growing worry that he might *actually* have to take the throne. He'd grown up knowing it could happen, but he'd *also* grown up wishing – desperately – that it never would. In his quiet moments, he'd assumed this hesitance was because a king couldn't apply himself to things like dueling and ... well ... enjoying life.

What if it went deeper? What if he'd always known inconsistency lurked within him? He couldn't keep pretending he was the man his father wanted him to be.

Well, it was moot anyway – Alethkar, as a nation, had fallen. He accompanied Ico back out of the captain's cabin onto the deck, walking over to Shallan, Kaladin, and Azure, who stood by the starboard wale. Each wore a shirt, trousers, and jacket they'd bought off the Reachers with dun spheres. Dun gemstones weren't worth nearly as much on this side, but apparently trade with the other side *did* happen, so they had some value.

Kaladin gaped at Adolin, looking down at his boots, then up at the neck scarf, then focusing on the waistcoat. That befuddled expression alone made the work worthwhile.

'How?' Kaladin demanded. 'Did you *sew* that?'

Adolin grinned. Kaladin looked like a man trying to wear his childhood suit; he'd never button that coat across his broad chest. Shallan fit her shirt and jacket better from a pure measurements standpoint, but the cut wasn't flattering. Azure looked far more . . . normal without her dramatic breastplate and cloak.

'I'd practically kill for a skirt,' Shallan noted.

'You're kidding,' Azure said.

'No. I'm getting tired of the way trousers rub my legs. Adolin, could you sew me a dress? Maybe stitch the legs of these trousers together?'

He rubbed his chin, which had begun to sprout a blond beard. 'It doesn't work that way – I can't magic more cloth out of nothing. It . . .'

He trailed off as, overhead, the clouds suddenly rippled, glowing with a strange mother-of-pearl iridescence. Another highstorm, their second since arriving in Shadesmar. The group stopped and stared up at the dramatic light show. Nearby, the Reachers seemed to stand up more straight, move about their sailing duties more vigorously.

'See,' Azure said. 'I told you. They *must* feed off it, somehow.'

Shallan narrowed her eyes, then grabbed her sketchbook and stalked over to begin interviewing some of the spren. Kaladin trailed away to join his spren at the prow of the ship, where she liked to stand. Adolin often noticed him looking southward, as if anxiously wishing the ship to move more quickly.

He lingered by the side of the ship, watching the beads crash away below. When he looked up, he found Azure studying him. 'Did you really sew that?' she asked.

'There wasn't much sewing involved,' Adolin said. 'The scarf and jacket hide most of the damage I did to the waistcoat – which used to be a smaller jacket.'

'Still,' she said. 'An unusual skill for a royal.'

'And how many royals have you known?'

'More than some might assume.'

Adolin nodded. 'I see. And are you enigmatic on *purpose*, or is it kind of an accidental thing?'

Azure leaned against the ship's wale, breeze blowing her short hair. She looked more youthful when not wearing the breastplate and cloak. Mid-thirties, maybe. 'A little of both. I discovered when I was younger that being too open with strangers . . . went poorly for me. But in answer to your question, I *have* known royals. Including one woman who left it behind. Throne, family, responsibilities . . .'

'She abandoned her duty?' That was practically inconceivable.

'The throne was better served by someone who enjoyed sitting on it.'

'Duty isn't about what you *enjoy*. It's about doing what is demanded of you, in serving the greater good. You can't just abandon responsibility because you *feel like it*.'

Azure glanced at Adolin, and he felt himself blush. 'Sorry,' he said, looking away. 'My father and my uncle might have . . . instilled me with a little passion on the topic.'

'It's all right,' Azure said. 'Maybe you're right, and maybe there's something in me that knows it. I always find myself in situations like in Kholinar, leading the Wall Guard. I get too involved . . . then abandon everyone. . . .'

'You *didn't* abandon the Wall Guard, Azure,' Adolin said. 'You couldn't have prevented what happened.'

'Perhaps. I can't help feeling that this is merely one in a long string of duties abdicated, of burdens set down, perhaps to disastrous results.' For some reason, she put her hand on the pommel of her Shardblade when she said that. Then she looked up at Adolin. 'But of all the things I've walked away from, the one I don't regret is allowing someone else to rule. Sometimes, the best way to do your duty is to let someone else – someone more capable – try carrying it.'

Such a *foreign* idea. Sometimes you took up a duty that wasn't yours, but abandoning one? Just . . . giving it to someone else?

He found himself musing on that. He nodded his thanks to Azure as she excused herself to get something to drink. He was still standing there when Shallan returned from interviewing – well, interrogating – the Reachers. She took his arm, and together they watched the shimmering clouds for a while.

'I look terrible, don't I?' she finally asked, nudging him in the side. 'No makeup, with hair that hasn't been washed in days, and now wearing a dumpy set of worker's clothing.'

'I don't think you're capable of looking terrible,' he said, pulling her closer. 'In all their color, even those clouds can't compete.'

They passed through a sea of floating candle flames, which represented a village on the human side. The flames were huddled together in patches. Hiding from the storm.

Eventually the clouds faded – but they were supposedly near the city now, so Shallan got excited, watching for it. Finally, she pointed to land on the horizon.

Celebrant nestled not far down its coast. As they drew closer, they spotted other ships entering or leaving the port, each pulled by at least two mandras.

Captain Ico walked over. 'We'll soon arrive. Let's go get your deadeye.'

Adolin nodded, patting Shallan on the back, and followed Ico down to the brig, a small room far aft in the cargo hold. Ico used keys to unlock the door, revealing the spren of Adolin's sword sitting on a bench inside. She looked at him with those haunting scratched-out eyes, her string face void of emotion.

'I wish you hadn't locked her in here,' Adolin said, stooping down to peer through the squat doorway.

'Can't have them on deck,' Ico said. 'They don't watch where they're walking and fall off. I'm not going to spend days trying to fish out a lost deadeye.'

She moved to join Adolin, then Ico reached over to shut the cell.

'Wait!' Adolin said. 'Ico, I saw something moving back there.'

Ico locked the door and hung the keys on his belt. 'My father.'

'Your *father*?' Adolin said. 'You keep your father locked up?'

'Can't stand the thought of him wandering around somewhere,' Ico said, eyes forward. 'Have to keep him locked away though. He'll go searching for the human carrying his corpse, otherwise. Walk right off the deck.'

'Your father was a Radiant spren?'

Ico started toward the steps up to the deck. 'It is rude to ask about such ones.'

'Rudeness doesn't imply untruth though, right?'

Ico turned and regarded him, then smiled wanly and nodded toward Adolin's spren. 'What is she to you?'

'A friend.'

'A tool. You use her corpse on the other side, don't you? Well, I won't blame you. I've heard stories of what they can do, and I am a pragmatic person. Just . . . don't pretend she is your friend.'

By the time they reached the deck, the ship was approaching the docks. Ico started calling orders, though his crew clearly knew what to do already.

The Celebrant docks were wide and large, longer than the city. Ships pulled in along stone piers, though Adolin couldn't figure out how they got back out again. Hook the mandras to the stern and pull them out that way?

The shore was marked by long warehouses set in rows, which marred the view of the city proper, in Adolin's opinion. The ship drew up at a berth on a specific pier, guided by a Reacher with semaphore. Ico's sailors unlatched a piece of the hull, which unfolded to steps, and a sailor hiked down immediately to greet another group of Reachers. These began unlatching the mandras with long hooks, leading them away.

As each flying spren was released from the rigging, the ship sank a little farther into the bead ocean. Eventually, it seemed to settle onto some braces and steady there.

Pattern came over, humming to himself and meeting the rest of them as they gathered on the deck. Ico stepped up, gesturing. 'A deal fulfilled, and a bond kept.'

'Thank you, Captain,' Adolin said, shaking Ico's hand. Ico returned the gesture awkwardly. He obviously knew what to do, but was unpracticed at it. 'You're sure you won't take us the rest of the way to the portal between realms?'

'I'm certain,' Ico said firmly. 'The region around Cultivation's Perpendicularity has gained a poor reputation of late. Too many ships vanishing.'

'What about Thaylen City?' Kaladin asked. 'Could you take us there?'

'No. I unload goods here, and then head east. Away from trouble. And if you'll accept a little advice, stay in Shadesmar. The Physical Realm is not a welcoming place these days.'

'We'll take that under advisement,' Adolin said. 'Is there anything we should know about the city?'

'Don't stray too far outside; with human cities nearby, there will be angerspren in the area. Try not to draw too many lesser spren, and maybe see if you can find a place to tie up that deadeye of yours.' He pointed. 'The dock registrar is that building ahead of us, with the blue paint. There you'll find a list of ships willing to take on passengers – but you'll have to go to each one individually and make sure they are equipped to take humans, and haven't already booked all their cabins.

'The building next to that is a moneychanger, where you can trade Stormlight for notes of exchange.' He shook his head. 'My daughter used to work there, before she ran off chasing stupid dreams.'

He bade them farewell, and the group of travelers walked down the gangway onto the docks. Curiously, Syl still wore an illusion, making her face an Alethi tan, her hair black, her clothing red. Was being an honorspren really that big a deal?

'So,' Adolin said as they reached the pier, 'how are we going to do this? In the city, I mean.'

'I've counted out our marks,' Shallan said, holding up a bag of spheres. 'It's been long enough since they were renewed, they'll almost certainly lose their Stormlight in the next few days. A few have already gone out. We might as well trade for supplies – we can keep the broams and the larger gemstones for Surgebinding.'

'First stop is the moneychanger, then,' Adolin said.

'After that, we should see if we can buy more rations,' Kaladin said, 'just in case. And we need to look for passage.'

'But to where?' Azure said. 'The perpendicularity, or Thaylen City?'

'Let's see what our options are,' Adolin decided. 'Maybe there will be a ship to one destination, but not the other. Let's send one group to inquire with ships, and another to get supplies. Shallan, do you have a preference which you'd rather do?'

'I'll look for passage,' she said. 'I have experience with it – I made a *lot* of trips when chasing down Jasnah.'

'Sounds good,' Adolin said. 'We should put one Radiant in each group, so bridgeboy and Syl, you'll go with me. Pattern and Azure will go with Shallan.'

'Maybe I should help Shallan –' Syl began.

'We'll need a spren with us,' Adolin said. 'To explain culture here. Let's go trade in those spheres first, though.'

CELEBRANT

*Moelach was said to grant visions of the future at different times –
but most commonly at the transition point between realms. When a
soul was nearing the Tranquiline Halls.*

—From Hessi's *Mythica*, page 144

K aladin hiked through the city with Adolin and Syl. The money-changing had gone quickly, and they'd left the spren of Adolin's sword with the others. After Shallan had taken the deadeye's hand, she had remained behind.

Reaching this city marked a welcome step forward, toward finally getting out of this place and reaching Dalinar. Unfortunately, a brand-new city full of unknown threats didn't encourage him to relax.

The city wasn't as densely populated as most human ones, but the variety of spren was stunning. Reachers like Ico and his sailors were common, but there were also spren that looked much like Adolin's sword – at least before she'd been killed. They were made entirely of vines, though they had crystal hands and wore human clothing. Equally common were spren with inky black skin that shone with a variety of colors when light hit them right. Their clothing seemed part of them, like that of the Cryptics and honorspren.

A small group of Cryptics passed nearby, huddling close together as they walked. Each had a head with a slightly different pattern. There were other spren with skin like cracked stone, molten light shining from within. Still others had skin the color of old white ashes – and when Kaladin saw one of these point toward something, the skin stretching at the joint of his arm disintegrated and blew away, revealing the joint and knobs of the humerus. The skin quickly regrew.

The variety reminded Kaladin of the costumes of the Cult of Moments – though he didn't spot a single honorspren. And it didn't seem like the other spren mixed much. Humans were rare enough that the three of them – including Syl, imitating an Alethi – turned heads.

Buildings were constructed using bricks in a variety of colors or blocks of many different types of stone. Each building was a hodgepodge of materials with no pattern Kaladin could determine.

'How do they get building materials?' Kaladin asked as they followed the moneychanger's instructions toward the nearby market. 'Are there quarries on this side?'

Syl frowned. 'I . . .' She cocked her head. 'You know, I'm not sure. I think maybe we make it appear on this side, somehow, from yours? Like Ico did with the ice?'

'They seem to wear whatever,' Adolin said, pointing. 'That's an Alethi officer's coat over an *Azish scribe's vest*. Tashikki wrap worn with trousers, and there's *almost* a full Thaylen tlmko, but they're missing the boots.'

'No children,' Kaladin noticed.

'There have been a few,' Syl said. 'They just don't look little, like human children.'

'How does that even *work*?' Adolin said.

'Well, it's certainly less messy than your method!' She scrunched her face up. 'We're made of power, bits of gods. There are places where that power coalesces, and parts start to be aware. You go, and then come back with a child? I think?'

Adolin chuckled.

'What?' Kaladin asked.

'That's actually not that different from what my nanny told me when I asked her where children come from. A nonsense story about parents baking a new child out of crem clay.'

'It doesn't happen often,' Syl said as they passed a group of the ash-colored spren sitting around a table and watching the crowds. They eyed the humans with overt hostility, and one flicked fingers toward Kaladin. Those fingers exploded to bits of dust, leaving bones that grew back the flesh.

'Raising children doesn't happen often?' Adolin asked.

Syl nodded. 'It's rare. Most spren will go hundreds of years without doing it.'

Hundreds of years. 'Storms,' Kaladin whispered, considering it. 'Most of these spren are that old?'

'Or older,' Syl said. 'But aging isn't the same with spren. Like time isn't. We don't learn as fast, or change much, without a bond.'

Towers in the city's center showed the time by way of fires burning in a set of vertical holes – so they could judge how to meet back with the others in an hour, as agreed. The market turned out to be mostly roofless stalls open to the air, with goods piled on tables. Even in comparison to the improvised market of Urithiru, this seemed . . . ephemeral to Kaladin. But there were no stormwinds to worry about here, so it probably made sense.

They passed a clothing stall, and of course Adolin insisted on stopping. The oily spren who managed the place had an odd, very terse way of talking, with a strange use of words. But it did speak Alethi, unlike most of Ico's crew.

Kaladin waited for the prince to finish, until Syl stepped up and presented herself in an oversized poncho tied with a belt. On her head she wore a large, floppy hat.

'What's that?' Kaladin asked.

'Clothes!'

'Why do you need clothes? Yours are built in.'

'Those are boring.'

'Can't you change them?'

'Takes Stormlight, on this side,' she said. 'Plus, the dress is part of my essence, so I'm actually walking around naked *all the time*.'

'It's not the same.'

'Easy for you to say. We bought *you* clothing. You have three sets!'

'Three?' he said, looking down at his clothing. 'I have my uniform, and this one Ico gave me.'

'Plus the one you're wearing underneath that one.'

'Underwear?' Kaladin said.

'Yeah. That means you have *three* sets of clothing, while I have *none*.'

'We need two sets so one can be washed while we wear the other.'

'Just so you won't be stinky.' She rolled her eyes in an exaggerated way. 'Look, you can give these to Shallan when I get bored with them. You know she likes hats.'

That was true. He sighed, and when Adolin returned with another set of underclothing for each of them – along with a skirt for Shallan – Kaladin had him haggle for the clothing Syl was wearing too. The prices were shockingly cheap, using a tiny fraction of the money from their writ.

They continued on, passing stalls that sold building materials. According to the signs Syl could read, some items were far more expensive than others. Syl seemed to think the difference had to do with how permanent the thing was in Shadesmar – which made Kaladin worry for the clothing they'd bought.

They found a place selling weapons, and Adolin tried to negotiate while Kaladin browsed. Some kitchen knives. A few hand axes. And sitting in a locked, glass-topped box, a long thin silvery chain.

'You like?' the shopkeeper asked. She was made of vines – her face formed as if from green string – and wore a havah with a crystal safehand exposed. 'Only a thousand broams of Stormlight.'

'A *thousand broams*?' Kaladin asked. He looked down at the box, which was locked to the table and guarded by small orange spren that looked like people. 'No thanks.' The pricing here really was bizarre.

The swords proved more expensive than Adolin wanted, but he did buy them two harpoons – and Kaladin felt a lot more secure once one was placed in his hands. Walking on, Kaladin noted that Syl was hunkered down in her oversized poncho, her hair tucked into the collar and her hat pulled down to shadow her face. It seemed like she didn't trust Shallan's illusion to keep her from being recognized as an honorspren.

The food stall they found had mostly more 'cans' like those on the ship. Adolin started haggling, and Kaladin settled in for another wait, scanning those who passed on the pathway for danger. He found his eyes drawn, however, to a stall across from them. Selling art.

Kaladin had never had much time for art. Either the picture depicted something useful – like a map – or it was basically pointless. And yet, nestled among the paintings for display was a small one painted from thick strokes of oil. White and red, with lines of black. When he looked away, he found himself drawn back toward it, studying the way the highlights played off those dark lines.

Like nine shadows . . . he thought. *With a figure kneeling in the middle . . .*

∴

The ashen spren waved excitedly, pointing to the east and then making a cutting motion. She spoke a language Shallan couldn't understand, but fortunately Pattern could interpret.

'Ah . . .' he said. 'Mmm, yes. I see. She will not sail back to Cultivation's Perpendicularity. Mmm. No, she will not go.'

'Same excuse?' Shallan asked.

'Yes. Voidspren sailing warships and demanding tribute from any who approach. Oh! She says she would rather trade with honorspren than take another trip to the perpendicularity. I think this is an insult. Ha ha ha. Mmm . . .'

'Voidspren,' Azure said. 'Can she at least explain what that means?'

The ashen spren began speaking quickly after Pattern asked. 'Hmm . . . There are many varieties, she says. Some of golden light, others are red shadows. Curious, yes. And it sounds like some of the Fused are with them – men with shells that can fly. I did not know this.'

'What?' Azure prompted.

'Shadesmar has been changing these last months,' Pattern explained. 'Voidspren have arrived mysteriously just west of the Nexus of Imagination. Near Marat or Tukar on your side. Hmm . . . and they have sailed up and seized the perpendicularity. She says, ahem, "You need but spit into a crowd, and you'll find one, these days." Ha ha ha. I do not think she actually has spit.'

Shallan and Azure shared a look as the sailor retreated onto her ship, to which mandras were being harnessed. The spren of Adolin's sword lingered nearby, seeming content to stay where told. Passersby looked away from her, as if embarrassed to see her there.

'Well, the dock registrar was right,' Azure said, folding her arms. 'No ships sailing toward the peaks *or* toward Thaylen City. Those destinations are too close to enemy holdings.'

'Maybe we should try for the Shattered Plains instead,' Shallan said. That meant going east – a direction ships were more likely to travel, these days. It would mean going away from both what Kaladin *and* Azure wanted, but at least it would be something.

If they got there, she'd still need to find a way to engage the Oathgate on this side. What if she failed? She imagined them trapped in some far-off location, surrounded by beads, slowly starving. . . .

'Let's keep asking the ships on our list,' she said, leading the way. The next ship in line was a long, stately vessel made of white wood with golden trim. Its entire presentation seemed to say, *Good luck affording me.* Even the mandras being led toward it from one of the warehouses wore gold harnesses.

According to the list from the dock registrar, this was heading someplace called Lasting Integrity – which was to the southwest. That was *kind of* the direction Kaladin wanted to go, so Shallan had Pattern stop one of the grooms and ask if the captain of the ship would be likely to take human passengers.

The groom, a spren that looked like she was made of fog or mist, merely laughed and walked off as if she'd heard a grand joke.

'I suppose,' Azure said, 'we should take that for a no.'

The next ship in line was a sleek vessel that looked fast to Shallan's untrained eyes. A good choice, the registrar had noted, and likely to be welcoming toward humans. Indeed, a spren working on the deck waved as they approached. He put one booted foot up on the side of his ship and looked down with a grin.

What kind of spren, Shallan thought, *has skin like cracked rock?* He glowed deep within, as if molten on the inside. 'Humans?' he called in Veden, reading Shallan's hair as a sign of her heritage. 'You're far from home. Or close, I suppose, just in the wrong realm!'

'We're looking for passage,' Shallan called up. 'Where are you sailing?'

'East!' he said. 'Toward Freelight!'

'Could we potentially negotiate passage?'

'Sure!' he called down. 'Always interesting to have humans aboard. Just don't eat my pet chicken. Ha! But negotiations will have to wait. We've got an inspection soon. Come back in a half hour.'

The dock registrar had mentioned this; an official inspection of the ships happened at first hour every day. Shallan and the team backed off, and she suggested returning to their meeting place near the dock registrar. As they approached, Shallan could see that Ico's ship was already under inspection by a dock official – another spren made of vines and crystal.

Maybe we could convince Ico to take us, if we just tried harder. Perhaps—

Azure's breath caught and she grabbed Shallan by the shoulder, yanking her into an alley between two warehouses, out of sight of the ship. 'Damnation!'

'What?' Shallan demanded as Pattern and, lethargically, Adolin's spren joined them.

'Look up there,' Azure said. 'Talking with Ico, on the poop deck.'

Shallan frowned, then peeked out, spotting what she'd missed earlier: A figure stood up there, with the marbled skin of a parshman. He floated a foot or two off the deck next to Ico, looming like a stern tutor over a foolish student.

The spren with the vines and crystal body walked up, reporting to this one.

'Perhaps,' Azure said, 'we should have asked *who runs* the inspections.'

∴

Kaladin's harpoon drew nervous glances as he crossed the pathway between stalls, to get a closer look at the painting.

Can spren even be hurt in this realm? a part of him wondered. *The sailors wouldn't carry harpoons if things couldn't be killed on this side, right?* He'd have to ask Syl, once she was done interpreting for Adolin.

Kaladin stepped up to the painting. The ones beside it showed far more technical prowess – they were capable portraits, perfectly capturing their human subjects. This one was sloppy by comparison. It looked like the painter had simply taken a knife covered in paint and slopped it onto the canvas, making general shapes.

Haunting, *beautiful* shapes. Mostly reds and whites, but with a figure at the center, throwing out nine shadows . . .

Dalinar, he thought. *I failed Elhokar. After all we went through, after the rains and confronting Moash, I've failed. And I lost your city.*

He reached up his fingers to touch the painting.

'Marvelous, isn't it!' a spren said.

Kaladin jumped, sheepishly lowering his fingers. The proprietor of this stall was a Reacher woman, short, with a bronze ponytail.

'It's a unique piece, human,' she said. 'From the far-off Court of Gods, a painting intended only for a divinity to see. It is exceptionally rare that one escapes being burned at the court, and makes its way onto the market.'

'Nine shadows,' Kaladin said. 'The Unmade?'

'This is a piece by Nenefra. It is said that each person who sees one of his masterworks sees something different. And to think, I charge such a minuscule price. Only three hundred broams' worth of Stormlight! Truly, times are difficult in the art market.'

'I . . .'

Haunting images from Kaladin's vision overlapped the stark wedges of paint on the canvas. He needed to reach Thaylen City. He had to be there on time –

What was that disturbance behind him?

Kaladin shook out of his reverie and glanced over his shoulder, just in time to see Adolin jogging toward him.

'We have a problem,' the prince said.

.*.

'How could you not mention this!' Shallan said to the little spren at the registrar office. 'How could you *neglect* to point out that *Voidspren* ruled the city?'

'I thought everyone knew!' he said, vines curling and moving at the corners of his face. 'Oh dear. Oh my! Anger is *not* helpful, human. I am a *professional*. It is not my job to explain things you should already know!'

'He's still on Ico's ship,' Azure said, looking out the office window. 'Why is he still on Ico's ship?'

'That *is* odd,' the spren said. 'Each inspection usually takes only thirteen minutes!'

Damnation. Shallan breathed out, trying to calm herself. Coming back to the registrar had been a calculated risk. He was probably working with the Fused, but they hoped to intimidate him into talking.

'When did it happen?' Shallan asked. 'My spren friend told us this was a free city.'

'It's been months now,' the vine spren said. 'Oh, they don't have *firm* control here, mind you. Just a few officials, and promises from our leaders to follow. Two Fused check in on us now and then. I think the other is quite insane. Kyril – who is running the inspections – well, he might be mad too, actually. You see, when he gets angry—'

'Damnation!' Azure cursed.

'What?'

'He just set Ico's ship on fire.'

⁘

Kaladin ran back across the street to find Syl a center of activity. She had pulled her oversized hat down to obscure her face, but a collection of spren stood around the food stall, pointing at her and talking.

Kaladin shoved his way through, took Syl by the arm, and pulled her away from the stall. Adolin followed, holding his harpoon in one hand and a sack of food in the other. He looked threateningly toward the spren in the gathered crowd, who didn't give chase.

'They recognize you,' Kaladin said to Syl. 'Even with the illusory skin color.'

'Uh . . . maybe . . .'

'*Syl.*'

She held to her hat with one hand, her other arm in his hand as he towed her through the street. 'So . . . you know how I mentioned I snuck away from the other honorspren . . .'

'Yes.'

'So, there *might* have been an enormous reward for my return. Posted in basically every port in Shadesmar, with my description and some pictures. Um . . . yeah.'

'You've been forgiven,' Kaladin said. 'The Stormfather has accepted your bond to me. Your siblings are watching Bridge Four, investigating potential bonds themselves!'

'That's kind of recent, Kaladin. And I doubt I've been forgiven – the others on the Shattered Plains wouldn't talk to me. As far as they're concerned, I'm a disobedient child. There's still an incredible reward in Stormlight to be given to the person that delivers me to the honorspren capital, Lasting Integrity.'

'And you didn't think this was important to tell me?'

'Sure I did. Right now.'

They stopped to allow Adolin to catch up. The spren back at the food stall were still talking. Storms. This news would spread throughout Celebrant before long.

Kaladin glared at Syl, who pulled down into the oversized poncho she'd bought. 'Azure is a *bounty hunter,*' she said in a small voice. 'And

I'm ... I'm kind of like a spren lighteyes. I didn't want you to know. In case you hated me, like you hate them.'

Kaladin sighed, taking her by the arm again and pulling her toward the docks.

'I should have known this disguise wouldn't work,' she added. 'I'm obviously too beautiful and interesting to hide.'

'News of this might make it hard to get passage,' Kaladin said. 'We ...' He stopped in the street. 'Is that smoke up ahead?'

⁘

The Fused touched down on the quay, tossing Ico to the ground of the docks. Behind, Ico's ship had become a raging bonfire – the other sailors and inspectors scrambled down the gangway in a frantic jumble.

Shallan watched from the window. Her breath caught as the Fused lifted a few inches off the ground, then glided toward the registrar's building.

She sucked in Stormlight by reflex. 'Look frightened!' she said to the others. She grabbed Adolin's spren by the arm and pulled her to the side of the clerk's room.

The Fused burst in and found them cringing, wearing the faces of sailors that Shallan had sketched. Pattern was the oddest one, his strange head needing to be covered by a hat to have any semblance of looking realistic.

Please don't notice we're the same sailors as on the ship. Please.

The Fused ignored them, gliding up to the frightened vine spren behind the desk.

'That ship was hiding human criminals,' Pattern whispered, translating the Fused's conversation with the registrar. 'They had a hydrator and remnants of human food – eaten – on the deck. There are two or three humans, one honorspren, and one inkspren. Have you seen these criminals?'

The vine spren cringed down by the desk. 'They went to the market for needed supplies. They asked me for ships that would get them passage to the perpendicularity.'

'You *hid* this from me?'

'Why does everyone assume I'll just tell them things? Oh, I need *questions*, not assumptions!'

433

The Fused regarded him with a cold glare. 'Put that out,' he said, gesturing toward the fire. 'Use the city's sand stores, if needed.'

'Yes, great one. If I might say, starting fires on the docks is an unwise—'

'You may *not* say. When you finish putting out the fire, clear your things from this office. You are to be replaced immediately.'

The Fused charged out of the room, letting in the scent of smoke. Ico's ship foundered, the blaze flaring high. Nearby, sailors from other ships were frantically trying to control their mandras and move their vessels away.

'Oh, oh *my*,' said the spren behind the desk. He looked to them. 'You . . . you are a Radiant? The old oaths are spoken again?'

'Yes,' Shallan said, helping Adolin's spren to her feet.

The frightened little spren sat up straighter. 'Oh, *glorious* day. Glorious! We have waited so long for the honor of men to return!' He stood up and gestured. 'Go, please! Get on a ship. I will stall, yes I will, if that one comes back. Oh, but go *quickly*!'

∴

Kaladin sensed something on the air.

Perhaps it was the flapping of clothing, familiar to him after hours spent riding the winds. Perhaps it was the postures of the people farther down the street. He reacted before he understood what it was, grabbing Syl and Adolin, pulling them all into a tent at the edge of the market.

A Fused soared past outside, its shadow trailing behind, pointing the wrong direction.

'Storms!' Adolin said. 'Nice work, Kal.'

The tent was occupied only by a single bewildered spren made of smoke, looking odd in a green cap and what seemed to be Horneater clothing.

'Out,' Kaladin said, the smell of smoke on the air filling him with dread. They hurried down an alleyway between warehouses, out onto the docks.

Farther down, Ico's ship burned brilliantly. There was chaos on the docks as spren ran in all directions, shouting in their strange language.

Syl gasped, pointing at a ship bedecked in white and gold. 'We have to hide. *Now.*'

'Honorspren?' Kaladin asked.

'Yeah.'

'Pull down your hat, go back into the alley.' Kaladin scanned the crowd. 'Adolin, do you see the others?'

'No,' he said. 'Ishar's soul! There's no water to put that fire out. It will burn for hours. What happened?'

One of Ico's sailors stepped from the crowd. 'I saw a flash from something the Fused was holding. I think he intended to frighten Ico, but started the fire by accident.'

Wait, Kaladin thought. *Was that Alethi?* 'Shallan?' he asked as four Reachers gathered around.

'I'm right here,' said a different one. 'We are in trouble. The only ship that might have agreed to give us passage is that one there.'

'The one sailing away at full speed?' Kaladin said with a sigh.

'Nobody else would consider taking us on,' Azure said. 'And they were all heading the wrong directions anyway. We're about to be stranded.'

'We could try fighting our way onto a ship,' Kaladin said. 'Take control of it, maybe?'

Adolin shook his head. 'I think that would take long enough – and make enough trouble – that the Fused would find us.'

'Well, maybe I could fight *him*,' Kaladin said. 'Only one enemy. I should be able to take him.'

'Using all our Stormlight in the process?' Shallan asked.

'I'm just trying to think of something!'

'Guys,' Syl said. 'I might have an idea. A great bad idea.'

'The Fused went looking for you,' Shallan said to Kaladin. 'It flew to the market.'

'It passed us.'

'Guys?'

'Not for long though. It's going to turn around soon.'

'Turns out Syl has a bounty on her head.'

'Guys?'

'We need a plan,' Kaladin said. 'If nobody . . .' He trailed off.

Syl had started running toward the majestic white and gold ship, which was slowly being pulled away from the docks. She threw down her poncho and hat, then screamed up at the ship while running along the pier beside it.

'Hey!' she screamed. 'Hey, look down here!'

The vessel stopped ponderously, handlers slowing its mandras. Three blue-white honorspren appeared at the side, looking down with utter shock.

'*Sylphrena,* the Ancient Daughter?' one shouted.

'That's me!' she shouted back. 'You'd better catch me before I scamper away! Wow! I'm feeling capricious today. I might just vanish again, off to where nobody can find me!'

It worked.

A gangway dropped, and Syl scrambled up onto the ship – followed by the rest of them. Kaladin went last, watching nervously over his shoulder, expecting the Fused to come after them at any moment. It did, but it stopped at the mouth of the alleyway, watching them board the ship. Honorspren gave it pause, apparently.

On board, Kaladin discovered that most of the sailors were those spren made of fog or mist. One of these was tying Syl's arms together with rope. Kaladin tried to intervene, but Syl shook her head. 'Not now,' she mouthed.

Fine. He would argue with the honorspren later.

The ship pulled away, joining others that fled the city. The honorspren didn't pay much mind to Kaladin and the others – though one did take their harpoons, and another went through their pockets, confiscating their infused gemstones.

As the city grew smaller, Kaladin caught sight of the Fused hovering over the docks, beside the smoke trail of a burning ship.

It finally streaked off in the other direction.

Many cultures speak of the so-called Death Rattles that sometimes overtake people as they die. Tradition ascribes them to the Almighty, but I find too many to be seemingly prophetic. This will be my most contentious assertion I am sure, but I think these are the effects of Moelach persisting in our current times. Proof is easy to provide: the effect is regionalized, and tends to move across Roshar. This is the roving of the Unmade.

—From Hessi's *Mythica*, page 170

D alinar started awake in an unfamiliar place, lying on a floor of cut stone, his back stiff. He blinked sleepily, trying to orient himself. Storms . . . where was he?

Soft sunlight shone through an open balcony on the far side of the room, and ethereal motes of dust danced in the streams of light. What were those sounds? They seemed like the voices of people, but muffled.

Dalinar stood, then fastened the side of his uniform jacket, which had come undone. It had been . . . what, three days since his return from Jah Keved? His excommunication from the Vorin church?

He remembered those days as a haze of frustration, sorrow, agony. And drink. A great deal of drink. He'd been using the stupor to drive away the

437

pain. A terrible bandage for his wounds, blood seeping out on all sides. But so far, it had kept him alive.

I know this room, he realized, glancing at the mural on the ceiling. *I saw it in one of my visions.* A highstorm must have come while he was passed out.

'Stormfather?' Dalinar called, his voice echoing. 'Stormfather, why have you sent me a vision? We agreed they were too dangerous.'

Yes, he remembered this place well. This was the vision where he'd met Nohadon, author of *The Way of Kings*. Why wasn't it playing out as it had before? He and Nohadon had walked to the balcony, talked for a time, then the vision had ended.

Dalinar started toward the balcony, but storms, that light was *so intense*. It washed over him, making his eyes water, and he had to raise his hand to shield his eyes.

He heard something behind him. Scratching? He turned – putting his back to the brilliance – and spotted a door on the wall. It swung open easily beneath his touch, and he stepped out of the loud sunlight to find himself in a circular room.

He shut the door with a click. This chamber was much smaller than the previous one, with a wooden floor. Windows in the walls looked out at a clear sky. A shadow passed over one of these, like something enormous moving in front of the sun. But . . . how could the sun be pointed this direction too?

Dalinar looked over his shoulder at the wooden door. No light peeked underneath it. He frowned and reached for the handle, then paused, hearing the scratching once more. Turning, he saw a large desk, heaped with papers, by the wall. How had he missed that earlier?

A man sat at the desk, lit by a loose diamond, writing with a reed pen. Nohadon had aged. In the previous vision, the king had been young – but now his hair was silver, his skin marked by wrinkles. It *was* the same man though, same face shape, same beard that came to a point. He wrote with focused concentration.

Dalinar stepped over. '*The Way of Kings*,' he whispered. 'I'm watching it be written. . . .'

'Actually,' Nohadon said, 'it's a shopping list. I'll be cooking Shin loaf bread today, if I can get the ingredients. It always breaks people's brains. Grain was not meant to be so fluffy.'

What . . . ? Dalinar scratched at the side of his head.

Nohadon finished with a flourish and tossed the pen down. He threw back his chair and stood, grinning like a fool, and grabbed Dalinar by the arms. 'Good to see you again, my friend. You've been having a hard time of it lately, haven't you?'

'You have no idea,' Dalinar whispered, wondering who Nohadon saw him as. In the previous vision, Dalinar had appeared as one of Nohadon's advisors. They'd stood together on the balcony as Nohadon contemplated a war to unite the world. A drastic resort, intended to prepare mankind for the next Desolation.

Could that morose figure have really become this spry and eager? And where had this vision come from? Hadn't the Stormfather told Dalinar that he'd seen them all?

'Come,' Nohadon said, 'let's go to the market. A little shopping to turn your mind from your troubles.'

'Shopping?'

'Yes, you shop, don't you?'

'I . . . usually have people to do that for me.'

'Ah, but of course you do,' Nohadon said. 'Very like you to miss a simple joy so you can get to something more "important." Well, come on. I'm the king. You can't very well say no, now can you?'

Nohadon led Dalinar back through the door. The light was gone. They crossed to the balcony, which – last time – had overlooked death and desolation. Now, it looked out on a bustling city full of energetic people and rolling carts. The sound of the place crashed into Dalinar, as if it had been suppressed until that moment. Laughing, chatting, calling. Wagons creaking. Chulls bleating.

The men wore long skirts, tied at the waists by wide girdles, some of which came all the way up over their stomachs. Above that they had bare chests, or wore simple overshirts. The outfits resembled the takama Dalinar had worn when younger, though of a far, far older style. The tubular gowns on the women were even stranger, made of layered small rings of cloth with tassels on the bottom. They seemed to ripple as they moved.

The women's arms were bare up to the shoulders. No safehand covering. *In the previous vision, I spoke the Dawnchant,* Dalinar remembered. *The words that gave Navani's scholars a starting point to translate ancient texts.*

'How do we get down?' Dalinar asked, seeing no ladder.

Nohadon leaped off the side of the balcony. He laughed, falling and sliding along a cloth banner tied between a tower window and a tent below. Dalinar cursed, leaning forward, worried for the old man – until he spotted Nohadon glowing. He was a Surgebinder – but Dalinar had known that from the last vision, hadn't he?

Dalinar walked back to the writing chamber and drew the Stormlight from the diamond that Nohadon had been using. He returned, then heaved himself off the balcony, aiming for the cloth Nohadon had used to break his fall. Dalinar hit it at an angle and used it like a slide, keeping his right foot forward to guide his descent. Near the bottom, he flipped off the banner, grabbing its edge with two hands and hanging there for an instant before dropping with a *thump* beside the king.

Nohadon clapped. 'I thought you wouldn't do it.'

'I have practice following fools in their reckless pursuits.'

The old man grinned, then scanned his list. 'This way,' he said, pointing.

'I can't believe you're out shopping by yourself. No guards?'

'I walked all the way to Urithiru on my own. I think I can manage this.'

'You didn't walk all the way to Urithiru,' Dalinar said. 'You walked to one of the Oathgates, then took that to Urithiru.'

'Misconception!' Nohadon said. 'I walked the whole way, though I did require some help to reach Urithiru's caverns. That is no more a cheat than taking a ferry across a river.'

He bustled through the market and Dalinar followed, distracted by the colorful clothing everyone was wearing. Even the stones of the buildings were painted in vibrant colors. He'd always imagined the past as . . . dull. Statues from ancient times were weathered, and he'd never considered that they might have been painted so brightly.

What of Nohadon himself? In both visions, Dalinar had been shown someone he did not expect. The young Nohadon, considering war. Now the elderly one, glib and whimsical. Where was the deep-thinking philosopher who had written *The Way of Kings*?

Remember, Dalinar told himself, *this isn't really him. The person I'm talking to is a construct of the vision.*

Though some people in the market recognized their king, his passing didn't cause much of a stir. Dalinar spun as he saw something move beyond the buildings, a large shadow that passed between two structures,

440

tall and enormous. He stared in that direction, but didn't see it again.

They entered a tent where a merchant was selling exotic grains. The man bustled over and hugged Nohadon in a way that *should* have been improper for a king. Then the two started haggling like scribes; the rings on the merchant's fingers flashed as he gestured at his wares.

Dalinar lingered near the side of the tent, taking in the scents of the grains in the sacks. Outside, something made a distant *thud*. Then another. The ground shook, but nobody reacted.

'Noh – Your Majesty?' Dalinar asked.

Nohadon ignored him. A shadow passed over the tent. Dalinar ducked, judging the form of the shadow, the sounds of crashing footfalls.

'Your Majesty!' he shouted, fearspren growing up around him. 'We're in danger!'

The shadow passed, and the footfalls grew distant.

'Deal,' Nohadon said to the merchant. 'And well argued, you swindler. Make sure to buy Lani something nice with the extra spheres you got off me.'

The merchant bellowed a laughing reply. 'You think you got the worse of that? Storms, Your Majesty. You argue like my grandmother when she wants the last spoonful of jam!'

'Did you see that shadow?' Dalinar asked Nohadon.

'Have I told you,' Nohadon replied, 'where I learned to make Shin loaf bread? It wasn't in Shin Kak Nish, if that's what you were going to reply.'

'I . . .' Dalinar looked in the direction the enormous shadow had gone. 'No. You haven't told me.'

'It was at war,' Nohadon said. 'In the west. One of those senseless battles in the years following the Desolation. I don't even remember what caused it. Someone invaded someone else, and that threatened our trade through Makabakam. So off we went.

'Well, I ended up with a scouting group on the edge of the Shin border. So you see, I tricked you just now. I said I wasn't in Shin Kak Nish, and I wasn't. But I was right next to it.

'My troops occupied a small village beneath one of the passes. The matron who cooked for us accepted my military occupation without complaint. She didn't seem to care which army was in charge. She made me bread every day, and I liked it so much, she asked if I wanted to learn . . .'

He trailed off. In front of him, the merchant set weights on one side of his large set of scales – representing the amount Nohadon had purchased – then started pouring grain into a bowl on the other side of the scale. Golden, captivating grain, like the light of captured flames. 'What happened to the cook woman?' Dalinar asked.

'Something very unfair,' Nohadon said. 'It's not a happy story. I considered putting it into the book, but decided my story would best be limited to my walk to Urithiru.' He fell silent, contemplative.

He reminds me of Taravangian, Dalinar suddenly thought. *How odd.*

'You are having trouble, my friend,' Nohadon said. 'Your life, like that of the woman, is unfair.'

'Being a ruler is a burden, not merely a privilege,' Dalinar said. '*You* taught me that. But storms, Nohadon. I can't see any way out! We've gathered the monarchs, yet the drums of war beat in my ears, demanding. For every step I make with my allies, we seem to spend weeks deliberating. The truth whispers in the back of my mind. I could best defend the world if I could simply *make* the others do as they should!'

Nohadon nodded. 'So why don't you?'

'You didn't.'

'I tried and failed. That led me to a different path.'

'You're wise and thoughtful. I'm a warmonger, Nohadon. I've never accomplished *anything* without bloodshed.'

He heard them again. The tears of the dead. Evi. The children. Flames burning a city. He heard the fire roar in delight at the feast.

The merchant ignored them, busy trying to get the grain to balance. The weighted side was still heavier. Nohadon set a finger on the bowl with the grain and pushed down, making the sides even. 'That will do, my friend.'

'But—' the merchant said.

'Give the excess to the children, please.'

'After all that haggling? You know I'd have donated some if you'd asked.'

'And miss the fun of negotiating?' Nohadon said. He borrowed the merchant's pen, then crossed an item off his list. 'There is satisfaction,' he said to Dalinar, 'in creating a list of things you can actually accomplish, then removing them one at a time. As I said, a simple joy.'

'Unfortunately, I'm needed for bigger things than shopping.'

'Isn't that always the problem? Tell me, my friend. You talk about your burdens and the difficulty of the decision. What is the cost of a principle?'

'The cost? There shouldn't *be* a cost to being principled.'

'Oh? What if making the right decision created a spren who instantly blessed you with wealth, prosperity, and unending happiness? What then? Would you still have principles? Isn't a principle about what you *give up*, not what you *gain*?'

'So it's all negative?' Dalinar said. 'Are you implying that nobody should have principles, because there's no benefit to them?'

'Hardly,' Nohadon said. 'But maybe you shouldn't be looking for life to be easier because you choose to do something that is right! Personally, I think life *is* fair. It's merely that often, you can't immediately see what balances it.' He wagged the finger he'd used to tip the merchant's scales. 'If you'll forgive a somewhat blatant metaphor. I've grown fond of them. You might say I wrote an entire book about them.'

'This . . . is different from the other visions,' Dalinar said. 'What's going on?'

The thumping from before returned. Dalinar spun, then charged out of the tent, determined to get a look at the thing. He saw it above the buildings, a stone creature with an angular face and red spots glowing deep in its rocky skull. Storms! And he had no weapon.

Nohadon stepped from the tent, holding his bag of grain. He looked up and smiled. The creature leaned down, then offered a large, skeletal hand. Nohadon touched it with its own, and the creature stilled.

'This is quite the nightmare you've created,' Nohadon said. 'What does that thunderclast represent, I wonder?'

'Pain,' Dalinar said, backing away from the monster. 'Tears. *Burdens.* I'm a lie, Nohadon. A hypocrite.'

'Sometimes, a hypocrite is nothing more than a man who is in the process of changing.'

Wait. Hadn't *Dalinar* said that? Back when he'd felt stronger? More certain?

Other thumps sounded in the city. Hundreds of them. Creatures approaching from all sides, shadows in the sun.

'All things exist in three realms, Dalinar,' Nohadon said. 'The Physical: what you are now. The Cognitive: what you see yourself as being.

The Spiritual: the perfect you, the person beyond pain, and error, and uncertainty.'

Monsters of stone and horror surrounded him, heads cresting roofs, feet crushing buildings.

'You've said the oaths,' Nohadon called. 'But do you understand the journey? Do you understand what it requires? You've forgotten one essential part, one thing that without which there can *be* no journey.'

The monsters slammed fists toward Dalinar, and he shouted.

'What is the most important step a man can take?'

Dalinar awoke, huddled in his bed in Urithiru, asleep in his clothing again. A mostly empty bottle of wine rested on the table. There was no storm. It hadn't been a vision.

He buried his face in his hands, trembling. Something bloomed inside of him: a recollection. Not really a *new* memory – not one he'd completely forgotten. But it suddenly became as crisp as if he'd experienced it yesterday.

The night of Gavilar's funeral.

STRENGTH

Ashertmarn, the Heart of the Revel, is the final of the three great mindless Unmade. His gift to men is not prophecy or battle focus, but a lust for indulgence. Indeed, the great debauchery recorded from the court of Bayala in 480 – which led to dynastic collapse – might be attributable to the influence of Ashertmarn.

—From Hessi's *Mythica,* page 203

Navani Kholin had some practice holding a kingdom together. During Gavilar's last days, he had gone strange. Few knew how dark he'd grown, but they had seen the eccentricity. Jasnah had written about that, of course. Jasnah somehow found time to write about everything, from her father's biography, to gender relations, to the importance of chull breeding cycles on the southern slopes of the Horneater Peaks.

Navani strode through the hallways of Urithiru, joined by a nice burly group of Bridge Four Windrunners. As Gavilar had grown more and more distracted, Navani herself had worked to keep squabbling lighteyes from sundering the kingdom. But that had been a different kind of danger from the one she faced today.

Today, her work had implications not only for one nation, but for the entire world. She burst into a room deep within the tower, and the four lighteyes seated there scrambled to their feet – all but Sebarial, who appeared to be flipping through a stack of cards bearing pictures of women in compromising positions.

Navani sighed, then nodded as Aladar gave her a respectful bow, light glinting off his bald head. Not for the first time, Navani wondered if his thin mustache and the tuft of beard on his bottom lip were compensation for his lack of hair. Hatham was there as well: refined, with rounded features and green eyes. As usual, his fashion choices stood out from everyone else. Orange today.

Brightness Bethab had come representing her husband. The men in the army tended to disrespect him for letting her do so – but that ignored the fact that marrying Mishinah for her political acumen had been a wise and calculated move.

The five men of Bridge Four arrayed themselves behind Navani. They had been surprised when she'd asked them to escort her; they didn't yet understand the authority they lent the throne. The Knights Radiant were the new power in the world, and politics swirled around them like eddies in a river.

'Brightlords and Brightlady,' Navani said. 'I've come at your request, and am at your service.'

Aladar cleared his throat, sitting. 'You know, Brightness, that we are the most loyal to your husband's cause.'

'Or at the least,' Sebarial added, 'we're the ones hoping to get rich by throwing in our lot with him.'

'My husband appreciates the support,' Navani said, 'regardless of motive. You create a stronger Alethkar, and therefore a stronger world.'

'What's left of either one,' Sebarial noted.

'Navani,' Brightlady Bethab said. She was a mousy woman with a pinched face. 'We appreciate that you've taken the initiative in this difficult time.' There was a glint to her orange eyes, as if she assumed Navani was enjoying her new power. 'But the highprince's absence is not advantageous for morale. We know that Dalinar has returned to his . . . distractions.'

'The highprince,' Navani said, 'is in mourning.'

'The only thing he seems to be mourning,' Sebarial said, 'is the fact that people won't bring him bottles of wine fast enough for—'

'Damnation, Turinad!' Navani snapped. 'That's *enough*!'

Sebarial blinked, then pocketed his cards. 'Sorry, Brightness.'

'My husband,' Navani said, 'is still this world's best chance for survival. He *will* push through his pain. Until then, our duty is to keep the kingdom running.'

Hatham nodded, beads on his coat glistening. 'This is, of course, our goal. But Brightness, can you define what you *mean* by kingdom? You do know that Dalinar ... came to us and asked what we thought of this highking business.'

That news wasn't commonly known yet. They'd planned an official announcement, and even had Elhokar seal the papers before leaving. Yet Dalinar had delayed. She understood; he wanted to wait until Elhokar and Adolin – who would become Kholin highprince in Dalinar's place – returned.

And yet, as more and more time passed, the questions began to grow more pressing. What had happened to them in Kholinar? Where *were* they?

Strength. They *would* return.

'The highking proclamation has not been made official,' Navani said. 'I think it's best to pretend you don't know about it, for now. And whatever you do, *don't* mention it to Ialai or Amaram.'

'Very well,' Aladar said. 'But Brightness, we have other problems. Surely you've seen the reports. Hatham does an excellent job as Highprince of Works, but there isn't proper infrastructure. The tower has plumbing, but it keeps getting clogged, and the Soulcasters work themselves to exhaustion dealing with the waste.'

'We can't continue pretending the tower can accommodate this population,' Brightness Bethab said. 'Not without a very favorable supply deal from Azir. Our emerald reserves, despite hunts on the Shattered Plains, are dwindling. Our water carts have to work nonstop.'

'Equally important, Brightness,' Hatham added, 'we might be facing a severe labor shortage. We have soldiers or caravan men filling in hauling water or packing goods, but they don't like it. Menial carrying is beneath them.'

'We're running low on lumber,' Sebarial added. 'I've tried to claim the forests back near the warcamps, but we used to have parshmen to cut them. I don't know if I can afford to pay men to do the work instead.

But if we don't start something, Thanadal might try to seize them. He's building himself quite the kingdom in the warcamps.'

'This is not a time,' Hatham said softly, 'when we can afford weak leadership. It is not a time when a would-be king can spend his days locked in his rooms. I'm sorry. We are not in rebellion, but we are *very* concerned.'

Navani drew in a breath. *Hold it together.*

Order was the very substance of rule. If things were organized, control could be asserted. She just had to give Dalinar time. Even if, deep down, a part of her was angry. Angry that his pain so overshadowed her growing fear for Elhokar and Adolin. Angry that *he* got to drink himself to oblivion, leaving her to pick up the pieces.

But she had learned that nobody was strong all the time, not even Dalinar Kholin. Love wasn't about being right or wrong, but about standing up and helping when your partner's back was bowed. He would likely do the same for her someday.

'Tell us honestly, Brightness,' Sebarial said, leaning forward. 'What does the Blackthorn want? Is this all secretly a way for him to dominate the world?'

Storms. Even *they* worried about it. And why shouldn't they? It made so much sense.

'My husband wants unity,' Navani said firmly. '*Not* dominion. You know as well as I do that we could have seized Thaylen City. That would have led to selfishness and loss. There is no path through conquest to facing our enemy together.'

Aladar nodded slowly. 'I believe you, and I believe in him.'

'But how do we survive?' Brightness Bethab said.

'This tower's gardens once grew food,' Navani said. 'We will figure out how it was done, and we will grow here again. The tower once flowed with water. The baths and lavatories prove that. We will delve into the secrets of their fabrials, and we will fix the plumbing problems.

'The tower is above the enemy's storm, supremely defensible and connected to the most important cities in the world. If there is a nation that can stand against the enemy, we will forge it here. With your help and my husband's leadership.'

They accepted that. Bless the Almighty, they accepted it. She made a mental note to burn a glyphward in thanks, then finally took a seat.

Together, they delved into the tower's most recent list of problems, talking through – as they'd done many times before – the dirty necessities of running a city.

Three hours later, she checked her arm fabrial – a mirror of the one Dalinar carried, with inset clock and newly designed painrials. Three hours and twelve minutes since the meeting had begun. Exhaustionspren had collected to swirl around them all, and she called an end. They'd hashed out their immediate problems, and would summon their various scribes to offer specific revisions.

This would keep everyone going a little longer. And, bless them, these four *did* want the coalition to work. Aladar and Sebarial, for all their flaws, had followed Dalinar into the dark of the Weeping and found Damnation waiting there. Hatham and Bethab had been at the advent of the new storm, and could see that Dalinar had been right.

They didn't care that the Blackthorn was a heretic – or even whether he usurped the throne of Alethkar. They cared that he had a plan for dealing with the enemy, long-term.

After the meeting broke, Navani walked off down the strata-lined hallway, trailed by her bridgeman guards, two of whom carried sapphire lanterns. 'I do apologize,' she noted to them, 'for how boring that must have been.'

'We like boring, Brightness,' Leyten – their leader today – said. He was a stocky man, with short, curly hair. 'Hey, Hobber. Anyone try to kill you in there?'

The gap-toothed bridgeman grinned his reply. 'Does Huio's breath count?'

'See, Brightness?' Leyten said. 'New recruits might get bored by guard duty, but you'll never find a veteran complaining about a nice quiet afternoon full of not being stabbed.'

'I can see the appeal,' she said. 'But surely it can't compare with soaring through the skies.'

'That's true,' Leyten said. 'But we have to take turns ... you know.' He meant using the Honorblade to practice Windrunning. 'Kal has to return before we can do more than that.'

To a man, they were absolutely certain he'd return, and showed the world jovial faces – though she knew not everything was perfect with them. Teft, for example, had been hauled before Aladar's magistrates two days ago. Public intoxication on firemoss. Aladar had quietly requested her seal to free him.

No, all was not well with them. But as Navani led them down toward the basement library rooms, a different issue gnawed at her: Brightlady Bethab's implication that Navani was eager for the chance to take over while Dalinar was indisposed.

Navani was not a fool. She knew how it looked to others. She'd married one king. After he died, she'd immediately gone after the next most powerful man in Alethkar. But she *couldn't* have people believing she was the power behind the throne. Not only would it undermine Dalinar, but it would grow tedious for her. She had no problem being a wife or mother to monarchs, but to be one herself – storms, what a dark path that would lead them all down.

She and the bridgemen passed no fewer than six squads of sentries on their way to the library rooms with the murals and – more importantly – the hidden gemstone records. Arriving, she idled in the doorway, impressed by the operation that Jasnah had organized down here since Navani had been forced to step back from the research.

Each gemstone had been removed from its individual drawer, catalogued, and numbered. While one group listened and wrote, others sat at tables, busy translating. The room buzzed with a low hum of discussion and scratching reeds, concentrationspren dotting the air like ripples in the sky.

Jasnah strolled along the tables, looking through pages of translations. As Navani entered, the bridgemen gathered around Renarin, who blushed, looking up from his own papers, which were covered in glyphs and numbers. He *did* look out of place in the room, the only man in uniform rather than in the robes of an ardent or stormwarden.

'Mother,' Jasnah said, not looking up from her papers, 'we need more translators. Do you have any other scribes versed in classical Alethelan?'

'I've lent you everyone I have. What is Renarin studying over there?'

'Hm? Oh, he thinks there might be a pattern to which stones were stored in which drawers. He's been working on it all day.'

'And?'

'Nothing, which is not surprising. He insists he can find a pattern if he looks hard enough.' Jasnah lowered her pages and looked at her cousin, who was joking with the men of Bridge Four.

Storms, Navani thought. *He truly looks happy.* Embarrassed as they ribbed him, but happy. She'd worried when he had first 'joined' Bridge Four. He was the son of a highprince. Decorum and distance were appropriate when dealing with enlisted soldiers.

But when, before this, had she last heard him *laugh*?

'Maybe,' Navani said, 'we should encourage him to take a break and go out with the bridgemen for the evening.'

'I'd rather keep him here,' Jasnah said, flipping through her pages. 'His powers need additional study.'

Navani would talk to Renarin anyway and encourage him to go out more with the men. There was no arguing with Jasnah, any more than there was arguing with a boulder. You just stepped to the side and went around.

'The translation goes well,' Navani asked, 'other than the bottleneck on numbers of scribes?'

'We're lucky,' Jasnah said, 'that the gemstones were recorded so late in the life of the Radiants. They spoke a language we can translate. If it had been the Dawnchant . . .'

'That's close to being cracked.'

Jasnah frowned at that. Navani had thought the prospect of translating the Dawnchant – and writings lost to the shadowdays – would have excited her. Instead, it seemed to trouble her.

'Have you found anything more about the tower's fabrials in these gemstone records?' Navani asked.

'I'll be certain to prepare a report for you, Mother, with details of each and every fabrial mentioned. So far, those references are few. Most are personal histories.'

'Damnation.'

'Mother!' Jasnah said, lowering her pages.

'What? I wouldn't have thought you would object to a few strong words now and—'

'It's not the language, but the dismissal,' Jasnah said. 'Histories.'

Oh, right.

'History is the key to human understanding.'

Here we go.

'We must learn from the past and apply that knowledge to our modern experience.'

Lectured by my own daughter again.

'The best indication of what human beings will do is not what they think, but what the record says similar groups have done in the past.'

'Of course, Brightness.'

Jasnah gave her a dry look, then set her papers aside. 'I'm sorry, Mother. I've been dealing with a lot of lesser ardents today. My didactic side might have inflated.'

'You have a didactic side? Dear, you *hate* teaching.'

'Which explains my mood, I should think. I—'

A young scribe called for her from the other side of the room. Jasnah sighed, then went to answer the question.

Jasnah preferred to work alone, which was odd, considering how good she was at getting people to do what she wanted. Navani liked groups – but of course, Navani wasn't a scholar. Oh, she knew how to *pretend*. But all she really did was nudge here and there, perhaps provide an idea. Others did all the real engineering.

She poked through the papers Jasnah had set aside. Perhaps her daughter had missed something in the translations. To her mind, the only scholarship of importance was stuffy, dusty writings of old philosophers. When it came to fabrials, Jasnah barely knew her pairings from her warnings. . . .

What was this?

The glyphs were scrawled in white on the highprince's wall, the paper read. *We quickly ascertained the implement of writing to be a stone pried free near the window. This first sign was the roughest of them, the glyphs malformed. The reason for this later became apparent, as Prince Renarin was not versed in writing glyphs, save the numbers.*

The other pages were similar, talking about the strange numbers found around Dalinar's palace in the days leading up to the Everstorm. They'd been made by Renarin, whose spren had given him warning that the enemy was preparing an assault. The poor boy, uncertain of his bond and frightened to speak out, had instead written the numbers where Dalinar would see them.

It was a little odd, but in the face of everything else, it didn't really register. And . . . well, it *was* Renarin. Why had Jasnah collected all of these?

I have a description for you, finally, Jasnah, another said. *We've convinced the Radiant that Lift found in Yeddaw to visit Azimir. Though she has not yet arrived, you can find sketches of her spren companion here. It looks like the shimmer you see on a wall when you shine light through a crystal.*

Troubled, Navani set the sheets down before Jasnah could return. She got a copy of the translated portions from the gemstones – several young scribes were assigned to making these available – then slipped out to go check on Dalinar.

SPIRIT, MIND, AND BODY

SIX YEARS AGO

Only the very most important people were allowed to watch Gavilar's holy interment.

Dalinar stood at the front of the small crowd, gathered in the royal catacombs of Kholinar, beneath the stone sight of kings. Fires burned at the sides of the room, a primal light, traditional. Distinctly more alive than the light of spheres, it reminded him of the Rift – but for once, that pain was overpowered by something new. A fresh wound.

The sight of his brother, lying dead on the slab.

'Spirit, mind, and body,' the wizened ardent said, her voice echoing in the stone catacomb. 'Death is the separation of the three. The body remains in our realm, to be reused. The spirit rejoins the pool of divine essence that gave it birth. And the mind . . . the mind goes to the Tranquiline Halls to find its reward.'

Dalinar's nails bit his skin as he clenched his hands into fists – tight, to keep him from trembling.

'Gavilar the Majestic,' the ardent continued, 'first king of Alethkar in the new Kholin Dynasty, thirty-second highprince of the Kholin princedom, heir of the Sunmaker and blessed of the Almighty. His accomplishments will be lauded by all, and his dominion extends to the hereafter. Already he leads men again on the battlefield, serving the Almighty in the true war against the Voidbringers.'

The ardent thrust a bony hand toward the small crowd. 'Our king's war has moved to the Tranquiline Halls. The end of our war for Roshar did not end our duty to the Almighty! Think upon your Callings, men and women of Alethkar. Think of how you might learn here, and be of use in the next world.'

Jevena would use any available opportunity to preach. Dalinar clenched his hands tighter, angry at her – angry at the *Almighty*. Dalinar should not have lived to see his brother die. This was *not* the way it should have gone.

He felt eyes on his back. Collected highprinces and wives, important ardents, Navani, Jasnah, Elhokar, Aesudan, Dalinar's sons. Nearby, Highprince Sebarial glanced at Dalinar, eyebrows raised. He seemed to be expecting something.

I'm not drunk, you idiot, Dalinar thought. *I'm not going to make a scene to amuse you.*

Things had been going better lately. Dalinar had started controlling his vices; he'd confined his drinking to monthly trips away from Kholinar, visiting outer cities. He said the trips were to let Elhokar practice ruling without Dalinar looking over his shoulder, as Gavilar had been spending more and more time abroad. But during those trips, Dalinar drank himself to oblivion, letting himself escape the sounds of children crying for a few precious days.

Then, when he returned to Kholinar, he controlled his drinking. And he'd never again yelled at his sons, as he had at poor Renarin during that day on the way back from the Shattered Plains. Adolin and Renarin were the only pure remnant of Evi.

If you control your drinking when back in Kholinar, a part of him challenged, *what happened at the feast? Where were you when Gavilar was fighting for his life?*

'We must use King Gavilar as a model for our own lives,' the ardent was saying. 'We must remember that our lives are not our own. This world is but the skirmish to prepare us for the true war.'

'And after that?' Dalinar asked, looking up from Gavilar's corpse.

The ardent squinted, adjusting her spectacles. 'Highprince Dalinar?'

'After that, what?' Dalinar said. 'After we win back the Tranquiline Halls? What then? No more war?'

Is that when we finally get to rest?

'You needn't worry, Blackthorn,' Jevena said. 'Once that war is won, the Almighty will certainly provide for you another conquest.' She smiled comfortingly, then moved on to the ritual sayings. A series of keteks, some traditional, others composed by female family members for the event. Ardents burned the poems as prayers in braziers.

Dalinar looked back down at his brother's corpse, which stared upward, lifeless blue marbles replacing his eyes.

Brother, he'd said, *follow the Codes tonight. There is something strange upon the winds.*

Dalinar needed something to drink, storm it.

'You, always about dreams. My soul weeps. Farewell, weeping soul. My dreams . . . about, always, You.'

The poem slapped him harder than the others. He sought out Navani, and knew instantly that the ketek had been hers. Gazing straight ahead, she stood with one hand on Elhokar's – *King Elhokar's* – shoulder. So beautiful. Next to her, Jasnah stood with arms wrapped around herself, eyes red. Navani reached toward her, but Jasnah pulled away from the others and stalked off toward the palace proper.

Dalinar wished he could do the same, but instead drew himself to attention. It was over. He'd never have a chance to live up to Gavilar's expectations. Dalinar would live the rest of his life as a failure to this man whom he had loved so dearly.

The hall grew still, quiet save for the crinkling sound of paper burning in the fires. The Soulcaster stood up, and old Jevena stepped hastily backward. She wasn't comfortable with what was coming next. None of them were, judging by the shuffling feet, the coughs into hands.

The Soulcaster might have been male, might have been female. Hard to say, with that hood up over their face. The skin beneath was colored like granite, cracked and chipped, and seemed to *glow* from within. The Soulcaster regarded the corpse, head cocked, as if surprised to find a body here. They ran their fingers along Gavilar's jaw, then brushed the hair off his forehead.

'The only part of you that is true,' the Soulcaster whispered, tapping a stone that had replaced one of the king's eyes. Then, light emerged as the Soulcaster drew their hand from their pocket, revealing a set of gemstones bound into a fabrial.

Dalinar didn't look away, despite how the light made his eyes water. He wished . . . he wished he'd taken a drink or two before coming. Was he really supposed to watch something like this while sober?

The Soulcaster touched Gavilar on the forehead, and the transformation happened instantly. One moment Gavilar was there. The next he had become a statue.

The Soulcaster slipped a glove onto their hand while other ardents hurried to remove the wires that had held Gavilar's body in position. They used levers to tip him carefully forward until he was standing, holding a sword with point toward the ground, his other hand outstretched. He stared toward eternity, crown on his head, the curls of his beard and hair preserved delicately in the stone. A powerful pose; the mortuary sculptors had done a fantastic job.

The ardents pushed him back into an alcove, where he joined the lines of other monarchs – most of them highprinces of the Kholin princedom. He would be forever frozen here, the image of a perfect ruler in his prime. Nobody would think of him as he'd been that terrible night, broken from his fall, his grand dreams cut short by treason.

'I'll have vengeance, Mother,' Elhokar whispered. 'I'll *have* it!' The young king spun toward the gathered lighteyes, standing before his father's outstretched stone hand. 'You've each come to me privately to give support. Well, I demand you swear it in public! Today, we make a pact to hunt those who did this. Today, Alethkar goes to *war!*'

He was greeted by stunned silence.

'I swear it,' Torol Sadeas said. 'I swear to bring vengeance to the traitorous parshmen, Your Majesty. You can depend upon my sword.'

Good, Dalinar thought, as others spoke up. This would hold them together. Even in death, Gavilar provided an excuse for unity.

Unable to stand that stone visage any longer, Dalinar left, stomping into the corridor toward the palace proper. Other voices echoed after him as highprinces swore.

If Elhokar was going to chase those Parshendi back toward the plains, he'd expect the Blackthorn's help. But . . . Dalinar hadn't been that man for years. He patted his pocket, looking for his flask. Damnation. He pretended he was better these days, kept telling himself he was in the process of finding a way out of this mess. Of returning to the man he'd once been.

But that man had been a monster. Frightening, that nobody had blamed him for the things he'd done. Nobody but Evi, who had seen what the killing would do to him. He closed his eyes, hearing her tears.

'Father?' a voice said from behind.

Dalinar forced himself to stand upright, turning as Adolin scrambled up to him.

'Are you well, Father?'

'Yes,' Dalinar said. 'I just . . . need to be alone.'

Adolin nodded. Almighty above, the boy had turned out well, through little effort of Dalinar's. Adolin was earnest, likable, and a master of the sword. He was truly capable in modern Alethi society, where how you moved among groups was even more important than strength of arm. Dalinar had always felt like a tree stump in those kinds of settings. Too big. Too stupid.

'Go back,' Dalinar said. 'Swear for our house on this Vengeance Pact.'

Adolin nodded, and Dalinar continued onward, fleeing those fires below. Gavilar's stare, judging him. The cries of people dying in the Rift.

By the time he reached the steps, he was practically running. He climbed one level, then another. Sweating, frantic, he raced through ornate hallways past carved walls, sedate woods, and accusatory mirrors. He reached his chambers and scrabbled in his pockets for the keys. He'd locked the place tight; no more would Gavilar sneak in to take his bottles. Bliss waited inside.

No. Not bliss. Oblivion. Good enough.

His hands wouldn't stop shaking. He couldn't – It—

Follow the Codes tonight.

Dalinar's hands trembled, and he dropped the keys.

There is something strange upon the winds.

Screams for mercy.

Get out of my head! All of you, get out!

In the distance, a voice . . .

'You must find the most important words a man can say.'

Which key was it? He got one into the lock, but it wouldn't turn. He couldn't see. He blinked, feeling dizzy.

'Those words came to me from one who claimed to have seen the future,' the voice said, echoing in the hallway. Feminine, familiar. '"How is this possible?" I asked in return. "Have you been touched by the void?"'

'The reply was laughter. "No, sweet king. The past is the future, and as each man has lived, so must you."

'"So I can but repeat what has been done before?"

'"In some things, yes. You will love. You will hurt. You will dream. And you will die. Each man's past is your future."

'"Then what is the point?" I asked. "If all has been seen and done?"

'"The question," she replied, "is not whether you will love, hurt, dream, and die. It is *what* you will love, *why* you will hurt, *when* you will dream, and *how* you will die. This is your choice. You cannot pick the destination, only the path."'

Dalinar dropped the keys again, sobbing. There was no escape. He would fall again. Wine would consume him like a fire consumed a corpse. Leaving only ash.

There was no way out.

'This started my journey,' the voice said. 'And this begins my writings. I cannot call this book a story, for it fails at its most fundamental to *be* a story. It is not one narrative, but many. And though it has a beginning, here on this page, my quest can never truly end.

'I wasn't seeking answers. I felt that I had those already. Plenty, in multitude, from a thousand different sources. I wasn't seeking 'myself.' This is a platitude that people have ascribed to me, and I find the phrase lacks meaning.

'In truth, by leaving, I was seeking only one thing.

'A journey.'

For years, it seemed that Dalinar had been seeing everything around him through a haze. But those words . . . something about them . . .

Could words give off light?

He turned from his door and walked down the corridor, searching for the source of the voice. Inside the royal reading room, he found Jasnah with a huge tome set before her at a standing table. She read to herself, turning to the next page, scowling.

'What is that book?' Dalinar asked.

Jasnah started. She wiped her eyes, smearing the makeup, leaving her eyes . . . clean, but raw. Holes in a mask.

'This is where my father got that quote,' she said. 'The one he . . .'

The one he wrote as he died.

Only a few knew of that.

'What book is it?'

'An old text,' Jasnah said. 'Ancient, once well regarded. It's associated with the Lost Radiants, so nobody references it anymore. There has to be some secret here, a puzzle behind my father's last words. A cipher? But what?'

Dalinar settled down into one of the seats. He felt as if he had no strength. 'Will you read it to me?'

Jasnah met his eyes, chewing her lip as she'd always done as a child. Then she read in a clear, strong voice, starting over from the first page, which he'd just heard. He had expected her to stop after a chapter or two, but she didn't, and he didn't want her to.

Dalinar listened, rapt. People came to check on them; some brought Jasnah water to drink. For once, he didn't ask them for anything. All he wanted was to listen.

He understood the words, but at the same time he seemed to be missing what the book said. It was a sequence of vignettes about a king who left his palace to go on a pilgrimage. Dalinar couldn't define, even to himself, what he found so striking about the tales. Was it their optimism? Was it the talk of paths and choices?

It was so unpretentious. So different from the boasts of society or the battlefield. Just a series of stories, their morals ambiguous. It took almost eight hours to finish, but Jasnah never gave any indication she wanted to stop. When she read the last word, Dalinar found himself weeping again. Jasnah dabbed at her own eyes. She had always been so much stronger than he was, but here they shared an understanding. This was their send-off to Gavilar's soul. This was their farewell.

Leaving the book on the lectern, Jasnah walked over to Dalinar as he stood up. They embraced, saying nothing. After a few moments, she left.

He went to the book, touching it, feeling the lines of the writing stamped into its cover. He didn't know how long he'd been standing there when Adolin peeked in. 'Father? We're planning to send expeditionary forces to the Shattered Plains. Your input would be appreciated.'

'I must,' Dalinar whispered, 'go on a journey.'

'Yeah,' Adolin said. 'It's a long way. Might get some hunts in while we're on our way, if there's time. Elhokar wants these barbarians wiped out quickly. We could be gone and back in a year.'

Paths. Dalinar could not choose his end.

But perhaps his *path* . . .

The Old Magic can change a person, Evi had said. *Make something great of them.*

Dalinar stood up taller. He turned and stepped toward Adolin, seizing him by the shoulder. 'I've been a poor father these last few years,' Dalinar said.

'Nonsense,' Adolin said. 'You—'

'I've been a poor father,' Dalinar repeated, raising his finger. 'To you and your brother both. You should know how proud I am of you.'

Adolin beamed, glowing like a sphere right after a storm. Gloryspren sprang up around him.

'We will go to war together,' Dalinar said. 'Like we did when you were young. I will show you what it is to be a man of honor. But first, I need to take an advance force – without you, I'm afraid – and secure the Shattered Plains.'

'We talked about that,' Adolin said, eager. 'Like your elites, from before. Fast, quick! You'll march—'

'Sail,' Dalinar said.

'Sail?'

'The rivers should be flowing,' Dalinar said. 'I'll march south, then take a ship to Dumadari. From there, I'll sail to the Ocean of Origins and make landfall at New Natanan. I'll move in toward the Shattered Plains with my force and secure the region, preparing for the rest of you to arrive.'

'That would be a sound idea, I guess,' Adolin said.

It *was* sound. Sound enough that when one of Dalinar's ships was delayed – and Dalinar himself remained in port, sending most of his force on without him – nobody would think it strange. Dalinar did get himself into trouble.

He would swear his men and sailors to secrecy, and travel a few months out of his way before continuing on to the Shattered Plains.

Evi had said the Old Magic could transform a man. It was about time he started trusting her.

LAW IS LIGHT

I find Ba-Ado-Mishram to be the most interesting of the Unmade. She is said to have been keen of mind, a highprincess among the enemy forces, their commander during some of the Desolations. I do not know how this relates to the ancient god of the enemy, named Odium.

—From Hessi's *Mythica*, page 224

S zeth of Shinovar flew with the Skybreakers for three days, southward.

They stopped several times to recover hidden stockpiles in mountain peaks or remote valleys. To find doorways, they often had to hack through five inches of crem. That amount of buildup had probably taken centuries to accumulate, yet Nin spoke of the places as if he'd just left. At one, he was surprised to find the food long since decayed – though fortunately, the gemstone stockpile there had been hidden in a place where it remained exposed to the storms.

In these visits, Szeth finally began to grasp how *ancient* this creature was.

On the fourth day, they reached Marat. Szeth had been to the kingdom before; he had visited most of Roshar during the years of his exile. Historically, Marat wasn't truly a nation – but neither was it a place of nomads, like the backwaters of Hexi and Tu Fallia. Instead, Marat was a group of loosely connected cities, tribally run, with a highprince at their head – though in the local dialect, he was called 'elder brother.'

The country made for a convenient waystop between the Vorin kingdoms of the east and the Makabaki ones of the center west. Szeth knew that Marat was rich in culture, full of people as proud as you'd find in any nation – but of almost no value on the political scale.

Which made it curious that Nin chose to end their flight here. They landed on a plain full of strange brown grass that reminded Szeth of wheat, save for the fact that this pulled down into burrows, leaving visible only the small bob of grain on the top. This was casually eaten by wild beasts that were wide and flat, like walking discs, with claws only on the underside to shove the grain into their mouths.

The disclike animals would probably migrate eastward, their droppings containing seeds that – stuck to the ground – would survive storms to grow into first-stage polyps. Those would later blow to the west and become second-stage grain. All life worked in concert, he'd been taught in his youth. Everything but men, who refused their place. Who destroyed instead of added.

Nin spoke briefly with Ki and the other masters, who took to the air again. The others joined them – all but Szeth and Nin himself – and streaked toward a town in the distance. Before Szeth could follow, Nin took him by the arm and shook his head. Together, the two of them flew to a smaller town on a hill near the coast.

Szeth knew the effects of war when he saw them. Broken doors, ruins of a short, breached wall. The destruction looked recent, though any bodies had been cleaned out and the blood had been washed away by highstorms. They landed before a large stone building with a peaked roof. Mighty doors of Soulcast bronze lay broken off in the rubble. Szeth would be surprised if somebody didn't return to claim those for their metal. Not every army had access to Soulcasters.

Aw, the sword said from his back. *We missed the fun?*

'That tyrant in Tukar,' Szeth said, looking through the silent town. 'He decided to end his war against Emul, and expand eastward?'

'No,' Nin said. 'This is a different danger.' He pointed toward the building with the broken doors. 'Can you read that writing above the doorway, Szeth-son-Neturo?'

'It's in the local language. I don't know the script, aboshi.' The divine

464

honorific was his best guess of how to address one of the Heralds, though among his people it had been reserved for the great spren of the mountains.

'It says "justice," ' Nin said. 'This was a courthouse.'

Szeth followed the Herald up the steps and into the cavernous main room of the ruined courthouse. In here, sheltered from the storm, they found blood on the floor. No bodies, but plenty of discarded weapons, helms, and – disturbingly – the meager possessions of civilians. The people had likely taken refuge inside here during the battle, a last grasp at safety.

'The ones you call parshmen name themselves the singers,' Nin said. 'They took this town and pressed the survivors into labor at some docks farther along the coast. Was what happened here justice, Szeth-son-Neturo?'

'How could it be?' He shivered. The dark reaches of the room seemed to be filled with haunted whispers. He drew closer to the Herald for safety. 'Ordinary people, living ordinary lives, suddenly attacked and murdered?'

'A poor argument. What if the lord of this city had stopped paying his taxes, then forced his people to defend the city when higher authorities arrived and attacked? Is not a prince justified in maintaining order in his lands? Sometimes, it is just to kill ordinary people.'

'But that did not happen here,' Szeth said. 'You said this was caused by an invading army.'

'Yes,' Nin said softly. 'This is the fault of invaders. That is true.' He continued walking through the hollow room, Szeth staying close behind him. 'You are in a unique position, Szeth-son-Neturo. You will be the first to swear the oaths of a Skybreaker in a new world, a world where I have failed.'

They found steps near the back wall. Szeth got out a sphere for light, as Nin did not appear to be so inclined. That drove the whispers back.

'I visited Ishar,' Nin continued. 'You call him Ishu-son-God. He has always been the most wise of us. I did not ... want to believe ... what had happened.'

Szeth nodded. He had seen that. After the first Everstorm, Nin had insisted that the Voidbringers hadn't returned. He had given excuse after excuse, until eventually he'd been forced to admit what he was seeing.

'I worked for thousands of years to prevent another Desolation,' Nin continued. 'Ishar warned me of the danger. Now that Honor is dead, other Radiants might upset the balance of the Oathpact. Might undermine certain . . . measures we took, and give an opening to the enemy.'

He stopped at the top of the steps and looked down at his hand, where a glistening Shardblade appeared. One of the two missing Honorblades. Szeth's people had care of eight. Once, long ago, it had been nine. Then this one had vanished.

He'd seen depictions of it, strikingly straight and unornamented for a Shardblade, yet still elegant. Two slits ran the length of the weapon, gaps that could never exist in an ordinary sword, as they would weaken it.

They walked along a loft at the top of the courtroom. Records storage, judging by the scattered ledgers on the floor.

You should draw me, the sword said.

'And do what, sword-nimi?' Szeth whispered.

Fight him. I think he might be evil.

'He is one of the Heralds – one of the *least*-evil things in the world.'

Huh. Doesn't bode well for your world, then. Anyway, I'm better than that sword he has. I can show you.

Picking his way past the legal debris, Szeth joined Nin beside the loft's window. In the distance, farther along the coast, a large bay glistened with blue water. Many masts of ships gathered there, figures buzzing around them.

'I have failed,' Nin repeated. 'And now, for the people, justice must be done. A very difficult justice, Szeth-son-Neturo. Even for my Skybreakers.'

'We will endeavor to be as passionless and logical as you, aboshi.'

Nin laughed. It didn't seem to carry the mirth that it should have. 'Me? No, Szeth-son-Neturo. I am hardly passionless. This is the problem.' He paused, staring out the window at the distant ships. 'I am . . . different from how I once was. Worse, perhaps? Despite all that, a part of me wishes to be merciful.'

'And is . . . mercy such a bad thing, aboshi?'

'Not bad; merely chaotic. If you look through the records in this hall, you will find the same story told again and again. Leniency and mercy. Men set free despite crimes, because they were good fathers, or well-liked in the community, or in the favor of someone important.

'Some of those who are set free change their lives and go on to produce for society. Others recidivate and create great tragedies. The thing is, Szeth-son-Neturo, we humans are *terrible* at spotting which will be which. The *purpose* of the law is so we do not have to choose. So our native sentimentality will not harm us.'

He looked down again at his sword.

'You,' he said to Szeth, 'must choose a Third Ideal. Most Skybreakers choose to swear themselves to the law – and follow with exactness the laws of whatever lands they visit. That is a good option, but not the only one. Think wisely, and choose.'

'Yes, aboshi,' Szeth said.

'There are things you must see, and things you must know, before you can speak. The others must *interpret* what they have sworn before, and I hope they will see the truth. *You* will be the first of a new order of Skybreakers.' He looked back out the window. 'The singers allowed the people of this town to return here to burn their dead. A kinder gesture than most conquerors would allow.'

'Aboshi . . . may I ask you a question?'

'Law is light, and darkness does not serve it. Ask, and I will answer.'

'I know you are great, ancient, and wise,' Szeth said. 'But . . . to my lesser eyes, you do not seem to obey your own precepts. You hunted Surgebinders, as you said.'

'I obtained legal permission for the executions I performed.'

'Yes,' Szeth said, 'but you ignored many lawbreakers to pursue these few. You had motives beyond the law, aboshi. You were not impartial. You brutally enforced specific laws to achieve your ends.'

'This is true.'

'So is this just your own . . . sentimentality?'

'In part. Though I have certain leniencies. The others have told you of the Fifth Ideal?'

'The Ideal where the Skybreaker *becomes* the law?'

Nin held out his empty left hand. A *Shardblade* appeared there, different and distinct from the Honorblade he carried in the other hand. 'I am not only a Herald, but a Skybreaker of the Fifth Ideal. Though I was originally skeptical of the Radiants, I believe I am the only one who eventually joined his own order.

'And now, Szeth-son-Neturo, I must tell you of the decision we Heralds made, long ago. On the day that would become known as Aharietiam. The day we sacrificed one of our own to end the cycle of pain and death . . .'

467

There is very little information about Ba-Ado-Mishram in more modern times. I can only assume she, unlike many of them, returned to Damnation or was destroyed during Aharietiam.

—From Hessi's *Mythica*, page 226

Dalinar found a washbasin ready for him in the morning. Navani meticulously kept it filled, just as she cleaned up the bottles and allowed the servants to bring him more. She trusted him better than he trusted himself.

Stretching in his bed, Dalinar woke feeling far too . . . whole, considering the drinking he'd been doing. Indirect sunlight illuminated the room from the window. Normally they kept the shutters in this room closed to ward off the cold mountain air. Navani must have opened them after rising.

Dalinar splashed his face with water from the basin, then caught a hint of his own scent. *Right.* He looked into one of the connecting rooms, which they'd appropriated for a washroom, as it had a back entrance the servants could use. Sure enough, Navani had ordered the tub filled for him. The water was cold, but he'd known his share of cold baths. It would keep him from lingering.

A short time later, he took a razor to his face, peering at himself in a bedroom mirror. Gavilar had taught him to shave. Their father had been too busy getting himself cut apart in foolish duels of honor, including the one where he'd taken a blow to the head. He'd never been right after that.

Beards were unfashionable in Alethkar these days, but that wasn't why Dalinar shaved. He liked the ritual. The chance to prepare, to cut away the nightly chaff and reveal the real person underneath – furrows, scars, and harsh features included.

A clean uniform and underclothes waited for him on a bench. He dressed, then checked the uniform in the mirror, pulling down on the bottom of the coat to tighten any folds.

That memory of Gavilar's funeral ... so vivid. He'd forgotten parts. Had that been the Nightwatcher, or the natural course of memories? The more he recovered of what he had lost, the more he realized that the memories of men were flawed. He'd mention an event now fresh to his mind, and others who had lived it would argue over details, as each recalled it differently. Most, Navani included, seemed to remember him as more noble than he deserved. Yet he didn't ascribe any magic to this. It was simply the way of human beings, subtly changing the past in their minds to match their current beliefs.

But then ... that vision with Nohadon. Where had that come from? Just a common dream?

Hesitant, he reached out to the Stormfather, who rumbled distantly. 'Still there, I see,' Dalinar said, relieved.

Where would I go?

'I hurt you,' Dalinar said. 'When I activated the Oathgate. I was afraid you would leave me.'

This is the lot I have chosen. It is you or oblivion.

'I'm sorry, regardless, for what I did. Were you ... involved in that dream I had? The one with Nohadon?'

I know of no such dream.

'It was vivid,' Dalinar said. 'More surreal than one of the visions, true, but captivating.'

What was the most important step a man could take? The first, obviously. But what did it mean?

He still bore the weight of what he had done at the Rift. This recovery – this stepping away from the week spent drinking – wasn't a redemption.

What would he do if he felt the Thrill again? What would happen the next time the weeping in his mind became too difficult to bear?

Dalinar didn't know. He felt better today. Functional. For now, he would let that be enough. He picked a piece of lint off his collar, then belted on a side sword and stepped out of the bedroom, walking through his study and into the larger room with the hearth.

'Taravangian?' he said, surprised to find the elderly king seated there. 'Wasn't there to be a meeting of the monarchs today?' He vaguely remembered Navani telling him of it early that morning.

'They said I wasn't needed.'

'Nonsense! We're all needed at the meetings.' Dalinar paused. 'I've missed several, haven't I? Well, regardless, what are they talking about today?'

'Tactics.'

Dalinar felt his face go red. 'The deployment of troops and the defense of Jah Keved, your kingdom?'

'I think they believe that I will give up the throne of Jah Keved, once a suitable local man has been found.' He smiled. 'Do not be so outraged on my behalf, my friend. They didn't forbid me; they simply noted I wasn't needed. I wanted some time to think, so I came here.'

'Still. Let's go up, shall we?'

Taravangian nodded, standing. He wobbled on unsteady legs and Dalinar hurried over to help him. Stabilized, Taravangian patted Dalinar's hand. 'Thank you. You know, I've always felt old. But lately, it seems my body is determined to give me persistent reminders.'

'Let me summon a palanquin to carry you.'

'No, please. If I give up walking, I fear my deterioration will increase. I've seen similar things happen to people in my hospitals.' But he held Dalinar's arm as they walked toward the doorway. Outside, Dalinar collected some guards of his own along with Taravangian's large Thaylen bodyguard. They started toward the lifts.

'Do you know,' Dalinar said, 'if there's word . . .'

'From Kholinar?' Taravangian asked.

Dalinar nodded. He vaguely remembered updates from Navani. No news of Adolin, Elhokar, or the Radiants. But had he been of sound enough mind to listen?

'I'm sorry, Dalinar,' Taravangian said. 'So far as I know, we haven't had a message from them. But we must keep hope, of course! They might have lost their spanreed, or gotten trapped in the city.'

I . . . may have felt something, the Stormfather said. *During a recent highstorm, it felt like Stormblessed was there with me. I do not know what it means, for I cannot see him – or the others – anywhere. I presumed them dead, but now . . . now I find myself believing. Why?*

'You have hope,' Dalinar whispered, smiling.

'Dalinar?' Taravangian asked.

'Just whispering to myself, Your Majesty.'

'If I might say . . . You seem stronger today. You've decided something?'

'More, I've *remembered* something.'

'Is it something you can share with a worried old man?'

'Not yet. I'll try to explain once I have it figured out myself.'

After an extended trip up the lifts, Dalinar led Taravangian into a quiet, windowless chamber on the penultimate floor of the tower. They'd dubbed it the Gallery of Maps, after a similar location in the warcamps.

Aladar led the meeting, standing beside a table that was covered by a large map of Alethkar and Jah Keved. The dark-skinned Alethi man wore his war uniform – the mix of a traditional takama skirt and modern jacket that had been catching on among his officers. His bodyguard, Mintez, stood behind him in full Shardplate – Aladar preferred not to use the Shards personally. He was a general, not a warrior. He nodded to Dalinar and Taravangian when they entered.

Ialai sat nearby, and studied Dalinar, saying nothing. He'd almost have welcomed a wisecrack; in the old days, she'd been quick to joke with him. Her silence now didn't mean she was being respectful. It meant she was saving her barbs to whisper where he couldn't hear.

Highprince Ruthar – thick-armed and wearing a full beard – sat with Ialai. He'd opposed Dalinar from the start. The other Alethi highprince who had come today was Hatham, a long-necked man with light orange eyes. He wore a red and gold uniform of a type that Dalinar hadn't seen before, with a short jacket that buttoned only at the top. Silly-looking, but what did Dalinar know of fashion? The man was extremely polite, and he ran a tight army.

Queen Fen had brought the Thaylen high admiral, a scrawny old man with mustaches that drooped almost to the table. He wore a short sailor's saber and sash, and looked like exactly the type who would complain about being stuck on the land for too long. She'd also brought her son – the one Dalinar had dueled – who saluted Dalinar sharply. Dalinar saluted back. That boy would make an excellent officer, if he could learn to keep his temper.

The Azish emperor wasn't there, nor was their little Edgedancer. Instead, Azir had sent a collection of scholars. Azish 'generals' tended to be of the armchair type, military historians and theorists who spent their days in books. Dalinar was certain they had men with practical knowledge in their military, but those rarely ended up promoted. So long as you failed certain tests, you could remain in the field and command.

Dalinar had met the two Veden highprinces during his trip to their city. The brothers were tall, prim men with short black hair and uniforms much like those of the Alethi. Taravangian had appointed them after their predecessors had been poisoned, following the civil war. Jah Keved obviously still had many problems.

'Dalinar?' Aladar said. He stood up straighter, then saluted. 'Brightlord, you're looking better.'

Storms. How much did the rest of them know?

'I've spent some time in meditation,' Dalinar said. 'I see you've been busy. Tell me about the defensive array.'

'Well,' Aladar said, 'we—'

'That's it?' Queen Fen interrupted. 'What in Damnation was wrong with you? You ran all around Vedenar like a wildman, then locked yourself in your room for a week!'

'I was excommunicated from the Vorin church soon after hearing of Kholinar's fall. I took it poorly. Did you expect me to react by throwing a feast?'

'I expected you to lead us, not *sulk*.'

I deserved that. 'You are right. You can't have a commander who refuses to command. I'm sorry.'

The Azish whispered among themselves, looking surprised at the bluntness of the exchange. But Fen settled back and Aladar nodded. Dalinar's mistakes had needed to be aired.

Aladar began explaining their battle preparations. The Azish generals – all wearing robes and Western hats – crowded around, offering commentary through translators. Dalinar used a little Stormlight and touched one on the arm, to gain access to their language for a short time.

He found their advice surprisingly astute, considering that they were basically a committee of scribes.

They'd moved ten battalions of Alethi troops through the Oathgates, along with five battalions of Azish. That put fifteen thousand men on the ground in Jah Keved, including some of their most loyal Kholin and Aladar forces.

That seriously cut into his troop numbers. Storms, they'd lost so many at Narak – the companies that Dalinar had remaining at Urithiru were mostly recruits or men from other princedoms who had asked to join his military. Sebarial, for example, had cut back to maintaining only a single division, giving Dalinar the rest to wear Kholin colors.

Dalinar had interrupted a discussion of how to fortify the Jah Keved border. He offered some insights, but mostly listened as they explained their plans: stockpiles here, garrisons there. They hoped the Windrunners would be able to scout for them.

Dalinar nodded, but found that something bothered him about this battle plan. A problem he couldn't define. They'd done well; their lines of supply had been drawn realistically and their scout posts were spaced for excellent coverage.

What, then, was wrong?

The door opened, revealing Navani, who froze when she saw Dalinar, then melted into a relieved smile. He nodded to her, as one of the Veden highprinces explained why they shouldn't abandon the backwater strip of land running east of the Horneater Peaks. Aladar had been ready to cede it and use the Peaks as a barrier.

'It's not only about the opportunity to levy troops from His Majesty's Horneater subjects, Brightlord,' the highprince – Nan Urian – explained in Alethi. 'These lands are lush and well appointed, buffered from storms by the very Alethi highlands you've been speaking of. We've always fought desperately for them against invasions, because they will succor those who seize them – and provide staging areas for assaults on the rest of Jah Keved!'

Dalinar grunted. Navani stepped over to where most of them stood around the table map, so he reached out and put his arm around her waist. 'He's right, Aladar. I spent a long time skirmishing on that very border. That area is more important strategically than it first appears.'

'Holding it is going to be tough,' Aladar said. 'We'll get mired in an extended battle for that ground.'

'Which is what we want, isn't it?' the Veden highprince said. 'The longer we stall the invasion, the more time it will give my Veden brethren to recover.'

'Yes,' Dalinar said. 'Yes . . .' It *was* easy to get mired in battles along that vast Veden front. How many years had he spent fighting false bandits there? 'Let's take a break. I want to consider this.'

The others seemed to welcome the opportunity. Many stepped into the larger chamber outside, where attendants with spanreeds waited to relay information. Navani stayed beside Dalinar as he surveyed the map. 'It's good to see you up,' she whispered.

'You're more patient than I deserve. You should have dumped me out of bed and poured the wine on my head.'

'I had a feeling you'd push through.'

'I have for now,' he said. 'In the past, a few days – or even weeks – of sobriety didn't mean much.'

'You're not the man you were back then.'

Oh, Navani. I never grew beyond that man; I just hid him away. He couldn't explain that to her yet. Instead, he whispered thanks into her ear, and rested his hand on hers. How could he *ever* have been frustrated at her advances?

For now, he turned his attention to the maps, and lost himself in them: the fortresses, the storm bunkers, the cities, the drawn-in supply lines.

What's wrong? Dalinar thought. *What am I not seeing?*

Ten Silver Kingdoms. Ten Oathgates. The keys to this war. Even if the enemy can't use them, they can hinder us by seizing them.

One in Alethkar, which they already have. One in Natanatan – the Shattered Plains – which we have. One in Vedenar, one in Azimir, one in Thaylen City. All three ours. But one in Rall Elorim and one in Kurth, both the enemy's by now. One in Shinovar, belonging to neither side.

That left the one in Panatham in Babatharnam – which the combined Iriali and Riran armies might have captured already – and one in Akinah, which Jasnah was confident had been destroyed long ago.

Jah Keved made the most sense for the enemy to attack, didn't it? Only . . . once you engaged yourself in Jah Keved, you were stuck fighting a long war of attrition. You lost mobility, had to dedicate enormous resources to it.

He shook his head, feeling frustrated. He left the map, trailed by Navani, and stepped into the other room for refreshment. At the wine table, he forced himself to pour a warm, spiced orange. Something with no kick.

Jasnah joined the group, delivering a stack of papers to her mother.

'May I see?' Ialai asked.

'No,' Jasnah replied; Dalinar hid a smile in his drink.

'What secrets are you keeping?' Ialai asked. 'What happened to your uncle's grand talk of unification?'

'I suspect that each monarch in this room,' Jasnah said, 'would prefer to know that state secrets are allowed to remain their own. This is an alliance, not a wedding.'

Queen Fen nodded at that.

'As for these papers,' Jasnah continued, 'they happen to be a scholarly report which my mother has not yet reviewed. We will release what we discover, once we are certain that our translations are correct and that nothing in these notes might give our enemies an advantage against this city.' Jasnah cocked an eyebrow. 'Or would you prefer our scholarship be sloppy?'

The Azish seemed mollified by this.

'I just think,' Ialai said, 'you showing up here with them is a slap in the face for the rest of us.'

'Ialai,' Jasnah said, 'it is good you are here. Sometimes, an intelligent dissenting voice tests and proves a theory. I do wish you'd work harder on the *intelligent* part.'

Dalinar downed the rest of his drink and smiled as Ialai settled back in her chair, wisely not escalating a verbal battle against Jasnah. Unfortunately, Ruthar did not have similar sense.

'Don't mind her, Ialai,' he said, mustache wet with wine. 'The godless have no *concept* of proper decency. Everyone knows that the only reason to abandon belief in the Almighty is so that you can explore vice.'

Oh, Ruthar, Dalinar thought. *You can't win this fight. Jasnah has thought about the topic far more than you have. It's a familiar battleground to her—*

Storms, that was it.

'They aren't going to attack Jah Keved!' Dalinar shouted, interrupting Jasnah's rebuttal.

Those in the room turned to him, surprised, Jasnah's mouth half open.

'Dalinar?' Highprince Aladar asked. 'We decided that Jah Keved was the most likely—'

'No,' Dalinar said. 'No, we know the terrain too well! The Alethi and the Vedens have spent *generations* fighting over that land.'

'What, then?' Jasnah asked.

Dalinar ran back into the map room. The others flooded in around him. 'They went to Marat, right?' Dalinar asked. 'They cut through Emul and into Marat, silencing spanreeds nationwide. Why? Why go there?'

'Azir was too well fortified,' Aladar said. 'From Marat, the Voidbringers can strike at Jah Keved from both the west and the east.'

'Through the bottleneck in Triax?' Dalinar asked. 'We talk of Jah Keved's weakness, but that's *relative.* They still have a huge standing army, strong fortifications. If the enemy wades into Jah Keved now, while solidifying their own power, it will drain their resources and stall their conquest. That isn't what they want right now, when they still have the upper hand in momentum.'

'Where, then?' Nan Urian asked.

'A place that was hit hardest of all by the new storms,' Dalinar said, pointing at the map. 'A place whose military might was severely undermined by the Everstorm. A place with an Oathgate.'

Queen Fen gasped, safehand going to her lips.

'Thaylen City?' Navani asked. 'Are you sure?'

'If the enemy takes Thaylen City,' Dalinar said, 'they can blockade Jah Keved, Kharbranth, and what few lands in Alethkar we still own. They can seize command of the entire Southern Depths and launch naval assaults on Tashikk and Shinovar. They could swarm New Natanan and have a position from which to assault the Shattered Plains. Strategically, Thaylen City is *far* more important than Jah Keved – but at the same time, *far* worse defended.'

'But they'd need ships,' Aladar said.

'The parshmen took our fleet. . . .' Fen said.

'After that first terrible storm,' Dalinar said, 'how were there any ships *left* for them to take?'

Fen frowned. 'As I think about it, that's remarkable, isn't it? There were dozens remaining, as if the winds left them alone. Because the enemy needed them . . .'

Storms. 'I've been thinking too much like an Alethi,' Dalinar said. 'Boots on stone. But the enemy moved into Marat immediately, a *perfect* position from which to launch at Thaylen City.'

'We need to revise our plans!' Fen said.

'Peace, Your Majesty,' Aladar said. 'We have armies in Thaylen City already. Good Alethi troops. Nobody is better on the ground than Alethi infantry.'

'We have three divisions there right now,' Dalinar said. 'We'll want at least three more.'

'Sir,' Fen's son said. 'Brightlord. That's not enough.'

Dalinar glanced at Fen. Her wizened admiral nodded.

'Speak,' Dalinar said.

'Sir,' the youth said, 'we're glad to have your troops on the island. Kelek's breath! If you're going to get into a fight, you *definitely* want the Alethi on your side. But an enemy fleet is a *much* larger problem than you're assuming – one you can't easily fix by moving troops around. If the enemy ships find Thaylen City well defended, they'll just sail on and attack Kharbranth, or Dumadari, or any *number* of defenseless cities along the coast.'

Dalinar grunted. He *did* think too much like an Alethi. 'What, then?'

'We need our own fleet, obviously,' Fen's admiral said. He had a thick accent of mushed syllables, like a mouth full of moss. 'But most of our ships were lost to the blustering Everstorm. Half were abroad, caught unaware. My colleagues now dance upon the bottom of the depths.'

'And the rest of your fleet was stolen,' Dalinar said with a grunt. 'What else do we have?'

'His Majesty Taravangian has ships at our port,' the Veden highprince said.

All eyes turned toward Taravangian. 'Merchant ships only,' the old man said. 'Vessels that carried my healers. We haven't a true navy, but I did bring twenty ships. I could perhaps provide ten more from Kharbranth.'

'The storm took a number of our ships,' the Veden highprince said, 'but the civil war was more devastating. We lost hundreds of sailors. We have more ships than we have crew for right now.'

Fen joined Dalinar beside the map. 'We might be able to scrape together a semblance of a navy to intercept the enemy, but the fighting will be on the decks of ships. We'll need troops.'

'You'll have them,' Dalinar said.

'Alethi who've never seen a rough sea in their lives?' Fen asked, skeptical. She looked to the Azish generals. 'Tashikk has a navy, doesn't it? Staffed and supplemented by Azish troops.'

The generals conferred in their own language. Finally, one spoke through an interpreter. 'The Thirteenth Battalion, Red and Gold, has men who do a rotation on ships and patrol the grand waterway. Getting others here would take much time, but the thirteenth is already stationed in Jah Keved.'

'We'll supplement them with some of my best men,' Dalinar said. *Storms, we need those Windrunners active.* 'Fen, would your admirals present a suggested course for the gathering and deployment of a unified fleet?'

'Sure,' the short woman said. She leaned in, speaking under her breath. 'I warn you. Many of my sailors follow the Passions. You're going to have to do something about these claims of heresy, Blackthorn. Already there's talk among my people that this is – at long last – the right time for the Thaylens to break free from the Vorin church.'

'I won't recant,' Dalinar said.

'Even if it causes a wholesale religious collapse in the middle of a war?'

He didn't reply, and she let him withdraw from the table, thinking about other plans. He spoke with the others about various items, thanked Navani – again – for holding everything together. Then eventually, he decided to go back down below and take a few reports from his stewards.

On his way out, he passed Taravangian, who had taken a seat by the wall. The old man looked distracted by something.

'Taravangian?' Dalinar said. 'We'll leave troops in Jah Keved too, in case I'm wrong. Don't worry.'

The old man looked to Dalinar, then strangely wiped tears from his eyes.

'Are . . . are you in pain?' Dalinar asked.

'Yes. But it is nothing you can fix.' He hesitated. 'You are a good man, Dalinar Kholin. I did not expect that.'

Ashamed by that, Dalinar hurried from the room, followed by his guards. He felt tired, which seemed unfair, considering he'd just spent a week basically sleeping.

Before seeking his stewards, Dalinar stopped on the fourth floor from the bottom. An extended walk from the lifts took him to the outer wall of the tower, where a small series of rooms smelled of incense. People lined the hallways, waiting for glyphwards or to speak with an ardent. More than he'd expected – but then, they didn't have much else to do, did they?

Is that how you think of them already? a part of him asked. *Only here to seek spiritual welfare because they don't have anything better to do?*

Dalinar kept his chin high, resisting the urge to shrink before their stares. He passed several ardents and stepped into a room lit and warmed by braziers, where he asked after Kadash.

He was directed onto a garden balcony, where a small group of ardents was trying to farm. Some placed seed paste while others were trying to get some shalebark starters to take along the wall. An impressive project, and one he didn't remember ordering them to begin.

Kadash was quietly chipping crem off a planter box. Dalinar settled down beside him. The scarred ardent glanced at him and kept working.

'It's very late coming,' Dalinar said, 'but I wanted to apologize to you for Rathalas.'

'I don't think I'm the one you need to apologize to,' Kadash said. 'Those who *could* bear an apology are now in the Tranquiline Halls.'

'Still, I made you part of something terrible.'

'I chose to be in your army,' Kadash said. 'I've found peace with what we did – found it among the ardents, where I no longer shed the blood of men. I suppose it would be foolish of me to suggest the same to you.'

Dalinar took a deep breath. 'I'm releasing you, and the other ardents, from my control. I won't put you in a position where you have to serve a heretic. I'll give you to Taravangian, who remains orthodox.'

'No.'

'I don't believe you have the option to—'

'Just listen for one *storming* moment, Dalinar,' Kadash snapped, then he sighed, forcibly calming himself. 'You assume that because you're a heretic, we don't want anything to do with you.'

'You proved that a few weeks ago, when we dueled.'

'We don't want to normalize what you've done or what you're saying.

That doesn't mean we will abandon our posts. Your people need us, Dalinar, even if *you* believe you don't.'

Dalinar walked to the edge of the garden, where he rested his hands on the stone railing. Beyond him, clouds mustered at the base of the peaks, like a phalanx protecting its commander. From up here, it looked like the entire world was nothing more than an ocean of white broken by sharp peaks. His breath puffed in front of him. Cold as the Frostlands, though it didn't seem as bad inside the tower.

'Are any of those plants growing?' he asked softly.

'No,' Kadash said from behind. 'We aren't sure if it's the cold, or the fact that few storms reach this high.' He kept scraping. 'What will it feel like when a storm goes high enough to engulf this entire tower?'

'Like we're surrounded by dark confusion,' Dalinar said. 'The only light coming in flashes we can't pinpoint or comprehend. Angry winds trying to tow us in a dozen different directions, or barring that, rip our limbs from our bodies.' He looked toward Kadash. 'Like always.'

'The Almighty was a constant light.'

'And?'

'And now you make us question. You make *me* question. Being an ardent is the only thing that lets me sleep at night, Dalinar. You want to take that from me too? If He's gone, there's only the storm.'

'I think there must be something beyond. I asked you before, what did worship look like before Vorinism? What did—'

'Dalinar. Please. Just . . . stop.' Kadash drew in a deep breath. 'Release a statement. Don't let everyone keep whispering about how you went into hiding. Say something pedantic like, "I'm pleased with the work the Vorin church does, and support my ardents, even if I myself no longer have the faith I once did." Give us permission to move on. Storms, this isn't the time for confusion. We don't even know what we're fighting. . . .'

Kadash didn't want to know that Dalinar had *met* the thing they were fighting. Best not to speak of that.

But Kadash's question did leave him considering. Odium wouldn't be commanding the day-to-day operations of his army, would he? Who did that? The Fused? The Voidspren?

Dalinar strolled a short distance from Kadash, then looked toward the sky. 'Stormfather?' he asked. 'Do the enemy forces have a king or a highprince? Maybe a head ardent? Someone other than Odium?'

The Stormfather rumbled. *Again, I do not see as much as you think I do. I am the passing storm, the winds of the tempest. All of this is me. But I am not all of it, any more than you control each breath that leaves your mouth.*

Dalinar sighed. It had been worth the thought.

There is one I have been watching, the Stormfather added. *I can see her, when I don't see others.*

'A leader?' Dalinar asked.

Maybe. Men, both human and singer, are strange in what or whom they revere. Why do you ask?

Dalinar had decided not to bring anyone else into one of the visions because he worried about what Odium would do to them. But that wouldn't count for people already serving Odium, would it?

'When is the next highstorm?'

⋯

Taravangian felt old.

His age was more than the aches that no longer faded as the day proceeded. It was more than the weak muscles, which still surprised him when he tried to lift an object that should have seemed light.

It was more than finding that he'd slept through yet another meeting, despite his best efforts to pay attention. It was even more than slowly seeing almost everyone he'd grown up with fade away and die.

It was the urgency of knowing that tasks he started today, he wouldn't finish.

He stopped in the hallway back to his rooms, hand resting on the strata-lined wall. It was beautiful, mesmerizing, but he only found himself wishing for his gardens in Kharbranth. Other men and women got to live out their waning hours in comfort, or at least familiarity.

He let Mrall take him by the arm and guide him to his rooms. Normally, Taravangian would have been bothered by the help; he did *not* like being treated like an invalid. Today though . . . well, today he would suffer the indignity. It was a lesser one than collapsing in the hallway.

Inside the room, Adrotagia sat amid six different scribbling spanreeds, buying and trading information like a merchant at market. She looked at him, but knew him well enough not to comment on his exhausted face or slow steps. Today was a good day, of average intelligence. Perhaps a little on the stupid side, but he'd take that.

He seemed to be having fewer and fewer intelligent days. And the ones he did have frightened him.

Taravangian settled down in a plush, comfortable seat, and Maben went to get him some tea.

'Well?' Adrotagia asked. She'd grown old too, with enormous bags around her green eyes, the persistent kind formed by drooping skin. She had liver spots and wispy hair. No man would look at her and see the mischievous child she'd once been. The trouble the two of them had gotten into . . .

'Vargo?' Adrotagia asked.

'My apologies,' he said. 'Dalinar Kholin has recovered.'

'A problem.'

'An enormous one.' Taravangian took the tea from Maben. 'More than you can guess, I should say, even with the Diagram before you. But please, give me time to consider. My mind is slow today. Have you reports?'

Adrotagia flipped over a paper from one of her stacks. 'Moelach seems to have settled in the Horneater Peaks. Joshor is on his way there now. We might again soon have access to the Death Rattles.'

'Very well.'

'We've found what happened to Graves,' Adrotagia continued. 'Scavengers found the storm-blown wreckage of his wagon, and there was an intact spanreed inside.'

'Graves is replaceable.'

'And the Shards?'

'Irrelevant,' Taravangian said. 'We won't win the prize through force of arms. I was reluctant to let him try his little coup in the first place.'

He and Graves had disagreed about the Diagram's instructions: to kill Dalinar or recruit him? And who was to be king of Alethkar?

Well, Taravangian had been wrong about the Diagram himself many times. So he'd allowed Graves to move forward with his own plots, according to his own readings of the Diagram. While the man's schemes had failed, so had Taravangian's attempt to have Dalinar executed. So perhaps neither of them had read the Diagram correctly.

He took some time to recover, frustrated that he should need to *recover* from a simple walk. A few minutes later, the guard admitted Malata. The Radiant wore her usual skirt and leggings, Thaylen style, with thick boots.

She took a seat across from Taravangian at the low table, then sighed in a melodramatic way. 'This place is awful. Every last idiot here is frozen, ears to toes.'

Had she been this confident before bonding a spren? Taravangian hadn't known her well then. Oh, he'd managed the project, full of eager recruits from the Diagram, but the individuals hadn't mattered to him. Until now.

'Your spren,' Adrotagia asked, getting out a sheet of paper. 'Has she anything to report?'

'No,' Malata said. 'Only the tidbit from earlier, about other visions Dalinar hasn't shared with everyone.'

'And,' Taravangian asked, 'has the spren expressed any . . . reservations? About the work you've given her?'

'Damnation,' Malata said, rolling her eyes. 'You're as bad as Kholin's scribes. Always poking.'

'We need to be cautious, Malata,' Taravangian said. 'We can't be certain what your spren will do as her self-awareness grows. She will surely dislike working against the other orders.'

'You're as frozen as the lot of them,' Malata said. She started glowing, Stormlight rising from her skin. She reached forward, whipping off her glove – safehand no less – and pressing it against the table.

Marks spread out from the point of contact, little swirls of blackness etching themselves into the wood. The scent of burning filled the air, but the flames didn't persist if she didn't will them to.

The swirls and lines extended across the tabletop, a masterwork of engraving accomplished in moments. Malata blew off the ash. The Surge she used, Division, caused objects to degrade, burn, or turn to dust.

It also worked on people.

'Spark is *fine* with what we're doing,' Malata said, pressing her finger down and adding another swirl to the table. 'I told you, the rest of them are *idiots*. They assume all the spren are going to be on their side. Never mind what the Radiants did to Spark's friends, never mind that *organized* devotion to *Honor* is what killed hundreds of ashspren in the first place.'

'And Odium?' Taravangian asked, curious. The Diagram warned that the personalities of the Radiants would introduce great uncertainty to their plans.

'Spark is game for whatever it takes to get vengeance. And what lets her break stuff.' Malata grinned. 'Someone should have warned me how fun this would be. I'd have tried *way* harder to land the job.'

'What we do is not *fun*,' Taravangian said. 'It is necessary, but it is *horrible*. In a better world, Graves would have been right. We would be allies to Dalinar Kholin.'

'You're too fond of the Blackthorn, Vargo,' Adrotagia warned. 'It will cloud your mind.'

'No. But I do wish I hadn't gotten to know him. That *will* make this difficult.' Taravangian leaned forward, holding his warm drink. Boiled ingo tea, with mint. Smells of home. With a start, he realized ... he'd probably never live in that home again, would he? He'd thought perhaps he would return in a few years.

He wouldn't be alive in a few years.

'Adro,' he continued, 'Dalinar's recovery convinces me we must take more drastic action. Are the secrets ready?'

'Almost,' she said, moving some other papers. 'My scholars in Jah Keved have translated the passages we need, and we have the information from Malata's spying. But we need some way to disseminate the information without compromising ourselves.'

'Assign it to Dova,' Taravangian said. 'Have her write a scathing, anonymous essay, then leak it to Tashikk. Leak the translations from the Dawnchant the same day. I want it all to strike at once.' He set aside the tea. Suddenly, scents of Kharbranth made him hurt. 'It would have been so, *so* much better for Dalinar to have died by the assassin's blade. For now we must leave him to the enemy's desires, and that will not be as kind as a quick death.'

'Will it be enough?' Malata asked. 'That old axehound is tough.'

'It will be enough. Dalinar would be the first to tell you that when your opponent is getting back up, you must act quickly to crush his knees. Then he will bow, and present to you his skull.'

Oh, Dalinar. You poor, poor man.

drawing is easy!

clearly it isn't.

seems that the spren we see ur physical world are only partial festations of more complex beings are part of an entire ecosystem their own.

uld spend er lifetime ying these n alone.

These are surprisingly stealthy, and can sense your anticipation from a great distance.

We saw many of these. They are tenacious.

Chemoarish, the Dustmother, has some of the most varied lore surrounding her. The wealth of it makes sorting lies from truths extremely difficult. I do believe she is not the Nightwatcher, contrary to what some stories claim.

—From Hessi's *Mythica,* page 231

S hallan sketched in her notepad as she stood on the deck of the honorspren ship, the wind of its passing ruffling her hair. Next to her, Kaladin rested his arms on the ship's railing, overlooking the ocean of beads.

Their current vessel, *Honor's Path,* was faster than Ico's merchant ship. It had mandras rigged not only at the front, but also to winglike rails jutting from the sides. It had five decks — including three below for crew and storage — but those were mostly empty. It felt like a war vessel intended to carry troops, but which didn't currently have a full complement.

The main deck was similar to the top deck of human ships, but this craft also had a high deck running down its center from prow to stern. Narrower than the main deck, it was supported by broad white pillars, and probably offered an excellent view. Shallan could no more than guess, as only the crew was allowed up there.

At least they'd been let out – Shallan and the others had spent their first week on board locked in the hold. The honorspren had given no explanation when, finally, the humans and Pattern had been released and allowed to move on deck, so long as they stayed off the high deck and did not make nuisances of themselves.

Syl remained imprisoned.

'Look here.' Shallan tipped her sketched map toward Kaladin. 'Pattern says there's an honorspren stronghold near Kharbranth in our world. They call it Unyielding Fidelity. We've *got* to be heading there. We went southwest after leaving Celebrant.'

'While we were in the hold,' Kaladin said softly, 'I saw a sea of tiny flames through the porthole. A town on our side?'

'That was here,' Shallan said, pointing at her map. 'See where the rivers meet, just southwest of the lake? There are towns there, on our side. The river peninsulas should have blocked our way, but the spren seem to have cut a canal through the stone. We wove east around the Icingway River, then swung west again.'

'So you're saying . . .'

She pointed at a spot with her charcoal pencil. 'We're right about here, heading toward Kharbranth across the Frostlands.'

Kaladin rubbed his chin. He glanced toward an honorspren passing above, and narrowed his eyes. He'd spent their first day of freedom arguing with the honorspren – which had ended with him locked up for *another* two days.

'Kaladin . . .' Shallan said.

'They need to let her out,' he said. 'Prisons are terrible for me – they'll be worse for her.'

'Then help me figure out a way off this ship.'

He looked back at her map and pointed. 'Thaylen City,' he said. 'If we continue this direction, we'll eventually pass just north of it.'

'"Just north" in this case meaning more than three hundred miles away from it, in the middle of a bead ocean.'

'Far closer than we've been to any other Oathgate,' he said. 'And if we can get the ship to swing south a little, we could maybe get to the coast of Longbrow's Straits, which will be stone on this side. Or do you think we should still be trying for Azure's phantom "perpendicularity" in the Horneater Peaks?'

'I . . .' He spoke with such authority, such a compelling sense of *motion*. 'I don't know, Kaladin.'

'We're heading in the right direction,' he said, firm. 'I *saw* it, Shallan. We just need to continue with the ship a few more days, then find a way to escape. We can hike to the Oathgate on this side, and you can transfer us to Thaylen City.'

It sounded reasonable. Well, except for the fact that the honorspren were watching them. And the fact that the Fused knew where they were now, and were probably gathering forces to give chase. And the fact that they had to somehow escape from a ship in the middle of a sea of beads, reach the shore, then hike two hundred miles to reach Thaylen City.

All of that could fade before Kaladin's passion. All but the worry that topped them all – could she even make the Oathgate work? She couldn't help feeling that too much of this plan depended on her.

Yet those eyes . . .

'We could try a mutiny,' Veil said. 'Maybe those mistspren who do all the work will listen. They can't be happy, always hopping about, following honorspren orders.'

'I don't know,' Kaladin said, voice hushing as one of these spren – made entirely of mist, save for the hands and face – walked past. 'Could be reckless. I can't fight them all.'

'What if you had Stormlight?' Veil asked. 'If I could pinch it back for you? What then?'

He rubbed at his chin again. Storms, he looked good with a beard. All ragged and untamed through the face, contrasted by his sharp blue uniform. Like a wild spren of passion, trapped by the oaths and codes . . .

Wait.

Wait, had that been *Veil*?

Shallan shook free of the momentary drifting of personality. Kaladin didn't seem to notice.

'Maybe,' he said. 'You really think you can steal the gemstones back for us? I'd feel a lot more comfortable with some Stormlight in my pocket.'

'I . . .' Shallan swallowed. 'Kaladin, I don't know if . . . Maybe it would be best not to fight them. They're honorspren.'

'They're *jailers*,' he said, but then calmed. 'But they are taking us the right direction, if only inadvertently. What if we stole back our Stormlight, then simply jumped off the ship? Can you find a bead to make us a passage toward land, like you did at Kholinar?'

'I ... guess I could try. But wouldn't the honorspren simply swing around and pick us up again?'

'I'll think about that,' Kaladin said. 'Try and find some beads that we can use.' He walked across the deck, passing by Pattern – who stood with hands clasped behind his back, thinking number-filled thoughts. Kaladin eventually settled beside Azure, speaking softly with her, probably outlining their plan.

Such that it was.

Shallan tucked her sketchpad under her arm and looked over the side of the ship. So many beads, so many souls, piled on top of each other. Kaladin wanted her to search through all of *that* for something helpful?

She glanced toward a passing sailor, a mistspren who had gaseous limbs that ended in gloved hands. Her feminine face was the shape of a porcelain mask, and she – like the others of her kind – wore a vest and trousers that seemed to float on a body made of swirling, indistinct fog.

'Is there a way for me to get some of those beads?' Shallan asked.

The mistspren stopped in place.

'Please?' Shallan asked. 'I—'

The sailor jogged off, and then returned a short time later with the captain: a tall, imperious-looking honorspren named Notum. He glowed a soft blue-white, and wore an outdated – but sharp – naval uniform, which was part of his substance. His beard was of a cut she hadn't seen before, with the chin shaved, almost like a Horneater, but with a thin mustache and a sculpted line of hair that ran from it up his cheeks and blended into his sideburns.

'You have a request?' he asked her.

'I would like some beads, Captain,' Shallan said. 'To practice my art, if you please. I need to do *something* to pass the time on this trip.'

'Manifesting random souls is dangerous, Lightweaver. I would not have you doing it wantonly upon my decks.'

Keeping the true nature of her order from him had proven impossible, considering how Pattern followed her around.

'I promise not to manifest anything,' she said. 'I merely want to practice visualizing the souls inside the beads. It's part of my training.'

He studied her, clasping his hands behind his back. 'Very well,' he said – which surprised her. She hadn't expected that to work. He gave an order, however, and a mistspren lowered a bucket on a rope to get her some beads.

'Thank you,' Shallan said.

'It was a simple request,' the captain said. 'Just be careful. I suppose you'd need Stormlight to manifest anyway, but still . . . be careful.'

'What happens if we carry the beads away too far?' Shallan asked, curious as the mistspren handed her the bucket. 'They are tied to objects in the Physical Realm, right?'

'You can carry them anywhere in Shadesmar you wish,' the captain said. 'Their tie is through the Spiritual Realm, and distance doesn't matter. However, drop them – let them free – and they'll work their way back to the general location of their physical counterpart.' He eyed her. 'You are very new to all of this. When did it begin again? Radiants, swearing Ideals?'

'Well . . .'

Her mother's dead face, eyes burned.

'It hasn't been going on for long,' Shallan said. 'A few months for most of us. A few years for some . . .'

'We had hoped this day would never come.' He turned to march toward the high deck.

'Captain?' Shallan asked. 'Why did you let us out? If you're so worried about Radiants, why not just keep us locked away?'

'It wasn't honorable,' the captain said. 'You are not prisoners.'

'What are we, then?'

'Stormfather only knows. Fortunately, I don't have to sort it out. We'll deliver you and the Ancient Daughter to someone with more authority. Until then, please try not to break my ship.'

⁑

As days passed, Shallan fell into a routine on the honorspren ship. She spent most days sitting on the main deck, near the wale. They let her have beads in plenitude to play with, but most of them were useless things. Rocks, sticks, bits of clothing. Still, it was useful to visualize them. Hold them, meditate on them. Understand them?

Objects had desires. Simple desires, true, but they could adhere to those desires with passion – as she'd learned during her few attempts at Soulcasting. Now, she didn't try to change those desires. She just learned to touch them, and to listen.

She felt a familiarity to some of the beads. A growing understanding that, perhaps, she could make their souls blossom from beads into full-fledged objects on this side. Manifestations, they were called.

Between practices with the beads, she did sketches. Some worked, some didn't. She wore the skirt that Adolin had purchased for her, hoping it would make her feel more like Shallan. Veil kept poking through, which could be useful – but the way it just kind of *happened* was frightening to her. This was the opposite of what Wit had told her to do, wasn't it?

Kaladin spent the days pacing the main deck, glaring at honorspren he passed. He looked like a caged beast. Shallan felt some of his same urgency. They hadn't seen any sign of the enemy, not since that day in Celebrant. But she slept uneasily each night, worried that she'd wake to calls of an enemy ship approaching them. Notum had confirmed that the Voidspren were creating their own empire in Shadesmar. And they controlled Cultivation's Perpendicularity, the easiest way to get between realms.

Shallan sorted through another handful of beads, feeling the impression of a small dagger, a rock, a piece of fruit that had started to see itself as something new – something that could grow into its own identity, rather than merely a part of the whole.

What would someone see when looking at her soul? Would it give a single, unified impression? Many different ideas of what it was to be her?

Nearby, the ship's first mate – an honorspren woman with short hair and an angular face – left the hold. Curiously, she was carrying Azure's Shardblade. She stepped onto the main deck, beneath the shadow of the high deck, and went hiking toward Azure, who stood watching the ocean pass nearby.

Curious, Shallan pocketed the bead representing a knife – just in case – then left the bucket on top of her sketchbook and walked over. Nearby, Kaladin was pacing again, and he also noticed the sword.

'Draw her carefully,' Azure said to Borea, the first mate, as Shallan approached. 'Don't pull her out all the way – she doesn't know you.'

Borea wore a uniform like the captain's, all stiff and no-nonsense. She undid a small latch on the Shardblade, eased it from its sheath a half inch, then drew in a sharp breath. 'It . . . tingles.'

'She's investigating you,' Azure said.

'It really is as you say,' Borea said. 'A Shardblade that requires no spren – no enslavement. This is something else. How did you do it?'

'I will trade knowledge, per our deal, once we arrive.'

Borea snapped the Blade closed. 'A good bond, human. We accept your offer.' Surprisingly, the woman held the weapon toward Azure, who took it.

Shallan stepped closer, watching as Borea walked off toward the steps up to the high deck.

'How?' Shallan asked as Azure belted on the sword. 'You got them to give your weapon back?'

'They're quite reasonable,' Azure said, 'so long as you make the right promises. I've negotiated for passage and an exchange of information, once we reach Lasting Integrity.'

'You've done *what*?' Kaladin said. He stalked over. 'What did I just hear?'

'I've made a deal, Stormblessed,' Azure said, meeting his gaze. 'I'll be free, once we reach their stronghold.'

'We're not *going* to reach their stronghold,' Kaladin said softly. 'We're going to escape.'

'I'm not your soldier, or even Adolin's subject. I'm going to do what gets me to the perpendicularity – and, barring that, I'm going to find out what these people know about the criminal I'm hunting.'

'You'd throw away honor for a *bounty*?'

'I'm only here because you two – through no fault of your own, I admit – trapped me. I don't blame you, but I'm *also* not indebted to your mission.'

'Traitor,' he said softly.

Azure gave him a flat look. 'At some point, Kal, you need to admit that the *best* thing you can do right now is go with these spren. At their stronghold, you could clear up this misunderstanding, then move on.'

'That could take weeks.'

'I wasn't aware we were on a schedule.'

'Dalinar is in danger. Don't you care?'

'About a man I don't know?' Azure said. 'In danger from a threat you can't define, happening at a time you can't pinpoint?' She folded her arms. 'Forgive me for not sharing in your anxiety.'

Kaladin set his jaw, then turned and stalked away – right *up* the steps toward the high deck. They weren't supposed to go up there, but sometimes rules didn't seem to apply to Kaladin Stormblessed.

Azure shook her head, then turned and gripped the ship railing.

'He's just having a bad day, Azure,' Shallan said. 'I think he feels anxious because his spren is imprisoned.'

'Maybe. I've seen a lot of young hotheads in my time, and young Stormblessed feels like another color altogether. I wish I knew what it was he was so desperate to prove.'

Shallan nodded, then glanced again at Azure's sword. 'You said . . . the honorspren have information on your bounty?'

'Yeah. Borea thinks the weapon I'm chasing passed through their fortress a few years ago.'

'Your bounty is a . . . *weapon?*'

'And the one who brought it to your land. A Shardblade that bleeds black smoke.' Azure turned toward her. 'I don't mean to be callous, Shallan. I realize you're all eager to return to your lands. I can even believe that – through some tide of Fortune – Kaladin Stormblessed has foreseen some danger.'

Shallan shivered. *Be wary of anyone who claims to be able to see the future.*

'But,' Azure continued, 'even if his mission *is* critical, it doesn't mean mine isn't as well.'

Shallan glanced toward the high deck, where she could faintly hear Kaladin making a disturbance. Azure turned and clasped her hands, adopting a far-off look. She seemed to want to be alone, so Shallan trailed back toward where she'd left her things. She settled down and removed the bucket from her sketchpad. The pages fluttered, showing various versions of herself, each one wrong. She kept drawing Veil's face on Radiant's body, or vice versa.

She started back into her latest bucket of beads. She found a shirt and a bowl, but the next bead was a fallen tree branch. This brought up memories of the last time she'd dipped into Shadesmar – freezing, near death, on the banks of the ocean.

Why . . . why hadn't she tried to Soulcast since then? She'd made excuses, avoided thinking about it. Had focused all her attention on Lightweaving.

She'd ignored Soulcasting. Because she'd failed.

Because she was afraid. Could she invent someone who wasn't afraid? Someone new, since Veil was broken, and had been since that failure in the Kholinar market . . .

'Shallan?' Adolin asked, coming over to her. 'Are you all right?'

She shook herself. How long had she been sitting there? 'I'm fine,' she said. 'Just . . . remembering.'

'Good things or bad?'

'All memories are bad,' she said immediately, then looked away, blushing.

He settled down next to her. Storms, his overt concern was annoying. She didn't want him worrying about her.

'Shallan?' he asked.

'Shallan will be fine,' she said. 'I'll bring her back in a moment. I just have to recover . . . her . . .'

Adolin glanced at the fluttering pages with the different versions of her. He reached out and hugged her, saying nothing. Which turned out to be the right thing to say.

She closed her eyes and tried to pull herself together. 'Which one do you like the most?' she finally asked. 'Veil is the one who wears the white outfit, but I'm having trouble with her right now. She peeks out sometimes when I don't want, but then won't come when I need her. Radiant is the one who practices with the sword. I made her prettier than the others, and you can talk to her about dueling. But some of the time, I'll have to be someone who can Lightweave. I'm trying to think of who she should be. . . .'

'Ash's eyes, Shallan!'

'Shallan's broken, so I think I'm trying to hide her. Like a cracked vase, where you turn the nice side toward the room, hiding the flaw. I'm not doing it on purpose, but it's happening, and I don't know how to stop it.'

He held her.

'No advice?' she asked, numb. 'Everyone always seems to have loads.'

'You're the smart one. What can *I* say?'

'It's confusing, being all these people. I feel like I'm presenting different faces all the time. Lying to everyone, because I'm different inside. I . . . That doesn't make sense, does it?' She squeezed her eyes shut again. 'I'll pull it back together. I'll be . . . someone.'

'I . . .' He pulled her tight again as the ship rocked. 'Shallan, I killed Sadeas.'

She blinked, then pulled back and looked him in the eyes. '*What?*'

'I killed Sadeas,' Adolin whispered. 'We met in the corridors of the tower. He started insulting Father, talking about the terrible things he was going to do to us. And . . . and I couldn't listen anymore. Couldn't stand there and look at his smug red face. So . . . I attacked him.'

'So all that time we were hunting a killer . . .'

'It was me. I'm the one the spren copied the first time. I kept thinking about how I was lying to you, to Father, and to everyone. The honorable Adolin Kholin, the consummate duelist. A murderer. And Shallan, I . . . I don't think I'm *sorry*.

'Sadeas was a monster. He *repeatedly* tried to get us killed. His betrayal caused the deaths of many of my friends. When I formally challenged him to a duel, he wiggled out of it. He was smarter than me. Smarter than Father. He'd have won eventually. So I killed him.'

He pulled her to him and took a deep breath.

Shallan shivered, then whispered, 'Good for you.'

'Shallan! You're a Radiant. You're not supposed to condone something like this!'

'I don't know what I'm *supposed* to do. I only know that the world is a better place for the death of Torol Sadeas.'

'Father wouldn't like it, if he knew.'

'Your father is a great man,' Shallan said, 'who is, perhaps, better off not knowing everything. For his own good.'

Adolin breathed in again. With her head pressed to his chest, the air moving in and out of his lungs was audible, and his voice was different. More resonant. 'Yeah,' he said. 'Yeah, maybe. In any case, I think I know what it's like to feel like you're lying to the world. So maybe if you figure out what to do, you could tell me?'

She leaned into him, listening to his heartbeat, his breathing. She felt his warmth.

'You never did say,' she whispered, 'which one you prefer.'

'It's obvious. I prefer the real you.'

'Which one is that, though?'

'She's the one I'm talking to right now. You don't have to hide, Shallan. You don't have to push it down. Maybe the vase is cracked, but that only means it can show what's inside. And I *like* what's inside.'

So warm. Comfortable. And strikingly *unfamiliar*. What was this peace? This place without fear?

Noises from above spoiled it. Pulling back, she looked toward the upper deck. 'What *is* the bridgeboy doing up there?'

'Sir,' the misty sailor spren said in broken Alethi. 'Sir! Not. Please, not!'

Kaladin ignored her, looking through the spyglass he'd taken from the chain nearby. He stood on the rear section of the high deck, searching the sky. That Fused had watched them leave Celebrant. The enemy would find them eventually.

Dalinar alone. Surrounded by nine shadows . . .

Kaladin finally handed the spyglass to the anxious mistspren. The captain of the ship, in a tight uniform that probably would have been uncomfortable on a human, approached and dismissed the sailor, who scuttled away.

'I would prefer,' Captain Notum said, 'if you would refrain from upsetting my crew.'

'I would prefer that you let Syl go,' Kaladin snapped, feeling her anxiety through their bond. 'As I told you, the Stormfather has condoned what she did. There is no crime.'

The short spren clasped his hands behind his back. Of all the spren they'd interacted with on this side, the honorspren seemed to share the most human mannerisms.

'I could lock you away again,' the captain said. 'Or even have you tossed overboard.'

'Yeah? And what would *that* do to Syl? She told me that losing a bonded Radiant was hard on their spren.'

'True. But she would recover, and it might be for the best. Your relationship with the Ancient Daughter is . . . inappropriate.'

'It's not like we eloped.'

'It is worse, as the Nahel bond is far more intimate a relationship. The linking of spirits. This is not a thing that should be done lightly, unsupervised. Besides, the Ancient Daughter is too young.'

'Young?' Kaladin said. 'Didn't you just call her *ancient?*'

'It would be difficult to explain to a human.'

'Try anyway.'

The captain sighed. 'The honorspren were created by Honor himself, many thousands of years ago. You call him the Almighty, and . . . I'm afraid he's dead.'

'Which makes sense, as it's pretty much the only excuse I would have accepted.'

'That wasn't levity, human,' Notum said. 'Your god is *dead*.'

'Not my god. But please continue.'

'Well ...' Notum frowned; he'd obviously thought the concept of Honor's death would have been more difficult for Kaladin to accept. 'Well, sometime before his death, Honor stopped creating honorspren. We don't know why, but he asked the Stormfather to do it instead.'

'He was setting up an heir. I've heard that the Stormfather is a kind of image of the Almighty.'

'More like a weak shadow,' Notum said. 'You ... actually understand this?'

'Understand, no. Follow? Mostly.'

'The Stormfather created only a handful of children. All of these, save Sylphrena, were destroyed in the Recreance, becoming deadeyes. This loss stung the Stormfather, who didn't create again for centuries. When he was finally moved to remake the honorspren, he created only ten more. My great-grandmother was among them; she created my grandfather, who created my father, who eventually created me.

'It was only recently, even by your reckoning, that the Ancient Daughter was rediscovered. Asleep. So, in answer to your question, yes, Sylphrena is both old and young. Old of form, but young of mind. She is not ready to deal with humans, and certainly not ready for a bond. I wouldn't trust *myself* with one of those.'

'You think we're too changeable, don't you? That we can't keep our oaths.'

'I'm no highspren,' the captain spat. 'I can see that the variety of humankind is what gives you strength. Your ability to change your minds, to go *against* what you once thought, can be a great advantage. But your bond is dangerous, without Honor. There will not be enough checks upon your power – you risk disaster.'

'How?'

Notum shook his head, then looked away, off into the distance. 'I cannot answer. You should not have bonded Sylphrena, either way. She is too precious to the Stormfather.'

'Regardless,' Kaladin said, 'you're about half a year too late. So you might as well accept it.'

'Not too late. Killing you would free her – though it would be painful for her. There are other ways, at least until the Final Ideal is sworn.'

'I can't imagine you'd be willing to kill a man for this,' Kaladin said. 'Tell me truthfully. Is there *honor* in that, Notum?'

He looked away, as if ashamed.

'You know Syl shouldn't be locked away like this,' Kaladin said softly. 'You're an honorspren too, Notum. You must know how she feels.'

The captain didn't speak.

Finally, Kaladin gritted his teeth and strode off. The captain didn't demand that Kaladin go down below, so he took up a position at the very front of the high deck, hanging out over the bow.

With one hand on the flagpole, Kaladin rested a boot on the low railing, overlooking the sea of beads. He wore his uniform today, since he'd been able to wash it the previous night. *Honor's Path* had good accommodations for humans, including a device that made a great deal of water. The design – if not the vessel itself – probably stretched back centuries to when Radiants traveled Shadesmar with their spren.

Beneath him, the ship creaked as sailors shifted her heading. To the left, he could see land. Longbrow's Straits – on the other side of which they'd find Thaylen City. Tantalizingly close.

Technically, he was no longer Dalinar's bodyguard. But storms, during the Weeping, Kaladin had nearly abandoned his duty. The thought of Dalinar needing him now – while Kaladin was trapped and unable to help – brought a pain that was almost *physical*. He'd failed so many people in his life. . . .

Life before death. Strength before weakness. Journey before destination. Together, these Words formed the First Ideal of the Windrunners. He'd said them, but he wasn't certain he understood them.

The Second Ideal made more direct sense. *I will protect those who cannot protect themselves.* Straightforward, yes . . . but overwhelming. The world was a place of suffering. Was he really supposed to try to prevent it all?

I will protect even those I hate, so long as it is right. The Third Ideal meant standing up for anyone, if needed. But who decided what was 'right'? Which side was he supposed to protect?

The Fourth Ideal was unknown to him, but the closer he drew to it, the more frightened he became. What would *it* demand of him?

Something crystallized in the air beside him, a line of light like a pinprick in the air that trailed a long, soft luminescence. A mistspren sailor near him gasped, then nudged his companion. She whispered something in awe, then both scrambled away.

What have I done now?

A second pinprick of light appeared near him, spinning, coordinated with the other. They made spiral trails in the air. He'd have called them spren, but they weren't any he'd seen before. Besides, spren on this side didn't seem to vanish and appear – they were always here, weren't they?

K-Kaladin? a voice whispered in his head.

'Syl?' he whispered.

What are you doing? It was rare that he heard her directly in his mind.

'Standing on the deck. What's happened?'

Nothing. I can just . . . feel your mind right now. Stronger than usual. They let you out?

'Yes. I've tried to get them to set you free.'

They're stubborn. It's an honorspren trait which I, fortunately, escaped.

'Syl. What is the Fourth Ideal?'

You know you have to figure that out on your own, silly.

'It's going to be hard, isn't it?'

Yes. You're close.

He leaned forward, watching the mandras float beneath them. A small flock of gloryspren zipped past. They took a moment to fly up and spin about him before heading to the south, faster than the ship.

The strange pinpricks of light continued to whirl around him. Sailors gathered behind, making a ruckus until the captain pushed through and gaped.

'What are they?' Kaladin asked, nodding toward the pinpricks of light.

'Windspren.'

'Oh.' They did remind him a little of the way windspren would fly on gusts of wind. 'They're common. Why is everyone so upset?'

'They're not common on this side,' the captain said. 'They live on your side, almost completely. I . . . I've never seen them before. They're beautiful.'

Perhaps I haven't been giving Notum enough credit, Kaladin thought. Perhaps he would listen to a different kind of plea.

'Captain,' Kaladin said. 'I have taken an oath, as a Windrunner, to protect. And the Bondsmith who leads us is in danger.'

'*Bondsmith?*' the captain asked. 'Which one?'

'Dalinar Kholin.'

'No. Which Bondsmith, of the three?'

'I don't know what you mean,' Kaladin said. 'But his spren is the Stormfather. I told you I'd spoken to him.'

It seemed, from the captain's aghast expression, that perhaps Kaladin should have mentioned this fact earlier.

'I must keep my oath,' Kaladin said. 'I need you to let Syl go, then take us to a place where we can transfer between realms.'

'I've sworn an oath myself,' the captain said. 'To Honor, and to the truths we follow.'

'Honor is dead,' Kaladin said. 'But the Bondsmith is *not*. You say that you can see how human variety gives us strength – well, I challenge you to do the same. See beyond the letter of your rules. You must understand that my need to defend the Bondsmith is more important than your need to deliver Syl – especially considering that the Stormfather is well aware of her location.'

The captain glanced at the windspren, which were still spinning about Kaladin, leaving trails that drifted the entire length of the ship before fading.

'I will consider,' the captain said.

⁘

Adolin stopped at the top of the steps, just behind Shallan.

Kaladin, the storming bridgeman, stood at the bow of the ship, surrounded by glowing lines of light. They illuminated his heroic figure – determined, undaunted, one hand on the prow's flagpole, wearing his crisp Wall Guard uniform. The ship's spren gazed upon him as if he were a storming Herald come to announce the reclamation of the Tranquiline Halls.

Just ahead of him, Shallan seemed to change. It was in her bearing, the way she stopped resting lightly on one foot, and stood solidly on two feet instead. The way her posture shifted.

And the way that she seemed to melt upon seeing Kaladin, lips rising to a grin. Blushing, she adopted a fond – even eager – expression.

Adolin breathed out slowly. He'd caught those glimpses from her before – and seen the sketches of Kaladin in her book – but looking at her now, he couldn't deny what he was seeing. She was practically *leering*.

'I need to draw that,' she said. But she just stood there instead, staring at him.

Adolin sighed and made his way up onto the high deck. Seemed they weren't forbidden here any longer. He joined Pattern, who had come up another set of steps, and was humming happily to himself.

'Kind of hard to compete with *that*,' Adolin noted.

'Mmm,' Pattern said.

'You know, I've never really felt like this before? It's not just Kaladin, it's all of this. And what's happening to us.' He shook his head. 'We certainly are an odd bunch.'

'Yes. Seven people. Odd.'

'It's not like I can blame him. It's not as if he's *trying* to be like he is.'

Nearby, a sailor spren – one of the few who hadn't gathered around Stormblessed and his halo of glowing lights – lowered a spyglass. She frowned, then raised it again. Then she began to call out in the spren language.

People tore themselves away from Kaladin and crowded around. Adolin stepped back, watching until Kaladin and Shallan joined him. Azure crested the steps nearby, looking concerned.

'What is it?' Kaladin asked.

'No idea,' Adolin said.

The captain waved for the mistspren and honorspren to make space, then took the spyglass. He finally lowered it and looked back at Kaladin. 'You were right, human, when you said you might be followed.' He waved Kaladin and Adolin forward. 'Look low on the horizon, at two hundred ten degrees.'

Kaladin looked through the spyglass, then breathed out. He extended it toward Adolin, but Shallan snatched it first.

'Storms!' she said. 'There's at least six of them.'

'Eight, my scout says,' the captain replied.

Adolin finally got his turn. Because of the black sky, it took him forever to spot the distant specks flying toward the ship. The Fused.

Re-Shephir, the Midnight Mother, is another Unmade who appears to have been destroyed at Aharietiam.

—From Hessi's *Mythica,* page 250

Dalinar ran his fingers along a line of red crystal embedded in the stone wall. The little vein started at the ceiling and wound all the way down the wall – within the pattern of the light green and grey strata – to the floor. It was smooth to the touch, distinct in texture from the rock around it.

He rubbed his thumb across the crystal. *It's like the other strata lines ripple out from this one, getting wider as they move away from it.*

'What does it mean?' he asked Navani. The two of them stood in a storage room near the top of the tower.

'I don't know,' Navani said, 'but we're finding more and more of them. What do you know of Essential Theology?'

'A thing for ardents and scribes,' he said.

'And Soulcasters. That is a garnet.'

Garnet? Let's see . . . Emeralds for grain, that was the most important, and heliodors for flesh. They raised animals for their gemhearts to provide those two. He was pretty sure diamonds made quartz, and . . . storms, he didn't know much about the others. Topaz made stone.

They'd needed those for the bunkers on the Shattered Plains.

'Garnets make blood,' Navani said. 'We don't have any Soulcasters that use them.'

'Blood? That sounds useless.'

'Well, scientifically, we think Soulcasters were able to use garnets to make any liquid that was soluble in water, as opposed to oil-based ... Your eyes are crossing.'

'Sorry.' He felt at the crystals. 'Another mystery. When will we find answers?'

'The records below,' Navani said, 'speak of this tower like a living thing. With a heart of emerald and ruby, and now these veins of garnet.'

He stood up, looking around the darkened room, which held the monarchs' chairs between meetings. It was lit by a sphere he'd set on a stone ledge by the door.

'If this tower was alive,' Dalinar said, 'then it's dead now.'

'Or sleeping. But if that's the case, I have no idea how to wake it. We've tried infusing the heart like a fabrial, even had Renarin try to push Stormlight into it. Nothing's worked.'

Dalinar picked up a chair, then pushed the door open. He held the door with his foot – shooing away a guard who tried to do it for him – while Navani collected the sphere and joined him in the conference room, in front of the glass wall looking toward the Origin.

He set down the chair and checked his forearm clock. Stupid thing. He was growing *far* too dependent upon it. The arm device had a painrial in it too: a kind of fabrial with a spren that feasted upon pain. He'd never yet remembered to use the thing. *Twelve minutes left.* Assuming Elthebar's calculations were correct. With spanreeds confirming the storm's arrival hours before in the east, the calculations were down to judging the speed of the storm.

A runner arrived at the door. Creer – the duty sergeant for guards today – accepted it. He was a bridgeman from ... Bridge Twenty, was it? He and his brother were both guards, though Creer wore spectacles, unlike his twin.

'Message from Brightness Khal, sir,' Creer said, handing the note to Navani. It looked like it had come from a spanreed. It had marks on the sides from the clips that had held it to the board, and the tight letters covered only the center of the page.

'From Fen,' Navani said. 'A merchant ship vanished in the Southern Depths this morning, just off Marat. They went ashore at what they hoped was a safe distance – to use the spanreed – and reported a large number of ships at dock along the coast. Glowing figures rose from a nearby city and descended upon them, and the communication cut off.'

'Confirmation,' Dalinar said, 'that the enemy is building up a navy.' If that fleet launched from Marat before his own ships were ready, or if the winds were wrong when his armada *did* launch . . .

'Have Teshav write back to the Thaylens,' Dalinar said. 'Suggest to Queen Fen and our other allies that we hold the next meeting in Thaylen City. We'll want to inspect fortifications and shore up the ground defenses.'

He sent the guards to wait outside, then approached the window and checked his wrist clock. Just a few minutes left. He thought he could see the stormwall below, but it was difficult to be sure from this height. He wasn't accustomed to looking *down* on a highstorm.

'Are you sure you want to do this?' Navani asked.

'The Stormfather asked me something similar this morning. I asked him if he knew the first rule of warfare.'

'Is that the one about terrain, or the one about attacking where the enemy is weak?'

He could pick it out now, a dark ripple surging through the sky below.

'Neither,' Dalinar said.

'Ah, right,' Navani said. 'I should have guessed.' She was nervous, with good cause. It was the first time he'd stepped back into the visions since meeting Odium.

But Dalinar felt blind in this war. He didn't know what the enemy wanted, or how they intended to exploit their conquests.

The first rule of war. Know your enemy.

He raised his chin as the storm slammed into Urithiru, roughly at the height of its third tier.

All went white. Then Dalinar appeared in the ancient palace – the large open room with sandstone pillars and a balcony that looked out on an antiquated version of Kholinar. Nohadon strode through the center of the pillared chamber. This was the youthful Nohadon, not the elderly version from his recent dream.

Dalinar had taken the place of a guardsman, near the doors. A slender Parshendi woman appeared beside the king, in the spot Dalinar had occupied so long ago. Her skin was marbled red and white in a complex pattern, and she had long orange-red hair. She looked down with red eyes, surprised by her sudden appearance and the robes she wore, those of an advisor to the king.

Nohadon began speaking to her as if she were his friend Karm. 'I don't know what to do, old friend.'

Odium sees that a vision has begun, the Stormfather warned Dalinar. *The enemy is focusing on us. He comes.*

'Can you hold him back?'

I am but a shadow of a god. His power vastly outstrips my own. He sounded smaller than Dalinar was accustomed to. Like the quintessential bully, the Stormfather didn't know how to face someone stronger than himself.

'Can you *hold him back*? I need time to talk to her.'

I will . . . try.

Good enough. Unfortunately, it meant that Dalinar didn't have time to let this Parshendi woman experience the vision in full. He strode toward her and Nohadon.

．∴．

Venli turned around. Where was she? This wasn't Marat. Had Odium summoned her again?

No. It's the wrong storm. He doesn't come during highstorms.

A young Alethi male in robes was blathering at her. She ignored him, biting her hand to see if she could feel the pain.

She could. She shook her hand and looked down at the robes she wore. This couldn't be a dream. It was too real.

'My friend?' the Alethi man asked. 'Are you well? I realize that events have taken their toll on us all, but—'

Footsteps rang loudly on the stone as another Alethi man approached, wearing a crisp blue uniform. White dusted the hair at his temples, and his face wasn't as . . . round as other human faces. His features could almost have been those of a listener, even if that nose was wrong and the face bore far more creases than a listener's ever would.

Wait . . . she thought, attuning Curiosity. *Is that . . .*

'Disturbance on the battlefield, sir,' the older man said to her companion. 'You are needed immediately.'

'What is this? I didn't hear—'

'They didn't say what it was, Your Majesty, only that you are urgently requested.'

The human king drew his lips to a tight line, and then – obviously frustrated – stalked toward the doorway. 'Come,' he said to Venli.

The older man grabbed her arm above the elbow. 'Don't,' he said softly. 'We need to talk.'

This is the Alethi warlord.

'My name is Dalinar Kholin,' the man said. 'I lead the Alethi, and you're seeing a vision of past events. Only your mind has been transported, not your body. We two are the only real people here.'

She yanked her arm out of his hand and attuned Irritation. 'How ... why have you brought me here?'

'I want to talk.'

'Of course you do. Now that you're losing, now that we've seized your capital, *now* you want to talk. What of the years spent slaughtering my people on the Shattered Plains?' It had been a *game* to them. Listener spy reports had shown the humans had *enjoyed* the sport on the Shattered Plains. Claiming wealth, and listener lives, as part of a grand contest.

'We were willing to talk, when you sent your emissary,' Dalinar said. 'The Shardbearer. I'm willing to talk again now. I want to forget old grievances, even those personal to me.'

Venli walked away, still attuned to Irritation. 'How have you brought me to this place? Is this a prison?' *Is this your work, Odium? Testing my loyalty with a false vision of the enemy?*

She was using the old rhythms. She'd never been able to do that when Odium's attention had been on her.

'I'll send you back soon,' Kholin said, catching up to her. Though he was not short for a human, her current form was a good six inches taller than he was. 'Please, just hear me out. I need to know. What would a truce between our people cost?'

'A truce?' she asked to Amusement, stopping near the balcony. 'A *truce*?'

'Peace. No Desolation. No war. What would it cost?'

'Well, for a start, it would cost your kingdom.'

He grimaced. His words were dead, like those of all humans, but he wore his feelings on his face. So much passion and emotion.

Is that why the spren betrayed us for them?

'What is Alethkar to you?' he said. 'I can help you build a new nation on the Shattered Plains. I will give you laborers to raise cities, ardents to teach any skill you want. Wealth, as payment in ransom for Kholinar and its people. A formal apology. Whatever you demand.'

'I demand that we keep Alethkar.'

His face became a mask of pain, his brow furrowed. 'Why must you live there? To you, Alethkar is a place to conquer. But it's *my* homeland.'

She attuned Reprimand. 'Don't you understand? The people who live there – the singers, my cousins – are *from* Alethkar. That is their homeland too. The only difference between them and you is that they were born as slaves, and you as their master!'

He winced. 'Perhaps some other accommodation, then. A . . . dividing of the kingdom? A parshman highprince?' He seemed shocked to be considering it.

She attuned Resolve. 'Your tone implies you know that would be impossible. There can be no accommodation, human. Send me from this place. We can meet on the battlefield.'

'No.' He seized her arm again. 'I don't know what the accommodation will be, but we *can* find one. Let me prove to you that I want to negotiate, instead of fight.'

'You can start,' she said to Irritation, pulling away from him, 'by not assaulting me.'

She wasn't certain she could fight him, honestly. Her current body was tall, but fragile. And in truth, she'd never been proficient at battle, even during the days when she'd taken an appropriate form.

'At least let us try a negotiation,' he said. 'Please.'

He didn't sound very pleading. He'd grown stern, face like a stone, *glaring*. With the rhythms, you could infuse your tone with the mood you wished to convey, even if your emotions weren't cooperating. Humans didn't have that tool. They were as dull as the dullest slave.

A sudden *thump* resounded in the vision. Venli attuned Anxiety and rushed out onto the balcony. A half-destroyed city stretched below, where a battle had happened, dead heaped in piles.

That pounding sounded again. The . . . the *air* was breaking. The clouds and sky seemed to be a mural painted on an enormous dome ceiling, and as the pounds continued, a web of cracks appeared overhead.

Beyond them shone a vivid yellow light.

'He's here,' she whispered, then waved toward it. 'That's why there can't be a negotiation, human. He knows we don't need one. You want peace? Surrender. Give yourselves up and *hope* that he doesn't care to destroy you.'

A faint hope, considering what Rine had said to her about exterminating the humans.

With the next pound, the sky fractured and a hole appeared overhead, a powerful light shining beyond. The very shards of the air – broken like a mirror – were sucked into that light.

A *pulse* of power blasted from the hole, shaking the city with a terrible vibration. It tossed Venli to the balcony's floor. Kholin reached to help her, but a second pulse caused him to fall as well.

The bricks in the room's wall *separated* from one another and began to float apart. The boards that made up the balcony began to lift, nails floating into the sky. A guard ran to the balcony, but stumbled, and his very skin started to separate into water and a dried husk.

Everything just . . . came apart.

A wind rose around Venli, pulling debris toward that hole in the sky, and the brilliant, terrible light beyond. Boards shredded to splinters; bricks floated past her head. She growled, the Rhythm of Resolve thumping inside her as she grabbed and clung to parts of the floor that hadn't yet separated.

That *burning*. She knew it well, the terrible pain of Odium's heat scalding her skin, scorching her until her very bones – somehow still able to feel – became ash. It happened every time he gave her orders. What worse thing would he do if he found her fraternizing with the enemy?

She attuned Determination and crawled away from the light. *Escape!* She reached the chamber beyond the balcony and lurched to her feet, trying to run. The wind pulled at her, making each step a struggle.

Overhead, the ceiling separated in a single magnificent burst – each brick exploding away from the others, then streaming toward the void. The pieces of the unfortunate guard rose after them, a sack drained of grain, a puppet with no controlling hand.

Venli dropped to the ground again and continued crawling, but the stones of the floor separated, floating upward with her on them. Soon, she was scrambling precariously from one floating piece of stone to another. The Rhythm of Resolve still attuned, she dared to glance backward. The hole had widened, and the all-consuming light feasted on the streams of refuse.

She turned away, desperate to do what she could to delay her own burning. Then ... she stopped and looked back again. Dalinar Kholin stood on the balcony. And he was glowing.

Neshua Kadal. Radiant Knight.

Without meaning to, she attuned the Rhythm of Awe. Around Kholin, the balcony was stable. Boards trembled and quivered at his feet, but did not move into the sky. The balcony railing had ripped apart to either side of him, but where he held to it with a firm grip, it remained secure.

He was her enemy, and yet ...

Long ago, these humans had resisted her gods. Yes, the enslavement of her cousins – the singers – was impossible to ignore. Still, the humans had fought. And had *won.*

The listeners remembered this as a song sung to the Rhythm of Awe. *Neshua Kadal.*

The calm, gentle light spread from Dalinar Kholin's hand to the railing, then down into the floor. Boards and stones sank down from the air, reknitting. Venli's current block of stone settled back into place. All through the city, buildings burst apart and zoomed upward, but the walls of this tower returned to their positions.

Venli immediately made for the steps downward. If whatever Kholin was doing stopped, she wanted to be on solid rock. She wound her way to the ground floor, then – once on the street – she positioned herself near the balcony and Kholin's influence.

Above, Odium's light went out.

Stones and splinters rained down on the city, crashing about her. Dried bodies dropped like discarded clothing. Venli pressed back against the tower wall, attuning Anxiety, raising her arm against the dust of the debris.

The hole remained in the sky, though the light was gone from behind it. Below, the rubbled remains of the city seemed ... a sham. No cries of fear, no moans of pain. Bodies were just husks, skins lying empty on the ground.

A sudden *pounding* broke the air behind her, opening another hole, lower down and near the edge of the city. The sky crumbled into the gap, revealing that hateful light again. It consumed everything near it – wall, buildings, even the *ground* disintegrating and flowing into the maw.

Dust and debris washed over Venli in a furious wind. She pressed against the stone wall, clinging to one of the balcony's supports. Terrible heat washed across her from the distant hole.

Clamping her eyes shut, she tightened her grip. He could come claim her, but she would not let go.

And what of the grand purpose? What of the power he offers? Did she still want those things? Or was that merely something to grasp onto, now that she had brought about the end of her people?

She gritted her teeth. In the distance, she heard a quiet rhythm. Somehow it sounded over the roar of the wind, the clacking of dust and stones. The Rhythm of Anxiety?

She opened her eyes, and saw Timbre fighting against the wind in an attempt to reach her. Bursts of light exploded from the little spren in frantic rings.

Buildings crumbled along the street. The entire city was collapsing away – even the palace broke apart, all save this one patch near the balcony.

The little spren changed to the Rhythm of the Lost and began to slide backward.

Venli shouted and released the pillar. She immediately was pushed with the wind – but although she wasn't in stormform any longer, this *was* a form of power, incredibly nimble. She controlled her fall, going down on her side and skidding on the stones, feet toward the oppressive light. As she neared the little spren, Venli jammed her foot into a cleft in the street, then grabbed a crack in a broken stone, pulling herself to a halt. With her other hand, she twisted and snatched Timbre from the air.

Touching Timbre felt like touching silk being blown by a wind. As Venli folded her left hand around the spren, she felt a pulsing warmth. Timbre pulsed to Praise as Venli pulled her close to her breast.

Great, Venli thought, lowering her head against the wind, her face against the ground, holding on to the cleft in the rock with her right hand. *Now we can fall together.*

She had one hope. To hold on, and hope that eventually . . .

The heat faded. The wind stilled. Debris came clattering back to the ground, though the fall was less clamorous this time. Not only had the wind been pulling sideways rather than up, there simply wasn't much debris left.

Venli rose, covered in dust, her face and hands cut by chips of stone. Timbre pulsed softly in her hand.

The city was basically gone. No more than the occasional outline of a building foundation and the remains of the strange rock formations known as the windblades. Even those had been weathered down to knobs five or six feet tall. The only structure in the city that remained was a quarter of the tower where Kholin had been standing.

Behind her was a black, gaping hole into nothingness.

The ground trembled.

Oh no.

Something beat against the stones underneath her. The very ground began to shake and crumble. Venli ran toward the broken palace right as everything – at last – fell apart. The ground, the remaining foundations, even the air seemed to disintegrate.

A chasm opened beneath her, and Venli leaped, trying to reach the other side. She came up a few feet short, and plummeted into the hole. Falling, she twisted in the air, reaching for the collapsing sky with one hand and clutching Timbre in the other.

Above, the man in the blue uniform leaped into the chasm.

He fell beside the hole's perimeter, and stretched one hand toward Venli. His other ground against the rock wall, hand scraping the stone. Something flashed around his arm. Lines of light, a framework that covered his body. His fingers didn't bleed as they scraped the stone.

Around her, the rocks – the air itself – became more substantial. In defiance of the heat below, Venli slowed just enough that her fingers met those of Kholin.

Go.

She crashed to the floor of her cave back in Marat, the vision gone. Sweating, panting, she opened her left fist. To her relief, Timbre floated out, pulsing with a hesitant rhythm.

⁂

Dalinar dissolved into pure pain.

He felt himself being ripped apart, flayed, shredded. Each piece of him

511

removed and allowed to hurt in isolation. A punishment, a retribution, a personalized torment.

It could have persisted for an eternity. Instead, blessedly, the agony faded, and he came to himself.

He knelt on an endless plain of glowing white stone. Light coalesced beside him, forming into a figure dressed in gold and white, holding a short scepter.

'What *were* you seeing?' Odium asked, curious. He tapped his scepter on the ground like a cane. Nohadon's palace – where Dalinar had been moments before – materialized out of light beside them. 'Ah, this one again? Looking for answers from the dead?'

Dalinar squeezed his eyes shut. What a fool he had been. If there had ever been a hope of peace, he'd probably destroyed it by pulling that Parshendi woman into a vision and subjecting her to Odium's horrors.

'Dalinar, Dalinar,' Odium said. He settled down on a seat formed from light, then rested one hand on Dalinar's shoulder. 'It hurts, doesn't it? Yes. I know pain. I am the only god who does. The only one who *cares*.'

'Can there be peace?' Dalinar asked, his voice ragged. Speaking was hard. He'd felt himself being ripped apart in the light moments before.

'Yes, Dalinar,' Odium said. 'There can be. There *will* be.'

'After you destroy Roshar.'

'After *you* destroy it, Dalinar. I am the one who will rebuild it.'

'Agree to a contest between champions,' Dalinar forced out. 'Let us . . . let us find a way to . . .' He trailed off.

How could he fight this thing?

Odium patted Dalinar's shoulder. 'Be strong, Dalinar. I have faith in you, even when you don't have it in yourself. Though it will hurt for a time, there is an end. Peace is in your future. Push *through* the agony. Then you will be victorious, my son.'

The vision faded, and Dalinar found himself back in the upper room of Urithiru. He collapsed into the seat he'd placed there, Navani taking his arm, concerned.

Through his bond, Dalinar sensed weeping. The Stormfather had kept Odium back, but storms, he had paid a price. The most powerful spren on Roshar – embodiment of the tempest that shaped all life – was crying like a child, whispering that Odium was too strong.

A MILLION STARS

The Midnight Mother created monsters of shadow and oil, dark imitations of creatures she saw or consumed. Their description matches no spren I can find in modern literature.

—From Hessi's *Mythica,* page 252

Captain Notum gave the command, and two of the sailors unlatched a section of the hull, exposing the crashing waves of beads just beyond.

Shallan put her freehand on the frame of the open cargo door and leaned out over the churning depths. Adolin tried to tug her back, but she remained in place.

She'd chosen to wear Veil's outfit today, in part for the pockets. She carried three larger gemstones; Kaladin carried four others. Their broams had all run out of Stormlight. Even these larger, unset gems were getting close to failing. Hopefully they would last long enough to get them to Thaylen City and the Oathgate.

Beyond the waves – so close that the sailors feared hidden rocks beneath the beads – a dark landscape interrupted the horizon. The inverse of Longbrow's Straits, a place where trees grew tall, forming a black jungle of glass plants.

A sailor clomped down the steps into the hold and barked something at Captain Notum. 'Your enemies are close now,' the captain translated.

Honor's Path had made a heroic effort these last few hours, pushing its mandras to exhaustion – and it hadn't been nearly enough. The Fused were slower than Kaladin could go, but they were still far faster than the ship.

Shallan looked at the captain; his bearded face, which glowed with a soft, phantom light, betrayed nothing of what must have been a powerful conflict for him. Turn over the captives to the enemy and perhaps save his crew? Or set them free, and hope the Ancient Daughter could escape?

A door at the back of the hold opened, and Kaladin led Syl from her cabin. The captain had only now given permission to release her, as if wishing to delay the decision until the last possible moment. Syl's color seemed muted, and she clung to Kaladin's arm, unsteady. Was she going to be able to make it to shore with them?

She's a spren. She doesn't need air. She'll be fine. Hopefully.

'Go, then,' the captain said. 'And be swift. I cannot promise that my crew, once captured, will be able to keep this secret for long.' Apparently it was difficult to kill spren, but *hurting* them was quite easy.

Another sailor released Adolin's sword spren from her cabin. She didn't look as weathered as Syl – one place seemed as good as another to her.

Kaladin led Syl over.

'Ancient Daughter,' the captain said, bowing his head.

'Won't meet my eyes, Notum?' Syl said. 'I suppose locking me away here isn't too different from all those days you spent running about at Father's whims back home.'

He didn't reply, but instead turned away.

With Syl and the deadeye joining them, that only left one person. Azure lounged by the steps, wearing her breastplate and cloak, arms folded.

'You *sure* you won't change your mind?' Shallan asked.

Azure shook her head.

'Azure,' Kaladin said. 'I was too harsh earlier. That doesn't mean I—'

'It's not that,' she said. 'I simply have a different thread to chase, and besides, I left my men to fight these monsters in Kholinar. Doesn't feel right to do the same again.' She smiled. 'Don't fear for me, Stormblessed. You will have a much better chance if I stay here – as will these sailors.

When you boys next meet the swordsman who taught you that morning kata, warn him that I'm looking for him.'

'Zahel?' Adolin said. 'You know *Zahel*?'

'We're old friends,' she said. 'Notum, have your sailors been cutting those bales of cloth into the shapes I requested?'

'Yes,' the captain said. 'But I don't understand—'

'You soon will.' She gave Kaladin a lazy salute. He returned it, sharper. Then she nodded to them and walked up toward the main deck.

The ship crashed through a large wave of beads, sending some through the open cargo deck doors. Sailors with brooms started brushing them back toward the opening.

'Are you going?' the captain said to Shallan. 'Every moment you delay increases the danger to us all.' He still wouldn't look at Syl.

Right, Shallan thought. Well, someone had to start the party. She took Adolin by one hand and Pattern by the other. Kaladin linked hands with Pattern and Syl, and Adolin grabbed his spren. They crowded into the opening into the cargo hold, looking at the glass beads below. Churning, catching the light of a distant sun, sparkling like a million stars . . .

'All right,' she said. 'Jump!'

Shallan threw herself off the ship, joined by the others. She crashed into the beads, which swallowed her. They seemed to slip too easily into them – like before, when she'd fallen into this ocean, it felt like something was pulling her down.

She sank into the beads, which rolled against her skin, overwhelming her senses with thoughts of trees and rocks. She fought the sensations, struggling to keep herself from thrashing too much. She clung to Adolin, but Pattern's hand was pulled from her grip.

I can't do this! I can't let them claim me. I can't—

They hit the bottom, which was shallow, here near the shore. Then Shallan finally let herself draw in Stormlight. One precious gemstone's worth. It sustained her, calmed her. She fished in her pocket for the bead she'd picked from the bucket earlier.

When she fed the bead Stormlight, the other beads around her trembled, then pulled *back,* forming the walls and ceiling of a small room. The Stormlight curling from her skin illuminated the space with a faint glow. Adolin let go of her hand and fell to his knees, coughing and gasping. His deadeye just stood there, as always.

'Damnation,' Adolin said, wheezing. 'Drowning with no water. It shouldn't be so hard, should it? All we had to do was hold our breath. . . .'

Shallan stepped to the side of the room, listening. Yes . . . it was almost like she could hear the beads whispering to her beneath their clattering. She plunged her hand through the wall and her fingers brushed cloth. She grabbed hold, and a moment later Kaladin seized her arm and pulled himself into the room made from beads, stumbling and falling to his knees.

He wasn't glowing.

'You didn't use a gemstone?' Shallan asked.

'Almost had to,' he said. He took a few deep breaths, then stood up. 'But we need to conserve those.' He turned around. 'Syl?'

A disturbance at the other side of the chamber announced someone approaching. Whoever it was wasn't able to get in until Shallan walked over and broke the surface of the bead wall with her hand. Pattern entered and looked around the room, humming happily. 'Mmm. A nice pattern, Shallan.'

'Syl,' Kaladin repeated. 'We jumped hand-in-hand, but she let go. Where—'

'She'll be fine,' Shallan said.

'Mmm,' Pattern agreed. 'Spren need no air.'

Kaladin took a deep breath, then nodded. He started pacing anyway, so Shallan settled down on the ground to wait, pack in her lap. They each carried a change of clothing, three water jugs, and some of the food Adolin had purchased. Hopefully it would be enough to reach Thaylen City.

Then she'd have to make the Oathgate work.

They waited as long as they dared, hoping the Fused had passed them by, chasing the ship. Finally, Shallan stood up and pointed. 'That way.'

'You sure?' Kaladin asked.

'Yes. Even the slope agrees.' She kicked at the obsidian ground, which ran at a gentle incline.

'Right,' Adolin said. 'Lock hands.'

They did so and – heart fluttering – Shallan recovered the Stormlight from her shell of a room. Beads came crashing down, enveloping her.

They started up the slope, against the tide of beads. It was more difficult than she'd imagined; the current of the shifting beads seemed determined to hold them back. Still, she had Stormlight to sustain her. They soon reached a place where the ground was too steep to walk on easily. Shallan let go of the men's hands and scrambled up the incline.

A moment after her head broke the surface, Syl appeared on the bank, reaching down and helping Shallan up the last few feet. Beads rolled off her clothing, clattering against the ground, as the others pulled themselves onto the shore.

'I saw the enemy fly past,' Syl said. 'I was hiding by the trees here.'

At her urging, they entered the forest of glass plants before settling down to recover from their escape. Shallan immediately felt herself itching for her sketchpad. These trees! The trunks were translucent; the leaves looked like they were blown from glass in a multitude of colors. Moss drooped from one branch, like melted green glass, strands hanging down in silky lines. When she touched them, they broke off.

Overhead, the clouds rippled with the mother-of-pearl iridescence that marked another highstorm in the real world. Shallan could barely see it through the canopy, but the effect on Pattern and Syl was immediate. They stood up straighter, and Syl's wan color brightened to a healthy blue-white. Pattern's head shifted more quickly, spinning through a dozen different cycles in a matter of minutes.

Stormlight still trailed from Shallan's skin. She'd taken in a rather large amount of it, but hadn't lost *too* much. She returned it to the gemstone, a process she didn't quite understand, but which felt natural at the same time.

Nearby, Syl looked to the southwest with a kind of wistful, far-off expression. 'Syl?' Shallan asked.

'There's a storm that way too . . .' she whispered, then shook herself and seemed embarrassed.

Kaladin dug out two gemstones. 'All right,' he said, 'we fly.'

They'd decided to use two gemstones' worth of Stormlight to fly inward, a gamble to get a head start on their hike – and to get away from the coast. Hopefully the Fused wouldn't treat the honorspren *too* harshly. Shallan worried for them, but equally for what would happen if the Fused doubled back to search for her group.

A short flight now should deposit them far enough inland that they'd be tough to locate. Once they landed, they would hike across several days' worth of Shadesmar landscape before reaching the island of Thaylenah, which would manifest as a lake here. Thaylen City, and its Oathgate, were on the very rim of that lake.

Kaladin Lashed them one at a time – and fortunately, his arts worked on the spren as they did humans. They took to the air and started the last leg of their journey.

III

EILA STELE

It will not take a careful reader to ascertain I have listed only eight of the Unmade here. Lore is confident there were nine, an unholy number, asymmetrical and often associated with the enemy.

—From Hessi's *Mythica*, page 266

Dalinar stepped out of the Oathgate control building into Thaylen City and was met by the man he most wanted to punch in all Roshar.

Meridas Amaram stood straight in his House Sadeas uniform, clean-shaven, narrow-faced, square-jawed. Tall, orderly, with shining buttons and a sharp posture, he was the very image of a perfect Alethi officer.

'Report,' Dalinar said, hopefully keeping the dislike out of his voice.

Amaram – Sadeas – fell into step with Dalinar, and they walked to the edge of the Oathgate platform, overlooking the city. Dalinar's guards gave them space to converse.

'Our crews have done wonders for this city, Brightlord,' Amaram said. 'We focused our initial attentions on the debris outside the walls. I worried that would give an invading force too much cover – not to mention rubble to construct a ramp up to the wall.'

Indeed, the plain before the city walls – which had once housed the markets and warehouses of the docks – was completely clear. A killing field, interrupted by the occasional outline of a broken foundation. The Almighty only knew how the Thaylen military had allowed a collection of buildings *outside* the walls in the first place. That would have been a nightmare to defend.

'We shored up positions where the wall was weakened,' Amaram continued, gesturing. 'It's not high by Kholinar standards, but is an impressive fortification nonetheless. We cleared out the buildings right inside to provide staging and resource dumps, and my army is camped there. We then helped with general reconstruction.'

'The city looks far better,' Dalinar said. 'Your men did well.'

'Then maybe our penance can be over,' Amaram said. He said it straight, though angerspren – a pool of boiling blood – spread from beneath his right foot.

'Your work here was important, soldier. You didn't only rebuild a city; you built the trust of the Thaylen people.'

'Of course.' Amaram added, more softly, 'And I *do* see the tactical importance of knowing the enemy fortifications.'

You fool. 'The Thaylens are not our enemies.'

'I misspoke,' Amaram said. 'Yet I cannot ignore that the *Kholin* troops have been deployed to the border between our kingdom and Jah Keved. Your men get to liberate our homeland, while *mine* spend their days digging in rocks. You do realize the effect this has on their morale, particularly since many of them still assume you assassinated their highprince.'

'I *hope* that their current leader has worked to disabuse them of such false notions.'

Amaram finally turned to look Dalinar in the eyes. Those angerspren were still there, though his tone was crisp and militaristic. 'Brightlord. I know you for a realist. I've modeled my career after yours. Frankly, even if you *did* kill him – which I know you must deny – I would respect you for it. Torol was a liability to this nation.

'Let me *prove* to you that I am not the same. Storms, Dalinar! I'm your best frontline general, and you know it. Torol spent years wasting me because my reputation intimidated him. Don't make the same mistake. *Use* me. Let me fight for Alethkar, not kiss the feet of Thaylen merchants! I—'

'Enough,' Dalinar snapped. 'Follow your orders. *That* is how you'll prove yourself to me.'

Amaram stepped back, then – after a deliberate pause – saluted. He spun on his heel and marched down into the city.

That man ... Dalinar thought. Dalinar had intended to tell him that this island would host the front lines in the war, but the conversation had slipped from him. Well, Amaram might quickly get the fighting he wanted – a fact he would discover soon enough, at the planning meeting.

Boots on stone sounded behind him as a group of men in blue uniforms joined him at the rim of the plateau. 'Permission to stab him a little, sir,' said Teft, the bridgeman leader.

'How do you stab someone "a little," soldier?'

'I could do it,' Lyn said. 'I've only started training with a spear. We could claim it was an accident.'

'No, no,' Lopen said. 'You want to stab him a little? Let my cousin Huio do it, sir. He's the expert on little things.'

'Short joke?' Huio said in his broken Alethi. 'Be glad not short temper.'

'I'm just trying to involve you, Huio. I know that most people overlook you. It's very easy to do, you see. . . .'

'Attention!' Dalinar snapped, though he found himself smiling. They scrambled into ranks. Kaladin had trained them well.

'You've got' – Dalinar checked the clock on his arm – 'thirty-seven minutes until the meeting, men. And, er, women. Don't be late.'

They rushed off, chatting among themselves. Navani, Jasnah, and Renarin joined him soon after, and his wife gave him a sly smile as she noticed him checking his arm clock again. Storming woman had gotten him to start arriving early for appointments just by strapping a device to his arm.

As they gathered, Fen's son climbed up onto the Oathgate platform and greeted Dalinar warmly. 'We have rooms for you, above the temple where we'll be meeting. I . . . well, we know you don't *need* them, since you can simply Oathgate home in an instant . . .'

'We'll take them gladly, son,' Dalinar said. 'I could use a little refreshment and time to think.'

The young man grinned. Dalinar never *would* get used to those spiked eyebrows.

They climbed down from the platform, and a Thaylen guard gave the all clear. A scribe sent word via spanreed that the next transfer could take place. Dalinar paused to watch. A minute later a flash occurred, surrounding the Oathgate with light. The Oathgates were under almost perpetual use these days – Malata was running the device today, as was becoming her duty more often.

'Uncle?' Jasnah said as he lingered.

'Merely curious about who's coming in next.'

'I could pull the records for you . . .' Jasnah said.

The new arrivals turned out to be a group of Thaylen merchants in pompous clothing. They made their way down the larger ramp, surrounded by guards and accompanied by several men carrying large chests.

'More bankers,' Fen's son said. 'The quiet economic collapse of Roshar continues.'

'Collapse?' Dalinar said, surprised.

'Bankers all across the continent have been pulling out of cities,' Jasnah said, pointing. 'See that fortress of a building at the front of the Ancient Ward down below? That's the Thaylen Gemstone Reserve.'

'Local governments are going to have difficulty financing troops after this,' Fen's son said with a grimace. 'They'll have to write here with authorized spanreeds and get spheres shipped to them. It's going to be a nightmare of logistics for anyone not close to an Oathgate.'

Dalinar frowned. 'Couldn't you encourage the merchants to stay and support the cities they were in?'

'Sir!' he replied. 'Sir, force the merchants to obey *military* authority?'

'Forget I asked,' Dalinar said, sharing a look with Navani and Jasnah. Navani smiled fondly at what was probably a huge social misstep, but he suspected Jasnah agreed with him. She'd probably have seized the banks and used them to fund the war.

Renarin lingered, watching the merchants. 'How big are the gemstones they've brought?' he asked.

'Brightlord?' Fen's son asked, glancing toward Dalinar for help. 'They'll be spheres. Normal spheres.'

'Any larger gemstones?' Renarin asked. He turned toward them. 'Anywhere in the city?'

'Sure, lots of them,' Fen's son said. 'Some really nice pieces, like in every city. Um . . . why, Brightlord?'

'Because,' Renarin said. He didn't say anything more.

Dalinar splashed water onto his face from a basin in his rooms, which were in a villa above the temple of Talenelat, on the top tier of the city – the Royal Ward. He wiped his face with the towel and reached out to the Stormfather. 'Feeling any better?'

I do not feel like men. I do not sicken like men. I am. The Stormfather rumbled. *I could have been destroyed, though. Splintered into a thousand pieces. I live only because the enemy fears exposing himself to a strike from Cultivation.*

'So she lives still, then? The third god?'

Yes. You've met her.

'I . . . I *have*?'

You do not remember. But normally, she hides. Cowardice.

'Perhaps wisdom,' Dalinar said. 'The Nightwatcher—'

Is not her.

'Yes, you've said. The Nightwatcher is like you. Are there others, though? Spren like you, or the Nightwatcher? Spren that are shadows of gods?'

There is . . . a third sibling. They are not with us.

'In hiding?'

No. Slumbering.

'Tell me more.'

No.

'But—'

No! Leave them alone. You hurt them enough.

'Fine,' Dalinar said, setting aside the towel and leaning against the window. The air smelled of salt, reminding him of something not yet clear in his mind. One last hole in his memory. A trip by sea.

And his visit to the Valley.

He glanced at the dresser beside the washbasin, which held a book written in unfamiliar Thaylen glyphs. A little note beside it, in Alethi glyphs, read, 'Pathway. King.' Fen had left him a gift, a copy of *The Way of Kings* in Thaylen.

'I've done it,' Dalinar said. 'I've united them, Stormfather. I've kept my oath, and have brought men together, instead of dividing them. Perhaps this can be penance in some small way, for the pain I've caused.'

The Stormfather rumbled in reply.

'Did he . . . care about what we felt?' Dalinar asked. 'Honor, the Almighty? Did he truly care about men's pain?'

He did. Then, I didn't understand why, but now I do. Odium lies when he claims to have sole ownership of passion. The Stormfather paused. *I remember ... at the end ... Honor was more obsessed with oaths. There were times when the oath itself was more important than the meaning behind it. But he was not a passionless monster. He loved humankind. He died defending you.*

Dalinar found Navani entertaining Taravangian in the common area of their villa. 'Your Majesty?' Dalinar asked.

'You could call me Vargo, if you wish,' Taravangian said, pacing without looking at Dalinar. 'It is what they called me as a youth. . . .'

'What's wrong?' Dalinar asked.

'I'm just worried. My scholars ... It is nothing, Dalinar. Nothing. Silliness. I am ... I am well today.' He stopped and squeezed his pale grey eyes shut.

'That's good, isn't it?'

'Yes. But it is not a day to be heartless. So I worry.'

Heartless? What did he mean?

'Do you need to sit out the meeting?' Navani asked.

Taravangian shook his head quickly. 'Come. Let us go. I will be better ... better once we've started. I'm sure.'

·᛫·

As Dalinar stepped into the temple's main chamber, he found that he was looking *forward* to the meeting.

What a strange revelation. He'd spent so much of his youth and middle years dreading politics and the endless rambling of meetings. Now he was *excited.* He could see the outlines of something grand in this room. The Azish delegation warmly greeted Queen Fen, with Vizier Noura even giving Fen a poem she'd written as thanks for the Thaylen hospitality. Fen's son made a point of sitting next to Renarin and chatting with him. Emperor Yanagawn looked comfortable on his throne, surrounded by allies and friends.

Bridge Four joked with the guards of Highprince Aladar, while Lift the Edgedancer perched on a windowsill nearby, listening with a cocked head. In addition to the five scout women in uniform, two women in havahs had joined Bridge Four. They carried notepads and pencils, and had sewn Bridge Four patches to the upper sleeves of their dresses – the place where scribes commonly wore their platoon insignia.

Alethi highprinces, Azish viziers, Knights Radiant, and Thaylen admirals all in one room. The prime of Emul talking tactics with Aladar, who had been aiding the beleaguered country. General Khal and Teshav speaking with the princess of Yezier, who was eyeing Halam Khal – their eldest son – standing tall in his father's Shardplate by the door. There was talk of a political union there. It would be the first in centuries between an Alethi and a Makabaki princedom.

Unite them. A voice whispered the words in Dalinar's mind, echoing with the same resonant sound from months ago, when Dalinar had first started seeing the visions.

'I'm doing so,' Dalinar whispered back.

Unite them.

'Stormfather, is that you? Why do you keep saying this to me?'

I said nothing.

It was growing hard to distinguish between his own thoughts and what came from the Stormfather. Visions and memories struggled for space in Dalinar's brain. To clear his mind, he strode around the perimeter of the circular temple chamber. Murals on the walls – ones he had healed with his abilities – depicted the Herald Talenelat during several of his many, many last stands against the Voidbringers.

A large map had been mounted on one wall depicting the Tarat Sea and surrounding areas, with markers noting the locations of their fleet. The room quieted as Dalinar stepped up and studied this. He glanced for a moment out the doors of the temple, toward the bay. Already, a few of the faster ships of their fleet had arrived, flying the flags of both Kharbranth and Azir.

'Your Excellency,' Dalinar said to Yanagawn. 'Could you share news of your troops?'

The emperor gave leave for Noura to report. The main fleet was less than a day away. Their outriders – or scout ships, as she called them – had spotted no indications of the enemy advance. They'd worried that this window between storms would be when the enemy would move, but so far there was no sign.

The admirals began to discuss how to best patrol the seas while keeping Thaylen City safe. Dalinar was pleased by the conversation, mostly because the admirals seemed to think that the real danger to Thaylen City had passed. A Veden highprince had managed to get a foot scout close enough to Marat to count the ships at the docks. Well over a hundred vessels were waiting in the various coves and ports along the coast. For whatever reason, they weren't ready to launch yet, which was a blessing.

The meeting progressed, with Fen belatedly welcoming everyone – Dalinar realized he should have let her take charge from the start. She described the defenses in Thaylen City and raised concerns from her guildmasters about Amaram's troops. Apparently they'd been carousing.

Amaram stiffened at that. For all his faults, he liked to run a tight army.

Sometime near the end of this discussion, Dalinar noticed Renarin shifting uncomfortably in his seat. As the Azish scribes began explaining their code of rules and guidelines for the coalition, Renarin excused himself in a hoarse voice, and left.

Dalinar glanced at Navani, who seemed troubled. Jasnah stood to follow, but was interrupted by a scribe bringing her a small sheaf of documents. She accepted them and moved to Navani's side so they could study them together.

Should we break? Dalinar thought, checking his forearm clock. They'd only been going for an hour, and the Azish were obviously excited by their guidelines.

The Stormfather rumbled.

What? Dalinar thought.

Something . . . something is coming. A storm.

Dalinar stood up, looking about the room, half expecting assassins to attack. His sudden motion caught the attention of one of the Azish viziers, a short man with a very large hat.

'Brightlord?' the interpreter asked at a word from the vizier.

'I . . .' Dalinar could feel it. 'Something's wrong.'

'Dalinar?' Fen asked. 'What are you talking about?'

Spanreeds suddenly started blinking throughout the room. A dozen flashing rubies. Dalinar's heart sidestepped. Anticipationspren rose around him, streamers whipping from the ground, as the various scribes grabbed the blinking spanreeds from boxes or belts and set them out to begin writing.

Jasnah didn't notice that one of hers was blinking. She was too distracted by what she and Navani were reading.

'The Everstorm just hit Shinovar,' Queen Fen finally explained, reading over a scribe's shoulder.

'Impossible!' Ialai Sadeas said. 'It has only been five days since the last one! They come at nine-day intervals.'

'Yes, well, I think we have enough confirmation,' Fen said, nodding toward the spanreeds.

'The storm is too new,' Teshav said. She pulled her shawl closer as she read. 'We don't know it well enough to truly judge its patterns. The reports from Steen say it is particularly violent this time, moving faster than before.'

Dalinar felt cold.

'How long until it reaches us?' Fen asked.

'Hours yet,' Teshav said. 'It can take a full day for the highstorm to get from one side of Roshar to the other, and the Everstorm is slower. Usually.'

'It's moving faster though,' Yanagawn said through his interpreter. 'How far away are our ships? How are we going to shelter them?'

'Peace, Your Excellency,' Fen said. 'The ships are close, and the new docks miles farther along the coast are sheltered from both east and west. We merely need to make sure the fleet goes directly there, instead of stopping here to drop off troops.'

The room buzzed with conversations as the various groups received reports from their contacts in Tashikk, who in turn would be relaying information from contacts in Iri, Steen, or even Shinovar.

'We should break for a short time,' Dalinar told them. The others agreed, distracted, and separated into groups scattered about the room. Dalinar settled back in his seat, releasing a held breath. 'That wasn't so bad. We can deal with this.'

That wasn't it, the Stormfather said. He rumbled, his concerned voice growing very soft as he continued, *There's more.*

Dalinar jumped back to his feet, instincts prompting him to thrust his hand to the side, fingers splayed, to summon a Blade he no longer possessed. Bridge Four responded immediately, dropping food from the table of victuals, grabbing spears. Nobody else seemed to notice.

But . . . notice what? No attack came. Conversations continued on all sides. Jasnah and Navani were still huddled side by side, reading. Navani

527

gasped softly, safehand going to her mouth. Jasnah looked at Dalinar, lips drawn to a line.

Their message wasn't about the storm, Dalinar thought, pulling his chair over to them. 'All right,' he whispered, though they were far enough from other groups to have some privacy. 'What is it?'

'A breakthrough was made in translating the Dawnchant,' Navani whispered. 'Teams in Kharbranth and the monasteries of Jah Keved have arrived at the news separately, using the seed we provided through the visions. We are finally receiving translations.'

'That's good, right?' Dalinar said.

Jasnah sighed. 'Uncle, the piece that historians have been *most* eager to translate is called the Eila Stele. Other sources claim it is old, perhaps the oldest document in written memory, said to be scribed by the Heralds themselves. From the translation that finally came in today, the carving appears to be the account of someone who witnessed the very *first* coming of the Voidbringers, long, long ago. Even before the first Desolation.'

'Blood of my fathers,' Dalinar said. Before the first Desolation? The *last* Desolation had happened more than four thousand years ago. They were speaking of events lost to time. 'And . . . we can read it?'

'"They came from another world," Navani said, reading from her sheet. '"Using powers that we have been forbidden to touch. Dangerous powers, of spren and Surges. They destroyed their lands and have come to us begging.

'"We took them in, as commanded by the gods. What else could we do? They were a people forlorn, without home. Our pity destroyed us. For their betrayal extended even to our gods: to spren, stone, and wind.

'"Beware the otherworlders. The traitors. Those with tongues of sweetness, but with minds that lust for blood. Do not take them in. Do not give them succor. Well were they named Voidbringers, for they brought the void. The empty pit that sucks in emotion. A new god. Their god.

'"These Voidbringers know no songs. They cannot hear Roshar, and where they go, they bring silence. They look soft, with no shell, but they are hard. They have but one heart, and it cannot ever live."'

She lowered the page.

Dalinar frowned. *It's nonsense,* he thought. *Is it claiming that the first parshmen who came to invade had no carapace? But how would the writer know that parshmen* should *have carapace? And what is this about songs. . . .*

It clicked. 'That was not written by a human,' Dalinar whispered.

'No, Uncle,' Jasnah said softly. 'The writer was a Dawnsinger, one of the original inhabitants of Roshar. The Dawnsingers weren't spren, as theology has often postulated. Nor were they Heralds. They were parshmen. And the people they welcomed to their world, the otherworlders . . .'

'Were us,' Dalinar whispered. He felt cold, like he'd been dunked in icy water. 'They named *us* Voidbringers.'

Jasnah sighed. 'I have suspected this for a time. The first Desolation was the invasion of *humankind* onto Roshar. We came here and seized this land from the parshmen – after we accidentally used Surgebinding to destroy our previous world. That is the truth that destroyed the Radiants.'

The Stormfather rumbled in his mind. Dalinar stared at that sheet of paper in Navani's hand. Such a small, seemingly unimportant object to have created such a pit inside of him.

It's true, isn't it? he thought at the Stormfather. *Storms . . . we're not the defenders of our homeland.*

We're the invaders.

Nearby, Taravangian argued softly with his scribes, then finally stood up. He cleared his throat, and the various groups slowly stilled. The Azish contingent had servants pull their chairs back toward the group, and Queen Fen returned to her place, though she didn't sit. She stood, arms folded, looking perturbed.

'I have had disconcerting news,' Taravangian said. 'Over the spanreed, just now. It involves Brightlord Kholin. I don't wish to be objectionable . . .'

'No,' Fen said. 'I've heard it too. I'm going to need an explanation.'

'Agreed,' Noura said.

Dalinar stood up. 'I realize this is troubling. I . . . I haven't had time to adjust. Perhaps we could adjourn and worry about the storm first? We can discuss this later.'

'Perhaps,' Taravangian said. 'Yes, perhaps. But it *is* a problem. We have believed that ours is a righteous war, but this news of mankind's origins has me disconcerted.'

'What are you talking about?' Fen said.

'The news from the Veden translators? Ancient texts, manifesting that humans came from another world?'

'Bah,' Fen said. 'Dusty books and ideas for philosophers. What *I* want to know about is this highking business!'

'*Highking?*' Yanagawn asked through an interpreter.

'I've an essay,' Fen said, slapping papers against her hand, 'from Zetah the Voiced claiming that before King Elhokar left for Alethkar, he *swore* to Dalinar to accept him as emperor.'

Noura the vizier leaped to her feet. '*What?*'

'Emperor is an exaggeration!' Dalinar said, trying to reorient toward this unexpected attack. 'It's an internal Alethi matter.'

Navani stood beside him. 'My son was merely concerned about his political relation to Dalinar. We have prepared an explanation for you all, and our highprinces can confirm that we are *not* looking to expand our influence to your nations.'

'And this?' Noura said, holding up some pages. 'Were you preparing an explanation for *this* as well?'

'What is that?' Dalinar asked, bracing himself.

'Accounts of two visions,' Noura said, 'that you *didn't* share with us. In which you supposedly met and fraternized with a being known as Odium.'

Behind Dalinar, Lift gasped. He glanced toward her, and the men of Bridge Four, who were muttering among themselves.

This is bad, Dalinar thought. *Too much. Too fast for me to control.*

Jasnah leaped to her feet. 'This is obviously a concentrated attempt to destroy our reputation. Someone *deliberately* released all this information at the same time.'

'Is it true?' Noura asked in Alethi. 'Dalinar Kholin, *have you met with our enemy?*'

Navani gripped his arm. Jasnah subtly shook her head: *Don't answer that.*

'Yes,' Dalinar said.

'Did he,' Noura asked pointedly, 'tell you you'd destroy Roshar?'

'What of this ancient record?' Taravangian said. 'It claims that the Radiants *already* destroyed one world. Is that not what caused them to disband? They worried that their powers could not be controlled!'

'I'm still trying to wrap my mind around this highking nonsense,' Fen said. 'How is it merely an "internal Alethi matter" if you've allowed another king to swear to you?'

Everyone started talking at once. Navani and Jasnah stepped forward, responding to the attacks, but Dalinar only sank into his seat. It was all falling apart. A sword, as keen as any on a battlefield, had been rammed into the heart of his coalition.

This is what you feared, he thought. *A world that turns not upon force of armies, but upon the concerns of scribes and bureaucrats.*

And in that world, he had just been deftly outflanked.

I am certain there are nine Unmade. There are many legends and names that I could have misinterpreted, conflating two Unmade into one. In the next section, I will discuss my theories on this.

—From Hessi's *Mythica,* page 266

Kaladin remembered a woman's kiss.

Tarah had been special. The darkeyed daughter of an assistant quartermaster, she had grown up helping with her father's work. Though she was a hundred percent Alethi, she preferred dresses of an old-fashioned Thaylen style, which had an apronlike front with straps over the shoulders and skirts that ended right below the knee. She'd wear a buttoned shirt underneath, often in a bright color – brighter than most darkeyes could afford. Tarah knew how to squeeze the most out of her spheres.

That day, Kaladin had been sitting on a stump, shirt off, sweating. The evening was growing cold as the sun set, and he basked in the last warmth. His spear resting across his lap, he toyed with a rock of white, brown, and black. Alternating colors.

The warmth from the sun was mirrored as someone warm hugged him from behind, wrapping her arms across his chest. Kaladin rested a callused hand on Tarah's smooth one, drinking in her scent – of starched uniforms, new leather, and other clean things.

'You're done early,' he said. 'I thought there were greenvines to outfit today.'

'I have the new girl doing the rest.'

'I'm surprised. I know how much you like this part.'

'Storms,' she said, slipping around in front of him. 'They get *so* embarrassed when you measure them. "Hold on, kid. I'm not making a pass at you because I'm putting a measuring tape up against your chest, I swear...."' She lifted his spear, looking it over with a critical eye, testing the balance. 'I wish you'd let me requisition a new one for you.'

'I like that one. Took me forever to find one long enough.'

She peered along the length of the weapon, to make sure it was straight. She would never trust it, as she hadn't personally requisitioned it for him. She wore green today, under a brown skirt, her black hair tied back in a tail. Slightly plump, with a round face and firm build, Tarah's beauty was a subtle thing. Like an uncut gemstone. The more you saw of it – the more you discovered of its natural facets – the more you loved it. Until one day it struck you that you'd never known anything as wonderful.

'Any young boys among the greenvines?' Kaladin asked, standing up and pocketing Tien's stone.

'I didn't notice.'

He grunted, waving to Gol – one of the other squadleaders. 'You know I like to watch for kids who might need a little extra looking out for.'

'I know, but I was busy. We got a caravan from Kholinar today.' She leaned close to him. 'There was real flour in one of the packages. I traded in some favors. You know I've been wanting you to try some of my father's Thaylen bread? I thought maybe we'd fix it tonight.'

'Your father hates me.'

'He's coming around. Besides, he loves anyone who compliments his bread.'

'I have evening practice.'

'You just got done practicing.'

'I just got done warming up.' He looked to her, then grimaced. 'I organized the evening practice, Tarah. I can't just skip it. Besides, I thought you were going to be busy all evening. Maybe tomorrow, lunch?'

He kissed her on the cheek and reclaimed his spear. He'd taken only a step away when she spoke.

'I'm leaving, Kal,' she said from behind.

He stumbled over his own feet, then spun about. '*What?*'

'I'm transferring,' she said. 'They offered me a scribe's job in Mourn's Vault, with the highprince's house. It's a good opportunity, particularly for someone like me.'

'But . . .' He gaped. '*Leaving?*'

'I wanted to tell you over dinner, not out here in the cold. It's something I have to do. Father's getting older; he's worried he'll end up being shipped to the Shattered Plains. If I can get work, he can join me.'

Kaladin put a hand to his head. She couldn't just leave, could she?

Tarah walked over, stood on the tips of her toes, and kissed him lightly on the lips.

'Could you . . . not go?' he asked.

She shook her head.

'Maybe I could get a transfer?' he said. 'To the highprince's standing house guard?'

'Would you do that?'

'I . . .'

No. He wouldn't.

Not while he carried that stone in his pocket, not while the memory of his brother dying was fresh in his mind. Not while lighteyed highlords got boys killed in petty fights.

'Oh, Kal,' she whispered, then squeezed his arm. 'Maybe someday you'll learn how to be there for the living, not just for the dead.'

After she left, he got two letters from her, talking about her life in Mourn's Vault. He had paid someone to read them to him.

He never sent responses. Because he was stupid, because he didn't understand. Because men make mistakes when they're young and angry.

Because she had been right.

·❖·

Kaladin shouldered his harpoon, leading his companions through the strange forest. They'd flown part of the way, but needed to conserve what little Stormlight they had left.

So, they'd spent the last two days hiking. Trees and more trees, lifespren floating among them, the occasional bobbing souls of fish. Syl kept saying that they were lucky they hadn't encountered any angerspren or other predators. To her, this forest was strangely silent, strangely empty.

The jungle-style trees had given way to taller, more statuesque ones with deep crimson trunks and limbs like burnt-red crystals that, at the ends, burst into small collections of minerals. The rugged obsidian landscape was full of deep valleys and endless towering hills. Kaladin was beginning to worry that – despite the motionless sun to provide an unerring way to gauge their heading – they were going in the wrong direction.

'Storms, bridgeboy,' Adolin said, hiking up the incline after him. 'Maybe a break?'

'At the top,' Kaladin said.

Without Stormlight, Shallan trailed farthest behind, Pattern at her side. Exhaustionspren circled in the air above, like large chickens. Though she tried to push herself, she wasn't a soldier, and often was the biggest limitation to their pace. Of course, without her mapmaking skills and memory of Thaylen City's exact location, they probably wouldn't have any idea which way to go.

Fortunately, there was no sign of pursuit. Still, Kaladin couldn't help worrying that they were moving too slowly.

Be there, Tarah had told him. *For the living.*

He urged them up this hillside, past a section of broken ground, where the obsidian had fractured like layers of crem that hadn't hardened properly. Worry pulled him forward. Step after relentless step.

He *had* to get to the Oathgate. He would *not* fail like he had in Kholinar.

A single glowing windspren burst alight next to him as he reached the top of the hill. Cresting it, he found himself overlooking a sea of souls. Thousands upon thousands of candle flames bobbed about in the next valley over, moving above a grand ocean of glass beads.

Thaylen City.

Adolin joined him, then finally Shallan and the three spren. Shallan sighed and settled to the ground, coughing softly from the effort of the climb.

Amid the sea of lights were two towering spren, much like the ones they'd seen in Kholinar. One sparkled a multitude of colors while the other shimmered an oily black. Both stood tall, holding spears as long as a building. The sentries of the Oathgate, and they didn't look corrupted.

Beneath them, the device itself manifested as a large stone platform with a wide, sweeping white bridge running over the beads and to the shore.

That bridge was guarded by an entire army of enemy spren, hundreds – perhaps thousands – strong.

If I'm correct and my research true, then the question remains. Who is the ninth Unmade? Is it truly Dai-Gonarthis? If so, could their actions have actually caused the complete destruction of Aimia?

—From Hessi's *Mythica,* page 307

D alinar stood alone in the rooms Queen Fen had given him, staring out the window, looking west. Toward Shinovar, far beyond the horizon. A land with strange beasts like horses, chickens. And humans.

He'd left the other monarchs arguing in the temple below; anything he said only seemed to widen the rifts among them. They didn't trust him. They'd never really trusted him. His deception proved them right.

Storms. He felt *furious* with himself. He should have released those visions, should have immediately told the others about Elhokar. There had simply been so much piling on top of him. His memories ... his excommunication ... worry for Adolin and Elhokar ...

Part of him couldn't help but be impressed by how deftly he'd been outmaneuvered. Queen Fen worried about Dalinar being genuine; the enemy had delivered perfect proof that Dalinar had hidden political motives. Noura and the Azish worried that the powers were dangerous, whispering of Lost Radiants. To them, the enemy indicated that Dalinar was being manipulated by evil visions. And to Taravangian – who spoke so often of philosophy – the enemy suggested that their moral foundation for the war was a sham.

Or maybe that dart was for Dalinar himself. Taravangian said that a king was justified in doing terrible things in the name of the state. But Dalinar . . .

For once, he'd assumed what he was doing was *right*.

Did you really think you belonged here? the Stormfather asked. *That you were native to Roshar?*

'Yes, maybe,' Dalinar said. 'I thought . . . maybe we came from Shinovar originally.'

That is the land you were given, the Stormfather said. *A place where the plants and animals you brought here could grow.*

'We weren't able to confine ourselves to what we were given.'

When has any man ever been content with what he has?

'When has any tyrant ever said to himself, "This is enough"?' Dalinar whispered, remembering words Gavilar had once spoken.

The Stormfather rumbled.

'The Almighty kept this from his Radiants,' Dalinar said. 'When they discovered it, they abandoned their vows.'

It is more than that. My memory of all this is . . . strange. First, I was not fully awake; I was but the spren of a storm. Then I was like a child. Changed and shaped during the frantic last days of a dying god.

But I do remember. It was not only the truth of humankind's origin that caused the Recreance. It was the distinct, powerful fear that they would destroy this world, as men like them had destroyed the one before. The Radiants abandoned their vows for that reason, as will you.

'I will *not*,' Dalinar said. 'I *won't* let my Radiants retread the fate of their predecessors.'

Won't you?

Dalinar's attention was drawn to a solemn group of men leaving the temple below. Bridge Four, spears held on slumped shoulders, heads bowed as they quietly marched down the steps.

Dalinar scrambled out of his villa and ran down the steps to intercept the bridgemen. 'Where are you going?' he demanded.

They halted, falling into ranks at attention.

'Sir,' Teft said. 'We thought we'd head back to Urithiru. We left some of the men behind, and they deserve to know about this business with the ancient Radiants.'

'What we've discovered doesn't change the fact that we are being invaded,' Dalinar said.

'Invaded by people trying to reclaim their homeland,' Sigzil said. 'Storms. I'd be mad too.'

'We're supposed to be the good guys, you know?' Leyten said. 'Fighting for a good cause, for once in our storming lives.'

Echoes of his own thoughts. Dalinar found he couldn't formulate an argument against that.

'We'll see what Kal says,' Teft replied. 'Sir. All respect, sir. But we'll see what he says. He knows the right of things, even when the rest of us don't.'

And if he never returns? Dalinar thought. *What if none of them return?* It had been four weeks. How long could he keep pretending that Adolin and Elhokar were alive out there somewhere? That pain hid behind the rest, taunting him.

The bridgemen gave Dalinar their unique cross-armed salute, then left without waiting to be dismissed.

In the past, Honor was able to guard against this, the Stormfather told him. *He convinced the Radiants they were righteous, even if this land hadn't originally been theirs. Who cares what your ancestors did, when the enemy is trying to kill you right now?*

But in the days leading to the Recreance, Honor was dying. When that generation of knights learned the truth, Honor did not support them. He raved, speaking of the Dawnshards, ancient weapons used to destroy the Tranquiline Halls. Honor . . . promised that Surgebinders would do the same to Roshar.

'Odium claimed the same thing.'

He can see the future, though only cloudily. Regardless, I . . . understand now as I never did before. The ancient Radiants didn't abandon their oaths out of pettiness. They tried to protect the world. I blame them for their weakness, their broken oaths. But I also understand. You have cursed me, human, with this capacity.

The meeting in the temple seemed to be breaking up. The Azish contingent started down the steps.

'Our enemy hasn't changed,' Dalinar said to them. 'The need for a coalition is as strong as ever.'

The young emperor, being carried in a palanquin, didn't look at him. Oddly, the Azish didn't make for the Oathgate, instead taking a path down into the city.

Only Vizier Noura idled to speak to him. 'Jasnah Kholin might be right,' she said in Azish. 'The destruction of our old world, your secret visions, this business with you being highking – it seems too great a co-incidence for it all to come at once.'

'Then you can see that we're being manipulated.'

'Manipulated by the truth, Kholin,' she said, meeting his eyes. 'That Oathgate is dangerous. These powers of yours are *dangerous*. Deny it.'

'I cannot. I will not found this coalition on lies.'

'You *already have*.'

He drew in a sharp breath.

Noura shook her head. 'We will take the scout ships and join the fleet carrying our soldiers. Then we will wait out this storm. After that . . . we shall see. Taravangian has said we may use his vessels to return to our empire, without needing to use the Oathgates.'

She walked off after the emperor, eschewing the palanquin waiting to carry her.

Others drifted down the steps around him. Veden highprinces, who gave excuses. Thaylen lighteyes from their guild councils, who avoided him. The Alethi highprinces and scribes expressed solidarity – but Al-ethkar couldn't do this on its own.

Queen Fen was one of the last to leave the temple.

'Will you leave me too?' Dalinar asked.

She laughed. 'To go where, old hound? An army is coming this way. I still need your famous Alethi infantry; I can't afford to throw you out.'

'Such bitterness.'

'Oh, did it show? I'm going to check on the city's defenses; if you decide to join us, we'll be at the walls.'

'I'm sorry, Fen,' Dalinar said, 'for betraying your trust.'

She shrugged. 'I don't really think you intend to conquer me, Kholin. But oddly . . . I can't help wishing I *did* have to worry. Best I can tell, you've become a good man right in time to bravely sink with this ship. That's commendable, until I remember that the Blackthorn would have long since murdered everyone trying to sink him.'

Fen and her consort climbed into a palanquin. People continued to trickle past, but eventually Dalinar stood alone before the quiet temple.

'I'm sorry, Dalinar,' Taravangian said softly from behind. Dalinar turned, surprised to find the old man sitting on the steps. 'I assumed everyone had the same information, and that it would be best to air it. I didn't expect all of this. . . .'

'This isn't your fault,' Dalinar said.

'And yet . . .' He stood up, then walked – slowly – down the steps. 'I'm sorry, Dalinar. I fear I can no longer fight beside you.'

'Why?' Dalinar said. 'Taravangian, you're the most pragmatic ruler I've met! Aren't you the one who talked to me about the importance of doing what was politically necessary!'

'And that is what I must do now, Dalinar. I wish I could explain. Forgive me.'

He ignored Dalinar's pleas, limping down the stairs. Moving stiffly, the old man climbed into a palanquin and was carried away.

Dalinar sank down on the steps.

I tried my best to hide this, the Stormfather said.

'So we could continue living a lie?'

It is, in my experience, the thing men do best.

'Don't insult us.'

What? Is this not what you've been doing, these last six years? Pretending that you aren't a monster? Pretending you didn't kill her, Dalinar?

Dalinar winced. He made a fist, but there was nothing here he could fight. He dropped his hand to his side, shoulders drooping. Finally, he climbed to his feet and quietly trudged up the stone steps to his villa.

THE END OF

Part Four

INTERLUDES

◆ ◆

VENLI • RYSN • TEFT

After living for a week in a cave in Marat, Venli found herself missing the stone hermitage she'd been given outside Kholinar. Her new dwelling was even more austere, with only a single blanket for sleeping, and a simple cookfire upon which she prepared fish the crowds brought her.

She was growing dirty, rough. That was what the Fused seemed to want: a hermit living in the wilds. Apparently that was more convincing for the local crowds they brought to listen to her – most of whom were former Thaylen slaves. She was instructed to speak of 'Passion' and emotion more often than she had in Alethkar.

'My people are dead now,' Venli said to Destruction, repeating the now-familiar speech. 'They fell in that last assault, singing as they drew the storm. I remain, but my people's work is done.'

Those words *hurt*. Her people couldn't be *completely* gone ... could they?

'The day now belongs to your Passion,' she continued to Command. 'We had named ourselves "listeners" because of the songs we heard. These are your heritage, but you are not to just listen, but sing. Adopt the rhythms and Passions of your ancestors! You must sail to battle. For the future, for your children! And for us. Those who died that you might exist.'

She turned away, as instructed that she do after the end of each speech. She wasn't allowed to answer questions any longer, not since she'd talked with some of these singers about the specific history of her people. It made her wonder. Did the Fused and the Voidspren *fear* the heritage of her people, even as they used her for their purposes? Or did they not trust her for other reasons?

She put her hand to her pouch. Odium didn't seem to know that she'd been in that vision with Dalinar Kholin. Behind, a Voidspren led the Thaylen singers away. Venli moved toward her cave, but then hesitated. A Fused sat on the rocks just above the opening.

'Ancient One?' she asked.

He grinned at her and giggled.

Another one of those.

She started into the cave, but he dropped and seized her under the arms, then carried her into the sky. Venli prevented herself – with difficulty – from trying to batter him away. The Fused never touched her, not even the crazy ones, without orders. Indeed, this one flew her down to one of the many ships at the harbor, where Rine – the tall Fused who had accompanied her during her first days preaching in Alethkar – stood at the prow. He glanced toward her as she was landed – roughly – on the deck.

She hummed to Conceit at her treatment.

He hummed to Spite. A small acknowledgment of a wrong done, the best she'd get out of him, so she hummed to Satisfaction in response.

'Ancient One?' she asked to Craving.

'You are to accompany us as we sail,' he said to Command. 'You may wash yourself in the cabin as we go, if you wish. There is water.'

Venli hummed to Craving and looked toward the main cabin. Craving slipped into Abashment as she considered the sheer *size* of the fleet that was launching around her. Hundreds of ships, which must have been filled with thousands of singers, were sailing from coves all along the coast. They dotted the seas like rockbuds on the plains.

'Now?' she asked to Abashment. 'I wasn't prepared! I didn't know!'

'You may wish to grab hold of something. The storm will soon arrive.'

She looked to the west. A storm? She hummed to Craving again.

'Ask,' Rine said to Command.

'I can easily see the strength of the grand assault force we've gathered. But ... why do we need such? Are not the Fused enough of an army themselves?'

'Cowardice?' he asked to Derision. 'You do not wish to fight?'

'I simply seek to understand.'

Rine changed to a new rhythm, one she rarely heard. The Rhythm of Withdrawal – one of the only new rhythms that had a calm tone. 'The strongest and most skilled of our number have yet to awaken – but even if we were all awake, we would not fight this war alone. This world will not be ours; we fight to give it to you, our descendants. When it is won, our vengeance taken and our homeland secured at long last, we will sleep. Finally.'

He then pointed at the cabin. 'Go prepare. We will sail swiftly, with Odium's own storm to guide us.'

As if in agreement with his words, red lightning flashed on the western horizon.

RYSN

R ysn was bored.

Once she'd walked to the farthest reaches of Roshar, trading with the isolationist Shin. Once she'd sailed with her babsk to Icewater and cut a deal with pirates. Once she'd climbed Reshi greatshells, which were as large as towns.

Now she kept Queen Fen's ledgers.

It was a good job, with an office in the Thaylen Gemstone Reserve. Vstim – her former babsk – had traded favors to get her the job. Her apprenticeship finished, she was a free woman. No longer a student. Now a master.

Of boredom.

She sat in her chair, doodling at the edges of a Liaforan word puzzle. Rysn could balance while sitting, though she couldn't feel her legs and embarrassingly couldn't control certain bodily functions. She had to rely upon her porters to move her.

Career, over. Freedom, over. Life, *over*.

She sighed and pushed away her word puzzle. Time to get back to work. Her duties included annotating the queen's pending mercantile contracts with references to previous ones, keeping the queen's personal vault in the Gemstone Reserve, preparing weekly expenditure reports, and accounting the queen's salary as a portion of taxable income from various Thaylen interests at home and abroad.

Wheeeeeeeee.

She had an audit today, which had prevented her from attending Fen's meeting with the monarchs. She might have enjoyed seeing the Blackthorn and the Azish emperor. Well, the other aides would bring her word once the meeting was through. For now, she prepared for her audit, working by spherelight, as the reserve didn't have windows.

The walls of her office were blank. She'd originally hung souvenirs from her years traveling, but those had reminded her of a life she could no longer have. A life full of promise. A life that had ended when she'd stupidly fallen from the head of a greatshell, and landed here, in this cripple's chair. Now, the only memento she kept was a single pot of Shin grass.

Well, that and the little creature sleeping among the blades. Chiri-Chiri breathed softly, rippling the too-dumb grass, which didn't pull into burrows. It grew in something called soil, which was like crem that never hardened.

Chiri-Chiri herself was a small winged beast a little longer than Rysn's outstretched palm. The Reshi named her a larkin, and though she was the size of a large cremling, she had the snout, carapace, and build of a creature far more grand. An axehound, perhaps, with wings. A lithe little flying predator – though, for all her dangerous appearance, she sure did like to nap.

As Rysn worked, Chiri-Chiri finally stirred and peeked out from the grass, then made a series of clicking sounds with her jaw. She climbed down onto the desk and eyed the diamond mark Rysn was using for light.

'No,' Rysn said, double-checking numbers in her ledger.

Chiri-Chiri clicked again, slinking toward the gem.

'You *just* ate,' Rysn said, then used her palm to shoo the larkin back. 'I need that for light.'

Chiri-Chiri clicked in annoyance, then flew – wings beating very quickly – to the upper reaches of the room, where she settled onto one of her favorite perches, the lintel above the doorway.

A short time later, a knock at the door interrupted Rysn's tedium. 'Come,' she said. Her man, Wmlak – who was half assistant, half porter – poked his head in.

'Let me guess,' Rysn said, 'the auditor is early.' They always were.

'Yes, but . . .'

Behind Wmlak, Rysn caught sight of a familiar flat-topped, conical

549

hat. Wmlak stepped back and gestured toward an old man in blue and red robes, his Thaylen eyebrows tucked behind his ears. Spry for a man past his seventieth year, Vstim had a wise but unyielding way about him. Inoffensively calculating. He carried a small box under his arm.

Rysn gasped in delight; once, she would have leaped to her feet to embrace him. Now she could only sit there and gape. 'But you were off to trade in New Natanan!'

'The seas are not safe these days,' Vstim said. 'And the queen requested my aid in difficult negotiations with the Alethi. I have returned, with some reluctance, to accept an appointment from Her Majesty.'

An appointment . . .

'In the *government*?' Rysn asked.

'Minister of trade, and royal liaison to the guild of shipping merchants.'

Rysn could only gape further. That was the highest civilian appointment *in the kingdom*. 'But . . . Babsk, you'll have to *live* in Thaylen City!'

'Well, I *am* feeling my age these days.'

'Nonsense. You're as lively as I am.' Rysn glanced at her legs. 'More.'

'Not so lively that I wouldn't mind a seat . . .'

She realized he was still standing in the doorway to her office. Even all these months after her accident, she pushed with her arms as if to spring up and fetch him a seat. Idiot.

'Please, sit!' she said, waving toward the room's other chair. He settled down and placed his box on the table while she twisted to do something to welcome him, leaning over – precariously – to get the teapot. The tea was cold, unfortunately. Chiri-Chiri had drained the gemstone in her fabrial hotplate.

'I can't believe you'd agree to settle down!' she said, handing him a cup.

'Some would say that the opportunity offered me is far too important to refuse.'

'Storm that,' Rysn said. 'Staying in one city will wilt you – you'll spend your days doing paperwork and being bored.'

'Rysn,' he said, taking her hand. 'Child.'

She looked away. Chiri-Chiri flew down and landed on her head, clicking angrily at Vstim.

'I promise I'm not going to hurt her,' the old man said, grinning and releasing Rysn's hand. 'Here, I brought you something. See?' He held up a ruby chip.

Chiri-Chiri considered, then hovered down above his hand – not touching it – and sucked the Stormlight out. It flew to her in a little stream, and she clicked happily, then zipped over to the pot of grass and wriggled into it, peeking out at Vstim.

'You still have the grass, I see,' he said.

'You ordered me to keep it.'

'You're now a master merchant, Rysn! You needn't obey the orders of a doddering old man.'

The grass rustled as Chiri-Chiri shifted. She was too big to hide in it, though that never stopped her from trying.

'Chiri-Chiri likes it,' Rysn said. 'Maybe because it can't move. Kind of like me . . .'

'Have you tried that Radiant who—'

'Yes. He can't heal my legs. It's been too long since my accident, which is appropriate. This is my consequence – payment for a contract I entered into willingly the moment I climbed down the side of that greatshell.'

'You *don't* have to lock yourself away, Rysn.'

'This is a good job. You yourself got it for me.'

'Because you refused to go on further trading expeditions!'

'What good would I be? One must trade from a position of power, something I can never do again. Besides, an exotic goods merchant who can't walk? You know how much hiking is required.'

Vstim took her hand again. 'I thought you were frightened. I thought you wanted something safe and secure. But I've been listening. Hmalka has told me—'

'You spoke to my superior?'

'People talk.'

'My work has been exemplary,' Rysn said.

'It isn't your work she's worried about.' He turned and brushed the grass, drawing Chiri-Chiri's attention to his hand. She narrowed her eyes at it. 'Do you remember what I told you, when you cut out that grass?'

'That I was to keep it. Until it no longer seemed odd.'

'You've always been so quick to make assumptions. About yourself, now, more than others. Here, perhaps this will . . . anyway, have a look.' Vstim handed her the box.

She frowned, then slid off the wooden lid. Inside was a wound-up cord of white rope. Beside that, a slip of paper? Rysn took out the sheet, reading it.

'A deed of ownership?' she whispered. 'To a *ship*?'

'Brand new,' Vstim said. 'A three-masted frigate, the largest I've ever owned – with fabrial stabilizers for storms, of the finest Thaylen engineering. I had her built in the shipyards of Klna City, which luckily sheltered her from both storms. While I've given the rest of my fleet – what's left of it – to the queen for use against the invasion, this one I reserved.'

'*Wandersail*,' Rysn said, reading the ship's name. 'Babsk, you *are* a romantic. Don't tell me you believe that old story?'

'One can believe in a story without believing it happened.' He smiled. 'Whose rules are you following, Rysn? Who is forcing you to stay here? Take the ship. Go! I wish to fund your initial trade run, as an investment. After that, you'll have to do well to maintain a vessel of this size!'

Rysn recognized the white rope now. It was a captain's cord some twenty feet long, used as a traditional Thaylen mark of ownership. She'd wrap it in her colors and string it in the rigging of her ship.

It was a gift worth a fortune.

'I can't take this,' she said, putting the box on the desk. 'I'm sorry. I—'

He pushed the cord into her hands. 'Just think about it, Rysn. Humor an old man who can no longer travel.'

She held the rope and found her eyes watering. 'Bother. Babsk, I have an *auditor* coming today! I need to be composed and ready to account the queen's vault!'

'Fortunately, the auditor is an old friend who has seen much worse from you than a few tears.'

'. . . But you're the minister of trade!'

'They were going to make me go to a stuffy meeting with old Kholin and his soldiers,' Vstim said, leaning in, 'but I insisted on coming to do this. I've always wanted to see the queen's vault in person.'

Rysn wiped her tears, trying to recover some of her decorum. 'Well, let's be to it then. I assure you, everything is in order.'

⁂

The Sphere Vault's thick steel door required three numbers to open, each rolled into a different dial, in three separate rooms. Rysn and other scribes knew one number, the door guards protected another, and an auditor

– like Vstim – was typically given a third by the queen or the minister of the treasury. All were changed at random intervals.

Rysn knew for a fact that this was mostly for show. In a world of Shardblades, the real defense of the vault was in the layers of guards who surrounded the building, and – more importantly – in the careful auditing of its contents. Though novels were full of stories of the vault being robbed, the only real thefts had occurred through embezzlement.

Rysn moved her dial to the proper number, then pulled the lever in her room. The vault door finally opened with a resounding thump, and she scrambled her dial and called for Wmlak. Her porter entered, then pushed down on the back handles of her chair, lifting the front legs so he could wheel it out to meet the others.

Vstim stood by the now-open vault door with several soldiers. Today's inner door guard – Tlik – stood with crossbow at the ready, barring entry. There was a slot that let the men stationed in the vault communicate with those outside, but the door couldn't be opened from within.

'Scheduled accounting of the queen's personal vault,' Rysn said to him. 'Daily passcode: lockstep.'

Tlik nodded, stepping back and lowering his crossbow. Vstim entered with ledger in hand, trailed by a member of the Queen's Guard: a rough-looking man with a shaved head and spiked eyebrows. Once they were in, Wmlak wheeled Rysn through the vault door, down a short corridor, and into a little alcove, where another guard – Fladm, today – waited.

Her porter brushed off his hands, then nodded to her and retreated. Tlik shut the vault door after him, the metal making a deep *thump* as it locked into place. The inner vault guards didn't like anyone coming in who wasn't specifically authorized – and that included her servant. She'd have to rely on the guards to move her now – but unfortunately, her large wheeled chair was too bulky to fit between the rows of shelves in the main vault.

Rysn felt a healthy dose of shame in front of her former babsk as she was taken – like a sack of roots – from her chair with rear wheels to a smaller chair with poles along the sides. Being carried was the most humiliating part.

The guards left her usual chair in the alcove, near the steps down to the lower level. Then, Tlik and the guardsman the queen had sent – Rysn didn't know his name – took the poles and carried her into the main vault chamber.

Even here, in this job where she sat most of the time, her inability was a huge inconvenience. Her embarrassment was exacerbated as Chiri-Chiri – who wasn't allowed in the vault for practical reasons – flitted by in a buzz of wings. How had *she* gotten in?

Tlik chuckled, but Rysn only sighed.

The main vault chamber was filled with metal racks, like bookcases, containing display boxes of gemstones. It smelled stale. Of a place that never changed, and was never intended to change.

The guards carried her down one of the narrow rows, light from spheres tied to their belts providing the only illumination. Rysn carried the captain's rope in her lap, and fingered it with one hand. Surely she couldn't take this offer. It was too generous. Too incredible.

Too difficult.

'So dark!' Vstim said. 'A room full of a million gemstones, and it's *dark*?'

'Most gems never leave,' Rysn said. 'The personal merchant vaults are on the lower level, and there's some light to those, with the spheres every-one has been bringing lately. These, though . . . they're always here.'

Possession of these gems changed frequently, but it was all done with numbers in a ledger. It was a quirk of the Thaylen system of underwrit-ing trades; as long as everyone was confident that these gemstones were here, large sums could change hands without risk of anything being stolen.

Each gemstone was carefully annotated with numbers inscribed both on a plate glued to its bottom and on the rack that held it. Those num-bers were what people bought and sold – Rysn was shocked by how few people actually asked to come down and view the thing they were trading to own.

'0013017-36!' Vstim said. 'The Benval Diamond! I owned that way back when. Memorized the number even. Huh. You know, it's smaller than I thought it would be.'

She and the two guards led Vstim to the back wall, which held a series of smaller metal vault doors. The main vault behind them was silent; no other scribes were working today, though Chiri-Chiri did flit past. She hovered down toward the queen's guardsman – eyeing the spheres on his belt – but Rysn snatched her from the air.

Chiri-Chiri griped, buzzing her wings against Rysn's hand and clicking. Rysn blushed, but held tight. 'Sorry.'

'Must be like a buffet for her down here!' Tlik said.

'A buffet of empty plates,' Rysn said. 'Keep an eye on your belt, Tlik.'

The two guards set her chair down near a specific vault. With her free hand, Rysn dug a key from her pocket and handed it to Vstim. 'Go ahead. Vault Thirteen.'

Vstim unlocked and swung open the smaller vault-within-the-vault, which was roughly the size of a closet.

Light poured from it.

The shelves inside were filled with gemstones, spheres, jewelry, and even some mundane objects like letters and an old knife. But the most stunning item in the collection was obviously the large ruby on the center shelf. The size of a child's head, it glowed brightly.

The King's Drop. Gemstones of its size weren't unheard of – most greatshells had gemhearts as big. What made the King's Drop unique was that it was still glowing – over *two hundred* years after being first locked into the vault.

Vstim touched it with one finger. The light shone with such brilliance that the room seemed almost to be in daylight, though shaded bloodred by the gemstone's color.

'Amazing,' Vstim whispered.

'As far as scholars can tell,' Rysn said, 'the King's Drop never loses its Stormlight. A stone this large *should* have run out after a month. It's something about the crystal lattice, the lack of flaws and imperfections.'

'They say it's a chunk off the Stone of Ten Dawns.'

'Another story?' Rysn said. 'You *are* a romantic.'

Her former babsk smiled, then placed a cloth shade over the gemstone to reduce its glare so it wouldn't interfere with their work. He opened his ledger. 'Let's start with the smaller gemstones and work our way up, shall we?'

Rysn nodded.

The queen's guard killed Tlik.

He did it with a knife, right into the neck. Tlik dropped without a word, though the sound of the knife being ripped free shocked Rysn. The treacherous guard knocked against her chair, toppling her over as he slashed at Vstim.

The enemy underestimated the merchant's spryness. Vstim dodged backward into the queen's vault, screaming, 'Murder! Robbery! Raise the alarm!'

Rysn untangled herself from her toppled chair and, panicked, pulled herself away by her arms, dragging legs like cordwood. The murderer reached into the vault to deal with her babsk, and she heard a grunt.

A moment later, the traitor stepped out, carrying a large red light in his hand. The King's Drop, shining brightly enough despite its black wrapping cloth. Rysn caught a glimpse of Vstim collapsed on the floor inside the vault, holding his side.

The traitor kicked the door closed – locking the old merchant away. He glanced toward her.

And a crossbow bolt hit him.

'Thief in the vault!' Fladm's voice said. 'Alarm!'

Rysn pulled herself to a row of gemstone racks. Behind her, the thief took a *second* crossbow bolt, but didn't seem to notice. How . . .

The thief stepped over and picked up poor Tlik's crossbow. Footsteps and calls indicated that several guards from the lower level had heard Fladm, and were coming up the steps. The thief fired the crossbow once down a nearby row, and a shout of pain from Fladm indicated it had connected. Another guardsman arrived a second later and attacked the thief with his sword.

He should have run for help! Rysn thought as she huddled by the shelf. The thief took a cut along the face from the sword, then set his prize down and caught the guard's arm. The two struggled, and Rysn watched the cut on the thief's face reknit.

He was *healing*? Could . . . could this man be a *Knight Radiant*?

Rysn's eyes flicked toward the large ruby the thief had set down. Four more guards joined the fight, obviously assuming they could subdue one man on their own.

Sit back. Let them handle it.

Chiri-Chiri suddenly darted past, ignoring the combatants and making for the glowing gemstone. Rysn lunged forward – well, more *flopped* forward – to grab at the larkin, but missed. Chiri-Chiri landed on the cloth containing the enormous ruby.

Nearby, the thief stabbed one of the guards. Rysn winced at the awful sight of their struggle, lit by the ruby, then crawled forward – dragging her legs – and snatched the gemstone.

Chiri-Chiri clicked at her in annoyance as Rysn dragged the ruby with her around the corner. Another guard screamed. They were dropping quickly.

Have to do something. Can't just sit here, can I?

Rysn clutched the gemstone and looked down the row between shelves. An impossible distance, hundreds of feet, to the corridor and the exit. The door was locked, but she could call through the communication slot for help.

But why? If five guards couldn't handle the thief, what could one crippled woman do?

My babsk is locked in the queen's vault. Bleeding.

She looked down the long row again, then used the cord Vstim had given her to tie the ruby's cloth closed around it, and attached it to her ankle so she wouldn't have to carry it. Then she started pulling herself along the shelves. Chiri-Chiri rode behind on the ruby, and its light dimmed. Everyone else was struggling for their lives, but the little larkin was feasting.

Rysn made faster progress than she had expected to, though soon her arms began to ache. Behind, the fighting stilled, the last guard's shout cutting off.

Rysn redoubled her efforts, pulling herself along toward the exit, reaching the alcove where they'd left her chair. Here, she found blood.

Fladm lay at the threshold of the entry corridor, a bolt in him, his own crossbow on the floor beside him. Rysn collapsed a couple of feet from him, muscles burning. Spheres on his belt illuminated her chair and the steps down to the lower vault level. No more help would be coming from down there.

Past Fladm's body, the corridor led to the door out. 'Help!' she shouted. 'Thief!'

She thought she heard voices on the other side, through the communication slot. But . . . it would take the guards outside time to get it open, as they didn't know all three codes. Maybe that was good. The thief couldn't get out until they opened it, right?

Of course, that meant she was trapped inside with him while Vstim bled. . . .

The silence from behind haunted her. Rysn heaved herself to Fladm's corpse and took his crossbow and bolts, then pulled herself toward the steps. She turned over, putting the enormous ruby beside her, and pushed up so that she was seated against the wall.

She waited, sweating, struggling to point the unwieldy weapon into the darkness of the vault. Footsteps sounded somewhere inside, coming closer. Trembling, she swung the crossbow back and forth, searching for motion. Only then did she notice that the crossbow *wasn't loaded*.

She gasped, then hastily pulled out a bolt. She looked from it to the crossbow, helpless. You were supposed to cock the weapon by stepping into a stirrup on the front, then pulling it upward. Easy to do, if you could *step* in the first place.

A figure emerged from the darkness. The bald guard, his clothing ripped, a sword dripping blood in his shadowed hand.

Rysn lowered the crossbow. What did it matter? Did she think she could fight? That man could just heal anyway.

She was alone.

Helpless.

Live or die. Did she care?

I . . .

Yes. Yes, I care! I want to sail my own ship!

A sudden blur darted out of the darkness and flew around the thief. Chiri-Chiri moved with blinding speed, hovering about the man, drawing his attention.

Rysn frantically placed the crossbow bolt, then took the captain's cord off the ruby's sack and tied one end to the stirrup at the front of the crossbow. She tied the other end to the back of her heavy wooden chair. That done, she spared a glance for Chiri-Chiri, then hesitated.

The larkin was *feeding* off the thief. A line of light streamed from him, but it was a strange dark *violet* light. Chiri-Chiri flew about, drawing it from the man, whose face *melted* away, revealing marbled skin underneath.

A parshman? Wearing some kind of disguise?

No, a Voidbringer. He growled and said something in an unfamiliar language, batting at Chiri-Chiri, who buzzed away into the darkness.

Rysn gripped the crossbow tightly with one hand, then with the other she shoved her chair down the long stairway.

It fell in a clatter, the rope playing out after it. Rysn grabbed on to the crossbow with the other hand. The cord pulled taut as the chair jerked to a stop partway down the steps, and she yanked back on the crossbow at the same time, hanging on for all she was worth.

Click.

She cut the rope free with her belt knife. The thief lunged for her, and she twisted – screaming – and pulled the firing lever on the crossbow. She didn't know how to aim properly, but the thief obligingly loomed over her.

The crossbow bolt hit him right in the chin.

He dropped and, blessedly, fell still. Whatever power had been healing him was gone, consumed by Chiri-Chiri.

The larkin buzzed over and landed on her stomach, clicking happily.

'Thank you,' Rysn whispered, sweat streaming down the sides of her face. 'Thank you, *thank you.*' She hesitated. 'Are you . . . bigger?'

Chiri-Chiri clicked happily.

Vstim. I need the second set of keys.

And . . . that ruby, the King's Drop. The Voidbringers had been trying to steal it. Why?

Rysn tossed aside the crossbow, then pulled herself toward the vault door.

TEFT

Teft could function.

You learned how to do that. How to cling to the normal parts of your life so that people wouldn't be *too* worried. So that you wouldn't be *too* undependable.

He stumbled sometimes. That eroded trust, to the point where it was hard to keep telling himself that he could handle it. He knew, deep down, that he'd end up alone again. The men of Bridge Four would tire of digging him out of trouble.

But for now, Teft functioned. He nodded to Malata, who was working the Oathgate, then led his men across the platform and down the ramp toward Urithiru. They were a subdued group. Few grasped the meaning of what they'd learned, but they all sensed that something had *changed*.

Made perfect sense to Teft. It couldn't be easy, now, could it. Not in his storming life.

A winding path through corridors and a stairwell led them back toward their barracks. As they walked, a woman appeared in the hallway beside Teft, roughly his height, glowing with soft blue-white light. Storming spren. He pointedly did not look at her.

You have Words to speak, Teft, she said in his mind.

'Storm you,' he muttered.

You have started on this path. When will you tell the others the oaths you have sworn?

'I didn't—'

She turned away from him suddenly, becoming alert, looking down the corridor toward the Bridge Four barracks.

'What?' Teft stopped. 'Something wrong?'

Something is very wrong. Run quickly, Teft!

He charged out in front of the men, causing them to shout after him. He scrambled to the door into their barracks and threw it open.

The scent of blood immediately assaulted him. The Bridge Four common room was in shambles, and blood stained the floor. Teft shouted, rushing through the room to find three corpses near the back. He dropped his spear and fell to his knees beside Rock, Bisig, and Eth.

Still breathing, Teft thought, feeling at Rock's neck. *Still breathing. Remember Kaladin's training, you fool.*

'Check the others!' he shouted as more bridgemen joined him. He pulled off his coat and used it on Rock's wounds; the Horneater was sliced up good, a half dozen cuts that looked like they'd come from a knife.

'Bisig's alive,' Peet called. 'Though . . . storms, that's a Shardblade wound!'

'Eth . . .' Lopen said, kneeling beside the third body. 'Storms . . .'

Teft hesitated. Eth had been the one carrying the Honorblade today. Dead.

They came for the Blade, he realized.

Huio – who was better at field medicine than Teft – took over ministering to Rock. Blood on his hands, Teft stumbled back.

'We need Renarin,' Peet said. 'It's Rock's best chance!'

'But where did he go?' Lyn said. 'He was at the meeting, but left.' She looked toward Laran, one of the other former messengers – fastest among them. 'Run for the guard post! They should have a spanreed to contact the Oathgate!'

Laran dashed out of the room. Nearby, Bisig groaned. His eyes fluttered open. His entire arm was grey, and his uniform had been sliced through.

'Bisig!' Peet asked. 'Storms, what happened!'

'Thought . . . thought it was one of us,' Bisig muttered. 'I didn't really look – until he attacked.' He leaned back, groaning, closing his eyes. 'He had on a bridgeman coat.'

'Stormfather!' Leyten said. 'Did you see the face?'

Bisig nodded. 'Nobody I recognize. A short man, Alethi. Bridge Four coat, lieutenant's knots on the shoulder . . .'

Lopen, nearby, frowned, then glanced toward Teft.

A Bridge Four officer's coat, worn as a disguise. *Teft's* coat, which he'd sold weeks ago in the market. To get a few spheres.

He stumbled back as they hovered around Rock and Bisig, then fled through a falling patch of shamespren into the hallway outside.

PART
FIVE

New Unity

THE KNIGHTS RADIANT • ASH • NAVANI •
ADOLIN • TARAVANGIAN • YANAGAWN •
PALONA • VYRE • WIT

FIVE AND A HALF YEARS AGO

Dalinar came to himself, gasping, in the cabin of a stormwagon. Heart pounding, he spun about, kicking aside empty bottles and lifting his fists. Outside, the riddens of a storm washed the walls with rain.

What in the Almighty's tenth name had *that* been? One moment, he'd been lying in his bunk. The next, he had been ... Well, he didn't rightly remember. What was the drink doing to him now?

Someone rapped on his door.

'Yes?' Dalinar said, his voice hoarse.

'The caravan is preparing to leave, Brightlord.'

'Already? The rain hasn't even stopped yet.'

'I think they're, um, eager to be rid of us, sir.'

Dalinar pushed open the door. Felt stood outside, a lithe man with long, drooping mustaches and pale skin. Had to have some Shin blood in him, judging by those eyes.

Though Dalinar hadn't expressly said what he intended to do out here in Hexi, his soldiers seemed to understand. Dalinar wasn't sure whether he should be proud of their loyalty, or scandalized by how easily they accepted his intention to visit the Nightwatcher. Of course, one of them – Felt himself – had been this way before.

Outside, the caravan workers hitched up their chulls. They'd agreed to drop him off here, along their path, but refused to take him farther toward the Valley.

'Can you get us the rest of the way?' Dalinar asked.

'Sure,' Felt said. 'We're less than a day off.'

'Then tell the good caravan master that we will take our wagons and split from him here. Pay him what he asked, Felt, and then some on top.'

'If you say so, Brightlord. Seems that having a Shardbearer along with him should be payment enough.'

'Explain that, in part, we're buying his silence.'

Dalinar waited until the rain had mostly stopped, then threw on his coat and stepped out to join Felt, walking at the front of the wagons. He didn't feel like being cooped up any longer.

He'd expected this land to look like the Alethi plains. After all, the windswept flatlands of Hexi were not unlike those of his homeland. Yet strangely, there wasn't a rockbud in sight. The ground was covered in wrinkles, like frozen ripples in a pond, perhaps two or three inches deep. They were crusty on the stormward side, covered with lichen. On the leeward side, grass spread on the ground, flattened.

The sparse trees here were scrawny, hunched-over things with this-tle leaves. Their branches bent so far leeward, they almost touched the ground. It was like one of the Heralds had strolled through this place and bent everything sideways. The nearby mountainsides were bare, blasted and scoured raw.

'Not far now, sir,' Felt said. The short man barely came up to the middle of Dalinar's chest.

'When you came before,' Dalinar said. 'What . . . what did you see?'

'To be frank, sir, nothing. She didn't come to me. Doesn't visit every-one, you see.' He clapped his hands, then breathed on them. It had been winter, lately. 'You'll want to go in right after dark. Alone, sir. She avoids groups.'

'Any idea why she didn't visit you?'

'Well, best I could figure, she doesn't like foreigners.'

'I might have trouble too.'

'You're a little less foreign, sir.'

Up ahead, a group of small dark creatures burst from behind a tree and shot into the air, clumped together. Dalinar gaped at their speed and agility. 'Chickens?' he said. Little black ones, each the size of a man's fist.

Felt chuckled. 'Yes, wild chickens range this far east. Can't see what they'd be doing on this side of the mountains though.'

The chickens eventually picked another bent-over tree and settled in its branches.

'Sir,' Felt said. 'Forgive me for asking, but you sure you want to do this? You'll be in her power, in there. And you don't get to pick the cost.'

Dalinar said nothing, feet crunching on fans of weeds that trembled and rattled when he touched them. There was so much emptiness here in Hexi. In Alethkar, you couldn't go more than a day or two without running into a farming village. They hiked for a good three hours, during which Dalinar felt both an anxiety to be finished and – at the same time – a reluctance to progress. He had enjoyed his recent sense of purpose. Simultaneously, his decision had given him excuses. If he was going to the Nightwatcher anyway, then why fight the drink?

He'd spent much of the trip intoxicated. Now, with the alcohol running out, the voices of the dead seemed to chase him. They were worst when he tried to sleep, and he felt a dull ache behind his eyes from poor rest.

'Sir?' Felt eventually asked. 'Look there.' He pointed to a thin strip of green painting the windswept mountainside.

As they continued, Dalinar got a better view. The mountains split into a valley here, and since the opening pointed to the northeast, foothills shielded the interior from highstorms.

So plant life had *exploded* inside. Vines, ferns, flowers, and grasses grew together in a wall of underbrush. Trees stretched above them, and these weren't the durable stumpweights of his homeland. These were gnarled, tall, and twisted, with branches that wound together. They were overgrown with draping moss and vines, lifespren bobbing about them in plenitude.

It all piled atop itself, reeds and branches sticking out in all directions, ferns so overgrown with vines that they drooped beneath the weight. It reminded Dalinar of a battlefield. A grand tapestry, depicting people locked in mortal combat, each one struggling for advantage.

'How does one enter?' Dalinar asked. 'How do you pass through *that*?'

'There are some trails,' Felt said. 'If you look hard enough. Shall we camp here, sir? You can scout out a path tomorrow, and make your final decision?'

He nodded, and they set up at the edge of the breach, close enough he could smell the humidity inside. They set up the wagons as a barrier between two trees, and the men soon had tents assembled. They were quick to get a fire going. There was a . . . feeling to the place. Like you could hear all of those plants growing. The valley shivered and cracked. When wind blew out, it was hot and muggy.

The sun set behind the mountains, plunging them into darkness. Soon after, Dalinar started inward. He couldn't wait another day. The sound of it lured him. The vines rustling, moving as tiny animals scampered between them. Leaves curling. The men didn't call after him; they understood his decision.

He stepped into the musty, damp valley, vines brushing his head. He could barely see in the darkness, but Felt had been right – trails revealed themselves as vines and branches bent away from him, allowing Dalinar entrance with the same reluctance as guards allowing an unfamiliar man into the presence of their king.

He had hoped for the Thrill to aid him here. This was a challenge, was it not? He felt nothing, not even a hint.

He trudged through the darkness, and suddenly felt stupid. What was he doing here? Chasing a pagan superstition while the rest of the highprinces gathered to punish Gavilar's killers? He should be at the Shattered Plains. *That* was where he'd change himself, where he would go back to the man he'd been before. He wanted to escape the drink? He just needed to summon Oathbringer and find someone to fight.

Who knew what was out there in this forest? If he were a bandit, this was certainly where he would set up. People must flock here. Damnation! He wouldn't be surprised to discover that someone had started all this simply to draw in unsuspecting marks.

Wait. What was that? A sound different from scurries in the underbrush or vines withdrawing. He stopped in place, listening. It was . . .

Weeping.

Oh, Almighty above. No.

He heard a boy weeping, pleading for his life. It sounded like Adolin. Dalinar turned from the sound, searching the darkness. Other screams and pleas joined that one, people burning as they died.

In a moment of panic, he turned to run back the way he'd come. He immediately tripped in the underbrush.

He collapsed against rotten wood, vines twisting under his fingers.

People screamed and howled all around, the sounds echoing in the near-absolute darkness.

Frantic, he summoned Oathbringer and stumbled to his feet, then began slashing, trying to clear space. Those *voices*. All around him!

He pushed past a tree trunk, fingers digging into the hanging moss and wet bark. Was the entrance this way?

Suddenly he saw himself in the Unclaimed Hills, fighting those traitorous parshmen. He saw himself killing, and hacking, and murdering. He saw his lust, eyes wide and teeth clenched in a dreadful grin. A skull's grin.

He saw himself strangling Elhokar, who had never possessed his father's poise or charm. Dalinar took the throne. It should have been his anyway.

His armies poured into Herdaz, then Jah Keved. He became a king of kings, a mighty conqueror whose accomplishments far overshadowed those of his brother. Dalinar forged a unified Vorin empire that covered half of Roshar. An unparalleled feat!

And he saw them burn.

Hundreds of villages. Thousands upon *thousands* of people. It was the only way. If a town resisted, you burned it to the ground. You slaughtered any who fought back, and you left the corpses of their loved ones to feed the scavengers. You sent terror before you like a storm until your enemies surrendered.

The Rift would be but the first in a long line of examples. He saw himself standing upon the heaped corpses, laughing. Yes, he had escaped the drink. He had become something grand and terrible.

This was his future.

Gasping, Dalinar dropped to his knees in the dark forest and allowed the voices to swarm around him. He heard Evi among them, crying as she burned to death, unseen, unknown. Alone. He let Oathbringer slip from his fingers and shatter to mist.

The crying faded until it was distant.

Son of Honor . . . a new sound whispered on the winds, a voice like the rustling of the trees.

He opened his eyes to find himself in a tiny clearing, bathed in starlight. A shadow moved in the darkness beyond the trees, accompanied by the noise of twisting vines and blowing grass.

Hello, human. You smell of desperation. The feminine voice was like a hundred overlapping whispers. The elongated figure moved among the trees ringing the clearing, stalking him like a predator.

'They . . . they say you can change a man,' Dalinar said, weary.

The Nightwatcher *seeped* from the darkness. She was a dark green mist, vaguely shaped like a crawling person. Too-long arms reached out, pulling her along as she floated above the ground. Her essence, like a tail, extended far behind her, weaving among tree trunks and disappearing into the forest.

Indistinct and vaporous, she flowed like a river or an eel, and the only part of her with any specific detail was her smooth, feminine face. She glided toward him until her nose was mere inches from his own, her silken black eyes meeting his. Tiny *hands* sprouted from the misty sides of her head. They reached out, taking his face and touching it with a thousand cold – yet gentle – caresses.

What is it you wish of me? the Nightwatcher asked. *What boon drives you, Son of Honor? Son of Odium?*

She started to circle him. The tiny black hands kept touching his face, but their arms stretched out, becoming tentacles.

What would you like? she asked. *Renown? Wealth? Skill? Would you like to be able to swing a sword and never tire?*

'No,' Dalinar whispered.

Beauty? Followers? I can feed your dreams, make you glorious.

Her dark mists wrapped around him. The tiny tendrils tickled his skin. She brought her face right up to his again. *What is your boon?*

Dalinar blinked tears, listening to the sounds of the children dying in the distance, and whispered a single word.

'Forgiveness.'

The Nightwatcher's tendrils dodged away from his face, like splayed fingers. She leaned back, pursing her lips.

Perhaps it is possessions you wish, she said. *Spheres, gemstones. Shards. A Blade that bleeds darkness and cannot be defeated. I can give it to you.*

'Please,' Dalinar said, drawing in a ragged breath. 'Tell me. Can I . . . can I ever be forgiven?'

It wasn't what he'd intended to request.

He couldn't remember what he'd intended to request.

The Nightwatcher curled around him, agitated. *Forgiveness is no boon.*

What should I do *to you. What should I give you? Speak it, human. I—*

THAT IS ENOUGH, CHILD.

This new voice startled them both. If the Nightwatcher's voice was like whispering wind, this one was like tumbling stones. The Nightwatcher backed away from him in a sharp motion.

Hesitant, Dalinar turned and found a woman with brown skin – the color of darkwood bark – standing at the edge of the clearing. She had a matronly build and wore a sweeping brown dress.

Mother? the Nightwatcher said. *Mother, he came to me. I was going to bless him.*

THANK YOU, CHILD, the woman said. BUT THIS BOON IS BEYOND YOU. She focused on Dalinar. YOU MAY ATTEND ME, DALINAR KHOLIN.

Numbed by the surreal spectacle, Dalinar stood up. 'Who are you?'

SOMEONE BEYOND YOUR AUTHORITY TO QUESTION. She strode into the forest, and Dalinar joined her. Moving through the underbrush seemed easier now, though the vines and branches pulled *toward* the strange woman. Her dress seemed to meld with it all, the brown cloth becoming bark or grass.

The Nightwatcher curled along beside them, her dark mist flowing through the holes in the underbrush. Dalinar found her distinctly unnerving.

YOU MUST FORGIVE MY DAUGHTER, the woman said. THIS IS THE FIRST TIME IN CENTURIES I'VE COME PERSONALLY TO SPEAK WITH ONE OF YOU.

'Then this isn't how it happens every time?'

OF COURSE NOT. I LET HER HOLD COURT HERE. The woman brushed her fingers through the Nightwatcher's misty hair. IT HELPS HER UNDER-STAND YOU.

Dalinar frowned, trying to make sense of all this. 'What . . . why did you choose to come out now?'

BECAUSE OF THE ATTENTION OTHERS PAY YOU. AND WHAT DID I TELL YOU OF DEMANDING QUESTIONS?

Dalinar shut his mouth.

WHY HAVE YOU COME HERE, HUMAN? DO YOU NOT SERVE HONOR, THE ONE YOU CALL ALMIGHTY? LOOK UNTO HIM FOR FORGIVENESS.

'I asked the ardents,' Dalinar said. 'I didn't get what I wanted.'

YOU GOT WHAT YOU DESERVED. THE TRUTH YOU HAVE CRAFTED FOR YOURSELVES.

'I am doomed then,' Dalinar whispered, stopping in place. He could still hear those voices. 'They weep, Mother.'

She looked back at him.

'I hear them when I close my eyes. All around me, begging me to save them. They're driving me mad.'

She contemplated him, the Nightwatcher twining around her legs, then around Dalinar's, then back again.

This woman . . . she was more than he could see. Vines from her dress curled into the earth, permeating everything. In that moment he knew that he was not seeing *her*, but instead a fragment with which he could interact.

This woman extended into eternity.

THIS WILL BE YOUR BOON. I WILL NOT MAKE OF YOU THE MAN YOU CAN BECOME. I WILL NOT GIVE YOU THE APTITUDE, OR THE STRENGTH, NOR WILL I TAKE FROM YOU YOUR COMPULSIONS.

BUT I WILL GIVE YOU . . . A PRUNING. A CAREFUL EXCISION TO LET YOU GROW. THE COST WILL BE HIGH.

'Please,' Dalinar said. 'Anything.'

She stepped back to him. IN DOING THIS, I PROVIDE FOR HIM A WEAPON. DANGEROUS, VERY DANGEROUS. YET, ALL THINGS MUST BE CULTIVATED. WHAT I TAKE FROM YOU WILL GROW BACK EVENTUALLY. THIS IS PART OF THE COST.

IT WILL DO ME WELL TO HAVE A PART OF YOU, EVEN IF YOU ULTI-MATELY BECOME HIS. YOU WERE ALWAYS BOUND TO COME TO ME. I CONTROL ALL THINGS THAT CAN BE GROWN, NURTURED.

THAT INCLUDES THE THORNS.

She seized him, and the trees descended, the branches, the vines. The forest curled around him and crept into the crevices around his eyes, under his fingernails, into his mouth and ears. Into his *pores*.

A BOON AND A CURSE, the Mother said. THAT IS HOW IT IS DONE. I WILL TAKE THESE THINGS FROM YOUR MIND. AND WITH THEM, I TAKE HER.

'I . . .' Dalinar tried to speak as plant life engulfed him. 'Wait!'

Remarkably, the vines and branches stopped. Dalinar hung there, speared by vines that had somehow pushed through his skin. There was no pain, but he felt the tendrils writhing inside his very veins.

SPEAK.

'You'll take . . .' He spoke with difficulty. 'You'll take Evi from me?'

ALL MEMORIES OF HER. THIS IS THE COST. SHOULD I FORBEAR?

Dalinar squeezed his eyes shut. Evi . . .

He had never deserved her.

'Do it,' he whispered.

The vines and branches surged forward and began to rip away pieces of him from the inside.

∴

Dalinar crawled from the forest the next morning. His men rushed to him, bringing water and bandages, though strangely he needed neither.

But he *was* tired. Very, *very* tired.

They propped him in the shade of his stormwagon, exhaustionspren spinning in the air. Malli – Felt's wife – quickly scribed a note via spanreed back to the ship.

Dalinar shook his head, memory fuzzy. What . . . what had happened? Had he really asked for *forgiveness*?

He couldn't fathom why. Had he felt that bad for failing . . . He stretched for the word. For failing . . .

Storms. His wife. Had he felt so bad for failing her by letting assassins claim her life? He searched his mind, and found that he couldn't recall what she looked like. No image of her face, no memories of their time together.

Nothing.

He did remember these last few years as a drunkard. The years before, spent in conquest. In fact, everything about his past seemed clear *except* her.

'Well?' Felt said, kneeling beside him. 'I assume it . . . happened.'

'Yes,' Dalinar said.

'Anything we need to know about?' he asked. 'I once heard of a man who visited here, and from then on, every person he touched fell *upward* instead of down.'

'You needn't worry. My curse is for me alone.' How strange, to be able to remember scenes where she had been, but not remember . . . um . . . storms take him, her *name*.

'What was my wife's name?' Dalinar asked.

'*Shshshsh*?' Felt said. It came out as a blur of sounds.

573

Dalinar started. She'd been taken completely? Had that . . . that been the cost? Yes . . . grief had caused him to suffer these last years. He'd suffered a breakdown at losing the woman he loved.

Well, he assumed that he'd loved her. Curious.

Nothing.

It seemed that the Nightwatcher had taken memories of his wife, and in so doing, given him the boon of peace. However, he *did* still feel sorrow and guilt for failing Gavilar, so he wasn't completely healed. He still wanted a bottle to numb the grief of losing his brother.

He would break that habit. When men abused drink under his command, he'd found that the solution was to work them hard, and not let them taste strong wines. He could do the same to himself. It wouldn't be easy, but he could manage it.

Dalinar relaxed, but felt like something else was missing inside of him. Something he couldn't identify. He listened to his men breaking camp, telling jokes now that they could leave. Beyond that, he heard rustling leaves. And beyond that, nothing. Shouldn't he have heard . . .

He shook his head. Almighty, what a foolish quest this had been. Had he really been so weak that he needed a *forest spren* to relieve his grief?

'I need to be in communication with the king,' Dalinar said, standing. 'Tell our men at the docks to contact the armies. By the time I arrive, I want to have battle maps and plans for the Parshendi conquest.'

He'd moped long enough. He had not always been the best of brothers, or the best of lighteyes. He'd failed to follow the Codes, and that had cost Gavilar his life.

Never again.

He straightened his uniform and glanced at Malli. 'Tell the sailors that while they're in port, they're to find me an Alethi copy of a book called *The Way of Kings*. I'd like to hear it read to me again. Last time, I wasn't in my right mind.'

They came from another world, using powers that we have been forbidden to touch. Dangerous powers, of spren and Surges. They destroyed their lands and have come to us begging.

—From the Eila Stele

A spry ocean wind blew in through the window, shaking Dalinar's hair as he stood in his villa in Thaylen City. The wind was sharply chill. Crisp. It didn't linger, but passed him by, turning the pages of his book with a quiet ruffling sound.

It fled from the Everstorm.

Crimson. Furious. *Burning.* The Everstorm's clouds flowed in from the west. Like blood billowing in water, each new thunderhead spurted from the one behind it, hemorrhaging fits of lightning. And beneath the storm – within its shadow, and upon those tempestuous seas – *ships* dotted the waves.

'Ships?' he whispered. 'They sailed *during* the storm?'

He controls it, the Stormfather said, his voice diminutive – like the pattering of rain. *He uses it, as Honor once used me.*

So much for stopping the enemy in the ocean. Dalinar's fledgling armada had fled to take shelter from the storm, and the enemy had sailed in uncontested. The coalition had shattered anyway; they wouldn't defend this city.

The storm slowed as it darkened the bay in front of Thaylen City — then seemed to stop. It dominated the sky to the west, but strangely did not proceed. Enemy ships landed in its shadow, many ramming right up onto the shores.

Amaram's troops flooded out of the gates to seize the ground between bay and city; there wasn't enough room for them to maneuver on top of the wall. The Alethi were field troops, and their best chance of victory would involve hitting the parshmen while they disembarked. Behind them, Thaylen troops mounted the wall, but they were not veterans. Their navy had always been their strength.

Dalinar could faintly hear General Khal on the street below, shouting for runners and scribes to send word to Urithiru, calling up the Alethi reinforcements. *Too slow*, Dalinar thought. Suitably deploying troops could take hours, and though Amaram was hustling his men, they weren't going to get together in time for a proper assault on the ships.

And then there were the Fused, dozens of which launched into the skies from the ships. He imagined his armies bottlenecked as they left the Oathgate, assaulted from the air as they tried to fight through the streets to reach the lower portion of the city.

It came together with a frightening beauty. Their armada fleeing the storm. Their armies unprepared. The sudden evaporation of support . . .

'He's planned for everything.'

It is what he does.

'You know, Cultivation warned me that my memories would return. She said she was "pruning" me. Do you know why she did that? Did I *have* to remember?'

I do not know. Is it relevant?

'That depends upon the answer to a question,' Dalinar said. He carefully closed the book atop the dresser before the window, then felt the symbols on its cover. 'What is the most important step that a man can take?'

He straightened his blue uniform, then slipped the tome off the table. With *The Way of Kings* a comfortable weight in his hand, he stepped out the door and into the city.

'All this way,' Shallan whispered, 'and they're already *here*?'

Kaladin and Adolin stood like two statues to either side of her, their faces twin stoic masks. She could see the Oathgate distinctly; that round platform at the edge of the bridge was the exact size of the control buildings.

Hundreds upon hundreds of strange spren stood in the lake of beads that marked the shore of Thaylen City. They looked vaguely humanoid, though they were twisted and odd, like shimmering dark light. More the scribbled outlines of people, like drawings she'd done in a maddened state.

On the shore, a large dark mass of living red light surged across the obsidian ground. It was something more terrible than all of these – something that made her eyes *hurt* to look upon. And as if that weren't enough, a half dozen Fused passed overhead, then landed on the bridge that led to the Oathgate platform.

'They knew,' Adolin said. 'They led us here with that cursed vision.'

'Be wary,' Shallan whispered, 'of *anyone* who claims to be able to see the future.'

'No. No, that wasn't from him!' Kaladin looked between them, frantic, and finally turned to Syl for support. 'It was like when the Stormfather . . . I mean . . .'

'Azure warned us from this path,' Adolin said.

'And what else could we have done?' Kaladin said, then hushed his voice, pulling back with the rest of them into the shadowed concealment of the trees. 'We couldn't go to the Horneater Peaks, like Azure wanted. The enemy waits there too! Everyone says their ships patrol there.' Kaladin shook his head. 'This was our only option.'

'We don't have enough food to return . . .' Adolin said.

'Even if we did,' Syl whispered, 'where would we go? They hold Celebrant. They're watching this Oathgate, so they're probably watching the others. . . .'

Shallan sank down on the obsidian ground. Pattern put his hand on her shoulder, humming softly with concern. Her body yearned for Stormlight to wash away her fatigue. Light could make an illusion, change this world into something else – at least for a few moments – so she could pretend . . .

577

'Kaladin is right,' Syl said. 'We *can't* back down now. Our remaining gemstones won't last much longer.'

'We have to try,' Kaladin said with a nod.

'Try what, Kal?' Adolin said. 'Take on an army of Voidbringers by ourselves?'

'I don't know how the portal works,' Shallan added. 'I don't even know how much Stormlight it might require.'

'We'll . . . we'll try something,' Kaladin said. 'We have Stormlight still. An illusion? A distraction? We could get you to the Oathgate, and you could . . . find out how to free us.' He shook his head. 'We can make it work. We *have* to.'

Shallan bowed her head, listening to Pattern hum. Some problems could not be fixed with a lie.

⁖

Jasnah carefully stepped out of the way of a troop of soldiers running for the Oathgate. She had been informed via spanreed that troops were gathering in Urithiru to come help. Unfortunately, they would soon have to acknowledge what she already knew.

Thaylen City was lost.

Their adversary had played this hand too well. That angered her, but she kept that emotion in check. At the very least, she hoped that Amaram's band of malcontents would soak up arrows and spears long enough to let the Thaylen civilians evacuate.

Lightning from the storm lit the city red.

Focus. She had to focus on what she *could* do, not what she had *failed* to do. First, she had to see that her uncle didn't get himself killed fighting a useless battle. Second, she needed to help evacuate Thaylen City; she had already warned Urithiru to prepare for refugees.

Both these goals would wait a short time as she dealt with a matter even more pressing.

'The facts align,' Ivory said. 'The truth that has always been, will now soon manifest to all.' He rode upon the high collar of her dress, tiny, holding on with one hand. 'You are correct. A traitor *is.*'

Jasnah undid the buttons on her safehand sleeve and pinned it back, exposing the gloved hand underneath. In preparation, she'd also worn a scout's yellow and gold havah, with shorter skirts slit at the

578

sides and front, trousers underneath. Sturdy boots.

She turned out of the path of another group of cursing soldiers and strode up the steps to the doorway of the temple of Pailiah'Elin. True to the information she'd been given, she found Renarin Kholin kneeling on the floor inside, head bowed. Alone.

A spren rose from his back, bright red, shimmering like the heat of a mirage. A crystalline structure, like a snowflake, though it dripped light upward toward the ceiling. In her pouch, she carried a sketch of the proper spren of the Truthwatchers.

And this was something different.

Jasnah put her hand to the side, then – taking a deep breath – summoned Ivory as a Shardblade.

⁙

Venli hopped down from the ship's improvised gangway. The city before her was yet another marvel. Built up the side of a mountain, it looked almost like it had been cut from the stone – sculpted like the winds and rain had shaped the Shattered Plains.

Hundreds of singers streamed around her. Hulking Fused walked among them, bearing carapace armor as impressive as any Shardplate. Some of the ordinary singers wore warform – but unlike their Alethi counterparts, they had not been through combat training.

Azish, Thaylen, Marati . . . a host of nationalities, these newly awakened singers were frightened, uncertain. Venli attuned Agony. Would they force her to march to the front line? She didn't have much battle training either; even with a form of power, she'd be cut to ribbons.

Like my people, on the field of Narak, who were sacrificed to birth the Everstorm. Odium seemed very quick to expend the lives of both listener and singer.

Timbre pulsed to Peace in her pouch, and Venli rested her hand on it. 'Hush,' she whispered to Agony. '*Hush.* Do you want one of them to hear you?'

Timbre reluctantly softened her pulsings, though Venli could still feel a faint vibration from her pouch. And that . . . that relaxed her. She almost thought that she could hear the Rhythm of Peace herself.

One of the hulking Fused called for her. 'You! Listener woman! Come!'

Venli attuned the Rhythm of Destruction. She would *not* be intimidated by these, gods though they be. She stepped up to this one and kept her head high.

The Fused handed her a sword in a sheath. She took it, then attuned Subservience. 'I've used an axe before, but not—'

'Carry it,' he said, eyes glowing softly red. 'You may need to defend yourself.'

She did not object further. There was a fine line between respectful confidence and defiance. She belted the sword on her slender body, wishing she had some carapace.

'Now,' the Fused said to Conceit, striding forward and expecting her to keep up, 'tell me what this little one is saying.'

Venli followed him to a gathering of singers in workform, holding spears. She had been speaking to the Fused in the ancient language, but these were speaking in Thaylen.

I'm an interpreter, she thought, relaxing. *That's why they wanted me on the battlefield.*

'What was it,' Venli said to Derision, addressing the one the Fused had indicated, 'you wished to say to the holy one?'

'We ...' The singer licked his lips. 'We aren't soldiers, ma'am. We're fishers. What are we doing here?' Though a shade of the Rhythm of Anxiety laced his words, his cringing form and face were the stronger indication. He spoke and acted like a human.

She interpreted.

'You are here to do as you are told,' the Fused told them, through Venli. 'In return, you are rewarded with further opportunities to serve.' Though his rhythm was Derision, he didn't seem angry. More ... as if he were lecturing a child.

She passed that along, and the sailors looked to each other, shuffling uncomfortably.

'They wish to object,' she told the Fused. 'I can read it in them.'

'They may speak,' he said.

She prompted them, and their leader looked down, then spoke to Anxiety. 'It's just that ... Thaylen City? This is our home. We're expected to attack it?'

'Yes,' the Fused said after Venli interpreted. 'They enslaved you. They tore your families apart, treated you like dumb animals. Do you not thirst for vengeance?'

'Vengeance?' the sailor said, looking to his fellows for support. 'We're glad to be free. But ... I mean ... some of them treated us pretty nice. Can't we just go settle somewhere, and leave the Thaylens alone?'

'No,' the Fused said. Venli interpreted, then jumped to follow him as he stalked off.

'Great one?' she asked to Subservience.

'These have the wrong Passion,' he said. 'The ones who attacked Kholinar did so gladly.'

'The Alethi are a warlike people, great one. It's not surprising they passed this on to their slaves. And perhaps these were better treated?'

'They were slaves for far too long. We need to show them a better way.'

Venli stuck close to the Fused, happy to have found one that was both sane and reasonable. He didn't shout at the groups they visited, many of whom shared similar complaints. He merely had her repeat the same sorts of phrases.

You must seize vengeance, little ones. You must earn *your Passion.*

Qualify yourselves for greater service, and you will be elevated to the place of a Regal, given a form of power.

This land was yours long ago, before they stole it. You have been trained to be docile. We will teach you to be strong again.

The Fused remained calm, but fierce. Like a smoldering fire. Controlled, but ready to burst alight. He eventually walked to join some of his fellows. Around them, the singer army formed up awkwardly, coating the land just east of the bay. Alethi troops mustered across a short battlefield, banners flapping. They had archers, heavy infantry, light infantry, even some outriders on horses.

Venli hummed to Agony. This was going to be a *slaughter.*

She suddenly felt something odd. Like a rhythm, but oppressive, *demanding.* It shook the very air, and the ground beneath her feet trembled. Lightning in the clouds behind seemed to flash to this rhythm, and in a moment she saw that the area around her was filled with ghostly spren.

Those are the spirits of the dead, she realized. *Fused who haven't yet chosen a body.* Most were twisted to the point that she barely recognized them as singers. Two were roughly the size of buildings.

One dominated even these: a creature of swirling violence, tall as a small hill, seemingly made up entirely of red smoke. She could see these overlaid on the real world, but somehow knew they would be invisible to most. She could see into the other world. That happened sometimes right before . . .

A blistering heat shone behind her.

Venli braced herself. She usually only saw him during the storms. But . . . this *was* a storm. It hovered behind, immobile, churning the seas.

Light crystallized beside her, forming an ancient parshman with a face marbled gold and white, and a regal scepter he carried like a cane. For once, his presence didn't vaporize her immediately.

Venli released a relieved breath. This was more an *impression* than his true being. Still, power streamed from him like the tendrils of a vinebud waving in the wind, vanishing into infinity.

Odium had come to personally supervise this battle.

⁂

Teft hid.

He couldn't face the others. Not after . . . after what he'd done.

Rock and Bisig bleeding. Eth dead. The room destroyed. The Honorblade stolen.

He had . . . he had on a Bridge Four . . . uniform. . . .

Teft scrambled through the rock hallways, passing shamespren in bursts, looking for a place where nobody could see him. He'd done it again, to yet another group that trusted him. Just like with his family, whom he'd sold out in a misguided attempt at righteousness. Just like with his squad in Sadeas's army, whom he'd abandoned for his addiction. And now . . . and now Bridge Four?

He tripped on an uneven bit of stone in the dark hallway and fell, grunting, scraping his hand against the floor. He groaned, then lay there, knocking his head against the stone.

Would that he could find someplace hidden, and squeeze inside, never *ever* to be found again.

When he looked up, she was standing there. The woman made of light and air, with curls of hair that vanished into mist.

'Why are you following me?' Teft growled. 'Go pick one of the others. Kelek! Pick *anyone* but me.'

He rose and pushed past her – she had barely any substance – and continued down the hallway. Light from ahead showed that he'd accidentally made his way to the outer ring of the tower, where windows and balconies overlooked the Oathgate platforms.

He stopped by a stone doorway, puffing, holding on with a hand that bled from the knuckles.

'Teft.'

'You don't want me. I'm *broken*. Pick Lopen. Rock. Sigzil. Damnation, woman. I . . .'

What was that?

Drawn by faint sounds, Teft walked into the empty room. Those sounds . . . Shouts?

He walked out onto the balcony. Below, figures with marbled skin flooded across one of the Oathgate platforms, the one that led to Kholinar. That was supposed to be locked, unusable.

Scouts and soldiers began to shout in panic down below. Urithiru was under attack.

⁘

Puffing from her run, Navani scrambled up the last few steps onto the wall of Thaylen City. Here, she found Queen Fen's retinue. *Finally.*

She checked her arm clock. If only she could find a fabrial that would manipulate exhaustion, not just pain. Wouldn't *that* be something. There were exhaustionspren, after all . . .

Navani strode along the wall walk toward Fen. Below, Amaram's troops flew the new Sadeas banner: the axe and the tower, white on forest green. Anticipationspren and fearspren – the eternal attendants of the battlefield – grew up around them. Sadeas's men were still streaming through the gates, but already blocks of archers moved forward. They'd soon start pelting the disorganized parshman army.

That storm though . . .

'The enemy only keeps coming,' Fen said as Navani approached, her admirals making room. 'I'll soon get to judge your famed Alethi troops firsthand – as they fight an impossible battle.'

'Actually,' Navani said, 'we're better off than it looks. The new Sadeas is a renowned tactician. His soldiers are well rested and – if lacking in discipline – known for their tenacity. We can attack the enemy before it finishes deploying. Then, if they rebound and overwhelm us with numbers, we can pull back into the city until we get reinforcements.'

Kmakl, Fen's consort, nodded. 'This is winnable, Fen. We might even be able to capture some of our ships back.'

The ground shook. For a moment, Navani felt that she was on a swaying ship. She cried out, grabbing the battlement to keep from falling.

Out in the field, between the enemy troops and the Alethi ones, the ground *shattered*. Lines and cracks split the stone, and then an enormous stone *arm* pulled itself from the ground – the fractures having outlined its hand, forearm, elbow, and upper arm.

A monster easily thirty feet tall pulled itself from the stone, dropping chips and dust on the army below. Like a skeleton made of rock, it had a wedge-shaped head with deep, molten red eyes.

⁂

Venli got to watch the thunderclasts awaken.

Among the waiting spirits were two larger masses of energy – souls so warped, so mangled, they didn't seem singer at all. One crawled into the stone ground, somehow inhabiting it like a spren taking residence in a gemheart. The stone *became* its form.

Then it ripped itself free of the rock. Around her, the parshmen stumbled back in awe, so surprised that they actually drew spren. The thing loomed over the human forces, while its companion climbed into the stone ground, but didn't rip out immediately.

There was one other, mightier than even these. It was out in the water of the bay, but when she looked into the other world, she couldn't help but glance toward it. If those two lesser souls had created such daunting stone monsters, then what was *that* mountain of power?

In the Physical Realm, the Fused knelt and bowed their heads toward Odium. So they could see him too. Venli knelt quickly, knocking her knees against the stone. Timbre pulsed to Anxiety, and Venli put her hand on the pouch, squeezing it. *Quiet. We can't fight him.*

'Turash,' Odium said, resting fingers upon the shoulder of the Fused she had been following. 'Old friend, you look well in this new body.'

'Thank you, master,' Turash said.

'Your mind holds firm, Turash. I am proud of you.' Odium waved toward Thaylen City. 'I have prepared a grand army for our victory today. What do you think of our prize?'

'An excellent position of great import, even without the Oathgate,' Turash said. 'But I fear for our armies, master.'

'Oh?' Odium asked.

'They are weak, untrained, and frightened. Many may refuse to fight. They don't crave vengeance, master. Even with the thunderclast, we may be outmatched.'

'These?' Odium asked, looking over his shoulder at the gathered singers. 'Oh, Turash. You think too *small*, my friend! These are not my army. I brought them here to watch.'

'Watch what?' Venli asked, looking up. She cringed, but Odium paid her no mind. Odium held his hands to the sides, yellow-gold power streaming behind his figure like a wind made visible. Beyond him, in the other place, that red churning power became more *real*. It was pulled into this realm completely, and the ocean boiled.

Something came surging out. Something primeval, something Venli had felt but never truly known. Red mist. Ephemeral, like a shadow you see on a dark day and mistake for something real. Charging red horses, angry and galloping. The forms of men, killing and dying, shedding blood and reveling in it. Bones piled atop one another, making a hill upon which men struggled.

The red mist climbed up from the surging waves, rolling out onto an empty section of rock, northward along the rim of the water. It brought to her a lust for the battlefield. A beautiful focus, a Thrill for the fight.

.·.

The largest of the spren, the roiling mass of red light, vanished from Shadesmar.

Kaladin gasped and walked closer to the outer edge of the trees, feeling that power vacate this place and . . . go to the other?

'Something's happening,' he said to Adolin and Shallan, who were still discussing what to do. 'We might have an opening!'

They joined him and watched as the strange army of spren began to vanish too, winking out in waves.

'The Oathgate?' Shallan asked. 'Maybe they're using it?'

In moments, only the six Fused remained, guarding the bridge.

Six, Kaladin thought. *Can I defeat six?*

Did he need to?

'I can challenge them as a distraction,' he said to the others. 'Maybe we can use some illusions as well? We can draw them off while Shallan sneaks over and figures out how to work the Oathgate.'

'I suppose we don't have any other choice,' Adolin said. 'But . . .'

'What?' Kaladin said, urgent.

'Aren't you worried about where that army went?'

.•.

'Passion,' Odium said. 'There is great Passion here.'

Venli felt cold.

'I've prepared these men for decades,' Odium said. 'Men who want nothing so much as something to *break,* to gain vengeance against the one who killed their highprince. Let the singers watch and learn. I've prepared a different army to fight for us today.'

Ahead of them on the battlefield, the human ranks slumped, their banner wavering. A man in glittering Shardplate, sitting upon a white horse, led them.

Deep within his helm, something started glowing red.

The dark spren flew toward the men, finding welcoming bodies and willing flesh. The red mist made them lust, made their minds open. And the spren, then, *bonded* to the men, slipping into those open souls.

'Master, you have learned to inhabit humans?' Turash said to Subservience.

'Spren have always been able to bond with them, Turash,' Odium said. 'It merely requires the right mindset and the right environment.'

Ten thousand Alethi in green uniforms gripped their weapons, their eyes glowing a deep, dangerous red.

'Go,' Odium whispered. 'Kholin would have sacrificed you! Manifest your anger! Kill the Blackthorn, who murdered your highprince. Set your Passion free! Give me your pain, and seize this city in my name!'

The army turned and – led by a Shardbearer in gleaming Plate – attacked Thaylen City.

Jo Shore - 1400

ALONE

We took them in, as commanded by the gods. What else could we do? They were a people forlorn, without a home. Our pity destroyed us. For their betrayal extended even to our gods: to spren, stone, and wind.

—From the Eila Stele

K aladin thought he could hear the wind as he stepped from beneath the obsidian trees. Syl said this place had no wind. Yet was that the tinkling of glass leaves as they quivered? Was that the sigh of cool, fresh air coursing around him?

He'd come far in the last half year. He seemed a man distant from the one who carried bridges against Parshendi arrows. That man had welcomed death, but now – even on the bad days, when everything was cast in greys – he *defied* death. It could not have him, for while life was painful, life was also sweet.

He had Syl. He had the men of Bridge Four. And most importantly, he had purpose.

Today, Kaladin *would* protect Dalinar Kholin.

He strode toward the sea of souls that marked the existence of Thaylen City on the other side. Many of those souls' flames, in ranks, had turned sharply *red*. He shivered to think what that meant. He stepped up onto the bridge, beads churning below, and reached the highest point in its arc before the enemy noticed him.

Six Fused turned and rose into the air, arraying to regard him. They raised long spears, then looked to the sides, seeming shocked.

One man, alone?

Kaladin set one foot back – gently scraping the tip of his boot against the white marble bridge – and fell into a combat posture. He hooked the harpoon in a one-handed underarm grip, letting out a long breath.

Then he drew in all of his Stormlight, and burst alight.

Within the power's embrace, a lifetime's worth of moments seemed to snap into place. Throwing Gaz to the ground in the rain. Screaming in defiance while charging at the front of a bridge. Coming awake in the practice grounds during the Weeping. Fighting the assassin on the stormwall.

The Fused leaped for him, trailing long cloaks and robes. Kaladin Lashed himself straight upward, and took to the sky for the first time in what had been far, far too long.

∴

Dalinar stumbled as the ground shook again. A second sequence of cracks sounded outside. He was too low down in the city now to see past the city wall, but he feared he knew what that breaking stone must signify. A second thunderclast.

Violet fearspren sprouted from the streets all around as civilians shouted and screamed. Dalinar had made his way down through the central section of the city – the part called the Ancient Ward – and had just entered the Low Ward, the bottom portion nearest the city wall. The steps behind him were filling with people who fled upward, toward the Oathgate.

As the trembling subsided, Dalinar grabbed the arm of a young mother who was pounding frantically on the door of a building. He sent her running up the steps with her child in her arms. He needed these people off the streets, preferably taking shelter at Urithiru, so they wouldn't get caught between clashing armies.

Dalinar felt his age as he jogged past the next row of buildings, still clutching *The Way of Kings* under his arm. He had barely any spheres on him, an oversight, but neither did he have Plate or Blade. This would be his first battle in many, many years without Shards. He'd insisted on stepping out of those boots, and would have to let Amaram and other Shardbearers command the field.

How was Amaram faring? Last Dalinar had seen, the highprince had been arranging his archers – but from this low in the city, Dalinar couldn't see the troops outside.

A sudden feeling slammed into him.

It was focus and passion. An eager energy, a warmth, a promise of strength.

Glory.

Life.

To Dalinar, this thirst for the battle felt like the attentions of a lover you'd turned away long ago. The Thrill was here. His old, *dear* friend.

'No,' he whispered, sagging against a wall. The emotion struck him harder than the earthquake had. '*No.*'

The taste was so, *so* appealing. It whispered that he could save this city all on his own. Let the Thrill in, and the Blackthorn could return. He didn't need Shards. He only needed this passion. Sweeter than any wine.

No.

He shoved the Thrill aside, scrambling to his feet. As he did, however, a shadow moved beyond the wall. A monster of stone, one of the beasts from his visions, standing some thirty feet tall – looming over the twenty-foot city wall. The thunderclast clasped its hands together, then swung them low, *crashing* them through the city wall, flinging out chunks of stone.

Dalinar leaped toward cover, but a falling boulder pounded into him, crushing him into a wall.

Blackness.

Falling.

Power.

He gasped, and Stormlight flooded into him – he shook awake to find his arm pinned by the boulder, rocks and dust falling on a rubble-strewn street before him. And . . . not just rubble. He coughed, realizing some of those lumps were bodies coated in dust, lying motionless.

He struggled to pull his arm from under the boulder. Nearby, the thunderclast kicked at the broken wall, opening a hole. Then it stepped through, footfalls shaking the ground, approaching the shelf that made up the front of the Ancient Ward.

A massive stone foot *thumped* to the ground by Dalinar. Storms! Dalinar hauled on his arm, heedless of the pain or the damage to his body, and finally got it free. The Stormlight healed him as he crawled away, ducking as the monster ripped the roof off a building at the front of the Ancient Ward and sent debris raining down.

The Gemstone Reserve? The monster cast the roof aside, and several Fused that he'd missed before – they were riding on its shoulders – slipped down into the building. Dalinar was torn between heading for the battlefield outside, and investigating whatever was going on here.

Any idea what they're after? he asked the Stormfather.

No. This is odd behavior.

In a flash decision, Dalinar yanked his book out from under some rubble nearby, then went running back up the now-empty steps to the Ancient Ward, dangerously close to the thunderclast.

The monster released a sudden piercing roar, like a thunderclap. The shock wave almost knocked Dalinar off his feet again. In a fit of rage, the titanic creature *attacked* the Gemstone Reserve, ripping apart its walls and innards, tossing chunks backward. A million sparkling bits of glass caught the sunlight as they fell over the city, the wall, and beyond.

Spheres and gemstones, Dalinar realized. *All the wealth of Thaylenah. Scattered like leaves.*

The thing seemed increasingly angry as it pounded the area around the reserve. Dalinar put his back to a wall as two Fused darted past, led by what appeared to be a glowing yellow spren. These two Fused didn't seem to be able to fly, but there was a startling grace to their motion. They slid along the stone street with no apparent effort, as if the ground were greased.

Dalinar gave chase, squeezing past a group of scribes huddled in the street, but before he could catch up, the Fused attacked one palanquin among the many trying to move through the crowds. They knocked it over, shoving aside the porters, and dug inside.

The Fused ignored Dalinar's shouts. They soon streaked away – one tucking a large object under its arm. Dalinar drew in Stormlight from some fleeing merchants, then ran the rest of the distance to the palanquin.

Amid the wreckage he found a young Thaylen woman alongside an elderly man who appeared to have been previously wounded, judging by the bandages.

Dalinar helped the dazed young woman to a sitting position. 'What did they want?'

'Brightlord?' she said in Thaylen. She blinked, then seized his arm. 'The King's Drop . . . a ruby. They tried to steal it before, and now, now they've taken it!'

A ruby? A simple gemstone? The porters attended to the old man, who was barely conscious.

Dalinar looked over his shoulder at the retreating thunderclast. The enemy had ignored the wealth of the Gemstone Reserve. Why would they want a specific ruby? He was about to press for more details when something else drew his attention. From this higher vantage, he could see through the hole the thunderclast had broken in the wall.

Figures outside with glowing red eyes arrayed themselves on the battlefield – but they weren't parshmen.

Those were *Sadeas* uniforms.

⁘

Jasnah moved into the temple, gripping her Shardblade, stepping on slippered feet. The red spren rising from Renarin – like a snowflake made of crystal and light – seemed to sense her and panicked, disappearing into Renarin with a puff.

A spren is, Ivory said. *The wrong spren is.*

Renarin Kholin was a liar. He was no Truthwatcher.

That is *a spren of Odium,* Ivory said. *Corrupted spren. But . . . a human, bonded to one? This thing is not.*

'It is,' Jasnah whispered. 'Somehow.'

She was now close enough to hear Renarin whispering. 'No . . . Not Father. No, *please* . . .'

⁘

Shallan wove Light.

A simple illusion, recalled from the pages of her sketchpad: some soldiers from the army, people from Urithiru, and some of the spren she'd sketched on her trip. Around twenty individuals in total.

'Taln's nails,' Adolin said as Kaladin shot upward through the sky. 'The bridgeboy is really into it.'

Kaladin drew away four of the Fused, but two remained behind. Shallan added an illusion of Azure to her group, then some of the Reachers she'd drawn. She hated using up so much Stormlight – what if she didn't have enough left to get through the Oathgate?

'Good luck,' she whispered to Adolin. 'Remember, I won't be controlling these directly. They will make only rudimentary motions.'

'We'll be fine.' Adolin glanced at Pattern, Syl, and the spren of his sword. 'Right, guys?'

'Mmmm,' Pattern said. 'I do not like being stabbed.'

'Wise words, friend. Wise words.' Adolin gave Shallan a kiss, then they took off running toward the bridge. Syl, Pattern, and the deadeye followed – as did the illusions, which were bound to Adolin.

This force drew the attention of the last two Fused. As those were distracted, Shallan slipped over to the base of the bridge, then eased herself down into the beads. She crossed silently beneath the bridge, using precious Stormlight to make herself a safe walking platform with one of the beads she'd found while on *Honor's Path*.

She made her way across to the small island platform that represented the Oathgate on this side. Two enormous spren stood above it.

Judging by the shouting on the bridge, Adolin and the others were doing their job. But could Shallan do hers? She stepped up beneath the two sentinels, which stood tall as buildings, reminiscent of statues in armor.

One mother-of-pearl, the other black with a variegated oily shimmer. Did they guard the Oathgate, or did they – somehow – facilitate its workings?

At a loss for what else to do, Shallan simply waved her hand. 'Um, hello?'

Steadily, two heads turned down toward her.

⁖

The air around Venli – once crowded by the spirits of the dead – was now empty save for the single black figure of swirling smoke. She'd missed that one at first, as it was the size of a normal person. It stood near Odium, and she did not know what it represented.

The second thunderclast dragged arms as long as its body, with hands like hooks. It crossed the field eastward, toward the city walls and the human army of turncoats. Just behind Venli, to the west, the common singers stood arrayed before their ships. They stayed far from the red mist of the Unmade coating the north side of the battlefield.

Odium stood beside Venli, a glowing force of burning gold. The first thunderclast left the city and placed something down on the ground: two of the Fused – gods with lithe bodies and little armor. They skirted the turncoat army, sliding along the rock with an uncanny grace.

'What is that they carry?' Venli asked. 'A gemstone? Is *that* why we came here? A rock?'

'No,' Odium said. 'That is merely a precaution, a last-minute addition I made to prevent a potential disaster. The prize I claim today is far greater – even more grand than the city itself. The conduit of my freedom. The bane of Roshar. Forward, child. To the gap in the wall. I may need you to speak for me.'

She swallowed, then started hiking toward the city. The dark spirit followed, the one of swirling mists, the last who had yet to inhabit a body.

❖

Kaladin soared through this place of black heavens, haunted clouds, and a distant sun. Only four of the Fused had chosen to take off after him. Adolin would have to deal with the other two.

The four flew with precision. They used Lashings like Kaladin did, though they didn't seem to be able to vary their speed as much as he could. It took them longer to build up to greater Lashings, which should have made it easy to stay ahead of them.

But *storms*, the way they flew! So graceful. They didn't jerk this way or that, but flowed lithely from one motion to the next. They used their entire bodies to sculpt the wind of their passing and control their flight. Even the Assassin in White hadn't been so fluid as these, so like the winds themselves.

Kaladin had claimed the skies, but storms, it looked like he'd moved into territory where someone had a prior entitlement.

I don't have to fight them, he thought. *I only have to keep them busy long enough for Shallan to figure out how to activate the portal.*

Kaladin Lashed himself upward, toward those strange, too-flat clouds.

He twisted in the air, and found one of the Fused almost upon him – a male with pale white skin swirled through with a single marbling of red, like smoke blown across the cheeks. The creature stabbed its long spear at him, but Kaladin Lashed himself to the side just in time.

Lashing *wasn't* flying, and that was part of its strength. Kaladin didn't have to be facing any specific direction to move in the air. He fell up and slightly to the north, but fought while facing downward, battering away the enemy lance with his harpoon. The Fused's weapon was far longer, with sharpened sides rather than a single fine point. Kaladin's harpoon was at a severe disadvantage.

Right. Time to change that.

As the Fused rammed the lance upward again, Kaladin reached out with both hands on his harpoon's haft, holding it sideways. He let the enemy spear pass into the opening between his arms, chest, and harpoon.

He Lashed his own weapon downward with multiple Lashings. Then he dropped it.

It slid along the length of the lance and smacked into the Fused's arms. The creature shouted in pain, letting go of his weapon. At the same moment Kaladin dove, canceling all upward Lashings and binding himself downward instead.

The sudden, jarring change made his stomach lurch and his vision go black. Even with Stormlight, this was almost too much. His ears ringing, he gritted his teeth, riding the momentary loss of sight until – blessedly – his vision returned. He spun in the air, then pulled up and snatched the falling lance as it dropped past him.

The four Fused swooped after him, more cautious. The wind of his passing chilled the sweat on his face from his near blackout.

Let's . . . not try that again, Kaladin thought, hefting his new weapon. He'd practiced with things like this in pike walls, but they were normally too long to maneuver in one-on-one combat. Flying would negate that.

The Fused he'd disarmed swooped down to fetch the harpoon. Kaladin waved his hand toward the others palm upward, then took off toward some nearby dark obsidian mountains, forested on the sides – the direction he and the others had come. Down below, he could see Shallan's illusions engaging the two Fused on the bridge.

Eyes forward, Kaladin thought as the four others chased after him. He belonged in the skies with these creatures.

Time to prove it.

◆

Prime Aqasix Yanagawn the First, emperor of all Makabak, paced in the cabin of his ship.

He was actually starting to *feel* like an emperor. He wasn't embarrassed talking to the viziers and scions any longer. He understood much of what they discussed now, and didn't jump when someone called him 'Your Majesty.' Remarkably, he was starting to forget that he'd ever been a frightened thief sneaking through the palace.

But then, even an emperor had limits to his rule.

He paced back the other way. Regal robes – of Azish patterns – weighed him down, along with the Imperial Yuanazixin: a fancy hat with sweeping sides. He'd have taken the thing off, but he felt he needed its authority when talking to his three most important advisors.

'Lift thinks we should have stayed,' he said. 'War is coming to Thaylen City.'

'We're merely protecting our fleet from the storm,' Noura said.

'Pardon, Vizier, but that's a load of chull dung, and you know it. We left because you're worried that Kholin is being manipulated by the enemy.'

'That is not the *only* reason,' Scion Unoqua said. He was an old man with a full paunch. 'We have always been skeptical of the Lost Radiants. The powers that Dalinar Kholin wishes to harness are extremely dangerous, as now proven by the translations of an ancient record!'

'Lift says –' Yanagawn said.

'Lift?' Noura said. 'You listen to her far too much, Your Imperial Majesty.'

'She's smart.'

'She once tried to *eat* your cummerbund.'

'She ... thought it sounded like a type of dessert.' Yanagawn took a deep breath. 'Besides, she's not *that* kind of smart. She's the other kind.'

'What other kind, Your Imperial Majesty?' Vizier Dalksi asked. Her hair was powder white, peeking out beneath her formal headdress.

'The kind that knows when it's wrong to betray a friend. I think we should go back. Am I emperor or not?'

'You *are* emperor,' Noura said. 'But, Your Majesty, remember your lessons. The thing that *separates* us from the monarchies of the east – and the chaos they suffer – is that our emperor is held in check. Azir can, and will, withstand a change in dynasty. Your power is absolute, but you do not exercise it all. You must not.'

'You were chosen,' Unoqua said, 'by Yaezir himself to lead—'

'I was *chosen*,' Yanagawn cut in, 'because nobody would shed a tear if the Assassin in White came for me! Let's not play games, all right?'

'You performed a miracle,' Unoqua said.

'*Lift* performed a miracle. Using powers you now say are too dangerous to trust!'

The three – two viziers, one scion – looked to each other. Unoqua was their religious leader, but Noura had most seniority by year of passing the tests for master office, which she'd done – remarkably – at age *twelve*.

Yanagawn stopped by the cabin window. Outside, waves chopped, churning, rocking their ship. His smaller ship had met up with the main fleet, then joined them in taking shelter in Vtlar Cove, along the Thaylen coast. But reports via spanreed said that the Everstorm had *stopped* near Thaylen City.

A knock came at the door. Yanagawn let Dalksi – least senior, despite her age – call admittance. Yanagawn settled in his regal chair as a guardsman with light brown skin entered. Yanagawn thought he recognized the man, who held a cloth to the side of his face and winced as he gave the formal bow of admittance to the emperor.

'Vono?' Noura asked. 'What happened to your charge? You were to keep her busy and distracted, yes?'

'I was, Your Grace,' Vono said. 'Until she kicked me in my spheres and stuffed me under the bed. Um, Your Grace. Don't right know how she moved me. She's not real big, that one. . . .'

Lift? Yanagawn thought. He almost cried out, demanding answers, but that would have shamed this man. Yanagawn held himself back with difficulty, and Noura nodded to him in appreciation of a lesson learned.

'When was this?' Noura asked.

'Right before we left,' the guard said. 'Sorry, Your Grace. I've been down since then, only now recovered.'

Yanagawn turned toward Noura. Surely *now* she would see the importance of returning. The storm had yet to advance. They could go back if . . .

Another figure approached the door, a woman in the robes and pattern of a second-level scribe, seventh circle. She entered and quickly gave the formal bows to Yanagawn, so hasty she forgot the third gesture of sub-servient obedience.

'Viziers,' she said, bowing in turn to them, then to Unoqua. 'News from the city!'

'Good news?' Noura asked hopefully.

'The Alethi have turned against the Thaylens, and now seek to conquer them! They've been allied with the parshmen all along. Your Grace, by fleeing, we have narrowly avoided a trap!'

'Quickly,' Noura said. 'Separate our ships from any that bear Alethi troops. We must not be caught unaware!'

They left, abandoning Yanagawn to the care of a dozen young scribes who were next in line for basking in his presence. He settled into his seat, worried and afraid, feeling a sickness in his gut. The Alethi, traitors?

Lift had been wrong. He had been wrong.

Yaezir bless them. This really was the end of days.

··

We are the gatekeepers, the two enormous spren said to Shallan, speaking with voices that overlapped, as if one. Though their mouths did not move, the voices reverberated through Shallan. *Lightweaver, you have no permission to use this portal.*

'But I *need* to get through,' Shallan cried up to them. 'I have Stormlight to pay!'

Your payment will be refused. We are locked by the word of the parent.

'Your parent? Who?'

The parent is dead now.

'So . . .'

We are locked. Travel to and from Shadesmar was prohibited during the parent's last days. We are bound to obey.

Behind Shallan, on the bridge, Adolin had devised a clever tactic. He acted like an illusion.

Her false people had instructions to act like they were fighting – though without her direct attention, that meant they just stood around and slashed at the air. To avoid revealing himself, Adolin had chosen to do the same, slashing about with his harpoon randomly. Pattern and Syl did likewise, while the two Fused hovered overhead. One held her arm, which had been hit – but now seemed to be healing.

They knew *someone* in that mass was real, but they couldn't ascertain who.

Shallan's time was short. She looked back up at the gatekeepers. 'Please. The other Oathgate – the one at Kholinar – let me through.'

Impossible, they said. *We are bound by Honor, by rules spren cannot break. This portal is closed.*

'Then why did you let those others through? The army that stood around here earlier?'

The souls of the dead? They did not need our portal. They were called by the enemy, pulled along ancient paths to waiting hosts. You living cannot do the same. You must seek the perpendicularity to transfer. The enormous spren cocked their heads in concert. *We are apologetic. We have been . . . alone very long. We would enjoy granting passage to men again. But we cannot do that which was forbidden.*

⁂

Szeth of the Skybreakers hovered far above the battlefield.

'The Alethi have changed sides, aboshi?' Szeth asked.

'They have seen the truth,' Nin said, hovering beside him. Only the two of them watched; Szeth did not know where the rest of the Skybreakers had gone.

Nearby, the Everstorm rumbled its discontent. Red lightning rippled across the surface, passing from one cloud to the next.

'All along,' Szeth said, 'this world belonged to the parshmen. My people watched not for the return of an invading enemy, but for the masters of the house.'

'Yes,' Nin said.

'And you sought to stop them.'

'I knew what must happen if they returned.' Nin turned toward him. 'Who has jurisdiction over this land, Szeth-son-Neturo? A man can rule his home until the citylord demands his taxes. The citylord controls his lands until the highlord, in turn, comes to him for payment. But the highlord must answer to the highprince, when war is called in his lands. And the king? He . . . must answer to God.'

'You said God was dead.'

'*A* god is dead. Another won the war by right of conquest. The original masters of this land have returned, as you so aptly made metaphor, with the keys to the house. So tell me, Szeth-son-Neturo – he who is about to swear the Third Ideal – whose law should the Skybreakers follow? That of humans, or that of the *real* owners of this land?'

There seemed to be no choice. Nin's logic was sound. No choice at all . . .

Don't be stupid, the sword said. *Let's go fight those guys.*

'The parshmen? They are the rightful rulers of the land,' Szeth said.

Rightful? Who has a right to land? Humans are always claiming things. But nobody asks the things, now do they? Well, nobody owns me. Vivenna told me. I'm my own sword.

'I have no choice.'

Really? Didn't you tell me you spent a thousand years following the instructions of a rock?

'More than seven years, sword-nimi. And I didn't follow the rock, but the words of the one who held it. I . . .'

. . . Had no choice?

But it had always been nothing more than a rock.

⁘

Kaladin swooped downward and passed above the treetops, rattling the glass leaves, sending a spray of broken shards behind himself. He turned upward with the slope of the mountain, adding another Lashing to his speed, then another.

When he passed the tree line, he Lashed himself closer to the rock, skimming with obsidian only inches from his face. He used his arms to sculpt the wind around himself, angling toward a crack through the glossy black rock where two mountains met.

Alive with Light and wind, he didn't care if the Fused were gaining on him or not.

Let them watch.

His angle was wrong to get through the crack, so Kaladin Lashed himself back away from the mountain slope in an enormous loop, continuously changing his Lashings one after another. He made a circle in the air, then darted past the Fused and straight through the crack, close enough to the walls that he could feel them pass.

He broke out the other side, exhilarated. Should he have run out of Stormlight by now? He didn't use it up as quickly as he had during his early months training.

Kaladin dove along the slopes as three Fused popped out of the crack to follow him. He led them around the base of the obsidian mountain, then wound back toward the Oathgate to check on Shallan and the others. As he approached, he let himself drop among the trees, still moving at incredible speed. He oriented himself as if he were diving through the chasms. Dodging these trees wasn't so different from that.

He wove between them, using his body more than Lashings to control his direction. His wake caused a melody of breaking glass. He exploded free of the forest, and found the fourth Fused – the one with his harpoon – waiting. The creature attacked, but Kaladin dodged and tore across the ground until he was passing over the sea of beads.

A quick glance showed him Shallan on the platform, waving her hands over her head – the prearranged signal that she needed more time.

Kaladin continued out over the sea, and beads reacted to his Stormlight, rattling and surging like a wave behind him. The last Fused slowed to hover in place, and the other three slowly emerged from the forest.

Kaladin spun in another loop, beads rising in the air behind him like a column of water. He curved in an arc and came in toward the harpoon-wielding Fused. Kaladin slapped the parshman's weapon aside, then swung the butt of his own lance up, catching the harpoon on the haft while he kicked his enemy in the chest.

The harpoon went upward. The Fused went backward.

The creature pulled himself to a stop in the air with a Lashing, then looked down at his hands, dumbfounded as Kaladin caught the harpoon in his free hand. The disarmed enemy barked something, then shook his head and took out his sword. He glided backward to join the other three, who approached with fluttering robes.

One of these – the male with the white face swirled with red – moved forward alone, then pointed at Kaladin with his lance and said something.

'I don't speak your language,' Kaladin called back. 'But if that was a challenge, you against me, I accept. Gladly.'

At that moment, his Stormlight ran out.

◆◆

Navani finally got the rock unwedged, and shoved it out of the remnants of the doorway. Other stones fell around it, opening a path out onto the wall.

What was left of it.

About fifteen feet from where she stood, the wall ended in a ragged, broken gap. She coughed, then tucked back a lock of hair that had escaped her braid. They'd run for cover inside one of the stone guard towers along the wall, but one side had collapsed in the shaking.

It had fallen on the three soldiers who had come to protect the queen. The poor souls. Behind, Fen led her consort – who nursed a cut scalp – out over the rubble. Two other scribes had taken shelter with Navani and the queen, but most of the admirals had run in the other direction, taking shelter in the next guard tower along.

That tower was now missing. The monster had swept it away. Now the creature stomped across the plain outside, though Navani couldn't see what had drawn its attention.

'The stairway,' Fen said, pointing. 'Looks like it survived.'

The stairway down was fully enclosed in stone, and would lead into a small guard chamber at the bottom. Maybe they could find soldiers to help the wounded and search the rubble for survivors. Navani pulled open the door, letting Fen and Kmakl head down first. Navani moved to follow, but hesitated.

Damnation, that sight beyond the wall was mesmerizing. The red lightning storm. The two monsters of stone. And the boiling, churning red mist along the right coast. It had no distinct shape, but somehow gave the impression of charging horses with the flesh ripped away.

One of the Unmade, certainly. An ancient spren of Odium. A thing beyond time and history. Here.

A company of soldiers had just finished pouring into the city through the gap. Another formed up outside to enter next. Navani felt a growing chill as she looked at them.

Red eyes.

Gasping softly, she left the stairwell and stumbled along the wall, reaching the broken stone edge. *Oh, dear Almighty, no . . .*

The ranks outside split, making way for a single parshwoman. Navani squinted, trying to see what was so special about her. One of the Fused? Behind her, the red mist surged, sending tendrils to weave among the men – including one wearing Shardplate, riding a brilliant white stallion. Amaram had changed sides.

He joined an overwhelming force of Voidbringers in all shapes and sizes. How could they fight this?

How could anyone *ever* fight this?

Navani fell to her knees above the broken edge of the wall. And then she noticed something else. Something incongruous, something her mind refused – at first – to accept. A solitary figure had somehow gotten around the troops who had already entered the city. He now picked his way across the rubble, wearing a blue uniform, carrying a *book* tucked under his arm.

Unaided and defenseless, Dalinar Kholin stepped into the gap in the broken wall, and there faced the nightmare alone.

CHAMPION WITH NINE SHADOWS

Beware the otherworlders. The traitors. Those with tongues of sweetness, but with minds that lust for blood. Do not take them in. Do not give them succor. Well were they named Voidbringers, for they brought the void. The empty pit that sucks in emotion. A new god. Their god.

—From the Eila Stele

D alinar stepped onto the rubble, boots scraping stone. The air felt too still out here near the red storm. Stagnant. How could the air be so motionless?

Amaram's army hesitated outside the gap. Some men had already gotten in, but the bulk had been forming up to wait their turn. When you rushed a city like this, you wanted to be careful not to push your own forces too hard from behind, lest you crush them up against the enemy.

These kept uneven ranks, snarling, eyes red. More telling, they ignored the wealth at their feet. A field of spheres and gemstones – all dun – that had been thrown out onto this plain by the thunderclast that destroyed the reserve.

They wanted blood instead. Dalinar could *taste* their lust for the fight, the challenge. What held them back?

Twin thunderclasts stomped toward the wall. A red haze drifted

604

among the men. Images of war and death. A deadly storm. Dalinar faced it alone. One man. All that remained of a broken dream.

'So . . .' a sudden voice said from his right. 'What's the plan?'

Dalinar frowned, then looked down to find a Reshi girl with long hair, dressed in a simple shirt and trousers.

'Lift?' Dalinar asked in Azish. 'Didn't you leave?'

'Sure did. What's wrong with your army?'

'They're his now.'

'Did you forget to feed them?'

Dalinar glanced at the soldiers, standing in ranks that felt more like packs than they did true battle formations. 'Perhaps I didn't try hard enough.'

'Were you . . . thinkin' you'd fight them all on your own?' Lift said. 'With a book?'

'There is someone else for me to fight here.'

'. . . With a book?'

'Yes.'

She shook her head. 'Sure, all right. Why not? What do you want me to do?'

The girl didn't match the conventional ideal of a Knight Radiant. Not even five feet tall, thin and wiry, she looked more urchin than soldier.

She was also all he had.

'Do you have a weapon?' he asked.

'Nope. Can't read.'

'Can't . . .' Dalinar looked down at his book. 'I meant a real weapon, Lift.'

'Oh! Yeah, I've got one a those.' She thrust her hand to the side. Mist formed into a small, glittering Shardblade.

. . . Or no, it was just a pole. A silver pole with a rudimentary crossguard.

Lift shrugged. 'Wyndle doesn't like hurting people.'

Doesn't like . . . Dalinar blinked. What kind of world did he live in where *swords* didn't like *hurting people*?

'A Fused escaped from this city a short time ago,' Dalinar said, 'carrying an enormous ruby. I don't know why they wanted it, and I'd rather not find out. Can you steal it back?'

'Sure. Easy.'

'You'll find it with a Fused who can move with a power similar to your own. A woman.'

'Like I said. Easy.'

'Easy? I think you might find—'

'Relax, grandpa. Steal the rock. I can do that.' She took a deep breath, then exploded with Stormlight. Her eyes turned a pearly, glowing white. 'It's just us two, then?'

'Yes.'

'Right. Good luck with the army.'

Dalinar looked back at the soldiers, where a figure materialized, wearing gold, holding a scepter like a cane.

'It's not the army that worries me,' Dalinar said. But Lift had already scampered away, hugging the wall and running quickly to round the outside of the army.

Odium strolled up to Dalinar, trailed by a handful of Fused – plus the woman Dalinar had sucked into his visions – and a shadowy spren that looked like it was made of twisting smoke. What was that?

Odium didn't address Dalinar at first, but instead turned to his Fused. 'Tell Yushah I want her to stay out here and guard the prison. Kai-garnis did well destroying the wall; tell her to return to the city and climb toward the Oathgate. If the Tisark can't secure it, she is to destroy the device and recover its gemstones. We can rebuild it as long as the spren aren't compromised.'

Two Fused left, each running toward one of the towering thunderclasts. Odium placed both hands on the top of his scepter and smiled at Dalinar. 'Well, my friend. Here we are, and the time has arrived. Are you ready?'

'Yes,' Dalinar said.

'Good, good. Let us begin.'

⁘

The two Fused hovered near Adolin, out of easy reach, admiring Shallan's illusory handiwork. He did his best to blend in, waving his harpoon around crazily. He wasn't sure where Syl had gone, but Pattern seemed to be enjoying himself, humming pleasantly and swinging a glass branch.

One of the Fused nudged the other, then pointed at Shallan, whom they'd just noticed. Neither appeared worried that she'd open the Oathgate – which was a bad sign. What did they know about the device that Adolin's team did not?

The Fused turned from Shallan and continued a conversation in a language Adolin couldn't understand. One pointed at each illusion in turn, then thrust with his spear. The other shook her head, and Adolin could almost interpret her answer. *We tried stabbing each one. They keep mixing about, so it's hard to keep track.*

Instead, the female took out a knife and cut her hand, then flung it toward the illusions. Orange blood fell through the illusions, leaving no stain, but splattered against Adolin's cheek. Adolin felt his heart flutter, and he tried to covertly wipe the blood off, but the female gestured toward him with a satisfied grin. The male saluted her with a finger to his head, then lowered his lance and flew straight toward Adolin.

Damnation.

Adolin scrambled away, passing through an illusion of Captain Notum and causing it to diffuse. It formed back together, then blew apart a second later as the Fused soared through it, lance pointed at Adolin's back.

Adolin spun and flung his harpoon up to block, deflecting the lance, but the Fused still smashed into him, tossing him backward. Adolin hit the stone bridge hard, smacking his head, seeing stars.

Vision swimming, he reached for his harpoon, but the Fused slapped the weapon away with the butt of his lance. The creature then alighted softly on the bridge, billowing robes settling.

Adolin yanked out his belt knife, then forced himself to his feet, unsteady. The Fused lowered its lance to a two-handed, underarm grip, then waited.

Knife against spear. Adolin breathed in and out, worried about the other Fused – who had gone for Shallan. He tried to dredge up Zahel's lessons, remembering days on the practice yard running this exact exchange. Jakamav had refused the training, laughing at the idea that a Shardbearer would ever fight knife to spear.

Adolin flipped the knife to grip it point down, then held it forward so he could deflect the spear thrusts. Zahel whispered to him. Wait until the enemy thrusts with the spear, deflect it or dodge it, then grab the spear with your left hand. Pull yourself close enough to ram the knife into the enemy's neck.

Right. He could do that.

He'd 'died' seven times out of ten doing it against Zahel, of course.

Winds bless you anyway, you old axehound, he thought. Adolin stepped in, testing, and waited for the thrust. When it came, Adolin shoved the lance's point aside with his knife, then grabbed at—

The enemy floated backward in an unnatural motion, too fast – no ordinary human could have moved in such a way. Adolin stumbled, trying to reassess. The Fused idly brought the lance back around, then fluidly rammed it right through Adolin's stomach.

Adolin gasped at the sharp spike of pain, doubling over, feeling blood on his hands. The Fused seemed almost *bored* as he yanked the lance out, the tip glistening red with Adolin's blood, then dropped the weapon. The creature landed and instead unsheathed a wicked-looking sword. He advanced, slapped away Adolin's weak attempt at a parry, and raised the sword to strike.

Someone leaped onto the Fused from behind.

A figure in tattered clothing, a scrabbling, angry woman with brown vines instead of skin and scratched-out eyes. Adolin gaped as his deadeye raked long nails across the Fused's face, causing him to stumble backward, *humming* of all things. He rammed his sword into the spren's chest, but it didn't faze her in the least. She just let out a screech like the one she'd made at Adolin when he'd tried to summon his Blade, and kept attacking.

Adolin shook himself. *Flee, idiot!*

Holding his wounded gut – each step causing a shock of pain – he lurched across the bridge toward Shallan.

⁂

Employing subterfuge will not deceive us or weaken our resolve, Lightweaver, the guardians said. *For indeed, this is not a matter of decision, but one of nature. The path remains closed.*

Shallan let the illusion melt around her, then slumped down, exhausted. She'd tried pleading, cajoling, yelling, and even Lightweaving. It was no use. She had failed. Her illusions on the bridge were wavering and vanishing, their Stormlight running out.

Through them shot a Fused trailing dark energy, lance leveled directly toward Shallan. She dove to the side, barely getting out of the way. The creature passed in a whoosh, then slowed and turned for another pass.

Shallan leaped to her feet first. 'Pattern!' she yelled, sweeping her hands forward by instinct, trying to summon the Blade. A part of her was impressed that was her reaction. Adolin would be proud.

It didn't work, of course. Pattern shouted in apology from the bridge, panicked. And yet in that moment – facing the enemy bearing down, its lance pointed at her heart – Shallan felt *something*. Pattern, or something like him, just beyond her mental reach. On the other side, and if she could just tug on it, feed it . . .

She screamed as Stormlight flowed through her, raging in her veins, reaching toward something in her pocket.

A wall appeared in front of her.

Shallan gasped. A sickening *smack* from the other side of the wall indicated that the Fused had collided with it.

A wall. A storming *wall* of worked stones, broken at the sides. Shallan looked down and found that her pocket – she was still wearing Veil's white trousers – was connected to the strange wall.

What on Roshar? She pulled out her small knife and sawed the pocket free, then stumbled back. In the center of the wall was a small bead, melded into the stone.

That's the bead I used to cross the sea down below, Shallan thought. What she'd done felt like Soulcasting, yet different.

Pattern ran up to her, humming as he left the bridge. Where were Adolin and Syl?

'I took the soul of the wall,' Shallan said, 'and then made its physical form appear on this side.'

'Mmm. I think these beads are more minds than souls, but you did manifest it here. Very nice. Though your touch is unpracticed. Mmm. It will not stay for long.'

The edges were already starting to unravel to smoke. A scraping sound on the other side indicated that the Fused had not been defeated, merely stunned. Shallan turned from it and scrambled over the bridge, away from the towering sentinels. She passed some of her illusions and recovered a little of their Stormlight. Now, where was—

Adolin. Bleeding!

Shallan dashed over and grabbed him by the arm, trying to keep him upright as he stumbled.

'It's just a little cut,' he said. Blood seeped out between his fingers, which were pressed to his gut, right below the navel. The back of his uniform was bloody too.

'Just a little cut? Adolin! You—'

'No time,' he said, leaning against her. He nodded toward the Fused she'd fought, who rose into the air over Shallan's wall. 'The other one is back behind me somewhere. Could be on us at any moment.'

'Kaladin,' Shallan said. 'Where—'

'Mmm . . .' Pattern said, pointing. 'He ran out of Stormlight and fell into the beads over that way.'

Great.

'Take a deep breath,' Shallan said to Adolin, then pulled him off the bridge with her and leaped for the beads.

∴

Lift became awesome.

Her powers manifested as the ability to slide across objects without truly touching them. She could become really, really slick – which was handy, because soldiers tried to snatch her as she rounded the Alethi army. They grabbed at her unbuttoned overshirt, her arm, her hair. They couldn't hold her. She just slid away. It was like they were trying to grab hold of a song.

She burst from their ranks and fell to her knees, which she'd slicked up real good. That meant she kept going, sliding on her knees away from the men with the glowing red eyes. Wyndle – who she knew by now was almost certainly not a Voidbringer – was a little snaking line of green beside her. He looked like a fast-growing vine, jutting with small crystals here and there.

'Oh, I don't like this,' he said.

'You don't like nothin'.'

'Now, that is *not* true, mistress. I liked that nice town we passed back in Azir.'

'The one that was deserted?'

'So peaceful.'

There, Lift thought, picking out a *real* Voidbringer – the type that looked like parshmen, only big and scary. This one was a woman, and moved across the rock smoothly, like she was awesome too.

'I've always wondered,' Lift said. 'Do you suppose they got those marble colorings on *all* their parts?'

'Mistress? Does it matter?'

'Maybe not now,' Lift admitted, glancing at the red storm. She kept her legs slick, but her hands not slick, which let her paddle and steer

610

herself. Going about on your knees didn't look as deevy as standing up – but when she tried being awesome while standing, she usually ended up crashed against a rock with her butt in the air.

That Fused *did* seem to be carrying something large in one hand. Like a big gemstone. Lift paddled in that direction – which was taking her dangerously close to that parshman army and their ships. Still, she got up pretty close before the Voidbringer woman turned and noticed.

Lift slid to a halt, letting her Stormlight run out. Her stomach growled, so she took a bite of some jerky she'd found in her guard's pocket.

The Voidbringer said something in a singsong voice, hefting the enormous ruby – it didn't have any Stormlight, which was good, since one that big would have been *bright*. Like, redder and brighter than Gawx's face when Lift told him about how babies was made. He should know stuff like that already. He'd been a starvin' thief! Hadn't he known any whores or anything?

Anyway . . . how to get that ruby? The Voidbringer spoke again, and while Lift couldn't figure out the words, she couldn't help feeling that the Voidbringer sounded amused. The woman pushed off with one foot, then slid on the other, easy as if she were standing on oil. She coasted for a second, then looked over her shoulder and grinned before kicking off and sliding to the left, casually moving with a grace that made Lift seem super stupid.

'Well starve me,' Lift said. 'She's *more* awesome than I am.'

'Do you *have* to use that term?' Wyndle asked. 'Yes, she appears to be able to access the Surge of—'

'Shut it,' Lift said. 'Can you follow her?'

'I might leave you behind.'

'I'll keep up.' Maybe. 'You follow her. I'll follow you.'

Wyndle sighed but obeyed, streaking off after the Voidbringer. Lift followed, paddling on her knees, feeling like a pig trying to imitate a professional dancer.

⁂

'You must choose, Szeth-son-Neturo,' Nin said. 'The Skybreakers will swear to the Dawnsingers and their law. And you? Will you join us?'

Wind rippled Szeth's clothing. All those years ago, he'd been correct. The Voidbringers *had* returned.

Now . . . now he was to simply accept their rule?

'I don't trust myself, aboshi,' Szeth whispered. 'I cannot see the right any longer. My own decisions are not trustworthy.'

'Yes,' Nin said, nodding, hands clasped behind his back. 'Our minds are fallible. This is why we must pick something external to follow. Only in strict adherence to a code can we approximate justice.'

Szeth inspected the battlefield far below.

When are we going to actually fight someone? asked the sword on his back. *You sure do like to talk. Even more than Vasher, and he could go on and on and on. . . .*

'Aboshi,' Szeth said. 'When I say the Third Ideal, can I choose a *person* as the thing I obey? Instead of the law?'

'Yes. Some of the Skybreakers have chosen to follow me, and I suspect that will make the transition to obeying the Dawnsingers easier for them. I would not suggest it. I feel that . . . I am . . . am getting worse. . . .'

A man in blue barred the way into the city below. He confronted . . . something else. A force that Szeth could just barely sense. A hidden fire.

'You followed men before,' Nin continued. 'They caused your pain, Szeth-son-Neturo. Your agony is because you did not follow something unchanging and pure. You picked men instead of an ideal.'

'Or,' Szeth said, 'perhaps I was simply forced to follow the wrong men.'

∴

Kaladin thrashed in the beads, suffocating, coughing. He wasn't that deep, but which way . . . which way was out? *Which way was out?*

Frantic, he tried to swim toward the surface, but the beads didn't move like water, and he couldn't propel himself. Beads slipped into his mouth, pushed at his skin. Pulled at him like an invisible hand. Trying to drag him farther and farther into the depths.

Away from the light. Away from the wind.

His fingers brushed something warm and soft among the beads. He thrashed, trying to find it again, and a hand seized his arm. He brought his other arm around and grabbed hold of a thin wrist. Another hand took him by the front of the coat, pulling him away from the darkness, and he stumbled, finding purchase on the bottom of the sea.

Lungs burning, he followed, step by step, eventually bursting from the beads to find Syl pulling him by the front of the coat. She led him up the bank, where he collapsed in a heap, spitting out spheres and wheezing. The Fused he'd been fighting landed on the Oathgate platform near the two they'd left behind.

As Kaladin was recovering his breath, beads nearby pulled back, revealing Shallan, Adolin, and Pattern crossing the seafloor through some kind of passage she'd made. A hallway in the depths? She was growing in her ability to manipulate the beads.

Adolin was wounded. Kaladin gritted his teeth, forcing himself to his feet and stumbling over to help Shallan get the prince up onto the shore. The prince lay on his back, cursing softly, holding his gut with bloodied hands.

'Let me see it,' Kaladin said, prying Adolin's fingers out of the way.

'The blood –' Shallan started.

'The blood is the least of his worries,' Kaladin said, prodding at the wound. 'He's not going to bleed out from a gut wound anytime soon, but sepsis is another story. And if internal organs got cut . . .'

'Leave me,' Adolin said, coughing.

'Leave you to go *where*?' Kaladin said, moving his fingers in the wound. Storms. The intestines were cut. 'I'm out of Stormlight.'

Shallan's glow faded. 'That was the last of what I had.'

Syl gripped Kaladin's shoulder, looking toward the Fused, who launched up and flew toward them, lances held high. Pattern hummed softly. Nervously.

'What do we do then?' Shallan asked.

No . . . Kaladin thought.

'Give me your knife,' Adolin said, trying to sit up.

It can't be the end.

'Adolin, no. Rest. Maybe we can surrender.'

I can't fail him!

Kaladin looked over his shoulder toward Syl, who held him lightly by the arm.

She nodded. 'The Words, Kaladin.'

⁂

Amaram's soldiers parted around Dalinar, flooding into the city. They ignored him – and unfortunately, he had to ignore them.

'So, child . . .' Odium nodded toward the city, and took Dalinar by the shoulder. 'You did something marvelous in forging that coalition. You should feel proud. *I'm* certainly proud.'

How could Dalinar fight this thing, who thought of every possibility, who planned for every outcome? How could he face something so vast, so incredible? Touching it, Dalinar could *sense* it stretching into infinity. Permeating the land, the people, the sky and the stone.

He would break, go insane, if he tried to comprehend this being. And somehow he had to defeat it?

Convince him that he can lose, the Almighty had said in vision. *Appoint a champion. He will take that chance. . . . This is the best advice I can give you.*

Honor had been slain resisting this thing.

Dalinar licked his lips. 'A test of champions,' he said to Odium. 'I demand that we clash over this world.'

'For what purpose?' Odium asked.

'Killing us won't free you, will it?' Dalinar said. 'You could rule us or destroy us, but either way, you'd still be trapped here.'

Nearby, one of the thunderclasts climbed over the wall and entered the city. The other stayed behind, stomping around near the rearguard of the army.

'A contest,' Dalinar said to Odium. 'Your freedom if you win, our lives if humans win.'

'Be careful what you request, Dalinar Kholin. As Bondsmith, you can offer this deal. But is this truly what you wish of me?'

'I . . .'

Was it?

⁂

Wyndle followed the Voidbringer, and Lift followed him. They slipped back among the men of the human army. The front ranks were pouring into the city, but the opening wasn't big enough for them to all go at once. Most waited out here for their turn, cursing and grumbling at the delay.

They took swipes at Lift as she tried to follow the trail of vines Wyndle left. Being little helped her avoid them, fortunately. She liked being little. Little people could squeeze into places others couldn't, and could go unnoticed. She wasn't supposed to get any older; the Nightwatcher had promised her she wouldn't.

The Nightwatcher had lied. Just like a starvin' human would have. Lift shook her head and slipped between the legs of a soldier. Being little was nice, but it *was* hard not to feel like every man was a mountain towering overhead. They smashed weapons about her, speaking guttural Alethi curses.

I can't do this on my knees, she thought as a sword chopped close to her shirt. *I have to be like her. I have to be free.*

Lift zipped over the side of a small rise in the rock, and managed to land on her feet. She ran for a moment, then slicked the bottoms of her feet and went into a slide.

The Voidbringer woman passed ahead. She didn't slip and fall, but performed this strange walking motion – one that let her control her smooth glide.

Lift tried to do the same. She trusted in her awesomeness – her Stormlight – to sustain her as she held her breath. Men cursed around her, but sounds slid off Lift as she coated herself in Light.

The wind itself couldn't touch her. She'd been here before. She'd held for a beautiful moment between crashes, sliding on bare feet, moving free, untouched. Like she was gliding between worlds. She could do it. She could—

Something crashed to the ground nearby, crushing several soldiers, throwing Lift off balance and sending her into a heap. She slid to a stop and rolled over, looking up at one of the huge stone monsters. The skeletal thing raised a spiked hand and slammed it down.

Lift threw herself out of the way, but the shaking from the impact sent her sprawling again. Soldiers nearby didn't seem to care that their fellows had been crushed. Eyes glowing, they scrambled for her, as if it were a contest to see who could kill her first.

Her only choice was to dodge *toward* the stone monster. Maybe she could get so close that it—

The creature pounded again, mashing three soldiers, but also slamming into Lift. The blow snapped her legs in the blink of an eye, then crushed her lower half, sending her into a screaming fit of pain. Eyes watering, she curled up on the ground.

Heal. Heal.

Just had to weather the pain. Just had to . . .

Stones ground against one another overhead. She blinked away tears, looking up at the creature raising its spike high in the sky, toward the sun, which was slipping behind the clouds of the deadly storm.

'Mistress!' Wyndle said. His vines climbed over her, as if trying to cradle her. 'Oh, mistress. Summon me as a sword!'

The pain in her legs started to fade. Too slowly. She was growing hungry again, her Stormlight running low. She summoned Wyndle as a rod, twisting against the pain and holding him toward the monster, her eyes watering with the effort.

An explosion of light appeared overhead, a ball of expanding Radiance. Something dropped from the middle of it, trailing smoke both black and white. Glowing like a star.

'Mother!' Wyndle said. 'What is—'

As the monster raised its fist to strike Lift, the spear of light hit the creature in the head and *cut straight through*. It divided the enormous thing in two, sending out an explosion of black smoke. The halves of the monster fell to the sides, crashing into the stone, then *burned away*, evaporating into blackness.

Soldiers cursed and coughed, backing up as something resolved in the center of the tempest. A figure in the smoke, glowing white and holding a jet-black Shardblade that seemed to *feed* on the smoke, sucking it in, then letting it pour down beneath itself as a liquid blackness.

White and black. A man with a shaved head, eyes glowing a light grey, Stormlight rising from him. He straightened and strode through the smoke, leaving an afterimage behind. Lift had seen this man before. The Assassin in White. Murderer.

And apparently savior.

He stopped beside her. 'The Blackthorn assigned you a task?'

'Uh . . . yeah,' Lift said, wiggling her toes, which seemed to be working again. 'There's a Voidbringer who stole a large ruby. I'm supposed to get it back.'

'Then stand,' the assassin said, raising his strange Shardblade toward the enemy soldiers. 'Our master has given us a task. *We shall see it completed.*'

·•·

Navani scrambled across the top of the wall, alone except for crushed corpses.

Dalinar, don't you dare become a martyr, she thought, reaching the stair-well. She pulled open the door at the top and started down the dark steps.

What was he thinking? Facing an entire army on his own? He wasn't a young man in his prime, outfitted in Shardplate!

She fumbled for a sphere in her safepouch, then eventually undid the clasp on her arm fabrial instead, using its light to guide her down the steps and into the room at the base. Where had Fen and—

A hand grabbed her, pulling her to the side and slamming her against the wall. Fen and Kmakl lay here, gagged, bound tightly. A pair of men in forest green, eyes glowing red, held knives to them. A third one, wearing the knots of a captain, pressed Navani against the wall.

'What a handsome reward you'll earn me,' the man hissed at Navani. 'Two queens. Brightlord Amaram will enjoy this gift. That almost makes up for not being able to kill you personally, as justice for what your husband did to Brightlord Sadeas.'

❖

Ash stumbled to a stop before a brazier. It bore delicate metalwork around the rim, a finer piece than one expected to find in such a common location.

This improvised camp was where the Alethi troops had bivouacked while repairing the city; it clogged multiple streets and squares of the Low Ward. The unlit brazier that had stopped Ash was in front of a tent, and had perhaps been used for warmth on cold Thaylen nights. Ten figures ringed the bowl. Her fingers *itched*. She couldn't move on, no matter how desperate her task, until she'd done it.

She seized the bowl and turned it until she found the woman depicting her, marked by the iconography of the brush and the mask, symbols of creativity. Pure absurdity. She pulled out her knife and sawed at the metal until she'd managed to scratch out the face.

Good enough. Good enough.

She dropped the brazier. Keep going. What that man, Mraize, had told her had better be true. If he had lied . . .

The large tent near the wall was completely unguarded, though soldiers had run past her a short time ago, eyes glowing with the light of corrupted Investiture. *Odium has learned to possess men.* A dark, dangerous day. He'd always been able to tempt them to fight for him, but sending spren to bond with them? Terrible.

And how had he managed to start a *storm* of his *own?*

Well, this land was finally doomed. And Ash ... Ash couldn't find it inside herself to care any longer. She pushed into the tent, forcibly keeping herself from looking at the rug in case it bore depictions of the Heralds.

There she found him, sitting alone in the dim light, staring ahead sightlessly. Dark skin, even darker than hers, and a muscled physique. A king, for all the fact that he'd never worn a crown. He was the one of the ten who was never supposed to have borne their burden.

And he'd borne it the longest anyway.

'Taln,' she whispered.

⁘

Renarin Kholin knew he wasn't actually a Knight Radiant. Glys had once been a different kind of spren, but something had changed him, corrupted him. Glys didn't remember that very well; it had happened before they had formed their bond.

Now, neither knew what they'd become. Renarin could feel the spren trembling inside him, hiding and whispering about the danger. Jasnah had found them.

Renarin had seen that coming.

He knelt in the ancient temple of Pailiah, and to his eyes it was full of colors. A thousand panes of stained glass sprouted on the walls, combining and melting together, creating a panorama. He saw himself coming to Thaylen City earlier in the day. He saw Dalinar talking to the monarchs, and then he saw them turning against him.

She will hurt us! She will hurt us!

'I know, Glys,' he whispered, turning toward a specific section of stained glass. This showed Renarin kneeling on the floor of the temple. In the sequence of stained glass panels, Jasnah approached him from behind, sword raised.

And then ... she struck him down.

Renarin couldn't control what he saw or when he saw it. He had learned to read so he could understand the numbers and words that appeared under some of the images. They had shown him when the Everstorm would come. They had shown him how to find the hidden compartments in Urithiru. Now they showed his death.

The future. Renarin could see what was forbidden.

He wrenched his eyes away from the glass pane showing himself and Jasnah, turning toward one even worse. In it, his father knelt before a god of gold and white.

'No, Father,' Renarin whispered. 'Please. Not that. Don't do it. . . .'

He will not be resisted, Glys said. *My sorrow, Renarin. I will give you my sorrow.*

.•.

A pair of gloryspren swung down from the skies, golden spheres. They floated and spun around Dalinar, brilliant like drops of sunlight.

'Yes,' Dalinar said. 'This is what I wish.'

'You wish a contest of champions?' Odium repeated. 'This is your true desire, not forced upon you? You were not beguiled or tricked in any way?'

'A contest of champions. For the fate of Roshar.'

'Very well,' Odium said, then sighed softly. 'I agree.'

'That easily?'

'Oh, I assure you. This won't be easy.' Odium raised his eyebrows in an open, inviting way. A *concerned* expression. 'I have chosen my champion already. I've been preparing him for a long, long time.'

'Amaram.'

'Him? A passionate man, yes, but hardly suited to this task. No, I need someone who dominates a battlefield like the sun dominates the sky.'

The Thrill suddenly returned to Dalinar. The red mist – which had been fading – roared back to life. Images filled his mind. Memories of his youth spent fighting.

'I need someone stronger than Amaram,' Odium whispered.

'No.'

'A man who will win no matter the cost.'

The Thrill overwhelmed Dalinar, choking him.

'A man who has served me all his life. A man I trust. I believe I warned you that I knew you'd make the right decision. And now here we are.'

'*No.*'

'Take a deep breath, my friend,' Odium whispered. 'I'm afraid that this will hurt.'

These Voidbringers know no songs. They cannot hear Roshar, and where they go, they bring silence. They look soft, with no shell, but they are hard. They have but one heart, and it cannot ever live.

—From the Eila Stele

No,' Dalinar whispered again, voice ragged as the Thrill thrummed inside of him. '*No.* You are wrong.'

Odium gripped Dalinar's shoulder. 'What does *she* say?'

She?

He heard Evi crying. Screaming. Begging for her life as the flames took her.

'Don't blame yourself,' Odium said as Dalinar winced. 'I made you kill her, Dalinar. I caused *all* of this. Do you remember? I can help. Here.'

Memories flooded Dalinar's mind, a devastating onslaught of images. He lived them all in detail, somehow squeezed into a moment, the Thrill raging inside of him.

He saw himself stab a poor soldier in the back. A young man trying to crawl to safety, crying for his mother ...

'I was with you then,' Odium said.

He killed a far better man than himself, a highlord who had held

Teleb's loyalty. Dalinar knocked him to the ground, then slammed a poleaxe into his chest.

'I was with you then.'

Dalinar fought atop a strange rock formation, facing another man who knew the Thrill. Dalinar dropped him to the ground with burning eyes, and called it a mercy.

'I was with you then.'

He raged at Gavilar, anger and lust rising as twin emotions. He broke a man in a tavern, frustrated that he'd been held back from enjoying the fight. He fought on the borders of Jah Keved, laughing, corpses littering the ground. He remembered every moment of the carnage. He felt each death like a spike driven into his soul. He began to weep for the destruction.

'It's what you needed to do, Dalinar,' Odium said. 'You made a better kingdom!'

'So ... much ... *pain*.'

'Blame me, Dalinar. It wasn't you! You saw red when you did those things! It was *my* fault. Accept that. You don't have to hurt.'

Dalinar blinked, meeting Odium's eyes.

'Let me have the pain, Dalinar,' Odium said. 'Give it to me, and never feel guilty again.'

'No.' Dalinar hugged *The Way of Kings* close. 'No. I can't.'

'Oh, Dalinar. What does *she* say?'

No ...

'Have you forgotten? Here, let me help.'

And he was back in that day. The day he killed Evi.

⁖

Szeth found purpose in wielding the sword.

It screamed at him to destroy evil, even if evil was obviously a concept that the sword itself could not understand. Its vision was occluded, like Szeth's own. A metaphor.

How was a twisted soul like his to decide who should die? Impossible. And so he put his trust in someone else, someone whose light peeked through the shadow.

Dalinar Kholin. Knight Radiant. *He* would know.

This choice was not perfect. But ... Stones Unhallowed ... it was the best he could manage. It brought him some small measure of peace as he swept through the enemy army.

The sword screamed at him. *DESTROY!*

Anyone he so much as nicked *popped* into black smoke. Szeth laid waste to the red-eyed soldiers, who kept coming, showing no fear. Screaming, as if they thirsted for death.

It was a drink that Szeth was all too good at serving.

He wielded Stormlight in one hand, Lashing any men who drew too close, sending them flipping into the air or crashing backward into their fellows. With the other hand he swept the sword through their ranks. He moved on nimble feet, his own body Lashed upward just enough to lighten him. Skybreakers didn't have access to all of the Lashings, but the most useful – and most deadly – were still his.

Remember the gemstone.

A phantom sense called to him, a desire to continue killing, to revel in the butchery. Szeth rejected it, sick. He had never enjoyed this. He *could* never enjoy this.

The Voidbringer with the gemstone had slipped away, moving on too-swift feet. Szeth pointed the sword – a piece of him terrified by how quickly it was chewing through his own Stormlight – and Lashed himself to follow. He plowed through soldiers, men bursting into smoke, seeking that one individual.

The Voidbringer turned at the last moment, dancing away from his sword. Szeth Lashed himself downward, then spun in a sweeping arc towing black smoke – almost liquid – behind his sword as he destroyed men in a grand circle.

EVIL! the sword cried.

Szeth leaped for the Voidbringer woman, but she dropped to the ground and slid on the stone as if it were greased. His sword swung over her head, and she pushed herself backward toward him, sliding right past his legs. There, she swept gracefully to her feet and seized the *sheath* off Szeth's back, where he'd tied it for safekeeping.

It broke free. When Szeth turned to attack, she blocked the sword with its own sheath. How had she done that? Was there something about the silvery metal that Szeth didn't know?

She blocked his next few attacks, then ducked away from his attempts to Lash her.

The sword was growing frustrated. *DESTROY, DESTROY, DE-STROY!* Black veins began to grow around Szeth's hand, creeping toward his upper arm.

He struck again, but she simply slipped away, moving across the ground as if natural laws had no purchase on her. Other soldiers piled in, and the pain started up Szeth's arm as he worked death among them.

⁂

Jasnah stopped one pace behind Renarin. She could hear his whispers clearly now. 'Father. Oh, Father . . .' The young man whipped his head in one direction, then another, seeing things that weren't there.

'He sees not what *is,* but what *is to come,*' Ivory said. 'Odium's power, Jasnah.'

⁂

'Taln,' Ash whispered, kneeling before him. 'Oh, Taln . . .'

The Herald stared forward with dark eyes. 'I am Talenel'Elin, Herald of War. The time of the Return, the Desolation, is near at hand. . . .'

'Taln?' Ash took his hand. 'It's me. It's Ash.'

'We must prepare. You will have forgotten much. . . .'

'Please, Taln.'

'Kalak will teach you to cast bronze. . . .'

He just continued on, repeating the same words over and over and over.

⁂

Kaladin fell to his knees on the cold obsidian of Shadesmar.

Fused descended around them, six figures in brilliant, flapping clothing.

He had a single slim hope. Each Ideal he'd spoken had resulted in an outpouring of power and strength. He licked his lips and tried whispering it. 'I . . . I will . . .'

He thought of friends lost. Malop. Jaks. Beld and Pedin.

Say it, storm you!

'I . . .'

Rod and Mart. Bridgemen he'd failed. And before them, slaves he'd tried to save. Goshel. Nalma, caught in a trap like a beast.

A windspren appeared near him, like a line of light. Then another.

A single hope.
The Words. Say the Words!

⁘

'Oh, Mother! Oh, Cultivation!' Wyndle cried as they watched the assassin murder his way across the field. 'What have we done?'

'We've pointed *him* away from *us*,' Lift said as she perched on a boulder, her eyes wide. 'You'd rather he was close by?'

Wyndle continued to whimper, and Lift kinda understood. That was a *lot* of killing that the assassin did. Red-eyed men who seemed to have no light left in them, true, but . . . storms.

She'd lost track of the woman with the gemstone, but at least the army seemed to be flowing away from Szeth, leaving him fewer people to kill. He stumbled, slowing, then dropped to his knees.

'Uh-oh.' Lift summoned Wyndle as a rod in case the assassin lost his starvin' mind – what was left of it – and attacked her. She slipped off the rock, then ran over.

He held the strange Shardblade before himself. It continued to leak black liquid that vaporized as it streamed toward the ground. His hand had gone all black.

'I . . .' Szeth said. 'I have lost the sheath. . . .'

'Drop the sword!'

'I . . . can't. . . .' Szeth said, teeth gritted. 'It holds to me, feasting upon my . . . my Stormlight. It will soon consume me.'

Stormsstormsstormsstorms. 'Right. Right. Ummmmm . . .' Lift looked around. The army was flooding into the city. The second stone monster was stomping across the Ancient Ward, stepping on buildings. Dalinar Kholin still stood before the gap. Maybe . . . maybe he could help?

'Come on,' Lift said.

⁘

'Kill the man,' said the captain holding Navani. He swept his hand toward old Kmakl, Fen's consort. 'We don't need him.'

Fen screamed against her gag, but she was held tightly. Navani carefully wiggled her safehand fingers out of her sleeve, then touched her other arm and the fabrial there, flipping a latch. Small knobs extended from the front of the device, just above her wrist.

Kmakl struggled to stand. He seemed to want to face his death with dignity, but the other two soldiers didn't give him that honor. They pushed him back against the wall, one pulling out a dagger.

Navani seized the arm of the man holding her, then pressed the knobs of her pain fabrial against his skin. He screamed and dropped, writhing in agony. One of the others turned toward her, and she pressed the painrial against his uplifted hand. She'd tested the device on herself, of course, so she knew what it felt like. A thousand needles being shoved into your skin, under your nails, into your *eyes*.

The second man wet himself as he dropped.

The last one managed to cut a gash in her arm before she sent him to the ground, spasming. Bother. She flipped the switch on the painrial, drawing away the agony of the cut. Then she took the knife and quickly cut Fen's bonds. As the queen freed Kmakl, Navani bound her painless wound.

'These will recover soon,' Navani said. 'We may need to dispatch them before that happens.'

Kmakl kicked the man who had almost slit his throat, then cracked the door into the city. A troop of men with glowing eyes rushed past. The entire area was overrun with them.

'These are the least of our trouble, it seems,' the aging man said, shutting the door.

'Back up to the wall, then,' Fen said. 'We might be able to spot friendly troops from that vantage.'

Navani nodded, and Fen led the way up. At the top, they barred the door. There were bars on both sides; you wanted to be able to lock out enemies who had seized the wall, and also ones who had broken through the gates.

Navani surveyed their options. A quick glance revealed that the streets were indeed held by Amaram's troops. Some groups of Thaylens held ground farther up, but they were falling quickly.

'By Kelek, storms, and Passions alike,' Kmakl said. 'What is *that*?'

He'd noticed the red mist on the north side of the battlefield, with its horrific images forming and breaking apart. Shadows of soldiers dying, of skeletal features, of charging horses. It was a grand, intimidating sight.

But Dalinar . . . *Dalinar* drew her eyes. Standing alone, surrounded by enemy soldiers, and facing something she could just *barely* sense. Something vast. Something unimaginable.

Something angry.

∴

Dalinar lived in two places.

He saw himself crossing a darkened landscape, dragging his Shardblade behind him. He was on the field at Thaylen City with Odium, but he was also in the past, approaching Rathalas. Urged on by the boiling red anger of the Thrill. He returned to the camp, to the surprise of his men, like a spren of death. Coated in blood, eyes glowing.

Glowing red.

He ordered the oil brought. He turned toward a city where Evi was imprisoned, where children slept, where innocent people hid and prayed and burned glyphwards and wept.

'Please . . .' Dalinar whispered in Thaylen City. 'Don't make me live it again.'

'Oh, Dalinar,' Odium said. 'You will live it again and again until you let go. You can't carry this burden. Please, give it to me. *I* drove you to do this. *It wasn't your fault.*'

Dalinar pulled *The Way of Kings* close against his chest, clutching it, like a child with his blanket in the night. But a sudden *flash* of light blasted in front of him, accompanied by a deafening crack.

Dalinar stumbled backward. Lightning. That had been *lightning*. Had it struck him?

No. It had somehow struck only the book. Burned pages fluttered around him, singed and smoldering. It had been blasted right from his hands.

Odium shook his head. 'The words of a man long dead, long failed.'

Overhead, the sun finally passed behind the clouds of the storm, and all fell into darkness. Slowly, the flames of the burning pages went out.

∴

Teft huddled someplace dark.

Maybe the darkness would hide his sins. But in the distance, he heard shouting. Men fighting.

Bridge Four dying.

626

Kaladin stuttered, the Words stumbling.

He thought of his men from Amaram's army. Dallet and his squad, slain either by Shallan's brother or by Amaram. Such good friends who had fallen.

And then, of course, he thought of Tien.

···

Dalinar fell to his knees. A few gloryspren swirled around him, but Odium batted them away, and they faded.

In the back of his mind, the Stormfather wept.

He saw himself step up to where Evi was imprisoned. That tomb in the rock. Dalinar tried to look away, but the vision was everywhere. He didn't merely see it, he *lived* it. He ordered Evi's death, and listened to her screams.

'Please . . .'

Odium wasn't done with him. Dalinar had to watch the city burn, hear the children die. He gritted his teeth, groaning in agony. Before, his pains had driven him to drink. There was no drink now. Just the Thrill.

He had always craved it. The Thrill had made him live. Without it . . . he'd . . . he'd been dead. . . .

He slumped, bowing his head, listening to the tears of a woman who had believed in him. He'd *never* deserved her. The Stormfather's weeping faded as Odium somehow shoved the spren away, separating them.

That left Dalinar alone.

'So alone . . .'

'You're *not* alone, Dalinar,' Odium said, going down on one knee beside him. 'I'm here. I've always been here.'

The Thrill boiled within. And Dalinar knew. He *knew* he'd always been a fraud. He was the same as Amaram. He had an honest reputation, but was a murderer on the inside. A destroyer. A child killer.

'Let go,' Odium whispered.

Dalinar squeezed his eyes shut, trembling, hands tense as he hunched over and clawed the ground. It hurt so badly. To know that he'd failed them. Navani, Adolin, Elhokar, Gavilar. He couldn't live with this.

He couldn't live with her *tears*!

627

'Give it to me,' Odium pled.

Dalinar ripped his fingernails off, but the pain of the body couldn't distract him. It was nothing beside the agony of his soul.

Of knowing what he truly was.

⁘

Szeth tried to walk toward Dalinar. The darkness had grown up his arm, and the sword drank his last wisps of Stormlight.

There was ... was a lesson in this ... wasn't there? There had to be. Nin ... Nin wanted him to learn. ...

He fell to the ground, still holding the sword as it screamed mindlessly. *DESTROY EVIL.*

The little Radiant girl scrambled to him. She looked toward the sky as the sun vanished behind clouds. Then she took Szeth's head in her hands.

'No ...' he tried to croak. *It will take you too. ...*

She breathed life into him somehow, and the sword drank of it freely. Her eyes went wide as the black veins began to grow up her fingers and hands.

⁘

Renarin didn't want to die. But strangely, he found himself welcoming Jasnah's strike.

Better to die than to live to see what was happening to his father. For he saw the future. He saw his father in black armor, a plague upon the land. He saw the Blackthorn return, a terrible scourge with nine shadows.

Odium's champion.

'He's going to fall,' Renarin whispered. 'He's already fallen. He belongs to the enemy now. Dalinar Kholin ... is no more.'

⁘

Venli shivered on the plain, near Odium. Timbre had been pulsing to Peace, but now she quieted. Twenty or thirty yards away, a figure in white clothing collapsed to the ground, a little girl at his side.

Nearer to her, Dalinar Kholin – the man who had resisted – slumped forward, head bowed, holding one hand against his chest and trembling.

Odium stepped back, his appearance that of a parshman with golden

628

carapace. 'It is done,' he said, looking toward Venli and the gathered group of Fused. 'You have a leader.'

'We must follow one of them?' Turash asked. 'A human?'

Venli's breath caught. There had been no respect in that tone.

Odium smiled. 'You will follow me, Turash, or I will reclaim that which gives you persistent life. I care not for the shape of the tool. Only that it cuts.'

Turash bowed his head.

Stone crunched as a figure in glittering Shardplate walked up to them, carrying a Shardblade in one hand and – strangely – an empty sheath in the other. The human had his faceplate up, exposing red eyes. He tossed the silvery sheath to the ground. 'I was told to deliver that to you.'

'Well done, Meridas,' Odium said. 'Abaray, could you provide this human with an appropriate housing for Yelig-nar?'

One of the Fused stepped forward and proffered a small, uncut smokestone toward the human, Meridas.

'And what is *this*?' Meridas asked.

'The fulfillment of my promise to you,' Odium said. 'Swallow it.'

'*What?*'

'If you wish for the promised power, ingest that – then try to control the one who follows. But be warned, the queen at Kholinar tried this, and the power consumed her.'

Meridas held up the gemstone, inspecting it, then glanced toward Dalinar Kholin. 'So, you've been speaking to him all this time too?'

'Even longer than I've been speaking to you.'

'Can I kill him?'

'Someday, assuming I don't let him kill you.' Odium rested his hand on the shoulder of the huddled Dalinar Kholin. 'It's done, Dalinar. The pain has passed. Stand up and claim the station you were born to obtain.'

.·.

Kaladin thought, finally, of Dalinar.

Could Kaladin do it? Could he really say these Words? Could he *mean* them?

The Fused swept close. Adolin bled.

'I . . .'

You know what you need to do.

'I . . . can't,' Kaladin finally whispered, tears streaming down his cheeks. 'I can't lose him, but . . . oh, Almighty . . . I can't save him.' Kaladin bowed his head, sagging forward, trembling.

He couldn't say those Words.

He wasn't strong enough.

Syl's arms enfolded him from behind, and he felt softness as her cheek pressed against the back of his neck. She pulled him tight as he wept, sobbing, at his failure.

⁕

Jasnah raised her Blade over Renarin's head.

Make it quick. Make it painless.

Most threats to a dynasty came from within.

Renarin was obviously corrupted. She'd known there was a problem the moment she'd read that he had predicted the Everstorm. Now, Jasnah had to be strong. She had to do what was *right*, even when it was so, so hard.

She prepared to swing, but then Renarin turned and looked at her. Tears streaming down his face, he met her eyes, and he *nodded.*

Suddenly they were young again. He was a trembling child, weeping on her shoulder for a father who didn't seem to be able to feel love. Little Renarin, always so solemn. Always misunderstood, laughed at and condemned by people who said similar things about Jasnah behind her back.

Jasnah froze, as if standing at the edge of a cliff. Wind blew through the temple, carrying with it a pair of spren in the form of golden spheres, bobbing in the currents.

Jasnah dismissed her sword.

'Jasnah?' Ivory said, appearing back in the form of a man, clinging to her collar.

Jasnah fell to her knees, then pulled Renarin into an embrace. He broke down crying, like he had as a boy, burying his head in her shoulder.

'What's wrong with me?' Renarin asked. 'Why do I see these things? I thought I was doing something right, with Glys, but somehow it's all wrong. . . .'

'Hush,' Jasnah whispered. 'We'll find a way through it, Renarin. Whatever it is, we'll fix it. We'll survive this, somehow.'

Storms. The things he'd said about Dalinar . . .

'Jasnah,' Ivory said, becoming full size as he stepped free of her collar. He leaned down. 'Jasnah, this is right. Somehow it *is*.' He seemed completely stunned. 'It is not what makes sense, yet it is still right. How. How *is* this thing?'

Renarin pulled back from her, his tearstained eyes going wide. 'I saw you kill me.'

'It's all right, Renarin. I'm not going to.'

'But don't you *see*? Don't you understand what that means?'

Jasnah shook her head.

'Jasnah,' Renarin said. 'My vision was wrong about you. What I see . . . it *can be wrong*.'

·:·

Alone.

Dalinar held a fist to his chest.

So alone.

It hurt to breathe, to think. But something stirred inside his fist. He opened bleeding fingers.

The most . . . the most important . . .

Inside his fist, he somehow found a golden sphere. A solitary gloryspren.

The most important step a man can take. It's not the first one, is it?

It's the next *one. Always the next step, Dalinar.*

Trembling, bleeding, agonized, Dalinar forced air into his lungs and spoke a single ragged sentence.

'You cannot have my pain.'

UNITY

As I began my journey, I was challenged to defend why I insisted on traveling alone. They called it irresponsible. An avoidance of duty and obligation.

Those who said this made an enormous mistake of assumption.

—From *The Way of Kings*, postscript

O dium stepped back. 'Dalinar? What is this?'

'You cannot have my pain.'

'Dalinar—'

Dalinar forced himself to his feet. 'You. Cannot. Have. My. Pain.'

'Be sensible.'

'I killed those children,' Dalinar said.

'No, it—'

'I burned the people of Rathalas.'

'I was there, influencing you—'

'*YOU CANNOT HAVE MY PAIN!*' Dalinar bellowed, stepping toward Odium. The god frowned. His Fused companions shied back, and Amaram raised a hand before his eyes and squinted.

Were those gloryspren spinning around Dalinar?

'I *did* kill the people of Rathalas,' Dalinar shouted. 'You might have been there, but *I* made the choice. *I* decided!' He stilled. 'I killed her. It urts so much, but I did it. I accept that. You cannot have her. You *cannot* ake her from me again.'

'Dalinar,' Odium said. 'What do you hope to gain, keeping this burden?'

Dalinar sneered at the god. 'If I pretend ... If I pretend I *didn't* do hose things, it means that I can't have grown to become someone else.'

'A failure.'

Something stirred inside of Dalinar. A warmth that he had known nce before. A warm, calming light.

Unite them.

'Journey before destination,' Dalinar said. 'It cannot be a journey if it *loesn't have a beginning.*'

A thunderclap sounded in his mind. Suddenly, awareness poured back nto him. The Stormfather, distant, feeling frightened – but also surprised.

Dalinar?

'I will take responsibility for what I have done,' Dalinar whispered. 'If must fall, I will rise each time a better man.'

∴

Renarin ran after Jasnah through the Loft Wards of the city. People logged the streets, but she didn't use those. She leaped off buildings, lropping onto rooftops of the tiers below. She ran across each of these, hen leaped down to the next street.

Renarin struggled to follow, afraid of his weakness, confused by the hings he'd seen. He dropped to a rooftop, feeling sudden pain at the fall - though Stormlight healed that. He limped after her until the pain left.

'Jasnah!' he called. 'Jasnah, I can't keep up!'

She stopped at the edge of a rooftop. He reached her, and she took his rm. 'You *can* keep up, Renarin. You're a Knight Radiant.'

'I don't think I'm a Radiant, Jasnah. I don't know *what* I am.'

An entire *stream* of gloryspren flew past them, hundreds in a sweeping ormation that curved toward the base of the city. Something was glow-ng down there, a beacon in the dim light of an overcast city.

'I know what you are,' Jasnah said. 'You're my cousin. Family, Renarin. Iold my hand. Run with me.'

He nodded, and she towed him after her, leaping from the rooftop, gnoring the monstrous creature that climbed up nearby. Jasnah seemed ocused on only one thing.

That light.

.·.

Unite them!

Gloryspren streamed around Dalinar. Thousands of golden spheres, more spren than he'd ever seen in one place. They swirled around him in a column of golden light.

Beyond it, Odium stumbled back.

So small, Dalinar thought. *Has he always looked that small?*

.·.

Syl looked up.

Kaladin turned to see what had drawn her attention. She looked past the Fused who had landed to attack. She was staring toward the ocean of beads, and the trembling lights of souls above it.

'Syl?'

She pulled him tight. 'Maybe you don't have to save anyone, Kaladin. Maybe it's time for someone to save *you.*'

.·.

UNITE THEM!

Dalinar thrust his left hand to the side, plunging it between realms, grabbing hold of the very fabric of existence. The world of minds, the realm of thought.

He thrust his right hand to the other side, touching something vast, something that wasn't a place – it was all places in one. He'd seen this before, in the moment when Odium had let him glimpse the Spiritual Realm.

Today, he held it in his hand.

The Fused scrambled away. Amaram pushed down his faceplate, but that wasn't enough. He stumbled back, arm raised. Only one person remained in place. A young parshwoman, the one that Dalinar had visited in the visions.

'What are you?' she whispered as he stood with arms outstretched, holding to the lands of mind and spirit.

He closed his eyes, breathing out, listening to a sudden stillness. And within it a simple, quiet voice. A woman's voice, so familiar to him.

I forgive you.

Dalinar opened his eyes, and knew what the parshwoman saw in him. Swirling clouds, glowing light, thunder and lightning.

'I am Unity.'

He slammed both hands together.

And combined three realms into one.

⁜

Shadesmar exploded with light.

Fused screamed as a wind blasted them away, though Kaladin felt nothing. Beads clattered and roared.

Kaladin shaded his eyes with his hand. The light faded, leaving a brilliant, glowing pillar in the middle of the sea. Beneath it, the beads locked together, turning into a highway of glass.

Kaladin blinked, taking Shallan's hand as she helped him to his feet. Adolin had forced himself to sit up, holding his bloodied stomach. 'What . . . what is it?'

'Honor's Perpendicularity,' Syl whispered. 'A well of power that pierces all three realms.' She looked to Kaladin. 'A pathway home.'

⁜

Taln gripped Ash's hand.

Ash looked at his fingers, thick and callused. Thousands of years could come and pass, and she could lose lifetimes to the dream, but those hands . . . she'd never forget those hands.

'Ash,' he said.

She looked up at him, then gasped and raised her fingers to her lips.

'How long?' he asked.

'Taln.' She gripped his hand in both of hers. 'I'm sorry. I'm so, *so* sorry.'

'How long?'

'They say it's been four millennia. I don't always . . . note the passing of time. . . .'

'Four thousand years?'

She held his hand tighter. 'I'm sorry. I'm *sorry*.'

He pulled his hand from hers and stood up, walking through the tent. She followed, apologizing again – but what good were words? They'd betrayed him.

Taln brushed aside the front drapes and stepped out. He looked up at the city expanding above them, at the sky, at the wall. Soldiers in breast-plates and chain rushed past to join a fight farther along.

'Four thousand years?' Taln asked again. 'Ash . . .'

'We couldn't continue – I . . . we thought . . .'

'Ash.' He took her hand again. 'What a *wonderful* thing.'

Wonderful? 'We *left* you, Taln.'

'What a gift you gave them! Time to recover, for once, between Desolations. Time to progress. They never had a chance before. But this time . . . yes, maybe they do.'

'No, Taln. You can't be like this.'

'A wonderful thing indeed, Ash.'

'You *can't* be like this, Taln. You have to hate me! Hate me, *please.*'

He turned from her, but still held her hand, pulling her after him. 'Come. He's waiting.'

'Who?' she asked.

'I don't know.'

⁜

Teft gasped in the darkness.

'Can you see it, Teft?' the spren whispered. 'Can you feel the Words?'

'I'm *broken.*'

'Who isn't? Life breaks us, Teft. Then we fill the cracks with something stronger.'

'I make myself sick.'

'Teft,' she said, a glowing apparition in the darkness, 'that's what the Words are *about.*'

Oh, Kelek. The shouts. Fighting. His friends.

'I . . .'

Storm you! Be a man for once in your life!

Teft licked his lips, and spoke.

'I will protect those I hate. Even . . . even if the one I hate most . . . is . . . *myself.*'

⁜

Renarin fell to the last level of the city, the Low Ward. He stumbled to a stop there, his hand slipping from Jasnah's. Soldiers marched through these streets, with eyes like embers.

'Jasnah!' he called. 'Amaram's soldiers changed sides. They serve Odium now! I saw it in vision!'

She ran right toward them.

'Jasnah!'

The first soldier swung his sword at her. Jasnah ducked the weapon, then shoved her hand against him, throwing him backward. He *crystallized* in the air, slamming into the next man, who caught the transformation like a disease. He slammed into *another* man, knocking him back, as if the full force of Jasnah's shove had transferred to him. He crystallized a moment later.

Jasnah spun, a Shardblade forming in her gloved safehand, her skirt rippling as she sliced through six men in one sweep. The sword vanished as she slapped her hand into the wall of a building behind her, and that wall *puffed away* into smoke, causing the roof to crash down, blocking the alley between buildings, where other soldiers had been approaching.

She swept her hand upward, and air coalesced into stone, forming steps that she took – barely breaking her stride – to climb to the rooftop of the next building.

Renarin gaped. That – How—

It will be . . . great . . . vast . . . wonderful! Glys said from within Renarin's heart. *It will be beautiful, Renarin! Look!*

A well blossomed inside of him. Power like he'd never before felt, an awesome, overwhelming *strength*. Stormlight unending. A source of it so vast, he was stunned.

'Jasnah?' he shouted, then belatedly ran up the steps she'd created, feeling so *alive* that he wanted to dance. Wouldn't that be a sight? Renarin Kholin dancing on a rooftop while . . .

He slowed, gaping again as he looked through a gap in the wall and saw a column of light. Rising higher and higher, it stretched toward the clouds.

⁂

Fen and her consort backed away from the storm of light.

Navani exulted in it. She leaned out far over the side of the wall, laughing like a fool. Gloryspren streamed around her, brushing her hair, flowing toward the already impossible number that coursed around Dalinar in a pillar that stretched hundreds of feet into the air.

Then *lights* sparked to life in a wave across the field, the top of the wall, the street below. Gemstones that had been lying ignored, scattered from the broken bank, drank in Stormlight from Dalinar. They lit the ground with a thousand pinpricks of color.

⁛

'No!' Odium screamed. He stepped forward. 'No, we killed you. WE KILLED YOU!'

Dalinar stood within a pillar of light and spinning gloryspren, one hand to each side, clutching the realms that made up reality.

Forgiven. The pain he'd so recently insisted that he would keep started to fade away on its own.

These Words . . . are accepted, the Stormfather said, sounding stunned. *How? What have you done?*

Odium stumbled back. 'Kill him! *Attack him!*'

The parshwoman didn't move, but Amaram lethargically lowered his hand from his face, then stepped forward, summoning his Shardblade.

Dalinar took his hand from the glowing pillar and held it out. 'You *can* change,' he said. 'You can become a better person. I did. Journey before destination.'

'No,' Amaram said. 'No, he'll never forgive me.'

'The bridgeman?'

'Not him.' Amaram tapped his chest. 'Him. I'm sorry, Dalinar.'

He raised a familiar Shardblade. Dalinar's Shardblade, Oathbringer. Passed from tyrant to tyrant to tyrant.

A portion of light split from Dalinar's column.

Amaram swung Oathbringer with a shout, but the light met the Shardblade with an explosion of sparks, throwing Amaram backward – as if the strength of Shardplate were no more than that of a child. The light resolved into a man with shoulder-length wavy hair, a blue uniform, and a silvery spear in his hand.

A second glowing form split off into Shallan Davar, brilliant red hair streaming behind her, a long thin Shardblade with a slight curve forming in her hands.

And then, blessedly, Adolin appeared.

'Mistress!' Wyndle said. 'Oh, mistress!'

For once, Lift didn't have the will to tell him to shut up. She focused everything on those tendrils creeping up her arms, like deep, dark vines.

The assassin lay on the ground, staring upward, practically *covered* in those vines. Lift held them at bay, teeth gritted. Her will against the darkness until . . .

Light.

Like a sudden detonation, a force of light flashed across the field. Gemstones on the ground flared up, capturing Stormlight, and the assassin screamed, drawing in Light like glowing mist.

The vines shriveled, as the sword's thirst was slaked by the Stormlight. Lift fell back on the stone and pried her hands off Szeth's head.

I knew I liked you, a voice said in Lift's mind.

The sword. So it was a spren? 'You almost *ate* him,' Lift said. 'You almost starvin' ate *me*!'

Oh, I wouldn't do that, the voice said. She seemed completely baffled, voice growing slow, like she was drowsy. *But . . . maybe I was just really, really hungry. . . .*

Well, Lift supposed she couldn't blame someone for that.

The assassin climbed unsteadily to his feet. His face was crisscrossed with lines where the vines had been. That somehow left his skin grey in streaks, the color of stone. Lift's arms bore the same. Huh.

Szeth walked toward the glowing column of light, leaving an afterimage behind him. 'Come,' he said.

❖

Elhokar? Dalinar thought. But no one else came through the column of light. And he knew. Knew, somehow, that the king was not coming.

He closed his eyes, and accepted that grief. He had failed the king in many ways.

Stand up, he thought. *And do better.*

He opened his eyes, and slowly his column of gloryspren faded. The power within him withdrew, leaving him exhausted. Fortunately, the field was covered in glittering gemstones. Stormlight in plenty.

A direct conduit to the Spiritual Realm, the Stormfather said. *You renew spheres, Dalinar?*

'We are Connected.'

I was bonded to men before. This never happened then.

'Honor was alive then. We are something different. His remnants, your soul, my will.'

Kaladin Stormblessed stepped up beside Dalinar before the rubble of the wall, and Shallan Davar stood on the other side. Jasnah emerged from the city and surveyed the scene with a critical air, while Renarin popped out behind her, then cried out and ran for Adolin. He grabbed his older brother in an embrace, then gasped. Adolin was wounded?

Good lad, Dalinar thought as Renarin immediately set to healing his brother.

Two more people crossed the battlefield. Lift he had anticipated. But the assassin? Szeth scooped the silvery sheath off the ground and slammed his black Shardblade into it, before stepping up to join Dalinar.

Skybreaker, Dalinar thought, counting them off. *Edgedancer.* That was seven.

He would have expected three more.

There, the Stormfather said. *Behind your niece.*

Two more people appeared in the shadow of the wall. A large, powerful man with an impressive physique, and a woman with long, dark hair. Their dark skin marked them as Makabaki, perhaps Azish, but their eyes were wrong.

I know them, the Stormfather said, sounding surprised. *I know them from long, long ago. Memories of days when I did not fully live.*

Dalinar, you are in the presence of divinities.

'I've grown accustomed to it,' Dalinar said, turning back toward the field. Odium had retreated into nothingness, though his Fused remained, as did most of the troops, and one strange spren – the one like black smoke. Beyond it, of course, the Thrill still encompassed the north side of the landing, near the water.

Amaram had ten thousand men, and maybe half of those had made it into the city so far. They had wilted before Dalinar's display, but now . . .

Wait.

Those two only make nine, he thought to the Stormfather. Something told him there should be one more.

I don't know. Perhaps they haven't been found yet. Regardless, even with the bond you are just one man. Radiants are not immortal. How do you face this army?

'Dalinar?' Kaladin said. 'Orders, sir?'

The enemy ranks were recovering. They lifted weapons, eyes glowing deep red. Amaram stirred as well, some twenty feet away. The Thrill had Dalinar most worried, however. He knew what it could do.

He glanced down at his arm, and noticed something. The lightning that had struck him earlier, shredding *The Way of Kings*, had broken his arm fabrial. The clasp was undone, and Dalinar could see the tiny gemstones Navani had placed to power it.

'Sir?' Kaladin asked again.

'The enemy is trying to crush this city, Captain,' Dalinar said, lowering his arm. 'We're going to hold it against his forces.'

'Seven Radiants?' Jasnah said, skeptical. 'Uncle, that seems a tall order, even if one of us is – apparently – the storming *Assassin in White.*'

'I serve Dalinar Kholin,' Szeth-son-son-Vallano whispered. His face, for some reason, was streaked with grey. 'I cannot know truth, so I follow one who does.'

'Whatever we do,' Shallan said, 'we should do it quickly. Before those soldiers—'

'Renarin!' Dalinar barked.

'Sir!' Renarin said, scrambling forward.

'We need to hold out until troops arrive from Urithiru. Fen doesn't have the numbers to fight alone. Get to the Oathgate, stop that thunderclast up there from destroying it, and open the portal.'

'Sir!' Renarin saluted.

'Shallan, we don't have an army yet,' Dalinar said. 'Lightweave one up for us, and keep these soldiers busy. They're consumed by a bloodlust that I suspect will make them easier to distract. Jasnah, the city we're defending happens to have a big storming hole in its wall. Can you hold that hole and stop anyone who tries to get through?'

She nodded, thoughtful.

'What about me?' Kaladin asked.

Dalinar pointed at Amaram, who was climbing to his feet in his Shardplate. 'He's going to try to kill me for what I do next, and I could use a bodyguard. As I recall, you have a score to settle with the highlord.'

'You could say that.'

'Lift, I believe I already gave you an order. Take the assassin and *get me that ruby*. Together, we hold this city until Renarin returns with troops. Any questions?'

'Um ...' Lift said. 'Could you maybe ... tell me where to get something to eat ...?'

Dalinar glanced at her. Something to *eat*? 'There ... should be a supply dump just inside the wall.'

'Thanks!'

Dalinar sighed, then started walking toward the water.

'Sir!' Kaladin called. 'Where are you going?'

'The enemy brought a very big stick to this battle, Captain. I'm going to take it away.'

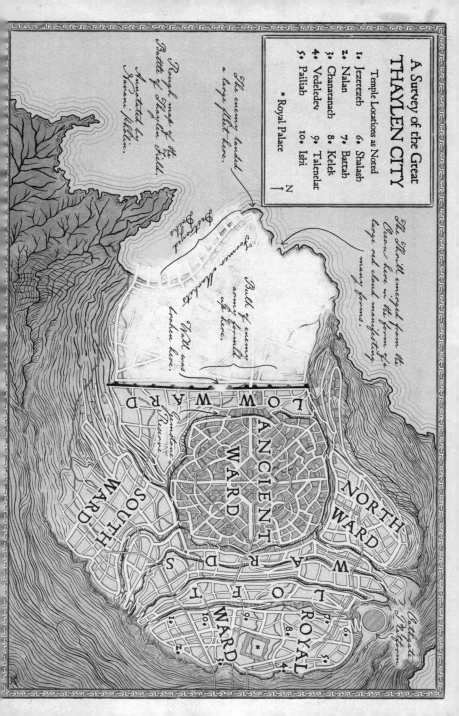

A Survey of the Great
THAYLEN CITY

Temple Locations as Noted

1. Jezerezeh   6. Shalash
2. Nalan   7. Battah
3. Chanaranach   8. Kelek
4. Vedeledev   9. Talenelat
5. Pailiah   10. Ishi

* Royal Palace

→ N

The Unmade emerged from the
Rboar line in the form of a
large red cloud manifesting
many forms.

Bulk of enemy
army formed
up here.

Wall was
broken here.

The enemy landed
a large fleet here.

Rough map of the
Battle of Thaylen Field.

Annotated by
Navani Kholin.

*If the journey itself is indeed the most important piece, rather than
the destination itself, then I traveled not to avoid duty – but to seek it.*

—From *The Way of Kings,* postscript

Kaladin rose into the sky, alive with Stormlight.

Below him, Dalinar walked toward the red mist. Though tendrils of it moved among the soldiers of Amaram's army, the bulk of it swirled closer to the coast, to the right of the bay and the destroyed docks.

Storms, Kaladin felt good to be in the real world again. Even with the Everstorm dominating the sun, this place felt so much more *bright* than Shadesmar. A group of windspren dodged around him, though the air was relatively still. Perhaps they were the ones who had come to him on the other side, the ones he had failed.

Kaladin, Syl said. *You* don't *need another reason to berate yourself.*

She was right. Storms, he *could* be down on himself sometimes. Was that the flaw that had prevented him from speaking the Words of the Fourth Ideal?

For some reason, Syl sighed. *Oh, Kaladin.*

'We'll talk about it later,' he said.

For now, he'd been given a second chance to protect Dalinar Kholin.

Stormlight raging inside of him, the Sylspear a comfortable weight in his hand, he Lashed himself downward and crashed to the stones near Amaram.

The highlord, in turn, fell to his knees.

What? Kaladin thought. Amaram was coughing. He tipped his head back, faceplate up, and groaned.

Had he just *swallowed* something?

٭

Adolin prodded at his stomach. Beneath the bloodstained rip, he felt only smooth, new skin. Not even a hint of an ache.

For a time, he'd been sure he would die.

He'd been there before. Months ago, he'd felt it when Sadeas had withdrawn, leaving the Kholin troops alone and surrounded on the Shattered Plains. This had been different. Staring up at that black sky and those unnatural clouds, feeling suddenly, *appallingly* fragile . . .

And then light. His father – the great man Adolin could never match – somehow embodying the Almighty himself. Adolin couldn't help feeling that he hadn't been worthy to step into that light.

Here he was anyway.

The Radiants broke apart to do Dalinar's bidding, though Shallan knelt to check on Adolin. 'How do you feel?'

'Do you realize how fond I was of this jacket?'

'Oh, Adolin.'

'Really, Shallan. Surgeons should take more care with the clothing they cut open. If a man's going to live, he'll want that shirt. And if he dies . . . well, he should *at least* be well dressed on his deathbed.'

She smiled, then glanced over her shoulder toward the troops with red eyes.

'Go,' he said. 'I'll be fine. Save the city. Be *Radiant*, Shallan.'

She kissed him, then turned and stood. That white clothing seemed to glow, the red hair a striking swatch, as Stormlight rose from her. Pattern appeared as a Shardblade with a faint, almost invisible latticework running up the length. She wove her power, and an *army* climbed from the ground around her.

In Urithiru, she'd made an army of a score to distract the Unmade. Now, *hundreds* of illusions rose around her: soldiers, shopkeepers, washwomen, scribes, all drawn from her pages. They glowed brilliantly, Light streaming from them – as if each were a Knight Radiant.

Adolin climbed to his feet, and came face-to-face with an illusion of himself wearing a Kholin uniform. The illusory Adolin glowed with Stormlight and floated a few inches off the ground. She'd made him a Windrunner.

I . . . I can't take that. He turned toward the city. His father had been focused on the Radiants, and had neglected to give Adolin a specific duty. So maybe he could help the defenders inside.

Adolin picked his way across the rubble and through the broken wall. Jasnah stood right inside, hands on hips, as if she were surveying a mess left by rampaging children. The gap opened into an unremarkable city square dominated by barracks and storehouses. Fallen troops wearing either Thaylen or Sadeas uniforms indicated a recent clash here, but most of the enemy seemed to have moved on. Shouts and clangs sounded from nearby streets.

Adolin reached for a discarded sword, then paused, and – feeling a fool – summoned his Shardblade. He braced himself for a scream, but none came, and the Blade fell into his hand after ten heartbeats.

'I'm sorry,' he said, lifting the glistening weapon. 'And thank you.'

He headed toward one of the nearby clashes, where men were shouting for help.

∴

Szeth of the Skybreakers envied Kaladin, the one they called Storm-blessed, in the honor of protecting Dalinar Kholin. But of course, he would not complain. He had chosen his oath.

And he would do as his master demanded.

Phantoms appeared, created from Stormlight by the woman with the red hair. These were the shadows in the darkness, the ones he heard whispering of his murders. How she brought them to life, he did not know. He landed near the Reshi Surgebinder, Lift.

'So,' she said to him. 'How do we find that ruby?'

Szeth pointed with his sheathed Shardblade toward the ships docked in the bay. 'The creature carrying it ran back that way.' The parshmen still clustered there, deep within the shadow of the Everstorm.

'Figures,' Lift said, then glanced at him. 'You aren't gonna try to eat me again, right?'

Don't be silly, said the sword in Szeth's hand. *You aren't evil. You're nice. And I don't eat people.*

'I will not draw the sword,' Szeth said, 'unless you are already dead and I decide to accept death myself.'

'Greaaaaaaaaaaat,' Lift said.

You're supposed to contradict me, Szeth, the sword said, *when I say I don't eat people. Vasher always did. I think he was joking. Anyway, as people who have carried me go, you aren't very good at this.*

'No,' Szeth said. 'I am not good at being a person. It is . . . a failing of mine.'

It's all right! Be happy. Looks like there's a lot of evil to slay today! That's greaaaaaaaaaaaat, right?

Then the sword started humming.

⁜

The brands on Kaladin's head seemed a fresh pain as he dove to strike Amaram. But Amaram recovered quickly from his fit, then slammed his faceplate down. He rebuffed Kaladin's attack with an armored forearm.

Those red eyes cast a crimson glow through the helm's slit. 'You should thank me, boy.'

'*Thank* you?' Kaladin said. 'For what? For showing me that a person could be even *more* loathsome than the petty lighteyes who ruled my hometown?'

'I created you, spearman. I *forged* you.' Amaram pointed at Kaladin with the wide, hook-ended Shardblade. Then he extended his left hand, summoning a *second* Blade. Long and curved, the back edge rippled like flowing waves.

Kaladin knew that Blade well. He'd won it – saving Amaram's life – then refused to bear it. For when he looked at his reflection in the silvery metal, all he could see were the friends it had killed. So much death and pain, caused by that rippling Blade.

It seemed a symbol of all he'd lost, particularly held now in the hand of the man who had lied to him. The man who had taken Tien away.

Amaram presented a sword stance, holding two Blades. One taken in bloodshed, at the cost of Kaladin's crew. The other, Oathbringer. A sword given to ransom Bridge Four.

Don't be intimidated! Syl whispered in Kaladin's mind. *History notwithstanding, he's only a man. And you're a Knight Radiant.*

The vambrace of Amaram's armor *pulsed* suddenly on his forearm, as if something were pushing it from beneath. The red glow from the helm deepened, and Kaladin got the distinct impression of something enveloping Amaram.

A black smoke. The same that Kaladin had seen surrounding Queen Aesudan at the end, as they'd fled the palace. Other sections of Amaram's armor began to rattle or pulse, and he suddenly moved with a violent burst of speed, swinging with one Shardblade, then the other.

.⁎.

Dalinar slowed as he approached the main core of the Thrill. The red mist churned and boiled here, nearly solid. He saw familiar faces reflected in it. He watched the old highprince Kalanor fall from the heights of a rock formation. He saw himself fight alone on a field of stone after a rockslide. He watched as he caught the claw of a chasmfiend on the Shattered Plains.

He could hear the Thrill. A thrumming, insistent, warming pulse. Almost like the beating of a drum.

'Hello, old friend,' Dalinar whispered, then stepped into the red mist.

.⁎.

Shallan stood with arms outstretched. Stormlight expanded from her on the ground, a pool of liquid light, radiant mist swirling above it. It became a gateway. From it, her collection emerged.

Every person she'd ever sketched – from the maids in her father's house to the honorspren who had held Syl captive – grew from Stormlight. Men and women, children and grandparents. Soldiers and scribes. Mothers and scouts, kings and slaves.

Mmm, Pattern said as a sword in her hand. *MMMMMMM.*

'I've lost these,' Shallan said as Yalb the sailor climbed from the mist and waved to her. He drew a glowing Shardspear from the air. 'I lost these pictures!'

You are close to them, Pattern said. *Close to the realm of thought ...*

648

and beyond. All the people you've Connected to, over the years . . .

Her brothers emerged. She'd buried worries about them in the back of her mind. Held by the Ghostbloods . . . No word from any spanreed she tried . . .

Her father stepped from the Light. And her mother.

The illusions immediately started to fail, melting back to Light. Then, someone seized her by the left hand.

Shallan gasped. Forming from mist was . . . was *Veil*? With long straight black hair, white clothing, brown eyes. Wiser than Shallan – and more focused. Capable of working on small pieces when Shallan grew overwhelmed by the large scale of her work.

Another hand took Shallan's on the right. Radiant, in glowing garnet Shardplate, tall, with braided hair. Reserved and cautious. She nodded to Shallan with a steady, determined look.

Others boiled at Shallan's feet, trying to crawl from the Stormlight, their glowing hands grabbing at her legs.

'. . . No,' Shallan whispered.

This was enough. She had created Veil and Radiant to be strong when she was weak. She squeezed their hands tight, then hissed out slowly. The other versions of Shallan retreated into the Stormlight.

Then, farther out, figures by the hundred surged from the ground and raised weapons at the enemy.

∴

Adolin, now accompanied by some two dozen soldiers, charged through the streets of the Low Ward.

'There!' one of his men shouted with a thick Thaylen accent. 'Brightlord!' He pointed toward a group of enemy soldiers disappearing down an alley back toward the wall.

'Damnation,' Adolin said, waving his troops to follow as he gave chase. Jasnah was alone in that direction, trying to hold the gap. He charged down the alleyway to—

A soldier with red eyes suddenly hurtled through the air overhead. Adolin ducked, worried about Fused, but it was an ordinary soldier. The unfortunate man crashed into a rooftop. What on Roshar?

As they approached the end of the alleyway, another body smashed into the wall right by the opening. Gripping his Shardblade, Adolin peeked around the corner, expecting to find another stone monster like the one that had climbed into the Ancient Ward.

Instead, he found only Jasnah Kholin, looking completely nonplussed. A glow faded around her, different from the smoke of her Stormlight. Like geometric shapes outlining her . . .

All right then. Jasnah didn't need help. Adolin instead waved for his men to follow the sounds of battle to the right. There they found a small group of beleaguered Thaylen soldiers backed up against the base of the wall, facing a much larger force of men in green uniforms.

Well. This Adolin could fix.

He waved his own soldiers back, then charged the enemy in Smokestance, sweeping with his Shardblade. The enemy had packed in close to try to get at their prey, and had a hard time adjusting to the miniature storm that crashed into them from behind.

Adolin stepped through the sequence of swipes, feeling immense satisfaction at finally being able to do something. The Thaylens let out a cheer as he dropped the last group of enemies, red eyes going black as they burned out. His satisfaction lasted until, glancing down at the corpses, he was struck by how *human* they looked.

He'd spent years fighting Parshendi. He didn't think he'd actually killed another Alethi since . . . well, he couldn't remember.

Sadeas. Don't forget Sadeas.

Fifty men dead at his feet, and some three dozen killed while gathering his other troops. Storms . . . after feeling so useless in Shadesmar, now this. How much of his reputation was him, and how much of it was – and had always been – the sword?

'Prince Adolin?' a voice called in Alethi. 'Your Highness!'

'Kdralk?' Adolin said as a figure emerged from the Thaylens. The queen's son had seen better days. His eyebrows were bloodied from a cut across his forehead. His uniform was torn, and there was a bandage on his upper arm.

'My mother and father,' Kdralk said. 'They're trapped on the wall a little farther down. We were pushing to reach them, but we got cornered.'

'Right. Let's move, then.'

⁘

Jasnah stepped over a corpse. Her Blade vanished in a puff of Stormlight, and Ivory appeared next to her, his oily black features concerned as he regarded the sky. 'This place is three, still,' he said. 'Almost three.'

'Or three places are nearly one,' Jasnah replied. Another batch of gloryspren flocked past, and she could see them as they were in the Cognitive Realm: like strange avians with long wings, and a golden sphere in place of the head. Well, being able to see into the Cognitive Realm without trying was one of the *least* unnerving things that had happened so far today.

An incredible amount of Stormlight thrummed inside her – more than she'd ever held before. Another group of soldiers broke through Shallan's illusions and charged over the rubble through the gap in the wall. Jasnah casually flipped her hand toward them. Once, their souls would have resisted mightily. Soulcasting living things was difficult; it usually required care and concentration – along with proper knowledge and procedure.

Today, the men puffed away to smoke at her barest thought. It was so easy that a part of her was horrified.

She felt invincible, which was a danger in itself. The human body wasn't meant to be stuffed this full of Stormlight. It rose from her like smoke from a bonfire. Dalinar had closed his perpendicularity, however. He had been the storm, and had somehow recharged the spheres – but like a storm, his effects were passing.

'Three worlds,' Ivory said. 'Slowly splitting apart again, but for now, three realms *are* close.'

'Then let's make use of it before it fades, shall we?'

She stepped up before the rent portion of the wall, a gap as wide as a small city block.

Then raised her hands.

⁘

Szeth of the Skybreakers led the way toward the parshman army, the child Edgedancer following.

Szeth feared not pain, as no physical agony could rival the pain he already bore. He feared not death. That sweet reward had already been snatched from him. He feared only that he had made the wrong choice.

Szeth expunged that fear. Nin was correct. Life could not be lived making decisions at each juncture.

The parshmen standing on the shore of the bay did not have glowing eyes. They looked much like the Parshendi who had used him to assassinate King Gavilar. When he drew close, several of them ran off and boarded one of the ships.

'There,' he said. 'I suspect they are going to warn the one we seek.'

'I'm after it, crazyface,' Lift said. 'Sword, don't eat anyone unless they try to eat you first.' She zipped off in her silly way – kneeling and slapping her hands on the ground. She slid among the parshmen. When she reached the ship, she somehow scrambled up its side, then squeezed through a tiny porthole.

The parshmen here didn't seem aggressive. They shied away from Szeth, murmuring among themselves. Szeth glanced at the sky and picked out Nin – as a speck – still watching. Szeth could not fault the Herald's decision; the law of these creatures *was* now the law of the land.

But . . . that law was the product of the many. Szeth had been exiled because of the consensus of the many. He had served master after master, most of them using him to attain terrible or at least selfish goals. You could not arrive at excellence by the average of these people. Excellence was an individual quest, not a group effort.

A flying Parshendi – 'Fused' was a term Lift had used for them – shot out of the ship, carrying the large dun ruby that Dalinar sought. Lift followed the Fused out, but couldn't fly. She clambered up onto the prow of the ship, releasing a loud string of curses.

Wow, the sword said. *That's impressive vocabulary for a child. Does she even know what that last one means?*

Szeth Lashed himself into the air after the Fused.

If she does know what it means, the sword added, *do you think she'd tell me?*

The enemy swooped down low across the battlefield, and Szeth followed, a mere inch above the rocks. They soon passed among the fighting illusions. Some of these appeared as enemy soldiers, to further add confusion. A clever move. The enemy would be less likely to retreat if they thought most of their companions were still fighting, and it made the battle look far more real. Except that when Szeth's quarry zipped past, her fluttering robes struck and disturbed illusory shapes.

Szeth followed close, passing through a pair of fighting men he had seen were illusions. This Fused was talented, better than the Skybreakers had been, though Szeth had not faced their best.

652

The chase took him in a long loop, eventually swinging back down near where Dalinar was walking through the edge of the red mist. The whispered voices grew louder, and Szeth put his hands to his ears as he flew.

The Fused was smooth and graceful, but sped up and slowed less quickly than Szeth did. He took advantage of this, anticipating the enemy's move, then cutting to the side as they turned. Szeth collided with the enemy, and they twisted in the air. The Fused – gemstone in one hand – stabbed Szeth with a wicked knife.

Fortunately, with Stormlight, that didn't do anything but cause pain.

Szeth Lashed them both downward, holding tight, and sent them crashing to the stone. The gemstone rolled free as the Fused groaned. Szeth Lashed himself gracefully to his feet, then slipped along the stone at a standing glide. He scooped up the ruby with his free hand, the one not carrying his sheathed sword.

Wow, the sword said.

'Thank you, sword-nimi,' Szeth said. He restored his Stormlight from nearby fallen spheres and gemstones.

I meant that. *To your right.*

Three more Fused were swooping down toward him. He appeared to have gotten the enemy's attention.

.•.

Adolin and his men reached a covered stairwell leading up onto the wall. Aunt Navani waved from up above, then gestured urgently. Adolin hurried inside the stairwell, and at the top found a jumble of Sadeas troops chopping at the door with hand axes.

'I can probably get through that a little easier,' Adolin said from behind them.

A short time later, he stepped onto the wall walk, leaving five more corpses on the steps. These didn't make him feel quite so melancholy. They'd been minutes from reaching Aunt Navani.

Navani hugged him. 'Elhokar?' she asked, tense.

Adolin shook his head. 'I'm sorry.'

She pulled him tight, and he dismissed his Blade, holding her as she shook, letting out quiet tears. Storms . . . he knew how that felt. He hadn't really been able to take time to think since Elhokar's death. He'd felt the oppressive hand of responsibility, but had he grieved for his cousin?

He pulled his aunt tighter, feeling her pain, mirror to his own. The stone monster crashed through the city, and soldiers shouted from all around – but in that moment, Adolin did what he could to comfort a mother who had lost her son.

Finally they broke, Navani drying her eyes with a handkerchief. She gasped as she saw his bloodied side.

'I'm fine,' he explained. 'Renarin healed me.'

'I saw your betrothed and the bridgeman down below,' Navani said. 'So everyone . . . everyone but him?'

'I'm sorry, Aunt. I just . . . We failed him. Elhokar and Kholinar both.'

She blotted her eyes and stiffened with determination. 'Come. Our focus now has to be on keeping this city from suffering the same fate.'

They joined Queen Fen, who was surveying the battle from atop the wall. 'Estnatil was on the wall with us when that thing hit,' she was saying to her son. 'He got thrown down and likely died, but there's a Shardblade in that rubble somewhere. I haven't seen Tshadr. Perhaps at his manor? I wouldn't be surprised to find him gathering troops at the upper tiers.'

Counting Shardbearers. Thaylenah had three sets of Plate and five Blades – a solid number of Shards for a kingdom of this size. Eight houses passed them down, father to son, each of whom served the throne as a highguard.

Adolin glanced over the city, assessing the defense. Fighting in city streets was difficult; your men got divided up, and were easily flanked or surrounded. Fortunately, the Sadeas troops seemed to have forgotten their battle training. They didn't hold ground well; they had broken into roving bands, like axehound packs, loping through the city and looking for contests.

'You need to join your troops,' Adolin said to the Thaylens. 'Block off a street below, coordinate a resistance. Then—'

A sudden whooshing sound cut him off.

He stumbled back as the wall shook, then the broken gap in it *mended*. Metal grew like crystals to fill the hole, springing into existence out of a tempest of rushing, howling air.

The end result was a beautiful, brilliant section of polished bronze melding with the stonework and completely sealing the gap.

'Taln's *palms*,' Fen said. She and her consort stepped closer to the edge and looked down at Jasnah, who dusted off her hands, then rested them on her hips in a satisfied posture.

'So . . . change of tactics,' Adolin said. 'With the gap filled, you can get archers in position to harry the army outside *and* hold the inside square. Set up a command position here, clear the street below, and then hold this wall at *all costs.*'

Below, Jasnah strode away from the marvel she'd created, then knelt beside some rubble and cocked her head, listening to something. She pressed her hand against the rubble and it vanished into smoke, revealing a corpse beneath – and a brilliant Shardblade beside it.

'Kdralk,' Adolin said, 'how are your Shardblade stances?'

'I . . . I've practiced with them, like other officers, and – I mean—'

'Great. Take ten soldiers, go get that Blade, then rescue that cluster of troops over there at the base of the Ancient Ward. Next try to rescue that other group fighting on the steps. Station every archer you can up here on the wall, and put the rest of the soldiers to work guarding the streets.' Adolin glanced over his shoulder. Shallan's distraction was working well, for now. 'Don't stretch too far, but as you rescue more men, make a coordinated effort to hold the entire Low Ward.'

'But Prince Adolin,' Fen said, 'what will *you* be doing?'

Adolin summoned his Blade and pointed with it toward the back of the Ancient Ward, where the gigantic stone monstrosity swept a group of soldiers from a rooftop. Others tried – in futility – to trip it with ropes.

'Those men seem like they could use the help of a weapon designed *specifically* to cut through stone.'

∴

Amaram fought with striking fury – a frenetic kind of harmony, an unending assault of weaving Shardblades and beautiful stances. Kaladin blocked one Blade with the Sylspear, and they locked for a moment.

A sharp violet *crystal* burst out of Amaram's elbow, cracking the Shardplate there, glowing with a soft inner light. Storms! Kaladin flung himself backward as Amaram swung his other Blade, nearly connecting.

Kaladin danced away. His training with the sword had been short, and he'd never seen anyone use two Blades at once. He would have considered it unwieldy. Amaram made it look elegant, mesmerizing.

That deep red glow within Amaram's helm grew darker, bloody, somehow even more sinister. Kaladin blocked another hit, but the power of the blow sent him skidding backward on the stone. He'd made himself lighter for the fight, but that had repercussions when facing someone in Plate.

Puffing, Kaladin launched himself into the air to get some distance. That Plate prevented him from using Lashings against Amaram, and it blocked hits from the Sylspear. Yet, if Amaram landed a single strike, that would immobilize Kaladin. Healing the wound from a Shardblade was possible, but was slow and left him horribly weakened.

This was all complicated by the fact that, while Amaram could focus only on their duel, Kaladin had to keep watching Dalinar in case—

Damnation!

Kaladin Lashed himself to the side, streaking through the air to engage one of the Fused who had started hovering near Dalinar. She struck toward Kaladin – but that only let him change Syl to a Blade midswing, and cut her long spear in half. She hummed an angry song and floated backward, sliding her sword from its sheath. Below, Dalinar was a mere shadow against the shifting crimson cloud. Faces emerged within, screaming with rage, fury, bloodlust – like the billowing front of a thunderhead.

Being near the mist made Kaladin feel nauseous. Fortunately, the enemy didn't seem eager to enter it either. They hovered outside, watching Dalinar. A few had ducked in closer, but Kaladin had managed to drive them back.

He pressed his advantage against his current foe, using Syl as a spear. The Fused was nimble, but Kaladin was flush with Stormlight. The field below was still littered with a fortune in glowing spheres.

After he got in close with a strike – cutting the Fused's robes – she zipped away to join a group that was focusing on Szeth. Hopefully the assassin could stay ahead of them.

Now, where had Amaram gotten to. ... Kaladin glanced over his shoulder, then yelped and Lashed himself backward, Stormlight puffing before him. A thick black arrow shot right through that, dispersing the Light.

Amaram stood near his horse, where he'd unhooked a massive Shardbow that used arrows as thick as a spear's haft. Amaram raised it to loose again, and a line of crystals *jutted* out along his arm, cracking his Shardplate. Storms, what was happening to that man?

Kaladin zipped out of the way of the arrow. He could heal from a hit like that, but it would distract him – potentially let some of the Fused seize him. All the Stormlight in the world wouldn't save him if they simply bound him, then hacked at him until he stopped healing.

Amaram launched another arrow, and Kaladin blocked it with Syl, who became a shield in his grip. Then, Kaladin Lashed himself into a dive, summoning Syl as a lance. He swooped down on Amaram, who hooked his Shardbow back onto the horse's saddle and dodged to the side, moving with incredible speed.

Amaram grabbed the Syllance as Kaladin dove past, flinging Kaladin to the side. Kaladin was forced to dismiss Syl and slow himself, spinning and sliding across the ground until his Lashing ran out and he settled down.

Teeth gritted, Kaladin summoned Syl as a short spear, then rushed Amaram – determined to bring the highlord down before the Fused returned to attack Dalinar.

⁂

The Thrill was happy to see Dalinar.

He had imagined it as some evil force, malignant and insidious, like Odium or Sadeas. How wrong he was.

Dalinar walked through the mist, and each step was a battle he relived. Wars from his youth, to secure Alethkar. Wars during his middle years, to preserve his reputation – and to sate his lust for the fight. And ... he saw times when the Thrill withdrew. Like when Dalinar had held Adolin for the first time. Or when he'd grinned with Elhokar atop a rocky spire on the Shattered Plains.

The Thrill regarded these events with a sad sense of abandonment and confusion. The Thrill didn't hate. Though some spren could make decisions, others were like animals – primal, driven by a single overpowering directive. Live. Burn. Laugh.

Or in this case, *fight*.

⁂

Jasnah existed halfway in the Cognitive Realm, which made everything a blurry maze of shadows, floating souls of light, and beads of glass. A thousand varieties of spren churned and climbed over one another in Shadesmar's ocean. Most did not manifest in the physical world.

She willed steps to Soulcast beneath her feet. Individual axi of air lined up and packed next to each other, then Soulcast into stone – though in spite of the realms being linked, this was difficult. Air was amorphous, even in concept. People thought of it as the sky, or a breath, or a gust of wind, or a storm, or just 'the air.' It *liked* to be free, difficult to define.

Yet, with a firm command and a concept of what she wanted, Jasnah made steps form beneath her feet. She reached the top of the wall and found her mother there with Queen Fen and some soldiers. They had made a command station at one of the old guard posts. Soldiers huddled outside with pikes pointed toward two Fused in the sky.

Bother. Jasnah strode along the wall, taking in the melee of illusions and men outside. Shallan stood at the back; most of the spheres around her had been drained already. She was burning through Stormlight at a terrible rate.

'Bad?' she asked Ivory.

'It is,' he said from her collar. 'It is.'

'Mother,' Jasnah called, approaching where Fen and Navani stood by the guard post. 'You need to rally the troops within the city and clear the enemy inside.'

'We're working on it,' Navani said. 'But – Jasnah! In the air—'

Jasnah raised an absent hand without looking, forming a wall of black pitch. A Fused crashed through it, and Jasnah Soulcast a flick of fire, sending the thing screaming and flailing, burning with a terrible smoke.

Jasnah Soulcast the rest of the pitch on the wall to smoke, then continued forward. 'We must take advantage of Radiant Shallan's distraction and cleanse Thaylen City. Otherwise, when the assault comes from outside once more, our attention will be divided.'

'From outside?' Fen said. 'But we have the wall fixed, and – Storms! Brightness!'

Jasnah stepped aside without looking as the second Fused swooped down – the reactions of spren in Shadesmar allowed her to judge where it was. She turned and swung her hand at the creature. Ivory formed and sliced through the Fused's head as it passed, sending it curling about itself – eyes burning – and tumbling along the wall top.

'The enemy,' Jasnah said, 'will not be stopped by a wall, and Brightness

Shallan has feasted upon almost all of the spheres Uncle Dalinar recharged. My Stormlight is nearly gone. We have to be ready to hold this position through conventional means once the power is gone.'

'Surely there aren't enough enemy troops to . . .' Fen's consort said, but trailed off as Jasnah pointed with Ivory – who obligingly formed again – toward the waiting parshman armies. Neither the hovering red haze nor the breaking lightning of the storm was enough to drown out the red glows beginning to appear in the parshmen's eyes.

'We must be ready to hold this wall as long as it takes for troops to arrive from Urithiru,' Jasnah said. 'Where is Renarin? Wasn't he to deal with that thunderclast?'

'One of my soldiers reported seeing him,' Fen said. 'He had been slowed by the crowds. Prince Adolin expressed an intention to go help.'

'Excellent. I will trust that task to my cousins, and instead see what I can do to keep my ward from getting herself killed.'

⁝

Szeth wove and dodged between the attacks of five enemy Fused, carrying the large dun ruby in his left hand, the sheathed black sword in his right. He tried to approach Dalinar in the red mist, but the enemy cut him off, and he was forced to turn east.

He skimmed the now-repaired wall and crossed over the city, eventually soaring past the monster of stone. It flung several soldiers into the air, and for a moment they soared with Szeth.

Szeth Lashed himself downward, diving for the city streets. Behind him, Fused broke around the monster and swarmed after. He shot through a doorway and into a small home – and heard a thump above as a soldier's body fell onto the roof – then crashed out the back door and Lashed himself upward, narrowly avoiding the next building.

'Was I supposed to save those soldiers, sword-nimi?' Szeth said. 'I am a Radiant now.'

I think they would have flown like you instead of falling down, if they'd wanted to be saved.

There was a profound puzzle in the words, one which Szeth could not consider. The Fused were deft, more skilled than he was. He dodged among the streets, but they kept on him. He swung around, left the Ancient Ward, and shot for the wall – trying to get back to Dalinar.

Unfortunately, a swarm of the enemies cut him off. The rest surrounded him.

Looks like we're cornered, the sword said. *Time to fight, right? Accept death, and die slaying as many as possible? I'm ready. Let's do it. I'm ready to be a noble sacrifice.*

No. He did not win by dying.

Szeth lobbed the gemstone away as hard as he could.

The Fused went after it, leaving him an avenue to escape. He dropped toward the ground, where spheres glistened like stars. He drew in a deep breath of Stormlight, then spotted Lift waiting on the field between the fighting illusions and the waiting parshmen.

Szeth settled down lightly beside her. 'I have failed to carry this burden.'

'That's okay. Your weird face is burden enough for one man.'

'Your words are wise,' he said, nodding.

Lift rolled her eyes. 'You're right, sword. He's not very fun, is he?'

I think he's deevy anyway.

Szeth did not know this word, but it sent Lift chortling in a fit of amusement, which the sword mimicked.

'We have not fulfilled the Blackthorn's demands,' Szeth snapped at the two of them, Stormlight puffing from his lips. 'I could not stay ahead of those Fused long enough to deliver the stone to our master.'

'Yeah, I saw,' Lift said. 'But I've got an *idea.* People are always after stuff, but they don't really like the *stuff* – they like *having* the stuff.'

'These words are . . . not so wise. What do you mean?'

'Simple. The best way to rob someone is leave them thinking that nothing is wrong. . . .'

❖

Shallan clung to Veil's and Radiant's hands.

She'd long since fallen to her knees, staring ahead as tears leaked from her eyes. Taut, her teeth gritted. She'd made *thousands* of illusions. Each one . . . each one was her.

A portion of her mind.

A portion of her soul.

Odium had made a mistake in flooding these soldiers with such thirst for blood. They didn't care that Shallan fed them illusions – they just wanted a battle. So she provided one, and somehow her illusions *resisted* when the enemy hit them. She thought maybe she was combining Soul-casting with her Lightweaving.

The enemy howled and sang, exulting in the fray. She painted the ground red and sprayed the enemy with blood that felt real. She serenaded them with the sounds of men screaming, dying, swords clashing and bones breaking.

She absorbed them in the false reality, and they drank it in; they *feasted* on it.

Each one of her illusions that died hit her with a little *shock*. A sliver of her dying.

Those were reborn as she pushed them out to dance again. Enemy Fused bellowed for order, trying to rally their troops, but Shallan drowned out their voices with sounds of screaming and metal on metal.

The illusion absorbed her entirely, and she lost track of everything else. Like when she was drawing. Creationspren blossomed around her by the hundred, shaped like discarded objects.

Storms. It was beautiful. She gripped Veil's and Radiant's hands tighter. They knelt beside her, heads bowed within her painted tapestry of violence, her—

'Hey,' a girl's voice said. 'Could you, uh, stop hugging yourself for a minute? I need some help.'

∴

Kaladin ducked toward Amaram, thrusting with his spear one-handed. That was usually a good tactic against an armored man with a sword. His spear hit right on target, where it would have dug into the armpit of an ordinary opponent. Here, unfortunately, the spear just slid off. Shardplate didn't have traditional weak points, other than the eye slit. You had to break it open with repeated hits, like cracking into a crab's shell.

Amaram laughed, a startlingly genuine mirth. 'You have great form, spearman! Do you remember when you first came to me? Back in that village, when you begged me to take you? You were a blubbering child who wanted so badly to be a soldier. The glory of the battle! I could see the lust in your eyes, boy.'

Kaladin glanced toward the Fused, who rounded the cloud, timid, looking for Dalinar.

Amaram chuckled. With those deep red eyes and the strange crystals growing from his body, Kaladin hadn't expected him to sound so much like himself. Whatever hybrid monster this was, it still had the mind of Meridas Amaram.

Kaladin stepped back, reluctantly changing Syl into a Blade, which would be better for cracking Plate. He fell into Windstance, which had always seemed appropriate. Amaram laughed again and surged forward, his second Shardblade appearing in his waiting grip. Kaladin dodged to the side, ducking under one Blade and getting at Amaram's back – where he got in a good hit on the Plate, cracking it. He raised his Blade to attack again.

Amaram slammed his foot down, and his Shardplate boot *shattered*, exploding outward in bits of molten metal. Beneath, his ripped sock revealed a foot overgrown with carapace and deep violet crystals.

As Kaladin came in for his attack, Amaram tapped his foot, and the stone ground became *liquid* for a moment. Kaladin stumbled, sinking down several inches, as if the rock were crem mud. It hardened in a moment, locking Kaladin's boots in place.

Kaladin! Syl cried in his mind as Amaram swung with two Shard-blades, parallel to one another. Syl became a halberd in Kaladin's hands, and he blocked the blows – but their force threw him to the ground, snapping his ankles.

Teeth gritted, Kaladin hauled his pained feet out of the boots and pulled himself away. Amaram's weapons sliced the ground behind, narrowly missing him. Then Amaram's other armored boot exploded, crystals from inside breaking it apart. The highlord pushed with one foot and *glided* across the ground, incredibly quick, approaching Kaladin and swinging.

Syl became a large shield, and Kaladin barely blocked the attack. He Lashed himself backward, getting out of range as Stormlight healed his ankles. Storms. *Storms!*

That Fused! Syl said. *She's getting very close to Dalinar.*

Kaladin cursed, then scooped up a large stone. He launched it into the air with several Lashings compounded, which sent it zipping off to slam into the head of the Fused. She shouted in pain, pulling back.

Kaladin scooped up another stone and Lashed it toward Amaram's horse.

'Beating up the animal because you can't defeat me?' Amaram asked.

He didn't seem to notice that the horse, in bolting away, carried off the Shardbow.

I've killed a man wearing that Shardplate before, Kaladin thought. *I can do it again.*

Only, he wasn't merely facing a Shardbearer. Amethyst crystals broke Amaram's armor all up the arms. How did Kaladin defeat ... whatever this thing was?

Stab it in the face? Syl suggested.

It was worth a try. He and Amaram fought on the battlefield near the red mist, on the western shore but between the main body of troops and the waiting parshmen. The area was mostly flat, except for some broken building foundations. Kaladin Lashed himself up a few inches, so he wouldn't sink into the ground if Amaram tried again to do ... whatever he'd done. Then he moved backward carefully, positioning himself where Amaram would likely leap across a broken foundation to get at him.

Amaram stepped up, chuckling softly. Kaladin raised Syl as a Shardblade, but shifted his grip, preparing for the moment when she'd become a thin spear he could ram right through that faceplate—

Kaladin! Syl cried.

Something hit Kaladin with the force of a falling boulder, flinging him to the side. His body broke, and the world spun.

By instinct, Kaladin Lashed himself upward and forward, opposite the way he'd been flung. He slowed and released the Lashings right as his momentum ran out, touching down, then slid to a stop on the stone, pain fading from a healed shoulder and side.

A brawny Fused – taller even than Amaram in his Plate – dropped a shattered club that he'd used on Kaladin. His carapace was the color of stone; he must have been crouching near that foundation, and Kaladin had taken him for merely another part of the stony field.

As Kaladin watched, the creature's brown carapace crusted up his arms, covering his face like a helm, growing to thick armor in a matter of moments. He raised his arms, and carapace spurs grew above and below the hands.

Delightful.

Adolin heaved himself up over the rim of a broken rooftop onto a small alley between two buildings. He'd made it to the Loft Wards of the city, right above the Ancient Ward. Here, buildings were constructed practically atop one another in tiers.

The building to his left had been completely flattened. Adolin crept across rubble. To his right, a main city thoroughfare led upward – toward the Royal Ward and the Oathgate – but was clogged with people fleeing from the enemy troops below. This was compounded by the local merchant guards and platoons of Thaylen military, who struggled against the tide.

Moving on the streets was extremely slow – but Adolin had found one corridor that was empty. The thunderclast had crossed the Ancient Ward, kicking down buildings, then had stepped on roofs as it climbed up to the Loft Wards. This swath of destruction made almost a roadway. Adolin had managed to follow, using rubble like stairs.

Now he was right in the thing's shadow. The corpse of a Thaylen soldier drooped from a rooftop nearby, tangled in ropes. It hung there, eyebrows dangling to brush the ground. Adolin swept past, peeking out between buildings onto a larger street.

A handful of Thaylens fought here, trying to bring the thunderclast down. The ropes had been a great idea, but the thing was obviously too strong to be tripped that way. In the street beyond Adolin, a soldier got in close and tried to hit the monster's leg with a hammer. The weapon bounced off. That was old hardened cremstone. The plucky soldier ended up getting stomped.

Adolin gritted his teeth, summoning his Shardblade. Without Plate, he'd be as squishy as anyone else. He had to be careful, tactical.

'This is what you were designed for, isn't it?' Adolin said softly as his Blade dropped into his hand. 'It was for fighting things like that. Shardblades are impractically long for duels, and Plate is overkill even on the battlefield. But against a monster of stone . . .'

He felt something. A stirring on the wind.

'You want to fight it, don't you?' Adolin asked. 'It reminds you of when you were alive.'

Something tickled his mind, very faint, like a sigh. A single word: *Mayalaran*. A . . . name?

'Right, Maya,' Adolin said. 'Let's bring that thing down.'

Adolin waited for it to turn toward the small group of defending soldiers, then he bolted out along the rubbled street, dashing straight for the thunderclast. He was barely as tall as its calf.

Adolin didn't use any of the sword stances – he just hacked as if he were attacking a wall, slicing right along the top of the thing's ankle.

A sudden *bang* sounded above, like two stones *slamming* against one another, as the thing cried out. A shock wave of air washed over Adolin and the monster turned, thrusting a hand down toward him. Adolin dodged to the side, but the monster's palm smashed the ground with such force that Adolin's boots left the ground momentarily. He dismissed Maya as he fell, then rolled.

He came up puffing on one knee with his hand out, summoning Maya again. Storms, he was like a rat gnawing on the toes of a chull.

The beast regarded him with eyespots like molten rock just beneath the surface. He'd heard the descriptions of these things from his father's visions – but looking up at it, he was struck by the shape of its face and head.

A chasmfiend, he thought. *It looks like a chasmfiend.* The head, at least. The body was vaguely like a thick human skeleton.

'Prince Adolin!' one of the few living soldiers shouted. 'It's the son of the Blackthorn!'

'Protect the prince! Distract the monster from the Shardbearer. It's our only chance to—'

Adolin lost the last part as the monster swept its hand across the ground. He barely dodged, then threw himself through the doorway of a low building. Inside, he leaped over a few bedding pallets, pushed into the next room, then attacked the brick wall with Maya, cutting in four quick strikes. He slammed his shoulder against the wall, breaking through the hole.

As he did, he heard a whimper from behind.

Adolin gritted his teeth. *I could use one of those storming Radiants about now.*

He ducked back into the building and flipped over a table, finding a young boy huddled underneath. That was the only person Adolin saw in the building. He hauled the boy out right as the thunderclast smashed a fist down through the roof. Dust billowing after him, Adolin shoved the child into the arms of a soldier, then pointed both toward the street to the south. Adolin took off running east, around the side of the building. Maybe he could climb up to the next level of the Loft Wards and circle the creature.

For all the troops' calls to distract the thing, however, it obviously knew who to focus on. It stepped over the broken house and thrust a fist toward Adolin – who leaped through a window into another house, across a table, then out an open window on the other side.

Crash.

The building fell in behind him. The thing was doing damage to its own hands with the attacks, leaving the wrists and fingers scored with white scrapes. It didn't seem to care – and why should it? It had ripped itself right from the ground to make this body.

Adolin's only advantage, other than his Blade, was his ability to react faster than the thing. It swung for the next building beyond him, trying to smash it before he got inside – but he was already doubling back. He ran underneath the monster's swing, sliding on the chips and dust as the fist passed narrowly overhead.

That put him in position to run between the thunderclast's legs. He slashed at the ankle he'd already cut once, digging his Blade deep into the stone, then whipping it out the other side. *Just like a chasmfiend,* he thought. *Legs first.*

When the thing stepped again, the ankle cracked with a sharp sound, then its foot broke free.

Adolin braced himself for the pained thunderclap from above, but still winced at the shock wave. Unfortunately, the monster balanced easily on the stump of its leg. It was a little clumsier than before, but it was in no real danger of falling. The Thaylen soldiers had regrouped and gathered up their ropes, however, so maybe—

A hand in Shardplate reached out of a building nearby, grabbed Adolin, and pulled him inside.

⁖

Dalinar held his hands out to the sides, enveloped by the Thrill. It returned every memory he hated about himself. War and conflict. Times when he'd shouted Evi into submission. Anger that had driven him to the brink of madness. His shame.

Though he had once crawled before the Nightwatcher to beg for

release, he no longer wished to forget. 'I em__
what I was.'

The Thrill colored his sight red, inflicting a deep longing
the conflict, the challenge. If he rejected it, he would drive t c
away.

'Thank you,' Dalinar said, 'for giving me strength when I needed it.'

The Thrill thrummed with a pleased sound. It drew in closer to him,
the faces of red mist grinning with excitement and glee. Charging horses
screamed and died. Men laughed as they were cut down.

Dalinar was once again walking on the stone toward the Rift, intent
on murdering everyone inside. He felt the heat of anger. The yearning so
powerful, it made him ache.

'I *was* that man,' Dalinar said. 'I *understand* you.'

∴

Venli crept away from the battlefield. She left the humans to struggle
against shadows in a mess of anger and lust. She walked deeper into the
darkness beneath Odium's storm, feeling strangely sick.

The rhythms were going *crazy* inside her, merging and fighting. A
fragment from Craving blended into Fury, into Ridicule.

She passed Fused arguing about what to do, now that Odium had
withdrawn. Did they send the parshmen in to fight? They couldn't control
the humans, consumed by one of the Unmade as they were.

Rhythms piled over rhythms.

Agony. Conceit. Destruction. Lost—

There! Venli thought. *Grab that!*

She attuned the Rhythm of the Lost. She clung to the solemn beat,
desperate – a rhythm one attuned to remember those you missed. Those
who had gone before.

Timbre thrummed to the same rhythm. Why did that feel different
from before? Timbre vibrated *through* Venli's entire being.

Lost. What had Venli lost?

Venli missed being someone who cared about something other than
power. Knowledge, favoritism, forms, wealth – it was all the same to her.
Where had she gone wrong?

Timbre pulsed. Venli dropped to her knees. Cold stone reflected lightning from above, red and garish.

e her own eyes in the polished wet

chem.

had reached out toward her. Dalinar Kholin,
they'd killed. But he'd reached from the pillar of
ne, and spoken to her.

eath.'

You   *ome a better person.*

'Strength before ... before weakness ...'

I did.

'Jou—'

Someone grabbed Venli roughly and spun her over, slamming her to the ground. A Fused with the form that grew carapace armor like Shardplate. He looked Venli up and down, and for a panicked moment she was sure he'd kill her.

The Fused seized her pouch, the one that hid Timbre. She screamed and clawed at his hands, but he shoved her back, then ripped open the pouch.

Then he turned it inside out.

'I could have sworn . . .' he said in their language. He tossed the pouch aside. 'You failed to obey the Word of Passion. You did not attack the enemy when commanded.'

'I . . . I was frightened,' Venli said. 'And weak.'

'You cannot be weak in his service. You must choose who you will serve.'

'I choose,' she said, then shouted, 'I *choose!*'

He nodded, evidently impressed by her Passion, then stalked back toward the battlefield.

Venli climbed to her feet and made her way to one of the ships. She stumbled up the gangway – yet felt crisper, more awake, than she'd been in a long, long time.

In her mind played the Rhythm of Joy. One of the old rhythms her people had learned long ago – after casting out their gods.

Timbre pulsed from *within* her. Inside her gemheart.

'I'm still wearing one of their forms,' Venli said. 'There was a Voidspren in my gemheart. How?'

Timbre pulsed to Resolve.

'You've done *what*?' Venli hissed, stopping on the deck.

Resolve again.

'But how can you . . .' She trailed off, then hunched over, speaking more softly. 'How can you keep a Voidspren *captive*?'

Timbre pulsed to Victory within her. Venli rushed toward the ship's cabin. A parshman tried to forbid her, but she glared him to submission, then took the ruby sphere from his lantern and went inside, slamming the door and locking it.

She held up the sphere, and then – heart fluttering – she drank it in. Her skin started glowing with a soft white light.

'Journey before destination.'

∴

Adolin was confronted by a figure in glistening black Shardplate, a large hammer strapped to its back. The helm had stylized eyebrows like knives sweeping backward, and the Plate was skirted with a triangular pattern of interlocking scales. *Cvaderln,* he thought, remembering his lists of Thaylen Shards. It meant, roughly, 'shell of Cva.'

'Are you Tshadr?' Adolin guessed.

'No, Hrdalm,' the Shardbearer said in a thick Thaylen accent. 'Tshadr holds Court Square. I come, stop monster.'

Adolin nodded. Outside, the thing sounded its angry call, confronting the remaining Thaylen troops.

'We need to get out and help those men,' Adolin said. 'Can you distract the monster? My Blade can cut, while you can take hits.'

'Yes,' Hrdalm said. 'Yes, good.'

Adolin quickly helped Hrdalm get the hammer untied. Hrdalm hefted it, then pointed at the window. 'Go there.'

Adolin nodded, waiting by the window as Hrdalm charged out the doorway and went running straight for the thunderclast, shouting a Thaylen battle cry. When the thing turned toward Hrdalm, Adolin leaped out the window and charged around the other side.

Two flying Fused swooped in behind Hrdalm, slamming spears into his back, tossing him forward. Plate ground against stone as he fell, face-first. Adolin ran for the thunderclast's leg – but the creature ignored Hrdalm and fixated on Adolin. It crashed a palm down on the ground nearby, forcing Adolin to dance backward.

Hrdalm stood up, but a Fused swooped down and kicked him over. The other landed on his chest and began pounding on his helm with a hammer, cracking it. As Hrdalm tried to grab her and throw her free, the other one swooped down and used a spear to pin the hand down. Damnation!

'All right, Maya,' Adolin said. 'We've practiced this.'

He wound up, then hurled the Shardblade, which spun in a gleaming arc before slamming into the Fused on Hrdalm's chest, piercing her straight through. Dark smoke trailed from her eyes as they burned away.

Hrdalm sat up, sweeping away the other Fused with a Shard-enhanced punch. He turned toward the dead one, then looked back at Adolin with a posture that somehow expressed amazement.

The thunderclast called, sending a wave of sound across the street, rattling chips of stone. Adolin swallowed, then started counting heartbeats as he dashed away. The monster crashed along the street behind – but Adolin soon pulled to a stop in front of a large section of rubble, which blocked the street. Storms, he'd run the wrong way.

He shouted, spinning around. He hit a count of ten, and Maya returned to him.

The thunderclast loomed overhead. It thrust its palm down, and Adolin managed to judge the shadow and dodge between two fingers. As its palm crashed to the ground, Adolin leaped, trying to avoid being knocked over. He grabbed a massive finger with his left arm, desperately holding Maya to the side in his right.

As before, the thunderclast began to rub its palm across the ground, an attempt to grind Adolin to the stones. He hung from the finger, feet lifted a few inches off the ground. The sound was terrible, like Adolin was trapped in a rockslide.

As soon as the thunderclast ended its sweep of the hand, Adolin dropped off, then raised Maya in a double-handed grip and chopped straight through the finger. The beast released a thunderclap of anger and pulled its hand back. The tip of an unbroken finger connected with Adolin and flung him backward.

Pain.

It hit him like a flash of lightning. He struck the ground and rolled, but the agony was so sharp, he barely noticed. As he came to a rest, he coughed and trembled, his body seizing up.

Storms. Stormsstormsstorms . . . He squeezed his eyes shut against the pain. He'd . . . he'd gotten too accustomed to the invincibility of Plate. But his suit was back in Urithiru – or hopefully coming here soon on Gaval, his Plate standby.

Adolin somehow crawled to his feet, each move causing a spear of agony from his chest. Broken rib? Well, at least his arms and legs were working.

Move. That thing was still behind him.

One.

The roadway in front of him was piled with rubble from a broken building.

Two.

He limped to the right – toward the ledge down to the next tier of homes.

Three. Four.

The thunderclast trumped and followed, its steps shaking the ground.

Five. Six.

He could hear stone grinding just behind.

He fell to his knees.

Seven.

Maya! he thought, truly desperate. *Please!*

Blessedly, as he raised his hands, the Blade materialized. He slammed it into the rock wall – the edge pointed to the side, not down – then rolled off the ledge, holding on to the hilt. The thunderclast's fist came down again, crashing to the rock. Adolin dangled from Maya's hilt over the edge, a drop of some ten feet to the rooftop below.

Adolin gritted his teeth – his elbow was hurting badly enough to make his eyes water. But, once the thunderclast had rubbed its hand to the side, Adolin grabbed the cliff edge with one hand and swept Maya out to the side, freeing her from the stone. He reached down and rammed her into the stone below, then let go and swung from this new handhold a moment before releasing the Blade and dropping the rest of the way to the rooftop.

His leg screamed in pain. He collapsed to the rooftop, eyes watering. As he lay there in agony, he felt something – a faint *panic* on the wind. He forced himself to roll to the side, and a Fused swept past, its lance barely missing him.

Need . . . a weapon . . .

He started counting again and climbed, shakily, to his knees. But the thunderclast loomed on the tier overhead, then rammed its stump leg down into the center of the stone roof Adolin was on.

Adolin fell in a jumble of broken stone and dust, then hit hard on the floor inside, chunks of rock clattering around him.

Everything went black. He tried to gasp, but his muscles couldn't make the motions. He could only lie there, straining, groaning softly. A part of him was aware of the sounds made as the thunderclast pulled its stump out of the broken home. He waited for it to smash him, but as his vision slowly returned, he saw it stepping down from that upper tier onto the street outside.

At least . . . at least it wasn't continuing on toward the Oathgate.

Adolin shifted. Chips from the shattered roof streamed off him. His face and hands bled from a hundred scrapes. He recovered his breath, gasping in pain, and tried to move, but his leg . . . *Damnation,* that hurt.

Maya brushed his mind.

'I'm trying to get up,' he said through gritted teeth. 'Give me a sec. Storming sword.' He had another coughing fit, then finally rolled off the rubble. He crawled out onto the street, half expecting Skar and Drehy to be there to pull him to his feet. Storms, he missed those bridgemen.

The street was empty around him, though maybe twenty feet away people crowded, trying to get up the thoroughfare to safety. They called and shouted in fear and urgency. If Adolin ran that way, the thunderclast would follow. It had proven *determined* to bring him down.

He sneered at the looming monster and – leaning against the wall of the small home he'd fallen into – pulled himself to his feet. Maya dropped into his hand. Though he was covered in dust, she still shone bright.

He steadied himself, then held Maya in two hands – his grip wetted by blood – and fell into Stonestance. The immovable stance.

'Come and get me, you bastard,' he whispered.

'Adolin?' a familiar voice called from behind. 'Storms, Adolin! What are you doing!'

Adolin started, then glanced over his shoulder. A glowing figure pushed through the crowd onto his street. Renarin carried a Shardblade, and his blue Bridge Four uniform was unstained.

Took you long enough.

As Renarin approached, the thunderclast actually took a step back, as if *afraid*. Well, that might help. Adolin clenched his teeth, trying to hold in his agony. He wobbled, then steadied himself. 'All right, let's—'

'Adolin, don't be foolhardy!' Renarin grabbed his arm. A burst of healing moved through Adolin like cold water in his veins, causing his pains to retreat.

'But—'

'Get *away*,' Renarin said. 'You're unarmored. You'll get yourself killed fighting this thing!'

'But—'

'I can handle it, Adolin. Just go! Please.'

Adolin stumbled back. He'd never heard such forceful talk from Renarin – that was almost more amazing than the monster. Renarin, shockingly, *charged* at the thing.

A clatter announced Hrdalm climbing down from above, his Plate's helm cracked, but otherwise in good shape. He had lost his hammer, but carried one of the lances from the Fused, and his Plate fist was covered in blood.

Renarin! He didn't have Plate. How—

The thunderclast's palm crashed down on Renarin, smashing him. Adolin screamed, but his brother's Shardblade cut up through the palm, then separated the hand from the wrist.

The thunderclast trumpeted in anger as Renarin climbed from the rubble of the hand. He seemed to heal more quickly than Kaladin or Shallan did, as if being crushed wasn't even a bother.

'Excellent!' Hrdalm said, laughing inside his helm. 'You, rest. Okay?'

Adolin nodded, stifling a groan of pain. Renarin's healing had stopped his insides from aching, and it was no longer painful to put weight on his leg, but his arms still ached, and some of his cuts hadn't closed.

As Hrdalm stepped toward the fight, Adolin took the man by the arm, then lifted Maya.

Go with him for now, Maya, Adolin thought.

He almost wished she'd object, but the vague sensation he received was a resigned agreement.

Hrdalm dropped his lance and took the Blade reverently. 'Great Honor in you, Prince Adolin,' he said. 'Great Passion in me at this aid.'

'Go,' Adolin said. 'I'll go see if I can help hold the streets.'

Hrdalm charged off. Adolin chose an infantry spear from the rubble, then made toward the roadway behind.

.•.

Szeth of the Skybreakers had, fortunately, trained with all ten Surges.

The Fused transferred the enormous ruby to one of their number who could manipulate Abrasion – a woman who slid across the ground like Lift did. She infused the ruby, making it glow with her version of a Lashing. That would make the thing impossibly slick and difficult to carry for anyone but the Fused woman herself.

She seemed to think her enemies would have no experience with such a thing. Unfortunately for them, Szeth had not only carried an Honorblade that granted this power, he had practiced with skates on ice, a training exercise that somewhat mimicked an Edgedancer's movements.

And so, as he chased down the gemstone, he gave the Fused woman plenty of opportunities to underestimate him. He let her dodge, and was slow to reorient, acting surprised when she slipped this way, then that.

Once the Fused was confident she controlled this race, Szeth struck. When she leaped off a ledge of stone – soaring a short time in the air – Szeth swooped in with a sudden set of Lashings. He collided with her right as she landed. As his face touched her carapace, he Lashed her upward.

That sent her flying into the air with a scream. Szeth landed and prepared to follow, then cursed as the Fused *fumbled* with the gemstone. He whipped his jacket off as she dropped it. Though one of the flying Fused swept in to grab it, the ruby slipped out of his fingers.

Szeth caught it in the jacket, held like a pouch. A lucky turn; he had assumed he would need to attack her again to get it out of her hands.

Now, the real test. He Lashed himself eastward, toward the city. Here, a chaotic mix of soldiers fought on a painted battlefield. The Lightweaver was good; even the corpses looked authentic.

A Fused had begun gathering glowing-eyed soldiers who were real, then putting them with their backs to the city wall. They'd made ranks with spears bristling outward and yelled for soldiers to join them, but touched each one who approached. Illusions that tried to get in were disrupted. Soon the enemy would be able to ignore this distraction, regroup, and focus on getting through that wall.

Do what Dalinar told you. Get him this gemstone.

The ruby had finally stopped glowing, making it no longer slick. Above, many Fused swooped to intercept Szeth; they seemed happy to play this game, for as long as the gemstone was changing hands, it was not being delivered to Dalinar.

As the first Fused came for him, Szeth ducked into a roll and canceled his Lashing upward. He collided with a rock, acting dazed. He then shook his head, took up his pouch with the ruby, and launched into the air again.

Eight Fused gave chase, and though Szeth dodged between them, one eventually got close enough to seize his pouch and rip it out of his fingers. They swept away as a flock, and Szeth slowly floated down and landed beside Lift, who stepped out of the illusory rock. She held a bundle wrapped in clothing: the real gemstone, which she'd taken from his pouch during his feigned collision. The Fused now had a false ruby – a rock cut into roughly the same shape with a Shardblade, then covered in an illusion.

'Come,' Szeth said, grabbing the girl and Lashing her upward, then towing her after him as he swept toward the northern edge of the plain. This place nearest the red mist had fallen into darkness – the Windrunner had consumed all of the Stormlight in gemstones on the ground. He fought against several enemies nearby.

Shadowed darkness. Whispered words. Szeth slowed to a halt.

'What?' Lift asked. 'Crazyface?'

'I ...' Szeth trembled, fearspren bubbling from the ground below. 'I cannot go into that mist. I must be away from this place.'

The whispers.

'I got it,' she said. 'Go back and help the redhead.'

He dropped Lift to the ground and backed away. That churning red mist, those faces breaking and re-forming and screaming. Dalinar was still in there, somewhere?

The little girl with the long hair stopped at the border of the mist, then stepped inside.

⁘

Amaram was screaming in pain.

Kaladin sparred with the Fused who had the strange overgrown

675

carapace, and couldn't spare a glance. He used the screaming to judge that he was staying far enough from Amaram to not be immediately attacked.

But storms, it was distracting.

Kaladin swept with the Sylblade, cutting through the Fused's forearms. That sheared the spurs completely free and disabled the hands. The creature backed up, growling a soft but angry rhythm.

Amaram's screaming voice approached. Syl became a shield – anticipating Kaladin's need – as he raised her toward his side, blocking a set of sweeping blows from the screaming highlord.

Stormfather. Amaram's helm was cracked from the wicked, sharp amethysts growing out of the sides of his face. The eyes still glowed deeply within, and the stone ground somehow *burned* beneath his crystal-covered feet, leaving flaming tracks behind.

The highprince battered against the Sylshield with two Shardblades. She, in turn, grew a latticework on the outside – with parts sticking out like the tines of a trident.

'What are you doing?' Kaladin asked.

Improvising.

Amaram struck again, and Helaran's sword got tangled in the tines. Kaladin spun the shield, wrenching the sword out of Amaram's grip. It vanished to smoke.

Now, press the advantage.

Kaladin!

The hulking Fused charged him. The creature's cut arms had regrown, and – even as it swung its hands – a large club formed there from carapace. Kaladin barely got Syl in place to block.

It didn't do much good.

The force of the club's sideways blow flung Kaladin against the remnants of a wall. He growled, then Lashed himself upward into the sky, Stormlight reknitting him. Damnation. The area around where they were fighting had grown dark and shadowed, the gemstones drained. Had he really used so much?

Uh-oh, Syl said, flying around him as a ribbon of light. *Dalinar!*

The red mist billowed, ominous in the gloom. Red on black. Within it Dalinar was a shadow, with two flying Fused besetting him.

Kaladin growled again. Amaram had gone hiking for his bow, which had fallen from the horse's saddle some ways off. Damnation. He couldn't defeat them all.

He shot down toward the ground. The hulking Fused came for him, and instead of dodging, Kaladin let the creature ram a knifelike spur into his stomach.

He grunted, tasting blood, but didn't flinch. He grabbed the creature's hand and Lashed him upward and toward the mist. The Fused flipped past his companions in the air, shouting something that sounded like a plea for help. They zipped after him.

Kaladin stumbled after Amaram, but his footsteps steadied as he healed. He got a little more Stormlight from some gemstones he'd missed earlier, then took to the sky. Syl became a lance, and Kaladin swooped down, causing Amaram to turn away from the bow – still a short distance from him – and track Kaladin. Crystals had broken through his armor all along his arms and back.

Kaladin made a charging pass. He wasn't accustomed to flying with a lance though, and Amaram batted the Syllance aside with a Shardblade. Kaladin rose up on the other side, considering his next move.

Amaram launched himself into the air.

He soared in an incredible leap, far higher and farther than even Shardplate would have allowed. And he *hung* for a time, sweeping close to Kaladin, who dodged backward.

'Syl,' he hissed as Amaram landed. 'Syl, that was a *Lashing*. What is he?'

I don't know. But we don't have much time before those Fused return.

Kaladin swept down and landed, shortening Syl to a halberd. Amaram spun on him, eyes within the helm trailing red light. 'Can you feel it?' he demanded of Kaladin. 'The beauty of the fight?'

Kaladin ducked in and rammed Syl at Amaram's cracked breastplate.

'It could have been so glorious,' Amaram said, swatting aside the attack. 'You, me, Dalinar. Together on the same side.'

'The wrong side.'

'Is it wrong to want to help the ones who truly own this land? Is it not *honorable*?'

'It's not Amaram I speak to anymore, is it? Who, or what, are you?'

'Oh, it's me,' Amaram said. He dismissed one of his Blades, grabbed his helm. With a tug of the hand, it finally shattered, exploding away and revealing the face of Meridas Amaram – surrounded by amethyst crystals, glowing with a soft and somehow dark light.

He grinned. 'Odium promised me something grand, and that promise has been kept. With honor.'

'You still pretend to speak of honor?'

'Everything I do is for honor.' Amaram swept with a single Blade, making Kaladin dodge. 'It was honor that drove me to seek the return of the Heralds, of powers, and of our god.'

'So you could join the *other side*?'

Lightning flashed behind Amaram, casting red light and long shadows as he resummoned his second Blade. 'Odium showed me what the Heralds have become. We spent years trying to get them to return. But they were *here all along*. They *abandoned* us, spearman.'

Amaram carefully circled Kaladin with his two Shardblades.

He's waiting for the Fused to come help, Kaladin thought. *That's why he's being cautious now.*

'I hurt, once,' Amaram said. 'Did you know that? After I was forced to kill your squad, I . . . hurt. Until I realized. It wasn't my fault.' The color of his glowing eyes intensified to a simmering crimson. 'None of this is my fault.'

Kaladin attacked – unfortunately, he barely knew what he was facing. The ground rippled and became liquid, almost catching him again. Fire trailed behind Amaram's arms as he swung with both Shardblades. Somehow, he briefly ignited the very *air*.

Kaladin blocked one Blade, then the other, but couldn't get in an attack. Amaram was fast and brutal, and Kaladin didn't dare touch the ground, lest his feet freeze to the liquefied stone. After a few more exchanges, Kaladin was forced to retreat.

'You're outclassed, spearman,' Amaram said. 'Give in, and convince the city to surrender. That is for the best. No more need die today. Let me be merciful.'

'Like you were merciful to my friends? Like you were merciful to me, when you gave me these brands?'

'I left you alive. I *spared* you.'

'An attempt to assuage your conscience.' Kaladin clashed with the highprince. 'A failed attempt.'

'*I* made you, Kaladin!' Amaram's red eyes lit the crystals that rimmed his face. '*I* gave you that granite will, that warrior's poise. This, the person you've become, was *my gift!*'

'A gift at the expense of everyone I loved?'

'What do you care? It made you strong! Your men died in the name of battle, so that the strongest man would have the weapon. Anyone would have done what I did, even Dalinar himself.'

'Didn't you tell me you'd given up that grief?'

'Yes! I'm beyond guilt!'

'Then why do you still hurt?'

Amaram *flinched.*

'Murderer,' Kaladin said. 'You've switched sides to find peace, Amaram. But you won't ever have it. He'll *never* give it to you.'

Amaram roared, sweeping in with his Shardblades. Kaladin Lashed himself upward, then – as Amaram passed underneath – twisted and came back down, swinging in a powerful, two-handed grip. In response to an unspoken command, Syl became a hammer, which crashed against the back of Amaram's Plate.

The cuirass-style breastplate – which was all one piece – exploded with an unexpected force, pushing Kaladin backward across the stone. Overhead, the lightning rumbled. They were fully in the Everstorm's shadow, which made it even more ghastly as he saw what had happened to Amaram.

The highprince's entire chest had collapsed inward. There was no sign of ribs or internal organs. Instead, a large violet crystal pulsed inside his chest cavity, overgrown with dark veins. If he'd been wearing a uniform or padding beneath the armor, it had been consumed.

He turned toward Kaladin, heart and lungs replaced by a gemstone that glowed with Odium's dark light.

'Everything I've done,' Amaram said, blinking red eyes, 'I've done for Alethkar. I'm a patriot!'

'If that is true,' Kaladin whispered, '*why do you still hurt?*'

Amaram screamed, charging him.

Kaladin raised Syl, who became a Shardblade. 'Today, what I do, I do for the men you killed. I am the man I've become because of *them.*'

'*I* made you! I *forged* you!' He leaped at Kaladin, propelling himself off the ground, hanging in the air.

And in so doing, he entered Kaladin's domain.

Kaladin launched at Amaram. The highprince swung, but the winds themselves curled around Kaladin, and he anticipated the attack. He Lashed himself to the side, narrowly avoiding one Blade. Windspren streaked past him as he dodged the other by a hair's width.

Syl became a spear in his grip, matching his motions perfectly. He spun and slammed her against the gemstone at Amaram's heart. The amethyst cracked, and Amaram faltered in the air – then dropped.

Two Shardblades vanished to mist as the highprince fell some twenty feet to crash into the ground.

Kaladin floated downward toward him. 'Ten spears go to battle,' he whispered, 'and nine shatter. Did that war *forge* the one that remained? No, Amaram. All the war did was *identify the spear that would not break.*'

Amaram climbed to his knees, howling with a bestial sound and clutching the flickering gemstone at his chest, which went out, plunging the area into darkness.

Kaladin! Syl shouted in Kaladin's mind.

He barely dodged as two Fused swooped past, their lances narrowly missing his chest. Two more came in from the left, one from the right. A sixth carried the hulking Fused back, rescued from Kaladin's Lashing.

They'd gone to fetch friends. It seemed the Fused had realized that their best path to stopping Dalinar was to first remove Kaladin from the battlefield.

∴

Renarin puffed in and out as the thunderclast collapsed – crushing houses in its fall, but also breaking off its arm. It reached upward with its remaining arm, bleating a plaintive cry. Renarin and his companion – the Thaylen Shardbearer – had cut off both legs at the knees.

The Thaylen tromped up and slapped him – carefully – on the back with a Plated hand. 'Very good fighting.'

'I just distracted it while you cut chunks of its legs off.'

'You did good,' the Thaylen said. He nodded toward the thunderclast, which got to its knees, then slipped. 'How to end?'

It will fear you! Glys said from within Renarin. *It will go. Make it so that it will go.*

'I'll see what I can do,' Renarin said to the Thaylen, then carefully picked his way over to the street and up a level to get a better view of the thunderclast's head.

'So . . . Glys?' he asked. 'What do I do?'

Light. You will make it go with light.

The thing pulled itself up across the rubble of a destroyed building. Stone rubbed stone as its enormous, wedge-shaped head turned to Renarin. Recessed molten eyes fluttered, like a sputtering fire.

It was in pain. It could hurt.

It will go! Glys promised, excitable as ever.

Renarin raised his fist and summoned Stormlight. It glowed as a powerful beacon. And . . .

The red molten eyes faded before that light, and the thing settled down with a last extinguishing sigh.

His Thaylen companion approached with a soft clinking of Plate. 'Good. Excellent!'

'Go help with the fighting,' Renarin said. 'I need to open the Oathgate in person.' The man obeyed without question, running for the main thoroughfare leading down to the Ancient Ward.

Renarin lingered with that stone corpse, troubled. *I was supposed to have died. I saw myself die. . . .*

He shook his head, then hiked toward the upper reaches of the city.

∴

Shallan, Veil, and Radiant held hands in a ring. The three flowed, faces changing, identities melding. Together, they had raised an army.

It was dying now.

A hulking variety of Fused had organized the enemy. These refused to be distracted. Though Veil, Shallan, and Radiant had made copies of themselves – to keep the real ones from being attacked – those died as well.

Wavering. Stormlight running out.

We've strained ourselves too far, they thought.

Three Fused approached, cutting through the dying illusions, marching through evaporating Stormlight. People fell to their knees and puffed away.

'Mmmm . . .' Pattern said.

'Tired,' Shallan said, her eyes drowsy.

'Satisfied,' Radiant said, proud.

'Worried,' Veil said, eyeing the Fused.

They wanted to move. Needed to move. But it hurt to watch their army die and puff into nothing.

One figure didn't melt like the others. A woman with jet-black hair that had escaped its usual braids. It blew free as she stepped between the enemy and Shallan, Radiant, and Veil. The ground turned glossy, the surface of the stone Soulcast into oil. Veil, Shallan, and Radiant were able to glimpse it in the Cognitive Realm. It changed so easily. How did Jasnah manage that?

Jasnah Soulcast a spark from the air, igniting the oil and casting up a field of flames. The Fused raised hands before their faces, stumbling back.

'That should buy us a few moments.' Jasnah turned toward Radiant, Veil, and Shallan. She took Shallan by the arm – but Shallan wavered, then puffed away. Jasnah froze, then turned to Veil.

'Here,' Radiant said, tired, stumbling to her feet. She was the one Jasnah could feel. She blinked away tears. 'Are you . . . real?'

'Yes, Shallan. You did well out here.' She touched Radiant's arm, then glanced toward the Fused, who were venturing into the fires despite the heat. 'Damnation. Perhaps I should have opened a pit beneath them instead.'

Shallan winced as the last of her army – like the shredded light of a setting sun – vanished. Jasnah proffered a gemstone, which Radiant drank eagerly.

Amaram's troops had begun to form ranks again.

'Come,' Jasnah said, pulling Veil back to the wall, where steps grew from the stone itself.

'Soulcast?' Shallan asked.

'Yes.' Jasnah stepped onto the first, but Shallan didn't follow.

'We shouldn't have ignored this,' Radiant said. 'We should have practiced this.' She slipped – for a moment – into viewing Shadesmar. Beads rolled and surged beneath her.

'Not too far,' Jasnah warned. 'You can't bring your physical self into the realm, as I once assumed you could, but there are things here that can feast upon your mind.'

'If I want to Soulcast the air. How?'

'Avoid air until you practice further,' Jasnah said. 'It is convenient, but difficult to control. Why don't you try to turn some stone into oil, as I did? We can fire it as we climb the steps, and further impede the enemy.'

'I . . .' So many beads, so many *spren*, churning in the lake that marked Thaylen City. So overwhelming.

'That rubble near the wall will be easier than the ground itself,' Jasnah said, 'as you'll be able to treat those stones as distinct units, while the ground views itself all as one.'

'It's too much,' Shallan said, exhaustionspren spinning around her. 'I can't, Jasnah. I'm sorry.'

'It is well, Shallan,' Jasnah said. 'I merely wanted to see, as it seemed you were Soulcasting to give your illusions weight. But then, concentrated Stormlight has a faint mass to it. Either way, up the steps, child.'

Radiant started up the stone steps. Behind, Jasnah waved her hand toward the approaching Fused – and stone formed from air, completely encasing them.

It was brilliant. Any who saw it in only the Physical Realm would be impressed, but Radiant saw so much more. Jasnah's absolute command and confidence. The Stormlight rushing to do her will. The air itself responding as if to the voice of God himself.

Shallan gasped in wonder. 'It obeyed. The air obeyed your call to transform. When I tried to make a *single little stick* change, it refused.'

'Soulcasting is a practiced art,' Jasnah said. 'Up, up. Keep walking.' She sliced the steps off as they walked. 'Remember, you mustn't order stones, as they are more stubborn than men. Use coercion. Speak of freedom and of movement. But for a gas becoming a solid, you must impose discipline and will. Each Essence is different, and each offers advantages and disadvantages when used as a substrate for Soulcasting.'

Jasnah glanced over her shoulder at the gathering army. 'And perhaps . . . this is one time when a lecture isn't advisable. With all my complaints about not wanting wards, you'd think I would be able to resist instructing people at inopportune times. Keep moving.'

Feeling exhausted, Veil, Shallan, and Radiant trudged up and finally reached the top of the wall.

⁖

After how hard it had been for Renarin to get up to fight the thunderclast – he'd spent what seemed like an eternity caught in the press of people – he'd expected to have to work to cover the last distance to the Oathgate. However, people were moving more quickly now. The ones up above must have cleared off the streets, hiding in the many temples and buildings in the Royal Ward.

He was able to move with the flow of people. Near the top tier, he ducked into a building and walked to the back, past some huddled merchants. Most of the buildings here were a single story, so he used Glys to cut a hole in the roof. He then hollowed out some handholds in the rock wall and climbed up on top.

Beyond, he was able to get onto the street leading to the Oathgate platform. He was ... unaccustomed to being able to do things like this. Not only using the Shardblade, but being physical. He'd always been afraid of his fits, always worried that a moment of strength would instantly become a moment of invalidity.

Living like that, you learned to stay back. Just in case. He hadn't suffered a fit in a while. He didn't know if that was just a coincidence – they could be irregular – or if they had been healed, like his bad eyesight. Indeed, he still saw the world differently from everyone else. He was still nervous talking to people, and didn't like being touched. Everyone else saw in each other things he never could understand. So much noise and destruction and people talking and cries for help and sniffles and muttering and whispering all like buzzing, buzzings.

At least here, on this street near the Oathgate, the crowds had diminished. Why was that? Wouldn't they have pressed up here, hoping for escape? Why ...

Oh.

A dozen Fused hovered in the sky above the Oathgate, lances held formally before themselves, clothing draping beneath them and fluttering.

Twelve. *Twelve.*

This, Glys said, *would be bad.*

Motion caught his attention: a young girl standing in a doorway and waving at him. He walked over, worried the Fused would attack him. Hopefully his Stormlight – which he'd mostly used up fighting the thunderclast – wasn't bright enough to draw their ire.

He entered the building, another single-story structure with a large open room at the front. It was occupied by dozens of scribes and ardents, many of whom huddled around a spanreed. Children that he couldn't see crowded the back rooms, but he could hear their whimpers. And he heard the scratching, scratching, scratching of reeds on paper.

'Oh, bless the Almighty,' Brightness Teshav said, appearing from the mass of people. She pulled Renarin deeper into the room. 'Have you any news?'

'My father sent me up here to help,' Renarin said. 'Brightness, where are General Khal and your son?'

'In Urithiru,' she said. 'They transferred back to gather forces, but then . . . Brightlord, there's been an attack at Urithiru. We've been trying to get information via spanreed. It appears that a strike force of some kind arrived at the advent of the Everstorm.'

'Brightness!' Kadash called. 'Spanreed to Sebarial's scribes is responding again. They apologize for the long delay. Sebarial pulled back, following Aladar's command, to the upper levels. He confirms that the attackers are parshmen.'

'The Oathgates?' Renarin asked, hopeful. 'Can they reach those, and open the way here?'

'Not likely. The enemy is holding the plateau.'

'Our armies have the advantage at Urithiru, Prince Renarin,' Teshav said. 'Reports agree that the enemy strike force isn't nearly large enough to defeat us there. This is obviously a delaying tactic to keep us from activating the Oathgate and bringing help to Thaylen City.'

Kadash nodded. 'Those Fused above the Oathgate held even when the stone monster outside was falling. They know their orders – keep that device from being activated.'

'Radiant Malata is the only way for our armies to reach us through the Oathgate,' Teshav said. 'But we can't contact her, or any of the Kharbranth contingent. The enemy struck them first. They knew exactly what they had to do to cripple us.'

Renarin took a deep breath, drawing in Stormlight that Teshav was carrying. His glow lit the room, and eyes all through the chamber looked up from spanreeds, turning toward him.

'The portal has to be opened,' Renarin said.

'Your Highness . . .' Teshav said. 'You can't fight them all.'

'There's nobody else.' He turned to go.

Shockingly, nobody called for him to stop.

All his life they'd done that. No, Renarin. That's not for you. You can't do that. You're not *well*, Renarin. Be *reasonable*, Renarin.

He'd always been reasonable. He'd always listened. It felt wonderful and terrifying at once to know that nobody did that today. The spanreeds continued their scratching, moving on their own, oblivious to the moment.

Renarin stepped outside.

Terrified, he strode down the street, summoning Glys as a Shardblade. As he approached the ramp up to the Oathgate, the Fused descended. Four landed on the ramp before him, then gave him a gesture not unlike a salute, humming to a frantic tune he did not know.

Renarin was so frightened, he worried he'd wet himself. Not very noble or brave, now was he?

Ah ... what will come now? Glys said, voice thrumming through Renarin. *What emerges?*

One of his fits struck him.

Not the old fits, where he grew weak. He had new ones now, that neither he nor Glys could control. To his eyes, glass grew across the ground. It spread out like crystals, forming lattices, images, meanings and pathways. Stained-glass pictures, panel after panel.

These had always been right. Until today – until they had proclaimed that Jasnah Kholin's love would fail.

He read this latest set of stained-glass images, then felt his fear drain away. He smiled. This seemed to confuse the Fused as they lowered their salutes.

'You're wondering why I'm smiling,' Renarin said.

They didn't respond.

'Don't worry,' Renarin said. 'You didn't miss something funny. I ... well, I doubt you'll find it amusing.'

Light exploded from the Oathgate platform in a wave. The Fused cried out in a strange tongue, zipping into the air. A luminous wall expanded from the Oathgate platform in a ring, trailing a glowing afterimage.

It faded to reveal an entire division of Alethi troops in Kholin blue standing upon the Oathgate platform.

Then, like a Herald from lore, a man rose into the air above them. Glowing white with Stormlight, the bearded man carried a long silver Shardspear with a strange crossguard shape behind the tip.

Teft.

Knight Radiant.

⁘

Shallan sat with her back against the battlement, listening to soldiers shout orders. Navani had given her Stormlight and water, but was currently distracted by reports from Urithiru.

Pattern hummed from the side of Veil's jacket. 'Shallan? You did well, Shallan. Very well.'

'An honorable stand,' Radiant agreed. 'One against many, and we held our ground.'

'Longer than we should have,' Veil said. 'We were *already* exhausted.'

'We're still ignoring too much,' Shallan said. 'We're getting too good at pretending.' She had decided to stay with Jasnah in the first place to *learn*. But when the woman returned from the dead, Shallan had – instead of accepting training – immediately fled. What had she been thinking?

Nothing. She'd been trying to hide away things she didn't want to face. Like always.

'Mmm ...' Pattern said, a concerned hum.

'I'm tired,' Shallan whispered. 'You don't have to worry. After I rest, I'll recover and settle down to being just one. I actually ... actually don't think I'm quite as lost as I was before.'

Jasnah, Navani, and Queen Fen whispered together farther along the wall. Thaylen generals joined them, and fearspren gathered around. The defense, in their opinion, was going poorly. Reluctantly, Veil pushed herself to her feet and surveyed the battlefield. Amaram's forces were gathering beyond bow range.

'We delayed the enemy,' Radiant said, 'but didn't defeat them. We still have an overwhelming army to face. ...'

'Mmmm ...' Pattern said, high pitched, worried. 'Shallan, look. Beyond.'

Out nearer the bay, thousands upon thousands of fresh parshman troops had begun to carry ladders off their ships to use in a full-on assault.

⁘

'Tell the men not to give chase to those Fused,' Renarin said to Lopen. 'We need to hold the Oathgate, first and foremost.'

'Good enough, sure,' Lopen said, launching into the sky and going to relay the order to Teft.

The Fused clashed with Bridge Four in the air over the city. This group of enemies seemed more skilled than the ones Renarin had seen below, but they didn't *fight* so much as *defend themselves*. They were progressively moving the clash farther out over the city, and Renarin worried they were deliberately drawing Bridge Four away from the Oathgate.

The Alethi division marched into the city with shouts of praise and joy from the surrounding people. Two thousand men wasn't going to do much if those parshmen outside joined the battle, but it was a start – plus, General Khal had brought not one, but *three* Shardbearers. Renarin did his best to explain the city situation, but was embarrassed to tell the Khals that he didn't know his father's status.

As they reunited with Teshav – turning her scribe station into a command post – Rock and Lyn landed next to Renarin.

'Ha!' Rock said. 'What happened to uniform? Is needing my needle.'

Renarin looked down at his tattered clothing. 'I got hit by a large block of stone. Twenty times ... You're not one to complain, anyway. Is that *your* blood on your uniform?'

'Is nothing!'

'We had to carry him all the way down to the Oathgate,' Lyn said. 'We were trying to get him to you, but he started drawing in Stormlight as soon as he got here.'

'Kaladin is close,' Rock agreed. 'Ha! I feed him. But here, today, he fed me. With light!'

Lyn eyed Rock. 'Storming Horneater weighs as much as a chull. . . .' She shook her head. 'Kara will fight with the others – don't tell anyone, but she's been practicing with a spear since childhood, the little cheater. But Rock won't fight, and I've only been handling a spear for a few weeks now. Any idea where you want us?'

'I'm ... um ... not really in command or anything. . . .'

'Really?' Lyn said. 'That's your best Knight Radiant voice?'

'Ha!' Rock said.

'I think I used up all my Radianting for the day,' Renarin said. 'Um, I'll work the Oathgate and get more troops here. Maybe you two could go down and help on the city wall, pull wounded out of the front lines?'

'Is good idea,' Rock said. Lyn nodded and flew off, but Rock lingered, then grabbed Renarin in a very warm, suffocating, and *unexpected* embrace.

Renarin did his best not to squirm. It wasn't the first hug he'd endured from Rock. But ... storms. You weren't supposed to just grab someone like that.

'Why?' Renarin said after the embrace.

'You looked like person who needed hug.'

'I assure you, I *never* look like that. But, um, I am glad you guys came. Really, *really* glad.'

'Bridge Four,' Rock said, then launched into the air.

Renarin settled down nearby on some steps, trembling from it all, but grinning anyway.

⁂

Dalinar drifted in the Thrill's embrace.

He'd once believed he had been four men in his life, but he now saw he'd grossly underestimated. He hadn't lived as two, or four, or six men – he had lived as thousands, for each day he became someone slightly different.

He hadn't changed in one giant leap, but across a million little steps.

The most important always being the next, he thought as he drifted in the red mist. The Thrill threatened to take him, control him, rip him apart and shred his soul in its eagerness to please him – to give him something it could never understand was dangerous.

A small hand gripped Dalinar's.

He started, looking down. 'L-Lift? You shouldn't have come in here.'

'But I'm the *best* at going places I'm not supposed to.' She pressed something into his hand.

The large ruby.

Bless you.

'What is it?' she said. 'Why do you need that rock?'

Dalinar squinted into the mists. *Do you know how we capture spren, Dalinar?* Taravangian had said. *You lure the spren with something it loves. You give it something familiar to draw it in ...*

Something it knows deeply.

'Shallan saw one of the Unmade in the tower,' he whispered. 'When she got close, it was afraid, but I don't think the Thrill comprehends like

689

it did. You see, it can only be bested by someone who deeply, sincerely, *understands it.*'

He lifted the gemstone above his head, and – one last time – embraced the Thrill.

War.

Victory.

The contest.

Dalinar's entire life had been a competition: a struggle from one conquest to the next. He accepted what he had done. It would always be part of him. And though he was determined to resist, he would not cast aside what he had learned. That very thirst for the struggle – the fight, the *victory* – had also prepared him to refuse Odium.

'Thank you,' he whispered again to the Thrill, 'for giving me strength when I needed it.'

The Thrill churned close around him, cooing and exulting in his praise.

'Now, old friend, it is time to rest.'

⁖

Keep moving.

Kaladin dodged and wove, avoiding some strikes, healing from others.

Keep them distracted.

He tried to take to the skies, but the eight Fused swarmed about him, knocking him back down. He hit the stone ground, then Lashed himself laterally, away from the stabbing lances or crushing clubs.

Can't actually escape.

He had to keep their attention. If he managed to slip away, all of these would turn against Dalinar.

You don't have to beat them. You simply have to last long enough.

He dodged to the right, skimming a few inches above the ground. But one of the hulking Fused – there were four fighting him now – grabbed him by the foot. She slammed him down, then carapace grew down along her arms, threatening to bind Kaladin to the ground.

He kicked her off, but another grabbed him by the arm and flung him to the side. Flying ones descended, and while he warded away their lances with the Sylshield, his side throbbed with pain. The healing was coming more slowly now.

Two other Fused swept along, scooping up nearby gemstones, leaving Kaladin in an ever-expanding ring of darkness.

Just buy time. Dalinar needs time.

Syl sang in his mind as he spun, forming a spear and ramming it through the chest of one of the hulking ones. Those could heal unless you stabbed them in exactly the right spot in the sternum, and he'd missed. So, he made Syl into a sword and – the weapon still embedded in the Fused woman's chest – swept upward through the head, burning her eyes. Another hulking Fused swung, but as it hit – the club being part of the thing's actual body – Kaladin used much of his remaining Stormlight to Lash this man upward, crashing him into a Fused above.

Another clobbered him from the side, sending him rolling. Red lightning pulsed overhead as he came to a rest on his back. He immediately summoned Syl as a spear, pointing straight up. That impaled the Fused dropping down to attack him, cracking its sternum within, causing its eyes to burn.

Another grabbed him by the foot and lifted him, then slammed him face-first into the ground. That knocked Kaladin's breath out. The monstrous Fused stomped a carapace-encrusted foot onto his back, shattering ribs. Kaladin screamed, and though the Stormlight healed what it could, the last of it fluttered inside.

Then went out.

A sudden sound rose behind Kaladin, like that of rushing air – accompanied by wails of pain. The Fused stumbled backward, muttering to a quick, worried rhythm. Then, remarkably, it *turned and ran.*

Kaladin twisted, looking behind himself. He couldn't make out Dalinar anymore, but the mist itself had begun to thrash. Surging and pulsing, it whipped about like it was caught in a powerful wind.

More Fused fled. That wailing grew louder, and the mist seemed to roar – a thousand faces stretching from it, mouths opened in agony. They were sucked back together, like rats pulled by their tails.

The red mist imploded, vanishing. All went dark, with the storm overhead growing still.

Kaladin found himself lying broken on the ground. Stormlight had healed his vital functions; his organs would probably be intact, though his cracked bones left him gasping with pain when he tried to sit up. The spheres around the area were dun, and the darkness prevented him from spotting whether Dalinar lived.

The mist was entirely gone. That seemed a good sign. And in the darkness, Kaladin could see something streaking from the city. Brilliant white lights flying in the air.

A scraping sound came from nearby, and then a violet light flickered in the darkness. A shadow stumbled to its feet, dark purple light pulsing alive in its chest cavity, which was empty save for that gemstone.

Amaram's glowing red eyes illuminated a distorted face: his jaw had broken as he'd fallen, and gemstones had pushed out the sides of his face at awkward angles, making the jaw hang limp from his mouth, drool leaking out the side. He stumbled toward Kaladin, gemstone heart pulsing with light. A Shardblade formed in his hand. The one that had killed Kaladin's friends so long ago.

'Amaram,' Kaladin whispered. 'I can see what you are. What you've always been.'

Amaram tried to speak, but his drooping jaw only let out spittle and grunts. Kaladin was struck by a memory of the first time he'd seen the highlord at Hearthstone. So tall and brave. Seemingly perfect.

'I saw it in your eyes, Amaram,' Kaladin whispered as the husk of a man stumbled up to him. 'When you killed Coreb and Hab and my other friends. I *saw* the guilt you felt.' He licked his lips. 'You tried to break me as a slave. But you failed. They rescued me.'

Maybe it's time for someone to save you, Syl had said in Shadesmar. But someone already had.

Amaram raised the Shardblade high.

'Bridge Four,' Kaladin whispered.

An arrow slammed into Amaram's head from behind, going right through the skull, coming out his inhuman mouth. Amaram stumbled forward, dropping his Shardblade, the arrow stuck in his head. He made a choking sound, then turned about just in time to catch another arrow straight in the chest – right through the flickering gemstone heart.

The amethyst exploded, and Amaram dropped in a crumbled wreck beside Kaladin.

A glowing figure stood on some rubble beyond, holding Amaram's enormous Shardbow. The weapon seemed to match Rock, tall and brilliant, a beacon in the darkness.

Amaram's red eyes faded as he died, and Kaladin had the distinct impression of a dark smoke escaping his corpse. Two Shardblades formed beside him and clanged to the stone.

⁂

The soldiers made a space for Radiant on the wall as they prepared for the enemy assault. Amaram's army formed assault ranks while parshmen carried ladders, ready to charge.

It was hard to step atop the wall without squishing a fearspren. Thaylens whispered of Alethi prowess in battle, recalling stories like when Hamadin and his fifty had withstood ten thousand Vedens. This was the first battle the Thaylens had seen in a generation, but Amaram's troops had been hardened by constant war on the Shattered Plains.

They looked to Shallan as if she could save them. The Knights Radiant were the only edge this city had. Their best hope of survival.

That terrified her.

The armies started charging the wall. No pause, no breather. Odium would keep pushing forces at this wall as long as it took to crack Thaylen City. Bloodlusty men, controlled by . . .

The lights in their eyes started to go out.

That clouded sky made it unmistakable. All across the field, red faded from the eyes of Amaram's soldiers. Many immediately fell to their knees, retching on the ground. Others stumbled, holding themselves upright by sagging against spears. It was like the very life had been sucked out of them – and it was so abrupt and unexpected that Shallan had to blink several times before her mind admitted that – yes – this was happening.

Cheers erupted along the wall as the Fused inexplicably retreated back toward the ships. The parshmen rushed to follow, as did many of Amaram's troops – though some just lay on the broken stones.

Lethargically, the black storm faded until it was a mere overcast stain, rippling with drowsy red lightning. It finally rolled across the island – impotent, bereft of wind – and vanished to the east.

⁂

Kaladin drank Stormlight from Lopen's gemstones.

'Be lucky the Horneater was looking for you, gon,' Lopen said. 'The rest of us thought we'd just fight, you know?'

Kaladin glanced toward Rock, who stood over Amaram's body, looking down, the enormous bow held limply in one hand. How had he drawn it? Stormlight granted great endurance, but it didn't vastly improve strength.

'Whoa,' Lopen said. 'Gancho! Look!'

The clouds had thinned, and sunlight peeked through, illuminating the field of stone. Dalinar Kholin knelt not far away, clutching a large ruby that glowed with the same strange phantom light as the Fused. The Reshi girl stood with her diminutive hand resting on his shoulder.

The Blackthorn was crying as he cradled the gemstone.

'Dalinar?' Kaladin asked, worried, jogging over. 'What happened?'

'It is over, Captain,' Dalinar said. Then he smiled. So were they tears of joy? Why had he seemed so grieved? 'It's over.'

It becomes the responsibility of every man, upon realizing he lacks the truth, to seek it out.

—From *The Way of Kings*, postscript

Moash found it easy to transition from killing men to breaking apart rubble.

He used a pick to hack at pieces of fallen stone in the former east wing of the Kholinar palace, smashing fallen columns so they could be carried off by other workers. Nearby, the floor was still red with dried blood. That was where he'd killed Elhokar, and his new masters had ordered the blood to not be cleaned. They claimed that the death of a king was a thing to regard with reverence.

Shouldn't Moash have felt pleasure? Or at least satisfaction? Instead, killing Elhokar had only made him feel . . . cold. Like a man who had hiked across half of Roshar with a caravan of stubborn chulls. At the top of the last hill, you didn't feel satisfaction. You just felt tired. Maybe a sliver of relief at being done.

He slammed his pick into a fallen pillar. Near the end of the battle for Kholinar, the thunderclast had knocked down a large portion of the palace's eastern gallery. Now, human slaves worked to clear out the rubble. The others would often break down crying, or work with hunched shoulders.

Moash shook his head, enjoying the peaceful rhythm of pick on stone.

A Fused strode past, covered in carapace armor as brilliant and wicked as Shardplate. There were nine orders of them. Why not ten?

'Over there,' the Fused said through an interpreter. He pointed at a section of wall. 'Break this down.'

Moash wiped his brow, frowning as other slaves began work there. Why break down that wall? Wouldn't it be needed to rebuild this portion of the palace?

'Curious, human?'

Moash jumped, startled to find a figure hovering down through the broken ceiling, swathed in black. Lady Leshwi still visited Moash, the man who had killed her. She was important among the singers, but not in a highprince sort of way. More like a field captain.

'I guess I am curious, Ancient Singer,' Moash said. 'Is there a reason you're ripping apart this section of the palace? More than just to clear away the rubble?'

'Yes. But you do not yet need to know why.'

He nodded, then returned to his work.

She hummed to a rhythm he associated with being pleased. 'Your passion does you credit.'

'I have no passion. Just numbness.'

'You have given him your pain. He will return it, human, when you need it.'

That would be fine, so long as he could forget the look of betrayal he'd seen in Kaladin's eyes.

'Hnanan wishes to speak with you,' the ancient one said. The name wasn't fully a word. It was more a hummed sound, with specific beats. 'Join us above.'

She flew off. Moash set aside his pick and followed in a more mundane manner, rounding to the front of the palace. Once away from the picks and the clatter of rocks, he could hear sobs and whimpers. Only the most destitute humans sheltered here, in the broken buildings near the palace.

Eventually, these would be rounded up and sent to work farms. For now, however, the grand city was a place of wails and heartache. The people thought the world had ended, but they were only half right. *Their* world had.

He entered the palace uncontested, and started up the stairwell. Fused didn't need guards. Killing them was difficult, and even if you succeeded, they would simply be reborn at the next Everstorm, assuming a willing parshman could be found to take the burden.

Near the king's chambers, Moash passed two Fused reading books in a library. They'd removed their lengthy coats, floating with bare feet peeking from loose, rippling trousers, toes pointed downward. He eventually found Hnanan out beyond the king's balcony, hovering in the air, her train blowing and rippling in the wind beneath.

'Ancient Singer,' he said from the balcony. Though Hnanan was the equivalent of a highprince, they did not demand that Moash bow even to her. Apparently, by having killed one of their better fighters, he had obtained a level of respect.

'You did well,' she said, speaking Alethi, her voice thickly accented. 'You felled a king in this palace.'

'King or slave, he was an enemy to me and mine.'

'I have called myself wise,' she said, 'and felt pride for Leshwi at picking you out. For years, my brother, sister, and I will boast of having chosen you.' She looked to him. 'Odium has a command for you. This is rare for a human.'

'Speak it.'

'You have killed a king,' she said, removing something from a sheath within her robes. A strange knife, with a sapphire set into the pommel. The weapon was of a bright golden metal, so light it was almost white. 'Would you do the same to a god?'

⁂

Navani left through the sally port in the Thaylen City wall, and ran across the broken field, heedless of the calls of soldiers who scrambled after her. She'd waited as long as was reasonable to let the enemy army withdraw.

Dalinar walked with help from Lopen and Captain Kaladin, one under each arm. He towed jets of exhaustionspren like a swarm. Navani took him in a powerful embrace anyway. He was the Blackthorn. He'd survive a forceful hug.

Kaladin and Lopen hovered nearby. 'He's mine,' she said to them.

They nodded, and didn't move.

'People need your help inside,' she said. 'I can handle him, boys.'

Finally they flew off, and Navani tried to get under Dalinar's arm. He shook his head, still holding her in the embrace, a large stone – wrapped in his coat – held in one hand and pressing against her back. What was that?

'I think I know why the memories came back,' he whispered. 'Odium was going to make me remember once I faced him. I needed to learn to stand up again. All my pain these last two months was a blessing.'

She held to him on that open field of rock, broken by the thunderclasts, littered with men who wailed toward the empty sky, screaming for what they'd done, demanding to know why they'd been abandoned.

Dalinar resisted Navani's attempts to tug him toward the wall. Instead, teary eyed, he kissed her. 'Thank you for inspiring me.'

'Inspiring you?'

He released her and held up his arm, which was strapped with the clock and painrial she'd given him. It had cracked open, exposing the gemstones. 'It reminded me,' he said. 'Of how we make fabrials.'

He lethargically unwrapped his uniform jacket from around a large ruby. It glowed with a bizarre light, deep and dark. Somehow, it seemed to be trying to pull the light around it *in*.

'I want you to keep this safe for me,' Dalinar said. 'Study it. Find out why this gemstone specifically was capable of holding one of the Unmade. Don't break it though. We dare not let it out again.'

She bit her lip. 'Dalinar, I've seen something like this before. Much smaller, like a sphere.' She looked up at him. 'Gavilar made it.'

Dalinar touched the stone with his bare finger. Deep within it, something seemed to stir. Had he really trapped an entire *Unmade* inside this thing?

'Study it,' he repeated. 'And in the meantime, there's something else I want you to do, dearest. Something unconventional, perhaps uncomfortable.'

'Anything,' she said. 'What is it?'

Dalinar met her eyes. 'I want you to teach me how to read.'

⁖

Everyone started celebrating. Shallan, Radiant, and Veil just settled down on the wall walk, back to the stone.

Radiant worried they'd leave the city undefended in their reverie. And what had become of the enemy that had been fighting in the streets?

The defenders had to make certain this wasn't an elaborate feint.

Veil worried about looting. A city in chaos often proved how feral it could become. Veil wanted to be out on the streets, looking for people likely to be robbed, and making sure they were cared for.

Shallan wanted to sleep. She felt . . . weaker . . . more tired than the other two.

Jasnah approached along the wall walk, then leaned down beside her. 'Shallan? Are you well?'

'Just tired,' Veil lied. 'You have no idea how draining that was, Brightness. I could use a stiff drink.'

'I suspect that would help very little,' Jasnah said, rising. 'Rest here a while yet. I want to make absolutely certain the enemy is not returning.'

'I swear to do better, Brightness,' Radiant said, taking Jasnah's hand. 'I wish to fulfill my wardship – to study and learn until *you* determine I am ready. I will not flee again. I've realized I have very far to go yet.'

'That is well, Shallan.' Jasnah moved off.

Shallan. *Which . . . which am I . . . ?* She'd insisted she would be better soon, but that didn't seem to be happening. She grasped for an answer, staring into the nothingness until Navani approached and knelt down beside her. Behind, Dalinar accepted a respectful bow from Queen Fen, then bowed back.

'Storms, Shallan,' Navani said. 'You look like you can barely keep your eyes open. I'll get you a palanquin to the upper reaches of the city.'

'The Oathgate is likely clogged,' Radiant said. 'I would not take a place from others who might be in greater need.'

'Don't be foolish, child,' Navani said, then gave her an embrace. 'You must have been through so much. Devmrh, would you get a palanquin for Brightness Davar?'

'My own feet are good enough,' Veil said, glaring at the scribe who jumped to obey Navani. 'I'm stronger than you think – no offense, Brightness.'

Navani pursed her lips, but then was pulled away by Dalinar and Fen's conversation; they were planning to write the Azish and explain what had happened. Veil figured he was rightly worried that today's events would spread as rumors of Alethi betrayal. Storms, if she hadn't been here herself, she'd have been tempted to believe them. It wasn't every day that an entire army went rogue.

Radiant decided they could rest for ten minutes. Shallan accepted that, leaning her head back against the wall. Floating . . .

'Shallan?'

That voice. She opened her eyes to find Adolin scrambling across the wall to her. He skidded a little as he fell to his knees beside her, then raised his hands – only to hesitate, as if confronted by something very fragile.

'Don't look at me like that,' Veil said. 'I'm not some delicate piece of crystal.'

Adolin narrowed his eyes.

'Truly,' Radiant said. 'I'm a soldier as much as the men atop this wall. Treat me – other than in obvious respects – as you would treat them.'

'Shallan . . .' Adolin said, taking her hand.

'What?' Veil asked.

'Something's wrong.'

'Of course it is,' Radiant said. 'This fighting has left us all thoroughly worn out.'

Adolin searched her eyes. She bled from one, to the other, and back. A moment of Veil. A moment of Radiant. Shallan peeking through—

Adolin's hand tightened around her own.

Shallan's breath caught. *There,* she thought. *That's the one. That's the one I am.*

He knows.

Adolin relaxed, and for the first time she noticed how ragged his clothing was. She raised her safehand to her lips. 'Adolin, are you all right?'

'Oh!' He looked down at his ripped uniform and scraped hands. 'It's not as bad as it looks, Shallan. Most of the blood isn't mine. Well, I mean, I guess it is. But I'm feeling better.'

She cupped his face with her freehand. 'You'd better not have gotten too many scars. I'm expecting you to remain pretty, I'll have you know.'

'I'm barely hurt, Shallan. Renarin got to me.'

'Then it's all right if I do this?' Shallan asked, hugging him. He responded, pulling her tight. He smelled of sweat and blood – not the gentlest of scents, but this was *him* and she was *Shallan.*

'How are you?' he asked. '*Really?*'

'Tired,' she whispered.

'You want a palanquin . . .'

'Everyone keeps asking that.'

'I could carry you up,' he said, then pulled back and grinned. 'Course, you're a Radiant. So maybe you could carry me instead? I've already been all the way up to the top of the city and back down once. . . .'

Shallan smiled, until farther down the wall a glowing figure in blue landed on the battlements. Kaladin settled down, blue eyes shining, flanked by Rock and Lopen. Soldiers all along the walk turned toward him. Even in a battle with multiple Knights Radiant, there was something about the way Kaladin flew, the way he moved.

Veil immediately took over. She pulled herself to her feet as Kaladin strode along the wall to meet with Dalinar. *What happened to his boots?*

'Shallan?' Adolin asked.

'A palanquin sounds *great*,' Veil said. 'Thanks.'

Adolin blushed, then nodded and strode toward one of the stairwells down into the city.

'Mmm . . .' Pattern said. 'I'm confused.'

'We need to approach this from a logical position,' Radiant said. 'We've been dancing around a decision for months, ever since those days we spent in the chasms with Stormblessed. I've begun to consider that a relationship between two Knights Radiant is likely to accomplish a more equitable union.'

'Also,' Veil added, 'look at those *eyes*. Simmering with barely bridled emotion.' She walked toward him, grinning.

Then slowed.

Adolin knows me.

What was she doing?

She shoved Radiant and Veil aside, and when they resisted, she stuffed them into the back part of her brain. They were not her. She was occasionally them. But they were *not her*.

Kaladin hesitated on the wall walk, but Shallan just gave him a wave, then went the other way, tired – but determined.

⁘

Venli stood by the railing of a fleeing ship.

The Fused boasted from within the captain's cabin. They talked about next time, promising what they'd do and how they'd win. They spoke of past victories, and subtly hinted at why they'd failed. Too few of them had awakened so far, and those who had awakened were unaccustomed to having physical bodies.

What a strange way to treat a failure. She attuned Appreciation anyway. An old rhythm. She loved being able to hear those again at will – she could attune either old or new, and could make her eyes red, except when she drew in Stormlight. Timbre had granted this by capturing the Voidspren within her.

This meant she could hide it from the Fused. From Odium. She stepped away from the cabin door and walked along the side of the ship, which surged through the water, heading back toward Marat.

'This bond was supposed to be impossible,' she whispered to Timbre.

Timbre pulsed to Peace.

'I'm happy too,' Venli whispered. 'But why me? Why not one of the humans?'

Timbre pulsed to Irritation, then the Lost.

'That many? I had no idea the human betrayal had cost so many of your people's lives. And your own grandfather?'

Irritation again.

'I'm not sure how much I trust the humans either. Eshonai did though.'

Nearby, sailors worked on the rigging, speaking softly in Thaylen. Parshmen, yes, but also Thaylens. 'I don't know, Vldgen,' one said. 'Yeah, some of them weren't so bad. But what they did to us . . .'

'Does that mean we have to kill them?' his companion asked. She caught a tossed rope. 'It doesn't seem right.'

'They took our culture, Vldgen,' the malen said. 'They blustering took our *entire identity*. And they'll never let a bunch of parshmen remain free. Watch. They'll come for us.'

'I'll fight if they do,' Vldgen said. 'But . . . I don't know. Can't we simply enjoy being able to *think*? Being able to *exist*?' She shook her head, lashing a rope tight. 'I just wish I knew who we were.'

Timbre pulsed to Praise.

'The listeners?' Venli whispered to the spren. 'We didn't do that good a job of resisting Odium. As soon as we got a *hint* of power, we came running back to him.' That had been her fault. She had driven them toward new information, new powers. She'd always hungered for it. Something new.

Timbre pulsed to Consolation, but then it blended, changing once again to Resolve.

Venli hummed the same transformation.

Something new.

But also something old.

She walked to the two sailors. They immediately stood at attention, saluting her as the only Regal on the ship, holding a form of power. 'I know who you were,' she said to the two of them.

'You . . . you do?' the femalen asked.

'Yes.' Venli pointed. 'Keep working, and let me tell you of the listeners.'

∴

I think you did a great job, Szeth, the sword said from Szeth's hand as they rose above Thaylen City. *You didn't destroy many of them, yes, but you just need some more practice!*

'Thank you, sword-nimi,' he said, reaching Nin. The Herald floated with toes pointed downward, hands clasped behind his back, watching the disappearing ships of the parshmen in the distance.

'I am sorry, master,' Szeth finally said. 'I have angered you.'

'I am not your master,' Nin said. 'And you have not angered me. Why would I be displeased?'

'You have determined that the parshmen are the true owners of this land, and that the Skybreakers should follow their laws.'

'The very reason that we swear to something external is because we acknowledge that our own judgment is flawed. *My* judgment is flawed.' He narrowed his eyes. 'I used to be able to feel, Szeth-son-Neturo. I used to have compassion. I can remember those days, before . . .'

'The torture?' Szeth asked.

He nodded. 'Centuries spent on Braize – the place you call Damnation – stole my ability to feel. We each cope somehow, but only Ishar survived with his mind intact. Regardless, you are certain you wish to follow a man with your oath?'

'It is not as perfect as the law, I know,' Szeth said. 'But it feels right.'

'The law is made by men, so it is not perfect either. It is not perfection we seek, for perfection is impossible. It is instead consistency. You have said the Words?'

'Not yet. I swear to follow the will of Dalinar Kholin. This is my oath.'

At the Words, snow crystallized around him in the air, then fluttered down. He felt a surge of something. Approval? From the hidden spren who only rarely showed itself to him, even still.

'I believe that your Words have been accepted. Have you chosen your quest for the next Ideal?'

'I will cleanse the Shin of their false leaders, so long as Dalinar Kholin agrees.'

'We shall see. You may find him a harsh master.'

'He is a good man, Nin-son-God.'

'That is precisely why.' Nin saluted him quietly, then began to move away through the air. He shook his head when Szeth followed, and then he pointed. 'You must protect the man you once tried to kill, Szeth-son-Neturo.'

'What if we meet on the battlefield?'

'Then we will both fight with confidence, knowing that we obey the precepts of our oaths. Farewell, Szeth-son-Neturo. I will visit you again to oversee your training in our second art, the Surge of Division. You may access that now, but take care. It is dangerous.'

He left Szeth alone in the sky, holding a sword that hummed happily to itself, then confided that it had never really liked Nin in the first place.

⁘

Shallan had found that no matter how bad things got, *someone* would be making tea.

Today it was Teshav, and Shallan gratefully took a cup, then peeked through the command post at the top of the city, still looking for Adolin. Now that she was moving, she found she could ignore her fatigue. Momentum could be a powerful thing.

Adolin wasn't here, though one of the runner girls had seen him a short time ago, so Shallan was on the right track. She walked back to the main thoroughfare, passing men carrying stretchers full of the wounded. Otherwise, the streets were mostly empty. People had been sent to storm-shelters or homes as Queen Fen's soldiers gathered gemstones from the reserve, rounded up Amaram's troops, and made certain there was no looting.

Shallan idled in the mouth of an alleyway. The tea was bitter, but good. Knowing Teshav, it probably had something in it to keep her on her feet and alert – scribes always knew the best teas for that.

She watched the people for a time, then glanced upward as Kaladin landed on a rooftop nearby. He was next up for working the Oathgate, taking over from Renarin.

The Windrunner stood like a sentinel, surveying the city. Was that going to become a *thing* for him? Always standing around up high somewhere? She'd seen how envious he'd been as he'd watched those Fused, with their flowing robes, moving like the winds.

Shallan glanced toward the thoroughfare as she heard a familiar voice. Adolin hiked down the street, led by the messenger girl, who pointed him toward Shallan. Finally. The messenger girl bowed, then scampered off back toward the command post.

Adolin stepped over and ran his hand through his mop of hair, blond and black. It looked fantastic, despite his ripped uniform and scraped face. Perhaps that was the advantage to persistently messy hair – he managed to make it go with anything. Though she had no idea how he'd gotten so much dust on his uniform. Had he fought a bag of sand?

She pulled him against her in the mouth of the alleyway, then twisted and put his arm around her shoulders. 'Where did you get off to?'

'Father asked me to check on each of the Thaylen Shardbearers and report. I left you a palanquin.'

'Thank you,' she said. 'I've been surveying the aftermath of the fight. I think we did a good job. Only half the city destroyed – which is quite the step up from our work in Kholinar. If we keep this up, some people might actually live through the end of the world.'

He grunted. 'You seem in higher spirits than earlier.'

'Teshav fed me tea,' she said. 'I'll probably be bouncing off the clouds soon. Don't get me laughing. I sound like an axehound puppy when I'm hyper.'

'Shallan . . .' he said.

She twisted up to look at his eyes, then followed his gaze. Above, Kaladin rose into the air to inspect something that they couldn't see.

'I didn't mean to abandon you earlier,' Shallan said. 'I'm sorry. I should never have let you run off.'

He took a deep breath, then removed his arm from her shoulders.

I've screwed it up! Shallan thought immediately. *Stormfather. I've gone and ruined it.*

'I've decided,' Adolin said, 'to step back.'

'Adolin, I didn't mean to—'

'I have to say this, Shallan. Please.' He stood up tall, stiff. 'I'm going to let him have you.'

She blinked. '*Let* him *have* me.'

'I'm holding you back,' Adolin said. 'I see the way you two look at each other. I don't want you to keep forcing yourself to spend time with me because you feel sorry for me.'

Storms. Now he's *trying to ruin it!* 'No,' Shallan said. 'First off, you don't get to treat me like some kind of prize. You don't decide who *gets* me.'

'I'm not trying to . . .' He took another deep breath. 'Look, this is hard for me, Shallan. I'm trying to do the right thing. Don't make it harder.'

'I don't get a choice?'

'You've made your choice. I see how you look at him.'

'I'm an *artist*, Adolin. I appreciate a nice picture when I see one. Doesn't mean I want to pull it off the hook and go get intimate.'

Kaladin landed on a roof in the distance, still looking the other way. Adolin waved toward him. 'Shallan. He can *literally* fly.'

'Oh? And is that what women are supposed to seek in a mate? Is it in the *Polite Lady's Handbook to Courtship and Family*? The Bekenah edition, maybe? 'Ladies, you can't *possibly* marry a man if he can't fly.' Never mind if the other option is as handsome as sin, kind to everyone he meets regardless of their station, passionate about his art, and genuinely humble in the weirdest, most confident way. Never mind if he actually seems to get you, and remarkably listens to your problems, encouraging you to be you – not to hide yourself away. Never mind if being *near* him makes you want to rip his shirt off and push him into the nearest alleyway, then kiss him until he can't breathe anymore. If he can't *fly*, then well, you just have to call it off!'

She paused for breath, gasping.

'And . . .' Adolin said. 'That guy is . . . me?'

'You are such a fool.' She grabbed his ripped coat and pulled him into a kiss, passionspren crystallizing in the air around them. The warmth of the kiss did more for her than the tea ever could. It made her bubble and boil inside. Stormlight was nice, but this . . . *this* was an energy that made it dun by comparison.

Storms, she loved this man.

When she let him out of the kiss, he grabbed her and pulled her close, breathing heavily.

'Are you . . . are you sure?' he asked. 'I just . . . Don't glare at me, Shallan. I have to say this. The world is full of gods and Heralds now, and you're one of them. I'm practically a nobody. I'm not used to that feeling.'

'Then it's probably the best thing that's ever happened to you, Adolin Kholin. Well. Except for *me*.' She snuggled against him. 'I will admit to you, in the interest of full honesty, that Veil *did* have a tendency to fawn over Kaladin Stormblessed. She has terrible taste in men, and I've convinced her to fall in line.'

'That's worrisome, Shallan.'

'I won't let her act on it. I promise.'

'I didn't mean that,' Adolin said. 'I meant . . . you, Shallan. Becoming other people.'

'We're all different people at different times. Remember?'

'Not the same way as you.'

'I know,' she said. 'But I . . . I think I've stopped leaking into new personas. Three for now.' She turned around, smiling at him, his hands still around her waist. 'How do you like that, though? Three betrotheds instead of one. Some men drool over the idea of such debauchery. If you wanted, I could be practically anyone.'

'But that's the thing, Shallan. I don't want anyone. I want *you*.'

'That might be the hardest one. But I think I can do it, Adolin. With some help, maybe?'

He grinned that goofy grin of his. Storms, how could his hair look so good with *gravel* in it? 'So . . .' he said. 'You mentioned something about kissing me until I can't breathe. But here I am, not even winded—'

He cut off as she kissed him again.

.*.

Kaladin settled down on the edge of a roof, high at the top of Thaylen City.

This poor city. First the Everstorm, and its subsequent returns. The Thaylens had only just started figuring out how to rebuild, and now had to deal with more smashed buildings leading up to the corpse of the thunderclast, which lay like a toppled statue.

We can win, he thought. *But each victory scars us a little more.*

707

In his hand he rubbed a small stone with his thumb. Down below, in an alleyway off the main thoroughfare, a woman with flowing red hair kissed a man in a ragged and ripped uniform. Some people could celebrate despite the scars. Kaladin accepted that. He merely wished he knew how they did it.

'Kaladin?' Syl said. She wove around him as a ribbon of light. 'Don't feel bad. The Words have to come in their own time. You'll be all right.'

'I always am.'

He squinted down at Shallan and Adolin, and found that he couldn't be bitter. He didn't feel resignation either. Instead he felt . . . agreement?

'Oh, them,' Syl said. 'Well, *I* know that you don't back down from fights. You've lost the round, but—'

'No,' he said. 'Her choice is made. You can see it.'

'I can?'

'You should be able to.' He rubbed his finger on the rock. 'I don't think I loved her, Syl. I felt . . . something. A lightening of my burdens when I was near her. She reminds me of someone.'

'Who?'

He opened his palm, and she landed on it, forming into the shape of a young woman with flowing hair and dress. She bent down, inspecting the rock in his palm, cooing over it. Syl could still be shockingly innocent – wide-eyed and excited about the world.

'That's a nice rock,' she said, completely serious.

'Thank you.'

'Where did you get it?'

'I found it on the battlefield below. If you get it wet it changes colors. It looks brown, but with a little water, you can see the white, black, and grey.'

'Oooooh.'

He let her inspect it for a moment more. 'It's true, then?' he finally said. 'About the parshmen. That this was their land, their *world*, before we arrived? That . . . that *we* were the Voidbringers?'

She nodded. 'Odium is the void, Kaladin. He draws in emotion, and doesn't let it go. You . . . you brought him with you. I wasn't alive then, but I know this truth. He was your first god, before you turned to Honor.'

Kaladin exhaled slowly, closing his eyes.

The men of Bridge Four were having trouble with this idea. As well they should. Others in the military didn't care, but his men . . . they knew.

708

You could protect your home. You could kill to defend the people inside. But what if you'd stolen that house in the first place? What if the people you killed were only trying to get back what was rightfully theirs?

Reports from Alethkar said that the parshman armies were pushing north, that Alethi armies in the area had moved into Herdaz. What would happen to Hearthstone? His family? Surely in the face of the invasion, he could convince his father to move to Urithiru. But what then?

It got so complicated. Humans had lived upon this land for thousands of years. Could anyone really be expected to let go because of what ancient people had done, no matter how dishonorable their actions?

Who did he fight? Who did he protect?

Defender? Invader?

Honorable knight? Hired thug?

'The Recreance,' he said to Syl. 'I always imagined it as a single event. A day the knights all gave up their Shards, like in Dalinar's vision. But I don't think it actually happened like that.'

'Then . . . how?' Syl asked.

'Like this,' Kaladin said. He squinted, watching the light of a setting sun play on the ocean. 'They found out something they couldn't ignore. Eventually they had to face it.'

'They made the wrong choice.'

Kaladin pocketed the stone. 'The oaths are about perception, Syl. You confirmed that. The only thing that matters is whether or not we are confident that we're obeying our principles. If we lose that confidence, then dropping the armor and weapons is only a formality.'

'Kal—'

'I'm not going to do the same,' he said. 'I'd like to think that the past of Bridge Four will make us a little more pragmatic than those ancient Radiants. We won't abandon you. But finding out what we *will* do might end up being messy.'

Kaladin stepped off the building, then Lashed himself so he soared in a wide arc over the city. He landed on a rooftop where most of Bridge Four was sharing a meal of flatbread with kuma – crushed lavis and spices. They could have demanded something far better than travel rations, but they didn't seem to realize it.

Teft stood apart, glowing softly. Kaladin waved to the other men, then walked up to join Teft at the edge of the rooftop, staring out over the ocean beyond.

'Almost time to get the men back to work,' Teft noted. 'King Taravangian wants us to fly wounded up from the triage stations to the Oathgate. The men wanted a break for food, not that they storming did much. You'd already won this battle when we got here, Kal.'

'I'd be dead if you hadn't activated the Oathgate,' Kaladin said softly. 'Somehow I knew that you would, Teft. I knew you'd come for me.'

'Knew better than I did, then.' Teft heaved a breath.

Kaladin rested his hand on Teft's shoulder. 'I know how it feels.'

'Aye,' Teft said. 'I suppose you do. But isn't it supposed to feel better? The longing for my moss is still storming there.'

'It doesn't change us, Teft. We're still who we are.'

'Damnation.'

Kaladin looked back at the others. Lopen was currently trying to impress Lyn and Laran with a story about how he lost his arm. It was the seventh rendition Kaladin had heard, each a little different.

Beard . . . Kaladin thought, feeling the loss like a stab to his side. *He and Lopen would have gotten along well.*

'It doesn't get easier, Teft,' he said. 'It gets harder, I think, the more you learn about the Words. Fortunately, you *do* get help. You were mine when I needed it. I'll be yours.'

Teft nodded, but then pointed. 'What about him?'

For the first time, Kaladin realized that Rock wasn't with the rest of the team. The large Horneater was sitting – Stormlight extinguished – on the steps of one of the temples down below. Shardbow across his lap. Head bowed. He obviously considered what he'd done to be an oath broken, despite it having saved Kaladin's life.

'We lift the bridge together, Teft,' Kaladin said. 'And we carry it.'

⁖

Dalinar refused to leave Thaylen City immediately – but in compromise with Navani, he agreed to return to his villa in the Royal Ward and rest. On his way, he stopped in the temple of Talenelat – which had been cleared of people to make space for the generals to meet.

Those hadn't arrived yet, so he had a short time to himself, looking at the reliefs dedicated to the Herald. He knew that he should go up and sleep, at least until the Azish ambassador arrived. But something about those images of Talenelat'Elin, standing tall against overwhelming forces . . .

Did he ever have to fight humans in one of these last stands? Dalinar thought. *Worse, did he ever wonder about what he had done? What we all had done, in taking this world?*

Dalinar was still standing there when a frail figure darkened the doorway to the temple. 'I brought my surgeons,' Taravangian said, voice echoing in the large stone chamber. 'They have already begun helping with the city's wounded.'

'Thank you,' Dalinar said.

Taravangian didn't enter. He stood, waiting, until Dalinar sighed softly. 'You abandoned me,' he said. 'You abandoned this city.'

'I assumed that you were going to fall,' Taravangian said, 'and so positioned myself in a way that I could seize control of the coalition.'

Dalinar started. He turned toward the old man, who stood silhouetted in the doorway. 'You *what?*'

'I assumed that the only way for the coalition to recover from your mistakes was for me to take command. I could not stand with you, my friend. For the good of Roshar, I stepped away.'

Even after their discussions together – even *knowing* how Taravangian viewed his obligations – Dalinar was shocked. This was brutal, utilitarian politics.

Taravangian finally stepped into the chamber, trailing a wizened hand along one of the wall reliefs. He joined Dalinar, and together they studied a carving of a powerful man, standing tall between two pillars of stone – barring the way between monsters and men.

'You . . . didn't become king of Jah Keved by accident, did you?' Dalinar asked.

Taravangian shook his head. It seemed obvious to Dalinar now. Taravangian was easy to dismiss when you assumed he was slow of thought. But once you knew the truth, other mysteries began to fit into place.

'How?' Dalinar asked.

'There's a woman at Kharbranth,' he said. 'She goes by the name Dova, but we think she is Battah'Elin. A Herald. She told us the Desolation was approaching.' He looked to Dalinar. 'I had nothing to do with the death of your brother. But once I heard of what incredible things the assassin did, I sought him out. Years later, I located him, and gave him specific instructions. . . .'

∴

Moash stepped down out of the Kholinar palace into the shadows of a night that had seemed far too long in coming.

People clogged the palace gardens – humans who had been cast out of homes to make way for parshmen. Some of these refugees had strung tarps between benches of shalebark, creating very low tents only a couple of feet tall. Lifespren bobbed among them and the garden plants.

Moash's target was a particular man who sat giggling in the darkness near the back of the gardens. A madman with eye color lost to the night.

'Have you seen me?' the man asked as Moash knelt.

'No,' Moash said, then rammed the strange golden knife into the man's stomach. The man took it with a quiet grunt, smiled a silly smile, then closed his eyes.

'Were you really one of them?' Moash asked. 'Herald of the Almighty?'

'Was, was, was . . .' The man started to tremble violently, his eyes opening wide. 'Was . . . no. No, what is this death? *What is this death!*'

Huddled forms stirred, and some of the wiser ones scuttled away.

'It's taking me!' the man screamed, then looked down at the knife in Moash's hand. 'What *is* that?'

The man trembled for a moment more, then jerked once, going motionless. When Moash pulled the yellow-white knife free, it trailed dark smoke and left a blackened wound. The large sapphire at the pommel took on a subdued glow.

Moash glanced over his shoulder toward the Fused hanging in the night sky behind the palace. This murder seemed a thing that they dared not do themselves. Why? What did they fear?

Moash held the knife aloft toward them, but there were no cheers. Nothing accompanied the act but a few muttered words from people trying to sleep. These broken slaves were the only other witnesses to this moment.

The final death of Jezrien. Yaezir. Jezerezeh'Elin, king of Heralds. A figure known in myth and lore as the greatest human who had ever lived.

∴

Lopen leaped behind a rock, then grinned, spotting the little spren in the shape of a leaf tucked there. 'Found you, naco.'

Rua transformed into the shape of a petulant young boy, maybe nine or ten years old. Rua was his name, but 'naco' was – of course – what Lopen called him.

Rua zipped into the air as a ribbon of light. Bridge Four stood near some tents at the bottom of Thaylen City, in the Low Ward, right in the shadow of the walls. Here, a massive surgeons' station was caring for the wounded.

'Lopen!' Teft called. 'Stop being crazy and get over here to help.'

'I'm not crazy,' Lopen yelled back. 'Sure, I'm the *least* crazy of this whole lot! And you all know it!'

Teft sighed, then waved to Peet and Leyten. Together, they carefully Lashed a large platform – easily twenty feet square – into the air. It was filled with recuperating wounded. The three bridgemen flew with it toward the upper part of the city.

Rua zipped onto Lopen's shoulder and formed into the shape of a young man, then thrust a hand toward the bridgemen and tried the gesture that Lopen had taught him.

'Nice,' Lopen said. 'But wrong finger. Nope! Not that one either. Naco, that's your foot.'

The spren turned the gesture toward Lopen.

'That's it,' Lopen said. 'You can thank me, naco, for inspiring this great advance in your learning. People – and little things made out of nothing too, sure – are often inspired near the Lopen.'

He turned and strolled into a tent of wounded, the far wall of which was tied right onto a nice, shiny bronze portion of wall. Lopen hoped the Thaylens would appreciate how nice it was. Who had a metal wall? Lopen would put one on his palace when he built it. Thaylens were strange though. What else could you say about a people who liked it so far south, in the cold? The local language was practically chattering teeth.

This tent of wounded was filled with the people who had been deemed too healthy to deserve Renarin's or Lift's healing, but still needed a surgeon's care. They weren't dying, sure, *right now*. Maybe later. But everyone was dying maybe later, so it was probably all right to ignore them for someone whose guts got misplaced.

The moans and whimpers indicated that they found not dying

immediately to be a small comfort. The ardents did what they could, but most of the real surgeons were set up higher in the city. Taravangian's forces had finally decided to join the battle, now that all the easy stuff – like dying, which really didn't take much skill – was through.

Lopen fetched his pack, then passed Dru – who was folding freshly boiled bandages. Even after all these centuries, sure, they did what the Heralds had told them. Boiling stuff killed rotspren.

Lopen patted Dru on the shoulder. The slender Alethi man looked up and nodded toward Lopen, showing reddened eyes. Loving a soldier was not easy, and now that Kaladin had returned from Alethkar alone . . .

Lopen moved on, and eventually settled down beside a wounded man in a cot. Thaylen, with drooping eyebrows and a bandage around his head. He stared straight ahead, not blinking.

'Want to see a trick?' Lopen asked the soldier.

The man shrugged.

Lopen lifted his foot up and put the boot on the man's cot. The laces had come undone, and Lopen – one hand behind his back – deftly grabbed the strings and looped them around his hand, twisted them, then pulled them tight, using his other foot to hold one end. He wound up with an excellent knot with a nice bow. It was even symmetrical. Maybe he could get an ardent to write a poem about it.

The soldier gave no reaction. Lopen settled back, pulling over his pack, which clinked softly. 'Don't look like that. It's not the end of the world.'

The soldier cocked his head.

'Well, sure. *Technically* it might be. But for the end of the world, it's not so bad, right? I figured that when everything ended, we'd sink into a noxious bath of pus and doom, breathing in agony as the air around us – sure – became molten, and we screamed a final burning scream, relishing the memories of the last time a woman loved us.' Lopen tapped the man's cot. 'Don't know about you, moolie, but my lungs aren't burning. The air doesn't seem very molten. Considering how bad this could have gone, you've got a lot to be thankful for. Remember that.'

'I . . .' The man blinked.

'I meant, remember those exact words. That's the phrase to tell the woman you're seeing. Helps a ton.' He fished in his pack and pulled out a bottle of Thaylen lavis beer he'd salvaged. Rua stopped zipping around the top of the tent long enough to float down and inspect it.

'Want to see a trick?' Lopen asked.

'A . . . another?' the man asked.

'Normally, I'd pop the cap off with one of my fingernails. I have great Herdazian ones, extra hard. You have weaker ones like most people. So here's the trick.'

Lopen rolled up his trouser leg with one hand. He pressed the bottle – top first – to his leg and then, with a quick flick, twisted off the cap. He raised the bottle toward the man.

The man reached for it with the bandaged stump of his right arm, which ended above the elbow. He looked at it, grimaced, then reached with the left hand instead.

'If you need any jokes,' Lopen said, 'I've got a few I can't use anymore.'

The soldier drank quietly, eyes flicking to the front of the tent, where Kaladin had entered, glowing softly, speaking with some of the surgeons. Knowing Kaladin, he was probably telling them how to do their jobs.

'You're one of them,' the soldier said. 'Radiant.'

'Sure,' Lopen said. 'But not *really* one of them. I'm trying to figure out the next step.'

'Next step?'

'I've got the flying,' Lopen said, 'and the spren. But I don't know if I'm good at saving people yet.'

The man looked at his drink. 'I . . . think you might be doing just fine.'

'That's a beer, not a person. Don't get those mixed up. Very embarrassing, but I won't tell.'

'How . . .' the man said. 'How does one join up? They say . . . they say it heals you. . . .'

'Sure, it heals everything except what's in the rockbud on the end of your neck. Which is great for me. I'm the only sane one in this group. That might be a problem.'

'Why?'

'They say you have to be broken,' Lopen said, glancing toward his spren, who made a few loops of excitement, then shot off to hide again. Lopen would need to go looking for the little guy – he did enjoy the game. 'You know that tall woman, the king's sister? The chortana with the glare that could break a Shardblade? She says that the power has to get into your soul somehow. So I've been trying to cry a lot, and moan about my life being so terrible, but I think the Stormfather knows I'm lying. Hard to act sad when you're the Lopen.'

'I might be broken,' the man said softly.

'Good, good! We don't have a Thaylen yet, and lately it looks like we're trying to collect one of everything. We even have a parshman!'

'I just ask?' the man said, then took a drink.

'Sure. Ask. Follow us around. Worked for Lyn. But you have to say the Words.'

'Words?'

'"Life before death, strength before weakness, journey before pancakes." That's the easy one. The hard one is, 'I will protect those who cannot protect themselves,' and—'

A sudden flash of coldness struck Lopen, and the gemstones in the room flickered, then went out. A symbol crystallized in frost on the stones around Lopen, vanishing under the cots. The ancient symbol of the Windrunners.

'What?' Lopen stood up. '*What? Now?*'

He heard a far-off rumbling, like thunder.

'NOW?' Lopen said, shaking a fist at the sky. 'I was saving that for a dramatic moment, you penhito! Why didn't you listen earlier? We were, sure, all about to die and things!'

He got a distinct, very distant impression.

You weren't quite ready.

'Storm you!' Lopen made a double obscene gesture toward the sky – something he'd been waiting a long time to use properly for the first time. Rua joined him, making the same gesture, then grew two *extra* arms to give it more weight.

'Nice,' Lopen said. 'Hey gancho! I'm a full Knight Radiant now, so you can start complimenting me.' Kaladin didn't seem to have even noticed. 'Just a moment,' Lopen said to the one-armed soldier, then stalked over to where Kaladin was speaking with a runner.

'You're sure?' Kaladin said to the scribe. 'Does Dalinar know about this?'

'He sent me, sir,' the woman said. 'Here's a map with the location the spanreed listed.'

'Gancho,' Lopen said. 'Hey, did you—'

'Congratulations, Lopen, good job. You're second-in-command after Teft until I return.'

Kaladin burst from the tent and Lashed himself to the sky, streaking away, the tent's front flaps rustling in the wind of his passing.

Lopen put his hands on his hips. Rua landed on his head, then made a little squeal of angry delight while proffering toward Kaladin a double rude gesture.

'Don't wear it out, naco,' Lopen said.

∴

'Come on,' Ash said, holding Taln's hand, pulling him up the last few steps.

He stared at her dully.

'Taln,' she whispered. '*Please.*'

The last glimmers of his lucidity had faded. Once, nothing would have kept him from the battlefield when other men died. Today, he had hidden and whimpered during the fighting. Now he followed her like a simpleton.

Talenel'Elin had broken like the rest of them.

Ishar, she thought. *Ishar will know what to do.* She fought down the tears – watching him fade had been like watching the sun go out. All these years, she'd hoped that maybe . . . maybe . . .

What? That he'd be able to redeem them?

Someone nearby cursed by her name, and she wanted to slap him. *Don't swear by us. Don't paint pictures of us. Don't worship at our statues.* She'd stamp it all out. She would ruin every depiction. She . . .

Ash breathed in and out, then pulled Taln by the hand again, getting him into line with the other refugees fleeing the city. Only foreigners were allowed out right now, to prevent the Oathgate from being overworked. She'd get back to Azir, where their skin tones wouldn't stand out.

What a gift you gave them! he'd said. *Time to recover, for once, between Desolations. Time to progress . . .*

Oh, Taln. Couldn't he have just hated her? Couldn't he have let her—

Ash stopped in place as something *ripped* inside of her.

Oh God. Oh, Adonalsium!

What was that? *What was that?*

Taln whimpered and collapsed, a puppet with cut strings. Ash stumbled, then sank to her knees. She wrapped her arms around herself, trembling. It wasn't pain. It was something far, far worse. A loss, a hole inside of her, a piece of her soul being excised.

'Miss?' a soldier asked, jogging up. 'Miss, are you all right? Hey, someone get one of the healers! Miss, what's wrong?'

'They . . . they killed him somehow. . . .'

'Who?'

She looked up at the man, tears blurring her vision. This wasn't like their other deaths. This was something horrible. She couldn't feel him at all.

They'd done something to Jezrien's soul.

'My father,' she said, 'is dead.'

They caused a stir in the refugees, and someone detached themselves from the group of scribes up ahead. A woman in deep violet. The Blackthorn's niece. She looked at Ash, then at Taln, then at a piece of paper she'd been carrying. It contained shockingly accurate sketches of the two of them. Not as they were presented in iconography, but real sketches. Who . . . why?

That's his drawing style, a part of Ash noted. *Why has Midius been giving away pictures of us?*

The ripping sensation finally ended. So abruptly that – for the first time in thousands of years – Ash fell unconscious.

Yes, I began my journey alone, and I ended it alone.
But that does not mean that I walked alone.

—From *The Way of Kings*, postscript

Kaladin flew across the churning ocean. Dalinar had been able to summon the strength to overcharge him with Stormlight, though it was obviously exhausting to do so.

Kaladin had used up that charge getting to Kharbranth, where he'd stopped for a night's sleep. Even Stormlight could only push the body so far. After a long flight the next day, he'd reached the Tarat Sea.

He flew now using gemstones requisitioned from the royal treasury in Kharbranth. Smoke rose from several places along the coast of Alethkar, where cities still resisted the parshman invasion. Kaladin's map fluttered in his fingers, and he watched the coast for the rock formation the scribe had sketched for him.

By the time he spotted it, he worried he wouldn't have enough Stormlight left to make it back to safety. He dropped there and continued on foot, per the instructions, crossing a cold and rocky land that reminded him of the Shattered Plains.

Along a dried-out river, he found a little group of refugees huddled by a cavern in the stone. A very small fire laced the air with smoke, and lit ten people in brown cloaks. Nondescript, like many others he'd passed during his search. The only distinctive feature was a small symbol they'd painted on an old tarp pinned up between two poles at the front of the camp.

The symbol of Bridge Four.

Two of the figures rose from the fire, pulling back hoods. Two men: one tall and lanky, the other short and scrappy, silver-haired at the temples.

Drehy and Skar.

They gave Kaladin a pair of sharp salutes. Drehy had old cuts on his face and Skar looked like he hadn't slept in weeks. They'd had to cover their foreheads in ash to hide their tattoos, an act that wouldn't have worked in simpler times. It basically marked them as runaway slaves.

Syl let out a laugh of pure delight, zipping over to them – and from the way they reacted, it seemed she'd let them see her. Behind them, Shallan's three servants emerged from their cloaks. Kaladin didn't know the other people, but one of them would be the merchant they'd found – a man who still possessed a spanreed.

'Kal,' Skar said as Kaladin slapped him on the back. 'There's something we didn't mention by spanreed.'

Kaladin frowned as Drehy returned to the fire and picked up one of the figures there. A child? In rags. Yes, a frightened little boy, maybe three or four years old, lips chapped, eyes haunted.

Elhokar's son.

'We protect those,' Drehy said, 'who cannot protect themselves.'

⁘

Taravangian was unable to solve the first page of the day's puzzles.

Dukar, the stormwarden, took the paper and looked it over. He shook his head. Stupid today.

Taravangian rested back against his seat in Urithiru. He seemed to be stupid more and more often. Perhaps it was his perception.

Eight days had passed since the Battle of Thaylen Field. He wasn't certain Dalinar would ever trust him again, but giving him some truth had been a calculated risk. For now, Taravangian was still part of the coalition. It was good, even if . . . It . . .

Storms. Trying to think through the fuzz in his brain was . . . bothersome.

'He is weak of mind today,' Dukar announced to Mrall, Taravangian's thick-armed bodyguard. 'He can interact, but should not make important policy decisions. We cannot trust his interpretation of the Diagram.'

'Vargo?' Adrotagia asked. 'How would you like to spend the day? In the Veden gardens, perhaps?'

Taravangian opened his eyes and looked to his faithful friends. Dukar and Mrall. Adrotagia, who looked so old now. Did she feel as he did, shocked every time she looked in the mirror, wondering where the days had gone? When they'd been young, they'd wanted to conquer the world.

Or save it.

'Your Majesty?' Adrotagia asked.

Oh. Right. His mind did wander sometimes. 'We cannot do anything until the Everstorm passes. Correct?'

Adrotagia nodded, proffering her calculations. 'It is nearly here.' People had spent the eight days since the battle vainly hoping that the Everstorm had blown itself out for good. 'It's not as strong as it was during its previous cycle, but it *is* coming. It has already reached Azir, and should hit Urithiru within the hour.'

'Then let us wait.'

Adrotagia gave him a few letters that had come from his grandchildren in Kharbranth. He could read, even when he was stupid, though it took him longer to make out some of the words. Gvori had been accepted to study at the School of Storms, which had legacy access to the Palanaeum for all scholars. Karavaniga, the middle granddaughter, had been accepted for wardship, and had sketched him a picture of the three of them. Little Ruli grinned a gap-toothed smile in the center. She had drawn him a picture of flowers.

Taravangian touched the tears on his cheek as he finished reading. None of the three knew anything of the Diagram, and he was determined to keep it that way.

Adrotagia and Dukar conversed quietly in the corner of the room, confused by portions of the Diagram. They ignored Maben, the room servant, who felt Taravangian's forehead, as he'd been coughing lately.

What fools we can be, Taravangian said, resting fingers on the picture of flowers. *We never know as much as we think. Perhaps in that, the smart me has always been the more stupid one.*

He knew the Everstorm's arrival only by a *ding* from Adrotagia's clock – a magnificently small piece, gifted by Navani Kholin.

'The Diagram has been wrong too often,' Mrall said to Adrotagia and Dukar. 'It predicted Dalinar Kholin would fall, if pressured, and become the enemy's champion.'

'Perhaps Graves was right,' Dukar said, rubbing his hands together nervously. He glanced toward the window, shuttered despite the fact that the Everstorm didn't reach this high. 'The Blackthorn could have been made an ally. This is what the Diagram meant.'

'No,' Taravangian said. 'That is not what it meant.'

They looked to him. 'Vargo?' Adrotagia asked.

He tried to find the argument to explain himself, but it was like trying to hold a cupful of oil in his fist.

'We're in a dangerous position,' Dukar said. 'His Majesty revealed too much to Dalinar. We will be watched now.'

. . . the . . . window . . .

'Dalinar doesn't know of the Diagram,' Adrotagia countered. 'Or that we brought the singers to Urithiru. He only knows that Kharbranth controlled the assassin – and thinks that the Herald's insanity prompted us. We're still well positioned.'

Open . . . the . . . window. . . . None of the others heard the voice.

'The Diagram is growing too flawed,' Mrall insisted. Though he was no scholar, he was a full participant in their scheme. 'We've deviated too much from its promises. Our plans need to change.'

'It's too late,' Adrotagia said. 'The confrontation will happen soon.'

OPEN IT.

Taravangian rose from his seat, trembling. Adrotagia was right. The confrontation predicted by the Diagram would happen soon.

Sooner, even, than she thought.

'We must trust in the Diagram,' Taravangian whispered, as he passed by them. 'We must trust the version of myself that knew what to do. We must have faith.'

Adrotagia shook her head. She didn't like it when any of them used words like 'faith.' He tried to remember that, and did remember it when he was smart.

Storms take you, Nightwatcher, he thought. *Odium's victory will kill you too. Couldn't you have just gifted me, and not cursed me?*

He'd asked for the capacity to save his people. He'd begged for compassion and acumen – and he'd gotten them. Just never at the same time.

He touched the window shutters.

'Vargo?' Adrotagia asked. 'Letting in fresh air?'

'No, unfortunately. Something else.'

He opened the shutters.

And was suddenly in a place of infinite light.

The ground beneath him glowed, and nearby, rivers flowed past, made of something molten colored gold and orange. Odium appeared to Taravangian as a twenty-foot-tall human with Shin eyes and a scepter. His beard was not wispy, like Taravangian's had been, but neither was it bushy. It almost looked like an ardent's beard.

'Now,' Odium said. 'Taravangian, is it?' He squinted, as if seeing Taravangian for the first time. 'Little man. Why did you write to us? Why did you have your Surgebinder unlock the Oathgate, and allow our armies to attack Urithiru?'

'I wish only to serve you, Great God,' Taravangian said, getting down onto his knees.

'Do not prostrate yourself,' the god said, laughing. 'I can see that you are no sycophant, and I will not be fooled by your attempts to seem one.'

Taravangian drew in a deep breath, but remained on his knees. Today of all days, Odium finally contacted him in person? 'I am not well today, Great God. I . . . um . . . am frail and of ill health. Might I meet with you again, when I am well?'

'Poor man!' Odium said.

A chair sprouted from the golden ground behind Taravangian, and Odium stepped over to him, suddenly smaller, more human sized. He gently pushed Taravangian up and into the chair. 'There. Isn't that better?'

'Yes . . . thank you.' Taravangian scrunched up his brow. This was not how he'd imagined this conversation.

'Now,' Odium said, lightly resting his scepter on Taravangian's shoulder. 'Do you think I will ever meet with you when you are feeling well?'

'I . . .'

'Do you not realize that I chose this day *specifically* because of your ailment, Taravangian? Do you really think you will *ever* be able to negotiate with me from a position of *power*?'

Taravangian licked his lips. 'No.'

'Good, good. We understand one another. Now, what is it you have been doing. . . .' He stepped to the side, and a golden pedestal appeared with a book on top of it. The Diagram. Odium began leafing through it, and the golden landscape changed, shifting to a bedroom with fine wooden furniture. Taravangian recognized it from the scribbled writing on every surface – from floor to ceiling, to the headboard of the bed.

'Taravangian!' Odium said. 'This is *remarkable*.' The walls and furniture faded, leaving behind the words, which hung in the air and started glowing with a golden light. 'You did this *without* access to Fortune, or the Spiritual Realm? Truly incredible.'

'Th-thank you?'

'Allow me to show you how far I see.'

Golden words exploded outward from the ones Taravangian had written in the Diagram. Millions upon millions of golden letters burned into the air, extending into infinity. Each took one small element that Taravangian had written, and expanded upon it in volumes and volumes' worth of information.

Taravangian gasped as, for a moment, he saw into eternity.

Odium inspected words that Taravangian had once written on the side of a dresser. 'I see. Take over Alethkar? Bold plan, bold plan. But why invite me to attack Urithiru?'

'We—'

'No need! I see. Give up Thaylen City to ensure that the Blackthorn fell, removing your opposition. An overture toward me, which worked, obviously.' Odium turned to him and smiled. A knowing, confident smile.

Do you really think you will ever be able to negotiate with me from a position of power?

All that writing loomed over Taravangian, blocking off the landscape with millions of words. A smarter him would have tried to read it, but this dumber version was simply intimidated. And . . . could that be for his . . . his good? Reading that would consume him. Lose him.

My grandchildren, he thought. *The people of Kharbranth. The good people of the world.* He trembled to think of what might happen to them all.

Somebody had to make the difficult decisions. He slipped off his golden seat as Odium studied another portion of the Diagram. There. Behind where the bed had stood. A section of words that had faded from golden to black. What was that? As he drew near, Taravangian saw that the words were blacked out into eternity starting from this point on his wall. As if something had happened here. A ripple in what Odium could see . . .

At its root, a name. Renarin Kholin.

'Dalinar was not supposed to Ascend,' Odium said, stepping up behind Taravangian.

'You need me,' Taravangian whispered.

'I need nobody.'

Taravangian looked up and there, glowing in front of him, was a set of words. A message from himself, in the past. Incredible! Had he somehow seen even this?

Thank you.

He read them out loud. 'You have agreed to a battle of champions. You must withdraw to prevent this contest from occurring, and so must not meet with Dalinar Kholin again. Otherwise, he can force you to fight. This means you must let your agents do your work. You need me.'

Odium stepped up, noting the words that Taravangian had read. Then he frowned at the tears on Taravangian's cheeks.

'Your Passion,' Odium said, 'does you credit. What is it you ask in barter?'

'Protect the people I rule.'

'Dear Taravangian, do you not think I can see what you are planning?' Odium gestured toward writing where the ceiling had once stood. 'You would seek to become king of all humans – and then I would need to preserve them all. No. If you help me, I will save your family. Anyone within two generations of you.'

'Not enough.'

'Then we have no deal.'

The words started to fade all around them. Leaving him alone. Alone and stupid. He blinked tears from the corners of his eyes. 'Kharbranth,' he said. 'Preserve only Kharbranth. You may destroy all other nations. Just leave my city. It is what I beg of you.'

The world was lost, humankind doomed.

They had planned to protect so much more. But . . . he saw now how little they knew. One city before the storms. One land protected, even if the rest had to be sacrificed.

'Kharbranth,' Odium said. 'The city itself, and any humans who have

725

been born into it, along with their spouses. This is whom I will spare. Do you agree to this?'

'Should we write . . . a contract?'

'Our word is the contract. I am not some spren of Honor, who seeks to obey only the strictest letter of a promise. If you have an agreement from me, I will keep it in spirit, not merely in word.'

What else could he do? 'I will take this deal,' Taravangian whispered. 'The Diagram will serve you, in exchange for the preservation of my people. But I warn you, the assassin has joined Dalinar Kholin. I was forced to reveal my association with him.'

'I know,' Odium said. 'You are still of use. First, I will require that Honorblade which you have so cleverly stolen. And then you will find out for me what the Alethi have discovered about this tower. . . .'

⁘

Shallan breathed out Stormlight, shaping an illusion possible only when she and Dalinar met. Spinning curls of mist swept out to form oceans and peaks – the entire continent of Roshar, a mass of vibrant colors.

Highprinces Aladar and Hatham waved for their generals and scribes to walk around the map, which filled the large room, hovering at about waist height. Dalinar stood in the very center of the thing, among the mountains near Urithiru, the illusion rippling and dissolving where it touched his uniform.

Adolin wrapped his arms around Shallan from behind. 'It looks beautiful.'

'*You* look beautiful,' she replied.

'You *are* beautiful.'

'Only because you're here. Without you, I fade.'

Brightness Teshav stood near them, and though the woman normally maintained a stoic professionalism, Shallan thought she caught a hint of an eye roll. Well, Teshav was so old she probably forgot what it was like to *breathe* most days, let alone what it was like to love.

Adolin made Shallan giddy. With his warmth so close, she had trouble maintaining the illusion of the map. She felt silly – they'd been betrothed for months now, and she'd grown so comfortable with him. Yet something had still changed. Something incredible.

It was *finally* time. The wedding date had been set for only one week away – once the Alethi put their minds to something, they made it happen. Well, that was good. Shallan wouldn't want to go too far in a relationship without oaths, and storms, even one week was starting to sound like an eternity.

She still needed to explain some things to Adolin. Most notably, the entire mess with the Ghostbloods. She'd done too good a job of ignoring that one lately, but it would be a relief to finally have someone she could talk to about it. Veil could explain – Adolin was growing accustomed to her, though he wouldn't be intimate with her. He treated her like a drinking buddy, which was actually kind of working for both of them.

Dalinar walked through the illusion, holding his hand over Iri, Rira, and Babatharnam. 'Change this part of the land to a burning gold.'

It took her a moment to realize he was talking to her. Stupid Adolin and his stupid arms. Stupid strong yet gentle arms pressing against her, right beneath her breasts ...

Right. Right. Illusion.

She did as Dalinar commanded, amused by how the scribes and generals pointedly did not look at her and Adolin. Some whispered about Adolin's Westerner heritage, which made him too public with his affection. His mixed parentage didn't seem to concern the Alethi in most cases – they were a pragmatic people, and saw his hair as a sign of other peoples conquered and brought into their superior culture. But they *would* look for excuses for why he didn't always act like they thought he should.

By reports via spanreed, most of the lesser kingdoms surrounding the Purelake had been captured by Iri – which had moved, accompanied by Fused, to secure land they'd eyed for generations. This secured for them three total Oathgates. Shallan painted those kingdoms on the map a vivid gold at Dalinar's request.

Azir and its protectorates she painted a pattern of blue and maroon, the symbol the Azish scribes had chosen for the coalition between their kingdoms. The emperor of Azir had agreed to continue negotiations; they weren't fully in the coalition. They wanted assurances that Dalinar could control his troops.

She continued shading the landscape colors at Dalinar's request. Marat and those around it went gold, as did – unfortunately – Alethkar. Lands that hadn't yet committed, like Shinovar and Tukar, she turned green. The result was a depressing view of a continent, with far too little of it colored the shades of their coalition.

The generals began discussing tactics. They wanted to invade Tu Bayla – the large land that stretched between Jah Keved and the Purelake. The argument was that if the enemy took that, they'd divide the coalition in two. The Oathgates allowed quick access to the capitals, but many cities were far from the centers of power.

Dalinar crossed the room, forming a ripple that followed in his wake. He stopped near where Adolin and Shallan stood by Herdaz. And Alethkar.

'Show me Kholinar,' he said softly.

'That's not how it works, Brightlord,' she said. 'I have to sketch something first, and . . .'

He touched her on the shoulder, and a thought entered her mind. Another pattern.

'This is what the Stormfather sees,' Dalinar said. 'It is not specific, so we won't be able to rely on the details, but it should give us an impression. If you please.'

Shallan turned and waved her hand toward the wall, painting it with Stormlight. When the illusion took, the side of the room seemed to vanish – letting them look out, as if from a balcony in the sky, toward Kholinar.

The gate nearest them still hung broken, exposing ruined buildings inside – but some progress had been made toward cleaning those up. Parshmen walked the streets and patrolled the unbroken sections of wall. Fused coursed overhead, trailing long clothing. A flag flew from the tops of buildings, red lines on black. A foreign symbol.

'Kaladin said they weren't here to destroy,' Adolin said, 'but to occupy.'

'They want their world back,' Shallan said, pushing against him, wanting to feel his body against hers. 'Could we . . . just let them have what they've taken?'

'No,' Dalinar said. 'So long as Odium leads the enemy, they will try to sweep us off this land, and make the world so it has no need of another Desolation. Because we'll be gone.'

The three of them stood as if on a precipice, overlooking the city. The humans toiling outside, preparing for a planting. The lines of smoke curling from inside, where lighteyed keeps had tried to hold out against the invasion. The sights haunted Shallan, and she could only imagine how Adolin and Dalinar felt. They had protected Thaylenah, but had lost their homeland.

'There's a traitor among us,' Dalinar said softly. 'Someone attacked Bridge Four specifically to get the Honorblade – because they needed it to unlock the Oathgates and let the enemy in.'

'That,' Shallan said softly, 'or it was unlocked by a Radiant who has changed sides.'

Inexplicably, the Assassin in White had joined them. He sat outside the room, guarding the door as Dalinar's new bodyguard. He'd explained, frankly and without concern, that the majority of the Order of the Sky-breakers had chosen to serve Odium. Shallan wouldn't have thought that possible, but that – and Renarin's bonding of a corrupted spren – indicated that they couldn't trust someone simply because they'd spoken Ideals.

'You think,' Adolin said, 'Taravangian might have done it?'

'No,' Dalinar said. 'Why would he work with the enemy? Everything he's done so far has been to secure a safe Roshar – if through brutal means. Still, I have to wonder. I can't afford to be too trusting. Hopefully that's one thing Sadeas cured in me.'

The Blackthorn shook his head, then looked to Shallan and Adolin. 'Either way, Alethkar needs a *king*. More so now than ever.'

'The heir – ' Adolin began.

'Too young. This isn't the time for a regency. Gavinor can be named your heir, Adolin, but we must see you two married and the monarchy secured. For the good of Alethkar, but also the world.' He narrowed his eyes. 'The coalition needs more than I can provide. I will continue to lead it, but I have never been good at diplomacy. I need someone on the throne who can inspire Alethkar *and* command the respect of the monarchs.'

Adolin grew tense, and Shallan took his hand, holding tight. *You can be this man, if you want,* she thought to him. *But you don't* have *to be what he makes of you.*

'I'll prepare the coalition for your coronation,' Dalinar said. 'Perhaps the day before the wedding.' He turned to walk away. Dalinar Kholin was a force like a storm. He simply blew you over, and assumed you'd always *wanted* to lie down in the first place.

Adolin looked to Shallan, then set his jaw and seized his father by the arm. 'I killed Sadeas, Father,' Adolin whispered.

Dalinar froze.

'It was me,' Adolin continued. 'I broke the Codes of War and killed him in the corridor. For speaking against our family. For betraying us time and time again. I stopped him because it needed to be done, and because I knew you would never be able to do it.'

Dalinar turned, speaking in a harsh whisper. 'What? Son, *why* did you hide this from me?'

'Because you're you.'

Dalinar took a deep breath. 'We can fix this,' he said. 'We can see that atonement is made. It will hurt our reputation. Storms, this is *not* what I needed now. Nonetheless, we will fix it.'

'It's already fixed. I'm not sorry for what I did – and I'd do it again, right now.'

'We'll talk about this further once the coronation—'

'I'm *not* going to be king, Father,' Adolin said. He glanced at Shallan, and she nodded to him, then squeezed his hand again. 'Didn't you listen to what I just said? I broke the Codes.'

'Everyone in this storming country breaks the Codes,' Dalinar said, loudly, then looked over his shoulder. He continued, more softly. '*I* broke the Codes hundreds of times. You don't have to be perfect, you only have to do your duty.'

'*No.* I'll be highprince, but not king. I just . . . no. I don't want that burden. And before you complain that none of us want it, I'd also be terrible at the job. You think the monarchs would listen to *me?*'

'I can't be king of Alethkar,' Dalinar said softly. 'I have to lead the Radiants – and need to divest myself of that power in Alethkar, to move away from that highking nonsense. We need a ruler in Alethkar who won't be pushed over, but who can also deal with diplomats in diplomatic ways.'

'Well, that's not me,' Adolin repeated.

'Who, then?' Dalinar demanded.

Shallan cocked her head. 'Hey. Have you boys ever considered . . .'

⁂

Palona skimmed through the latest gossip reports out of Tashikk, looking for the juicy stuff.

Around her in the grand conference room of Urithiru, kings and princes squabbled with one another. Some complained that they weren't allowed to join whatever meeting Dalinar was having on the floor above, with his generals. The Natans still complained that they should be given control of the Oathgate at the Shattered Plains, while the Azish were talking – again – about how God himself had apparently prophesied that Surgebinders would destroy the world.

Everyone was quite persistent, and quite loud – even those who didn't speak Alethi. You had to be very dedicated to your grousing to wait for interpretation.

Sebarial – Turi – snored softly beside Palona. That was an act. He did the same fake snore when she tried to tell him about the latest novel she'd read. Then when she quit, he got annoyed. He seemed to like hearing the stories, but only as long as he could comment on how trite and feminine they were.

She nudged him, and he cracked an eye as she turned one of her gossip reports toward him, pointing at a drawing it included. 'Yezier and Emul,' she whispered. 'The prince and princess were seen together in Thaylen City, speaking intimately while their guards worked on the rubble.'

Turi grunted.

'Everyone thinks their romance is back on, though they can't talk about it, as head monarchs in Azir are forbidden marriage without the emperor's consent. But the rumors are wrong. *I* think she's been courting Halam Khal, the Shardbearer.'

'You could just go *talk to* her,' Turi said, pointing a lazy finger toward the princess of Yezier, whose translators were complaining forcefully about the dangers of Surgebinding.

'Oh, Turi,' Palona said. 'You can't just *ask* people about gossip. This is why you're hopeless.'

'And here I thought I was hopeless because of my terrible taste in women.'

The doors to the room slammed open, the noise of it sending a shock through the room, complaints falling silent. Even Turi sat up to note Jasnah Kholin standing in the doorway.

She wore a small but unmistakable crown on her head. The Kholin family, it seemed, had chosen their new monarch.

Turi grinned at the looks of worry on the faces of many of the others in the room. 'Oh my,' he whispered to Palona. 'Now *this* should be interesting.'

Moash pounded the pickaxe down again.

Two weeks of work, and he was still here clearing out rubble. Kill a god. Get back to work.

Well, he didn't mind. It would take months, maybe years, to clear all the rubble from this city. All of it out of Alethkar.

Most days this week, he was the only one here working at the palace. The city was slowly being reversed, humans shipped out, singers moved in – but they left him alone to break stones, with no overseer or guard in sight.

So he was surprised when he heard another pick fall beside him. He spun, shocked. 'Khen?'

The beefy parshwoman started breaking rocks.

'Khen, you were freed from your slavery,' Moash said. 'Your assault on the palace earned you the Passion of Mercy.'

Khen kept working. Nam and Pal stepped in, wearing warform – two others who had survived with him during the assault. Only a handful had.

They lifted picks and started breaking stones too.

'Pal,' Moash said. 'You—'

'They want us to farm,' she said. 'I'm tired of farming.'

'And I'm no house servant,' Khen said. 'Running drinks.' They were starting to speak to rhythms, like proper singers.

'So you'll break rocks?' Moash asked.

'We heard something. Made us want to be near you.'

Moash hesitated, but then the numbness drove him to keep working, to hear that steady beat of metal on stone that let him pass between times.

It was maybe an hour later when they came for him. Nine flying Fused, rippling clothing pooling beneath them as they descended around Moash.

'Leshwi?' he asked. 'Ancient One?'

She held something before herself in two hands. A long, slender weapon. A Shardblade with a gentle curve, its metal largely unornamented. Elegant, yet somehow humble, as Shardblades went. Moash had known it as the sword of the Assassin in White. Now he recognized it as something else. The Blade of Jezerezeh. Honorblade.

Moash reached for it, hesitant, and Leshwi hummed a warning rhythm. 'If you take it, you die. Moash will be no more.'

'Moash's world is no more,' he said, taking the Blade by the hilt. 'He might as well join it in the tomb.'

'Vyre,' she said. 'Join us in the sky. You have a work.' She and the others Lashed themselves upward.

Join us in the sky. The Honorblades, Graves had told him, gave their powers to any who held them.

Hesitant, Moash took the sphere that Khen offered. 'What was that she said? Vyre?' She had said it in a way that rhymed with 'fire.'

'It's one of their names,' Khen said. 'I've been told it means He Who Quiets.'

Vyre, He Who Quiets, sucked in the light of the sphere.

It was sweet and beautiful, and – as he'd been promised – brought Passion with it. He held to it, then Lashed himself upward into the sky.

❖

Though Shallan had been given months to grow accustomed to the idea of getting married, on the actual day, she didn't feel ready.

It was such an ordeal and a hassle.

Everyone was determined that, after Dalinar and Navani's rushed wedding, they'd do this one *right*. So Shallan had to sit here and be fussed over, primped, her hair braided and her face painted by the royal Alethi makeup artists. Who'd known there even was such a thing?

She suffered it, then was deposited on a throne while scribes lined up and gave her piles of keteks and glyphwards. Noura delivered a box of incense from the Azish emperor, along with a dried fish from Lift. A Marati rug came from Queen Fen. Dried fruit. Perfumes.

A pair of boots. Ka seemed embarrassed as she opened the box and revealed them as a gift from Kaladin and Bridge Four, but Shallan just laughed. It was a much-needed moment of relief in the stress of the day.

She got gifts from professional organizations, family members, and one from each highprince except for Ialai – who had left Urithiru in disgrace. Though Shallan was grateful, she found herself trying to vanish into her dress. So many things that she didn't want – most of all, this attention.

Well, you're marrying an Alethi highprince, she thought as she squirmed on her wedding throne. *What did you expect?* At least she wasn't going to end up as queen.

Finally – after ardents arrived and pronounced blessings, anointings, and prayers – she was shuffled off into a little room by herself with a brazier, a window, and a mirror. The table held implements for her to paint a last prayer, so that she could meditate. Somewhere, Adolin was suffering gifts from the men. Probably swords. Lots and lots of swords.

The door closed, and Shallan stood facing herself in the mirror. Her sapphire gown was of an ancient style, with twin drooping sleeves that went far beyond her hands. Small rubies woven into the embroidery glowed with a complementary light. A golden vest draped over the shoulders, matched by the ornate headdress woven into her braids.

She wanted to shrink from it.

'Mmm . . .' Pattern said. 'This is a good you, Shallan.'

A good me. She breathed out. Veil formed on one side of the room, lounging against the wall. Radiant appeared near the table, tapping it with one finger, reminding her that she really should write a prayer – for tradition's sake, if nothing else.

'We're decided upon this,' Shallan said.

'A worthy union,' Radiant said.

'He's good for you, I suppose,' Veil said. 'Plus he knows his wine. We could do far worse.'

'But not much better,' Radiant said, giving Veil a pointed look. 'This is good, Shallan.'

'A celebration,' Veil said. 'A celebration of *you*.'

'It's okay for me to enjoy this,' Shallan said, as if discovering something precious. 'It's all right to celebrate. Even if things are terrible in the world, it's all right.' She smiled. 'I . . . I deserve this.'

Veil and Radiant faded. When Shallan looked back into the mirror, she didn't feel embarrassed by the attention any longer. It was all right.

It was *all right* to be happy.

She painted her glyphward, but a knock at the door interrupted burning it. What? The time wasn't up.

She turned with a grin. 'Come in.' Adolin had probably found an excuse to come steal a kiss. . . .

The door opened.

Revealing three young men in worn clothing. Balat, tallest and round faced. Wikim, still gaunt, with skin as pale as Shallan's. Jushu, thinner than she recalled, but still plump. All three were somehow younger than

734

she pictured them in her head, even though it had been over a year since she'd seen them.

Her brothers.

Shallan cried out in delight, throwing herself toward them, passing through a burst of joyspren like blue petals. She tried to embrace all three at once, heedless of what it might do to her carefully arranged dress. 'How? When? What happened?'

'It was a long trek across Jah Keved,' Nan Balat said. 'Shallan ... we didn't hear anything until we were transported here through that device. You're getting *married*? The son of the *Blackthorn*?'

So much to tell them. Storms, these tears were going to *ruin* her makeup. She'd have to go through it all again.

She found herself too overwhelmed to talk, to explain. She pulled them tight again, and Wikim even complained about the affection, as he always had. She hadn't seen them in how long, and he still complained? That made her even more giddy, for some reason.

Navani appeared behind them, looking over Balat's shoulder. 'I will call for a delay of the festivities.'

'No!' Shallan said.

No. She was going to *enjoy* this. She pulled her brothers tight, one after another. 'I'll explain after the wedding. So *much* to explain ...'

Balat, as she hugged him, handed her a slip of paper. 'He said to give you this.'

'Who?'

'He said you'd know.' Balat still had the haunted look that had always shadowed him. 'What is going on? How do you know people like *that*?'

She unfolded the letter.

It was from Mraize.

'Brightness,' Shallan said to Navani, 'will you provide my brothers with seats of honor?'

'Of course.'

Navani drew the three boys away, joining Eylita, who had been waiting. Storms. Her brothers were back. *They were alive.*

A wedding gift, Mraize's note read.

In payment for work done. You will find that I do keep my promises. I apologize for the delay.

I congratulate you on your upcoming nuptials, little knife. You have done well. You have frightened away the Unmade who was in this tower, and in payment, we forgive a part of your debt owed from the destruction of our Soulcaster.

Your next mission is equally important. One of the Unmade seems willing to break from Odium. Our good and that of your Radiant friends align. You will find this Unmade, and you will persuade it to serve the Ghostbloods. Barring that, you will capture it and deliver it to us.

Details will be forthcoming.

She lowered the note, then burned it in the brazier meant for her prayer. So Mraize knew about Sja-anat, did he? Did he know about Renarin accidentally bonding one of her spren? Or was that a secret Shallan actually had over the Ghostbloods?

Well, she could worry about him later. Today, she had a wedding to attend. She pulled open the door and strode out. Toward a celebration.

Of being herself.

⁜

Dalinar entered his rooms, full of food from the wedding feast, glad to finally get some peace after the celebrations. The assassin settled down outside his door to wait, as was becoming his custom. Szeth was the only guard Dalinar had for the moment, as Rial and his other bodyguards were all in Bridge Thirteen – and that whole crew had gone up as squires to Teft.

Dalinar smiled to himself, then walked to his desk and settled down. A Shardblade hung on the wall before him. A temporary place; he'd find it a home. For now, he wanted it near. It was time.

He picked up the pen and started writing.

Three weeks had seen him progress far, though he still felt uncertain as he scratched out each letter. He worked at it a good hour before Navani returned, slipping into their rooms. She bustled over, opening the balcony doors, letting in the light of a setting sun.

A son married. Adolin was not the man Dalinar had thought he was – but then, couldn't he forgive someone for that? He dipped his pen and continued writing. Navani walked up and placed hands on his shoulders, looking at his paper.

'Here,' Dalinar said, handing it to her. 'Tell me what you think. I've run into a problem.'

As she read, he resisted the urge to shift nervously. This was as bad as his first day with the swordmasters. Navani nodded to herself, then smiled at him, dipping her pen and making a few notes on his page to explain mistakes. 'What's the problem?'

'I don't know how to write "I."'

'I showed you. Here, did you forget?' She wrote out a few letters. 'No, wait. You used this several times in this piece, so you obviously know how to write it.'

'You said pronouns have a gender in the women's formal script, and I realized that the one you taught me says "I, being female."'

Navani hesitated, pen in her fingers. 'Oh. Right. I guess . . . I mean . . . Huh. I don't think there is a masculine 'I.' You can use the neuter, like an ardent. Or . . . no, here. I'm an idiot.' She wrote some letters. 'This is what you use when writing a quote by a man in the first person.'

Dalinar rubbed his chin. Most words in the script were the same as the ones from spoken conversation, but small additions – that you wouldn't read out loud – changed the context. And that didn't even count the undertext – the writer's hidden commentary. Navani had explained, with some embarrassment, that that was never read to a man requesting a reading.

We took Shardblades from the women, he thought, glancing at the one hung on the wall above his desk. *And they seized literacy from us. Who got the better deal, I wonder?*

'Have you thought,' Navani said, 'about how Kadash and the ardents will respond to you learning to read?'

'I've been excommunicated already. There's not much more they could do.'

'They could leave.'

'No,' Dalinar said. 'I don't think they will. I actually think . . . I think I might be getting through to Kadash. Did you see him at the wedding? He's been reading what the ancient theologians wrote, trying to find justification for modern Vorinism. He doesn't want to believe me, but soon he won't be able to help it.'

Navani seemed skeptical.

'Here,' Dalinar said. 'How do I emphasize a word?'

'These marks here, above and below a word you want to stress.'

He nodded in thanks, dipped his pen, then rewrote what he'd given to Navani, substituting the proper changes.

The most important words a man can say are, 'I will do better.' These are not the most important words *any* man can say. I am a man, and they are what I needed to say.

The ancient code of the Knights Radiant says 'journey before destination.' Some may call it a simple platitude, but it is far more. A journey will have pain and failure. It is not only the steps forward that we must accept. It is the stumbles. The trials. The knowledge that we will fail. That we will hurt those around us.

But if we stop, if we accept the person we are when we fall, the journey ends. That failure *becomes* our destination.

To love the journey is to accept no such end. I have found, through painful experience, that the most important step a person can take is always the *next* one.

I'm certain some will feel threatened by this record. Some few may feel liberated. Most will simply feel that it should not exist.

I needed to write it anyway.

He sat back, pleased. It seemed that in opening this doorway, he had entered a new world. He could read *The Way of Kings*. He could read his niece's biography of Gavilar. He could write down his own orders for men to follow.

Most importantly, he could write this. His thoughts. His pains. His *life*. He looked to the side, where Navani had placed the handful of blank pages he'd asked her to bring. Too few. Far, far too few.

He dipped his pen again. 'Would you close the balcony doors again, gemheart?' he asked her. 'The sunlight is distracting me from the other light.'

'Other light?'

He nodded absently. What next? He looked up again at the familiar Shardblade. Wide like him – and thick, also like him, at times – with a hook shape at the end. This was the best mark of both his honor and his disgrace. It should have belonged to Rock, the Horneater bridgeman. He'd killed Amaram and won it, along with two other Shards.

Rock had insisted that Dalinar take Oathbringer back. A debt repaid, the Windrunner had explained. Reluctantly, Dalinar had accepted, handling the Shardblade only through cloth.

As Navani shut the balcony doors, he closed his eyes and felt the warmth of a distant, unseen light. Then he smiled, and – with a hand still unsteady, like the legs of a child taking his first steps – he took another page and wrote a title for the book.

Oathbringer, My Glory and My Shame.
Written by the hand of Dalinar Kholin.

A ll great art is hated,' Wit said.

He shuffled in line – along with a couple hundred other people – one dreary step.

'It is obscenely difficult – if not impossible – to make something that nobody hates,' Wit continued. 'Conversely, it is incredibly easy – if not expected – to make something that nobody loves.'

Weeks after the fall of Kholinar, the place still smelled like smoke. Though the city's new masters had moved tens of thousands of humans out to work farms, complete resettlement would take months, if not years.

Wit poked the man in front of him in the shoulder. 'This makes sense, if you think about it. Art is about *emotion, examination,* and *going places people have never gone before to discover and investigate new things.* The only way to create something that nobody hates is to ensure that it can't be loved either. Remove enough spice from soup, and you'll just end up with water.'

The brutish man in front eyed him, then turned back to the line.

'Human taste is as varied as human fingerprints,' Wit said. 'Nobody will like everything, everybody dislikes something, someone loves that thing you hate – but at least being hated is better than nothing. To risk metaphor, a grand painting is often about contrast: brightest brights, darkest darks. Not grey mush. That a thing is hated is not proof that it's great art, but the lack of hatred is certainly proof that it is not.'

They shuffled forward another step.

He poked the man in the shoulder again. 'And so, dear sir, when I say that you are the very embodiment of repulsiveness, I am merely looking to improve my art. You look so ugly, it seems that someone tried – and failed – to get the warts off your face through aggressive application of sandpaper. You are less a human being, and more a lump of dung with aspirations. If someone took a stick and beat you repeatedly, it could only serve to improve your features.

'Your face defies description, but only because it nauseated all the poets. You are what parents use to frighten children into obedience. I'd tell you to put a sack over your head, but think of the poor sack! Theologians use you as proof that God exists, because such hideousness can *only* be intentional.'

The man didn't respond. Wit poked him again, and he muttered something in Thaylen.

'You . . . don't speak Alethi, do you?' Wit asked. 'Of course you don't.' Figured.

Well, repeating all that in Thaylen would be monotonous. So Wit cut in front of the man in line. This finally provoked a response. The beefy man grabbed Wit and spun him around, then punched him right in the face.

Wit fell backward onto the stone ground. The line continued its shuffling motion, the occupants refusing to look at him. Cautiously, he prodded at his mouth. Yes . . . it seemed . . .

One of his teeth popped out. 'Success!' he said in Thaylen, speaking with a faint lisp. 'Thank you, dear man. I'm glad you appreciate my performance art, accomplished by cutting in front of you.'

Wit flicked the tooth aside and stood up, starting to dust off his clothing. He then stopped himself. After all, he'd worked hard to place that dust. He shoved hands in the pockets of his ragged brown coat, then slouched his way through an alley. He passed groaning humans crying for deliverance, for mercy. He absorbed that, letting it reflect in him.

Not a mask he put on. Real sorrow. Real pain. Weeping echoed around him as he moved into the section of town nearest the palace. Only the most desperate or the most broken dared remain here, nearest the invaders and their growing seat of power.

He rounded to the courtyard out in front of the steps leading up. Was it time for his big performance? Strangely, he found himself reluctant.

Once he walked up those steps, he was committing to leave the city.

He'd found a much better audience among these poor people than he had among the lighteyes of Alethkar. He'd enjoyed his time here. On the other hand, if Rayse learned that Wit was in the city, he'd order his forces to level it – and would consider that a cheap price for even the slimmest chance of ending him.

Wit lingered, then moved through the courtyard, speaking softly with several of the people he'd come to know over the weeks. He eventually squatted next to Kheni, who still rocked her empty cradle, staring with haunted eyes across the square.

'The question becomes,' he whispered to her, 'how many people need to love a piece of art to make it worthwhile? If you're inevitably going to inspire hate, then how much enjoyment is needed to balance out the risk?'

She didn't respond. Her husband, as usual, hovered nearby.

'How's my hair?' Wit asked Kheni. 'Or lack thereof?'

Again, no response.

'The missing tooth is a new addition,' Wit said, poking at the hole. 'I think it will add that special touch.'

He had a few days, with his healing repressed, until the tooth grew back. The right concoction had made him lose his hair in patches.

'Should I put an eye out?'

Kheni looked at him, incredulous.

So you are *listening.* He patted her on the shoulder. *One more. One more, then I go.*

'Wait here,' he told her, then went walking along an alley to the north. He scooped up some rags – the remnants of a spren costume. He didn't see many of those around anymore. He took a cord from his pocket and twisted it around the rags.

Nearby, several buildings had fallen to the thunderclast's attacks. He felt life from one, and when he drew close, a dirty little face poked out from some rubble.

He smiled at the little girl.

'Your teeth look funny today,' she said to him.

'I take exception to that, as the funny part is not the teeth, but the lack of tooth.' He held out his hand to her, but she ducked back in.

'I can't leave Mama,' she whispered.

'I understand,' Wit said. He took the rags and cord he'd worked with earlier, forming them into the shape of a little doll. 'The answer to the question has been bothering me for some time.'

The little face poked out again, looking at the doll. 'The question?'

'I asked it earlier,' Wit said. 'You couldn't hear. Do you know the answer?'

'You're weird.'

'Right answer, but wrong question.' He walked the little doll along the broken street.

'For me?' the girl whispered.

'I need to leave the city,' he said. 'And I can't take her with me. Someone needs to care for her.'

A grimy hand reached toward the doll, but Wit pulled it back. 'She's afraid of the darkness. You've got to keep her in the light.'

The hand vanished into the shadows. 'I can't leave Mama.'

'That's too bad,' Wit said. He raised the doll to his lips, then whispered a choice set of words.

When he set it down, it started to walk on its own. A soft gasp sounded inside the shadows. The little doll toddled toward the street. Step by step by step . . .

The girl, maybe four years old, finally emerged from the shadows and ran to get the doll. Wit stood and dusted off his coat, which was now grey. The girl hugged the patchwork creation, and he picked her up, turning away from the broken building – and the bones of a leg sticking from the rubble just inside.

He carried the girl back to the square, then quietly pushed the empty cradle away from Kheni and knelt before her. 'I think, in answer to my question . . . I think it only takes one.'

She blinked, then focused on the child in his arms.

'I have to leave the city,' Wit said. 'And someone needs to take care of her.'

He waited until, at long last, Kheni held out her arms. Wit put the child into them, then rose. Kheni's husband took him by the arm, smiling. 'Can you not stay a little longer?'

'I should think you are the first to ever ask me that, Cob,' Wit said. 'And in truth, the sentiment frightens me.' He hesitated, then leaned down and touched the doll in the child's hands. 'Forget what I told you before,' he whispered. 'Instead, take care of *her*.'

He turned and started up the steps toward the palace.

He adopted the act as he walked. The twitch of madness, the shuffle to his step. He squinted one eye and hunched over, changed his breathing to come raggedly, with occasional sharp intakes. He muttered to himself, and exposed his teeth – but not the one that was missing, for that was impossible.

He passed into the shadow of the palace, and the sentry hovering in the air nearby, wind rippling her long clothing. Vatwha was her name. Thousands of years ago, he'd shared a dance with her. Like all the others, she'd later been trained to watch for him.

But not well enough. As he passed underneath, she gave him the barest of glances. He decided not to take that as an insult, as it was what he wanted. He needed to be soup so bland, it was water. What a conundrum. In this case, his art was best when ignored.

Perhaps he would need to revise his philosophy.

He passed the sentry post, and wondered if anyone else thought it irregular that the Fused spent so much time here near this fallen section of the palace. Did anyone wonder why they worked so hard, clearing blocks, breaking down walls?

It was good to know that his heart could still flutter at a performance. He ducked in close to the work project, and a pair of more mundane singer guards cursed at him to move on toward the gardens, with the other beggars. He bowed several times, then tried to sell them some trinkets from his pocket.

One shoved him away, and so he acted panicked, scrambling past them and up a ramp into the work project itself. Nearby, some workers broke rocks, and a patch of blood stained the ground. The two singer guards shouted at him to get out. Wit adopted a frightened look, and hurried to obey, but tripped himself so he fell against the wall of the palace – a portion that was still standing.

'Look,' he whispered to the wall, 'you don't have many choices right now.'

Above, the Fused turned to look at him.

'I know you'd rather have someone else,' Wit said, 'but it isn't the time to be picky. I'm certain now that the reason I'm in the city is to find you.'

The two singer guards approached, one bowing apologetically to the

744

Fused in the air. They still didn't realize that sort of behavior would not impress the ancient singers.

'It's either go with me now,' Wit said to the wall, 'or wait it out and get captured. I honestly don't even know if you've the mind to listen. But if you do, know this: I will give you truths. And I know some *juicy* ones.'

The guards reached him. Wit pushed against them, slamming himself against the wall again.

Something slipped from one of the cracks in the wall. A moving Pattern that dimpled the stone. It crossed to his hand, which he tucked into his rags as the guards seized him under the arms and hauled him out into the gardens, then tossed him among the beggars there.

Once they were gone, Wit rolled over and looked at the Pattern that now covered his palm. It seemed to be trembling.

'Life before death, little one,' Wit whispered.

THE END OF

Book Three of

THE STORMLIGHT ARCHIVE

United, new beginnings sing: "Defying truth, love.
Truth defy!" Sing beginnings, new unity.

Ketek written by Jasnah Kholin on the occasion of her
ward Shallan Davar's wedding celebration.

ARS ARCANUM

THE TEN ESSENCES AND THEIR HISTORICAL ASSOCIATIONS

NUMBER	GEMSTONE	ESSENCE	BODY FOCUS	SOULCASTING PROPERTIES	PRIMARY / SECONDARY DIVINE ATTRIBUTES
1 Jes	Sapphire	Zephyr	Inhalation	Translucent gas, air	Protecting / Leading
2 Nan	Smokestone	Vapor	Exhalation	Opaque gas smoke, fog	Just / Confident
3 Chach	Ruby	Spark	The Soul	Fire	Brave / Obedient
4 Vev	Diamond	Lucentia	The Eyes	Quartz, glass, crystal	Loving / Healing
5 Palah	Emerald	Pulp	The Hair	Wood, plants, moss	Learned / Giving
6 Shash	Garnet	Blood	The Blood	Blood, all non-oil liquid	Creative / Honest
7 Betab	Zircon	Tallow	Oil	All kinds of oil	Wise / Careful
8 Kak	Amethyst	Foil	The Nails	Metal	Resolute / Builder
9 Tanat	Topaz	Talus	The Bone	Rock and stone	Dependable / Resourceful
10 Ishi	Heliodor	Sinew	Flesh	Meats, flesh	Pious / Guiding

The preceding list is an imperfect gathering of traditional Vorin symbolism associated with the Ten Essences. Bound together, these form the Double Eye of the Almighty, an eye with two pupils representing the creation of plants and creatures. This is also the basis for the hourglass shape that was often associated with the Knights Radiant.

Ancient scholars also placed the ten orders of Knights Radiant on this list, alongside the Heralds themselves, who each had a classical association with one of the numbers and Essences.

I'm not certain yet how the ten levels of Voidbinding or its cousin the Old Magic fit into this paradigm, if indeed they can. My research suggests that, indeed, there should be another series of abilities that is even more esoteric than the Voidbindings. Perhaps the Old Magic fits into those, though I am beginning to suspect that it is something entirely different.

Note that I currently believe the concept of the 'Body Focus' to be more a matter of philosophical interpretation than an actual attribute of this Investiture and its manifestations.

THE TEN SURGES

As a complement to the Essences, the classical elements celebrated on Roshar, are found the Ten Surges. These, thought to be the fundamental forces by which the world operates, are more accurately a representation of the ten basic abilities offered to the Heralds, and then the Knights Radiant, by their bonds.

Adhesion: The Surge of Pressure and Vacuum
Gravitation: The Surge of Gravity
Division: The Surge of Destruction and Decay
Abrasion: The Surge of Friction
Progression: The Surge of Growth and Healing, or Regrowth
Illumination: The Surge of Light, Sound, and Various Waveforms
Transformation: The Surge of Soulcasting
Transportation: The Surge of Motion and Realmatic Transition
Cohesion: The Surge of Strong Axial Interconnection
Tension: The Surge of Soft Axial Interconnection

ON THE CREATION OF FABRIALS

Five groupings of fabrial have been discovered so far. The methods of their creation are carefully guarded by the artifabrian community, but they appear to be the work of dedicated scientists, as opposed to the more mystical Surgebindings once performed by the Knights Radiant. I am more and more convinced that the creation of these devices requires forced enslavement of transformative cognitive entities, known as 'spren' to the local communities.

Augmenters: These fabrials are crafted to enhance something. They can create heat, pain, or even a calm wind, for instance. They are powered – like all fabrials – by Stormlight. They seem to work best with forces, emotions, or sensations.

The so-called half-shards of Jah Keved are created with this type of fabrial attached to a sheet of metal, enhancing its durability. I have seen fabrials of this type crafted using many different kinds of gemstone; I am guessing that any one of the ten Polestones will work.

Diminishers: These fabrials do the opposite of what augmenters do, and generally seem to fall under the same restrictions as their cousins. Those artifabrians who have taken me into confidence seem to believe that even greater fabrials are possible than what have been created so far, particularly in regard to augmenters and diminishers.

PAIRING FABRIALS

Conjoiners: By infusing a ruby and using methodology that has not been revealed to me (though I have my suspicions), you can create a conjoined pair of gemstones. The process requires splitting the original ruby. The two halves will then create parallel reactions across a distance. Spanreeds are one of the most common forms of this type of fabrial.

Conservation of force is maintained; for instance, if one is attached to a heavy stone, you will need the same strength to lift the conjoined fabrial that you would need to lift the stone itself. There appears to be some sort of process used during the creation of the fabrial that influences how far apart the two halves can go and still produce an effect.

Reversers: Using an amethyst instead of a ruby also creates conjoined halves of a gemstone, but these two work in creating *opposite* reactions. Raise one, and the other will be pressed downward, for instance.

These fabrials have only just been discovered, and already the possibilities for exploitation are being conjectured. There appear to be some unexpected limitations to this form of fabrial, though I have not been able to discover what they are.

There is only one type of fabrial in this set, informally known as the Alerter. An Alerter can warn one of a nearby object, feeling, sensation, or phenomenon. These fabrials use a heliodor stone as their focus. I do not know whether this is the only type of gemstone that will work, or if there is another reason heliodor is used.

In the case of this kind of fabrial, the amount of Stormlight you can infuse into it affects its range. Hence the size of gemstone used is very important.

WINDRUNNING AND LASHINGS

Reports of the Assassin in White's odd abilities have led me to some sources of information that, I believe, are generally unknown. The Windrunners were an order of the Knights Radiant, and they made use of two primary types of Surgebinding. The effects of these Surgebindings were known – colloquially among the members of the order – as the Three Lashings.

BASIC LASHING: GRAVITATIONAL CHANGE

This type of Lashing was one of the most commonly used Lashings among the order, though it was not the easiest to use. (That distinction belongs to the Full Lashing below.) A Basic Lashing involved revoking a being's or object's spiritual gravitational bond to the planet below, instead temporarily linking that being or object to a different object or direction.

Effectively, this creates a change in gravitational pull, twisting the energies of the planet itself. A Basic Lashing allowed a Windrunner to run up walls, to send objects or people flying off into the air, or to create similar effects. Advanced uses of this type of Lashing would allow a Windrunner to make himself or herself lighter by binding part of his or her mass upward. (Mathematically, binding a quarter of one's mass upward would halve a person's effective weight. Binding half of one's mass upward would create weightlessness.)

Multiple Basic Lashings could also pull an object or a person's body downward at double, triple, or other multiples of its weight.

A Full Lashing might seem very similar to a Basic Lashing, but they worked on very different principles. While one had to do with gravitation, the other had to do with the force (or Surge, as the Radiants called them) of Adhesion – binding objects together as if they were one. I believe this Surge may have had something to do with atmospheric pressure.

To create a Full Lashing, a Windrunner would infuse an object with Stormlight, then press another object to it. The two objects would become bound together with an extremely powerful bond, nearly impossible to break. In fact, most materials would themselves break before the bond holding them together would.

REVERSE LASHING: GIVING AN OBJECT
A GRAVITATIONAL PULL

I believe this may actually be a specialized version of the Basic Lashing. This type of Lashing required the least amount of Stormlight of any of the three Lashings. The Windrunner would infuse something, give a mental command, and create a *pull* to the object that yanked other objects toward it.

At its heart, this Lashing created a bubble around the object that imitated its spiritual link to the ground beneath it. As such, it was much harder for the Lashing to affect objects touching the ground, where their link to the planet was strongest. Objects falling or in flight were the easiest to influence. Other objects could be affected, but the Stormlight and skill required were much more substantial.

LIGHTWEAVING

A second form of Surgebinding involves the manipulation of light and sound in illusory tactics common throughout the cosmere. Unlike the variations present on Sel, however, this method has a powerful Spiritual element, requiring not just a full mental picture of the intended creation, but some level of Connection to it as well. The illusion is based not simply upon what the Lightweaver imagines, but upon what they *desire* to create.

In many ways, this is the most similar ability to the original Yolish variant, which excites me. I wish to delve more into this ability, with the hope to gain a full understanding of how it relates to cognitive and spiritual attributes.

SOULCASTING

Essential to the economy of Roshar is the art of Soulcasting, in which one form of matter is directly transformed into another by changing its spiritual nature. This is performed on Roshar via the use of devices known as Soulcasters, and these devices (the majority of which appear to be focused on turning stone into grain or flesh) are used to provide mobile supply for armies or to augment local urban food stores. This has allowed kingdoms on Roshar – where fresh water is rarely an issue, because of highstorm rains – to field armies in ways that would be unthinkable elsewhere.

What intrigues me most about Soulcasting, however, are the things we can infer about the world and Investiture from it. For example, certain gemstones are requisite in producing certain results – if you wish to produce grain, however, your Soulcaster must both be attuned to that transformation *and* have an emerald (not a different gemstone) attached. This creates an economy based on the relative values of what the gemstones can create, not upon their rarity. Indeed, as the chemical structures are identical for several of these gemstone varieties, aside from trace impurities, the *color* is the most important part – not their actual axial makeup. I'm certain you will find this relevance of hue quite intriguing, particularly in its relationship to other forms of Investiture.

This relationship must have been essential in the local creation of the table I've included above, which lacks some scientific merit, but is intrinsically tied to the folklore surrounding Soulcasting. An emerald can be used to create food – and thus is traditionally associated with a similar Essence. Indeed, on Roshar there are considered to be ten elements; not the traditional four or sixteen, depending upon local tradition.

Curiously, these gemstones seem tied to the original abilities of the Soulcasters who were an order of Knights Radiant – but they don't seem *essential* to the actual operation of the Investiture when performed by a living Radiant. I do not know the connection here, though it implies something valuable.